BEAUTY

LOUISE MENSCH

headline
review

First published in Great Britain in 2014
by HEADLINE REVIEW
An imprint of HEADLINE PUBLISHING GROUP

1

Cataloguing in Publication Data is available from the British Library

ISBN 978 0 7553 5896 0 (Hardback)
ISBN 978 0 7553 5897 7 (Trade paperback)

Typeset in Meridien by Avon DataSet Ltd, Bidford-on-Avon,
Warwickshire

Printed and bound in Great Britain by Clays Ltd, St Ives plc

HEADLINE PUBLISHING GROUP
An Hachette UK Company
338 Euston Road
London NW1 3BH

www.headline.co.uk
www.hachette.co.uk

For Peter, my ideal of beauty

Chapter One

The maternity ward was having a bad day.

And so was little Dina Kane.

The newborn lay in her plastic cot, coughing and mewling; she was wrapped in a cotton blanket, and the little beanie on her head had slipped to cover one eye. Her mother lay on a bed a few feet away, passed out from the pain. Nurses rushed around, thankful that the mother was unconscious, the father at work on a building site somewhere in the Bronx. No question of a day off for him; this family needed the money.

In another room they had a woman bleeding after a botched C-section, and two breech deliveries were going on at the same time. Dina's mother, Ellen Kane, had screamed all the way through, like she was being tortured. This was her second child, and it arrived fast. By the time Ellen Kane got checked in to a bed, she was already seven centimetres dilated – too late for an epidural.

Too bad for Ellen.

It seemed every poverty-struck woman in Westchester County, New York, wanted to pop out a kid at the same time.

The midwives ignored Ellen's screeching. They were too busy trying to staunch the horrible flow of blood from the mother who was dying because of their obstetrician's mistake. Others were massaging and wrestling the breech deliveries round. Nobody cared about the regular birth – agonising or not.

1

No health insurance? No goddamned sympathy.

'Hell,' one of them hissed at Ellen, as she moaned and tossed on her sweat-soaked sheets, 'just push – push. Women have been doing this forever.'

'Please,' Ellen shrieked, but she was casting her voice into space.

Nobody feared a lawsuit. This was a Medicare family, too poor to sue. And so Dina Kane entered the world to the sound of her mother's horrible screams. As she slithered from the womb, a harassed nurse cut the cord, hung her upside down and slapped her tiny bottom.

Baby Dina screamed too – a thin little wail.

But it was the only sound left around the bed.

Her mother had fainted. The baby was roughly – incompetently – swaddled, dropped in her plastic cot and left alone.

Faintly, Dina cried, ignored. Making her first bid for attention. Trying to force the world to notice. Her tiny fingers, with their translucent nails, curled into her soft, wet palms.

Dina Kane was already making a fist.

The journey home was better. Dina slept in her carrycot in the back of the car, as Paul Kane tried to think of a few nice things to say to his wife.

'She's real pretty,' he lied. 'You did good.'

What the hell? His daughter looked like a hairless gnome, all wet and wrinkled – like all babies.

'Thanks, honey,' Ellen said, wearily.

She didn't look back at her daughter. Ellen excused herself with trauma and exhaustion. Before the birth, big as a house, she hadn't slept for days. Now, here Dina was, the fruit of all that effort.

Not like when Johnny was born: her firstborn, her son and the apple of her eye. Of course, Ellen had been younger then – four years younger – and the birth was OK and, besides, they'd both *wanted* a kid – and he was a boy, which everybody said was easier.

Turned out kids were expensive.

Ellen prided herself on running a tight ship. Paulie made good money on the construction site, and she had big dreams. They rented an apartment in Mount Vernon, but she wanted to own her own house one day. Maybe even something in Tuckahoe, a village a few miles away – but a world of difference. Ellen wanted the family to drive a better car, maybe go on a vacation to Florida once a year. She even had dreams of Catholic school for Johnny. Ellen could see herself, still trim and pretty, going to meetings of the PTA with those rich suburban moms, putting Christmas decorations on her own lawn, hosting her parents for Thanksgiving.

She wanted to stay pretty and young, not beat down like those other wives of the construction guys, the ones who got slobby and spent all day in sweat pants, or went to answer the door with their curlers in. Ellen Kane spent a bit of money on keeping herself groomed, as cheap as she could manage, and she had a gift for style. She could pick out the one pair of well-cut slacks donated to the charity store, she found the best cheap place to have her eyebrows plucked, and she dyed her own hair. Paulie was happy – he loved that his wife looked good, loved all the jokes the guys on the construction site made about it – and Ellen worked on her dream.

Johnny was a good boy. They loved him; they spoiled him. He took the breast, and didn't complain when Ellen switched him to the bottle aged three months.

'I want to keep myself nice,' she said, coyly, to Paulie, as the baby slept in his bassinet, out in their closet.

'Yeah.' Paulie nuzzled his face against her tits; they still felt full, bouncy. He was so relieved. He didn't want Ellen getting floppy and loose like all those women he saw around their way. 'Real nice, baby; real nice.'

3

He had a good marriage, mostly. Ellen wasn't the best cook, but she looked sexy. He valued that a lot more than a pot roast. Paulie earned the wage, his house looked neat, he had a wife that was a step above, and a boy. He was happy.

The trouble came as Johnny started to grow. Baby clothes – new ones every couple of weeks. Formula was expensive. The kid needed toys, bibs, diapers, a play mat . . . Paulie felt like every day he was being asked to shell out more cash.

They cut back. His night at the bowling alley became a once a fortnight thing. That truly sucked, and he wasn't happy. Paulie found himself working extra shifts, longer hours.

'Jesus! Borrow the fucking clothes,' he hissed at Ellen.

She pouted. 'I can't, Paulie. I don't want Susan DiAngelo's castoffs. She'll tell all the girls. They'll laugh at us.'

He nodded, grimly. Saving face was very important around the neighbourhood.

Then the teething started.

'Fuck!' Paulie tossed in his bed, staring at the ceiling, their bedside alarm clock saying 2:15 a.m. 'Won't that goddamned kid ever shut up? I have to *work*.'

Ellen dragged herself out from under the covers, teary-eyed from lack of sleep, and walked to the closet to pick the baby up. He was bigger now, and his cot filled almost all the small space.

'We need a bigger apartment,' she said, weakly. 'Like, with a second bedroom.'

Paulie couldn't disagree. He worked still more hours, took on a second job at weekends and went to his local *capo* for help. Paulie Kane was exactly the kind of guy the mob took care of, wanting little in return: he worked their sites, didn't bitch about joining any unions, took on overtime and kept his mouth shut about the things he saw there.

And he had *no* ambition. Guys like that, the fodder, prospered.

They gave him a rise. Then another. Within three months,

they were renting a bigger apartment, a place with a tiny second bedroom of its own.

Sex resumed, and Paulie liked it when Ellen was happier. He took on another job on Sundays, when most of the guys were resting. Six months moonlighting at the bowling alley added a little pot to their savings, and soon they had a deposit down on the longed-for three-bedroom colonial on the Tuckahoe borders. It was more Eastchester, the lousy end of town, but Ellen didn't care. She had a tiny scrap of garden and they could see a church spire from their bedroom window. The fence in the back was chain link, not picket, but this was their dream and everything was going so well. Ellen had plans to train as a hairdresser when Johnny went to nursery next year; she could make good pocket money doing a shampoo and set for the old ladies that wandered into the village's only salon during the daytime.

And then the disaster happened.

Just when they were on top of it. Just when he was getting straight. The baby was sleeping nights and Paulie was back to bowling in the alley, not cleaning up behind the bar.

Ellen got pregnant.

'Jesus! You're kidding?'

She whimpered, looking grey. 'The doctor ran the tests, Paulie.'

He was stunned. 'What the fuck happened?'

Ellen shrugged. 'The pills didn't work, I guess.'

No use saying Paulie should have used a condom. Ellen thought she'd been OK, taken most of her pills through the cycle, but she did forget things sometimes, got busy, got distracted by another diaper or the pasta on the stove . . .

'You forgot.' Her husband's voice was tight with accusation.

'No way, Paulie. I took them every day.' Ellen was so definite, she'd almost convinced herself.

'We can't. We don't need more.' Screw what his mother said; Paulie Kane had no intention of being a big Irish family. His small, neat family suited him down to the ground. With horror, he glanced at his wife – still slim, with those perky tits. Would they survive another go round? He liked Ellen's body, liked how she kept herself pretty, kept herself lithe and sweet in his bed. Soon that handspan waist would soften, grow, she would pack on the pounds, her tits would be milky, motherly, far from anything he wanted to know about.

A surge of fury bubbled deep within his belly.

'Get it seen to.'

Ellen's eyes widened. 'Paulie, no. No.'

'What are you, some kind of God-botherer?'

They were Catholics – sort of. Not that they went to Mass outside of Christmas and Easter, but that was the tribe – St Patrick's day and going to your friends' kids' Holy Communions. Paulie didn't know if he believed in God and he'd certainly not discussed it with Ellen. Their church wedding was fun, but so what?

Paulie believed in Paulie. And perky tits. And weekends off.

'We can't afford another kid. *Get it done.*'

And, although Ellen ran into the next room crying like a baby, he was unmoved. He went to the bar and got drunk, then spent the night crashed on his friend Mikey's couch, just so as to ram the message home.

Paulie thought that would do it. But, when he came back from work the next night, Ellen was waiting for him.

'I can't.'

She sat at the kitchen table, her hands twisted in her lap. Ellen had never defied Paulie before, but he could see instantly that she was about to now.

'I went down there,' she said, 'to the clinic. And they put me on the table and poked around and I said, "I need some time to think," and I got up and ran back here. I can't do it.'

Ellen Kane looked sick.

'You got pregnant on purpose,' Paulie accused.

'The hell I did! I don't want another baby, either.' Ellen turned her big green eyes towards her husband. 'But, Paulie, you know how it is. People know I'm pregnant.'

His heart sank. 'What people? How do they know?'

'Mona Ruffalo. And Agnes Monticello knows. They were in the doctor's when I got tested – congratulating me and such.'

Paulie was never going to graduate the Ivy League, but he had a good amount of native cunning. He saw immediately where this was going.

Mona and Agnes were both soldiers' wives, part of the Italian ruling clique that controlled all the sites locally. They were fat and greasy and wore too much make-up, not like his Ellen, but their husbands were mafiosi – made men – and they gave Paulie his orders.

Crime round here ran strictly on its own morals. Steal from the poor, but never show disrespect; fuck all the whores you want, but out of sight of the family; kill husbands, brothers, sons – but don't abort a baby.

He wasn't Italian. He would never rise, not really. But Paulie could be one of the best-paid worker bees, somebody the boys liked to drink with, trusted and rewarded. The *famiglia* didn't like abortion. Might give their own wives ideas.

'We have to do it,' Ellen said, and burst into tears.

Paulie kicked the garbage can, but made the best of it. He went to the *capo* again, explained the predicament, got a little more money and a stern shake of the head.

At least the house had three bedrooms.

'*No more mistakes,*' he hissed to Ellen.

The little mistake, Dina, grew unwanted and unconscious in her mother's belly. She didn't hear her father's sighs of disappointment when the scans reported back that it was a girl. She didn't hear her mother privately curse and rage at the gods because they had given her another baby.

There would be plenty of time for that once Dina kicked

painfully out of the womb and tried to make herself heard in a world that wanted to ignore her.

Paul Kane stopped at a red light and glanced back at the baby. She was sleeping – that was good. He related to babies best when they were sleeping.

'Hey, it's not so bad,' he said to his wife. 'We can make the best of it, right?'

'Right,' Ellen said, wearily.

The first thing she'd done when she came round was ask for her purse. Inside were her birth-control pills, the ones she'd lumbered to the pharmacy to purchase last month. They said breast-feeding protects you, but Ellen wasn't taking any chances – ever again.

She looked over at the sleeping baby and felt nothing but resentment. This one *was* going to ruin her figure, empty their bank account and keep her away from her little Johnny. Plus, the Italians always said girls were the difficult ones.

'A girl steals her mother's looks,' cackled Mary Kane, her mother-in-law. The old witch.

Ellen hoped to feel something for the baby, like she had when Johnny was born, but there was nothing. The most she could say for Dina was that labour was finally over.

'It's not so bad,' she lied. 'And the baby's beautiful.'

That was what you were supposed to say about girl babies, even when they looked like bald pink rats, like this one.

'She is, right?' Paul agreed, with equal enthusiasm.

Duty done, the new parents drove home, determined to forget about Dina as much as was humanly possible.

But she *was* beautiful.

The pink rat opened her big eyes and, after a little while, a soft thatch of dark hair appeared on the bald head. Even in her Baby-gro, Dina was something special: pale skin, raven dark hair and those wide blue eyes that started to deepen to green. Ellen had green eyes too, but not like this. Dina's were as bright as a clover field, richly coloured, striking in her soft little face. Her tiny nose was delicate and her lips were full; she was a gorgeous little baby.

Ellen enjoyed the compliments at first. Even if she didn't have those maternal feelings, nobody needed to know. She cuddled and kissed Dina and pushed her in her chair alongside little toddler Johnny, and everybody congratulated her on her 'beautiful family'. Johnny was the only one to truly love Dina, not that she understood it yet. He would stand for hours over her bouncer, trying to interest his sister in a threadbare stuffed dog or his old set of plastic keys. Dina loved Johnny back, and smiled and laughed whenever he was around – a little chortling baby laugh that even Ellen thought was cute. Dina kept Johnny quiet, so that was another plus for her. *Best toy ever*, Ellen thought to herself.

Dina was given her brother's stuff, even a navy blue romper suit with an anchor print. She looked good in everything.

Paulie went back to being ignorant. He couldn't worry about the home fires. The mortgage was a struggle, and the building trade wasn't going so well. There were extra jobs, moonlighting. He didn't want to hear his wife's complaints.

As Dina grew, her beauty just increased. There were angelic brown curls when she was three, and Ellen had to put her in little dresses. Dina loved to draw, to paint, to pick out clothes – just like Momma.

Maybe it would make them closer.

But Ellen was getting older. The sparkle was draining from her eyes. She was still stylish, but fewer of Paulie's friends ogled her when she visited the building site. He was irritable, snapping at her when he got home. More interested in dinner than sex.

And Dina grew bigger. So carefree. So pretty.

Ellen looked at her daughter resentfully.

She caused all this.

One stupid mistake, and they were back slaving for every cent.

'Oh, your little girl's so pretty.'

'What a cutie!'

'She's adorable. She's a real *beauty*. Where did she get those eyes?'

Ellen would force a smile. 'My eyes are green.'

'But not like that,' Tony Verzano said, admiring Dina as she romped around in her little pink dress. 'She's so stunning. You must be proud.'

Ellen wanted to be proud of *Ellen*. She wanted the attention, was used to it.

Why is Dina even here?

Nobody could see at night when Dina held out her little arms to her mother to be snuggled.

'I'm busy with supper.'

'Go get in your bath.'

'I have to practise Johnny's reading.'

The little girl would screw up her face and cry.

'Stop making that racket.' Her mother held up Rabby, Dina's favourite stuffed rabbit. 'If you don't behave, I'm throwing him in the trash.'

Dina's round mouth opened wider with horror. She lowered her arms from her mother and stumbled closer to save Rabby.

Ellen threw the toy at her. 'Behave, Dina. Go and be quiet.'

Clutching the rabbit to herself, little Dina Kane went to her tiny room to look at picture books and be quiet. She had dollies there – Daddy liked to buy her dollies; it assuaged some of his guilt.

She would dress the dollies up so they looked cute and stylish, like Mommy. If she was more like Mommy, perhaps Mommy and Daddy would like her.

And, meanwhile, she waited for Johnny to come back from pre-kindergarten. He always gave her a hug.

In the kitchen, Ellen Kane was cooking, whistling to herself to drown out the sounds of Dina's stifled sobs. But that girl was always there, hanging around like a ghost. Dina Kane was always a problem.

Chapter Two

'This is an excellent piece of work.'

Peter MacAllister handed the term paper back to Dina Kane. His eyes met those startling green ones, fringed with the thick black lashes.

'Thank you, Mr MacAllister.'

She smiled, and it was like the whole classroom lit up.

At sixteen, Dina had legs that went on for days. She had pale skin that never seemed to catch the sun, but that just played up the raven hair and bright green eyes. Her face was almost pre-Raphaelite with an even nose and full lips.

Peter MacAllister realised he was staring.

'You have an excellent grasp of algebra,' he blurted out. 'Have you thought about pursuing math later? At college?'

The green eyes clouded.

'I'm not sure about college, Mr MacAllister. We can't afford it.'

'Really? Surely your mother has money?'

'She needs all she's got,' Dina said, defensively. 'My mom works so hard.'

Her teacher hesitated. Perhaps he should drop it. But Dina Kane *deserved* to go to college. She was the one really motivated, driven student he had in his entire class.

Eastchester public schools didn't send many to the Ivy League.

They were underfunded and overcrowded. Dina was different. From her first days, the teachers had marked her out. Eager to please, to be liked, she sought more from them. She worked incredibly hard, always looking for approval, and she was bright – intensely so. She had a particular gift for creative writing, math and chemistry. Dina loved mixing up potions and experimenting; her enthusiasm was a bright spot in a room full of sullen, resentful pupils.

It didn't make her popular.

'Teacher's pet.'

'Suck-up.'

'Such a nerd.'

MacAllister felt bad for her. School was a struggle for Dina, as far as the kids went. First it was her great grades, next it was her beauty. The other girls got jealous and banded together. There was a lot of spite. Dina mostly sat on her own at lunch, and the girls that would eat with her were the losers. Boys would ask Dina out, but then succumb to peer pressure and slouch away from her in the playground.

Dina Kane didn't care. She was relentlessly focused. Her average grade was an A. And she stayed for every afterschool programme she could.

'Don't you have a home to go to?' asked Ms Segal in chess club.

'Oh, yes. My mom really misses me,' Dina said, brightly. 'She just wants me to do well in school.'

'Your brother's at St Joseph's, right?'

'Yes.' A tiny cloud, but she smiled it away. 'There was only enough money for one of us.'

The Catholic school in Bronxville had a great reputation; it charged a small fee; class sizes were much smaller; the kids wore a uniform. They mostly headed to college and became professionals.

You couldn't say the same for Dina's school.

'That doesn't seem fair,' said Ms Segal.

'Better one of us than neither of us,' Dina replied. 'I'm doing fine here.'

And she was.

Dina dreaded going home each night.

'Hey, Mom! How was your day?'

She would smile and give her mother a hug, hoping against hope that one day things would be different. One day the hug would be returned. One day Ellen would be interested in Dina.

'What do you care? I just stay here and look after the house, cleaning and shopping and cooking –' Ellen made it sound like hard labour in a penal camp – 'while you just swan about at school.'

'I got a five hundred in my PSATs.'

'What the hell does that mean?'

'You know, Mom. Next year I take the SATs? For college? I got a really good grade in my practice tests.'

Ellen looked at her blankly. 'What the hell for? You ain't going to college. Not unless you win the lottery. I can't afford two of you.'

Dina felt the tears prickle. Mostly she tried so hard to ignore her mother's cruelty – the detachment, the coldness – but sometimes it was tough.

College was her dream, her ticket out of a hellish childhood, her chance to make something of herself, something special, something real.

But Ellen Kane was standing in her way, like a demon on a bridge.

It was Johnny first – always Johnny.

Her father's death had started the spiral.

'Paulie! Look out on the goddamned crane!' His supervisor's

yell came floating up from the ground, but Paulie Kane didn't hear him.

He was balancing on the heavy iron bar, trying to swing it into place. It was night and he was cold, but he had that good antifreeze, right in his pocket. Saturday frigging night and here he was, working overtime.

Johnny had started school and it all cost: tuition, books, uniform, everything. At least Ellen was happy again for a little while. He loved how she lit up when she saw her son, so cute in his blue uniform with the white piping. She was the mom of a private-school kid. And she got to take him there every day.

But Paulie was paying the bills. Ellen was obsessed with their status. When he'd said maybe Johnny could head to the elementary school across the block, for free, Ellen had sulked and refused to have sex with him.

Everything *seemed* OK in their house. That was what all the neighbours thought.

But it wasn't. It wasn't.

Paulie barely saw the kids. On Sundays, he slept. He was packing on the pounds. When he was there, they clambered over him, not giving him any rest. And if he gave little Dina any compliments, Ellen scowled at him.

'She's demanding. She's spoiled. You're encouraging her.'

'Come on, now.' Paulie wasn't so fatherly himself, but his wife's barely-concealed hostility perplexed him. 'She's just a little kid.'

'If you give in to her, she'll always be whining for attention,' Ellen said. 'Don't you see how she plays up to it?'

'She's real pretty, that's all it is.'

Exactly the wrong thing to say. 'She's vain, Paulie – vain – already, at four. Don't make it any worse.'

So he would disengage the little hands from his neck, and then, when Dina cried and Ellen yelled, he'd feel even more guilty.

The bar seemed like a good place to go.

A real good place – where you could get your stress relief cheap and fast, at a few bucks for a glass of rye whiskey, his favourite.

Paulie started to spend a lot of time there. He came late to the building site, dropped bricks, made mistakes. A warning came back through the channels: *Cut it out.*

He was smart. From that day on, Paulie never went back to the bar. Instead, he worked Saturday nights, and he brought a hip flask.

Drinks tasted good when you were bored. Booze ran like antifreeze through your veins when you were cold. He had to work while the boys were out bowling or watching football, so at least there was a little bit of relief in his pocket. That made work more fun. And he didn't have to think about the kids. Or his wife. Or his bills . . .

Paulie unscrewed the top again and tilted the metal bottle towards his mouth. Sweet relief . . .

Drip. Drip. He swallowed nothing. *Fuck!* It couldn't be gone already?

He had four more hours in this dump.

His body was wedged against the corner of the bar as it swung over the street below.

'Paulie! Jesus Christ!' Marco DiCapello was calling.

Jesus? That's funny: they think I'm Jesus. Paulie swayed and giggled to himself, then stood up on one leg, bracing his arm against the crane, to shake the bottle and tip out the last drops . . .

He didn't see the ice, or even feel it. There was a split second when he realised his arm wasn't bracing. Was reaching into air. Like the rest of him.

Eighty foot was too short a fall to scream.

* * *

'So sorry for your loss.'

Sal Rispelli was the local *capo*. He was used to this scene and did it well. Ellen Kane was playing her part too – the grieving widow with two little children – wearing a fitted black dress. She had fixed her hair and put it up in a ladylike bun, and she had done her make-up carefully. Despite her age and cares, she looked good today. Maybe it was the adrenaline.

'He was everything to me.' Ellen looked truly distressed, even frightened. Of course, Paulie was working off the books. 'I don't know how our family will survive.'

'Don't worry.' Sal placed a hand over hers.

'But I have to worry. There's our mortgage . . . and Johnny's school. And what will we live on? I can't go out to work. My darling Dina needs me.'

Ellen missed Paulie some. But she missed her security a hell of a lot more. The mascara-thickened lashes batted themselves at the *capo*.

'Anything you can do for our family, Signor Rispelli,' she said, humbly.

There was something very sexy about a pleading woman, humble and submissive. The way they should be.

'Paulie was family.' *That stupid drunk.* 'We take care of our own. Don Angelo has already paid off your mortgage. And you are receiving a lump sum of two hundred thousand dollars.'

Ellen nearly fainted. She swayed in her chair.

'What?' she whispered.

'Two hundred grand,' he repeated. Hell, they hadn't put the workers in safety harnesses. It was a lot cheaper than workman's comp. He'd chewed out that jerk-off, DiCapello, at the site this morning, and *now* the worker grunts had harnesses. But they were grumbling over Paulie. Watching a man die will do that to you.

The *famiglia* didn't like deaths they hadn't ordered. It was in their interest now to take real good care of Ellen Kane.

18

'And, for yourself, a pension wage. You come down to the salon for an hour every lunch and style the ladies' hair. You'll get very well paid.' A pretend job made things easier than a stipend to her little schmuck bank account.

'I can't believe it!' Ellen gasped. For once, she wasn't faking her emotion. She grabbed Rispelli's hand and kissed the back of it, just like she'd seen them do in the movies. Softly, again and again.

He was starting to get uncomfortably aroused. Time to get out of here and over to a strip joint. One of their hookers could finish what Ellen had started.

'You and the kids won't miss a beat. Remember, you're under our protection. So act respectable,' he said, with a thin smile.

Ellen heard the warning: *No drinking. No screwing. A grateful client household.*

'Yes, Signor Rispelli. Thank you so much.'

Joy was rushing through her, joy she had to lower her eyes to contain. No more worry. No more fear. This was the best thing Paulie ever did for her.

'Better get back to your daughter, then,' Rispelli grunted, waving his hand to dismiss her. 'Like you said – she needs you.'

'I have to make this money last,' Ellen said. 'It's all I have.'

Dina looked round their house. There was all new furniture and a fancy TV and videotape machine. The garden was now planted with roses. Her mother wore a soft, pretty dress made of pink wool and her hair was piled up neatly on her head. She went out to the beauty salon each Thursday.

'We live pretty well, Momma,' she said, pleadingly.

'I know.' Ellen turned to study her reflection in a gilt-edged mirror. She didn't believe in making investments, hadn't tried to sell the house and move up the property ladder. But she did love stuff that made her life easier: pretty dresses, hairdressing appointments, manicures, expensive mirrors.

'I take you on holiday twice a year,' she said, proudly. 'Disneyland! How many other kids get to go to Disneyland around here?'

Dina sighed. At Disneyland, Mom had a great time. She and Johnny were bored out of their brains. But, no matter how much they asked to go someplace else, it was always Ellen's choice.

'Yes, Momma, thank you. But, you know, school's more important.'

'Johnny is at Catholic school.'

'I meant me.' Dina brushed her dark hair back behind her ears, nervously. 'You know they get much better results at St Joseph's. I want to go there too.'

'Honey, you know there isn't money for the both of you. You wouldn't want to deny Johnny his chance?'

Dina flushed. 'I love Johnny.'

'Well, I can't afford to pay twice. We all have to make sacrifices.'

'Maybe . . . Maybe you could get another job.'

Ellen's hour or two at the salon was hardly backbreaking.

Dina's green eyes begged. 'Momma, lots of parents work, you know? And maybe we could skip the vacations? Save our money for the fee for St Joseph's?'

'Dina, please stop *whining*. It's all about you. I work so hard raising you two kids without Daddy. All on my own, with nobody to help me.' Ellen's voice cracked with self-pity. 'Now you want me to slave till I drop for private school.'

'It's not fair.'

'What?'

'It's not fair,' Dina repeated, louder. She could hardly believe she had actually spoken the words. They had been swimming around her little head for so long. 'You treat Johnny better than me. You love him more than me.'

You love him would probably have been enough.

All her young life, Dina Kane had been wriggling away from

this moment, from admitting it: her mother didn't love her. Didn't really even like her.

And now, aged ten, it was staring her in the face.

'You're such a spoiled little madam. You think you're so special,' Ellen hissed. 'Asking a *widow* to work extra hours?'

'Don't you want me to get a good education?'

'The local public school is perfectly fine. Besides, Johnny needs it more. He's a man; he has to make his own way.'

'What does that mean?'

'You know well enough.' Ellen tossed her head. 'You're a girl. And you're not ugly.' It was as close as she would come to paying Dina a compliment. 'You can marry some poor schlub. Maybe he'll have more patience for your nonsense than I do.'

'Momma,' Dina's eyes filled with tears, 'I went to see the principal at St Joseph's and asked about aid. You know, for the poor kids. But she said we have money, so they can't pay it. The money we got when Daddy died?'

'You want me to give you my pension? Public school is good enough for you, Dina. Life's what you make it.'

Life's what you make it.

The taunt was seared into Dina Kane's mind.

Her mother had given her life, food to eat and shelter. Not too much else – cheap Christmas gifts and holidays that she didn't want.

But she had also been given the gift of determination – hard and cold as a diamond, deep inside her.

Johnny was the light of her life.

'Hey, sis! Looking beautiful.'

'Hi, Dinasaur! Have a great day at school?'

'How's my little princess? Still smarter than all her teachers, right?'

Johnny would hug Dina, kiss her, sweep her up. She'd clung to him ever since her tiny arms could snake around his neck.

Johnny made her childhood bearable. Dina knew she was loved, loved by someone, loved by family.

Often she wished that they were like all those orphan brothers and sisters in the fairy stories: no parents. Just two children out on their own.

A dead mommy could be mourned.

Dina constructed a fantasy world. Her mommy loved her. Her daddy watched over her from heaven. She was at PS 935 because it was the *best* school and Mommy wanted the *best*.

And so Dina worked to make it the best.

She occasionally got a few friends – at least for a while – but it never lasted. Girls would invite Dina to play. Then, as Ellen never reciprocated, the playdates dried up.

'But why can't we have Susan over?'

'I don't need my neat house wrecked by a gaggle of screaming kids. I have enough on my plate.'

Dina didn't argue. She suspected Ellen was as embarrassed as she was – any strangers might see how much her mother disliked her.

As she grew and blossomed, her friends drifted away. There was jealousy, cattiness – rumours about her mother.

'Did you see Ellen Kane in that short skirt yesterday?'

'God, I know. It's so ridiculous. She's, like, *thirty*.'

'Older than thirty.'

Priscilla Contratto turned on Dina as she walked past, carrying her books. 'Your mom looks like a tramp. Can't you do something about it?'

'Shut up, Prissy. My mom looks great.'

Truth was, Ellen feared the loss of her looks and had decided to do something about it. The skirts got shorter. The hair got blonder. She started wearing a red slash of lipstick to go grocery shopping.

Dina tried to speak to her about it.

'Mom, I think the grey skirt looks really chic on you.'

'The grey?' Ellen held it up. 'No fun.'

She was moving into a black leather mini. Dina gulped.

'You know, maybe that's more . . .'

The green eyes, duller than Dina's own, narrowed to chips of ice. 'More what?'

'More, like, for teenagers?'

Ellen flushed. 'Don't be stupid. And, anyway, my boyfriend likes it.'

Dina squirmed. 'Who is your boyfriend?'

'I keep my business private. I'll let you know if I decide to get serious.'

It wasn't long before Dina was doing her homework alone at night. Johnny would be at after-school programmes, or in his room, studying for SATs. Ellen would not be there.

A succession of black Lincoln town cars would pull up at the front of their place.

Different cars. Different licence plates.

Ellen avoided talking about it. She wore expensive jewellery and smiled a lot, except in the mornings when she was hung-over. Sometimes she talked about 'the boys' and snapped if Dina tried to ask her anything.

Her eyes got redder. Her skin developed a pallid tinge. Ellen was drinking and partying like she could make her tiny life go away.

'We have to do something,' Dina said to Johnny.

He was in his room, playing with his video games. 'Like what? She doesn't listen.'

'Maybe she'll listen to you. She likes you.'

Johnny shrugged. He was well-meaning, but saw no reason to get involved with lost causes – like his mother's relationship with Dina, or his mother's need for help. Johnny Kane wanted an easy life, and that mostly involved turning a blind eye. He gave little Dina affection and, in return, she didn't push him. On anything. It was their unspoken bargain.

'Hey, Mom's not talking. Let's leave her to her own life.'

'Johnny—'

'Drop it, Dina.'

But if Ellen wasn't talking, everybody else was.

Tramp. Bike. Plaything.

There was Sal Rispello – he was first, putting aside his earlier scruples. After all, she was offering it on a plate. Then there was Paolo Cottini, Giorgio Amalfi . . .

'Why's Dina's mom like table salt?' Lorna Fay shouted out in recess.

Dina scuffed her shoes in a corner of the playground, pretending to read her copy of *The Catcher in the Rye*.

'Because she gets passed around!' Lorna shrieked.

Dina heard the cackles of laughter, the hoots. Tears stung her eyes, but she didn't move. She wouldn't give them the satisfaction.

The next day, she skipped school for the first time in her life.

Angelo Tallarico sat by the pool, drinking coffee.

It was a serene scene. Angelo sat in his custom-designed chair, next to a side table made of marble. The lawns of the estate were so closely trimmed, the green grass looked like satin. Angelo wore a white summer suit, tailored in Savile Row, London. His Rolex was heavy, solid platinum, and his fingers were covered with enough diamond rings to make them look like a knuckle-duster. They sparkled as he lifted his crystal glass of ice tea to his mouth.

The infinity pool was perfectly blue; it lapped gently with its artificial current. The house behind him was white, Edwardian and huge. Angelo liked the English look. He'd had the place fitted out with rose gardens and topiary hedges. They had colour all four seasons.

You could barely see the bodyguards stationed around the place. All of them wearing back. All of them strapped to the nines.

Angelo loved to hire ex-military. The boys of the family were great, but, in a crisis, you wanted an accurate shot. Just one more way he was modernising his role.

They used the old terms: *Don Angelo*. But not in public. That was catnip to the FBI. Angelo despised the old guard who liked to court publicity. All they did was bring trouble on everyone's head.

He was training his new recruits in different techniques: arms trading, union corruption, public-sector payoffs.

Nobody does gangster like the politicians.

But Angelo didn't want to go too fast. He needed to carry the soldiers, the captains with him. The construction sites and gambling houses stayed open; the drug deals were still run on the corners – he was peeling back from them, but only slowly.

All in good time. Even if he hated that petty shit.

Angelo told himself he was patient. That was why he was now the Don. Two cousins shot, another doing twenty-five in maximum security. His uncle Claudio had been poisoned, so they thought. So Angelo avoided stupid mistakes, like trampling on the old ways, at least until he was ready.

He shifted in his chair, enjoying the sun. August was tremendous in New York. In retirement, he wanted to leave the bitter winters, head to Florida, maybe even further afield. Get a hacienda in Mexico, where they understood security.

There were two young girls waiting in the bedroom. A soldier had talent-spotted them at one of the family's strip joints. Legal age – he'd checked. Big tits, curvy asses and mouths that knew how to do stuff other than talk.

The soldier got a tip. The girls got a new assignment.

Angelo would keep them for a month, then send them packing.

He liked fresh meat, no involvement. There was no wife, nor did he want one. When he married, years from now, it would be a classy girl, not some painted screecher from round here.

'Signore?' This was a new take on *Don*. Angelo liked both. 'There is a girl here to see you.'

Angelo stretched. 'I didn't order another one yet. I like how that redhead grinds.'

'Yes, sir.' A grin. Sometimes the boss would order his girls down to the security barracks, with instructions to please every man in the room. It kept the men loyal, taught the females their place. 'It's not a whore, this one. A schoolgirl.'

Angelo looked up. 'What?'

'The daughter of one of your workers.' He shrugged. 'He died a few years ago.'

'Boohoo,' Angelo said. 'What the fuck does she want?'

'To see you. She said she won't leave till she does.'

'Jesus! Get rid of her.'

'Yes, sir.' The man straightened up, putting his hand on his gun. 'We'll escort her to the road.'

Angelo sipped his tea. 'Wait.'

His spider-sense was tingling, as if this could be a mistake, this could be trouble.

'How old is she?'

'Sixteen, seventeen . . . I think.'

'And whose kid?'

'His name was Paul Kane.'

A bell was ringing, but he couldn't place it. 'Pretty?'

The guy laughed and kissed his fingertips. 'Ass like a peach. Better than those two you got upstairs, signore.'

'I'll see her.' What the hell? He could give her five minutes, just to make sure this wasn't some problem. But better, older men than him had been assassinated by kids. 'Frisk her; frisk her thoroughly.'

'And if she refuses?' He licked his lips.

'She's somebody's daughter. But, if she refuses, throw her out.'

'Yes, sir.' The bodyguard walked off.

'Spread your legs, baby.' The guard ran his hands down her ribcage, pausing to cup her breasts under the bra. She tensed, and he jiggled them, then laughed. 'Full search. We don't know what you've got under there.'

Dina bit her tongue. She was facing a brick wall. There were bloodstains on it. Reluctantly, she widened her legs.

'Great ass,' his colleague said. 'Spread 'em a little wider.'

'Why?'

'Because I said so.'

He came behind her, ran his hands over her legs, starting at her ankles, squeezing tight. Then he felt her ass, briskly, and then, with more leisure, fondled it, cupped her pussy.

Dina gasped.

'You a virgin?' he said, idly.

'Joe, cut it out. She's not for us.'

The hands were removed and Dina was allowed to step back. She raised her head, scarlet with embarrassment.

Both guards laughed.

'She's clean.'

'Not for long,' his friend said. 'I'd give a week's pay to pop that cherry.'

The first guard smirked, then beckoned her. 'Follow me. Don't say shit. Understand?'

Angelo looked over the girl standing before him, with her curvy figure and come-hither eyes.

Marek was right. She was better than the hookers he had inside. Fresher. Prettier. Those cheap jeans and the white T-shirt did absolutely nothing to hide her assets. She was gorgeous looking, with a soft, aristocratic face.

'What was your father's name? Kane?'

'Paul Kane, Don Angelo. He was killed in a construction accident out in the Bronx.'

'Sorry to hear that.'

'You took care of our family, sent my mother money. My brother goes to Catholic school. We live in Eastchester.'

He nodded. 'You are here to ask for more money?'

The girl shook her dark head. 'No, sir. It's . . . It's my mother.'

Despite himself, Angelo Tallarico was starting to get interested. It was the courage of this little slip of a girl, standing before him. The guards would have had their fun, but she was still here.

'What about her?'

'She sees men.'

'That happens when you're a grown-up, kid.'

'No. She sees *your* men. A few of them. At night, in fancy cars. They give her presents. People talk.' A slow flush was making its way up Dina's neck, but she ploughed on. 'My mom is drinking more. These men don't care for her.'

Angelo hesitated. Why was this his problem? He should tell the feisty little piece of cooze to get back to whichever small-town hell she came from.

'Mr Rispello; Mr Cottini; Mr Amalfi.' Recklessly Dina named them. 'Mr Casini, I think.'

All captains. All married.

'Then maybe have a talk with your mother.'

'She doesn't listen. But you could tell the men, Don Angelo. Warn them off.'

'Honey –' he sipped his tea – 'interfering in people's private lives . . . is not what I do. Bad for business.'

Dina shook her dark head. 'See, Don Angelo, my daddy worked for you. And he died. You took care of us. All the other workers know it. But now people are talking bad. Like, your bosses will use a guy's widow. All the kids in school –' the blush got deeper – 'they all know. And some of them have fathers who used to work alongside Dad. Still work for you now. They won't like the thought of that happening to *their* wives.'

Angelo considered this. Then he turned away and rifled through the papers in front of him, on his white marble coffee table. He didn't trust computers. They could be hacked, traced, run through by the FBI. Reports were typed out and sent to him; he read the papers and burned them each night.

Construction site delays in Brooklyn, Bronx.
Workers quitting. Sickness. Retired. Morale low.
Experienced hands replaced. Younger guys making mistakes.
Costing money.
Project budget may need revision.

Angelo saw through the dry lines of old-fashioned ink. There were problems. The old guys were dropping out.

The girl is right.

'OK. I'll speak to the boys.' *And your mother*, but he didn't tell her that. It was time for Father Confessor Angelo Tallarico to pay a visit to Ellen Kane, and he would have a stern penance to deliver for her sins.

'You were right to come to me,' he said. She had stopped the rot. 'What's your name again, baby?'

'Dina.'

'You can leave school next year, right? Want to work for me? As a secretary?'

He could station her out of sight of her father's old gang, working the head offices in Jersey City. She was smart, and she had that look about her – that she'd fuck like a freight train once the right guy had warmed her up.

Dina's green eyes opened wide. 'Oh, no,' she said, like it was a stupid question.

Angelo was amused. Working right for the Don was an opportunity girls round here would kill to have. 'Why not?'

'Because I'm going to make something of myself,' Dina said, artlessly.

Angelo Tallarico laughed aloud. 'You know what, kid? I don't doubt it.'

The next night, in her room, Dina was hunched over her desk, working, waiting for the limousines.

They didn't come.

She heard her mom making calls. They were short; there was shouting. And after that, nothing.

Ellen sloped round the house, getting drunker, missing her days at work, lashing out. She stopped cooking, cleaning. Dina quietly did it all herself. She poured out the vodka bottles she found hidden under the sink, but her mother bought more.

Still, the kids at the school stopped talking. Dina went back to her schoolwork. Johnny looked a little less hunched, less defeated.

Ellen Kane was drunk.

She didn't know why. Just a little hair of the dog from last night. That was bad; she had the shakes. She needed it.

And then she felt so much better. One more wouldn't hurt. Anyway, she was quitting after this bottle. It cost money, it would be a waste to pour it away.

She deserved it. They were all bastards, all of them – using bastards. Something had happened, something bad. It worried her nights. She had anxiety – that was it, anxiety. And if a little martini made you feel better, so what? It was better than them shrink pills. They would kill you.

The doorbell rang.

'Comin'!' she yelled. Her words were slurry. *Shit!* Maybe it was Paolo, come back. He was her favourite. The way he caressed her ass . . . made her feel good, sexy, young again.

But she was already, well, a little bit nice.

Ellen stumbled to her bathroom and swilled the Listerine around her mouth. Yeah – great. Now she was set.

She opened the door, steadying herself on the handle.

It wasn't Paolo. It wasn't any of them.

But it was a younger man, handsome in a kind of fierce way, with a scar on his cheek. And a fancy suit and a *reeeal* nice watch. He was Italian, for sure.

Ellen glanced behind him. He didn't have a town car. He had a limo you could take a bath in.

Maybe one of the boys had recommended her. *Recommended her*. That was kind of humiliating, but sexy, too. Ellen tossed back her blond hair. She liked to party; she was a pretty girl who liked to party. Not a goddamned crime, right?

'Hey, baby,' she said, carefully enunciating. 'Come on in.'

Angelo Tallarico sat on the couch and stared at Ellen. She was a sloppy, drunken mess. Now she was sobbing, her small shoulders heaving, eyes and nose streaming.

He glanced around; the little house was neat. Dina had probably taken care of that.

Tallarico was a murderer and a drug dealer – with very particular ideas about how things should be done.

And Ellen Kane didn't fit the template.

'Stop crying,' he said, coldly. 'I'm not your shrink. You understand me?'

She mopped at her face.

'The boys aren't coming round. None of them. Ever. Don't call. Don't email. You're an embarrassment to the family.'

Ellen trembled. She thought she'd get more compassion from a snake.

'We support you. But one more incident and that money is cut off. One more embarrassment, so are you.'

She moaned.

'Do you understand?'

'Yes.'

'You've had your last drink. If I ever see you drinking again, ever hear reports of you drinking, you will wind up in an accident.'

Ellen's whole body shuddered. Never had she wanted booze as much as she did in that second.

'Don Angelo—'

'Don't call me that.'

'I can't stop drinking . . . not right away. Give me a week, a month . . .'

'You have the weekend to clean up. Lock yourself in your bedroom and order a pizza. Monday morning, you're back at work. Sober. For good. If not . . .' he shrugged.

'I . . . I . . .'

'Call it the fast-track twelve-step programme, lady –' a thin smile at his own joke – 'one step: you stop. Or you die.'

'And men?'

'Nobody from the family. If you can find a nice single, divorced guy, date him like a civilised broad; you can get married. Good luck with that.' He laughed cruelly. 'I wouldn't fuck you with my gardener's dick.'

'Oh, God,' Ellen said.

'Spend our money. Live clean. Live quiet. Then you live. Shit, you could consider looking after that pretty little daughter of yours.'

Ellen collapsed into sobs. When she looked up, Tallarico had gone.

She fled to the kitchen and picked up the vodka bottle.

Outside, in the street, the limousine flashed and dipped its headlights.

Fear gripped her. Fear worse than the craving. Ellen lifted the bottle, so he could see, and poured all that lovely, calming liquid right down the sink.

Then she collapsed on to the floor and crawled upstairs to her bedroom on her hands and knees.

That pretty little daughter of yours . . . Pretty little daughter . . .

Dina!

It was Dina. She was here to curse the mother that slaved for her. Here to ruin Ellen's life.

Ellen bit her lip. She dared not say anything to Dina. The man – the bastard, Tallarico – would not like it. And, like a threatened animal, Ellen scented danger.

He was angry. If she did anything to worsen that, she was dead. And not in a metaphorical sense.

Lying on her bedroom rug, watching the ceiling spin and dance as she gasped and sweated and longed for a drink, Ellen Kane held tight to one thing:

She would have her revenge.

Chapter Three

Dina Kane graduated from school a major success – that is, if you were looking at grades. She was top of the class.

Despite her mom, Dina had applied to the Ivy League – and got in. There were acceptances from Columbia, Vassar, even Stanford.

But Dina could not afford the fees. She was considered too well-off for financial aid – her mother had almost three hundred grand in the bank.

None of her pleading meant a goddamned thing.

'No, Dina.' Ellen was colder these days in her dismissal. Unable to compete as an aging sexpot, she had taken refuge in the clothing of the upright. Hair twisted into a severe bun, Ellen Kane favoured long, stout skirts, membership of community organisations and a disapproving frown at all times.

For some time now, she hadn't touched a drink. Or any drug stronger than caffeine.

Ellen joined the PTA at Johnny's Catholic school. She volunteered in the St Patrick's Society. She was on the town-beautification committee. Their house grew cleaner and neater and Ellen gave gifts to local organisations so she could be thanked at dinners.

At first, Dina was thrilled. That horrible trip to Tallarico had had its effects. Her mother had said she was sick and barely came out of her room all week, but when she did, she was changed. Older. Sober. No mascara. Plain, sensible pants. She looked like a mom.

Unfortunately, she still didn't act like one. Dina got a square meal at supper and new clothes when she'd worn out the last set. And that was it.

They were strangers. No people came to the house; no men visited at night. Dina Kane started to live for the moments her brother came home from school.

'There's no money for you to go to college. I need it for my pension. I won't be marrying again and there's no security in welfare. Besides, this place has property taxes . . .'

The list went on and on.

'But, Mom, you've got plenty – really.' Dina didn't want to cry, but she couldn't help it. 'I need you to help me out, Momma.'

Ellen looked blank. 'Johnny's at college. I'm paying for that.'

Johnny was at a pretty nondescript, local private university – the best he could get into with his so-so grades. But at least it was college.

'You can't just favour one of us over the other, Mom!'

Ellen smiled, very quickly, very slightly, then swallowed it. She turned to Dina, her face set once more. 'It's clear from your school success that I picked the right place for you. Johnny might have needed more help. Putting one kid in college is all that I can manage. You should respect that, Dina. You can always get a job, work your way through.'

'I can't work through Columbia's fees . . .'

'I'm sorry. There's nothing to discuss.'

'Mom –' Dina tried one last, desperate tactic – 'if you *lend* me the money for college, I'll graduate, I'll have a career and I can pay you back . . . I'll do well in life, Momma; I'm going to work hard.'

Her mother laughed. 'Really, honey, don't get ideas above

your station. You should go out with one of the local boys. Get married, have some children. Life's all about a happy home!'

'So what will you do?' The principal, Mr Rogers, looked at Ellen Kane's departing figure with withering contempt.

She'd turned up at graduation, sat there for the ceremony and clapped politely as Dina received her cap and gown, and the meaningless little scroll that made her a high-school graduate. Then, as soon as she'd posed for a photo with her desperately smiling daughter and the slothful elder brother lolling around next to her, Ellen had turned around and walked off.

Mr Rogers had no doubt that the photo would be framed. It would go on her mantelpiece. Ellen Kane: pillar of the community, single mom of the year. But she had no few minutes to spend with her daughter – the one whose incredible potential she was just throwing down the drain.

'There's always community college.'

'My mom's too poor to afford college,' Dina said again.

He smiled sympathetically. Now wasn't the time for the truth. 'Sure, Dina.'

'I think I want to move to the city. Get a job and save some money. Then maybe I can reapply next year.'

He wanted to tell her she was crazy, but he had no answers. 'What kind of job?'

'I'll figure something out,' she said.

'OK.' Mr Rogers hesitated. 'Is your momma setting you up in an apartment?'

'Of course.' Dina smiled. 'Momma does everything for me.'

She walked home, thinking about it. Letting the warmth of the sun on her back calm her. New York was great when it was baking hot. It could distract you from pain.

Johnny had left home now . . . He couldn't bear to be around Ellen and Dina, to see the cruelty, the tension. Johnny wasn't built for confrontation – or, really, effort of any kind. He wanted to hug his sister, have a good time. And he avoided acknowledging how he hadn't protected her, skipping out whenever a bad scene came up, which was more and more often these days.

Dina never quite believed it – that the mom who raised her would dump her like this. In a few months she'd be eighteen, a legal adult.

Ellen was finally shot of her.

And it showed. Her mother could barely contain her jubilation. 'I hope you've worked at finding a job,' she'd said. 'And can you make sure your things are packed? I need a real guest bedroom.'

'But where will I sleep?'

'Sleep?' Ellen arched a brow. 'Dina, adults have their own lives. It's healthy for you to get on with yours.'

'I don't know anyone in the city.'

'You know Johnny.' Her brother had a tiny apartment near his college. Ellen gave him an allowance, part of his college arrangements, so she told Dina. As a working woman, Dina could afford her own rent.

When she turned the corner into her street, Dina Kane had made up her mind.

She looked up at the house in which she'd been raised. It was neat, well kept and pretty – exactly the same as it always was. Her mother's big break meant nothing. She spent all that money on herself, and spent it just to stand still.

If Dina got a hundred grand, she would do something with it.

Momma was right. It was time to move on. But Dina would do it on her own terms.

'Hey, Momma.' Dina walked into the kitchen and set her graduation cap down on the counter. She carefully hung up her cape on the hook on the kitchen door.

Underneath, she wore a pair of jeans from Gap and a plain

white T-shirt. On her, this was an absolutely knock-out look. Her naturally tanned skin popped against the white, and her breasts, medium sized and sweetly shaped, were outlined perfectly. Dina had a narrow waist and was naturally slim. Even in flats, she was absolutely stunning.

'Well, I'm glad *that's* over,' said Ellen, brutally.

Dina breathed in. The casual cruelty, so normal, so painful, gave her strength to come out with what she had to say.

'So, I'm not eighteen for two months. But I'd like to move out now.'

A slight flicker of a smile; it hurt Dina like a punch to the gut.

Why do I still care?

I love her. I hate her.

'You found somewhere?'

'I'm going to. I have places to visit today.'

'Places to visit? Aren't you staying with a friend?'

Dina shook her head. 'Rentals. I found them in the *Village Voice*.'

Ellen paused. 'But you don't have a job. And rentals need a deposit.'

'Yes – two months' rent, and security. It's more for me, though, because I don't have a job yet, you're right. I plan to move to the city and job hunt from there.'

Her mother saw where this was going.

'Dina, we've spoken about money. You can't ask me for any.'

Dina took a deep breath. 'Not asking you, Momma – telling you. I need fifteen thousand dollars.'

Ellen laughed. 'I can't lend you fifteen grand.'

'It won't be a loan. It will be a gift. And you're going to give me fifteen thousand right now.'

Her mother looked up from the stove, startled. There was a fire in her daughter's green eyes that she had never seen before.

'Write me the cheque and I will be out of your hair – permanently. Don't write it, and I will go and see Don Tallarico.'

Ellen gasped. Adrenaline prickled across her skin like she'd been doused with water. 'My God. It *was* you.'

'Yes, it was. And it will be again. Give me the money now, Momma. There's a pen on the countertop. Write me that cheque.'

And Dina Kane held out her hand.

The apartment was vile. It was tiny, cramped and filthy. The bathroom had a stand-up shower in it with a dead bug resting against the drain. The paint was peeling and the kitchen alcove was barely big enough for a refrigerator and a hot plate. A rickety double bed took up most of the rest of the space. There was a chair wedged right up against a large TV, one closet and stains on the green rug. Plus, you had to walk up eight flights of stairs to get there.

'Are all the apartments in the building like this?'

The realtor sniffed. 'Honey, you couldn't afford any of the others. This used to belong to the super. He was from Mexico.'

'So, for him, it was a palace?'

She shrugged. 'Don't give me any of that equality crap. You want it?'

The building itself was in a backwater, but it was secure and it was Manhattan. And Dina wouldn't have to share.

'Not at this price,' she said.

Ten minutes and a five-hundred-dollar discount later, Dina Kane had a deal. As she folded up her copy of the lease papers, she took note of the landlord's address.

As soon as she got the keys, Dina moved in. She called a handyman to remove everything in the flat and dump it into storage. Next, she got on the subway to a cheap furniture store in Midtown.

She looked around, thinking carefully about what to buy. After two hours, she was satisfied with her purchases.

'We deliver,' the saleswoman said. 'Twenty-four hours' notice.'

'See you tomorrow.'

'You getting everything delivered?'

'All except this.' Dina held up a sleeping bag.

Next, she headed to the local grocery store. She bought bleach, roach traps, dust cloths, mops and several pairs of bright yellow rubber gloves.

Long into the night, Dina was on her knees, cleaning. The stench was so bad, she had to stop twice to throw up. Heaving, she managed to open a window; warm air floated up from the alley below, but at least there was some oxygen in it. The stale odour of booze and sweat and sex dissipated under her assault – washing, scrubbing, mopping, till the place smelled like a hospital.

She showered in her clean stall, clambered into her sleeping bag and lay down on the floor.

The filthy net curtain on the single window had already gone into the trash. The bright lights of Manhattan streamed into her apartment. But Dina was content.

She was in the big city now.

In the morning, Dina woke early. She had no choice – her curtainless window got her up with the sun.

She showered, dressed from her suitcase and raced to the nearest hardware store. A few more dollars for brushes and paint. White – that was all she needed.

Dina painted with rollers and brushes. She wasn't her dad, and she had no practice, but the colour was basic, and forgiving enough that she did a reasonable job.

Besides, she was motivated. This was home. In a way, it was her first.

She was finished by eleven. Starving, she headed out to eat – anywhere, as long as it was cheap.

Dina had about two thousand dollars left in the account, and it had to last her. There was a Greek place across the street, the Olympia Café. She picked it because it was the closest, and she was so tired her legs could hardly hold her up.

She ordered a pork gyro. It would be hot, and she needed the iron. She waited and waited, but it didn't come, so she meekly flagged down a waiter.

'Jeez, baby, I'm sorry.' His shirt was open and he looked stressed. 'Girl's off sick again. I'll bring it right now.'

Dina ate the pita; it was nothing remarkable, but she was so hungry, and it tasted good. As she chewed, she thought hard.

'Check, please.'

'Nothing else? No coffee?'

Coffee was a dollar fifty. Dina shook her head. The tap water came free.

'You got it.'

'Your waitress often sick?' she ventured.

'Sick? No, honey; it's a Sunday. Saturday night on the town.' He looked fed up. 'Rolls around every weekend.'

'I can waitress. I don't drink.'

He laughed.

'I'm serious,' Dina said.

'Are you? Then turn up here at eight tonight. We're an all-night operation. Minimum wage; no benefits. You keep the tips.'

'Aren't you a waiter too?'

'I own the place. We don't spend money we don't have. Rents are high.' He smiled. 'I'll try you out. Sandwich is on the house.'

Her furniture was delivered just after three. Dina got out a hammer, some nails and twenty whole dollars to tip the delivery guys, who cursed her as they set the heavy stuff down.

'Eight goddamned flights. What a dump!'

'Have a nice day,' said Dina.

'Whatever.' He snatched the money.

Dina loved it – Manhattan attitude. She rolled out her new rug: chocolate brown, to hide any stains. The old bed and chair were gone; in their place was a neat, compact couch that unfolded to a queen-sized bed. She hung a plain cream blind over the window and a large mirror on the opposite wall, to catch the tiny amount of light and reflect it – that gave an illusion of space. Add a new fridge and a toaster oven to the cleaned-up hot plate, and the tiny studio was chic and respectable.

Dina added wire baskets to the single closet; she couldn't magic up more room, but she could make it work. There wasn't space for a lot of clothes. Good – that would mean she couldn't make any mistakes.

When she was finished, it was six p.m. She napped for an hour, then got up, showered and put on flats and a simple black dress.

'You're back.'

'Yes, sir.'

He grinned. 'I can't believe it.'

'It's ten to eight,' Dina pointed out.

'What's she doing here?' A heavy-set girl, twenty-two or so, with thick black eyeliner and greasy hair swept back in a ponytail, had marched up to the man.

'Working. What you should be doing.'

'We don't need you.'

'Not your call, Aella. Get back in the kitchen.'

Dina hovered.

'You done this before?'

'No, sir. But I'm a quick learner.'

'You don't have to call me sir. My name's Gil Barberis. I own the restaurant with my brother Dimitri. You'll see him in the kitchen. He cooks.'

'OK.'

'There's a changing room behind there with an apron you

43

can put on. Dimitri will tell you what to do. If he's busy, ask Aella.'

'Got it.'

'Any questions?' Gil asked, but she had already disappeared, walking into the back.

He realised he didn't even know her name.

Dina set her back to it. Dimitri, the brother, was fat, made good food and cooked it fast. He shouted out orders and she tried to get the hang of it. Aella cursed her and jostled her and tried to make her spill platters, but Dina was quick and focused. She dropped two plates and served three customers the wrong orders.

'I guess it didn't work out,' she said, at the end of the shift.

'Are you kidding? You were great. Can you work tomorrow?'

By the end of the first week, Gil was really pleased. This girl was something else. She showed up on time and learned quick. Plus, she actually smiled at the customers, passed the time of day.

And, goddamn, she was pretty.

Women gave her tips. Men gave her even bigger tips. Plus, they started showing up on off-times, just to catch a glimpse of her.

Dina Kane was a real gorgeous girl. More than that, she had a certain way about her. She wore form-fitting, minimal black clothes under the diner apron, just a little make-up, so that she always looked smooth, but not a drop more. She wore her hair high, in a clean bun. It made her look out of place. It made her look expensive.

He knew she needed money. She was grateful for every tip – thanked the customers personally. Gil was afraid to lose her. He offered her more work, the pick of the sessions. Aella and Katrina bitched, but bad waitresses were a dime a dozen.

'I can't. I have to look for a job,' Dina said.

'You have one.'

'I mean a real job. I need to make rent. So I have to take time out for that.'

Gil sighed, but he couldn't push things. He didn't want Dina Kane to leave completely.

Dina worked her shifts diligently, collected her money, went home and slept. In her off hours, she tied on her trainers and her cheap running clothes and worked out every day, following the streets down to the Hudson River and racing alongside the water. Men whistled at her, stared; she ignored them all.

She was running – from her mother, from her heartbreak, from a tiny life.

The waitress job paid enough to feed her, buy her make-up and clothes. It couldn't touch the rent, and Dina was scared. She had assumed the money from her mother would buy space and time, and that she'd get a real career, a foot on the ladder.

School had been easy; work – not so much.

'I'm sorry; you need experience to be a paralegal.'

'Our internships are unpaid.'

'Assistants at our company all have college degrees.'

'When did you graduate college, Miss Kane?'

'Nanny? Do you have referrals? A child-related qualification of some kind?'

'Babysitter? Our agency only takes girls currently at university. Which is yours?'

Great jobs all had something in common – Dina wasn't qualified to do any of them.

Some men at the diner had advice for her.

'Get a boyfriend – he'll look after you.'

'Baby, if you're nice to me, I can do you favours.'

'Lots of girls who can't afford college go dance in the clubs. I know a guy—'

'I'm not a stripper,' Dina said. She smiled at the customer, but her eyes were ice.

'Who's talking stripper? This is exotic dancing – like, artistic shit. They make the real money over there.'

I hate you, Momma, Dina thought.

Desperately, she tried to make something more of the job she had.

'Dimitri, maybe you could experiment. Cook some more authentic dishes.'

'What?' Her boss stared at her blankly. 'People come for diner food.'

'There are lots of diners. Lots of delis. Not too many Greek restaurants, not proper ones. I reckon, if you made some real stuff, people would come. You could try adding a few items to the menu. And a promotion.'

Dimitri looked at Gil. They'd already learned to listen to Dina Kane. Her simple suggestion of photocopying colouring pages and bringing in a stack of crayons in plastic cups had led to a real surge in moms with kids. Now the dead times between lunch and dinner covers had a healthy number of tables occupied with spaghetti and meatballs, coffees and cookie plates. Even better, Dina had sectioned off a corner of the diner, and they sat all the happy families there. Working men went the other side, away from the coffee klatches, where they could ogle the waitresses.

'What kind of promotion?'

'Get it grandma tested. Do a one-day promotion. Seniors eat free if they bring one younger paying adult.'

'That will cost.'

Dina wasn't listening. 'See, you print a flyer – but you only print it *in Greek*. Put it up in the Orthodox churches, the community clubs. You want to get the community in to talk up your place. Like – it's a small market, but not much competition. What do you think?'

They tried it. It worked like a dream.

'I want a rise,' Dina said.

Gil sucked it up and gave her another fifty per cent. It still wasn't enough.

One evening, about a month later, when Dina was looking at another three weeks before she defaulted on her rent, an older man came into the restaurant. His suit was beautifully cut, and it was clear he didn't want to be there.

Dina ran over to seat his party. She knew the lady he was with – Olga Markos, one of their first senior customers. Olga loved Dimitri's *gavros marintos*, small, spiky fish fried with spices and served with ouzo.

'Wonderful to see you again. Your usual table?'

The man snorted, and Dina returned his contempt with a smile.

'Oh, sir, this lady prefers to sit right by the window.'

'I do.' Olga nodded emphatically. 'So I can see the world, Alexander. Young Dina remembers.'

'First name terms,' the man said, dryly.

'Oh, it's Dina – everybody knows Dina round here.'

'Do they indeed?' he said.

Dina showed them to their table. It was clean, with a fresh white rosebud in a jar on the table. Those got changed twice a week. Another Dina innovation. The restaurant stood out.

As she worked her covers, Dina noticed the man watching her. She was used to that. All the men liked to stare, but she couldn't let it get in her way. Saturday night was their busiest, the ouzo and retsina flowed, and the tips were fantastic.

At the end of the meal, she brought them their check. Olga tipped her normal ten per cent. Dina smiled brightly, to hide her disappointment. The man seemed rich; she'd hoped for a couple of extra bucks from him.

But he caught her glance at the dollars on the change tray.

'You wanted a tip?' he said.

She flushed, embarrassed to be caught out.

'Oh, no, sir. The lady already gave me a tip, thank you, ma'am.' Dina scooped it up. 'You have a great day.'

'Here's your tip.' He took a business card out of his wallet and handed it to Dina. 'Call me tomorrow.'

'I certainly will. Thank you.' She slipped it into her apron pocket, without looking at it. She got a hundred of those come-ons a night.

'I mean it,' he said shortly. Then he stood up, ignoring her, and helped Olga from the restaurant.

That night, just as she was about to clear the paper waste into the recycling, Dina paused. She fished the small card out of the recycling bag and read it again.

Alexander Markos, it said. *Mount Java.*

She started. Mount Java was the newest, hottest chain of coffee shops to hit Manhattan. They sold their coffee like Baskin-Robbins sold ice cream – forty-five flavours, all lined up in urns, freshly brewed every two hours. And tiny pastries, from every country in Europe: French macaroons, Italian biscotti, Greek baklava, German strudel, jam tarts from England.

The company was founded and run by an American – Alex Markos.

New York was lapping it up. A coffee there cost eight dollars – not one – and New Yorkers couldn't get enough of it. The city was rich, and it paid for quality.

Dina clutched the card to her chest. Her heart was pounding.

'New boyfriend?' Gil said, hopefully, although he knew what the answer would be.

'New job,' Dina said, tears in her eyes, like any other girl would have when she announced her marriage. Gil didn't understand the kid at times. She worked like a machine; she just wasn't normal. Jesus! The boys died for her – so did the men. She could have had her pick.

She passed the card over. Gil studied it for a second, then made the connection. He whistled. 'Goddamn. Guess he wants you for more than a waitress.'

'I hope you don't mind.'

Gil knew when he was beaten.

'Go with God.'

Chapter Four

The office was located on the thirty-fourth floor, and Dina had to pass through four sets of security guards just to reach the executive elevator.

The lobby had marble floors and high ceilings. The guards wore designer suits. The reception desk appeared to be carved from solid ebony. Dina's heartbeat quickened as she walked. The scent of money was in the air.

The elevator was brass, with velvet carpet, a mirror and a padded bench – bigger than her little bathroom at home – and it went straight to Alex Markos's office.

She breathed raggedly. This was her big chance to get exactly where she wanted to be.

The doors hissed open and Dina found herself in a dazzling palace of glass walls and sweeping views. Behind the sound-proofed window, the city went about its business. Dina walked up to the kidney-shaped desk of Mr Markos's secretary, an elegant fifty-something wearing what was unmistakably a Chanel suit.

I want to be like that, Dina thought, *only sitting in the inner office. Working for a big company. Chief Executive.* Visions of success danced in her head.

'Can I help you?'

'Dina Kane for Mr Markos.'

'He's expecting you. You can go right in.'

Dina walked up to the main door. The sound of her footfalls was muffled by carpet an inch thick, but the sound of her heartbeat crashed again and again in her ears.

She pulled the door open and walked in, trying to look more confident than she felt.

Markos was looking at a computer screen, his oak desk a small island in the vast room. Behind and below him, she saw the New York traffic crawling through the city's concrete canyons, flashes of sunlight glittering on the windscreens. This was money; this was power. Dina Kane felt it as a sexual thrill.

'Have a seat.'

There was a large chair right in front of him. Obediently, Dina sat, smoothing her dress on her lap. *Steady. Don't look nervous.*

'Thank you.'

'You impressed me yesterday. I asked my aunt about you. She told me some of the things you've done at that restaurant. How old are you?'

'Eighteen,' Dina lied.

'Why aren't you at college?'

She winced. 'It's a long story.'

'I see a lot of young people work tables. I make it my business to notice quality. It's pretty rare.'

'Thank you, Mr Markos.'

'What are your goals for yourself, Dina?'

'To make the rent next month. And then to go to college, when I have enough money.'

'And then?'

She grinned. 'I like your office, Mr Markos.'

He laughed. 'This job is taken. Found your own goddamned company. I have an opening for a junior manager in my new restaurant uptown. It pays thirty-five thousand a year, with a Christmas bonus.'

Dina quickly did the sums. That was almost three thousand

a month. But, of course, there were taxes. She would need the bonus.

'Do I get to keep the tips?'

He raised a brow. 'The words you're looking for are "thank you".'

'Thank you. Sir.'

Markos waited till she'd shut the door behind her. Maybe this was a mistake. They'd never hired a manager that young. Oh, and there was the question of her looks. Eighteen and all kinds of sexy, with a face that could stop traffic. As a waitress, she was an attraction. As a manager? Would they take her seriously?

He almost felt a stirring. Ludicrous. She was practically jail-bait. And he'd taken a fatherly interest because the kid reminded him of himself.

Guiltily, he tilted the black-framed picture of his wife, Athena, towards himself on the desk. She was the love of his life. He'd lost all interest in women when she died. All interest in everything, except the game of business: the thing that kept him sane.

His wife's forty-year-old face – so lovely, so classic – stared back at him, frozen in time, in that blessed year before she got sick.

Gently, he calmed himself. He would never take advantage of Dina Kane, teen beauty alone in the big city.

Other guys will do that, said the voice in his head.

'Susan –' he punched his intercom – 'get me the manager of the store at a hundred and twelfth. He's got a new colleague.'

Edward Johnson was a golden boy.

He was in his second year at Columbia – Ivy League – studying pre-med. His plan was to become a plastic surgeon, one of the most upmarket in the city. He wanted offices on Park Avenue and a string of starlets and news anchors begging him to perfect their faces and tits.

Not that he needed money. Edward, smoothly handsome with his dark hair and even features, was an only child. He was close to his mother, Penelope, and stood to inherit everything from his daddy one day – Shelby Johnson was president of the hugely successful Coldharbor Bank. They had a townhouse on Eighty-First Street and Amsterdam, close to Central Park, Zabar's and the best delis in town. Edward had already succeeded to a portion of his trust fund. There would be more when he turned twenty-one.

Edward Johnson liked pretty women. He was clever – the Columbia place proved it – but he was easily bored, too. Finding cute girls to fuck was his hobby. When everybody you knew was rich, how else could a fellow keep score?

Edward's family voted Democrat, like all middle-class New Yorkers, but he was strongly conservative. He believed in social strata. Edward Johnson had been to the right prep school. He worshipped on Sundays at a smart, Presbyterian church. He relished his parents' social acceptability and their place in the world.

After all, wouldn't it be his place too?

Edward dated occasionally – girls with parents like his, girls he treated with respect, took to dinner, to the private dining clubs in town. But he didn't want to get married yet; marriage was for a few years down the line. So dating was nothing special. And if those girls slept with him, neither of them talked about it. Edward was respected. The future was looking good.

No, when he wanted something, he was careful.

Edward Johnson liked downtown girls – girls he picked up in late-night clubs; girls he could hit on, working checkout at the supermarket; girls from the bridge-and-tunnel crowd; young Jersey chicks with big hair and big tits and too much make-up; girls he could wine, dine and bang once or twice and then drop without a trace.

'Hell, man, you're a stud.'

'Ed, you are such a player.'

'Jesus! Look at that piece of ass. How does he do it?'

'Watch and learn, boys,' Edward crowed. 'Watch and learn.'

He loved it – the notoriety. They called him a pussy-hound, a babe magnet, a player, the king of clubs.

And if the girls called him, crying, after he dumped them, so what? Edward cut them off. What the fuck? They gave it up; that was their problem.

'Jesus, honey, give it a rest. I'm not interested.'

'What are you bothering me for, Camilla? We're done.'

'Mercedes, you were a one-nighter. OK?'

'No, it's not OK! You bastard! I thought you were different!'

'I don't see no ring on your finger,' he said, with an accent, mocking her. Then he'd laugh and hang up.

Edward felt no guilt. Why should he? The girls were easy – not his problem. They sold themselves for the price of a meal or two in a nice restaurant, some flowers or a bottle of champagne. He was sowing his wild oats, like they used to say, working it out before he got serious. Edward Johnson believed that girls like that – low class, gullible girls – were the natural toys of men like him. They wanted to ride in the fast car with the rich guy, eat at places they could never afford, go to the best clubs in town. And he wanted a lay he could show off to his friends.

'It's the four _F_s,' Edward told the admiring guys who hung around him in the coffee shops as they nursed their hangovers. 'Find 'em, feel 'em, fuck 'em, forget 'em.'

And they all laughed their heads off.

Dina settled into the new job. It was steady pay, and she waitressed on the side.

'But you're a junior manager,' her boss, Mike, told her. 'You don't have to be out front.'

'I need the tips.' Dina smiled. 'And besides, that way I can hear what the customers are saying.'

She did everything she could. Showed up on time, worked hard, smiled, tried to remember the regulars. On the plus side, she was finally making her rent. There were no more night shifts and every couple of weeks, she could afford to take the subway out to Westchester to visit her brother at college. But she was no closer to her dream. With rent and food, she was still tapped out. College seemed a world – galaxies – away.

And Dina was frustrated. Helping run a coffee house like this was about half of a white-collar job. She did some accountancy, double-checked the takings, wrote up careful reports on what pastries did and didn't sell. But after she'd supervised staff – getting them to show up on time, be polite, follow procedures – there wasn't too much left to do.

Dimitri and Gil had *listened* to her. She'd made things happen at the Greek diner; she'd been innovative. But Mount Java was already a major company. It was expanding nationwide and Alex Markos didn't need much from her. There was only room to execute his ideas well – not bring in her own.

Dina knew she wanted more. Was she ungrateful? She hoped not. She was learning, soaking it up like a sponge. The simple importance of quality was what Markos's store taught her. They imported the best beans, ground them finer than most, used all-natural flavourings and changed the water often. That was the secret – sound expensive; be fresher than the other guy.

But what the customers didn't seem to get was that they were paying for flavoured water. And water was cheap.

It cost two dollars extra to go from regular to large, and less than a hundredth of a cent to pay for the extra coffee in the cup. The recycled cardboard cost more. But the range of flavours gave their shop an edge . . . Customers wanted to try walnut coffee, or Irish cream, or cinnamon. And through the seasons, Java brought in special-edition flavours: spiced apple in the fall, ginger nut in winter, Easter chocolate in the spring, raspberry in summer. The customers came back to the store, just for the special editions. They loved the idea, the brand.

Dina made sure her store was meticulously clean, that there were no scuffs on the burgundy leather seats. People bought luxury and, even if you couldn't afford a cashmere sweater or an Aston Martin, you could afford a warm cup of Java Mountain coffee, brewed fresh with Madagascar vanilla, served in a chic, recycled, green cup with the red mountain logo.

Dina learned. But she was stuck.

She applied to join the higher-management programme. Maybe the way to get on here was in the central company. But her application came back, struck through.

Employee employed for only four months. More experience required.

She didn't hear again from Alexander Markos. And, after three months of pouring and smiling and serving little pastries, Dina was starting to feel trapped.

One thing made it worse. Much worse.

At Mount Java, Dina served a good cross-section of New York: alpha males in their business suits, who stopped by at seven for a latte to take in the cab; mothers, who congregated after drop-off and before pick-up; lunchtime dieters, who didn't do lunch but stimulated their system with caffeine, not calories. But the crowd that hurt her feelings came in after the others had left, or in the dead hours – eleven o'clock in the morning, half-ten. Breakfast, for them.

College kids, either nursing hangovers, or recovering from pulling an all-nighter.

They liked the drinks large and sweet, full of punch. Dina would bring the cups to the table, smiling and chatting, and all the time dying inside. Those privileged girls were her age and just a little older. They had long glossy hair and Columbia scarves and sweatshirts. Carrying piles of books, dark folders and yellow legal pads, they laughed and talked to each other, placing their orders without eye contact, as if Dina was invisible.

Dina *felt* invisible, because they were going somewhere and she was not. They were on their way to the courthouse, the surgery theatre, the museum, the investment bank.

And she was serving them coffee.

Every day it beat up in her head an endless rhythm of shame and failure.

I've got to get on, Dina thought. *Got to get out.*

The college boys didn't see her as invisible. Goddamn, they were obnoxious.

'Hey baby. Get that cute ass over here.'

'What time do you get off, sweetie? I can get *you* off.'

'Honey, you want to earn the biggest tip of your life? Give me your phone number . . .'

Sometimes she had to swallow back tears. It was so hard, but she needed the job. Needed to make rent. Had no place else to go.

Dina didn't think about love. Not yet. Maybe one day she would meet somebody, settle down, get married. But the boys and men that catcalled and whistled didn't want a date. They wanted a lay.

The memory of her mom burned fiercely in Dina's heart: the cars, the laughter, the aging playgirl, drunk and drugged – available for rich, powerful men.

That wasn't going to be her. Dina hoped that one day a man would come, a guy who would blow her away, reduce her to rubble.

Trouble was, she didn't find men that impressive. Nobody had stepped up in her mother's life. Her darling brother was a flake. And the boys at school had been scared of being unpopular.

At seventeen, Dina Kane had learned the hard way.

Only rely on yourself.

'You want to hang out with me, sweetcakes?'

His name was George Linden, and he was one of the most persistent college boys. With a daddy in the oil business in Texas, bright blond hair and a footballer's physique, he could pick up almost any girl he wanted.

'Your coffee's coming right up,' Dina said, brightly. She hated him and his group of hangers-on, the boys that would crowd around the golden god and cackle at everything he said. She pivoted on one heel, back to the kitchen.

'Goddamn, that's a beautiful view,' Linden said loudly. 'I could watch that ass all day.'

'Mike –' Dina spat it out to the manager as he handed her the pitcher and the stoneware mugs – 'aren't you going to throw them out?'

'Come on, Dina. College is a big part of the store.' Mike shrugged; he hadn't liked having a teenage junior manager forced on him. As far as he was concerned, she wanted tips, so she was still just a glorified waitress. *He* didn't serve up coffees. 'You don't have to wait tables, you know. It's a choice.'

A choice she needed for rent. 'Sure. Right.' Dina gritted her teeth. She moved back to the table with the coffee, set it down, careful not to bend over too much at the waist. The dark pencil skirt of her uniform set her ass off nicely, and she hated the way the frat boys ogled and stared.

'Here's your coffee. Pastries?'

'No, baby. You've got all the sweetness I want right here,' Linden cackled. 'Do you serve private parties? Me and the boys are having one on Saturday.'

'Jesus, George! Cut it out.'

Dina lifted her head, blinking back tears, to see one of their number remonstrating loudly with his friend. He was slim and dark, with an intense look about him. 'You're such a giant douche bag,' he said, before turning to Dina. 'I apologise for our friend over here. He's a loser. When confronted with an actual

59

live woman, as opposed to a computer screen, he falls apart.'

More laughter, but now the group had turned on George. Dina flushed with relief as they looked away from her, jostling the blond kid.

'Hey, fuck you, Edward.' Linden jumped up and pushed his way out of the group, storming out of the store.

'I apologise again. He was raised in a barn. Evidently.'

'Thank you, sir,' Dina replied, quietly, and moved away.

When the gang of students left, Dina found a twenty-dollar tip on their table, and a note.

I'm so sorry about that incident. I'm embarrassed. Yours ever, Edward Fielding.

There was a business card attached, with a cellphone number.

Dina took the twenty bucks. She didn't call the number.

At the end of her shift the next lunchtime, her dark-haired saviour from the other day was waiting for her.

'Miss Kane?'

Dina jumped out of her skin. What was his name? Edward . . . *Fielding*, that was it.

'Yes?' she said.

She felt a little safer dressed in her dark coat, her black trousers, blouse and sweater – a better New York winter uniform than that tight skirt and pumps.

'I'm sorry, I didn't mean to startle you. I was wondering if I could see you for a second.'

'How did you know my name?'

'I asked the store manager. I hope that's OK.'

Dina looked at him warily. He was handsome, and wearing a thick brushed-wool coat over what looked like a bespoke suit. His shirt had gold cufflinks, and the shoes and watch were expensive. But he was looking at her humbly.

'I got your apology, Mr Fielding. Thanks for saying what you said. It's all right now.'

'I'd like to take you out to dinner.'

Another come-on. Her eyes clouded. 'No, thanks.'

Gently, he put his hand on her arm. 'Not as an apology. I'm asking you for a date. Really. After your hours. I've seen you work and deal with all the bullshit. I'd like to have a meal with you tonight. Or see a movie. Anything, really.'

Dina hesitated.

'Not if you don't want to,' he said, falling back. 'I don't mean to harass you any further.'

She thought about it. He was smoothly good-looking, slim, confident. Not her normal style, but . . . who was she kidding? She worked so hard she didn't even *have* a normal style. There hadn't been more than a handful of dates at school – all disastrous. Dina had always thought she'd meet someone at college. Only, she wasn't going to college. Edward Fielding was, though. And he liked her . . .

'Maybe a dinner wouldn't hurt. Sure, I guess.'

'Do you live round here?'

'Downtown.' She gave him the address.

'I'll pick you up at eight.'

He was there punctually, knocking on her door. He didn't bring flowers, which Dina appreciated. That would have been cheesy.

'Wow!' Edward glanced around the inside of her apartment. 'Stylish.'

'You can come in for a second.' Dina was wearing a simple red dress, one of her favourites: DKNY and bought at Saks in the sale. She loved the way it clung to her curves, sat at the knee. This was the first chance she'd had to show off her style since she left her mom's house.

Dina Kane had no jewels, and needed none. Her dark hair was piled on top of her head, swept up in a regal up-do. She wore heels with a platform and a rounded toe, mid-height, and carried a small hand-held purse in dark green mock crocodile.

He looked her up and down. 'Nice.'

Her elegance was one thing – almost incongruous on that young body – but her face was something else. Edward was used to the pretty girl at the café, rushed off her feet, her face almost make-up free, like a weapon against the catcalls. Tonight she had paid attention to her beauty – a wash of tinted moisturiser, sheer against that teenage skin; a slick of bronzer, high on her cheekbones; glittering golden shadow with bronze liner and unusual navy mascara that made her huge eyes stand out. On her lips, there was a pale golden-brown gloss. She looked almost Egyptian, like a supermodel, like somebody else.

Edward Johnson – a.k.a. Fielding – was taking an inventory of the night so far. His dumb-ass friends were like a bull in a china shop. You couldn't get a chick like this just by calling her out. She would need *work*, more than the average bridge-and-tunnel skirt.

Right now, he was totally sure she was worth it.

Dina Kane was full of surprises. She did some management work at the coffee shop – so she was not just a waitress. This apartment, well, it was the size of a postage stamp, but the interior looked like it had been designed by a pro. There was space to stretch; it was clean, bright, popped with colour. The dress looked great on those curves. The up-do was classy. The make-up . . . Well, she was transformed; she was a supermodel.

Edward had a brief moment of doubt. Wasn't this a different girl? One he could take home to Momma?

Then he put it aside. Mixed relationships didn't do well. Dina Kane was a glorified waitress. She had attitude in that shop. There was a bet on as to who would bang her first. He was about to win that bet.

The fellows had been throwing themselves right at her for *months*. Pulling this chick would seal his college legend. Nobody had even got to first base with Dina.

Watch and learn, boys. Watch and learn.

'The apartment is beautiful – but not nearly as beautiful as you.'

She smiled slightly. It annoyed him how she lifted that chin, took his compliments for granted. She wasn't *grateful*. She, a waitress, was treating Edward Johnson as her equal. Not for long.

'Shall we go?' he asked.

The first night he kept it low-key: dinner in a semi-nice Italian restaurant; a chaste kiss at the door to thank her for a lovely evening.

The next day, he sent over flowers: a small bunch of yellow roses – nothing spectacular.

Wednesday, he asked her out again. They watched a movie, laughed about it on the way home. He asked her about herself, and drifted into his own thoughts when she answered.

On Saturday, another dinner – French, this time. Edward could be patient. One false move and the game was up.

Dina was incredibly beautiful. Each night, she made herself up so differently, yet always the same pretty face; it was like dating a thousand girls.

He almost regretted that the game was nearly over.

'You seem happy,' Mike said, suspiciously.

This wasn't the Dina Kane he knew. She was less of a robot, moving around with a smile on her face. She'd started to take her lunchbreaks, sitting with a cup of cinnamon coffee and reading those crumpled little notes her boyfriend sent her.

Even in the daytime, she had begun to wear cosmetics. His male clientele was slowly enlarging. Moms liked to be around her, too. Now their restaurant wasn't just super-efficient, it was cheerful.

'I am happy.'

'The new man? Who *is* this lucky guy?' Mike asked.

'It's a mystery. I could tell you, but I'd have to kill you.' And Dina laughed.

After three weeks, Edward made his move. They had been kissing; first on the cheek, then the lips, then a little tongue. She was nervous, ungainly. He liked that; it made him laugh. What if she was a virgin? Dina Kane was the trophy of the year in his set. If he popped her cherry too . . . Christ, they would have to set up a statue for him.

He did it right: dinner at a local restaurant downtown; lots of talk about family. He said he might like to meet her brother, her mom. Yeah, right – the Johnsons didn't socialise with those kinds of people. Daddy was going to run for Congress next year; he had all the donors lining up. Momma was a socialite and only mixed with exactly the right group. She threw benefit dinners to help people like the Kanes. The thought made him laugh.

Edward Johnson was never going to mix with the Kanes.

Dina should be flattered that she was getting any attention at all from him. She was the finest piece of ass out there on the scene for months, a trophy lay, and so he was doing something unfamiliar: he was actually putting *work* into her.

He asked around among the other waiters, offering a few twenties here and there, and he'd soon found out a lot of what he needed to know. Dina came from Tuckahoe, Westchester. She had been a good student, no boyfriends, the daughter of a dead, drunk workman. Her mother had fucked around with some Italian boys for a while. He liked that idea; it made him kind of hard, knowing her weakness. Hey, she had that prissy attitude, but the apple doesn't fall far from the tree. Edward fantasised about fucking Dina, breaking her in and getting the credit, then maybe passing her around his friends. Girls like her and her mom were just hookers by another name. You dressed up the tips with dinners and flowers, but in the end they were leisure activities for powerful men. Edward Johnson considered himself just that – a powerful man, in training. Hunting the stuck-up waitress was just too much fun.

He thought about her slutty mother, and smiled.

'I'd like you to meet my family.' Dina was acting shy; it was sexy. 'And you can take me to meet yours . . . I'd like to say hello to the Fieldings.'

She still hadn't twigged to the false name. That was the beauty of it. He paid restaurant bills in cash, always plenty of cash, and he'd bought a cheap phone he would throw away after tonight, so no harassing calls on his mobile. Once he'd banged Dina, the boys would stop showing up at the coffee shop. There was no Edward Fielding lodged at Columbia, so she couldn't find him there. She would never see him again. No harm done.

'I told Mom about you last night. She's looking forward to cooking for you.' Edward chuckled to himself. His mom hadn't picked up a frying pan since her wedding night. She just gave the menus to the cook.

Dina smiled, relaxed. 'It's so good that you respect me like this, Edward.'

'Why wouldn't I?' Respect her? Funniest thing ever. He couldn't wait to slip into that tight little pussy. Now he just needed to close the deal. He flashed her that bright smile. 'Let's celebrate. Waiter? Can I get a bottle of champagne for the table? Veuve Cliquot – perfect.'

Dina hoped she didn't look drunk.

She rarely took in alcohol. So three glasses of champagne and she was weaving.

Edward was being so nice . . . so sweet. He paid for everything; he told her all about his worries in class. Now he wanted to bring her to his parents.

They were going back to her apartment. She felt light, happy.

The wine ran round her bloodstream, warming her, taking away the fear.

Dina glanced over at Edward. He was tall, aristocratic, slim. But she didn't feel any desire for him . . . That undeveloped body. Was that normal? Was she normal?

She was eighteen. Most of the girls at school had sex long ago. Maybe it was time. She trusted Edward, and they'd been dating almost a month, a few times each week. Wasn't that how you were supposed to do it?

Perhaps it was always this way. Virgins probably didn't feel any desire, didn't actually ever want the guy. The way the TV showed it, it was always the husbands trying to get the wives into bed. Like sex was not something women wanted. Perhaps this was normal, the price you paid.

Dina wanted to be like other girls – to have a nice boyfriend.

Edward stopped at her door and slipped his arm around her. Dina tried not to shrink back when he thrust his tongue into her mouth.

'Can I come in?' he asked, softly. 'Be with you tonight?'

She shuddered, and he took it as lust.

'OK,' Dina said. 'Sure. Sure, Edward.'

Yes. He was her boyfriend, and this was the price.

Dina lay in her bed, looking at the ceiling. Wanting to cry.

She hated this sex – hated the pain when he penetrated her, hated how unaroused she felt, hated his weird smile as he moved on top of her. There was blood on her thighs and all she could think about was getting into the shower.

'Oh, this is great. You're so hot,' Edward said, gasping. 'You're so sexy . . .'

'Mmm,' Dina managed. She just wanted him to get it over with.

'You like this, baby. You like it, don't you?'

Dina could hardly say, *No.*

He was thrusting on top of her with a strange, triumphal smile. 'A virgin . . . God . . . you're a virgin . . . That's a shock.'

Dina gasped, looking at him.

'Popped your cherry!' he grunted, his face contorted in a weird laugh. He wasn't even looking at her, just staring at the wall. 'Popped your fucking cherry! Bet you can't wait to get banged again. Jesus! You're so fucking tight.' He gasped, grinned. 'Don't worry, baby; I'll give you a great review . . .'

She twisted, moaning in pain. 'What the hell are you talking about? What do you mean?'

'It's what all you bridge-and-tunnel girls like. Just like your momma, aren't you? She fucked around. Yeah, spread those legs for me, baby.'

Dina shrieked, tried to force him off her. But he was a dead weight. She couldn't move him. She was pushing against concrete.

'My momma? Edward, what the hell—?'

'Fucking around with the Italians. After your pops died. That's a great reputation, right there. Town slut. She lives nice, right?' He thrust. 'You treat me and my friends right, and we'll take care of you, too. No more attitude; your pussy's opened up now . . . Oh, oh, *God* . . .' He gasped. 'Dina! So fucking hot.' Then he grunted, went limp and collapsed on her.

Dina moaned in distress, tears springing to her eyes.

'Yeah, you loved it,' Edward said. He rolled off her before she could push him again.

'Edward . . .' she said, sobbing. 'What was that? What do you know about my mom? Why are you talking about me that way?'

She was hot, dehydrated, her head spinning from the wine. Did that happen? Did he turn into that grinning, taunting monkey, grinding away on top of her? She wanted to be sick.

He rolled his eyes. 'Let's not *talk*. Why do girls always want to talk? I'm going to sleep, OK?'

In seconds, he had fallen asleep, mouth open, like a large wet fish. Dina crawled out of bed and showered in her tiny stall. Then she dried off and crept back under the covers.

Maybe she was frigid. It felt horrible, felt so wrong. What the hell was he doing? Was that just dirty talk? It was like he'd turned into someone else – someone new and evil.

Dina's head pounded. Hell, had she imagined it? Was she just drunk?

At least . . . at least she had a boyfriend, a relationship. She would get to know Edward's family – hadn't he said that? Maybe she'd misheard him. Maybe it would get better . . .

After a while, feeling ashamed, nasty, dirty and exhausted, the alcohol lulled her into a fitful sleep.

Dina woke before the sun was up. She rolled over in her bed. Then she realised she'd rolled over.

Edward was gone.

All morning, his words rattled in her head: *Popped your cherry . . . Just like your momma . . . Town slut.* Dina wanted to tell herself that it was the hangover, that he never said it. But she knew it had happened. And her body, already tense and bruised, had writhed in rejection, while he laughed and kept pumping.

She made excuses: it was some twisted fantasy – erotic talk; he would never be that way; he'd call, explain, take her to lunch with his mother. Everything would be OK.

Dina waited for her phone to ring. It didn't. That was weird, but she had work to do . . . Maybe he was ill. She went to the coffee shop, but none of the boys came in, none of Edward's friends.

By lunchtime, she was worried. She called his mobile.

This number is not in service. Please check the number, and try again.

'Hey, Dina.' Mike was looking at her. 'What are you doing? The books need checking from last night.'

'Oh. Nothing. Sorry, Mike.'

Dina scurried into the back office, feeling sick. She tried the number again; got the same result.

By five o'clock, she knew something was wrong. She called the college and asked to be put through to Edward Fielding.

'We have no students here of that name.'

Hands shaking, Dina pulled out Edward's card, the original one he'd given her. She typed up a quick email: *Edward – where are you? D.*

In seconds, it bounced back to her: *Mailer Daemon. Address not valid.*

Numbly, she worked through her shift. Edward . . . whoever he was had had sex with her and disappeared.

It was as old as time, and she was just that stupid.

Dumb waitress. Plaything. Just like Mom.

Dina ran into the bathroom, sank to her knees and threw up. Somewhere, he was laughing at her.

'Dude, you're so full of it.' George Linden saw a way to get his own back. 'There is no way she gave it up to you.'

The boys laughed. Edward looked at them – Ralph and Charlie, Gideon and Homer – he despised them, really. They were minions, who backed up the winner of the moment in the battles for supremacy between him and George. 'Sure she did. Right on her back, legs splayed.' He smirked. 'Sweet little cherry, too.'

'Bullshit, man. Nobody was getting shit from that chick.'

Edward was annoyed. This was the first time anybody had called his prowess into question. He'd given up the idea of passing her round as soon as he'd come inside her; the irritating wriggles of protest and teary eyes told him she wouldn't be hooking herself out like he wanted. But, no matter, he'd fucked her, and that was what counted. And now he was supposed to be getting his props, dammit, not taking shit from George Linden.

'I banged her.'

George lifted his eyebrows, annoyingly. 'Show us the photos, then.'

'Jesus, man! She was lying right next to me.'

'And you didn't snap a quick shot of that sweet ass? Come on, Ed. Give it up.'

He coloured. 'I'll show you, you prick. Let's go have a coffee.'

Ralph lifted a brow. 'I thought we couldn't go in there again.'

'Just once. Apparently Georgie here needs proof. What are they going to do? Ban me because the waitress opened her legs?'

'Fine.' Linden was a little red now, too. 'I *don't* believe you. Let's see how she reacts.'

'I'm not drinking the coffee, though.' Edward was light now, giddy at the thought of showing off. 'Bet she spits in it.'

'Hey, Dina.' Mike was on her case again, but she didn't mind. For two days, Dina had been working numbly, trying to get through it.

She felt so dumb – so used, so humiliated. Edward Fielding – whatever his real name was – had just fucked her and vanished. After all the catcalls she'd brushed off, all the hooting men, this rich kid was patient for a couple of weeks, and she fell for it . . .

She didn't even like him. Didn't want him. And this would be the story of her virginity for the rest of her life . . .

Just like your momma. Town slut.

'Yes, Mike?' She was mopping down the counter in the back. Her rage and shame needed channelling. Dina had called the landlord of her building yesterday and made him an offer, a low offer, for her apartment. He'd accepted . . . Last time he saw the place, it was a grubby little dive.

She had a mortgage lined up. Credit was easy, and Dina had a plan. No income verification, a couple of points extra on the interest rate, but it didn't matter. The landlord wanted to close this month and Dina was more than willing. Her tiny savings would be the deposit, and she would flip it as soon as the ink was dry.

She didn't want to live where Edward had been. She didn't want him to be able to find her. The shame was so intense, she didn't even want this job.

One day, he might come back . . .

She polished the countertop aggressively. And, just as she was thinking about it . . .

'Your boyfriend,' Mike said, with a smile.

Dina froze. She put the cloth down, carefully. 'What?'

'Over there. With his friends. Ready to make up, I expect . . . ?'

She didn't rise to the question. Screw him; what business was it of his?

'Thanks.' Dina moved to look, her heart thumping. Maybe she had Edward all wrong. Maybe he'd been injured, in an accident, got sick and was here now to make it right . . .

He was there in the corner, sitting at his usual table with that group of goons all around him – including the one that had barracked her, the guy Edward apologised for. What was his name . . . ? George Linden.

George was born in a barn . . .

Only now they were sitting together and laughing.

Like nothing happened.

Rage surged up in her, so intense, so white hot, she had to steady herself against the counter for a minute. She was dizzy.

'You going to take their order?'

'Sure. Just a second.' Dina picked up a pot of coffee.

'That's old. Get a fresh one.'

'It's fine,' she said. She marched away from Mike, towards the table. Edward was sitting there, looking nasty, laughing and leering at her.

'Hey, Dina,' he said, and the other boys nudged him and cackled under their breath. 'How you been?'

'Can I get you something?' she said, coldly.

'Now, don't get an attitude. Just because I didn't call after sex . . .' He shrugged, laughed. 'You were up for it. How was I to know you were still a virgin?'

The eyes of his companions opened with shock. One of them laughed aloud, then comically clapped a hand in front of his mouth. They were all staring at her, the pack of them, raking their eyes over her like she was naked.

The anger crystallised to a white-hot point in her.

'Hey, somebody had to pop that cherry. Be thankful it was a nice guy like me.'

'Jesus, you fucking dog,' George Linden said, with reluctant admiration.

And then they all laughed – all the college boys, the Ivy Leaguers, laughing at the coffee-shop girl with her high-school diploma and the face of a sucker.

Dina forced herself to wait till the cackling died down.

'Don't worry, Edward; I know why you didn't call. You shouldn't be *that* embarrassed. I hear it happens to a lot of guys. Especially drunks.'

'Wait, what?' George Linden asked.

'He is Edward, right? That fake card . . . Classy touch, though. What's your real name?'

'Edward Johnson,' one of the other frat boys blurted out.

'Shut the fuck up, Ralph,' said Edward.

'Johnson by name; Johnson by nature,' Ralph said. 'But you'd know all about that, wouldn't you, miss?' And they all laughed again.

'Actually, not so much – Ralph. See, Edward here couldn't actually get it up. I really felt bad for him, at least at first.' Dina smiled brightly. 'He was crying in the bathroom, but then, he was pretty out of it.'

'You lying bitch! We fucked,' Edward snarled.

'Honey, you weren't fucking *anything*. I've seen stiffer plates of Jell-O.'

More laughter. They were really amused now, looking at Edward, enjoying the tennis match.

'I took your virginity. You were a slut, like all the others,' Edward spat. 'Like your mom.'

Dina swallowed her hatred and forced a sympathetic-looking smile, instead.

'Maybe next time lay off the vodka. Or get some Viagra.'

'Hey, sugar, give me a try,' George Linden leered. 'I won't let you down like Edward.'

'Any problems here?' Mike arrived. He looked critically at Dina. These customers spent money in his store – lots of it.

'No problems. Just a bunch of rich, arrogant bastards with dicks the size of maggots,' Dina said.

The laughter stopped cold.

'Jesus! You can't speak to them like that,' Mike said.

'I just did. Step back a second, Mike.' Her voice was so fierce, he actually backed away. 'These boys just need to cool down,' Dina said, and she lifted the coffee pot high and started to pour it all over them. Black, warm, scented coffee flowed over Edward, over George, over Ralph, ruining their clothes, staining their hair.

'Fuck!'

'Bitch!'

'Fucking psycho!'

'I'll sue you,' Edward Johnson hissed. 'This is fucking *assault*!'

'You're fired!' Mike shrieked at Dina's departing back. She had already untied the strings of her apron and let it slither to the floor.

'No,' she said, without turning round. 'I already quit.'

Edward Johnson, dripping, jumped to his feet. His friends were laughing at him. He was soaked. The suit was ruined. Instead of celebrating his triumph, they were all pissed off. And worse – he looked *foolish*.

Edward hated to be thought a fool. It was his biggest fear – being mocked, ridiculed. He'd come in, just for a minute, for a light-hearted poke at the stupid waitress, and now this.

She was in the back room, changing. Her boss was at the table, trying to calm the fellows down, offering to pay for their dry-cleaning. Bad publicity, lawsuits, a small item in the *Post* – he didn't want any of it.

Edward waited until Dina emerged, minus her uniform, wearing her plain back pants and the tight sweater. She looked great, like he remembered. He hated her.

'Bitch!' He reached out and gripped her arm. 'You'll pay for that. I know where you live.'

Dina shook herself free.

Edward glared at her, bitterly. 'I'm coming to get you,' he threatened. 'Believe it.'

She smiled – and, for the first time that night, it reached her eyes. 'Oh, no, Mr Johnson, you don't understand. I'm coming to get *you*.'

Chapter Five

Shelby Johnson was having a wonderful evening.

His lecture series was going down so well. The students and young people were lapping it up. He loved to talk about his foundation, his charity work and his vision for the state. What they weren't doing up in Albany. How all New York's vast wealth never reached the poorest . . .

Of course, Shelby knew all about vast wealth. His charities were tax-efficient write-offs. Coldharbor Bank, where he was president, was doing so well; it was a private haven for the society rich, who all knew him socially. He had a marvellous wife who threw the most wonderful parties, and he arrived at all these events in his personal limousine, complete with vanity plates.

He hadn't announced for Congress yet; that was coming next week.

Frankly, the party machine didn't know what had hit it. He was just smarter than them – smarter than the lot of them, the striving State Senators and pushy little judges and district attorneys who thought they had a shot at the big time.

Shelby was self-financed. He didn't have to raise money – he could just write a cheque.

He had business success – a real track record.

And he'd donated to others long enough to have built up that reservoir of good will. People owed him favours, and Shelby was coming to collect.

This tour was the warm-up act. Nothing stirred voters' hearts like education, not here in New York. And Shelby loved receiving the adulation of the students and the educators. When he jumped on the platform at these community colleges or youth centres, they applauded like he was some kind of rock star. He especially loved it when the kids asked him for advice.

And if they were pretty girls . . .

His eyes slid across to the co-ed, perched on the back seat of his car. Goddamn. The way she looked at him with such hero-worship . . .

Her name was Laura . . . what was it? Oh, yes. Laura Fielding. She was a student at NYU, and she'd really taken to his politics – so to speak.

First he'd seen her in the front row at the Ninety-Second Street Y community centre. She'd asked a question, and smiled and clapped at his response, bouncing up and down in her seat, those firm little titties bouncing along with her.

Next, it was at the Lincoln Center, a free event, and she hung out afterwards.

'Mr Johnson . . . my name's Laura. Laura Fielding. I so admire your politics. Are you going to run? I'd love to volunteer.'

'Thank you . . .' He nearly said, 'honey,' but stopped himself in time. 'What are your contact details?'

She handed over a number on a piece of paper. That low-cut dress, modest below the knees, but – goddamn – what a pair!

He called that night – nothing special, just sounding her out. She was breathy, full of admiration. He was a great man. She wanted him to run. She wanted to help.

'How can I serve?' she said.

Shelby had invited her to the next event. She helped lay out programmes. She was diligent, and very discreet. She was also totally sexually available.

'I want an older man,' she said. 'Somebody who knows what he's doing.'

'I'm married,' he said, weakly.

She pouted and stuck out those fantastic breasts. 'Come on, Shelby, I can't be the first. Anyway, I want to come along for the *ride*. All the way to Washington.'

He couldn't resist. He didn't want to. And now, here she was, in his limo. His *aide* – in a fantastic short skirt, with old-fashioned stockings high up her thighs, and he could see a glimpse of milky-white flesh like a glimpse of heaven.

'We'll head to the hotel,' he told the driver.

'Oh my God.' He stared at the ceiling, panting. 'That was incredible . . . Unbelievable.'

None of the momentary distractions he'd been with before – and there had been one or two . . . hookers, strip-club hostesses – had given him anything like this amount of pleasure. Her firm, tight young body, the beautiful face . . . Echoes of lust were still throbbing in his groin.

'We have to do it again.' His mind was already on to the next time, the next campaign stop, the next hotel. Shelby indulged his fantasies. After he was elected a hero, she'd be given a nice safe job in his office. Nothing too big, of course, but something to keep her always available. Every powerful man should have a sexy mistress. He flashed on Laura Fielding in a silk blouse, tight pencil skirt, seamed stockings. Sucking on a pencil. Sucking on him. 'Maybe I'll see you next week? At Albany?'

'Oh, I can't come up to Albany.' She was across the room, already getting dressed, briskly pulling on some new clothes – a pair of jeans and a sweater. Not the clinging red number she'd been wearing earlier. Laura Fielding was the perfect lay – you banged her, and then she got right up and got *herself* out of the door. 'I'm busy.'

'When will I see you?' Shelby propped himself up on his elbows, looking after her.

'Don't worry.' Laura wasn't looking at him. 'You'll hear from me soon enough.'

The Johnson townhouse was a sedate fantasy of old money.

Walnut panelling lined the Victorian elevator. There was imported Italian marble in the bathrooms, a maid's apartment in the attic, a private garden and a library.

It was the perfect backdrop for the moneyed politician. Or for a bright young buck, launching himself into society – into the same glorious future his mother and father had enjoyed.

Edward Johnson loved his home. He especially loved how it smelled of his mother – the one perfect woman in the world. As her only child, Penelope Johnson had pampered and spoiled Edward since the day he was born. He loved wandering into her boudoir, drinking in the scent of her powder and rosewater. He loved seeing her dressed in evening gowns, tucking him into bed. He loved watching her give orders to the cook, kiss his father on the cheek and generally behave like the perfect wife. Edward loved perfection and his house and mother were the apex of it.

One day, Mrs Edward Johnson would be a replica of his sainted mother. He adored her and, when his friends called him Mommy's Boy, Edward replied, 'Absolutely!'

He was sitting on the covered terrace at the back of his bedroom, eating stuffed olives and sipping an iced tea. Edward regularly went back home for Sunday lunch; that was the great advantage of Columbia – he didn't need to stay in his student apartment any more than he wanted to.

'Darling! Lunch!' his mother called.

'Coming!' he shouted.

The housekeeper had set up their table al fresco, because his mother preferred to dine in the garden in spring. She was immensely proud of this ritual. Father was back from his travels, electioneering, and the three of them would sit around and chitchat over a glass or two of chilled Chablis, a Waldorf salad and some carved ham.

Shelby Johnson was already sitting down, the *New York Times* sports section laid out in front of him, when Edward arrived. His wife was hovering, wearing a light yellow silk dress and a smug expression. Shelby's ascent in the polling was smooth, her social dominance almost complete.

'Some wine, sir?' A butler hovered as Edward threw himself into his seat.

'Yes. Of course.'

'Oh, you're here, Mr Edward. There's a package for you.' The old housekeeper, Selina, came forward and handed him a manila envelope.

'What's this?' he asked.

'It was hand-delivered earlier, sir. There's one for you, too, Mrs Johnson.'

'Thank you, Selina. That's all for now,' his mother said.

'Wait.' Edward felt the first stirrings of unease. 'Hand-delivered? By whom?'

'A young lady.' The older woman turned to leave.

'Wait!' Edward said, sweating. 'Mom! Don't open that—'

Too late. Penny had already neatly ripped the paper and, as he stared in horror, the large, colourful, glossy pictures poured out – nearly twenty of them. They scattered over the table, across it, spilling everywhere, polluting his eyes.

Shelby Johnson – Edward's father.

Shelby Johnson – Penny's husband.

Shelby Johnson – for Congress.

There he was, in all his elderly glory, ridiculously naked, pink-faced, erect. A young woman was straddling him. Her face was blocked out, cut off, but there was no denying it. Shelby Johnson, handcuffed; Shelby Johnson, gagged; Shelby Johnson, licking a pair of stilettos.

Penny Johnson went ashen.

One of the butlers moved forward, to pick up the shots.

'Get back!' Edward barked. 'Leave it! Leave us!'

'Sir . . . ?'

'Now!'

There was a clatter as all the staff withdrew. Penny Johnson started to wail, a keen, high-pitched shriek.

'I . . . I don't know . . . These are faked . . .'

Shelby was puce, muttering. He felt sick. He was dizzy. He gripped the table, hoping not to faint.

'I need to lie down,' he whimpered.

A small, neatly folded piece of letter paper fluttered out of the dreadful envelope to the paving stones of their terrace. Mechanically, Edward picked it up. His mother snatched it from him, held it in trembling hands. Then she read it aloud – the worst words Edward had ever heard in his life:

'*Since your son fucked me for his amusement, I fucked your husband for mine.*'

There was no signature.

Penny Johnson screamed and ripped up the note. She rounded on Shelby. 'You goddamned bastard!'

'It was a mistake . . .'

But Penny was rifling through the pictures. 'A mistake? A mistake? These will wind up in the press. I'll be a laughing stock!'

Shelby looked, moaned in horror. It was worse than being caught cheating. He was ridiculous – totally ridiculous.

He thought of all his friends, laughing. The nudges at the club. The sly looks in the boardroom.

'I can find her, Mother . . .' Edward said. 'I can get her—'

'Get her? You *got* her already, whoever she is . . . You found the lowest whore in the world.'

'Mother!' His mother was swaying. He rushed to steady her. 'I won't . . . let her do anything . . .'

'Find the bitch. Her name is Laura Fielding,' his father said.

Edward moaned in his throat. *Fielding*. The name he'd used. 'That's not her real name.'

'Just find her. What will it take to buy her off?'

'I don't know,' Edward said.

'Find her.'

He looked. He looked for two days. But she was gone, vanished from his sight. The apartment was locked up – sold, so the super told him, twice in a month.

'She lived here.' A hundred-dollar bill loosened his throat. 'Sure, she bought the apartment from the landlord. Sold it three weeks later. She made a nice profit on it, real nice.' He was admiring. 'I couldn't believe . . . Used to be a dump, before her. That kid is going places.'

Yeah – going to jail. For blackmail.

He rang the coffee shop, but she hadn't gone back since she was fired. There was nothing registered in the phone book. And then, on day four, Edward had a bright idea.

He reconnected his old cellphone – the cheap one he'd bought to woo Dina Kane.

Almost instantly, the text came through. It had been waiting for him:

Missing me? You can call.

He rang the number and left a message. In an hour, she rang him back.

'You fucking bitch!'

'How are you, Edward? Don't tell me you've stopped laughing about our little tryst. I thought you and your friends were so amused by it?'

'What do you want? Money? Isn't that what whores want?' He was vicious in his contempt, his hatred. 'How much will it take?'

Edward's family was already shattered. His mother had demanded a divorce and locked herself in her room, throwing things and drinking. His dad had slunk off to the Pierre hotel. He wanted the nightmare to be over, but the pictures were burned into his brain. He blamed his father, and Shelby blamed him, and Penny was diving into the vodka.

'You think I'd ask for money?'

'We don't want those photos in the press.'

'And?' she replied, coolly.

'How much?' *Name a figure. I'll come after you till the end of time. Whatever it takes.*

'I'm not a blackmailer, Edward. That's a felony.'

He bit his lip; he had been hoping to go to the police. Edward's father had contacts there, lots of them.

'If I send those photos to the press, that's my right – first amendment, and all that stuff.'

'What do you *want*?'

'Nothing. But I'm happy to offer you some advice. If I were your father, I wouldn't run for office, and if I were you, I'd drop out of college. You don't deserve to study when girls like me can't.'

'Drop out of college?' He'd be nothing – a trust-fund brat who couldn't hack it.

'It's your choice, of course, but doesn't your mother need you?'

I hate you, he thought. 'You *are* blackmailing me.'

'Hey, you can ignore the advice if you want, Edward Johnson. Nothing you do will affect how I use the photos – or don't use them. What I want is for you to stay the hell out of my life. Got it?'

She was too clever to fall into his trap. He hated her.

'You used my father like a toy.'

'A toy? Like you used me? And how many other girls?' Dina's voice was ice. 'Was my mother a toy when you went hunting for information about my background, just so you could humiliate me in bed? You said my mom was the town slut. Well, what about your dad? Seems we have something in common, no?' She laughed, and he flinched, hearing the loathing in that sound. 'Get over it, Edward. Volunteer at a homeless shelter. You know – do something useful. Goodbye.'

And she hung up.

Edward Johnson looked at the phone for a long time.

Then he made two calls. By the end of the day, Shelby Johnson was no longer a candidate for office, and Edward Johnson had dropped out of college. He didn't ring Dina Kane to tell her.

He knew she would be checking up.

'You little prick,' Shelby Johnson said.

He stared down at his son, sitting there on the couch in his sterile hotel suite. Behind him, the television news channel had his face on it. His goddamned face – not in triumph, the way it was meant to be when he was elected, but grim, like a mug shot.

Shelby Johnson pulling out of Congressional Race. Shock exit by Shelby Johnson. Johnson leaves family home . . .

The headlines scrolled across the screen like a horrible ribbon of smut beneath the pretty, bland faces of the newsreaders, who were talking about him, talking about his family. His marriage. His disgrace.

'We don't know exactly what happened, Joanne, but we have to speculate that some kind of affair is possible. After all, Mr Johnson left the family home last night.'

'His wife briefly left the house this morning and was seen without her wedding ring.'

'The thought of a Shelby Johnson affair will go down very badly with the Democrats, and his employers, Coldharbor Bank, are known to be extremely cautious with their image in the community . . .'

He wanted to switch it off, but he couldn't. They were talking about him, and he was rubbernecking at his own car crash.

'Don't blame me, Pop. I'm not married.'

Shelby grimaced. Penelope was out of control, screeching at him. She wouldn't let him home and he didn't even want to go back. Facing the world seemed impossible. The Democrats wanted him to give a press conference. A press conference!

The thought of those pictures – him, tied down on the bed, legs spread, humbled, into bondage . . . Oh, God. He thought he would kill himself, except he was too cowardly for that.

'But you provoked her, didn't you?'

'I couldn't tell that she was a bunny boiler.' Edward loosened his collar. 'It's your fault; you gave her something to work with; you gave her the photos. The first piece of skirt to throw herself at you and you're off . . . You've humiliated Momma . . .'

'Please don't try to play the moralist with me.' Anger suffused him – at the girl, Edward, his screaming, drunken wife, himself. What the hell? Other men did it, even powerful men – *especially* powerful men, so they said – letting hookers tie them up. But they were *careful*. He hadn't been. It was all over. 'I've lost all the work I put in.' He mopped a tissue over his brow, sweating. The photos loomed in his mind again, as though they were already splashed over page one of the *Post*. 'You're such a self-righteous little jerk, Edward. You've never done a stroke of work in your life. It's my fault; I gave you too much. You should have been working a job this summer, not chasing pussy at some fucking coffee shop. Your grades were dire before this, anyway.'

Shelby thought of the awful phone call, worse by far than his wife's demented crying, from Conrad Peterson, Chairman of Coldharbor. 'We don't think you should resign. Just retire, Shelby. It's better this way, wouldn't you say? So many clients want discretion these days, not scandal, nothing flashy in the bank . . . What did you tell me? Others want publicity; Coldharbor runs from it.'

He hadn't said too much. A call to the lawyers first, perhaps. They couldn't fire him for having an affair. There was no morals clause in his contract.

But, whatever he thought, the ghastly image of the photos . . . being released in the press, passed round at work . . . sniggers, maybe a *bringing the bank into disrepute* line.

Jesus. He didn't know what to do. Shelby hated everybody in the world right now, and his feckless, entitled son most of all. *Edward brought this on him.*

'What are you going to do?' Edward asked.

'Do? What the hell can I do?' Shelby paced. 'Take retirement from the bank, I suppose. Work out a divorce settlement with your mother.'

'Divorce! You have to fight to get her back!'

Shelby rounded on his son. 'Do I? She hasn't exactly stood by me, after one goddamned mistake, has she? She threw me out! No. You know what, Edward? I don't think I owe either of you anything.' He imagined Dina Kane, as he now knew she was called: that firm young body, the ripeness of it. Compared to his wife's ultra-thin, waspish, menopausal flesh . . . Christ, why *should* he try to get her back? The loss of money, of status, of his political dreams – it was all bad enough. He couldn't tolerate months of apologies to Penny as well, just to be allowed back to that sterile bed.

'It'll blow over, Dad.'

'Not soon enough. When is she releasing the damned pictures?'

Edward ran his hands through his hair. 'I don't know. Maybe tomorrow, maybe never, if we give her what she wants: me leaving school; you leaving the race for Congress.'

'I wish she'd just get it over with. And she wouldn't take money?'

He shook his head. 'I offered.'

Shelby thought about it. Leaving, leaving . . . He still had some cards to play. Give Penny the house; take most of the cash. There was an irrevocable trust – she could live off that. He could offer Coldharbor a deal, too – a quiet exit in exchange for an extra couple of million on top of his retirement fund.

It was possible to disappear without resorting to suicide. Florida – it had year-round sun, very few bankers – he was always advising middle-class clients to buy mansions there. The Homestead laws meant your principal residence couldn't be touched, even if you went bankrupt and it was a six-acre palace with a pool.

Plus, nobody there knew him. In his current world, Florida was déclassé. The social registry preferred California for a winter haven – something chic in Malibu. He saw himself living large on half the money – living better, really – a pool, properly divorced, some good therapy, a few nubile girlfriends. And no fucking photos. It was an escape route, a fresh start at almost sixty.

Why the hell not? Let Edward make his own way. No family firm. No handouts. Penny would get the house and plenty for her needs.

He made his decision. Let them all rant and rave, he was going to drop out – in a very moneyed, sun-filled manner.

'The photos are of me. The marriage is over, Edward. You need to stand on your own feet. I'm going to call your mother tonight – or at least her lawyers – and offer a quick settlement.'

'But where will you go?' Edward yelped. 'What will happen to *me*?'

'You're an adult. Make your own decisions,' he said. God, how had he raised this snivelling wimp that wanted his hand held, even now? 'You should have thought about it before dumping on the mad girl. I'm going to leave the state. Nobody really knows me outside of New York. I will retire and go to Florida. And find myself, in peace.'

Damn, if it didn't sound noble, put like that . . . For a moment his mood lightened a little. Perhaps that vicious little tramp had done him a favour, after all.

Dina Kane smiled to herself. The photos were already erased from the memory card, the camera dumped from a car somewhere off the New Jersey turnpike. She'd bought a prepaid phone and called Edward from that – it was in a dumpster two minutes after their conversation.

Now, maybe, it was all over. Now, at last, she could have some peace.

Sleeping with Shelby had been disgusting. But, every second, she'd kept in mind the grinning, mocking face of his son, the way he'd threatened to pass her around his friends, like a piece of meat, called her mom the 'town slut', turned sex into rape, shoving himself deeper, even as she struggled to push him off her. Edward Johnson: a privileged yob who stood for every man who'd ever leered at, drooled over or assaulted her – the guards who'd felt her up in Don Angelo's gatehouse, the boss who'd let her be abused, as long as it kept the customers happy.

Dina no longer believed in love. Revenge was a much more achievable goal. She wasn't going to send those pictures any-where. Just let them sweat; let them all sweat – cheating, lying Shelby; Penny, who raised that pig of a son; and, most of all, Edward, who treated her like a joke.

I just want to level the field.

Shelby would be divorced – his political dreams over. She didn't want a rich, arrogant bastard like him anywhere near the halls of power.

Penny Johnson . . . Dina shrugged to herself. A woman who associated with these assholes was not her problem. There were lots of good divorce lawyers out there . . . And she was better off out of that fake marriage, anyway.

And Edward, the arrogant college boy who'd used her while she slaved just to make the rent. If there was no college for Dina, there would be none for him, either.

Edward Johnson screwed her. Now she'd screwed him back. It was time to move on, to put this behind her.

And Dina truly believed it would be that easy.

Chapter Six

Dina wanted a new start. With the profit from the sale of her studio, she had enough for a small nest egg and a deposit on a cute one-bedroom apartment. It was east of Fifth, but that was OK. Dina liked the neighbourhood, still home to artists, singers, poverty-stricken film-makers and their grim documentaries. The West Village was way too expensive; bankers and movie stars lived there now. But the East Village had its vintage clothing dens, its middle-eastern restaurants and its comic-book stores.

The fashionista in Dina loved it. It was up and coming – like she wanted to be.

The one-bedroom was another fixer-upper. She would insert a mezzanine platform – the ceilings were high – and sell it in six months as 'split level'. If she kept flipping like this, Dina thought, she could have money, real money, by the time she was twenty-one.

But, of course, a job would help.

No more coffee – she was through with waiting tables.

She thought about fashion, but starving new designers couldn't pay her anything and the glossy magazines were full of unpaid interns whose fathers came from the same social scene as Shelby Johnson. Dina experimented with photography, but she had no talent for it.

She hit the New York Public Library. It was no good trying to work her way up; she needed a qualification – some kind of badge. She knew she was good at investing in property and there were night classes to become a realtor, so Dina enrolled.

As ever, the nest egg wouldn't last. She would have to work to support her studying, but she wanted something better than waitressing. Maybe something secretarial . . . At least she could type . . .

The Green Apothecary was a certain type of store: one that did well in the East Village. It was small enough to keep the bills down, and it catered to freaks.

Dina Kane fitted right in.

'Do you like this brand?'

Dina glanced up. It was Hector Green, the old man with a German accent, who owned the store.

'I love it,' she said, honestly, turning over the small pot of cold cream in her hands. It was shipped direct from the Dead Sea, Jordan.

The tiny store had attracted her when she was out walking. Dina was tempted and had taken a break from looking for work. This was no ordinary pharmacist's. They didn't fill prescriptions here or sell Maybelline cosmetics. The higgledy-piggledy shelves were crammed with imported goods: perfume from Paris in dusty glass bottles, English hand-milled soaps, attar of roses from Egypt. Hipsters and old ladies in lace wandered in and out, buying mostly on the packaging, just to be cool. But Dina tried everything.

It was paradise, standing before the ancient, gold-framed mirrors, applying the creams, the buttery eye shadows, the bronze lipsticks. Aladdin's cave. Mostly, she couldn't afford it, but some-times Dina would treat herself. And Hector would give her tips.

'Try this one.' He offered up a plain-looking ceramic jar. 'Solid perfume from Iran. White musk – thickly scented.'

Dina dipped a finger, and was transported.

'Don't touch that cream.' He warned her off a beautifully

engraved compact from Paris. 'It's anti-aging; the acids will irritate you. All you need is this.'

She picked up the latest, examining it doubtfully. It was a cheap-looking plastic tube from Austria. 'What is it?'

'Primer. Once you apply a few drops, the foundation stays on for days.'

And he was always right.

Dina hung out in the store, spending a lot more time there than money, but Hector never seemed to mind. Hers was the perfect face, and the cosmetics looked wonderful on her – even strange, non-standard colours; she was a young beauty, experimenting.

'I need some concealer. Like, stat,' a girl bellowed.

She was lovely, under it all – Dina registered that at once. She had jet-black hair, run slightly wild, expensively artless clothes and a strong Roman nose that gave character to her face. But her pupils were tight, her skin was haggard, she had spots and her teeth were yellowed. Reddened eyes made her look a mess. She had money, but, boy, was she messed up.

Dina pegged her immediately: the unhappy daughter of one of those rich guys in the West Village; likely saw a therapist a few times a week; heir to a fortune; miserable; self-medicating with alcohol and pot. Pretty, young, up all night . . .

'You don't need concealer.' Hector looked at her like she was mad. 'You need to sleep.'

'Yeah, thanks, Grandpa,' she snapped.

'Actually, you might want to try this – very exclusive – from Milan.' Dina moved forward; she just couldn't bear Hector's hurt look. 'It's a combination: tighteners and brighteners. Use about a quarter's worth on your cheeks and neck and you'll look like you live on carrot juice and sleep in, daily.'

The girl laughed. 'Get out of here!'

'Seriously. Sleep in a bottle.' Dina held it out towards her. It was a marvellous cream; Hector had pointed her to it after she was up all night studying and needed to look fresh for a job interview in the morning.

It cost twenty-three dollars.

'It's expensive though. I don't know if you can afford it.'

Hector opened his mouth, but Dina's green eyes warned him to silence.

'How much?' the girl said, greedily. She was staring at the tube.

'It's a hundred and twenty-three dollars,' Dina said, coolly.

'*How* much? That's bullshit.'

'Hey –' Dina shrugged – 'this isn't a corner pharmacy. I understand; you might want to walk over to Avenue A. They have a store on the corner that sells Revlon. Best drugstore stick for under the eyes.'

She turned to put the tube back on the shelf.

'No. Wait. I can afford it.' The girl hesitated, Dina could see it. Even for the privileged, more than a hundred dollars was a big chunk out of her allowance. 'Can I try a sample?'

'We don't have sample tubes. Up to you, but this will work great on you. I use it myself. We have similar skin.'

The girl cast an expert, assessing eye over Dina. She was slightly older, but her skin was still amazing and it glowed with the perfection of youth and clean living. And Dina Kane epitomised beauty. She was what everybody wanted to be.

'Goddamn. I'll take it.'

Without asking, Dina moved behind the counter. 'A hundred and fifty dollars, please.'

'I thought you said a hundred and twenty-three!'

'Plus tax,' Dina replied. 'And handling.'

The girl meekly fished the bills out of her bag, and Dina handed over the precious cream.

'This stuff really is amazing. Not like the promises you see in the magazines. It works.'

'For how long?' the girl said, suspiciously. Now she'd parted with her cash, she was hovering, like she might ask for a refund.

'For two, maybe three hours. It tightens; it brightens – gets you through your hangover.' Dina smiled. 'Nothing lasts longer, you know. The skin is the biggest organ in your body; it can't be changed by external creams. Temporary tightening effects are just that. This one has light-reflecting pigments and a sunscreen. You will *love* it.' She was congratulating the girl like she'd just won the lottery.

'OK! Great. *Thank* you.'

'Come back; tell us how it worked out. Nobody else stocks it,' Dina said, brightly.

The girl waved; she was already out of the door.

'My God.' Hector breathed out. 'Dina, what the hell were you doing?'

'Selling it,' Dina said, grinning. 'She was so rude. Besides, I think it's underpriced. And it will look awesome on her. She'll be a happy bunny. You don't mind, do you, Hector?'

She laughed and offered him the little sheath of banknotes. Seven twenty-dollar bills and a ten, right there in her hands.

'No. I don't mind.' Numbly he took the money. 'Thank you.'

'I should get going. I have another interview at a secretarial agency. Midtown.' Dina looked hopeful. 'Of course, if you want to give me any free samples . . .'

'No. I don't want to give you free samples,' Hector Green said. 'I want to give you a job.'

She wasn't interested in shelf stacking; she made that clear. And he was equally clear. He wanted her.

'*Liebchen*, I know what works.' Hector sat her down in the back, in his little office. It was narrow, the desk piled high with papers and books. 'I am a research chemist. In my youth, I studied dermatology.'

'Then . . . no disrespect, but how come you're running a beauty store?'

'My wife loved cosmetics. It was our game. I would be horrified at the stuff she put on her skin; I looked at the bottles. Sometimes I mixed lotions just for her.' He sighed. 'Maybe this is a way to stay close.'

'To stay close?'

'She died – in a car crash with our baby daughter.' He looked directly at Dina. 'You know, sometimes they say you will die of a broken heart, but that is a lie. It keeps pumping. And the bills don't care. I wanted to die.'

'And you didn't . . .'

'Kill myself?' His smile never reached his eyes. 'I wanted to do that, too. But my mother was alive. I couldn't leave her with the same loss: a dead child. And by the time she died, I was too much of a coward.'

'It isn't brave to kill yourself, Hector.' Dina felt sick.

'Isn't it? Sometimes I wonder.' His old, thin frame shuddered a little, as though he was shaking something off. 'At any rate, the bills were still coming. I just wanted to live peaceably. So, I don't mix creams anymore, but I sell them. Not well, but I still sell them.'

Dina looked back into the shop, to the cluttered chaos on the shelves. 'You make a profit?'

'Every year.' He lifted his palms. 'Because I buy things that are effective. This is the big secret. I didn't want to work hard. Just to live.'

She chewed her lip. 'You make money despite everything. Because your stuff works.'

'I look at the ingredients.' He leaned in again, as though she had missed the point. 'I'm a chemist.'

'Then what has changed?'

'Dina Kane . . . *Liebchen*,' he said again, affectionately. 'I am sixty-nine. I would like, now, to make a little money so perhaps I can stop working, and still live quietly. Until God sends me to join my Helga.' He lifted a brow. 'This is too morbid for you?'

She shook her head. 'I have longer to live, Hector. You do have great stuff. You realise the store is a disaster?'

He shrugged. 'You can fix that, yes?'

'Yes.' Dina nodded. 'I want you to give me forty per cent of whatever extra we make, on top of your take last year. Fair deal?'

'Fine.' He chuckled. 'You remind me of her, with more fire.'

'I'm not your daughter, Hector. I'm your partner. Your junior partner, but your partner.'

'You want a contract?'

She grabbed a piece of paper, a receipt from a Swiss factory, and wrote on the back of it. 'There. Sign your name, and date it.'

He did so.

'Wonderful,' Dina said, and she felt a shiver of joy run down her spine. Something amazing had just happened. Better than getting a job as a secretary; better than being a paralegal. This – this dusty shop, these unglamorous tubes – this was what she was born to do.

Dina left the office with a key. And when Hector arrived at eight thirty the next morning, the place was transformed.

'I . . . I don't understand.' He gazed around. 'Where is every-thing?'

Dina smiled. 'I've been here since five. Don't worry.'

The cluttered shelves were no more. Half his products were removed, in the back office, stacked in boxes. The rest were laid out, cleanly, on the shelves. Dina had tacked up square, cardboard signs, handwritten in crayon: EYES – DAY CREAMS – NIGHT CREAMS – HANDS – BRONZER – BLUSH, and on and on. Under specific products, like a high-class vintner, she'd written up a little pitch:

Egyptian – smells sexy for days.

From Finland – best European sunscreen for perpetual summer days.

This is mascara that never flakes – with plastic proteins to separate lashes.

Try this when you're sick – better than a facial.

Dina had rigged up lamps, little spotlights from Ikea that beamed on to the shelves. There was wood, but no dust – the floor was swept, the office vacuumed, even the shelves had been gone over with a feather duster. The counter was bare of junk: nothing there but the register and a small black machine.

'What is this?' asked Hector.

Dina smiled. 'Now we take credit cards. Welcome to the modern world, partner.'

Hector Green couldn't believe his luck.

At first, it was disconcerting – the way he was pushed out, moved over, swept aside. The girl ripped through his store like a mini-tornado, as though he had hired six of her. The first day was just the start. As customers came back in, and marvelled, Dina was on them like a wasp at a picnic. She read people – that was her brilliance – standing back when a woman just wanted to browse; right there when she looked like she might buy something. And it was never a simple, 'Can I help you?'

Dina Kane didn't ask women what they wanted. She told them.

'Your skin tone is a perfect match for this lipstick.'

'That's a great bronzer. Have you considered a hand cream? This one has the most natural self-tanner on the market. So light you can hardly see it.'

'You want something for your neck as well? This will tighten the skin and protect the décolletage.'

'Don't use that moisturiser under the eyes – different skin. Try this cream.'

'This Swiss shampoo deposits silver tones in your hair – it will kill the brassiness.'

And they listened – they all listened. Within a week, word was spreading. Ladies came back with their friends. He had less on the shelves, and was selling twice as much.

For the first time in years, Hector Green sensed an unfamiliar feeling – excitement. He could not help it. There was an audible crackle inside his tiny store. Shoppers who browsed were picking up items, buying them, returning for more. He started to see money, real money, in the till. The rent was paid off earlier in the month. He was released from standing around, could go back to his office to take control of his books, do a little stocktaking. Reluctantly at first, then more confidently, he was able to leave the store by seven p.m. Then six. He started to sleep better, to wake sooner.

Dina made things easy. Dina made things interesting.

'We've sold out.' She marched into the back room. 'Give me some stock.'

'I . . . I haven't ordered the new pieces yet.' Hector was flummoxed; it normally took months for his little orders to sell through. Now five pale-pink lipsticks would go in days. He wasn't ready for this level of traffic.

'Don't panic. Here's a list.' Dina handed him a piece of paper, with order numbers neatly typed. 'We just put the other stuff on the shelves. You'll need more quantity next time.'

'OK.'

The next week, she came into the office. 'I'm going to spend some money. About four thousand dollars.'

Hector had never spent that much in his life. 'On what?'

'A computer, a printer, some professional stock-taking software.'

Dina looked so certain, he never thought of arguing. 'OK.'

'We're opening new files,' Dina said, 'on our best customers. I've already done most of it. Can I walk you through it?' She sounded confident, and she was. Three years in the city and already she felt like Tuckahoe was another world.

There was no college for Dina, only slavish hard work. She

might have suffered abuse and humiliation at the hands of Edward Johnson, but she had paid him back. His father, too. And the work she was doing now, at the Green Apothecary – it was far closer to her dreams. Dina Kane was putting herself through an MBA – not in a classroom, but right out in the field, taking this old, creaking business and letting the light in. Automating it. Making it work.

Hector looked at the young girl. He was sixty-three; she was twenty – and sometimes he wondered who was the adult, and who the juvenile in the relationship.

'You need to know how it works, in case you have to do it. If I'm not here.'

He felt a rush of panic. 'What do you mean, if you're not here? Why wouldn't you be here?'

'You know,' Dina said. 'In case I take a day off.'

'A day off?' he repeated, slowly.

She smiled. 'People sometimes have vacations.'

People, he felt like saying. *Not you*.

Dina Kane was a machine. She worked six days a week; maybe she slept all day Sunday. He never heard her talk men, never saw her with a friend. It was one of the reasons he liked the girl. She was just like him.

'So, let me show you,' she explained. 'Here are the names – with notes. It's linked to the credit cards. When they swipe it, this will pop up on your screen. Abigail Adams: she's first on the list. Spends about three hundred a month. Age: early forties. Best products for her: moisturisers, tighteners, Dead Sea hand cream. Colours: she likes to buy pinks; steer her to pink golds – they look better on her skin and will get her more compliments. Open to perfume – think naturals. Last thing she bought: natural-fibre brushes from Japan.'

'Wow.' He didn't know what else to say.

'Look.' Dina jumped from her seat and did a little pantomime. 'Abi! How nice to see you. Did you like the brushes? They hold

98

powders much better than the artificial stuff, don't they? Oh, Dina said that, if you came in, I should point out the new lip glosses from Portugal. A little company in Lisbon hand-makes them. Great rose-gold colours she thinks would suit your look. We only have a few in stock, though.'

He laughed. 'I'm almost ready for rose-gold lip gloss myself.'

'It's about getting to know them, so they feel it's personal.' Dina smiled, proudly, and her mentor felt the happiness, the glow of achievement, bouncing off her. Goddamn it, if he could bottle *that* look, he'd make his fortune.

'You told me once your shop worked because the products worked?' she said.

He nodded. 'Of course.'

'This takes it one step further: which products work best for which women. Beauty is personal; beauty is unique. So, when they feel you know them, they come back.'

My God, Hector thought. *She really is a little genius.*

'Little Sis!' Johnny exclaimed. 'It's so good to see you!'

'You too, Johnny.' She threw her arms around him. 'And Brad. How are you doing?'

'I'm good.' Brad came over and shook her hand, shyly. Johnny threw his arm around Brad, kissing him on the lips.

'I'm sorry. He gets all worked up about meeting family.'

Dina smiled at her brother's boyfriend. 'You tell Mom yet?'

A slight chill descended across the table. Johnny shook his head.

They were eating Sunday lunch together: dim sum at the Nom Wah Tea Parlour in Chinatown, tucked away in a little back street and with one of the best menus in the city.

'Are you sure you can afford it?' Johnny whined, when Dina offered to pay for his cab into the city. 'Taxi fares are horrendous.'

'Just get a car. I want to meet the new man.'

Johnny was her family, her life outside work. It was easier, these days, for Dina to hear about his time at college. It wasn't *his* fault that Mom played favourites; Dina hoped for Johnny to succeed. As weak and passive as he'd been, he at least liked her, loved her. She would head out to see him most Sundays, and they'd get a beer, or sit in a coffee house or the dorm and talk. Six months ago, he told her he was gay, and now he'd met someone serious.

'I guess it's a big shock,' Johnny had said, his voice trembling.

She was surprised at how obvious it suddenly seemed. 'Not at all. Good for you, Johnny. I just want you to be happy.'

He was scraping through his studies. He'd switched majors – and his GPA looked like alphabet soup: a B here, a C there. Now he was in Peace and Justice Studies, and had no idea what he was going to do when he graduated.

'Maybe go to business school,' Johnny said, vaguely.

'Mom doesn't have any more money.'

'Oh. Right. Well, I'll get a job in social work, I guess.'

'OK,' Dina said, anxiously. 'Have you thought about where?'

Johnny sighed. 'Don't bug me about it. I'm a student. Are you always so type A?'

Dina was happy to see Johnny, and at least she was getting to meet the boyfriend. Maybe Brad could save her brother – he was studying pre-law – maybe they would settle down, he could whip Johnny into shape . . .

She hoped so. Johnny was her only family. The only small piece of love in her life.

'So, Brad, you like dim sum?'

He rolled his eyes. 'Dina, please; I'm Jewish. I was *born* for dim sum.'

She laughed. She liked this guy already.

It was a pleasant meal; Dina found it hard to relax, but she was trying. Having Sundays with her brother said something important: that she was a person, not a machine; that she could feel, she could switch off.

Sometimes she asked herself why doing well mattered so much. But, mostly, she just didn't have time. Work consumed her; the Green Apothecary was everything. She wasn't going to be her layabout mom, depending on wise-guy money, or her dad, who worked and died on a building site.

She wanted more. Much more.

Sometimes, at night, when she was exhausted, Dina thought about a boyfriend. But Edward Johnson hung in her mind, as did the men that had swarmed round her drunken, wasted mom.

It all seemed pointless. She could only rely on herself.

Her big brother reminded her she was human. She had someone. It might be imperfect, but it was family.

'So, the store's doing well,' she said, brightly.

'That's good,' Johnny offered. 'Can I get some more pork buns?'

Brad passed them over. 'How long have you been there now?'

'Coming up for six months. We're making real money.' She already had her one-bedroom apartment fixed up and under offer; she was shopping for a new place. 'My guess is that, this year, I might make about fifty-five thousand.'

Johnny finally sat up. 'Who? You?'

Dina nodded with pride. God, it was *so good* to be able to tell somebody, to share this with her brother – someone who wasn't Hector.

'Goddamn. That's real money.' He nudged Brad. 'That's my sister!'

'I know, dude. That's awesome. Congratulations.'

'I'm getting a new apartment. There's a two-bedroom in Murray Hill I want.'

'Renting?' Johnny asked.

'Buying.' She blushed slightly. 'I've got a small nest egg, you see, from my other two places . . . Sold them both for a profit . . .'

'Two places?' Johnny's mouth was open. 'I don't get it. You only just got here.'

'It's been nearly two years, Johnny. I bought as soon as I could.'

Her brother reached over, pinched her. 'Are we really related?'

I wonder that sometimes myself, Dina thought. But she smiled indulgently.

'Hector.' Dina's voice was calling him from the back office.

He put down the tube of eye cream he was showing the young tourist from Tokyo. 'Excuse me.'

When his young partner called, he came. It didn't even occur to him to tell her to wait. Dina Kane never waited.

'It's crazy out there. It's just insane,' Dina said. 'Look at them.'

'*Ja*. I know.' The older man glanced back; his store was full. Women, and a few men, were crowding the place. For the last three weeks, it had been like this – after work, at lunch hour. People would flood in. The small store had no space.

'They're panic buying. Everybody wants in.'

'Isn't that a good thing?'

'Not really.' Dina scowled. 'We have a reputation, Hector. We're selling things that make women look good. *On them.*'

'Of course. Then they tell their friends.'

'Now women are just buying anything. I can't get out there to give advice. We're too busy.'

'So, we hire somebody. Just to stand behind the till.' He had thought about this for at least two weeks. 'You are more valuable than ringing up prices, Dina.'

She laughed. 'It's bigger than that. We need to expand. We need a new store.'

He blinked. 'What? I live here.'

'A second store. A system. Staff.'

The old man had a sinking feeling. 'Dina . . . this . . . this is not for me. I just want a quiet life.'

She gestured at the shoving, angry crowd; the moneyed women, all scared they were missing something.

'And how quiet is that?'

No matter how hard she worked, Dina could not persuade him. Hector didn't want the risk; his vision had been for a successful shop, nothing beyond that.

'We could run an online business. Sell from a website,' Dina suggested.

'I'm a chemist,' Hector muttered. 'I don't trust these things. And it's too complicated . . . how I pick my stuff . . .'

'But Hector—'

'No, Dina. Enough. I'm not you.'

'We think you'll love it here. Excellent access to First Avenue . . . and a view of the river.'

'Yes, thank you, I can see.'

'Would you like a little time to yourself?'

The realtor's smile froze on her face. *Bitch*, she thought. This young girl was so stuck-up, with her insistence that Laurel be exactly on time, and her sheaf of financials. She was probably some rich kid playing at living alone, anyway. This apartment was over a half million dollars. How would a girl like this even come close to the deposit?

'How big is the maintenance?'

'Oh, hardly anything. The building has a doorman, but rates are very low. Less than five hundred a month.'

'Offer four eighty-five.'

Laurel smirked. *Yeah, right.* She was hardly going to waste her seller's time. 'I'll need to see your financials.'

The girl looked her dead in the eyes. 'I have a mortgage commitment from Washington Mutual. I brought the pre-approval letter with me.'

She passed it over. Laurel Sloane scanned it quickly.

'This is a no income verification loan. You'd need a twenty per cent deposit for that, I'm afraid.'

'I have a twenty per cent deposit. And I'm liquid, ready to close in thirty days. Ms Sloane, I'm going to buy *something*, and you're obliged to pass my offer on. I'm sure your seller would want me to get this one.'

Laurel wavered. She disliked the girl, but there was some sort of certainty about her. Very disconcerting but, like the boss said, you never know who has the money . . .

'There are other places I could show you. More expensive, more space. There's one on Forty-Third with a balcony—'

'No. This is perfect.' Dina looked around the apartment again: one reasonable bedroom, a small second one, a bathroom with a shower, unremarkable small kitchen and a living room cramped with a couch and a TV. The windows were large, though, and the place was a block away from the UN. The East River was clearly visible, and the full west aspect would let light sink in there all day.

It was small – maybe a thousand square foot – and the décor was dark and overstuffed.

'Well – we all have our passions. If you've found your home . . .'

Dina wanted to laugh. Home? On Forty-First and First? She wouldn't be here above eight months. No, she looked around and she was already stripping the apartment, gutting it, adding light, space, and nearly a million dollars to its value.

'. . . Just buy it,' she said.

Dina didn't argue.

'I have the answer,' Dina told Hector a week later, 'if you really don't want to expand.'

She was stuck. She liked Hector Green; he was her friend – her mentor, in a way. He'd hired her and, in all this time, he never hit on her, never made an advance, never 'accidentally' groped her butt. With Hector, she'd found stability, success. She put Edward and Shelby Johnson behind her.

But Hector was doing something impossible for her to stomach. He was trying to stand between her and her goals. The old man wanted modest success, and then he wanted to pack up and go home. Already, Dina realised, her dreams were so much bigger than that. She didn't want to leave him, and she couldn't. Who knew of their success? Only Hector . . . and a few of their customers.

But his name was on the store. His name was on the bank accounts. She credited him for sourcing the products; she just sold them. Young Dina Kane wanted to be a businesswoman, but mostly now she was a talented shopgirl.

Hector was digging his heels in. The customers scared him. The pace . . . the ordering . . . even the money. Dina knew she was a great judge of beauty, of style, but she also believed in the fundamentals. What worked? She would not know that . . . not without a chemistry degree. Even if she walked out today, it wasn't as easy as quitting.

'Please, Dina. Not again.' Hector sat down heavily, rubbing his forehead. 'I am a scientist. This is *wunderbar*, *fantastisch*, really great. But you are going fast . . . very fast for me. I don't want to move. Not another shop . . .'

'Let's think differently. You're working hard . . .'

He nodded. So many things to order, calls to make. It had never been this quick. He was starting to feel overwhelmed.

'But you should concentrate on what you do best. You're a chemist; you analyse the ingredients.'

'Yes. That's what I do.'

'What if we didn't have three hundred products, and all these orders? What if we just had one product?'

Hector blinked. 'That's crazy. The women want skin, make-up, scent. Everything, everything.'

'Right now, yes. But, Hector, what if you, yourself, made up a cream? A day cream. Something revolutionary. Your own brand. And we got the packaging, we sold it.'

'*I* make a cream?'

'Yes. Later on, maybe, you could do more in the range – if you wanted. But for the start, just one cream.'

'We can't make profit by selling one product here,' Hector said, slowly. But his eyes were flickering; he was already thinking about it. For years it had frustrated him, picking the best creams of a bad bunch, the inconsistency in batches, everything.

'We wouldn't have to. If you make a great product, we can sell it other places, too. I can do that for you,' Dina said, confidently. 'I know I can.'

'Well, there is a place I can work. I have friends – chemists. I know a small laboratory in White Plains.' Hector's anxiety was already dissipating. He was thinking about the cream. 'There are ingredients most do not use, as they are too costly for the mass market, but they work. Topical peptides. Salicylic acid. Vitamin E . . . and I like the compounds found in the Dead Sea mud . . . with sunscreen, a light sunscreen . . .'

'What will it do?'

'Very mild exfoliation, hydration and sun. You see –' Hector began to get worked up – 'the commercial creams mostly over-exfoliate. You cannot use that every day. It will strip the skin of oils. They get dry . . . If you go gently, very gently, the skin will become cleaner, softer. And a strong sunscreen . . .'

'You see? You want to do it,' Dina said.

'Yes.' He looked back into the shop. 'But I will have to go away. It will take some time to formulate. To be perfect.'

'Work there three days a week,' Dina said. 'I can handle this.'

In the end, it took five months. Hector didn't spend three days a week there – he disappeared. Dina was on her own, and it was a liberation. Without asking, she took control of the books, the marketing, the merchandise. She hired a couple of beautiful, smart students from NYU to help on the till, and made them up so they looked like models.

Every day, Hector would call, or email.

'The mixing is smooth.'

'Acid balance not right yet.'

'I have a manufacturer . . . Test batches tomorrow.'

She wired him money from the store, money they could barely afford. The profit was dipping. Dina took decisions, only spending where she thought it best: staff wages; sanding the floors and painting them a light, pale green. She decorated the walls in eggshell and hung mirrors everywhere to reflect light; it also allowed customers to see themselves clearly. Dina chose real sunlight bulbs, and those were expensive. But she was committed to quality. *No-regret buying*, Dina thought; her customers would see the cosmetics in true light, not flattering store bulbs.

She sunk money into their accountant, into their computers. Finally, she began to get a grip on the stock, the income, the taxes. The Green Apothecary was ready. But the cash was gone.

Dina tried not to panic. It was her decision; Hector was absorbed in his batches and testing. They were ready now, ready for bigger things. But they had no money.

She reserved just a tiny amount. Not for petty cash – for packaging. And every Sunday she went back out to see Johnny, using Metro North, to eat in a Mount Vernon diner. No more dim sum. Neither she nor Johnny could afford it. For once, she had barely touched her new apartment. The refurb would take cash – and every red cent was sunk into the Green Apothecary.

Dina didn't tell Hector she was using her personal money. The cash-flow problem was hers to deal with; she wanted Hector as a chemist, with nothing on his mind but the cream.

'I'm coming home,' Hector informed her on the phone one Monday. 'I will be there tomorrow.'

'Fantastic,' Dina replied.

She couldn't eat much that evening, couldn't sleep. Both of their futures depended on this working.

Dina looked down at the jar.

It wasn't much – maybe an ounce. Plain, hard and grey. She tapped it with her elegant nail, painted in Chanel's *Rouge Argent*, a silvery pink she loved. It chimed, lightly.

'Vitreous glass,' Hector said. 'Porcelain will crack. Anyway, it needs to be dark, to stabilise the minerals.'

'Let me try it,' she said. Delicately, she dipped her finger in the jar. It was thick – really thick. Smooth. Cool. There was a faint scent, maybe violets, something watery and light.

'You must rub it in your palm.'

'Why?' Her heart sped up a little. People were not patient; they wanted immediate gratification.

'To loosen the oils and vitamins. Warm it in the palm, then rub it on your skin.'

She hesitated. 'Won't that put customers off, Hector?'

'Only if they are fools.'

'Right,' she said. 'Excellent.'

He shrugged. 'The best ingredients cannot be worked together into a simple paste. The binding agent will smother some of the effects. I use algae here – Dead Sea compounds.'

She did as she was told and the cream released more scent. Slowly, Dina rubbed it into her face. It felt wonderful: soft and perfect. She hadn't slept much, and immediately her skin was tautening, brightening. The ingredients were sinking in, different somehow from other creams.

'Wait. It is important to wait.' Hector instructed.

She took a little more, warmed it in her palm and spread it across her face, her neck. 'Eyes?'

Hector nodded. 'It is protective. It can work there too.'

Next she took a foundation, a liquid number from Berne, and applied it.

'Beautiful. See?' She turned her face to Hector. 'It goes on so matte. It's like a wonderful primer.'

'For you it will tighten. For older women, it temporarily softens wrinkles. The stuff is easily absorbed to the dermis. It gives a rosy look because it promotes blood flow to the skin. This will have knock-on effects: it will slow aging, environmental damage. The sunscreen is full.'

'Blood flow to the skin?'

'It has collagen.' He was almost not listening to her questions. 'It will add what city life takes out, like a day in the country.'

Dina looked at herself; her foundation was still airbrush perfect.

'Hector, you're a genius. That's what we call it: *Meadow*. Because it brings the countryside to you.'

'Meadow. I like that,' he said, and nodded. 'I tested it on people with severe acne – it helps; and on victims with scars and burns – it assists healing.'

She clenched her fist, trying not to get excited. 'How much does it cost to make?'

The old man looked shifty. 'Uh . . . That depends . . .'

'Hector. *How much*?'

'About sixty-five dollars a jar.' He looked defensive. 'There are costs . . . It will need chemists . . .'

Dina was quiet for a moment.

'Then this is a two-hundred-dollar cream. Top of the line. And we have to test it commercially, here, first.'

'We can borrow some money . . .'

'There is no money,' Dina said. 'Our customers will have to do the testing.'

She was cautious. At first, there were just whispers to their best, most respected customers: the older ones – the ones who spent all the money.

'Anti-age. Proprietary. Would you like a sample jar?'

'Oh, Mrs Cohen, it's really very expensive. Far more than La Prarie. Will you try it for us?'

When they loved it, Dina expanded just a touch. She gave small jars to students – the ones with the worst pimples; to a pretty girl with blotchy skin; to a rosacea sufferer; to a soccer mom in her thirties with a great look, nice skin, whom she asked to use it as a primer.

Everybody raved. They wanted more. Their friends dropped by, asked for samples of their own.

'Make up a batch,' Dina instructed. 'Five hundred jars.'

Hector was horrified. 'We don't have that kind of money. You wiped us out. We're barely making the bills . . .'

'Next month will be more. Hector, we have to have a real batch. Get me five hundred jars. I will take charge of the boxes.' She had the design already: pretty little stars and flowers scattered across recycled green cardboard, with the word MEADOW emblazoned in gold. *Bring fresh to your face*, was the slogan. *Meadow is different.*

'Dina.' Now Hector's nerves were returning. He loved going back to the lab, loved making the cream, adored the thankful women as they raved about what it did for their faces . . . But money . . .

He brought Dina in to fix that. For a while, she had. Now there was a black hole again. And she wanted him to borrow, to risk everything he had . . .

'Go to the bank. We need to sell this cream.'

'I can't.' As soon as he said the words, he knew. 'It's my home. I can't risk that.'

Dina put her head in her hands. 'Jesus! Then *I'll* do it. I'll go to the bank. There's money in my apartment.'

'But it's all you own.'

'Not for long.' Dina put her small hand over his large, wrinkled one. 'It's mine, though – if I get the cash. You need to give me the formula, let me control the marketing. I take half the profits for that; you take the other half, for inventing it. I'm going to get a lawyer to draw up the papers, and you need one, too. OK, Hector?'

Who could argue with her? He wasn't going to try. 'OK.'

By the time Dina came back to her apartment that evening, she was exhausted.

She'd visited five different banks, before she found one that'd lend her the money. Two different attorneys. A horrible meeting in a stuffy West Village office, as Hector passed over the paper, and they both signed in triplicate. Dina Kane was now down most of her life's savings and, in return, she had a piece of paper, the number of a small factory in New Jersey and half a pot of face cream.

She'd never felt happier. And, as she showered in her unpainted bathroom and scrubbed her body with plain carbolic soap, Dina Kane whistled to herself. She stepped out, towelled off and threw on her white waffle dressing gown. It was dark but, even on the edge of the city, electricity pulsed through her windows: the traffic driving up First Avenue, the lights of the barges on the East River, the looming towers of the UN.

This would be the last year she would see this view, Dina vowed. Next year – Fifth Avenue.

Nothing was going to stop her.

Chapter Seven

'Pass me that,' Edward said. He pointed.

The waiter bowed slightly. 'Yes, sir. Certainly.'

'No, man. Not the cigars. The paper.'

'Of course, sir.'

The older man handed over the *Times* with an inscrutable expression on his face. He had learned the hard way never to show any emotion, especially contempt. Johnson was just the latest in a long line of moneyed losers. He showed up to the club at eleven and was drunk by half past; cocktails before lunch, wine with his steak, a digestif with coffee, and an afternoon sherry to pass the time.

It ran in the family, so they said. After the big society divorce, Shelby Johnson had run out of town – left the state altogether. No more Congress. No more Coldharbor Bank. He stepped down with a modest payout and, rumour had it, he was living quietly in Florida. They had sun there, and a law that said they couldn't take your house. The gossips were having a field day.

Penelope Johnson had really fallen apart. During the divorce – and the huge settlement – ladies around town whispered that she had Shelby over a barrel. How else to explain the giant cash settlement, millions for the maintenance, the way she kept the house?

But Penny paid the price. Women, slowly but surely, stopped coming to her parties. Invitations dried up. After all, it was so much safer to invite couples. Penny was touched by some hint of scandal . . . Nobody knew exactly what yet. Why had Shelby left? Was it her? Was he gay? Besides, a single woman of fortune might tempt their menfolk . . .

She was drinking . . . even more. And now the doctor had given her pills, too: anti-stress; anti-anxiety; pills to sleep.

Penny showed up at town charity events wearing tight dresses, her hair suddenly dyed blond. She looked desperate. Her eyes shone with a chemical glow.

'Jesus, Mom.' Edward watched in horror as she clutched a champagne flute at the Metropolitan benefit. 'Seriously. You just *can't*. Stop.'

'And why shouldn't I have a little fun? You're such a party pooper.'

'Mom, you're forty-eight. Come on . . .'

'I'm still attractive. Surgeons can do incredible things these days.'

Edward called her doctor. 'My mother is sick. If you so much as touch her face, I'll file a malpractice suit that will knock you off your ass . . .'

It worked. Beaten, bowed, humiliated, Penelope just gave up. She retired to her bedroom and barely came out for weeks.

Edward was almost glad he was out of college. He couldn't take the snickering. Even now, his phone rang and he heard giggling at the end of it. He changed his mobile number. So they thought it was funny, did they? Fuckers . . .

He let his mother sit there, in the house, rotting with her booze and her pills. He couldn't take the actual work to get her 'better': the AA meetings, the humiliations of rehab. The perfect woman was ruined. He detested her now, like he detested the embarrassment, the weakness of his father.

And most of all, he detested Dina Kane.

The best you could say was that she was some poor little nothing, a shopgirl, a nobody. For weeks, he'd waited for those pictures to appear, waking every morning in a cold sweat, waiting for his phone to ring, for the emails to come in.

Nothing. Every time he picked up a copy of the *Post*, page six was empty. There was nothing.

So that was it. He dropped out; his father vanished. And so had that bitch of a waitress. *Forget it.*

Edward tried to. But his golden world had turned to tin.

He had no idea what to do. His so-called friends were gone; invitations were drying up. Edward was no longer a favoured heir. Instead, he was just the remnant of a family in a social death spiral. The only kids that wanted to know him now were the hangers-on, the poor ones, the middle-class thrusters who liked to be with the rich.

He had dreams, fantasies of revenge, of restoring his family name, acting the way his cowardly father refused to.

'No, Edward,' Shelby said on the phone. 'I'm not coming back up there.'

'Mom needs you.'

'She wanted the divorce. She got what she asked for.' His father's voice was distant, detached. 'Maybe it's all for the best. I'm enjoying my life down here now; I'm finding myself; the sun shines; you know . . .'

'Jesus! No, I don't know. I know you ran away.'

'Edward, my life up there is over. I don't want to see those people anymore.'

'Dad . . .'

'You're a young man. You have to make your own way.'

'At what?' Edward shrieked. 'I had to drop out of college! Because of you! I was supposed to work at the firm, but you quit! Now what am I to do?'

'It's not my problem. You're twenty-one now, Edward. When I was your age, I was working in Wall Street . . .'

'I didn't get to graduate,' Edward whined. 'I don't even have a liberal arts degree . . .'

'Then find a job. It's what most men do.'

Edward swallowed hard. 'I'm not most men, Daddy; that's not how you raised me.'

A long sigh. '"Daddy"! Listen to yourself. Come on, Edward, you need to discover your own purpose, not mooch off your mother and me.'

'With what? How?'

'I can't hold your hand. If you can't think of anything else to do, join the army. It's been the making of several young men.'

'The army!' Edward's shriek rose into hysterical, high-pitched giggles. 'The army! Right – that's good. Look, just wire me some fucking money.'

'I need what I have. Your mother has all the money.'

'I'm your son!'

'My grown son.' Another sigh. 'Obviously I failed you, Edward. You were meant to stand on your own two feet.'

'Spare me the fucking lecture, old man!' Edward screeched. But Shelby had already hung up.

There was the trust fund – but that was a pittance.

'Just advance me some cash,' Edward said, confidently. He was dressed in one of his best suits – Armani – with a crisp silk shirt. Rutger Helmand was his father's private banker; he had dined at the Johnson house many times over the years.

'From which account do you want it?' Rutger smiled sympathetically. They were meeting on Park Avenue, in his office, which resembled an English country drawing room. This was how the upper classes did their banking, with Persian rugs on the floor, oil paintings of pheasants on the walls; nothing so vulgar as a rack of terminals. He was glancing at the discreet computer monitor placed on his mahogany desk.

'The family trust.'

'Of course. I'm authorised to make disbursals. How much would you like, Edward?'

He shrugged. 'Not much. Just half a million dollars?'

Rutger's eyes widened. 'Oh, no. I can only allow you to have five thousand, every six months.'

Edward's eyes narrowed. 'I have a trust fund, don't I? Three million?'

'It matures when you're thirty-five.'

Thirty-five? He may as well be dead.

'And your father's sign-off will still be required.'

He buried his head in his hands. That only left his allowance. Ten thousand a month: it was a pittance.

'Goddamn it, Rutger.'

'You must talk to your parents. By the way, you do know your allowance has been stopped?'

The head shot up. 'Huh?'

'Your father wired me this morning. I'm afraid it's all in order. He says you will be earning your own money from now on.'

'That's . . . that's not right.' Edward started to panic. 'Call him!'

'I did.' Rutger began to squirm slightly, and Edward had that sinking feeling, that all too common feeling. He was in the middle of a scene. Only this time, he was causing it. 'Really, Edward, I can't interfere. Have you spoken to your mother?'

She was at home, no doubt, wearing a silk dressing down and downing her third vodka gimlet of the morning.

'No. But, of course, I will.' Edward pulled himself together, forced himself to stand up. 'How much is left in my own account?'

'Almost two hundred thousand,' Rutger replied, reassuringly.

Peanuts. That wouldn't get him to first base.

'Terrific,' Edward forced himself to say. 'I think I'll head out to the club.'

* * *

The waiter handed over the copy of the *Times*, and Edward snatched it closer.

His heart thumped. Now, even his sanctuary was about to be invaded. The club . . . He was listed on his father's membership. The Farmers' Club was one of the oldest in the city, with burgundy leather armchairs, fine wines, a smoking terrace for cigars and a reassuringly white, male and exclusive membership. Edward enjoyed the calm, the obsequiousness. His mother was nowhere about. He moved in the pleasant hush of old money, the hush he'd been born into. And nobody objected to his drinking.

If he wanted coke, he went elsewhere, stumbled out on to the street, fished the tiny glass vial and miniature spoon from a hidden inner pocket. Not in the Farmers' Club . . . Edward had no wish to get banned, not from his last, best home.

And now, there was that flash of recognition. His heart thumped. He snatched the paper off the silver tray, greedily holding the newsprint to him, reading it.

Dina Kane is a newcomer to the world of beauty. The twenty-year-old has impressed with early sales of the 'Meadow' facial cream, reported to deliver superior skin toning, priming and moisture benefits. Now stocked at Saks, Bergdorf's, Glamour and other high-end stores, 'Meadow' is already racking up healthy sales, with a local New Jersey factory struggling to keep pace.

'We're different. We're chemist-designed. This is beauty for all skins,' Ms Kane said.

Challenged on the soaring $300 price, she replied, 'Meadow isn't for everyone. With no compromise on ingredients, it means no compromise on price.'

Ms Kane reportedly has a fifty-per-cent interest in the new company. 'Meadow' cream is now obtainable at all fine stores, or direct via the company website. But, be warned: there's a waiting list.

Edward read the item twice, three times. His head was pounding. The dry text swam before his eyes.

Oh, it was her, all right. The grainy black-and-white photo showed that. The pretty, cruel young face next to the delicate jar of product. *Beauty*. Somehow it did not surprise him. Beauty was the one thing she had in abundance. Style on a shoestring. And, now, maybe not such a shoestring.

He hated the words 'Kane' and 'company'. That slut was nothing. She was a gold-digger like the rest of them, only more vicious. She was meant to be serving coffee – and more – to him and his friends.

Dina Kane had not gone away. Edward was here, drunk, lonely, almost broke. His mother was a slave to her addiction, his father a dropout. And she was attempting – actually managing – to move up in the world.

He hated her. He remembered her body. Underneath the drunkenness, it stirred him.

Edward pushed himself to his feet. He wanted women; he wanted pussy. There were drugs that could make the booze go away.

'I'll put it on your tab, sir, shall I?' asked the waiter.

But Edward Johnson was already gone.

'It's selling extremely well.'

Dina was standing in the executive offices of the Glamour store on Fifth Avenue. She nodded as Jane Bowes, the buying director, scrolled through her slides.

'As you can see, another seventy-five per cent volume in the first month. But our customers are complaining about wait times. It's bad for the store if we have to tell them to hold on.'

Dina nudged Hector, standing beside her, awkward in his new three-piece suit.

'We understand,' she said. 'We are shifting production. There's another factory lined up, in Canada. And one in Milan that will service Europe.'

'Glamour wants to be first in line.'

'You are a premium customer. We're going just as fast as we can.'

'Maybe you'd consider developing a new product, just for Glamour. Say, a night cream. We hold, as a chain, to ethical production methods . . .'

'We know that,' Dina said. 'No exclusives.'

The girl ignored her, addressing Hector directly. 'A million-dollar advance before you sell a single pot, Dr Green. And all your sales on top of that.'

Dina stood up. 'This meeting is over.'

'I understand you have an interest in Meadow cream, Ms Kane, and we respect that, but Dr Green is a free agent, isn't he? You don't own all his future work.'

Dina glared at Hector. 'We are leaving. Are you coming?'

He looked wildly from one woman to the other. Christ! *A million dollars.* He'd never have to work again. And before he sold a single pot . . .

And yet there was the girl, his young partner, glaring at him, like she was eighty years old and his mother . . .

'Yes. Coming.' He felt resentful. He had mentored this girl, offered her help, assistance. And she was ordering him around – had done from the start. Now his cream was working and Dina was taking half. Sure, he was grateful . . . and she was energetic . . . but if they wanted to give him a million . . .

She was in her twenties; he wanted to retire.

We are leaving. So easy for her to say.

But he got to his feet, and regretfully followed her out.

'We need to talk, Dina. I am not happy.'

She passed a hand over her forehead. 'Christ, Hector. It's all happening. Do you realise how much money you're making?'

'You don't understand. I just want to have enough – to stop – not to do this again.'

'And we will. It's going to be more than that; it's going to be millions . . . if you stay with me.'

He bristled. 'You treat me like a child. It's my cream.'

Dina saw red. 'Which you wouldn't market, Hector; you wouldn't borrow a dime. You'd have been happy to sell it in our cramped little store.'

He flushed. 'That shop is my home. You were happy enough when I hired you.'

She paused. 'This is stupid. We have to work as a team.'

But Hector was brooding. 'It was wrong of you to take half the rights. And now you want the rest of my work?'

'You have to be kidding. I put everything I have on the line for this cream.'

'I'm calling that woman back,' the older man said. 'I want a million dollars. It's my research; nothing to do with you.'

Dina blinked back tears. 'Hector—'

'Really,' he said. 'You are the one who brought in lawyers. Just let me be, now, Dina, OK? I have a life without you.'

'I'm worried about you,' Brad said.

Johnny's little sis, the model of control, of command, the workaholic – she looked a mess.

They had read about the beauty cream. Nice – Dina looked to be set up for life.

But here she was at his apartment, late at night and shaken. Her skin was grey and she was crying.

'It doesn't matter,' Dina lied. 'Just a business thing, breaking up. That's all. Hector's right: he can do what he wants.'

Brad, Johnny's boyfriend, came over. He was in awe of Dina Kane – so strong; so ferocious. Old beyond her years and, from what Johnny had told him, he could guess why. But today she looked just like a twenty-year-old: upset and lost, stiffed by the older guy.

'He can't, actually, Dina,' Brad said. 'I don't know what's gone wrong, but you have half of the Meadow product. Why don't you get yourself your own lawyer? I'm guessing he can't use the name, or anything in connection with the first cream, without you.'

She bit her lip. 'Yeah. Maybe.'

'You're not thinking straight.'

'I don't know. It hurts. Hector meant a lot to me.'

Because you never knew your father, Brad thought. But he wasn't a shrink. Johnny, his love, was a messed up, insecure, lazy, sexy delight, and that was OK – Brad was grounded enough for the both of them. But Dina was more like him, full of duty and responsibility and the need to get on. Besides, she was going places; you could tell that the second she walked in the room.

'I would just get a lawyer – not the local guy you had run up the contract – a good one.'

'I spent everything I had on this cream. The packaging, the manufacture, everything. My apartment is hocked up to the eyeballs. It's selling, but the money takes a while to flow in, and all the lab bills have to be paid first and—'

'I'm sorry.' Brad patted her on the shoulder. 'Just my two cents.'

He had his own worries. He looked over at her brother. Two weeks ago, he was planning to drive Johnny to Vermont, ask him to marry him. Gay marriage was legal there. They could get a little place. He had his first job lined up: tax law at a small firm in Manhattan. It was a good gig for an Iona graduate, and he figured he could do well, get a promotion, get more money. He wasn't going to wind up on the Supreme Court, but they could have a nice place together. Maybe Johnny would do social work; maybe he'd just be a hippy peace activist. Brad didn't really care when he had those smooth limbs wound around him and that handsome face purring in his ear. It was white-picket-fence time, and he couldn't wait. If he was boring, Johnny brought the fireworks.

But . . . maybe a few too many fireworks. Johnny was

drinking; that was nothing new – he'd been drinking since he arrived at college. It started out of relief about getting away from home, or maybe guilt over the little sister without any college tuition. Then, as Dina pulled herself up from the pit, it was just drinking to party. Brad told him off; Brad worried. For a while, he switched to weed. The grades were plummeting, so he got a prescription to treat ADHD and crushed his Adderall. Next it was cocaine, just a little, here and there, when they were offered it at parties . . .

'I'm OK,' Johnny said. 'I'm holding it together.'

But his grades were bumping along the bottom. Brad was anxious. Maybe he'd get chucked out. Maybe he'd get addicted . . .

Now here Dina was, and Brad didn't know if he had anything left in reserve.

'Poor little sis.' Johnny stumbled over and gave her a bear hug.

'Johnny, you stink of whiskey.'

'Jack Daniel's don't stink.' Johnny pouted. 'What's the problem? We don't all want to be a party pooper, like you . . .'

'Here, baby.' Brad came over with a big glass of ice water and two Alka-Seltzers. 'Take these.'

Dina looked up slowly, shaken out of her self-reflection. Suddenly, Meadow cream seemed miles away. Johnny was in trouble. Johnny – the only family she had. It was obvious from the look on Brad's face. She didn't want him to get sick, but maybe he was already.

'No way,' Johnny slurred. 'I'm getting some ecstasy; Stacey has some down the block. She works porn, did you know that? She always has the best fucking shit. We're here; we should party . . . You think too much, Dina. You worry too much . . .'

'Johnny –' her voice was sharp and commanding – 'take the glass from Brad.'

He tossed his head, but he took it.

'Now swallow the pills. And the water. *All* of it.'

He did.

'Thanks.' Brad passed a hand over his face. 'I'll take him to the bathroom, get him to bed. Can you stay a minute?'

He was back out in five, with Johnny moaning in their tiny bedroom like a stuck elephant.

'He needs help.'

Dina nodded. 'How long has this been going on?'

'Maybe a month, maybe two. But we have to stop it before it gets any worse. I don't know how.'

Neither did Dina. For once, her self-possession deserted her. 'I'll . . . I'll go and see Mom. She loves him.' *Even if she doesn't love me.* 'She can decide what to do.'

'Does she know yet . . . ?'

'Don't worry,' Dina said, with more confidence than she felt. 'I'll tell her.'

The train out to Tuckahoe was a long thirty minutes for Dina. Every stop was redolent with memories. Bad memories.

Her golden dream was going wrong all around her. Hector was drifting away from her, corrupted. There would be lawyers . . . lawsuits. Her job was gone, with all she'd ploughed into it. It might have been only a year, but to Dina it was an age – it was her life.

And now her darling Johnny needed help. Something was rotten in his soul, something from childhood. They dealt with it in different ways, he and she. He wanted to get along, quietly, and hope it went away. Booze made pain go away. So did drugs.

'Woodlawn,' said the conductor. 'Wakefield next . . .'

She shivered in her seat. It was January – icy cold in New York. Dina was dressed for it, though; the ticket inspectors did a double take; the louche teenage boys sprawling across the banquettes were openly leering. She didn't notice any of them.

Everybody else riding to the suburbs was bundled up in so many layers they looked like the Stay-Puft marshmallow man. Not this girl. Dina Kane was dressed with effortless style. Her silk T-shirt was copper, with a bronze cashmere sweater draped lightly over the top. The blinking ticket inspector didn't notice the thermal vest under that shirt, keeping her warm without thick layers; she was just stunning, her hair long and loose, her legs chic in chestnut leather trousers.

But the thing the ticket inspector noticed most was the determined look on that beautiful, minimally made-up face. He shot a warning look at the boys: *Leave the lady alone*. And then he walked on down the carriage. No catcalls on his train, no trouble, no thanks.

Dina was oblivious.

Even on bad days, she lived for beauty. She wasn't trying to attract attention – this was something she did for herself. Looking her best was her comfort, her armour. She felt stronger when she looked better. Today she wore Meadow cream – a perfect bulwark against the cold – and a light, airbrushed foundation from the store, a little number imported from Germany. Her eyes were playful: dark green shadow at the lashline, copper mascara, golds and browns up to the brow. And her lips were plain – nothing but a tangerine gloss. To her, this was as simple as putting on moisturiser. Why wouldn't everybody do it? Five minutes, and you could almost be someone else . . .

Today she wished she was someone else – someone with a normal family, a normal life. One of these kids, heading into the suburbs.

Oh, no, you don't, chided the small voice in her head. *Not at any price*.

'Tuckahoe.'

She grabbed her Mulberry purse and stepped out of the train. Good clothes, good cosmetics: these were luxuries for some, necessities for her. Dina invested, every time she stepped up the ladder. She bought key pieces, classics that worked, and let her face be her canvas.

It was her business. Had been, anyway.

She walked carefully up the stone steps by the platform and found herself at the centre of the village – the post office to her left, a diner to her right – just a few minutes' walk from Ellen's house. They hadn't spoken in a year, other than a snatched phone call on her mom's birthday and at Christmas. Dina hadn't gone back. What was the point in pretending things were great?

The house was there, much as she remembered it: tall, neat, well painted. Maybe there was some relief in that. Dina noticed that the curtains were open. She could see her old room; it had been repainted, and was now a garish pink.

She rang the bell.

'Yes?'

Her mom looked her up and down. There was a slight start of recognition, then shock.

'My God, look at you!' She couldn't keep the admiration out of her voice. Then it coloured with jealousy. 'What are you, some kind of model?'

'I work in beauty, Mom. In a store.'

'Right. You could never be a model. You're not tall enough. Not skinny, either.'

Ellen was wearing black slacks and a matching polo-neck, with ballet slippers. Her hair was a darker blond, cut straight; she wore a little powder, some blusher and mascara. Nothing on her lips, and Dina knew right away she was too proud to show the fine lines she had there, to let anything bleed. She was stylish, still, but nothing to match her daughter.

'Can I come in, Mom?'

'I guess.' She opened the door.

'Wow. Things are different.' Dina glanced around. Every trace of teenagers had vanished. There were pictures in frames, though, portraits of Ellen and Paul, the family together, lots of frames of Johnny. No pictures of Dina, unless she was with her brother.

'Yeah. This is the house my way.'

'You want to give me the grand tour?'

Ellen shrugged. 'You can go round if you want.'

Curious, Dina mounted the stairs. Johnny's room was there; the posters had been taken down, but his bed was the same, his rug, his framed artwork. In Dina's room, the pink walls were just the start; her bed, her carpet, her toys, everything had been removed. It was a Home Shopping Network fantasy, with a double bed made up in pink and gold, and matching drapes over the windows, a shagpile rug and silk roses in a glass vase.

'You got your guest room,' she said, lightly, once she'd returned downstairs. It only stung a little bit; she was hardened to her mother's hurtfulness at this point.

'Yes. Sometimes my friends stay – from church, or the Friends' Club.'

'That's great, Mom. Look, I didn't come to socialise . . .'

'Of course not; why would you want to see your mother?'

'You've never called me once—' Dina stopped herself, swallowed her anger. 'Whatever. This is about Johnny. Mom, he's sick.'

'Sick? What kind of sick?' Actual concern spread across her mother's face. 'Is it cancer?'

'No. No. He's OK; it's not that.'

'Jesus. You scared me, Dina. Always so overdramatic.'

'Mom, he's having a rough time at college. Like, maybe it's too hard for him . . . Anyway, he's getting into alcohol. And drugs.'

'A little pot and booze never hurt anybody.' There was anger in Ellen's eyes. 'You always were the goody two-shoes over that. You ruined my life, back then. You know that?'

'I saved your life. You were being passed round like popcorn, Mom.'

Ellen pursed her lips. 'Now I don't even dare to take a drink at New Year's Eve.'

'You're better off.' Dina couldn't stand the self-pity. 'You have an addictive personality. Johnny inherited it. He's drinking out of control and he's popping pills. Coke, ecstasy. Prescription pills.'

'Maybe he needs a good romance. I got one, you know,' Ellen said, triumphantly. 'I'm dating again. Oliver Guyden.'

'Of Guyden's Funeral Home?'

'It's a good business,' Ellen said, defensively. 'And his wife died. She was in the church group with us. Oliver and I have been going out for a while, since the summer. I think maybe he's going to pop the question.'

'That's great, Mom. Really.' Dina smiled at her mother. Despite it all, she still wanted her to be happy; maybe it would soften her a little.

'No thanks to you,' Ellen said.

'Let's sit down.'

'Why? Are you staying?'

'Jesus,' Dina said, softly. 'I'm your own daughter. Why can't you be nice to me?'

Ellen shrugged. 'I would if you ever showed any respect. But it was always all about Little Miss Perfect. Come on, Dina, I have work to do here. What do you expect me to do about Johnny?'

'Talk to him. Reason with him. He still loves you.' Dina took a deep breath. 'Mom, you need to give Johnny acceptance.'

'I've always accepted my son.'

'He's gay. He has a boyfriend – Brad Evans. He's steady, going to be a lawyer. He's just what Johnny needs.'

Ellen's face drained white. She stumbled and gripped the top of a chair.

'Bullshit,' she hissed. 'You're lying, lying just to hurt me. Johnny's not *gay*.'

'He is. He's with Brad.'

The whiteness drained and came back red. Ellen looked flushed, as if she'd just downed a fifth of Jack Daniel's. 'He's on drugs. You said so yourself. He's just confused. There's no way he's homosexual. His dad was always chasing strippers . . .'

'Mom!' Dina shouted. 'I don't have time for this. Johnny is gay; Johnny is almost addicted. He needs your compassion and your love. For once in your horrible life, think about somebody else. He was born gay and he's going to die gay. Put aside the nineteen seventies, focus on *your son*.'

Ellen sat heavily on her couch. 'What will Oliver say?'

'Nothing, if he loves you. And if he has a problem with Johnny, you should cut him loose.'

Ellen sat quietly for a few minutes, chewing on her bottom lip. Dina could see her mother thinking, see the hamster wheels turning as she chewed it over. 'I'll see my son; I'll see the boyfriend too. He's mine. I don't care. Whatever it is, that's what happens these days, right? Things are different.'

Dina breathed out with relief. *Thank God*. 'Yes, Mom, things are different. The ladies at church would judge you a lot worse if you abandoned your boy. You know that.'

Ellen was rocking to and fro, hugging herself. 'Why did he tell you? Why not me?'

'You never go to see him, Mom.'

'I pay for his college.'

'It's more than writing a cheque. I've been by most Sundays since I landed in the city. He was even nervous of telling me, at first. Then he met Brad and it kind of just happened.'

Ellen stared at Dina. 'You've been over there every Sunday. Trying to get in with him. Talking to him about me.'

'Mom, don't be crazy.'

'Crazy? I'm not crazy. Why is he talking to *you*? You're just trying to take him away from me. Encouraging him in all this drug-taking and gay stuff.'

'He can't be *encouraged*; he's just gay.'

'You'll do anything to be first – anything to make him drop me. Me – who raised you both from children, on my own.'

Dina breathed in, raggedly; her mother's cruelty was toxic to her. She found herself shaking; the lack of love was making her anxious, panicky.

'Do you want me to bring him to you?'

'No. He can come on his own. He doesn't need you, Dina. Johnny needs his mother.'

'You accepting Brad will be good. After that, you probably need to pay to put him in rehab.'

Ellen looked up again. 'Pay? I pay for college.'

'Rehab is expensive, Mom. Don't you have anything left?'

'I need my savings. Oliver and I are going to sell this place, buy something nice. It's all been discussed. We're going to move to Bronxville.'

Bronxville: the fancier village next door. Her mother had been talking about Bronxville for years before Dina left. It was her goal, her Shangri-la.

'But Johnny needs it.'

'Right. And he needed college, only he's blowing that. And so did you, but you have a job, correct?'

'I used to have a job. I'm kind of self-employed . . .'

Ellen wasn't listening. 'And what if I sink my savings into rehab and he comes right out and just starts up again? What's to stop him?'

'We just have to hope. There are no guarantees—'

'Well, I can *guarantee* that, if I don't spend my money on junk, I'll still have it.'

'Thanks, Mom.' Dina had had enough. 'I'll get Johnny to see you, at least. Maybe that'll do something.'

'I'll meet his boyfriend,' her mother said, grandly. 'I'll give them my blessing.'

But no money.

'That's great.' Dina stood up. Her mother didn't rise, not even for a peck on the cheek.

'I'm feeling faint,' she said. 'You can see yourself out.'

Brad took Johnny down the next day. Dina waited in her apartment; she had to think. She'd tried calling Hector, but he wouldn't pick up the phone. When she went round to the store and pressed the buzzer on his apartment, there was no reply; she'd seen his curtains twitching shut.

She moved to her windows, looking out over the street. This place was functional now, a little more her; even though there was no money to renovate as she wanted, Dina had decorated cheaply, had painted, hung a few mirrors. Already it looked more spacious. But she would have to do better if she wanted to sell.

She felt tired – so tired. She thought about Johnny, her mom, Hector, Meadow. Desperately, she wanted independence, to cut loose. There could not be any waiting, could not be any more limbo. Dina wanted a life, wanted power. She had come close, but something was standing in her way.

Hector Green looked about him. These were unfamiliar surroundings: the long, walnut panelled conference room; the green leather armchairs. Four lawyers sat opposite him with yellow legal pads, writing furiously, even though he hadn't said much. A young man with pallid skin and a foppish haircut sat next to them, wearing an expensive suit.

'And you are sure of this?' The chief lawyer was a white-haired man of Hector's own age, perhaps a touch younger. He was heavy around the middle and spoke with supreme confidence.

'I'm afraid so,' the young man said. 'Miss Kane is a fraudster. She was involved in an unfortunate blackmail attempt on my family.' Edward Johnson spread his hands. 'Mr Green, you were successful on your own terms before she came along.'

'She did bankroll the launch of Meadow.'

'After your sweat equity,' the lawyer said. 'You designed the product; you worked around the clock. She was back at the shop selling things you ordered. In essence, it wasn't bad for Ms Kane to ask to be paid. Our quarrel is with the ludicrous contract she had you sign.'

'She could have asked for recoupment of her loan – even ten times over,' Edward said, sadly. 'Instead, she took fifty per cent. It took you a lifetime of learning to devise Meadow.'

'She took advantage of an old man without proper represent-ation. It's eminently challengeable.'

Hector shook his head. He had no idea what to think. If only they would stop talking!

He blamed Dina for this. Why was she trying to stop him making money?

'I would like to do the night cream, and retire.' He shrugged. 'It is very simple. I wish to go somewhere warm. I am old, I cannot work any longer.'

'The problem is, it would be a Meadow night cream. And she co-owns the name – unless we fight in court.'

'I can make it a different name . . .'

'The Glamour store wants your branding: Meadow.'

Hector snapped 'Then why are we here? She owns half. She has a contract.'

'We can fight—'

'I am not interested in work; I am not interested in fight.'

'Mr Green, if you'll allow me,' Edward Johnson said, 'Ms Kane does not have the money to hire lawyers for a protracted period. She has a cash crisis. My suggestion would be that you merely threaten her. The firm here can serve her the notifications, file the actions. We can bury her in paperwork. She'll soon admit that you are the real owner of Meadow.' He laughed. 'You will be generous if you refrain from suing her for fraud – attempted theft.'

Hector gnawed on his knuckles, an old habit. 'I want this all to be over.'

'Do you think a twenty-year-old girl should steal a life's work?'
He shook his head.

'Then you have to do this. Are you willing? Mr Johnson is paying our fees.'

Dina was jogging down the street when the pretty student ran up to her.

'Are you Dina Kane?' she asked. 'You know, who makes the Meadow cream?'

'I'm Dina,' she answered, startled out of her thoughts of Johnny. Brad had found him in Chinatown that morning, badly beaten up and dumped on the side of the street. He was in a hospital, and sweating and puking through withdrawal.

They said it was narcotics.

Johnny Kane was going downhill like a teen on a helter-skelter, faster than anyone suspected. The visit to Ellen had not gone well. Brad told Dina everything over a plate of spaghetti: the tight lips, the wooden hugs. Ellen's new boyfriend was there, he said, and kept coughing every time Brad touched Johnny, or talked about their relationship. And Johnny asked for a drink, and left twenty minutes after realising there was nothing in the house.

'I don't know if she loves him. I don't know if she really loves anything.'

'She hates that he's gay. My mom cares how things look, always has.'

'Well, she's going to have a dead son, if she's not careful.'

Dina called up after that and begged one more time for money. She found a rehab centre up in the Catskills, a remote place with great therapists and a good reputation. Johnny should stay a month, maybe six weeks; that might cost sixty thousand bucks.

'You must be kidding, Dina. Oliver and I are starting our own lives. Let Brad take care of Johnny.'

'He's still a student, Mom.'

'Maybe his parents are richer than me. Anyway, Johnny needs to want this,' Ellen said, piously. 'I don't feel he's ready.'

Dina shivered. The gossamer thread she thought was there – Ellen's love for Johnny – was tearing, weakening. She wondered which was worse, the revelation he was gay, or the news that he spent time with his sister.

Dina didn't want to face that. She'd clung to the idea that at least Momma loved *one* of them. Today, she wasn't so sure. The jealousy . . . the pathology in Ellen Kane . . . But at least Mom was making her own decision easy. If Ellen wouldn't help – wouldn't support Johnny – Dina would.

'Well, I'm glad I found you, then,' the student said, jerking her back to the street and her jogging. She slowed up, looking at the girl. 'These are for you.'

She reached in a backpack and handed Dina some envelopes.

'Excuse me?' Dina gasped.

'You've been served. I'm sorry. Have a pleasant run.' And the girl took out a camera and, before Dina could move, snapped her holding the crisp white envelopes.

Dina looked up First Avenue, towards her apartment building, and her heart started to pound – with more than the exercise.

Shaman and Kebler, the envelopes were stamped. *Attorneys-At-Law.*

They were stiff, thick bond paper. She stopped and ripped one open.

Our client . . . fraudulent coercion . . . Intellectual property, rights and trademark . . . Advantage of the vulnerable . . . Suing for release of contract, costs and damages in the amount of ten million dollars . . .

Dina almost laughed. Ten million dollars? It felt like she barely had ten dollars. And, if she did, she'd need nine of them for Johnny.

Chapter Eight

'I'm sorry,' Eliza Sherman said.

She looked her young client over. Dina Kane was an interesting girl, one of the most unusual people ever to walk through her doors. She wanted to help her, but the kid had no money. Not enough to fight.

'It's just that they are such a big firm – corporate law experts. You have a great case, in my opinion, but they can file motion after motion. Without money, no firm is going to represent you. No-win, no-fee is a risk here, because they have so many lawyers.' She squirmed a little; here was a twenty-year-old who'd pulled herself up from nothing, got fifty per cent of a hot beauty product and was about to get skewered. 'Look, I can recommend some suburban firms, maybe. You'd need to try and get a bank loan. Or maybe you have a lawyer in your family . . . ?'

'So, what would you do, if you were me?'

'It's a tough break.' Sherman's small, cramped office on Third Street was full of law books, with a small window that looked out on to another building. She did bread-and-butter stuff, lawsuits at work, slips and falls, corporate liability. 'I think I'd hire a lawyer to write a couple of letters saying you'll fight it all the way, and then I'd settle.'

'Settle?'

'Give back your half of the Meadow line. For whatever price they offer.'

Dina leafed through the letters again. 'They don't sound like they want to settle. Unless I sign it back, they're going to sue.'

'And you can't persuade Dr Green?'

'Hector won't talk to me. The money stuff really changed him.'

'Yes,' said the lawyer. 'It can do that.'

Dina sighed. 'So, if I hire you to write the letters, how much could I get?'

Eliza shrugged. 'I'd try for something small – you're right, they don't want to settle – like, maybe, fifty thousand dollars, just to make the headache go away.'

Dina almost choked on the water she was sipping from a white plastic cup. 'Fifty thousand? That's it?'

'They're a serious firm.'

'Thank you,' Dina said. The older woman could see her thinking. 'Just one more question,' Dina continued. 'If I had the money to hire a firm like them, and I could fight it, would I get to keep my share?'

'Oh, sure. I really think so. The contract is tight, you persuaded him to develop the cream, you took over at the store – your fingerprints are on everything. And the fact that you re-mortgaged your apartment . . . it's all there.'

'I appreciate your time.' Dina rose to her feet. 'What do I owe you for the consultation?'

Eliza Sherman felt a pang of pity for the kid. 'Absolutely nothing,' she said. 'Good luck, Ms Kane.'

Dina sat at her kitchen table, an uneaten bowl of oatmeal by her side. She was lost in the *Wall Street Journal* and her laptop. Next to her was a simple white pad, with a list of names on it.

It was a short list.

So few men had the power to help her. And the name on the top of the list? Well, it was like approaching a legend.

Joel Gaines was one of Wall Street's major mavericks. He was forty-one years old and a venture capitalist of the old school – not a dot com in sight. Gaines bought companies, broke them up and sold them off. He founded his first hedge fund aged just twenty-five and, by the age of thirty, owned a Detroit automaker, a travel agency in New York and several citrus farms in California. He had a bad reputation as a brutal player, with a ruthless eye on the bottom line. Gaines cut jobs and made companies profitable. He also started with senior management first. He had married early, at twenty-three, to a society beauty, Susan, who threw legendary parties in the Hamptons and sat on several charity boards. There were two sons, seventeen and fifteen. His partner, Bob Goldstein, was older and very respected. He provided the prestige, and Gaines did the rest.

Dina loved the story. She wanted to be like him. One day – maybe.

Her fingers reached for her cellphone, then hesitated. It was such a long shot. Why on earth would a man like Gaines agree to see her?

But one thing she knew: in her place, at her age, Joel Gaines would have made this call. He would have made all the calls.

The letters from the law firm were piled up in front of her, their threats written clearly on the stiff cream paper. She wanted out, she had no choice.

'What's on the list today?' Gaines asked.

His assistant, Marian, placed a neatly typed list on his desk. Gaines always wanted a hard copy. He found screens distracting. Other bankers ran the numbers, did the algorithms; Gaines went out to the factories, talked to the workers, used the products. It was part of what made him the best.

'You have the Japanese team here for the breakfast meeting.'

'Very good.' He glanced out of his huge floor-to-ceiling windows. 'Bring them in shortly.'

'The *New Yorker* is here to profile you at ten.'

'We agreed to that?'

'Yes, sir.'

'Very well. Twenty minutes, max.'

'Yes, sir. Then you are talking to the union leaders from the plant in Milwaukee.'

'They can have an hour.'

'Lunch with Mr Goldstein.'

'OK. We'll go to Jean-Georges today.'

'Very good, sir. You have forty minutes after that for emails and calls. I'll have a sheet ready for you.'

'Then what?'

'Your personal trainer at half three and, at five, you are meeting the Mayor over the new construction site in TriBeCa. Your driver will take you directly home from City Hall at five forty.'

He nodded. Going home: that was the part of the day he liked least. 'Anything else?'

'Well . . . you did mention you might speak to that young woman who called, about the beauty cream.'

'Yes. Cute. What was her name again?'

'Dina Kane.'

'See if you can squeeze in an extra phone call somewhere. I'll take her pitch. Ten minutes.'

'Oh.'

'What is it?'

'She's waiting outside, sir.'

Joel blinked. 'Did I say a meeting?'

'No. She says she would prefer to speak to you face to face. She understands you will only have a few minutes for her; says she'll wait. Do you want me to tell her to go away?'

He laughed; he liked a kid – of either sex – with balls. Mostly they were eager young Ivy League grads who'd watched *Wall Street* one too many times. Mostly they were men.

'She can go away and come back after lunch, if she wants. Or she can wait. It may be several hours.'

'Very good, sir.' Marian didn't argue the point.

'Bring me some coffee, please.'

He had few vices these days, but caffeine was one of them.

Dina waited. She came prepared; she had her notes, her print-outs, her projections, the case summary. And she had her phone. As the hours ticked by, she didn't idly leaf through magazines, or stare out of the vast Gaines Goldstein windows at Sixth Avenue below. She read up and studied, digging through the *Journal*, the *New York Times*, *Forbes*, *Fortune*, whatever was out there, following all the deals that Joel Gaines had ever done.

It was gripping. Dina got it immediately. There was a beautiful logic to the way he worked, mixed with a gambler's touch that made it artful. The private jet, the exclusive prep schools, the house in the Hamptons – all of these were less interesting to her; they were just the natural result of the brilliant mind at work in the office behind her.

She watched as men were shown in to the inner sanctum and returned, hours or minutes later, awe-struck and babbling amongst themselves. From Japanese businessmen to a journalist and photographer to some hard-looking, weather-beaten guys in lumberjack shirts and jeans. It wasn't clear precisely what he was doing, but from their reactions when they came out, he was doing it brilliantly.

It was exciting. It was thrilling. Another time, she might have been happy just to be in his presence. But not today. This wasn't just a courtesy call, nor was she a mere fan. She needed him. She needed this deal.

Finally, at almost noon, his secretary emerged: immaculate in pencil skirt, silk shirt and kitten heels; an elegant fifty-year-old blonde.

'Ms Kane – Mr Gaines can see you.'

She jumped to her feet, trying to calm her ragged breathing.

'I must warn you, this was meant to be a phone call. Mr Gaines has an absolute maximum of ten minutes. Try to make it less.'

Dina knew better than to sass the assistant. She meekly nodded her head. 'Yes, ma'am.'

The door opened into a cavernous office, exactly as she had expected. But that didn't make it any less impressive. The soft woollen carpet in eggshell grey led up to a wall of windows at one end, and stark white walls on the other three sides, hung with enormous canvases of modern art; she recognised a Basquiat, a huge Warhol print, two others she didn't know, but that still reeked of money. There was a large Wall Street ticker moving across one wall relentlessly, in an electronic banner.

Dina swallowed dryly. She was impressed, even a little aroused, despite herself. It was so in-your-face.

Gaines was sitting behind his desk, reading through some papers as she approached him. Dina took him in – the square, powerful shoulders, the muscled body under the well-cut suit. He wore a plain steel watch, nothing fancy. His square-jawed profile was striking and he had salt-and-pepper hair cut very close to the head.

'Thank you for seeing me, Mr Gaines.' She sat down, without being asked. There was a chair, and Dina didn't have time to waste with pleasantries.

'We were supposed to do this over the phone.' Gaines turned and looked at her, and Dina flushed with surprise.

He was sexy. The eyes were dark, fringed with black lashes so thick it looked like he was wearing mascara. He had a large nose and a cruel, arrogant set to his mouth, which matched his aura of power and the muscles of his body. She flashed to imagining him in a gym, lifting weights.

'Yes, sir.' She dragged herself back to the present. 'I thought I could get the point across better if I could see you.'

The dark eyes flickered up and down her body, and Dina felt desire licking at her.

He leaned back in his chair. 'Go ahead, kid. Pitch me.'

'I partnered with a man who ran a small beauty store – a chemist who hadn't worked in years. I love beauty.'

He inclined his head a fraction of an inch, without paying her a compliment.

'We were doing too well for the store, but he didn't want to expand. I persuaded him to develop a great day cream. I put up the money for lab costs, packaging: a loan against my apartment, in exchange for half the product. It's called Meadow and early orders are really good. Here.'

She passed over her fact sheets. 'It could be a blockbuster, if we had the right distribution. A new Crème de la Mer.'

Gaines looked over them. 'Congratulations. What do you need me for?'

'My partner is suing me – for ten million dollars. They're saying I stole half the cream from him. He wants to make other products in the line, without paying me. Glamour Store offered him a million bucks for a night cream.'

'Messy.'

Dina swallowed hard. 'I saw a lawyer and she says I can't fight it. Even though I can prove I funded it, he hired this big-shot firm and they can file so much stuff, I have no money to defend the suit. I spent all I had on funding Meadow.'

'Why is he doing this to you?'

She was ashamed to find tears prickling in the corners of her eyes, and fiercely blinked them back.

'Maybe I pushed him too hard. Hector just wanted a quiet life. Now he wants money first, then a quiet life.'

Gaines glanced at her, and then down at the papers again. It was a solid little bundle, presented by somebody who had judged him well. She had included not just the sales figures and her contract, but costs, projections and – more than that – press.

There was a small sheaf of articles and reviews, neatly clipped from beauty magazines and supplements. From her package, he got a sense of a wonder cream breaking into the market, a product with legs.

'My lawyer said somebody with money could fight this suit easily. But I don't have any.'

'What's your background?'

He pushed back in his chair. The girl was intriguing, and not just because she was beautiful. As a very rich man, he was around pretty girls all the time; the models swarmed at the nightclubs and the country clubs, hoping to pick up a financier, married or not.

She was elegantly dressed, wearing fitted black trousers and flats, and a dark red silk blouse. No jewellery; she didn't need it. Her face looked like it had been made up by a pro: gorgeous light rose blusher on the tops of her cheekbones, a translucent pink gloss on the lips, some sheer kind of foundation, eye shadow the pale brown of lightly done toast. When a girl like this spoke about beauty, young as she was, he got the sense of talking to an expert.

'I started out as a waitress. Then got into beauty retail, like I said.'

'No college?'

'There was no money. My mom was widowed early.'

He arched a brow. 'You don't think a sob story will have an effect on me?'

Dina flushed again, this time with anger. 'What sob story? I've done well.'

'Up to now.' He liked her spirit. Loved it. He was just playing with her now, enjoying himself. 'You can't fight this case.'

'No, sir. But, for you, it would be peanuts. They would wet themselves if they saw you coming.'

'That's probably true.' Gaines smiled. 'When it comes to lawyers, I have depth on the bench.'

'And a reputation.'

He pushed his chair back a little, examined her more closely. 'What reputation is that?'

She blushed. 'I'm sure you know that, Mr Gaines.'

'Very well.' The plain speaking amused him. Nobody ever talked to him like this. They were craven, flattering, obsequious. This girl hadn't got the memo. 'And knowing my reputation, why do you think I would be interested?'

'In the *Journal* it said that L'Audace was looking to expand its beauty presence, to add to its brands. You need a skincare line.'

L'Audace was a tired luxury goods house with a glittering past behind it that Gaines Goldstein had bought out two months ago.

'Meadow could be a big part of that revival. I will sell you my fifty per cent, and all my interest in future products and brands in the line. When they know you'll fight, they will probably cave themselves. You can buy out Hector's half, and the formula. And you'll have a great product. You see, Meadow actually works, because Hector is a talented chemist. It's what made our store good.'

He nodded. 'How does a waitress get a property she can borrow against?'

'My mom made me a small loan and I saved; I bought a studio, fixed it up, flipped it, did the same with another place.' She tossed her hair, a proud gesture. 'I did very well.'

'Excuse me. Sir?' Marion Harris was at the door, tutting impatiently. 'Your lunch reservation.'

'Coming.' He stood up, and the girl did too, dismissed. 'The idea has some merit; the figures need to back it up. I'll make some calls, get back to you.'

'Would you like my phone number?' Dina said.

'No.' He didn't look back at her as he strode towards the door. 'We can reach you if we want to.'

* * *

She spent a depressing afternoon trudging around the banks.

'We can't help you.'

'Far too complicated.'

'You have no assets. That's a piece of paper.'

Nothing she could say would persuade them. And the other venture capitalists she tried would barely talk to her; one of them gave her an appointment, three weeks away. By then she'd be a dinosaur.

Weary, discouraged, she headed back to her apartment. If this didn't work out, if she had to defend the suit, she might go bankrupt. *Jesus*, Dina thought. *Back to square one, back to nothing.* Tomorrow she would call a realtor, try to dump her apartment as soon as possible. Maybe, if she was lucky, she would get a few thousand to put in trust for Johnny.

And then what? She had no references, no proof of success. Would she waitress again? Hector would brand her a thief, when she caved; what beauty brand would want to work with her?

She went into the bedroom and lay down on the bed. Really, she should stand up, shower, change. But there was no energy; Dina just couldn't move.

This morning she thought she was really getting somewhere. But he hadn't called. It was a hopeless, stupid, extravagant play . . .

The phone rang at the side of her bed. 'Dina Kane.'

'Joel Gaines.'

She sat bolt upright, immediately. Her palm holding the receiver started to sweat.

'Yes, sir.'

'Here's the deal: I will buy you out for half a million dollars.'

She gasped in shock. 'My God.'

'I'm not doing you a favour; I'm taking a gamble. That will include all your interest, not just in this cream, but in anything developed for the Meadow brand, the line, the intellectual property, everything. I will accept all liability belonging to you.'

'I don't know what to say.'

'"Yes," is my suggestion,' he said.

'Yes. Sir. Thank you.'

'You aren't listening to me. By making this deal, you are putting yourself in Hector Green's position. I'm advancing you a relatively small amount of money. If the cream takes off, you will have sold a half share that could be worth tens of millions, maybe more, because you need money now. And don't try to come after me when that happens. There is no crying in baseball.'

'Yes, sir.' Dina couldn't stop the huge smile spreading across her face. He was so fair, straight with her. But not giving an inch. She loved it. 'It may be worth tens of millions to you, but it isn't worth that to me. I can't fight the suits.'

'Are you going to try to bargain?'

'I'm not in a position to bargain.'

'That's right. You're not,' he said, softly, and again, Dina felt that squirming lick of desire trawling across her belly. *Cut that out,* she ordered herself, thankful that she was on the end of a phone and he couldn't see any of her reactions.

'I do need the money fast, though.'

'They always do. You can meet me for coffee tomorrow morning at eight. I'll have papers for you to sign.'

'Meet for breakfast? OK. Yes, sir.'

'I said coffee. This is a half-million-dollar deal. You don't rate breakfast.'

Dina smiled. 'Of course not. Where should I come?'

'French Roast,' he said. 'Sixth and Twelfth. Don't be late.'

'Yes, sir. Thank you, Mr Gaines.'

'See you tomorrow, Dina Kane.'

The hooker was one of his favourites. An exotic mix of black and Hispanic, skin the colour of creamy coffee, she bounced up and down on his cock with a lazy smile and enthusiasm. She went by the nom-de-fuck of Coco, which was all right by Edward.

'Ah. Yeah.' He shifted around, watching those perfect, huge fake tits jiggle. 'Work it. Come on, show me.'

'Ohhh,' she groaned, theatrically. He scowled, hating it when they said anything. What Edward wanted was an anonymous screw. Quickly, he closed his eyes and thought of Dina Kane, that slim, sexy, younger body. He thought of the lawyers, and of breaking her. Mostly he thought of having her, desperate and penniless, coming back to him, humbly, and kneeling down to suck. He groaned, and came.

Coco slipped off him. '*Chérie*, that was wonderful.'

She affected some Creole shit. Not that he gave a damn. She was already heading to the shower. This was a classy joint, and her little apartment saw a lot of action. The two o'clock was already on the way.

He tugged on his pants, not bothering to wash. By the bed lay his little silver-topped vial with the tiny spoon for the coke. He helped himself to another small hit. He was just like an English gentleman of the eighteen hundreds with his bottle of snuff. Edward liked that image; it made him feel good.

As he buttoned his shirt, the chemical rush hit him. Yes, things were fine; things were better. His weak-ass father had bailed, so fuck him. Edward had no intention of working for a living. And, as for the army – that stuff was for suckers.

He didn't need therapy. He just needed to bury Dina Kane. And it was happening sooner than he'd ever hoped. Hector Green, that stupid, confused old man, had told him what he wanted to know.

'She did offer finance, though, Mr Johnson. She mortgaged her apartment . . .'

'How did she get one of those?'

A sugar daddy no doubt. Like his father. *Whore.*

'I don't know. We didn't talk much outside of business. I'm a private person. So is she.'

Not that private.

146

'OK. Thanks, Hector.'

It was especially delicious hiring lawyers that could dump all over Dina's stupid little discovery from a great height. Now they would be able to steal her little face cream – Jesus, a *face cream* – and whatever she'd borrowed against that apartment. The middle-class dream, climbing the property ladder . . . That would have to go.

The letters got sent, and it made him hard. There were drinks in a nightclub, quiet words with a discreet dealer, and then a visit to a hooker.

No more chasing teenage pussy, poor students or bridge-and-tunnel girls. He was going to select a classy wife, and fuck call girls on the side. The cocaine sparkled in his blood; Coco seemed like a great decision. Discreet. Easy to hide. He was smart; he was going to stick to professionals – whores with Blackberries and health certificates you could view.

But he was done now.

'See you soon, sugar,' she called as Edward headed out the door, ignoring her. He hadn't come for the conversation.

The car – with his mother's chauffeur – was parked outside. So what if it was nearly two in the morning? Time to earn his money. Edward felt like hitting a club, but there would be time for the big party later, once Dina was officially bankrupt. He expected the capitulation from her lawyers tomorrow, a letter begging Hector for mercy. Edward couldn't wait to show the girl who was really pulling the strings.

Edward was getting his shit together. First, he'd come out of the club and gone home. If Daddy wasn't going to be his meal ticket, Momma would have to. He *deserved* it. It was his *father*'s stupidity that let Dina take advantage. Edward had to drop out of college to preserve the family honour. They owed him. He was the victim here!

'Momma.' He marched into her bedroom and pulled back the

ornate drapes; sunlight streamed into the dusty room. 'Get up.'

'Oh, God,' she moaned. There were bottles everywhere – beside the bed, on the bedside cabinet – champagne and whiskey and liqueurs. She didn't seem particular, just anything left in the cellars, anything she would not have to go outside the house for. 'Leave me alone.'

The room stank of sweat, even a little vomit. Edward wanted to gag. He tugged the covers off the bed; his mother was lying there, fully clothed in the slacks she'd put on two days ago.

'Get into the shower.' He ferociously yanked her to her feet as she gagged and gasped. There was a master bathroom attached, with a wet room, all in marble, that his father had designed.

'No! Leave me alone!' Her hand reached for a whiskey bottle on the side, but Edward knocked it back, hard. His mother disgusted him, they all did.

'Get your clothes off, or I'll do it for you.' He flung a bathrobe at her.

Choking, she peeled off her stinking jumper and shirt. Edward turned his back, ignoring her, and walked into the shower, twisting the taps on full blast, lukewarm.

'Get in.'

She stumbled in, still wearing underwear, and Edward went outside and summoned a maid.

'In ten minutes, go into Mrs Johnson's room. You will throw away every bottle, strip the bed, remake it, and thoroughly disinfect and clean.'

'Yes, sir. Of course.'

'Tell Rafael to go through this house and remove everything alcoholic, including mouthwash.'

'Yes, sir.'

'And have the chauffeur get the car ready.'

He went to his mother's chest of drawers and pulled out a bra, a T-shirt, underwear, socks and a pair of lounge pants, and laid them on the embroidered French bench in the dressing room.

'Mother – get out.'

There was the soft sound of Penelope crying. Edward ignored it. He was driven with rage, pure white rage that felt so good for the soul. When she didn't move, he stepped into the shower and turned the dial all the way down to ice-cold.

She shrieked with misery and stepped out.

'Edward! Why are you doing this to me?'

He flung one of the huge Egyptian cotton bath sheets at her; was anything more repellent than the sight of his mother, shivering and half-naked?

'It's over, Momma.'

'What's over? You are acting crazy . . . I need a drink.'

'No drinks. That's all gone. I'm afraid I can't afford for you to fall apart. Go and put your clothes on, in the dressing room. I'm taking you to the doctor.'

She dry-retched. 'I feel sick.'

'You are sick. Your skin looks like day old porridge, your eyes are bloodshot, your hair is matted. You're drinking yourself to death. I'm taking you to the doctor. If you refuse, I will go to a court and have you committed. I'll put you in Bellevue, Mother.'

Penelope limped out of his sight, the towel clutched pathetically around her. As she dressed, Edward called Dr Rathbone, their highly overpaid, but always available, family physician.

'Why are you doing this? I'm sick. I feel so ill. God, Edward, if you only knew how much it hurts . . .'

His mother stood before him, dressed, her wet hair still plastered against her head. How he acted now would be key to his future.

He pulled her close, kissed her on the head. 'Somebody has to look after you, Momma. Daddy's gone now. I'll be the one to help you.'

She sobbed.

Edward wrapped an Hermès silk scarf round her head and selected a fox fur coat from her closet. A pair of Versace sunglasses, a relic from their last vacation at the Four Seasons resort in Costa Rica, was lying in her jewellery case; he slipped them on, hiding her bloodshot eyes, and doused her with Aqua di Parma to conceal the reek of alcohol seeping from her pores, despite the merciful shower.

'Come along. I'll take you to the car.'

'I don't want to go . . . I don't want to be seen out.'

'Don't worry,' he said. 'Dr Rathbone is fantastically discreet.'

He was. He admitted Penelope to his private clinic, with three recovery suites, mostly for models and film stars after their facelifts.

'She will experience delirium tremens.'

Edward shuddered at the thought. His own mother, calling out about spiders crawling on her skin, hallucinating.

'I don't care. I want you to sedate her. Keep her as an inpatient for a week. Get her clean.'

'That's extremely costly. Is she in a position to pay the bill?'

Edward was not surprised at the lack of sensitivity. Bill paying first, compassion later: that was Manhattan society for you. 'You need to sign this,' he said. 'It's a statement that she is medically unfit, giving me power of attorney. My lawyers will have it ratified today, and then you'll be paid from the family trust.'

Rathbone scribbled immediately. Edward smirked; this stay was tens of thousands to the doc.

'After she's sober, she'll be fit again. You do understand that?'

Edward smiled. 'Of course, doctor.'

He wasn't stupid. He couldn't just shove his mother out of the way. She would need to be persuaded. She would need to *depend* on him.

Every day, he came to the clinic. He brought flowers, toiletries. He sat with his mother. As she shook and shuddered, he gripped her hand, spoke soothingly to her.

'Don't worry, Momma. You're here. You're safe.'

Edward made sure the lights were kept on, the walls were clean white – that there was nothing to promote hallucinations. When Penelope started to gibber and panic, he insisted on sedatives.

'She shouldn't have too many benzodiazepines. That could be a whole different problem.'

'I don't give a damn,' Edward replied. 'Put her under.'

And his mother looked at him with wild, grateful eyes as the nurse administered another white pill.

She came home two weeks later, shaken and nervous, but sober, and grateful to him.

'I can't believe it.' Penelope looked round at her house. It was transformed: all the mess had vanished, the doors and windows sparkling clean. The stench of sweat and failure and crisis had gone. Edward had arranged fresh flowers in every room and conducted a complete clean out of her wardrobe and shoe closet. The fridge was stocked with healthy foods. Get-well-soon cards from some of her friends were arrayed on the mantelpiece of the drawing room. The garden was weeded and tended, and all the domestic staff had been paid. 'It's wonderful. Oh, Edward, I never want to go back.'

'The tendency will never leave you, now. You do understand that? No alcohol, ever again.'

Penny nodded meekly.

'I've arranged a small dinner party tonight.'

Her face creased with anxiety. 'I couldn't.'

'You can. You must. I have a programme set up for you, Mother. We will face our friends – tell them the stress of the divorce made you sick. I have enrolled you, in a small way, in a few local charities. And you can attend the odd benefit. I'm carefully selecting those where no alcohol will be present. And I am putting together a programme of events: concerts, plays, some spa and therapy days. I don't see why you can't resume your position.'

Penelope's lip trembled. Now sober, she was hideously embarrassed. Shame at what she'd done crawled over her skin like hallucinatory bugs in the clinic's hellish detox room.

'Do you really think so?'

'Mother, there will be weekly visits to the hairdresser, to a terrific massage therapist, and some work with the Episcopalians.' This was the least religious church Edward had been able to find. 'It will give you a wonderful new lease of life. You do understand, though, that you are very fragile?'

'I feel fragile.' She pressed her fingers to her forehead, the nails stubbed and broken. 'Oh, Edward, I'm not sure I'm ready for any of it . . .'

'If you sit and brood, you will wind up back in that clinic. Is that what you want?'

She shuddered. 'No! God, no.'

'Then let me handle things. After tonight, we will need to have a little talk about finances.'

'Very well,' his mother said, distantly.

She was staring at herself in the mirror; her face was lined and wrinkled, her blond hair streaked with thick grey roots, her nails cracked. She was clean and neatly dressed, but the woman gazing back at her had aged a hundred years.

'Oh, Momma.' Edward took her hand. 'Come into the guest bathroom. There are some therapists waiting to welcome you home.'

'Therapists?'

'I've brought in a manicurist to do your hands and give you a pedicure, and Jason Quigley is making a house call to tint your hair. After that, Dr Westin is coming in.'

Penelope Johnson smiled a proper smile for the first time in weeks. Jason Quigley was her hair colourist. And Dr Westin was her very able dermatologist, from a few months ago, from another life.

'And then we have Emma Lucille, who will attend to your make-up after everybody else has finished. She's a freelancer, but comes highly recommended.'

'What do you know about beauty, Edward?'

'I did a little digging,' he said, modestly.

The dinner was a great success. Edward felt the stone lift a little off his chest. The days when he and his family were social pariahs were gone.

He had invited friends he knew would come: the lower echelons of his mother's social circle, the ones who would still be grateful for an invitation from Penelope Johnson, and two other divorcees. Next, he made sure that none of the eight or nine guests drank alcohol. Finally, he had included Itsy Moran, a second stringer from *Society* magazine's gossip pages, whom he dated briefly. She could be relied upon for a sympathetic write-up: 'The Return of the Johnsons'.

Penny swept into the room with something like confidence. Four hours in that bathroom had restored her to herself; her hair was back to a dark honey blond and swept up in an elegant chignon; her face had been smoothed with Botox, plumped with filler and then carefully made up, light and neutral for a woman in her fifties. Her fingers and toes were neatly trimmed and glistening with French polish, and she wore a pair of flat Louboutins and a plain satin evening dress in cornflower blue, with long sleeves to hide the bruises on her arms. Add in her large diamond-stud earrings, and Penny Johnson looked well, even elegant.

'Penny! How wonderful to see you,' Itsy gushed.

'Darling! You look perfect,' said Bobby Grantham.

'Kiss kiss,' his mother said, distributing air pecks, just as she used to. 'Shall we eat?'

When they all left – quite soon after nine thirty; without wine, guests had other things to do – Penny Johnson came over to

Edward and gripped his arm tightly. Her eyes glittered with tears, happy tears.

'Oh, my. That was . . . enjoyable,' she said, as though she had not expected anything to be enjoyable again.

'You see? You can do it.'

She was looking at herself in the ornate gold-rimmed mirror in their hallway, and smiling softly again. 'Oh, yes, Edward – thank you so much.'

He returned the smile, concealing his contempt and resentment. Up to him to fix his own parents – both of them.

'Just step into the parlour room here, Mother,' he said. 'I have some paperwork that needs signing.'

She followed him into a small office – once his father's, now redecorated to remove every trace of Shelby – and Edward pulled out the French armchair for her at the mahogany desk. The bank forms were there, pre-signed by him.

'What is this, darling?'

'Just sign it, Momma. It's a transfer of money, so that I can take care of the house and look after you. You aren't in a fit state to do it – not yet.'

Penelope looked at the papers, her eyes crunching. 'This looks like a million dollars . . .'

'Two million, for the year. That's what I need. Can you sign by the crosses?'

'But that's so much money . . .'

'We have ten in the bank, cash. Believe me, this covers basic expenses, allows me to care for you. I need to make decisions, Momma. Aren't you a little better tonight? It went well?'

She nodded, hesitating.

'Look, if you don't trust me, I'm happy to step away,' he said. 'You can sort everything out here on your own. I've devoted myself to you, Momma; I gave up college for you. This is the only way things work.'

The pen trembled.

'Very well. Of course, you mustn't feel forced. I'll leave,' Edward said.

'No – no. Stay, darling. You . . . you manage things so well.'

She signed, and Edward Johnson was finally a millionaire.

The next morning, he was in the offices of Shaman and Kebler, Attorneys-At-Law, with a retainer cheque for a hundred thousand dollars. First order of business – going after Dina Kane.

Chapter Nine

French Roast was one of her favourite coffee places. It was almost like he knew. She loved the rich scents of the flavoured beans and different syrups, the bohemian crowd that thronged through day and night, the way it sat on the very edge of the Village, across the border at Sixth Avenue, like a gateway.

But it wasn't the kind of place you'd expect to meet Joel Gaines. Nowhere fancy. Nothing to suit a billionaire.

Dina was there, waiting, by half past seven. She ordered a plain omelette, mostly to secure a table. She was too nervous to eat.

It was wrong to be turned on by this. It was a business deal. For him, barely worth noticing; for her, everything. She tried to think about Meadow, the cream, the potential. Hector Green was a good chemist. The product would work, would fit with what Gaines was trying to do . . .

It was no good. Her mind kept flashing back to him: the salt-and-pepper hair, the dark eyes, the air of complete confidence, complete power.

Goddamn, Dina thought. *I need a boyfriend.*

But how stupid and small that word seemed. Boyfriend. What? Some skinny youth with acne from a world she'd never entered? A student? *Edward Johnson*, or another rich boy just like him?

Gaines had blazed his own trail, conquered his own worlds.

Dina forced herself to dress down for this meeting. Gaines was not for her – obviously not. He was married, for a start. Two teenaged kids. Far too old for her. And he was her only hope in life, right now. This deal would save her ass.

She put on a uniform: a fitted grey woollen skirt from DKNY, cashmere tights in pewter, and gunmetal pumps, with a cream silk blouse and a crewneck sweater in oyster; a silver woollen scarf and a black military coat from Prada lay over the back of her chair, with her leather gloves. Her make-up was almost non-existent: a touch of powder, a little bronzer on the cheeks for health, concealer for her sleepless eyes. Neutral shadow and a clear gloss. As businesslike as she could be.

Dina was sipping her coffee – Irish Whiskey scent, the closest she ever got to alcohol – when he arrived. He was bang on time, walking purposefully through the doors. His greatcoat and dark suit did nothing to hide that body. When he spoke to the hostess, Dina could see the admiration in the girl's body language, and was instantly jealous.

She jumped to her feet and waved.

He saw her, and threaded his way through the tables. He was carrying a briefcase; she hadn't seen one of those on the street for years. In that briefcase was the key to her future. The dark eyes were fixed on her, and her heart started to thump. Fear, adrenaline. Something else, too, that she didn't want to think about.

'Ms Kane, good morning.'

'Mr Gaines.' She offered her hand, and he shook it, amused. 'Would you call me Dina?'

'Certainly.' He sat down and turned to the hovering waitress. 'Black cinnamon coffee. Grande. No sugar.'

'Yes, sir,' she said.

Gaines gestured to the omelette. 'I thought I told you we weren't eating.'

'You don't have to eat. I need the protein.'

He laughed. 'You have a lot of attitude for somebody who needs my help desperately.'

'Like you said, Mr Gaines, you're not doing me a favour. You're getting fifty per cent of a major beauty product for half a million dollars.'

Gaines looked the girl over, up and down. She was incredibly beautiful. The perfection of her make-up made her look better than a model: young, but put together. Underneath the bravado, he could see the nerves, and he liked her more for that. Her body, beneath the form-fitting clothes, was tempting – tight, lush, with plenty of curves, despite the slimness.

Jesus. Get a grip.

He thought of his wife, back home. They had quarrelled that morning – it was becoming too frequent, lately – an argument over her lack of desire to do much of anything: shop, arrange charity dinners. Susan was far more polished and groomed than Dina Kane; she worked on herself every day, from the Pilates classes to the private hairdresser. Nobody could rock an evening gown and a diamond collar like his carefully blonde wife. It all seemed OK, back when the boys were young.

'What's your problem? I have work to do – running our home.'

'Of course,' he replied, reaching for his work papers. He had been looking forward to seeing the kid this morning – the fighter.

'Really, Joel, what would be the point? I could study as a lawyer, and then we'd have five hundred million dollars *plus* another ninety thousand.' Susan laughed lightly. 'You have somebody home here; isn't that priceless?'

She picked up her tennis racket and blew him a kiss. Gaines tried to imagine having sex with her tonight. Susan never said no to him – part of the wifely code, so he gathered. But she came to his bed without enthusiasm these days, like it was just another chore, a workout.

Dina Kane did not remind him of his wife. Nor of the younger, sexier set that hung out in the Hamptons – on the tennis courts, in the country clubs – with their blond hair worn long. She wasn't a Park Avenue Princess. She reminded him of *him*. Back when he was poor. Back when it was fun . . .

'Here.' He reached for the briefcase, snapped it open. 'A letter, several forms . . .'

She took them, pulling a plastic pen from her purse.

'You can do better than that.' Gaines removed a pen from an inner pocket: Montblanc, pure gold. 'Sign your first deal; start as you mean to go on.'

Dina took it, delicately. The flamboyance of the gesture heated her. To hide it, she bowed her head, dark hair tumbling around her face as she signed.

'Done. Thank you.'

'One copy's for you.' Gaines pushed the papers towards her. 'And keep the pen.'

She started. 'I couldn't.'

'Do great things with it. Make more deals.' He stood up, before he looked too long at those green eyes. The schedule was busy today – like always. 'Call me again when you've made your first ten million.'

Dina's belly fluttered with desire. 'You joke with me, Mr Gaines.'

'Joel,' he said, standing up. 'And I never joke.'

She watched his back as he left the room.

Edward Johnson arrived punctually at his new office. Penelope had signed away part of the trust-fund management to him and he'd set up a shell company, EdJo Inc, listed as 'private wealth management'. Edward enjoyed printing up little cards that said *Director*, and leasing one smart room in a block off Columbus Circle.

He had no intention of actually doing any work. There were brokers, good ones, who handled the Johnson money, now his mother's money. This title gave him something to pretend to do. Screw Columbia. Screw Dina. Once she'd handed over Meadow, he was planning another little sit-down with Hector Green. It would be amusing to take a share in that product himself, run it and make a success of it. Women went crazy for beauty; it was a billion-dollar industry. He loved the idea of making money there – New York Fashion Week, fucking the models, front row at the shows, designers cosying up to him. *Far* more fun than some stuffy law office or Wall Street traders' shop.

For now, there was a boring, cheap secretary in her late forties – practically dead, but you don't shit where you eat – and a little desk with a view. He would make a few calls to some of the brokers to 'discuss investments'. More importantly, there would be lunches, dinners, cocktails . . . Ed Johnson had a list of every little fucker that abandoned him, all those Ivy League fair-weather friends. He had money, position again. And he would pursue some girl to marry – one with a lot of cash and no crazy ideas about business.

'Good morning, Mr Johnson,' said Faustina Kopek, his new assistant.

'Morning. Get me some coffee. Jamaican Blue Mountain with cream. And croissants. There's a Whole Foods downstairs.'

'OK.'

He preferred *Yes, sir*; they would have to work on that. 'First things first, put me through to Giles Shaman at Shaman and Kebler.'

'Right away.'

He closed the door so he wouldn't have to look at her pudgy ass, and right away the little red button lit up on his phone. Just like a real office. Edward smiled.

'Johnson,' he said, pompously.

'Edward. This is Giles. I'm afraid we have a little bit of a problem.'

Dina called her bank to make sure the money was there. Then she called Brad.

'I've got the money – for rehab. Can you help me get him there?'

'You're kidding?' Brad breathed out, a long, guttural sigh of relief. 'Did your mother change her mind?'

'I got it myself. It's a long story.'

'He's cut back some . . . just some. He still needs the help.'

Dina could hear the stress in his voice. 'I'll be right over.'

Johnny was dressed and out of bed; that was the good part about it. But Dina looked with horror at her brother's skinny, half-skeletal frame, the hollows under his eyes, his shaking hands. His hair was long, grown over the collar. No longer handsome, he looked years older than himself.

As soon as Dina walked in, he burst into tears.

'I can't stop it,' he sobbed. 'I'm out of control. Brad asked me to move out. He said he can't take it.'

Dina looked over at Brad, who stared at the floor. 'I'm sorry,' he said. 'It's too much. I wish I were stronger.'

Johnny wept, his frail shoulders shaking pathetically. Dina's heart creased with pity – for her brother, for Brad, for everybody.

'Johnny, you'll get better. I have a place for you. The best rehab in the state.'

'We can't afford it.'

'It's all taken care of. You just get strong – get better. I'll speak to the dean's office; get you a medical leave of absence. You can finish college next semester.'

'I can't go yet,' he pleaded. 'I need something. One hit. One last hit . . .'

'I've got a car waiting outside – to drive you.'

Johnny got to his feet, unsteadily. 'I don't have a case packed . . . No clothes; can't go . . .'

Brad moved back into the bedroom with a small red suitcase. 'All your stuff is in here. Go with your sister.'

Tears sprang to Johnny's eyes. 'You just want to get rid of me! I loved you.'

'But you loved that stuff more,' Brad said, his own voice cracking, and then he turned away. 'Dina . . . please go.'

She hefted up the case with one hand and her brother with the other, cradling his weight by draping one skinny arm around her shoulder. It felt as though the suitcase weighed more.

'Come on, Johnny.' She wanted to cry too, but somebody had to be strong. 'They're waiting for you. We'll get through this; we'll get through it all.'

'That can't be.'

Edward's heart was hammering a million miles an hour, like he'd done too much coke. He felt his face flush with blood, his ears buzzing. Perhaps he would faint. He gripped the desk in front of him.

'Mr Gaines' lawyers have been on the phone all morning. They can run this case till the end of time. We can't possibly fight them.'

'You have to.' His voice rose in a high-pitched squeal. 'You goddamned have to.'

'Actually, we don't. Dr Green is our client, not you.'

'I paid you bastards. A hundred thousand!'

'To represent Dr Green,' said Giles Shaman, smoothly. 'The proprieties were explained to you at the time. We have to give our client the best advice.'

'I'm the client!'

'Please calm yourself, Mr Johnson. There is nothing for it except to advise Dr Green to sell his share. The good news is he's content about that – even relieved. Mr Gaines has offered him two million dollars, to include all intellectual property, the trademark, the brand. He's going back to Austria, to retire.'

'I don't care where he's going. I don't care about him! He has to sue her!'

'You don't seem to understand. Dr Green can't sue Ms Kane. Her interest has been bought out by Gaines Goldstein. If he alleges she fraudulently claimed half of Meadow, it's Gaines Goldstein lawyers who will defend the case. And they could countersue. My advice was to settle. Dr Green didn't have any real appetite to litigate against Ms Kane in the first place.'

'Who gives a fuck what he wants?'

'I do. I'm his lawyer. I am, however, willing to give you some free advice, Mr Johnson.'

Edward heard the suppressed laughter, the mocking tone in his voice. Red rage surged up in him, a bilious taste in his mouth. He wanted to curse but found himself gasping for breath, unable to speak. He'd given these fuckers a *hundred grand* and they'd screwed him over. Just like that, man. Just like Dina Kane.

'I will take silence as consent. Very well, then: at present, nobody knows you were good enough to pay Dr Green's legal costs. He is heading back to Europe before questions can be asked. If I were you, Mr Johnson, I would want to keep very quiet about my role in this. Whatever your relationship with Dina Kane.'

'I don't care what they think,' Edward lied.

'Everybody cares what Joel Gaines thinks. He does not have a forgiving reputation. Now he's a player in this, speaking for myself, I would get the hell out of Dodge, so to speak.'

Edward felt sick. 'How much?'

'Excuse me?'

'How much did she get? For her share?'

'Not as much as Dr Green, but it came encumbered with a possible lawsuit.'

'Give me the number, not the fucking footnotes.'

'Half a million dollars, I believe. A fair price, but not a spectacular one.'

Half a million.

In a year, that whore had gone from coffee waitress to business-woman. She could pay back her loans, sell another apartment. In his world, here in Manhattan, a half mil only got you to first base. But Dina had made that base in record time. This would be a seed – seed money for something bigger, something better.

A nightmarish vision swam before him: Dina Kane, a big success, famous, rich. Maybe owning a better house than his mother's. Maybe even moving past him, in the fast lane. Laughing at him. *Ruining his life.*

It could happen now. She was playing, doing it deliberately to spite him.

Unless he did something to stop it.

Edward forced himself to be calm, to show control.

'Good advice. Thank you. It feels so unfair, to know that she cheated Dr Green, the way she blackmailed my father. He was gulled into taking less because of her.'

'Yes. Well.' The lawyer was discomfited. 'I can certainly understand that perspective, Mr Johnson.'

'Destroy all records of our correspondence, then. I will cease to pay your bills as of now. Dr Green should understand that.'

'His flight to Austria leaves next week. So this whole matter is at a rest.'

The hell it is.

'Goodbye, Mr Shaman.'

Edward Johnson hung up, put his head in his hands and thought of Dina Kane. His body shivered with pure hatred.

There was a knock on the door. His secretary entered with his coffee in a plain china mug.

'I'll just get your croissants,' she said. 'Shall I call anybody at the broker's?'

He looked at her with loathing. *Stupid bitch.* Like she couldn't see his stress. He didn't want coffee; he wanted pussy. Better, he wanted some girl to kneel and give head; no talking, no nothing. Most of all, he wanted a snort or a drink, but that's where the Kane slut had driven his mother.

Better to find a couple of hookers. Or a sex club, one of the fancier ones, with masks and screwed-up girls who liked to be beaten. He could get into that. Every blow would be for Dina, every thrust for Dina . . .

He was getting hard, feeling sick. He shook his head.

'Forget the croissants. I have an urgent investment meeting outside. I may not be back today. Cancel lunch.'

'OK, sure,' his assistant said, but Edward had already brushed past her to the door.

'Payment in advance. In full. That's the policy.'

'Of course,' Dina said. She was just so glad that they had space. Johnny had cried the whole drive up, mewled like a cat in the back of the hire car. Twice, the driver had had to pull over so Johnny could vomit.

'Sixty thousand for a month's stay. Special interventions may be more – any hospitalisations, operations. We don't take medical insurance, but we can give you a letter for reimbursement.'

Yeah, that's likely. Dina nodded in the quiet, plush lobby of the facility, built like a giant wooden lodge, a luxury ski chalet. The difference was the uniformed nurses, and the occasional shouts and cries from within, far away, like somebody being tortured down the hallway. Her dark head lifted nervously.

'Heroin withdrawal is very difficult. Methamphetamine is worse.'

'I understand.'

'Everybody is here voluntarily. The therapists' time is booked in advance – that's why we take payment in full.' The receptionist allowed a hint of a smile to show through. Gallows humour. 'Sometimes the money is the only thing that stops them walking out. You'd be surprised – even addicts don't want to blow tens of thousands.'

'It makes sense.'

'Your brother may well need additional treatment. Please sign here for the amount you are prepared to pay.'

Dina wrote down two hundred thousand. *Easy come, easy go,* she thought. Johnny was all the family she had in the world.

'Can I visit him?'

'We don't allow it during treatment, unless it's exceptional circumstances. Patients have to progress. Mr Kane may need hospitalisation, intravenous nutrition, physical therapy . . .'

She couldn't argue. Johnny was a skeleton.

'Just take care of him,' Dina said. She signed her name and left.

The next two weeks were amongst the busiest of her life.

After Johnny, there was little money left. She paid the taxes, set aside the cash for his treatment, and renovated her apartment the way she always wanted. The city clerks, the building board and the painters didn't know what had hit them.

'Which architectural firm are you with?' asked the clerk in the permit office, looking at Dina's beautifully printed plans.

'Kane and Kane,' she said, smiling.

'That's not the right paint colour. We ordered ecru, not eggshell.'

'Hang the door exactly on those hinges – you don't want to lose a millimetre of space.'

'Make sure the glass is treated against reflection – it lets far more light in.'

'Jesus, honey, you're a real hard case. The owner knew what she was doing hiring you.'

Dina smiled and said nothing.

Within a month, her plain, dull apartment was transformed. The kitchen wall was ripped out and the cramped living room combined into the space to form one large living area with a small, chic kitchen alcove. She compensated for the lack of space with luxury: a small counter-top, but Italian marble; a compact fridge-freezer, but SubZero; a microwave, high in the wall; a built-in Viking oven and small range. Every cupboard and shelf was maximised for space. The tiny den was sacrificed, and Dina created a huge single bedroom with a walk-in closet, beautifully laid out with shoe racks, shelves and dress hangers, mirrored walls and overhead lighting. In the loft-like living area, Dina mounted a huge flat-screen TV above her newly installed, remote-controlled gas fire, which produced dancing flames, just like the real thing. The small bathroom was a problem, but Dina ripped out the shower and created a medium-sized wet room, with a stone bench and a steam-free mirror, to make it look larger.

Then she called her realtor.

'You can't be finished already. If you want a higher price point, you need serious upgrades.'

'It's done. Come and see.'

'I can't be in for an assessment until Friday,' said Laurel Sloane.

'That's fine. I'll find another realtor.'

Sloane swallowed hard. This girl was unbelievable. 'You know, let me check my diary . . . something might have opened up earlier . . .'

'My window is two p.m. today.'

Laurel surrendered. 'Two p.m. That's fine. I appreciate your business, Ms Kane.'

When she walked into the apartment, hours later, the lie became the truth. Laurel Sloane was open-mouthed. She had never witnessed such a job, so fast. The cramped one-bedroom-plus-den standard unit was now a luxurious loft, packed with boys' toys, playing up its spectacular view.

'My God.' She didn't attempt to conceal her surprise. 'It's like a James Bond movie.'

The younger woman nodded, and Laurel took another look at her. She was quite something in her tight riding pants, knee-high flat boots and luxurious boyfriend sweater. The hair was twisted into a French plait and her make-up was delicately done in pinks and neutrals; you never saw a twenty-something so polished.

'This apartment is a reasonable size for two, but big for a one-bedroom. Plus, it's near the UN; you want to market it to a diplomat or a staffer. They have large budgets, and they want the best.'

'The best is Fifth Avenue.'

'Right, but now, for a lot less, they come here, get all the bells and whistles, and walk a block to work. No subway. It'll sell.'

It sure would. Laurel Sloane put aside her jealousy. This girl was a natural. She had zeroed in on the buyer perfectly. If she stuck with her, Dina Kane could make her tens of thousands, maybe more, in commissions. It was all about the deal.

'How much do you want for it?'

'One and a half million,' Dina Kane said.

That would mean it had doubled its value in six months.

Laurel didn't hesitate. 'Yes, ma'am. No problem.'

Dina was home, trying to relax. Until it sold, this was her place now. Johnny was in rehab. Hector had gone. The last of the workmen had departed. She had some money, not much, and things were expensive here.

I've been pushing myself too hard, she thought, pouring out a large glass of fresh pomegranate juice. *I need security. A home. I need to stop.*

Joel Gaines drifted into her mind. The way he looked her over, his dark eyes assessing her – so different from the boys, those immature, mocking youths her own age.

He's married. Get over it. Stop.

I need a more normal life, Dina thought. *A normal life, period. It's not like I've ever had one.*

Ellen – barely a mother. No father. No love. Her talent stifled.

The teenage girl appealing to the Mafia don.

Her escape to the city. Working round the clock. Trying to change her life. And then Edward Johnson taking her virginity, her self-respect – mocking her like it was a game.

Shelby Johnson – hypocrite and letch. Her anger had been enough to get her into his bed. Anything to confront that rich, powerful, selfish family that she hated so much.

Hector Green – success, opportunity . . . then another man she'd trusted turning against her.

And nobody in her life – nobody since Edward. *No wonder you're getting a crush. A stupid, infantile crush. If you don't stop pushing yourself, you'll crack up . . .*

Dina tried to be logical. There must be guys out there, guys her own age, marriage material, guys who weren't Edward Johnson. She needed to date, find a nice guy, get married, have some kids. Make that real family her momma had denied her.

People do that, she thought. *They meet at college – or socially.*

Only Dina Kane had no social life.

Then there's the job . . .

The obvious thought occurred to her, out of the blue: it was time to give up on the dream of being some kind of mogul. If this apartment sold, she could be comfortable. Time to get an enjoyable job, one she'd be good at, but where she could leave work at five p.m., make friends, have a life. Have a chance to meet guys. Catch up on her sleep.

Slowly, as she sipped, Dina thought it through.

Hector hadn't sued – Joel Gaines changed all that. So all that really happened was she'd sold her half of Meadow. The companies who'd been buying it all knew her. Her reputation was good.

Dina loved beauty. But, right now, the only person that appreciated it was herself. She wanted to run a boutique, to run it successfully – but for somebody else, for a big salary. Maybe she'd have to work her way up, but Meadow's success should get her through the door. Meadow was her reference, her college degree. *The University of Gorgeous.*

Dina laughed to herself. Saks, Glamour, Bloomingdales . . . She'd go to work in one of these places, and she'd show the store what the beauty business was all about. And after the job, she'd pick up a lover. And stop thinking about Joel Gaines.

Definitely stop thinking about him . . .

The punching bag reeled from the force of the blow.

'Man!' Shamek Ahmed, his trainer, stumbled back a little. 'That's good. That's real good. Something got into you?'

Joel Gaines was stripped to the waist. Beads of sweat dewed the muscles of his back and legs. Outside the walls of his office, the sun was low in the sky as it rose.

New York City was just waking up. Gaines had been working for nearly an hour.

Shamek liked Joel better than most of his celebrity clients. They said he was a son of a bitch, and he didn't tolerate lateness. Or softness. But he worked himself harder than he worked the staff. By seven thirty a.m., this workout would be done and he would have showered and changed into one of those limey-cut suits and be kicking Wall Street ass.

'Nah.' Another flurry of blows – like the punchbag insulted his mother. 'Same old shit, different day.'

'I hear ya,' Shamek said. He didn't do *Yes, sir* and Gaines didn't ask him to. When you bellowed at guys all day long, deference didn't come natural.

For the last month, Joel Gaines had been coming to the city earlier. Working harder – much harder. There was a gym set up in one corner of this cavernous office, better than many professional places Shamek worked. And it wasn't just for show, either. Gaines went for it. This morning he had piled on the weights, grunting, pushing, hefting everything up; thirty minutes fast on the treadmill – six, seven miles an hour; a hundred push ups; working the barbells, now the bag. He was like a man ten, fifteen years younger. Or like somebody very angry, very frustrated.

None of Shamek's business. He admired the dorsal muscles in Gaines' back, knotting, releasing.

His timer buzzed. 'OK. You're done. Make that shower hot, and get some aspirin. You're going to be pretty sore.'

A dark smile. 'That's how we know we're still alive, right?'

'Right.' Shamek grinned. 'Stretch.'

'No time.'

'At least five minutes or I'm cancelling tomorrow's session.'

'Fuck you!' grunted Joel, but he started stretching.

Shamek slapped his client on the back. If only they were all that way . . . 'Well done, Joel.'

Bob Goldstein looked at the spreadsheets projected on the wall in front of them. 'This was really first rate.'

'Yes, sir.' Leo Tsardis, L'Audace's interim chairman, spoke up. He had the face of a drowning man who's just been thrown a lifejacket. 'Meadow is a lead product already. Our early production run is sold out. The new factory is going to ship fifty thousand units for spring. We have a team of chemists taking the formula and working on a range.'

'It's rebranded Meadow – Audace,' chimed in his colleague, Tamara Miller. She ran the company PR, and that haunted look was gone from her face. 'The industry loves it; they're saying it's an extraordinary acquisition. Really, the business pages are full of it.'

'Stores are taking everything we can ship. We estimate five million in sales in the first six months.'

Goldstein thumped the table. 'Anchor product. Bought for peanuts.'

'The initial marketer made good contacts. Very young kid: Dina Kane was her name. Knew how to sell. We had an easy time going in.'

'Maybe we should hire her,' Bob Goldstein said.

'No.' Gaines spoke up. 'Definitely not. She's far too young.'

Goldstein arched a brow. 'I remember when they said that about you.'

Gaines shrugged. Dina Kane had been on his mind far too much. Nothing he did could erase her image. Not sex with his wife, beautiful and mundane as she was. Not work. Not the way Meadow was flying off the shelves. Everything brought her back, reminded him of her. If she came to work for the company, he wouldn't be able to control himself. And Joel Gaines was always in control.

'She's not the corporate type. She got more money than she ever dreamed of with Meadow. Leave it at that.'

'Maybe she needs a job,' Tamara volunteered. 'It would be a great story.'

Gaines' fingers curled into a fist. 'Drop it.'

She dropped it.

'We need some more products to sell – maybe not another Meadow, but still higher quality. The brand was pimping itself out; it lost its reputation for high-end. Do you have any more tricks up your sleeve, Joel?'

'L'Audace is our major focus for the year,' Goldstein said. 'You guys concentrate on cutting costs, making Meadow, growing the line. Other products will be joining it.' He looked at his partner. 'Joel will make that happen. We want to have the company healthy for sale by the end of the year.'

'Sure. No problem,' Gaines said. 'Let's wrap this up. I'm seeing our bankers in forty minutes on the airline deal. Car's waiting.'

The limousine purred through the traffic.

Gaines glanced out of his tinted windows. He enjoyed these rides, the cavernous seats, the buttery leather, not having to think. It was a small vacation from the chaos of his day. His habit was to switch the cellphone off and stare at the traffic flowing silently past his soundproofed car.

It was hypnotic. Meditation.

Maybe he shouldn't have done that – stopped the girl from getting a job. She was a good kid; ballsy as hell, hard working, inventive. And he'd spiked her just because he found it uncomfortable thinking about her. Because he, Gaines, feared a lack of control.

He winced at the thought.

There were all kinds of good reasons to call Dina Kane. He would find her a job – someplace else. That was the solution: get her work, but not too near him. Salve his conscience.

And then, products . . . The chemist had ducked out, headed back to Europe and a comfortable retirement. Gaines Goldstein wasn't interested in developing new products itself – the company had no research labs. He wanted to buy other little brands, ones like Meadow that worked out of the gate, that would make L'Audace a cosmetics house. And then he could dump it.

At Gaines Goldstein level, you moved forward or stepped aside. That was it.

Dina Kane knew where he could find the good stuff. Gaines much preferred to work that way, rather than through intermediaries.

Yeah. That was a perfect reason. In fact, he had to do it.

He pulled out his cellphone and turned it on.

Dina was running. The East River, to her left, was grey and cold, but the sight of the water still soothed her. She was dressed warmly – gloves, a hat – music pumping through her earphones; she would never swap the street for the gym. There would have to be a blizzard. You got the light here, the street, the people, skyscrapers, traffic, streetcars: all Manhattan's variety, pace and power.

It drove Dina. It pushed her. She felt like she was going somewhere, seeing something. There was a point. That's what made it so good.

Her music stopped. Incoming call. Her heart flipped in her chest. She prayed it wasn't the rehab centre calling to say Johnny was sick, or in hospital. Or worse.

'Hello?'

'Joel Gaines.'

She slowed to a halt, feeling the cool air on her face, calming the immediate blush. 'Mr Gaines. Yes, sir.'

'Joel.'

'OK.'

'You sound busy.'

'No! No, I'm just running. It's fine; I mean, I'd love to talk to you.' She winced, bit her lip. *I'd love to talk to you? Jesus.*

'I want some recommendations from you. The products you sourced at your little store. Do you still have access to a list?'

'Yes,' she said. 'You want to buy them?'

'Small producers.' Dina could almost hear the shrug at the end of the line. 'You told me you went into this because they worked. That's what I'm looking for. Will you send me the list?'

'Certainly, as soon as you send me two hundred thousand dollars.'

He laughed, and she could hear the shock. 'What?'

'Come on, Joel.' Dina paced, gripping the phone. 'You got a deal on Meadow. And now you want to save maybe six months of research by taking my list and making offers to European boutiques. If you say yes right away, I won't raise the price to two fifty.'

'My God,' he said. 'That's it. I give up.' There was a pause, then he added, 'Come to lunch. Come today. I'll cancel my appointment.'

'Where?'

'I'll book somewhere.'

'If you come to my apartment, I'll cook for you. I can also print you the full list, and you can hand me a cheque for the two hundred grand.'

'That's a deal, kid. One p.m. Give me your address.'

Dina returned home early. She was far too excited for anything else. Quickly, she peeled off her workout clothes, headed to the wet room, showered and washed her hair.

She towelled off frantically and selected an outfit: a simple, sleeveless woollen shift, scarlet red – bold, like she wanted to be with him – sheer Wolford hose and ballet flats. She was trying to look casual, when she felt anything but. Her make-up had to be perfect, in case he had second thoughts about buying her list. She dived into her old stock from the Green Apothecary, applying feather-light mousse foundation, putting bronze lipstick against olive-green shadow, a touch of ochre blush, high on the cheekbones, and then solid, Egyptian mascara, so her eyes popped like Cleopatra.

She applied fast – five minutes – then she set the table; thank God there was yesterday's chilli still in the fridge. Dina was no gourmet, but she'd learned to cook to save money – dishes that could last and be warmed through were a favourite. Chilli, a salad, sparkling water and she set the coffee grinds into her pot: done.

There was nothing fancy. She wasn't worried. Gaines wasn't that kind of guy.

Dina ran back into the dressing room and got out the hairdryer. It was super-pro; one of the Green Apothecary's clients, a girl who owned a salon, had lent it to her and it was ideal at a time like this, when she wanted to nuke herself.

She blasted the air, aiming the nozzle right at her English Mason Pearson brush . . .

The buzzer went.

Dina jumped out of her skin. Her hair was still damp and tousled against the chic little dress.

It buzzed again. She glanced at her watch. Twelve thirty. *Damn it.*

'Go away!' she called out. 'I have somebody coming round in half an hour.'

'You have somebody round now,' Gaines replied through the door.

She shuddered and hurried to open the door.

He was standing there in a light blue shirt and navy suit. Almost six foot, he loomed over her, the strong body looking even more developed than before. The dark eyes glittered with amusement.

Dina squirmed. 'Joel . . . I'm not . . . not ready.'

'You look ready to me. Can I come in?'

She surrendered. 'Yes. Of course.'

He stepped inside, glanced around her place. 'Stylish. Who's the designer?'

'Me. I buy tired apartments, put in a little cosmetic work . . .'

'I should have known.'

'It's on the market for one and a half, if you want a pied-à-terre,' she said boldly.

'I think you've taken quite enough of my money for now.'

He took her in: the sexy, nervous length of her; that stunning face and slender body framed by damp hair; the way she was looking at him – the challenge, the admiration. The desire. The obvious desire.

Susan never looked at him like that. Not anymore. Gaines didn't know that she ever had. There was fun once, mutual affection, friendship . . . But love? He wasn't so sure. And never passion. Susan was willing, welcoming, accommodating. When he was younger, with his eyes on the prize, achieving great things in business, it was more than enough. She made a great home, was an elegant hostess, a good mom. And that was marriage.

Passion was for the movies. Rich men's wives were a certain breed. Elegant, educated, active on their school boards, they played tennis in the Hamptons, remembered to send gifts on friends' birthdays; they remodelled their kitchens and maybe had some small job. What they did was a social enterprise, war on a thousand fronts that men didn't bother with.

Dina Kane was not that kind of girl.

And he was fascinated.

'What's for lunch?' he asked, to distract himself.

'Chilli and rice,' she said, still blushing.

'Really?' He smiled again. Nobody had served him a bowl of plain chilli in years. 'Goddamn, that sounds good.'

'Take a seat.'

He pulled up a chair at her sleek little dining table. His practised eye could see she had spent a few dollars well: a good omen for business.

Dina served them each a large steaming bowl of the meat and beans, with a little rice. After the workout that morning, he was starving.

'It's good.'

'Thank you.' She reached to pour him water, leaning over him. He breathed in the scent of her shampoo and bath soap.

Dina sat back down and lifted her fork. She ate, head bowed. She wouldn't look at him, almost like she couldn't look at him.

When he had finished, Joel said, 'That was excellent.' He stood and cleared his bowl away to the kitchen. 'You can always get a new career as a cook.'

'I don't think I'll ever be making morsels of salmon in a pomegranate coulis, or whatever they serve in the good restaurants these days.'

'Open a place on Wall Street that does chilli, steaks, lasagne. Most businessmen haven't had a proper meal in years. I could happily die without ever seeing *jus* on a menu ever again.'

Dina laughed. 'I'm better at what goes on people's faces than what goes into their mouths, Mr Gaines.'

'Joel.'

She blushed again. 'I know. I just find it difficult.'

'Why?'

'Because you're so . . .' Her voice trailed off. 'You know.'

'Enlighten me.'

'Powerful. Successful. A major figure.' Dina was now bright red, and she tried to cover it by jumping to her feet and clearing the table. 'You're a legend – as you know.'

'I do know. It's still enjoyable hearing you say it.'

Dina felt herself moisten with desire. He was so arrogant, so handsome, so cocky. And it was justified; who could say it wasn't?

'Do you have the list?'

'Yes. Of course.' She was relieved to be able to flee into her bedroom, to get the printout from her computer. It was thick – ten pages long. 'I've made entries in bold of the brands you should look at – small manufacturers; good sellers – I can send you some notes, too.'

'Excellent.' He took the sheaf of pages and flicked through it; a few companies there were already on his radar. 'You're quite right, of course. This will save us months of prep work.'

'Then you will give me the cheque?'

'You sound as though you doubt it.'

Dina shrugged. 'Two hundred grand for a computer printout.'

He looked at her. 'I made the deal. When I make deals, they happen: first rule of business.'

He snapped open his briefcase and handed her a neatly typed cheque. Dina looked at it, the figures swimming before her eyes. This was really happening, this, her life.

'Thank you, Mr— Joel.'

'You can't just bank it. How much is left of the half million?'

'Not much. There was this place. My brother needed rehab. Taxes.'

He nodded. 'You need a job.'

Dina's heart pounded. 'Can I work for you?'

'I'm not in the beauty business. This is just one of many for me.' His eyes swept over her. 'Besides, that might not be a good idea.'

'Why not?' she whispered.

'My turn to say, "you know".'

Dina's heart thudded in her chest. She thought she might gasp with longing. He'd acknowledged it, right there in her apartment – the electricity between them.

'I'm married,' he said.

'Of course.'

But he was still looking at her. Dina's knees trembled a little. She could not remember ever having wanted anything more than she wanted this guy.

'You need to work for somebody, however. I can mentor you a little. What do you want to do?'

'I'd like to be a director of beauty retail. One of the major stores. Something well-paid, where I can make an impact. Saks, Bloomingdale's . . .'

'How about Torch?'

Dina wrenched her eyes from Gaines' face and body. Torch was the veteran ladies' fashion emporium on the Upper West Side, with the Lady Liberty logo, packed into twelve floors of belle époque New York splendour. But the architecture of the venerable building was the sexiest thing about it. The store had a great past, but the future was kind of dusty. Big in the eighties, Torch had settled to become a sort of halfway house. It stocked everybody, but didn't get the hip collections. Saks and Bloomingdale's had all the luxe, Glamour was the ethical shopping destination of the liberal elite and Macy's, downtown, competed on mid-price and sheer space.

All Torch had going for it was that it was uptown, so it mopped up local shoppers who couldn't be bothered to get in a cab. And, living on past glory, its average customer was fifty plus. Big sellers were fur coats, shawls and a lot of jewelled sequin jackets.

Not Dina Kane's cup of tea. But a venerable New York name.

'If I had a free rein,' she said, carefully.

'It's perfect for you. Why would you want to go somewhere successful?'

Dina smiled.

'Very good. Bank your cheque. I know the old man that owns that store. He lives in California now, enjoying the sun. He'll take a recommendation from me.'

Dina didn't know what to say. Just like that, he could swoop in, swoop down and make her life better. The ease of it; the naked power on display.

'I . . . Thank you.'

'Thank me by proving how brilliant I am at sourcing staff.'

'Should I call them?'

'They'll call you.' He stood, picked up the briefcase. 'So, now we're done.'

'Joel, will I see you again?'

For a long, brutal second, he looked her over, wanting the girl, liking the girl, feeling her electricity, the desire, the lifeforce.

'Maybe one day.' The words he forced out, with supreme discipline, sounded like somebody else was saying them. 'After you get a boyfriend.'

'Then I'll get a boyfriend,' she said.

Gaines immediately wanted to kill him.

'Goodbye,' he said, and he walked out of her door before he said something he could never take back.

Chapter Ten

'Welcome to Torch.'

Regina Freeman was bored with her life, and it showed. African-American and passably elegant, she had reached fifty-one and the heights of high achievement in life: a big salary, director at a major store, a husband in tort law and two kids at college.

The fire of her early days was smothered in comfort: a nice two-bedroom in a tree-lined block just off Columbus; great health, dental and long-term care insurance; cruise vacations with the same people every year; visits to her folks in Jersey at Thanksgiving. You didn't rock the boat with your life like that. Not ever.

She ran Torch's day-to-day operations. Staff costs were low, volume was high; they carried just enough high-end clothes to remain a major store. Mostly, the matrons of the Upper West shopped here. The Morgan family owned it, and the business paid low rates and no rent. They could afford to coast, and that's exactly what they were doing. Regina's job was just to keep the bills paid.

'You come highly recommended,' she said.

She was wearing a neat little Ann Klein pantsuit with a pink cotton blouse and mules: safe, easy wear. The young girl before her was different. Startlingly well made-up, she was a beauty in chic green Prada with a Mulberry handbag and Kate Spade wedges. Her look said *fashion*. *Chic*. *New*. All the things Torch wasn't.

'Thank you, ma'am.'

Regina softened fractionally. She appreciated good manners; she hated how the youth of today usually stared at their iPhones and never looked at you.

'You have something to do with Meadow, by L'Audace? We stock that here.'

'I helped bring that to market. I sold it to Mr Gaines; I think he recommended me to Mr Morgan. I also ran a successful independent beauty store downtown.'

'Big retail is very different.'

'Yes, ma'am. I'm here to learn.'

'Quickly, I hope, since you're going to be directing our beauty sales. I must say, Ms Kane, I've never seen anybody as young as you hired for a major job like this.'

'I do understand, Mrs Freeman. Please, call me Dina. I'll do my best to show Mr Morgan it was a good hire.'

Regina wanted to ask the girl what she was getting paid, but restrained herself. It must have been into six figures, like her own salary. The kid was coming straight to management. One fluke with a face cream and she was jumping the queue. But Dina did seem different to most young kids. She had old eyes in that pretty face.

'Do you have what you need?' Regina asked.

'I'd like to spend today observing, and then tomorrow running through our sales sheets and the order book. And I'll come up with my recommendations next week.'

'Very good,' Regina said. 'So I'll see you around.'

She walked back to her office, up the marble staircase with its faded royal blue carpet, trying to figure out the puzzle. Ludo – it had to be him. Mr Peter Morgan's son was a New York playboy, top of the most-eligible list. He always had an eye for the pretty girls. Mostly they just scored jobs as eyebrow threaders or perfume spritzers, though. Not directors of beauty.

Well, Dina Kane was uncommonly attractive. But Ludo went through two girls a month – he would tire of the novelty soon.

She'd just be patient and let the girl hang herself with her own rope. No need to rock the boat. The retirement account in her IRA was looking exceptionally healthy right now. And everybody at Torch knew you didn't mess with Ludo Morgan.

Dina walked around the dull, boring store, and felt her heart thud with excitement.

Joel Gaines, you genius.

He was so right. This place was a disaster area, and she was thrilled at the thought of putting it right.

The shop floor was badly lit and crowded with stock. Bored shopgirls talked to each other all day, ignoring the customers. Items were marked at a discount everywhere – clothes piled on tables under red *SALE* signs. Brands were jumbled with haute couture designer items, as if the store was afraid of selling the goods.

Torch looked tired – old.

The beauty department was better – if you want to be average. The big cosmetics houses controlled their own displays. Torch carried most of them, so things were standard. There was almost nothing new. She smiled when she saw the small stand for Meadow, and the steady stream of customers it was attracting.

Dina looked at the assistants in their drab white coats with the square gold nametags. Some were talking to customers; most were staring into space. Beauty wasn't doing much business. This was an older crowd, who knew what they wanted. She watched women home in on Estée Lauder or Chanel, grab a product and take it to a counter.

Like a post office, she thought. *Like buying stamps.*

There was buying – no selling. No reason to be here and not down the street, except, at Torch, you could pick up lingerie down the hall, and a cushion on floor two.

In her head, Dina saw something completely different. Space. Light. Style. A building redesigned. Exclusive clothing. Classics mixing with hot new designers. The latest beauty hits. An event store. A destination. Teens, twenty-somethings, chic professionals in their thirties and forties. The older women, too – if they were hipsters, the ones that wore black and went to off-Broadway shows. And men – a small group, mixed in with the women. Hardcore luxury addicts.

It would be intense. Huge. It would own uptown.

And it would cost a lot of money.

'Do I have to?' Ludo Morgan sighed.

He had a fun afternoon planned: cigars at the Havana club with two of his friends; tennis; a phone call to his father; perhaps a trip to the helipad – there was a cottage in the Hamptons the broker wanted him to view.

'Your father wants you to see her, sir. Just to hear her first report. She came recommended by Joel Gaines.'

'Not interested in Gaines' cast-offs. Can't he find someplace else for his girlfriends to play?'

Eric Strom shook his head. The arrogance of the kid wasn't disappearing with age.

'Mr Gaines doesn't have girlfriends. She sold him a brand. Your father put her in as beauty director.'

Now he had Ludo's full attention. 'What? Beauty what?'

'Director. With a brief to revamp the cosmetics department.'

He coloured. 'I hire personnel.'

'Yes, sir, but your father put Ms Kane in direct.'

'What experience has she got?'

'None at this level.'

Ludo Morgan's annoyance increased. Why couldn't the old man enjoy retirement? It was his time now.

'This is a mistake. I'm going to fire her. Give her three months' salary and tell her it was some kind of miscommunication. I'll see her for that.'

Eric Strom smiled slightly. It wasn't often he got to put one over on the next generation of hyper-privileged kids, but he enjoyed it when it happened.

'No, sir. She actually filed her first report direct to your father, and he loved it. Thought it had potential. He wants you to see her to discuss how Torch can execute it.'

Ludo Morgan breathed in sharply. This girl was in her early twenties, according to the paper in front of him – and already going straight to the top, over his head.

This wasn't just an annoyance. It was a power play.

'Bring her to my office,' he said. 'Twenty minutes.'

Dina Kane was prepared.

She'd read up on her new boss, Ludo Morgan: twenty-eight years old; NYU and a business degree out in California. He looked set to succeed his father, who was taking that backseat out in the sun. He dated casually. One sister – married with two children – living in Paris, with no interest in the family store. Ludo managed Torch well enough to keep it in the black, but Dina sensed no commitment, no love of his grandfather's legacy.

That was OK. She just wanted to get on, make a change, prove herself to Joel Gaines . . . to the world. Prove herself to the *world*. Dina blushed a little bit. Gaines couldn't have been plainer in his rejection.

And she'd get over it. Any day now.

'This way,' Regina Freeman said. 'Mr Morgan has come in especially to see you.'

'That's great!'

'No, it isn't.' Regina patted her on the shoulder. The kid had talent, no doubt; Dina's paper had surprised her. And her ideas might actually work – somewhere fashion forward, like Sephora. At Torch – no chance. Dina Kane would have to learn to go along to get along, just like the rest of them. 'Good luck, honey.'

Dina knocked and entered the room.

She won't last a month, Regina thought.

The young man was sitting behind a hefty oak desk, with a small chair in front of it, designed to be uncomfortable – a contrast to the way Gaines did business. The office itself was like the rest of the store: wood panelling, faded European carpet, velvet-covered couch. There were filing cabinets up against one wall and a printer was perched on top of the one closest to the desk. It all felt fussy and cramped, despite the big pre-war windows.

He didn't look up as she entered; Dina saw he was scanning her report.

'What the hell did you think you were doing reporting direct to my father?'

'Mr Morgan hired me, sir.'

'Hired you as beauty director. I run this store. Once hired, everything goes to Regina first, then she decides whether or not to take it to me. Understand?'

Now he raised his head – and looked at her, with an involuntary jerk of surprise. Dina saw him registering, approving.

She was wearing tailored slacks and a blouse, with stacked wedge heels. Her hair was worn up in a modern bun with a chic Japanese chopstick driven through it, and her make-up was bronzed today, everything for a sun-kissed look – golden highlighters on the cheeks, copper on the lips, light browns and ochres on her eyes, with chestnut mascara – as though she would be heading to a yacht on the Mediterranean, any second.

She looked stunning. And Ludo Morgan was suitably stunned.

'Excuse me,' he said, as the moment became uncomfortable. 'I was taken aback. You look like a model.'

She blushed at the unexpected compliment. Morgan was wearing a good suit – relaxed, no tie – Armani. And at least he didn't play games.

He was handsome; smooth featured, with dark blond hair. Rather like he belonged on TV, or in a rock band. Matinée-idol looks and a dapper suit on top – she could see why a kid like this would be a playboy. The girls would lap it up.

'Thank you, Mr Morgan. Beauty is my expertise, so I take care of how I make myself up. If you're interacting with customers, the first thing they do is look at your own face. You wouldn't let a shabby tailor make you a suit, would you, sir?'

Ludo laughed aloud. 'Funny. No, I suppose I wouldn't.'

'I will definitely go to Regina next time with the work,' Dina said. 'But the store needs major changes, and I wanted Mr Morgan senior to see that . . . since he took a chance on hiring me.'

'These plans require an injection of cash.'

'Yes, sir. I know.'

'Too much cash. I'm not going to authorise it. This is too much of a punt. You're unproven, and for years our customer base has been much older. We need to cater to them.'

Dina chewed on her lip. 'But, Mr Morgan—'

'My father was taken by the report, but, at the end of the day, he isn't going to overrule me. Think again about how we can sell more cosmetics. No big upgrades. Bread and butter, that's what Torch is about.'

'I . . .' Dina swallowed – the young man's face was set. 'Yes, sir.'

'You can call me Ludo,' he said, genially. 'And, from now on, go only through me.'

She went home early, dispirited.

Damn it. This was life. Nobody had any vision; nobody took chances.

Except Joel Gaines.

Dina poured herself an apple juice and listened to her messages.

'Dina! This is Laurel Sloane. I've sold your apartment! Congratulations! A hundred thou over the asking price . . .'

'Dina Kane, this is Far Haven Fields. Can you call us about Johnny? He's been taken to hospital.'

She put the juice down on the table and called a car-rental company.

The facility was small, like a country hospital normally is, but well heeled and private. As Dina walked through the doors, she took note of the gleaming floors, soft lighting and fresh flowers in the waiting area.

Not cheap. But Johnny needed it.

There wasn't insurance to cover this. Half her gains from the apartment would go in his bills. *As long as I have my brother . . .*

'He's in here,' the nurse said, showing her to a private room. Dina didn't have the heart to ask if Johnny could go on a ward.

He lay on the bed, weak, hollowed out. He had bruised patches under his eyes, like he'd gone ten rounds with Mike Tyson.

'Baby sis!' he muttered, looking at her with a weak smile. 'Good to see you! Aren't you proud of me? I'm kicking it. It's gone.'

Dina patted his hands, gently. 'Sure, I'm proud of you, Johnny – so proud.' She blinked back tears.

'That's good.' He turned his head to the pillow and fell asleep.

'Ms Kane?' A doctor entered the room, tall and patrician. He nodded at her. 'Can I see you outside?'

Dina got up and followed the doctor into the corridor.

'There was a lot of methamphetamine – crack cocaine – in his system when you brought him in,' he told her. 'You don't recover from that. You almost certainly saved his life.'

Dina's heart thudded in her chest. 'Thank God. But why does he look like that? Wasn't he meant to recover, to put on weight?'

'Cold turkey is a rough process. Your brother's immune system is compromised. There has been vomiting, dehydration. He needs stabilisation with intravenous fluids, and then feeding. Possibly physical rehab as well. There has been some muscle wastage.'

'You make it sound like he was in a concentration camp.'

'Think of it as advanced anorexia. He has induced a kind of voluntary starvation.'

Dina felt faint. 'I hope I can afford all this.'

'I hope you can,' the physician said, blankly. 'Your brother needs the treatment. I suppose you could take him back to the city, and try a public hospital . . .'

'No.' Dina shook her head. 'I take care of my family.'

She thought of her careful renovation, and the ecstatic call from her broker. *Oh, well. Profit and loss – they were only numbers.* She would never be like her mother, hoarding what she owned. But, even so, now more than ever she needed the job. She needed Ludo Morgan.

Gaines looked at the email sitting on his computer.

It was only two sentences, but he must have read it a hundred times.

Hey Joel. Have started at Torch. Run into a problem. I could use some advice. Coffee?

'This has got to stop,' he said to himself.

Last night, making love to his wife, trying to ignore the faked lust on her face, trying to maintain an erection, he had closed his eyes and thought of Dina Kane.

'Wow,' Susan had said, afterwards. 'That was incredible. You must have really liked my dress.'

'Yeah.' He was lying on their silk sheets, panting. 'Great dress. You looked sexy.'

She went to the shower, humming, and he hated himself.

But the brilliant, feisty girl was still in his thoughts. Thank God for work – Gaines flung himself into it – but now this. It was like she had telepathy; she could read his goddamned thoughts.

He clicked reply on the message. Time to be firm. Tell the girl – no coffee, no advice, no meeting.

I'm uptown later, he wrote. *Come to Eightieth and Columbus at eleven – the café there.*

'Thank you for making the time.' Dina sat with a fresh-squeezed orange juice. 'It means a lot.'

'I was in the neighbourhood. What's up?'

She was dressed down today: tight blue jeans and a white shirt, with brown cowboy boots and her dark hair in a ponytail. Minimal make-up. She looked anxious, vulnerable and sexy as hell.

Gaines swallowed, hard.

'I know what the store needs. The owner seems willing, but not his son – who runs the place.'

'Remind me . . .'

'Ludo Morgan. Twenty-eight. Business degree from UCLA. He was polite enough.'

I bet he was, Gaines thought.

'But no money. He said I'm unproven—'

'Jesus.' She was so beautiful, sitting there, so hot. He couldn't have her, and he wanted her; maybe he was falling for her. Which was so much worse. Dina Kane would never be out of his system. Gaines felt trapped, old, out of control. And rage coursed through him. He spoke with anger. 'What? Do you need me to hold your hand? Prove yourself, then! Get a success – *his* way. After you do that, go for the major revamp. That or quit and start your own goddamned business.'

Her green eyes opened, shocked. 'Joel . . . I've offended you?'

He stared at her, furiously. 'Pointless! This is pointless. Treat him like you did me, like you want something out of him and you'll do what it takes to get it. The rest is noise.'

'I'm sorry. I didn't mean to waste your time. I just went to see my brother and—'

'We all have problems. Look. We're even. I'm married. Don't email me again. You're on your own.'

He stood up and walked out of the café.

Dina watched him go. The tears welled up and she covered herself by dabbing at her mouth with a napkin.

Why does it hurt so much? I hardly know him.

You're on your own. *So be it.*

As she walked back down to Torch, Dina tried to clear her head. Gaines was right; of course he was right. She was pursuing him. Why had she asked him for coffee? Why not stick to email? Or just figure it out . . . ?

I wanted to see him.

She'd seen him. And she'd got more than she bargained for.

Her apartment was in contract. She was going to have to hand over another two hundred thousand to Johnny's hospital. Time to grow up. If she wanted to be in business, she had to act like it.

'Come in,' Ludo said.

It was the girl, Dina. She was less made-up today, but just as pretty.

'Hi. I don't have long. Got a lunch date.'

Caroline was the daughter of one of his father's friends, and it would be their third time out together. She was blonde, stick thin, a social X-ray. She looked good on his arm, but had none of the curves of this one, none of the attitude. For a moment, Ludo imagined taking Dina out instead – working-class girl from nowhere; career woman on the make.

Don't be stupid. She works for you.

'I'm going to do a little revamp of our beauty department. Bring in some exclusive products. It doesn't need much money, just a few adverts. Would you be OK with that? I'd like a budget for samples.' She put a piece of paper on his desk, a modest enough sum.

'Fine. Go ahead.'

'I can make the ad buys?'

'Sure.'

'Thanks,' Dina said.

For the next month, Dina worked tirelessly. She negotiated with the cosmetics houses to reduce the size of their stands, limiting their range and increasing the stock of bestsellers. She imported several of her favourite products – the best performers – from the Green Apothecary, and hired some of the best make-up artists in the city. New mirrors and flattering lights were screwed in on every available surface, and the carpet in the beauty department was ripped up and replaced by light-stained woods.

The place started to look like a salon.

Dina called in the staff to talk to them. They assembled in the canteen, in their dull uniforms, looking mutinously at the much-younger girl who was disrupting all their lives.

'Ladies,' she said. 'You are being stifled. Believe me, I get it. Nobody wants to stand around all day, bored out of their minds.'

Slight nods.

'We have to do so much better. I know most of you dreamed of being in the fashion industry – maybe a spa therapist; maybe a beautician – today, we're going to make that happen. Torch is about to become a spa. You engage the customer, not pressing her; only offer your very best products for her. Then step back. When she's ready, encourage her. Always thank your customers, whether they buy or not. Don't be afraid to refer them to another company's products. We want to show women how beauty can transform their lives, their self-esteem. And, when you ladies step up, I'm going to go to Mr Morgan and get you all a ten per cent raise. Because sales will rise by twenty-five per cent. Understand?'

Bigger nods. Everybody understood ten per cent.

'This store is a dinosaur. Ladies, we're going to start our own little revolution. We're going to show them how it's done. We're going to show them what women really want. Are you with me?'

This time, Dina even got applause.

She stayed up nights, walking around the empty store, playing with lighting design, spacing. She designed poster advertisements, loyalty cards. And, finally, she pulled off her master list: bloggers – beauty mavens who sat on the internet – the ones with the cult following amongst editors at fashion magazines; the ones NYU students read on a daily basis.

Hi. I'm Dina Kane, who sold Meadow cream to L'Audace. Torch is relaunching its beauty division with brand new exclusives from Europe. These will only debut here at Torch. The launch will also feature major names, free gifts and a five-minute makeover for every customer next week. Come at lunch and leave looking like a goddess. Your man won't know what hit him. Torch – for the spark.

And finally it was ready.

The relaunch week started with a bang. Dina gave out her personal cell number, and the phone never stopped ringing.

'What's your job there?'

'Free makeovers for every customer? Every one?'

'What can you do in just five minutes?'

She was busy. Every time a blogger or a beauty writer turned up, Dina squired them round personally. She repeated the same spiel fifty times a day.

'Five minutes is plenty. New York girls don't have time to waste at work. Torch is the new beauty playground; we'll show you just what looks great on you.'

'It's toys for girls.'

No blogger left without gifts. And not just the standard samples. Dina boxed up full-size products – just two or three – ones that she thought would benefit the woman in question. No standard-issue press kit. Everything was tailored.

'Wow.' Kathy Rennet, the owner of BeautyBuyer.com, stared at herself in the mirror. The make-up artist had transformed her, with just two minutes on the clock and three products – a shiny gloss, a bronzer from Portugal and dark green Revlon mascara. 'That's incredible.'

'I love it.' Emily Jones wrote for *Marie Claire* and she was bombarded with junket invitations every day. But Dina's make-up girl had changed the look of her face with a soft powder foundation she would never have touched, rose on her cheekbones and thick black mascara that covered her short lashes. 'This is amazing.'

'Not all products are great for everyone. Torch believes in personalised beauty.' Dina gestured towards the Elizabeth Arden stand. 'Eight-hour cream? It's a classic, but it's not for you. Your skin would break out.'

'I've tried it. It does.'

'When women come to Torch, we will try to sell them what works. This isn't just a store; it's a retail beautician.'

'Love it,' the journalist said again, earnestly writing *retail beautician* on her little pad.

The reviews came out in the next few days. Dina watched at home, on her computer.

Torch has the Spark.

Try their free makeovers – the store has bussed in true experts. Not your normal push for products!

Dina Kane brings in finds – this is Aladdin's cave.

They know what works. Get on the subway!

But would it translate? She'd spent every last penny on the staff, the best makeovers, the goodie bags. All new customers had to do was give out their email address . . . Dina was going to capture a database: what they bought, how old they were. Targeted mail.

She felt as nervous as she'd been in her entire life. This had to work, or she was dead. Ludo Morgan would not give her another chance.

But she had placed her bets, and now she was all in.

Chapter Eleven

'Excuse me; excuse me.' Ludo struggled through the crowd. He couldn't believe it; only ten fifteen and the ground floor was packed. Women, girls, teenagers were shoving him aside, thrusting forwards. The route to his office was blocked. The staircase entrance was thronged with chicks.

He glanced upstairs; the store there looked the same as normal – a few scattered shoppers.

'Christ! What is this? Some kind of fire drill?'

'No, sir,' a shopgirl said. 'These are customers. It is kind of crazy.'

'Customers for what?'

'The beauty department. Miss Kane's promotion.'

Ludo looked at the women in disbelief. 'Is she handing out free Chanel lipsticks?'

This wasn't normal. This wasn't Torch. He was fearful Dina Kane had gone nuts 'No, sir. Just little samples, like normal. And the makeovers. Excuse me, they need some help.' And the woman vanished.

He fought his way through to the staircase, panting, and climbed up to the first-floor balcony for a second look.

Hell. It was true. The women looked a nest of termites, swarming over his beauty department. There was jostling, and big lines at the cash registers. He could see several of the new product stands totally empty, with *sold out* signs on them. Instead of standing around, his staff were right in there, talking to the women, showing them things. Girls were perched on stools, five or six of them, being made up. The hubbub reached right up across the store, to the other, empty floors.

Ludo Morgan went into his office and shut the door. Then he wrote a little email to his father.

'Dina.'

She jumped out of her skin.

It was quarter to nine, and the store had just closed. Dina Kane was wearing a red shift dress and an air of exhaustion.

'How long have you been here?'

'Since seven a.m.'

An hour before opening.

'It's been a long time since lunch,' Ludo said.

She smiled. 'I didn't eat lunch.'

'Lunch is for wimps?'

'Something like that.' She rolled her head on her neck, stretching the muscles. 'I need to eat now, though, I'm feeling a little dizzy.'

'Low blood sugar. Let's go to Chiang Mai Thai; it's not the best, but it is right next door.'

She just nodded, too tired to argue.

Ludo ordered champagne and Dina drank a glass. She needed the energy, needed to relax. Besides, it had gone well. No denying that.

She was too tired to look at the menu; she ordered a simple chicken curry and an iced tea. Anything. She was starving.

'That was excellent work, today. I admit it: I'm impressed.'

Simple praise. She glowed a little. 'Thanks. It won't be like that all week; that was first-day stuff, after the reviews. But we should get a steady stream. I'm ordering new products from Europe. It'll be a couple of days.'

'Dina, don't get too hung up on this. I don't see a future for Torch, not like you do. The highest and best use of the building isn't a creaky department store. I want to convert it into luxury apartments, then sell it.'

'Ahhh.' She lifted a brow. 'Now I see your plan. I couldn't understand why you didn't want to make money.'

'My father has a sentimental attachment.'

'It may not be as easy as all that, though. The building is zoned commercial. There are lots of fancy condo buildings round here, and not enough stores. And Torch is the only big department store north of Bergdorf's.'

He tilted his champagne flute towards her. 'At the moment, that is true. Our architects are having no joy with the building department. But permissions like this take years. You have to build relationships with politicians . . .'

'Bribes?'

'Campaign contributions.'

'Your father might not want to dismantle.'

'The family has a majority of the stock, it passes to me and my sister . . .' Ludo shrugged. 'Eventually he will see sense. Meanwhile, I work on City Hall. It's a medium-term project.'

Dina thought about this.

'You know, Ludo, you could have both.'

'What?' he said, draining his glass and pouring another. Goddamn, she was a pretty girl, hick or no hick. What if he could spruce her up? Get her cultured? If they were dating, maybe she wouldn't be so in his face. He was bored of Caroline already – just another Identikit blonde. None of them had one interesting thing to say. At least the girls out in Cali had big fake tits and a sense of fun, not like these society ball darlings whose personalities were ironed as flat as their flaxen hair.

'You could have both. I mean, if you turned Torch around.

You see, then you'd be known as a retailing genius, and the brand would be worth something.'

'The brand? We're a store.'

'Saks was a store. Now there are branches of Saks in malls across the country, and they have a website. Saks Fifth Avenue is the flagship, but they don't need it. With Torch, the uptown store isn't as well known. So you establish the brand, open new branches and head into online sales. And then your father lets you convert the building here, and he hasn't really lost anything. You cut down the apple tree and plant an orchard.'

'My God.' He stared at her. 'That's poetry, honey. Apples and orchards.'

'It's smart business.' She gave herself a second glass, too. What the hell? She deserved some relief from the endless tension, the workaholism. 'It's what I would do, if I owned Torch.'

Ludo raised a finger. 'You had a good day in the beauty department. *I* own Torch, don't forget.'

'It's your call.'

'See what happens this week. If sales stay strong, you can double the beauty department. Lose some of those accessory tables. We have too much old stock out.'

'You can say that again.'

He lifted a brow. 'Can you revamp the rest of the store? The same way?'

'Maybe, but I'd need a couple of years to study. Beauty is my passion; I don't know about table lamps and hosiery.'

'You can at least redesign the surrounds.'

'Yes. Of course. You need that desperately. The place looks like an abandoned theatre, all moth-eaten carpet and frayed velveteen. Ugh!'

'Done. Come to me tomorrow with a budget.'

She smiled, a broad, real smile that reached her eyes.

'You really are stunning,' Ludo said, idly. 'Who's the lucky boyfriend?'

'I haven't had time.'

'What, ever?' He was liking this more and more. There was something strange, something isolated about Dina Kane. She was rough clay and would be malleable.

'Of course I've had a boyfriend, just not one at the moment.'

So not a virgin, then. Pity.

'I think we should go out,' Ludo announced. 'Let's face it – you aren't going to have lots of time on your hands from now on. I'm in reasonably good shape; you know, a few careful drivers . . .' He smiled at his own joke.

'Am I fired if I say no?' Dina's eyes narrowed.

'Not at all. And you still get your budget.'

Her shoulders slumped a little, releasing tension. 'And you'd take me out? In public?'

'If we hide it, people will talk. They say you shouldn't date at work, but where the hell else can you meet people these days? Church? A nightclub? Please!'

Dina smiled back. He was a little smug, but not unpleasant, and at least he was asking her out, straight, with no blackmail. *Come on, sweetheart, Joel Gaines is taken. Are you going to be one of those desperate obsessives who pines over a guy for forty years then dies alone with her cats?*

Hell no. She wanted family. Some friends. To be normal, for once. And Ludo Morgan was a rich, goofy kind of normal. Maybe, with him, she could watch her troubled childhood disappear in the rear-view mirror. Along with Ellen, and Edward, and every other man who'd ever leered at her.

'OK,' she said. 'You can pick me up Friday night at eight. But first you have to ask your dad's permission. I need the job.'

'Sure.' He nodded.

Sweet. If she worked out, her job was going to be looking after him. But Ludo was happy with taking things one step at a time.

* * *

He got her into a cab, then went back into the store and rode the elevator to the penthouse floor, already the owner's apartment. It was the best thing about living in this city. Beverly Hills was sun-drenched, laid back, but Ludo liked to see the city and the park spread out around him through the pre-war windows on every side, like it all belonged to him.

One day it would. He wanted a life of ease and wealth, but also success – the heir who built his father's fortune up, greater than it was before. He wanted a pretty, sexy wife, well-behaved kids, the respect of his peers, the best of everything.

And the key to life was taking your opportunities.

He walked into his office, designed as a small library, with a flat-mount TV, speakers in the walls and the best gaming computer known to man. The monitor jumped to life and he sent his father an email.

> Beauty expansion going well. My programme will revamp the entire department and store. Dina Kane contributing a few ideas, too. A smart hire. I'd also like to date her, and she wanted your permission first. Seems like a sensible girl. A hard worker. I plan to expand our business once the brand is revitalised, to online and outlets. There will be a full year programme. Hope you're well, Dad. Love, Ludo.

That would hit the sweet spot: *Sensible. A few ideas. Hard worker.* His father hadn't taken to any of the women he'd got as far as introducing; found them dull and venal.

Dina would come up with her ideas, he would cherry pick and execute. Which meant he got the credit – the commander, not the sergeant major. She would be happy enough with her creative freedom, a big salary rise, bonus . . . As long as she didn't tread on his toes. Besides, once he picked up her rules, he could do it all himself. Dina would have other, more pleasant things to do by then: shopping – for herself; lounging by the pool; travelling with him. He wondered if she even had a passport. Probably never crossed the state line, unless it was to Jersey.

There was a whole world out there, and Ludo was prepared to show it to this girl.

As long as she understood the rules of the game. He was first; that wasn't even a question.

'Dina Morgan,' he said to himself.

It sounded good.

'Edward, you're sitting over there.'

Edward stared blankly at his mother. He had pulled out the chair at the top of the table, where he sat, where his father used to sit. It might be Momma's house, but he was head of the family now.

'No, Mother, this is my seat now, remember?'

He hoped it wasn't stress again. Wasn't any kind of crash. It wouldn't do for Penny Johnson to swap alcohol for pills, not when she was doing so well.

'Philippe is going to sit there.'

Edward almost laughed. 'What?'

Philippe Leclerc was his mother's boyfriend, if you could call it that. A Frenchman, a former violinist in the New York Symphony Orchestra, slim and dapper, if you liked pale grey suits. He was talented as a musician, but not first rank. Edward had no idea what he did for a living.

Philippe had been round far too often – laughing with Penelope in the dining room after dinner, playing bridge with her till all hours, taking her to the opera, the theatre, paying extravagant compliments. He gave enough bows and kisses on her hand for a Renaissance court.

'Yes,' said his mother, her eyes flashing unusually. 'I've asked Philippe to move in with me. So, while we're courting, I would prefer him at the head of the table. You do understand, darling?'

'Mother, I really think—'

'No, Edward.' His mother's voice was firm, even a little strident. 'I've been thinking hard, and you know I'll always be grateful to you, darling, but it's time I stepped back into life on my own. It's not healthy for you to be so *tied* to me. I know you'll be wanting your own place. You can move out now, because Philippe will take care of me.'

'Mother.' Edward saw the danger he was in. 'Philippe has no money – none at all.'

'Oh, I know that, dearest. But money isn't everything. He's a highly accomplished man.'

'He's a retired middle-chair violinist. Ten years ago he was accomplished. Now what does he do?'

'He lives simply,' his mother said. 'He's quite open about all that.'

'He's after your fortune.'

'Please don't be crass, Edward. You speak as though he couldn't be attracted to me on my own . . . His focus has been in music; not every man can be a banker.'

The doorbell rang.

'I know I can trust you not to make a scene,' Penelope Johnson said.

Edward reluctantly got up and moved to the side.

'Monsieur Philippe Leclerc,' the butler said.

Monsieur, my ass. He's about as French as a burger and fries. Probably born here.

Philippe entered the room, beaming, in his elegant suit, with a Louis Vuitton luggage set being received by the servants in the hall behind him.

'Penelope. *Chérie*. What a happy day.' He drew close and kissed her softly, on both cheeks. 'And the wonderful *Edouard*. *Salut*. I am so happy you could join us on this special evening.'

'I believe you're joining *us*, Mr Leclerc.'

Penny shot a look of daggers at him.

'*Bienvenue*,' Edward said.

'How charming! He speaks French. You have certainly raised a wonderful young man, Penelope. I look forward to getting to know you, Edward, as we live together now.'

'Isn't this wonderful!' Penny said. She looked eagerly at Edward. 'Aren't you two going to be such friends?'

'Ah! God! Not so rough! Angel! Angel!' shrieked the girl.

Edward looked down at her, splayed and tied over the table. Her buttocks were red – lacerated with the whip. *Angel* was her safe word.

He lashed her again. And again. The rage was thick in him. She was a hooker, undocumented; he could have her deported. His fury was all that counted. His fury at Dina, at his mother.

Strike.

Scream.

She was sobbing, begging. 'No more! No more! Please, I'll do anything. Anything …'

'You'll do anything, anyway,' he snarled, and hit her.

The girl moaned, then her head lolled as she fainted.

Edward Johnson unbuttoned his fly, and started to rape her.

The feeling subsided a bit, after that. It worked every time. But it always came back. He liked it, liked giving money-hungry sluts what they deserved. He would dress, drop a few hundred on the bed and leave.

Some men in the scene were dumb. They stuck with the same girls and the same places. They got caught – lawyers, police, lawsuits, names in the papers.

Edward bounced around – fake names, new clubs, paying only in cash. He went to motels, not the women's apartments. No cameras. They were hookers and they got money, enough for some quack to stitch them up.

Tonight, though, as he showered in his room in the hotel across the street, he already knew it wasn't enough. He wanted control, real control. Philippe Leclerc was sitting in his house, drinking his father's wine, fucking his mother, and all without a cent to his name.

The guy was dead meat. And he meant that literally.

'I think you should consider a prescription,' Dr Summers said.

Edward stared at him. 'What for? I'm not ill.'

'For anxiety. I'd like to put you on a course of Klonopin.'

Edward rolled his eyes. 'Please. Sedative pills? Do I look frightened?'

Yes, Dr Summers thought. *Very*.

'Edward, you have many issues to work through. They go back beyond your fling with the waitress, beyond the divorce. Your early behaviours with women . . . You have esteem issues, anger issues. This runs deeper than you know. I feel strongly that you need calm to begin the work.'

'I am calm, doctor. I'm just worried for my mother.'

'You're not sleeping, Edward. You're erratic.'

He sat on the couch, head bowed. 'OK, doctor, you can give me the prescription. Thank you.'

Always important to keep them happy. What the fuck did this guy know? Edward's mother insisted on this therapy, when she was the one who was insane.

Edward went to a pharmacy to fill the prescription. Who knew? It might come in useful. He wasn't sleeping, but then sleep was overrated. Besides, he had other ideas for those pills.

'Faustina?' His secretary was waiting in the little office space, sitting there, reading a magazine. 'What are you doing?'

'Oh, sorry, Edward; we haven't had any calls . . .'

She blinked; her boss hadn't darkened the door for days. Wasn't she supposed to sit here and be decorative?

'First of all, you call me *sir*. I'm the boss.'

'OK . . . sir.'

'Second of all, get me some real-estate brokers. I want to see apartments – between one and two million. And mortgage brokers, too.'

'Yes, sir.'

'Then get me a call sheet of all my mother's financial advisers. I want to check something.'

'Yes, sir.'

'And lastly, get Cabot Associates on the phone.'

The older woman blinked. What had got into Edward Johnson?

'Yes, sir,' she said, nervously.

This was a good job, where she mostly did nothing. She didn't want to lose it.

Edward went into his office and slammed the door, and Faustina picked up the phone. Better get dialling.

That shrink was right about one thing, Edward thought. He *was* angry. He was so angry, the rage was now cascading from his heart into a whirlpool of hate. His father. His friends. Dina Kane. His mother. He had *rescued* his mother, and now she treated him like this, moving him aside for some penniless Frenchman.

He hated her stupidity. He could hear them laughing on Park Avenue.

At first, Edward had been lazy . . . He'd only wanted the money and an easy life.

But now he wanted revenge. And it was going to require some work.

He thought about the girl, blubbering and moaning as he lashed her exposed buttocks, slammed into her unconscious, warm body. God, that felt good; the control felt good. It was a long time since Edward Johnson felt good.

He was going to take back what belonged to him – not his wastrel quitter of a father; not Philippe; not his treacherous mother, who valued a smooth tongue and a fake compliment over her own son – him. Edward. His mind drifted to his picture, his perfect-future picture. Edward Johnson on the lawn of his Hamptons beach house, kissing his wife goodbye as he headed off to a tennis tournament. He wore tennis whites and a Rolex. She was in cut slacks and a little cashmere sweater – a blonde in pearls. There was a dog and a maid. His friends were waiting for him. His company was back in the city. Everything was perfect. He was respected, admired . . .

Not like today.

They had forced him into this, forced him into the hookers, the drugs, the showdown with some French chancer. They'd taken away his position, everything he was. Time to put it back.

'Yes, Mr Johnson, of course I can show you some wonderful properties. Even in that lower price range, there are gems out there.'

Edward swallowed his annoyance. 'I want a perfect, single-bedroom apartment. With views.'

'What a pity you didn't come to us a week ago. I have a client who just sold her place overlooking the East River for one and a half. Real bachelor pad. She made a ton on it. She's that girl who founded the Meadow cream; you heard of her?'

He started. 'Dina Kane?'

'Oh, you know her?'

'I've just heard of the cream.'

'That's her. Great eye for real estate. She's buying someplace else. Anyway, we'll find you something.'

'I want to live on the West Side.' Close to his mother's house. 'Has the Kane property closed?'

'Not yet, but it is in contract.'

'I'd like to see it, just to take in her design ideas.'

'Sure. We can set that up for you.'

* * *

210

He ate a sandwich at his desk while the calls continued.

'I don't really know if I should discuss this with you, Mr Johnson.'

'Mr Traynor, you have to discuss it with me. My mother gave me power of attorney.'

'There have been changes just recently. Your family holding company, Johnson Columbus, has made moves to dispose of some of its stock and invest in properties.'

Edward sat bolt upright, although he already knew the answer to his next question.

'Properties? Where, exactly?'

'Paris.'

'Who authorised this?'

'Mrs Johnson did, last week. It's all quite proper. She came in with her fiancé, Monsieur Leclerc. Of course, you know he will be on the board of the company very shortly.'

Edward hesitated just a fraction. 'Yes, of course, I realise that. It's a family company, after all.'

When he hung up, he felt almost joyful. Good things were about to happen.

The last meeting of the afternoon came in at five p.m.

'Faustina, you can go home.'

'Yes, sir.'

Edward didn't want anybody listening in to this one.

Olivia Broadwell sat before him, rake thin, her hair mouse-brown and natural. She had clear skin and light eyes; no make-up of any kind. She sat there in her Burberry mackintosh, not bothering to take it off, like she had somewhere else to be, and Edward knew he'd found his salvation.

'What's the job?' she said.

'Dina Kane. I want to know everything about her. Where she lives; who she's fucking; what she earns; the content of her bank account; the car she drives; her friends – if she has any; family –

their addresses. Any vulnerabilities, business and personal. Medical conditions.'

'We work within the law,' she said, with a face that implied the opposite. 'We provide data. We never reveal to clients how we obtained that data.'

'I understand. I don't want the firm having any record of this transaction. Declare the income, but I prefer to pay cash.'

'Fine by us.' The rat-like girl smiled, flashing white teeth. Cabot operated on the very edge of the law. They weren't like any of the other white-collar spy firms. They were highly effective, very dirty. Not many lawsuits, either. Rumour was they had files on cops and judges in the city – files three inches thick.

Mostly, targets never knew they were investigated. He heard some bad bastards worked for Cabot. And that's exactly who he wanted to hire.

'How fast can you get me what I need?' Johnson said.

'Fee is three hundred k. Is she a cop? Military or intelligence?'

'She's a fucking beautician,' Johnson said, laughing. 'A girl.'

'Then you can get everything in a week's time. And I do mean everything.'

He smiled a rich, deep, smile, the warmth running through him like he'd just stepped into a hot tub.

'How would you like the money?' Edward asked. 'Hundred-dollar bills?'

He stopped off at a florist's before he went home. Roses and lilies: his mother's favourites.

'Oh, Mr Edward,' said one of the maids. 'She's waiting for you in the garden, sir.'

Penelope was indeed out there, wrapped in one of her silver fox coats – one that his father had given her. A fresh burst of pain wrapped itself around Edward's heart. Once his father and mother had been here together, and that vicious little bitch, Dina Kane, had destroyed them. Whatever happened now, it was Kane's fault.

'Oh, Edward! I'm so glad you came.'

He offered her the flowers, kissing her on both cheeks. The acrid scent of cheap aftershave hung about her. Edward's fingers curled into a fist.

'I've got some wonderful news, darling. Philippe proposed! He said he can't live without me.'

She turned to him and extended her left hand. On it, in the place of his father's giant emerald-cut diamond, was a small ruby, surrounded by seed pearls.

'It was his mother's. They love coloured stones in Europe . . . Oh, darling, I'm so happy. Philippe said he doesn't care about money; he just wants us to be together. We're going to honeymoon in Paris . . . Paris!'

'Mother . . . you hardly know Philippe. If he really loved you, he wouldn't ask you yet . . .'

'Edward, no.' She clutched the flowers, furiously. 'I've been dating Philippe quietly ever since I stopped drinking. You don't know everything about my life, darling. Now I must insist you don't spoil today for me, or I'll have to ask you to leave.'

Edward swallowed the bile in his throat. He was angry at himself for even trying. Didn't he know better?

'Of course. You understand it's my role to protect you, Mother. Philippe might be just the man for you.' He forced a smile. 'I do think Paris is a wonderful idea. You can get away for the spring . . .'

'Oh, yes. I can't wait to leave New York.' She clung to Edward's sleeve, almost desperately. 'And you'll give him a chance?'

He's had his chance.

'Absolutely, I will.'

'We're going to buy a place together, in fact. Philippe thinks it's a tremendous time to invest in Europe. You can trust bricks and mortar, whereas these stocks give us both a headache.'

'Paris has some wonderful properties.' Edward smiled. 'I can see you both on the left bank.'

'Darling, I'm so relieved you're going to be *reasonable*. He wants to see you, you know. He's waiting in the library . . .' She dropped her voice, conspiratorially. 'I think he's going to ask your permission. He wants to do everything the right way, just to please me.'

'Well, so he should, Momma. Don't worry, I'll give him my blessing.' He leaned in and kissed her on the cheek.

The servants had laid a fire in the library, the way his father used to do. It was maybe his single favourite thing about the house. A crackling log fire, old books: it gave the place that air of British refinement.

And now there was this bastard of a Frenchman standing in front of it, warming his ass. He saw Edward come in, and smiled warily.

'Edouard! I take it you've heard the happy news?'

'I have.' He frowned a little. Roll over too fast and the little weasel would get suspicious. 'Mother tells me you want my permission.'

'Her father is dead, so . . .' Philippe shrugged. 'This is the old-fashioned way, and if it would make your mother happy I ask.'

'Why don't we sit down?' Edward suggested.

Philippe settled into the old high-backed burgundy chair and Edward took the green leather armchair opposite it. The fire danced in the grate. How easy it would be to take up a poker and smash his head in, once, twice.

'You know, Philippe, I need to be sure you have Mother's interests at heart. It seems like a very early marriage, and she is a rich woman.'

'Of course, I will take no offence.' He smiled silkily. 'Your mother is of an age where she is not twenty-one anymore. After divorce, many women know what they want. I love her, and she needs a companion; it is not healthy for a young man such as you to remain in the house.'

'And a prenuptial agreement?'

His eyes widened innocently. 'Ah, we do not accept those. If one is not committed to marriage, why marry? Penelope seems very firm. She tells me, when she married your father she was a girl; now she is a woman. We will share what we have.'

'And you have . . . ?'

'My talent; my creativity. A lifetime of devotion. I can give Penelope guidance. Also, she wants to have a little fun, and this is my gift . . . The gift of laughter.'

Laughter, all the way to the bank.

He smiled warmly. 'She certainly deserves some laughter. Very good, you have my blessing, Philippe. Bring a smile back to my mother's face.'

Edward reached across and offered a handshake. The Frenchman's sweaty palm slipped into his, and he refrained from crushing it between his fingers.

The dinner was almost unendurable, but he endured it. It was good to see that Philippe liked to drink. Edward matched him, keeping his glass full, but taking only small sips, then calling for a different wine. But Philippe stopped at three glasses, looking sideways at his new fiancée, who stuck to water, gazing adoringly at him all the while.

'But it's so tremendous you get on so well,' Penelope exclaimed when they got to dessert. 'I couldn't be happier.' She pressed her fingers to her forehead. 'I may skip the coffee and petits fours, though; I have a headache.'

'Come on, Mother, you should go upstairs to rest. I'll send Philippe up soon, I promise.' Edward winked jovially at his stepfather-to-be. 'We'll just head to the drawing room for some conversation, a small brandy . . .'

Philippe perked up immediately. 'Well . . . if my *chérie* does not mind?'

'Oh, no! That sounds lovely. I will . . . I will be upstairs.' She pushed back her chair. Edward suspected a migraine, from the stress, which was fine by him. When those things came on, his mother could concentrate on nothing else.

'Philippe, come on through.' Edward nodded to the butler. 'Bring me some brandy – a special bottle from the cellar. Try the Hine & Co. champagne cognac – the 1934.'

'Very good, sir.'

'You know your wine,' Philippe said, admiringly. 'The 1934 is a masterpiece.'

Penelope walked slowly and painfully up the stairs, and Edward noted that Philippe did not so much as look back at her.

The drawing room was warm, the thick velvet drapes drawn against the cold. Edward poured himself a little brandy and swallowed and spluttered, pretending to have downed a great gulp. There was a fireplace here, too, and he passed Philippe a glass full of the amber liquid, enough of it to swim in. The warmth and the comfort was too much to resist.

'I must go to your mother,' the older man said, greedily eyeing the brandy. 'She will expect me.'

'No; I recognise the signs. She has a bad headache. She won't expect more than a kiss on the cheek. It's a special occasion; drink up.'

He took a deep sip. 'Fantastic. What a cognac. *Mon Dieu.*'

'We will have a better one served at the wedding. What do you think? A small affair, hosted here? Or something larger?'

'We want it done as soon as possible; we will head down to City Hall. Just on our own. Your mother doesn't want any fuss.'

And you don't want any delay, Edward thought.

'Oh, I agree, soon – but you must enjoy the moment. A few select friends. A society columnist, perhaps. Your entrée, Philippe,

216

into major society. Come, you don't want to stand there in a dingy room with a strip light.' He packed scorn into his voice. 'We can have a judge marry you, here, in a couple of weeks. First, you can fly Mother to Paris, see the apartment you're buying together . . .'

'There would be press coverage?'

'Lots of it,' Edward promised.

'I *would* like to see the apartment.'

'Make sure you're choosing the right one. You and Mother need to spend your money wisely when you invest together. And she would like a break. Paris has some marvellous couturiers for a second marriage; an elegant brocade coat, perhaps. I can organise the wedding here. The Johnsons do things the right way; I'm sure the Leclercs do, as well.'

'Absolutely. Yes.' He took another deep drink of the brandy. 'This stuff is *merveilleux*. I must stop, though, Edouard, or I will have a terrible hangover tomorrow.'

'No, no.' Edward suppressed his excitement. It was all going so well; it was easy. 'Take five or six of these.' He pulled out of his pocket a bottle of baby aspirin. 'Drink some water, and you will be absolutely fine.'

'*Merci*.' Philippe chucked them down like candy, and Edward poured him a large glass of water from the jug on the table, ice cubes clinking delicately. Then he took the brandy away.

'It's settled then. I will tell Mother and make the arrangements: a society wedding in two weeks. Oh, and I will have moved out of the house by the time you return – I'm buying a place of my own.'

'Fantastic!' Philippe said. 'You will be very happy in your own place.'

'I'm sure I will. Goodnight, Philippe.'

Edward worked steadily, and it was a thrill. He contacted gossip writers; he booked a judge, set a date. Invitations went out in the post, just a few trusted friends, enough to make a wedding. His mother was ecstatic; he went to the house for dinner every other night.

Enough to get Philippe a little drunk, to pass him the aspirins, to settle into a pattern.

'Darling, this is so kind of you,' Penelope said. 'I don't feel up to organising a wedding, but you're taking care of us so well.'

'Momma, you and Philippe need a proper sendoff.'

She would sit with them nights when Edward organised the digestifs, watch him hand over the headache pills, make small talk about the apartment search. He called the family travel agent, booked first-class tickets for them to Charles de Gaulle, praised the nineteenth-century penthouse Philippe was buying on the Rive Gauche. He even invited some reliable friends of his mother's around, so they could gossip over his wedding plans together.

'What do you think of these?'

Philippe sat in his father's armchair, lording it over proceedings, nursing his vintage brandy. Matthew and Jane Elliott, and Lourdes and Spencer McCain, two of their old crowd of couples, had been dragooned in, reluctantly, but Edward had persuaded them.

'Edward – I did a lot of business with your father,' Matthew said. 'And this French guy . . . I gotta be honest with you . . . not our kind of thing.'

'Matt, Dad's gone. He's finding himself. Mom needs to see Jane. You know she's gotten over substance abuse. The wedding means a lot to her. Just show up once, please.'

Sigh. 'OK, son, since you insist.'

'I don't think your mother should marry this man,' Lourdes McCain told him. 'Please don't be angry at me, Edward.'

'It's not our decision, though – and she's dead set. Look, I just want her to be happy. You can help. One dinner.'

And they showed.

Edward took no chances. He booked the airline tickets and paid for them in full. He found a small apartment, right on Central Park West, a block from his mother's. It was overpriced and tiny, but that location always sold. To the world, he was totally involved with the wedding, backing it to the hilt.

There were no whores, no girls to hit, no S&M clubs. Edward had grown up. He was focused now. There would be time for all that later. The thought of Philippe, taking his mother's hand, changing her name, stealing his money, peacocking in his father's place . . . It was enough; it was everything.

As the time for the trip approached, he went over there more frequently, biding his time. Waiting for the opportunity.

And it came.

'I think it's another migraine,' Penelope said.

Edward exhaled, softly. He'd been getting worried. If she hadn't felt sick soon, he would have had to make her sick, which was a second layer to his plan. But the gods were smiling, not that there were any gods.

'You head upstairs. Philippe and I will put the world to rights,' Edward said. 'There's an excellent Calvados we want to work on.'

He enjoyed the evening, enjoyed it hugely. The excitement was almost unbearable. He filled Philippe's glass again and again. No water this time. Every trick he had, he employed to keep him drinking.

The guy was sloppy, revolting. He forgot who he was talking to. He laughed about the apartment, the joys of real money. He didn't want to work, and Penelope would help him concentrate on his art. Although, of course, he would be managing the family money now, since half of it would be his.

'Don't worry, Edouard – *ne t'inquiètes pas*; we won't forget you; there will be an allowance, or something . . .'

'Whatever. I'm not concerned about money. Your job is to make Mother happy. Here – one more shot; one for luck?'

'I shouldn't . . . I'm a little drunk.'

'A nightcap, then,' Edward said. 'You can sleep it off tomorrow. No need to get up early; you aren't some worker drone.'

'No – that's right.'

Edward lifted his own glass. 'To the good life.'

Philippe tittered. 'Why not? The good life. And I always make the ladies happy. They are so kind to me . . .'

Edward digested that . . . *the ladies*. Of course, this was how the fool had lived before: other, desperate women; gifts of money; a place to stay. He was a charmer, a sponger – essentially a hooker. And his mother had offered that ticket to the big time.

'Drink up, Philippe.' He gave him a shove on the back and Philippe stumbled and blinked. 'Best to take it all down. Your bride is waiting.'

He took the stem of the glass, laughed, and upended it. '*Sacré bleu*! It burns the throat. You will get your new papa in trouble . . .'

Edward swallowed, hard. *His new papa*. 'Here, take the aspirin. You want to take a few extra tonight, don't you think?'

'God, yes.'

He passed him eight little round pills, curled into the palm of his hand, and Philippe tossed them back, swallowing them.

'Great. Thank God for that.'

'Here, let me help you upstairs,' Edward said. He took Philippe's arm, draped it around his shoulder. 'Perhaps you should sleep in my old room tonight, so as not to disturb Mother.'

'Yesss . . .' Philippe was already slurring. 'Sure . . . No problem . . .'

Edward dragged him up, step by step. He figured he had at least five minutes. He waved cheerfully to the servants as they passed, and hoisted Philippe through the door of his own suite, placing him face down on the bed and slipping his shoes off.

Then took the small bottle of Klonopin pills from his jacket. He took off the lid and carefully formed Philippe's hand into a fist around the bottle, pressing his thumb and forefingers over the label, and twisting his other hand around the lid. Philippe was already drooling; Edward paid him no attention.

He put the open bottle of aspirins down on the bathroom sink. Then he turned off the light and closed the door, and, humming to himself, he left the house.

Chapter Twelve

Dina was in heaven.

Torch was humming. Every day the beauty department got a little bigger, expanded its floor space. Workmen mixed with the shoppers, there was yellow tape around the construction as she moved her territory forwards, and nobody seemed to mind.

New brands. Bigger stands. New products. More lights, mirrors and more blond wood.

She planned her days carefully: product selection, stock review, staff observations, new hirings, press releases – and at least three hours on the phone and email, working every girl in town.

The beauty bloggers were just the start.

Dina hit the editors, the beauty writers on magazines and the segment producers on local TV shows. She sent samples to personal shoppers for some of the biggest players in town. And she wrote all the press releases herself.

The result was a steady stream of good news. Once the blogs had moved on, Dina sent thank-you gifts. Torch's name was posted on internet forums. There was a snippet in the *Daily News*, two minutes on 'colours of spring' for NY1 at breakfast and then small items appeared in the magazines. Suddenly Torch was a hot ticket.

Ludo was thrilled, and Dina finally had a boss who was backing her all the way.

'These results are terrific,' he said, after the first month. 'I think you should take over the handbag space.'

'Move into sunglasses. They can go upstairs.'

'We don't need jewellery on the ground floor.'

With every expansion, her stock rose. And Dina loved it. Ludo treated her with respect, paid her compliments, came and talked to her team. He gave her carte blanche on hirings and backed her to the hilt. As the cash registers rang and the shoppers poured in, he asked her to come up to his office, every morning.

'You're doing wonders.'

'Thank you.' She smiled at him, confidently.

'I want to leverage the success for Torch. You're right. I'm going to make a series of announcements in the business press. My name should be on the end of all press releases – let them come from the MD.'

Dina's smile widened. 'That's great! Thank you, Ludo.'

'You can draft them, just send them up to me and my office will sign them off and put them out. Emails to bloggers you can do yourself. I'm thinking about a social-media campaign, too.'

'That would be incredible. We need to be all over Facebook, Twitter, Tumblr . . .'

'It's Torch, though – so your photo will be in there, along with the other department heads.'

Dina rolled her eyes a little; the other department heads seemed as wooden as planks to her. Whatever. The beauty department was making all the strides. Her team was hot, and the other store sectors wanted some of the magic they were creating. Dina understood reflected glory. Plus, at the moment they were jealous that the spotlight was on one person. Maybe she should share it around, soothe some wounded egos.

Looking on the bright side, if Ludo wanted all his senior people featured together, maybe they would bitch about her a little less.

'Sure. Why not?'

'I also want detailed notes on everything you're doing. We may replicate some of it elsewhere in the store.'

'Absolutely.'

'I'll speak to your hires when you bring them in, and eat lunch with the team captains.'

Dina had separated her staff into their areas of expertise: skincare; eyes and mascara; tan and body; cosmetics application; fragrance. She ripped up the old way of doing business, where you hired a dull girl who liked free samples and was willing to work for low pay. Dina recruited beauty students, fashion-school graduates, models who wanted some set hours, and placed them under well-paid pros who ran their departments: a consultant dermatologist, who'd quit her practice to fit work around raising her teenage boys, directed skincare; a renowned make-up artist, who wanted a steady job, was in charge of cosmetics; a former pro from Bobbi Brown was evaluating brushes; and two spray-tan salon perfectionists were running the bronzer area.

As well as classic brand booths, selling everything, Dina ran grouped walls of smaller products, the ones she could control. Indie eye shadows were together, racked by colour and type; lipsticks, fading from scarlet to clear gloss, tumbled down the colour chart like a computer screen. Women loved it when they came in for pale pink lips and found fifty glosses and sticks racked next to each other.

Even the part-timers were passionate. The old staffers had shaped up, or shipped out. Dina had transferred them elsewhere, if they couldn't cut it – to lighting, or cushions, or outerwear.

'Torch is for beauty. Torch is for babes,' Dina said, when the human-resources people questioned her. 'We want the cool kids, the enthusiasts, the elite. I don't carry passengers.'

They muttered, but she was untouchable. Dina Kane was backed by Ludo Morgan, and she always got her way.

The beauty division was shaping up so well. Dina was on a roll, and the money kept pouring in. Employees got spot bonuses

– a hundred here, five hundred there. If Dina saw or heard something good, she just passed out cash. Morale was through the roof, and the job applications rolled in.

And she was making money. Every month, Ludo increased her salary. There were perks – the free store card, the company car, parking included. She now drove an Audi, could afford to dress designer without having to wait for the good pieces to be marked down in price in the sales. Everyone was happy, and Dina Kane was happiest of all.

Except on the little matter of Joel Gaines.

She waited for the congratulatory call, the email. It didn't happen. Radio silence. Sometimes Dina would drift off, thinking about him. She would fantasise about him coming into the store, walking around, looking for her. And they would laugh, and he'd hug her, pat her on the head . . . When her thoughts drifted like this, Dina caught herself and tried to stop. *Screw him*, she thought, trying to pretend it didn't hurt her so much.

After all, things were good – even great. She had a dream job, was a big success. Even with Johnny's bills, there was enough money. Her apartment had sold and she'd moved to a new one on Eightieth Street, a block from Central Park, with a great view of the museum. Finally, it was something for herself. No more fixing and decorating – Dina Kane no longer had time. She was a retail mogul, a maestro, and busy from dawn to dusk. And she loved it.

There was something incredible about buying new. Her apartment had a breakfast terrace just outside the window, a spare room for when Johnny got out, a lovely kitchen – small, sure, but with Sub-Zero fridges and a Viking cooker; the flat-screen TV was already on the living room wall, and Dina's windows there looked out on to the tree-lined street and the Victorian townhouses opposite, giving a sense of the older, grander New York, of the Manhattan she'd arrived in.

Dina just supervised a little bit of design, using the crew

employed at Torch. She installed blond wood floors to open up the light, bought Danish furniture with sleek lines; the bedroom was a fantasy of oyster-white and the bathroom, which had both a European tub and a walk-in shower, followed a beach-slate palette. The pops of colour on the gunmetal couch were orange and bronze, and it looked modern Mediterranean, chic as hell. She invested in a gas fireplace to keep her warm all winter: realistic flames, and no mess with the flue. They worked while she was out, and she came home to endless luxury.

None of it was enough to make her forget Joel Gaines completely. But, if he had lost interest in her, others hadn't. Ludo Morgan was her boss, and he was also her boyfriend.

Dina liked how he kept it professional at work – backing her up, putting his name on everything, regular meetings. He'd kept his word: they were open about it; nothing was hidden.

That first Friday, Ludo showed up right on time. No flowers; no chauffeur. He took her for dinner at Jean Georges, one of the most expensive restaurants in midtown, and they lingered over a tasting menu for three hours.

The next week, they went to a play; Ludo procured tickets to the hottest show on Broadway, sold out for months in advance.

After that, he invited her to his palatial apartment, above the store, and they ordered Chinese takeout. He didn't pressure her to go to bed. Dina was wary, but happy.

Ludo would kiss her on the cheek in full view of the other staff, then go about his business. The staff – especially those outside the beauty department – resented it, gossiped and bitched. She knew that. But Dina believed her results were unarguable.

For the first time in her life, Dina Kane was part of a couple.

And she liked it. She liked the sense of respect, of fitting in. She liked the way people tilted their heads and smiled indulgently when Ludo kissed her on the cheek. She liked the way it felt when he opened a door for her, or flagged down a cab – like regular people did, people with lives. And, because she worked at

Torch, she could throw herself into the job round the clock and still see enough of her boyfriend.

Boyfriend. Boss. A taboo, but it worked.

'Good. So you'll see more of my stamp on your remodel, Dina,' Ludo said, bringing Dina back into his office, tearing her from her thoughts. He reached forward and clicked his mouse, closing the window on the computer, then pushed back from his desk, indicating the meeting was over. 'How are you fixed for Saturday?'

'I can't this Saturday,' she said.

Ludo frowned. 'Wait. What? You have a previous engagement?'

He made it sound ridiculous. And, she had to admit, she was wedded to the job.

'I'm going upstate to check on my brother. He's been making progress; they say he can be released soon.'

'Your brother. You're going to have to introduce me.'

'Sure, one day. I'd like to.'

He didn't mention her mother. Dina had already explained how little there was there. She sent money back each month, and never got a thank you for it. Often, she berated herself for still looking through the mail, as though that would ever change.

'Meantime, how about you go see your brother on Friday? I have plans for Saturday. Big plans.'

Dina laughed. 'Ludo, we work on Fridays.'

'You deserve an afternoon off. Take one. It's an order, if that helps.'

She smiled; as though he could order her about!

They were companionable together, friendly. She'd gone to bed with him, about five weeks in, once it seemed respectable and the right thing to do. She was nervous; the almost-virgin, the workaholic; boyfriend-free since Edward; no sex since bringing down his father. But that trauma was almost forgotten, and Ludo was tender and patient, and made sure she'd had a couple of glasses of champagne and, even though Dina felt little pleasure, it wasn't actually painful. She enjoyed his desire, his sweating, gasping lust, the way she saw herself through his eyes. The only time she sensed anything, was when she started to get excited, and then her thoughts drifted helplessly, inevitably, towards Joel Gaines; her eyes closed, she felt wet, open, as if she was lifting out of herself . . .

'Come on, baby. Oh, that's good; you're so good,' Ludo panted. She heard his voice, and the vision shattered. But she moaned and whimpered a little, and he came, and was done with her.

Maybe things would get better in time. When she got more used to him, and less shy. For now, it was enough to have a young man who treated her well, prized her, took her out.

But the whispers at work continued.

'She's caught herself a nice one.'

'Set her target the day she walked in here. The job's just for show.'

'Dina's smart; she got close; she'll be out of here in six months.'

'Lucky bitch.'

'This whole place will be hers one day. Did you hear about the palace he's got on the fucking roof? They say it's ten thousand square foot of space with a garden and a goddamned pool.'

'He can't even drive. Daddy got him a chauffeur.'

'Why does she bust her ass like that? All he wants is a respectable version of a model.'

'She's not *that* pretty. She must be on fire in bed.'

'No wonder he signs off on everything.'

'She isn't even the force, she's just the front woman, you know? Where did she go to college? He's got the MBA and she's just like this sexy brunette, fronting it, playing with make-up.'

'You've got to give it to her – she knows how to climb. She's from the middle of fucking nowhere, out in Westchester.'

Dina heard that stuff every day, out on the shop floor, as she moved about unobtrusively, amongst the crowds of women browsing and snatching. She tried not to resent it. They couldn't conceive of a girl who wanted to make money, not marry it. Ludo was great, handsome, good to her, but she tried not to think about it too much because she wasn't sure he was the one. He was a boyfriend, a good boyfriend, and Dina was trying to live a normal life. But marriage . . . ?

She shuddered a little. That was the sound of freedom gone and iron gates clanging shut.

Maybe other girls would jump at the chance, and they were surely welcome to go right ahead. Dina concentrated on her work. She was so sunk in Torch, she dreamed about it. That buzz when a beauty editor ran a feature, or they cleared yet another fifteen square foot for her playground, it was electric, inspiring. She lived on the adrenaline, and the humdrum love life was fine; Ludo was her friend, her boss.

And now that friend was asking for a favour.

'OK. I could do with a break.'

It was true, she felt exhausted. You couldn't mainline this stuff around the clock. It would be nice to focus on Johnny, not on the latest brand of cream eye shadow, or the new low-heat hair tongs she was bringing in to her beauty-tools section. 'So where are we going on Saturday?'

'Out to the beach,' Ludo said. 'I want you to meet my parents.'

Dina smiled tightly, hoping her nerves didn't show. 'Your parents! Wow. That's so great.'

'I thought you'd be pleased.' He smiled, and Dina tried to ignore the sinking feeling in her stomach.

Joel Gaines looked at his wife, reluctantly.

Susan had come bounding in from the beauty salon, wearing the hideously expensive 'casual' wear from Prabal Gurung's resort collection and Jimmy Choo ballet flats, and her hair was as big and bouncy as Farrah Fawcett's. She was done up to the nines, her eyes thick with mascara, artfully applied bronze shadow and chocolate liner, and her face was immaculately made up with some kind of airbrushed foundation and a high pink blusher. She looked like a model, an older model, perhaps, but still with that stylised perfection.

He hated it. All the women in the Hamptons did this, whenever a celebrity threw a party. It wasn't enough to have a fifteen-million-dollar beach house; you had to compete on the 'best trophy wife' circuit, like you were entering a prize dog at Crufts.

And he was as guilty as anybody. For years, Susan had worked the trophy-wife thing perfectly, and Joel had not complained. He'd bought her jewels, an emerald and South Sea pearl necklace, a canary diamond ring the size of an M&M, a platinum watch studded with rubies. Not so much to see her wear them, but as a vehicle for boasting about his wealth and power.

'How do you like it?'

Susan pirouetted. She was always happiest when she felt great about herself, when she was the star. They did less and less together these days.

'Stunning,' he lied.

Make-up should be subtle, present but not present, barely there, so you could see the woman. All the men that piled on this 'jewel eyes' crap were gay – the same men that designed the curves out of catwalk models and pushed 'menswear' trends on the girls every season.

Dina Kane, for example, had it down perfectly. Always groomed, but with a touch as light as gossamer . . .

No – *no*.

'What do you say we skip the party? I mean, altogether. Just go for a moonlit walk on the beach. We could make a bonfire, roast s'mores or something.'

Susan laughed. 'You're funny. We could do that every day. This is Roxana Felix's party, you know – the supermodel. *Everybody* will be there.'

'Right,' he sighed.

'Hey, honey, look at this magazine; I stole it from the salon. Though, with what I tipped them, they could buy a hundred of them.' She triumphantly plunked down a copy of *Vogue*. 'See this? A double-page spread on Torch. You know Torch, that fusty old store uptown? It's been turned around, like *completely*. All my girlfriends are shopping there, in the beauty department. This is an interview with Ludo Morgan; isn't he cute? You know the father, right?'

Joel nodded.

'Ludo is the heir and he's really transformed the place. He's everywhere these days! Interviews in *Vogue*, in the *New York Times* . . . Haven't you noticed? He's really the coming man.'

'Let me see that,' Gaines said. He looked at the spread, the young man with the bland features photographed artfully against the blond, well-lit beauty department. The article raved about the revamp, the coming shock to other departments, the soaring bottom line. Ludo Morgan was given all the credit.

'I heard they had a new beauty director – Dina Kane. She's had something to do with this?' he asked, casually.

Saying her name aloud was exciting. Gaines had tried, with minimal success, to forget her. Shouting at her, storming out of the café . . . His plan worked, if you wanted to call it that.

She was humiliated enough. She never called him again.

That was meant to be a signal for him to turn the page, move on, concentrate on Susan.

It wasn't happening. Daily, he struggled for mastery. Daily, he stopped himself making the call.

And she showed no mercy. Her brand was everywhere – growing, expanding, filling the business pages. At first, he saw her name on a daily basis in the press releases and announcements.

Then it changed – to the boss, Ludo Morgan.

Gaines reserved judgement. He made discreet inquiries; Dina had been promoted, given hiring privileges, perks, a bigger salary. Nobody was ripping her off, like they had done with Meadow. And yet, she was getting the cash, but no longer getting the credit.

'Who? Oh, yes, she works in the beauty department. All Ludo's staff are shown right here.'

Susan flipped the page and pointed to a small, inset picture. Dina was standing in the back row of a group of staffers, smiling and wearing a chic white shift dress that set off her tanned, toned body. No rocks necessary, and no panda eyes allowed.

Goddamn, she was pretty. A butterfly among the moths. But she was also an afterthought – just a director; one of many.

'You know, I knew that name was familiar,' Susan said, suddenly, and Gaines gave a guilty start. She couldn't know anything, could she? Impossible.

'From the store?'

'I'm not that much of a beauty geek; I don't memorise the *staff*,' Susan said contemptuously. 'No, she's a smart cookie, that one; she's actually dating him. I saw it on "Page Six". You know, the hot young couple. She's pretty and he has the brains and the money.'

Adrenaline flushed through Gaines' system. He felt something wholly unfamiliar: jealousy; rage. Ludo Morgan was unmarried and fifteen years younger than him, with money of his own. Not in Joel Gaines' league, but more than enough to offer Dina a life of endless luxury.

He tried to feel happy for his protégée. He failed.

'That's nice,' he said, eventually.

'Well, try and show some enthusiasm tonight, won't you?'

Gaines tore his eyes away from the tiny picture of Dina and looked up. 'What?'

'They're going to be there tonight – two of the star guests. His folks have a compound in Amagansett, and Ludo bought his own place in Sagaponack, just back from the beach on Daniels' Lane.'

He stared at her. 'What are you? A realtor?'

'I like to keep up with what goes on around here,' Susan said, smugly. 'You need to be up to date.'

233

'No kidding.' He passed a hand over his sweating forehead. 'And they are coming tonight?'

'Sure are. I can't wait to introduce you. I'm really into Torch.'

He stood up. 'That's great. I think I need to get some fresh air. I'll take the dogs out on the beach.'

Boxer and Clive bounded happily along the sand. Gaines knew a lot of rich men who envied their dogs: no therapists, no mergers, no taxes.

No women.

He walked here often when he needed to think. The scent of salt from the ocean, the breezes on a hot day: it lifted him, helped him to focus.

I won't go to the goddamned party. That would be easiest, but there would be fights for days, and it was also the coward's way out. Susan would pout, and wonder . . . He didn't need her to wonder . . .

Jesus. Wonder about what? There he went again, overthinking it. He hadn't done anything with Dina Kane. She was a cute piece of ass with a brain. Men were programmed to want pieces of ass. He hadn't even kissed her, let alone fucked her. He'd been dwelling on her, OK, Gaines admitted that. It was too embarrassing to discuss with his shrink, even. Just another rich guy's midlife crisis . . . She was young enough to be his daughter, if he'd started early.

Being near the water helped put things in perspective: the immensity of the ocean, crashing against the grey sand, soothing but relentless. Gaines could have any young piece of tail he wanted, either on a date, or ordered in from the most discreet escort services in the city, the ones where they tested the girls for diseases on a daily basis. He was a billionaire, and ass was available to him round the clock, if he was that way inclined.

He wasn't. Never had been.

He was also, he understood, very unhappy.

The moment he got up his courage and yelled at Dina Kane was meant to be a good one. He was supposed to have walked out of that café a free man, still the master of himself, still right with his conscience, like a junkie kicking the habit. And when she didn't email, didn't call, stopped dead, that was meant to be his victory.

Temptation was behind him. He was back with Susan, their long marriage getting longer.

Only, 'back with Susan' wasn't so great. Before Dina, he'd been so consumed with work he hadn't really cared. Now he did care. It bothered him that his wife seemed to endure sex, not enjoy it. It bothered him that she never talked about anything but their celebrity neighbours, like he gave a flying fuck, or how the kids were doing in college. Gaines loved his boys, but they were separate to his wife. When he arranged romance, like a quiet dinner, or a beach walk, she never talked about him, never asked about him. *How was your day?* was the extent of it.

He hated the spend-as-sport. Hated the panoply of servants disguised as teachers: personal trainer; personal tennis coach; personal shopper; personal stylist. Susan collected an army of redundant hangers-on, like their garden designer, and then spent hours in 'meetings' with them, making a life. He disdained the conspicuous dresses and the bold make-up; where was that chic, simple girl he married?

The boys were gone. Was this his life, for the rest of his life?

Gaines didn't know if he could take it. Why it suddenly mattered, the companion at home, he wasn't sure. Dina Kane was a witch, an enchantress; after just a few encounters, he was thinking about her all the damned time.

And now she was coming tonight. Very good. He would go.

He couldn't divorce Susan; they had been together too long. Marriage counselling, maybe; a heart to heart. He could talk to her, tell her what was missing. She'd given him two children, a lifetime of service. It wasn't good enough to trade her in for a younger model, like some scumbag who changed wives the way he changed cars . . .

That's what he told himself, anyway. That was what a priest or rabbi would say.

He wanted it to ring true. But all he felt was a horrible, sinking feeling. Maybe this was a midlife crisis. Older men were meant to buy a red sports car, right? Only he already had a red sports car. And a blue one. And a Humvee . . .

Gaines smiled grimly to himself. *Forget it*. It was a problem he had to think through, like any other. Forgetting Dina Kane hadn't worked, and running from her wouldn't help. What if this was a business issue? He should break it down like that, the way he was used to doing.

'Clive!' he called, because the golden Labrador was too far away along the beach, chasing the waves and barking. OK, so he was a little obsessed. Maybe yelling at her in the coffee shop wasn't the end of the story. He should talk to Dina again, get to know her, let her fall from whatever stupid pedestal he'd constructed. She had a boyfriend. It was good, he could see them together: two kids, the right age for each other. All's well that ends well, right? He recalled he'd once told her that they'd speak again when she got herself a lover.

He needed to process that. He was married, and she was taken. Nothing could be better than seeing her and the golden boy at the dumb celebrity party tonight. No doubt she'd love it just as much as Susan did, would fit right in to the deluxe soccer-mom crowd, and the scales would fall from his eyes. Perhaps he could see her how he was meant to, as an unusual girl, a comer, somebody he liked, mentored.

The dog came bounding up to him, and Boxer, his chocolate mutt, next to him. They were both good dogs. He liked this part of his life. It would be crazy to divorce, to give it all up.

But the thought was so tempting.

He turned for home. He wanted to have sex with Susan, but

knew already that she wouldn't go for it. Not a chance. Not with her hair all done and the airbrushed make-up so perfectly set. Sex would be his best shot of denuding himself of desire, so he didn't gawp over Dina like some drunken student. He didn't want to do it himself; that seemed sterile and hopeless when he was married and his wife was there.

Joel Gaines was just going to have to grin and bear it.

Dina looked at herself in the mirror and sighed.

'We absolutely have to go to this party?'

Ludo frowned slightly. 'Honey, please stop asking me that.'

She was exquisite, and he was enjoying being with her. Every month that passed was a testament to his good taste. First and foremost, she was gorgeous, and she was pliant when he wanted to have sex; but she just dressed with such style; her make-up was perfect – exactly like you'd expect.

And the workaholic stuff was fine with Ludo. It meant she never clung on to him, gave him whatever space he needed. Flying to Florida to watch baseball spring training? No problem. Gore-fest movie with the boys? She didn't care. Dining at a gentleman's club? Dina would be in the office. They did things when *he* wanted to do things. He led in this relationship, and that suited him perfectly.

Dina Kane had a lot of energy. Her six months at Torch had turned the store around, but he thought he could take it from here. She would need to be occupied. He could see her planning the most stylish wedding for years, then taking time out to raise great-looking kids.

Torch was his – literally. Ludo understood her passion, but she could channel it into home, kids, charity work. He'd been detaching her from the store without her realising, so ploughed in was she to everyday results. There was another 'Dina' installed in fashion now – he'd hired this cute young thing from *W* magazine – and picked up a former editor of *Wallpaper* to work some magic on home furnishings. There was a proper PR department in place, staffed full of hungry young kids who'd worked in the big agencies. Torch wasn't just beauty. He, Ludo, had a system, and he was motoring.

His father was ecstatic.

Dad and Mom had both liked Dina that week she flew out to their place in California. She'd stayed in a guest room, swum in the pool, helped his mother cook. They were pleased she worked at the store, and regarded her tales of stocktaking indulgently. His father had said something about Joel Gaines, and Dina flushed and replied that she deserved the job, on her own merits.

A little aggressive, that, but nothing to worry about.

His friends were jealous. And that was half the battle. Their air-headed models had no tits, no ass, and were hooked on drugs. Dina was curvaceous, and she was interesting to talk to, once she got off the subject of work.

'You know tonight's important to me. I want to show you off to everybody – our summer neighbours.'

'*Your* summer neighbours,' she said, but smiled.

'If you play your cards right, baby . . .'

'OK. I'll pack an overnight case.'

'No need; I had some of your stuff shipped to the house. Everything's there. You just pick the dress you're going to wear, and we'll take a helicopter in.'

'A helicopter!'

He kissed her on the cheek. 'This is how people live, Dina. You know, when time is more important than money.'

Her smile was a bit warmer now. 'I get that.'

'I don't feel like being stuck in gridlocked traffic for three hours. We'll head to midtown, for the heliport. So pack what you need in your purse.'

Dina blinked. She was wearing a sexy, figure-hugging Roland Mouret dress in structured green velvet, with folds and twists, and a simple single pearl on a golden chain at the hollow of her throat, like a drop of water. Her heels were cheaper – Jessica Simpson – but that was his girl; she mixed labels and high street with an irrepressible charm. The Simpson heels were ones she could walk in, she said, and they kept her going all night. The green velvet worked fine, and she carried a Prada clutch in khaki leather. It all looked effortless, and her dark hair piled on top of her head gave her the regal style of a Greek goddess.

'OK then, honey,' she said.

He liked the endearment; she rarely handed them out. It was kind of pleasing how little Dina Kane seemed to be after him and his money. She was ambitious and material in one way, always pushing for a bigger salary, or a bonus, or even stock options; quite surprising how hard she demanded that; he wasn't used to it in women employees. Ludo gave her a rise, a nice car, but fobbed her off on the stock. She was new to the company still, he said, and it wasn't right. Maybe at the year end . . .

But Dina was blind to the bonus sitting right opposite her. He laughed when he thought about it. A couple of hundred grand a year barely made you middle class in Manhattan, and he was offering her tens of millions. What was the problem? If she married him, she would have a penthouse, a beach house, resort vacations at the Four Seasons, and a car and driver, plus all the designers she could wear. Yet she showed little interest in commuting by helicopter or the fancy restaurants he took her to.

Other girls on the shop floor would kill for the opportunity. But Ludo Morgan liked Dina's brains. She brought class to the whole thing. And she was a challenge in a way he loved.

Growing up rich meant having girls fling themselves at you – in the nightclub, at the polo match, seniors in high school. Word went round, and the rich boys were prey. That made you resentful, made you distrust women. Maybe the best thing about Dina Kane was that she genuinely didn't care. That was the silver lining to this pushy, aggressive alpha female.

Ludo was wearing a bespoke tailored suit, paired with a crisp

Armani shirt – white with thin navy stripes – and shoes hand-crafted by John Lobb in England. He looked good, hair freshly cut: the new entrepreneur on the block, finally getting the recognition he deserved. Beauty was motoring, but only because he'd provided the funds and the vision to make it happen. Lots of companies had talented employees; Steve Jobs hadn't invented the iPod, but it was his company, so he led the way. Ludo had rearranged everything; the entire Torch building was now light wooden floors, mirrors, soft lighting. The old tables, piled with goods, had gone. A few designers showcased in each department. He'd brought furniture, fashion and accessories up to date as well. And the press was good – sales would catch up. A big spend, and a big return. This was what chief execs did.

In his pocket lay Dina Kane's next chapter. A small blue velvet box from Tiffany, containing a colossal ring: seven carats of internally flawless, round, brilliant diamond, flanked by two azure Thai sapphires, just to be different.

Ludo had it all planned out: their triumphant debut on the Hamptons scene; Dina as belle of the ball; himself as the coming man in retail. There were going to be actors there, directors, Roxana Felix herself and several hedge-fund billionaires. Susan Gaines, doyenne of the scene, and her husband, Joel . . . the guy who'd sent Dina over in the first place. He should shake his hand.

After some mingling, some compliments, a few glasses of champagne, he would walk Dina out to the beach and propose, right there on the seashore, under the stars. He had the exact spot in mind . . . The floodlights in front of Roxana's gates reached fifty foot. After all, Dina needed to be able to see the bling.

Then back inside – to receive congratulations, show off her rock. And then he'd have the chauffeur drive them a little way to their cottage. It was all laid out and ready: heated, warm, champagne on ice in a silver bucket on the kitchen island, a fire crackling in the grate in the living room, fresh silk sheets on the engagement bed. Dina Kane would fall asleep to the sound of the ocean in the distance, knowing that, in the morning, she would wake up as chatelaine of all Ludo owned. She could swim in the pool, eat a breakfast of strawberries and fresh-baked croissants, and then he'd broach the fact she was stepping down from Torch.

He needed a wife, not a rival, and it was time for her to break from all that stress. Besides, men in his position kept the family. The wives didn't work. Not ever.

'You're completely sure you have stuff at the house?' Dina said, now, breaking into his thoughts.

'Toothbrush, clean underwear, ten different outfits, sports gear . . .' Ludo ticked them off. 'Believe me, I have it all. Right down to your favourite perfume. Jo Malone, right? Pear and Freesia.'

Dina actually laughed. 'Wow! Very good. I'll just grab my coat, then.'

'Me too; I'm ready.' He stood up and walked to the door.

It was a crisp spring night, still cool. Summer would be here soon, and it was an excellent time for a drive.

Edward Johnson was enjoying himself behind the wheel.

Things were rolling his way. His mother, wracked with grief, had been packed off to a health farm in the Florida Keys, part of an exclusive resort, where she could have sun, water, a bunch of well-paid fakers to get her in touch with her spiritual self, and be guaranteed to meet absolutely nobody she knew.

It was a dry resort. Edward didn't want her diving back into the vodka bottle. After all, he loved her. He'd killed for her.

Once again, his mind drifted back to the delicious memories. The shrieking call at seven fifteen the next morning. His mother, hysterical. His careful call to the family doctor, to see 'if anything could be done'. The police interview; the way the detectives trampled through the house, his mother sobbing, Edward frantically trying to comfort her.

But it was all good. The prints on the pill bottle were perfect.

The alcohol and clonazepam in Philippe's blood had induced a coma, sleep apnoea; he'd just gone under, stopped breathing.

'It's such a goddamned tragedy. I had no idea he would mix them up. He was drunk . . . I didn't think he was that drunk,' Edward said, shaking his head. 'I blame myself.'

The detectives wanted to blame him, too, but he came up clean. All that wedding planning, the first-class tickets on his credit card. The staff, his mother's friends . . . so many witnesses to the bonhomie, to the habit of knocking back aspirin after a night on the sauce.

It was death by misadventure. Edward loved that. He read the coroner's report again and again. As he organised the simple and elegant funeral – Philippe, as a successful gigolo and con man, had no family and no real friends – Edward felt the most incredible surge of power. He hadn't fucked this up. The threat to his money, his dignity, was dead. Edward had killed him, and he'd got away with it, scot-free. The whole episode was gloriously pleasurable and, for a while, he went back to banging whores, not hitting them. It was like the monkey had been lifted off his back, and he was whole again.

'I'm finished,' Penelope sobbed at the crematorium. She buried her head into Edward's shoulder. 'Oh God! I can't bear it. All those women coming around. I can't take it; I don't want to see them.' She shuddered and started to hyperventilate. 'I'm panicking, Edward; I'm going to have a panic attack.'

'Here.' He pressed her hand and gave her a clonazepam. It was thrilling to medicate his mother with the same pills he'd used to kill her lover. 'Take this, quickly. Now breathe deep. It'll work soon – you know it will. Fill your lungs; hold your breath. Great, Mom. Exhale . . . Exhale . . .'

Her panics had returned. She was a mess; wholly dependent. It was a week's work to persuade her to give him full power of attorney. Edward drew up papers, lots of them. There were the ones giving him controlling shares in the family trust. The change of her will, to name him as the sole beneficiary. The irrevocable trust set up to place half her wealth in Edward's hands. His name was added to the deed on the family house. Penelope was in no condition to fight. She was desperately, pathetically grateful that Edward would take care of 'business things', as she put it. And he doled out what she needed: drugs and a flight out to someplace warm, where her days would be regimented and she wouldn't have to think.

Edward was happy to spend big money on it. He wanted Penelope out of his hair, and wanted to be able to show any court that he had done the best by his mother, in case they challenged things down the line.

Once her plane departed, he got to work. He let go of all the domestic staff, one by one. They had all seen too much, and he was the master of the house now. Some of them cried and wept, but Edward was implacable; there was severance, a handshake and he was done.

'I'm not my father, Ronald. I don't need a valet.'

'Mrs Johnson will be living very simply when she returns, Lia. She prefers to be alone.'

'We will be using a cleaning service.'

'But, Mr Edward, I keep house for you twenty years,' Consuela sobbed. 'Is all I know. My family . . .'

'I will give you an excellent reference.' Edward patted her hands. 'And four months' pay. We all have to move on. You can find another household; I'm sure of it.'

'But not like this. Oh, *por favor*, did you speak to Mrs Johnson, Mr Edward . . . ?'

'No, I didn't, and nor will you. We never did get your immigration status sorted, did we?' he asked, silkily. 'Four months is generous; you have plenty of time to find good employment elsewhere. And you will need my word for that.'

She got the message. 'Yes, sir. Thank you; *gracias* for the four months.'

'It's nothing,' Edward said, nobly, and of course it really wasn't.

Once they were gone, he hired the decorators. Every old piece of art was catalogued and sold. His parents' fussy French style was gutted from the house; simple, modern masculinity went in. There was to be nothing that reminded him of either one of them. The father who had destroyed them; the mother who had betrayed him: he didn't know whom he despised more. When Penelope returned, she would be living elsewhere, in a small, chic apartment more suitable for an older woman.

Like the one he had left.

Edward cleared house. The money from the art more than paid for the redecoration, and left two million dollars in the trust account. He put seven hundred grand aside for his mother's modest retirement, and kept the rest for himself. All of a sudden, his little office in midtown hummed with real activity. Now Edward was managing his own money, he suddenly cared – cared hugely.

The brokers were summoned. This time, they all came to him. Edward was treated to slides and presentations and talks on wealth management over coffee at the Four Seasons.

'I want the highest income,' he told them. 'Screw growth. This is my time to have fun.'

'Very good. Yes, sir.'

He started to dress well, to drink less. He made a few calls to those old school friends he hated so much, the ones that walked away after Dina Kane's stunt, and invited them round for dinner.

It was his house now. They came; money talks.

Edward circulated, careful of his image. No violence, no drugs, no loose women. He wanted to take a leaf from the book of poor, dead Philippe. Taking his mother's money was a piece of cake. Next, he wanted a wife that could cement things: an heiress with a fortune of her own.

Why work? That was for suckers.

A girl who was loaded would reset his personal clock. Once he had her married and pregnant, and tied up with an unbreakable prenup, it would be time to step back into the life he should always have led. The life he was leading before that bitch, Dina Kane, ruined everything.

You could blame *her* for Philippe; she split the family.

Blame her for beating those sluts; she drove him to it.

Blame her for his stupid, broken mother, and her stupid betrayal; Dina had put a wedge between them all.

Blame her for his father's pathetic attempt to grasp back his youth, to run from his past.

Edward was doing just fine. But he did not forgive, and he did not forget.

Philippe Leclerc found that out the hard way. Dina Kane was about to do so, as well. An eye for an eye, sugar.

Edward smiled, and put his foot on the gas.

Chapter Thirteen

'How do I look?' Susan asked.

She spun before him, and the hem of her dress flared out. It was a stately sheath in azure velvet, strapless, that flattered her ample bosom, lifted and firmed after breast-feeding the boys. Around her neck she wore a filigree necklace of white diamonds and platinum, shaped like a leaf, and he could see some sort of jewelled slippers peeking out from under her hem.

'You look great,' Gaines answered. It was certainly dramatic. He supposed, if she was going strong on the make-up, this was the way to complement it.

'Thank you, darling.' She came over, swishing as she walked, and kissed the air at the side of his cheek, so as not to disrupt her make-up.

'Let's go,' Gaines said. He didn't know if he was dreading this, or longing for it. Only that it had to be done.

Ludo held his hand out mutely, the wind from the chopper blades whipping round his coat and jacket. It was no use talking; the roar of the helicopter was too loud. Dina stepped out carefully, one hand on her head, steadying that up-do against the torrent of air; her coat lifted behind her like a cloak and her skirt moved deliciously up those legs. *Goddamn!* Those calves in old-fashioned silk stockings . . . the ladder to paradise, to those firm, milky thighs above them. He got a stir just looking at them.

He tugged her along, off the helipad and down the steps to where their chauffeur was waiting, hired for the night. It didn't pay to keep one in the Hamptons, but maybe in the future, once his shares in Torch were worth more, maybe double, he could upgrade the house . . . A bigger place, a proper estate, with a servant's quarters and a cook/driver to live in, year round. Everything on tap.

For now, though, he kept a Mercedes at the cottage, and this guy was from a decent service. He touched his cap and held open the door for them. As it shut behind him, he saw Dina fixing her hair, smoothing herself down; she was so pretty, so simple. He gave her a quick kiss on the cheek, and she squeezed his hand.

'You know the address.'

'Yes, sir,' the driver said. The limousine purred off into the darkness, the low lights of the Hamptons houses all around them, so different from Manhattan's endless neon towers. He was really looking forward to this.

'Who's going to be there . . . ? I mean, that we know?'

Ludo smiled. 'Not my parents. They went back to LA. I know a few people from the tennis club. There's Paul Turman and his wife, Mindy, and Luke Herlihy with Sophia, and I think my friend Emmett Lewis is coming along. Oh, and Joel and Susan Gaines; you've met Joel, haven't you? So that's at least one person you know yourself. Roxana Felix is a friend of my father's. As is her rock-star husband.' He looked over at her. 'What's wrong? You've gone all tense.'

Dina was sitting bolt upright, rigid, staring straight ahead. Underneath her perfect, light make-up, she had paled.

'Nothing,' she said. 'Nothing wrong.'

'What? You've fallen out with Gaines? Or you just feel overwhelmed? Come on, baby, you can eat all these people for breakfast back at the office. I know you can handle a social setting. They're our neighbours. And, besides, Joel Gaines is big business, major league. Much bigger even than my father. He could buy and sell us all a hundred times over.'

'I . . . I know that. It just might be a little awkward.'

'I can't afford for you to fall out with someone so powerful. His wife is a main mover in everything social round here. So be nice, OK?'

Dina swallowed hard. 'Fine. OK. I expect it'll be a big party.'

'It will, but I want to get us introduced. Anyway, didn't he call my dad about you? That's why you got hired.'

'Yes, I . . . he did. It was before we fell out.'

'Over what? He was making eyes at you or something?'

She blushed deeply. 'No! Of course not. I was just angry that he made so much money on Meadow – my cream. I only got half a million for it, you know. He . . . he ripped me off.'

That wasn't true, wasn't anything like true. But what could she say? She was so embarrassed at his casual joke. Making eyes . . . She had made them at Joel, and he'd told her to go jump in a lake. And now she had to see him again, here, tonight, with his wife.

Dina tried to collect herself. Come on, she would have to face him some time. Why not now? And see the woman he belonged to. And always would. She felt a moment of real thankfulness for Ludo, felt her ambivalence vanish; he was here beside her, her partner, boyfriend, whatever; she was with a man of her own, so she wouldn't look like some desperate bunny-boiling freak. Gratefully, she reached out and squeezed his arm. He wasn't muscular like Joel, but he was hers, he was there.

Perhaps she wanted too much, and this was real love. That sick, squirmy, sexual feeling she got with Joel couldn't be love; that was obsession . . . imagination. They hadn't ever even made love. Most couples weren't crazy about each other, right? They were fond of each other. Friends . . .

'Well, that's all forgotten now. Right? Promise me you'll be nice.' Joel squeezed her hand. 'This is a special night for me. I don't want anything to ruin it.'

'I'll be nice,' Dina managed. 'He probably won't even remember me.'

The mansion was incredible. Flaming torches were stacked across the wide sweep of the drive; lit candles, sunk into the lawn; the soaring modern architecture of the grand, thirty-million-dollar beach house was breathtaking. Dina clutched Ludo's arm as they fell in line with younger girls wearing Gucci, Prada, Prabal Gurung – all haute couture – and older women in St. John and fussy clouds of silk and taffeta.

The jewels all around her flashed and sparkled like strings of fairy lights. Dina had never seen such a concentration of wealth and power. Even as they waited to go in, party staff wearing chic light-green dresses or tailored suits hovered around them with flutes of vintage champagne, pink and white, and trays of hors d'oeuvres that looked meltingly delicious: tiny chunks of real honeycomb pierced with white Cheshire cheese, little paper flutes of home-made French fries, tiny quiches, little pear tartlets, caviar and chopped egg on whole-wheat blinis, and everything clever in between.

'Dina! This is Malcolm Bruce, the director . . .'

'Oh. Hi. I loved *Marianne* . . .'

'And you know Solomon Perry, the banker? And his wife, Sarah.'

'Hi.'

'And here's Jake Carter, the best tort litigator on the East Coast . . .'

One after another, Ludo hit her with them: actresses, models, hedge-fund guys, a defence contractor, an award-winning architect. These were the rich people and, she realised as she looked at the women, those pretty enough to hang out with them: the plus ones. You were either a wife with a string of pearls the size of gulls' eggs and a smug look of adoration for your husband, or a jittery model type, nervous and hoping to get lucky.

At least it kept her busy. Dina was shaking hands and smiling, and coming up with quick one-liners, fast enough to make her head spin. But that was good – she could see Ludo glowing – it was as if she were back on opening day at Torch, with all the beauty bloggers and the new customers pushing and shoving and trying to buy every product she could put out there.

And the girls, those eager girls who all looked at her, with Ludo on her arm, so enviously – it made her want to laugh – but they actually did a double take, and wanted to speak to her.

'Wait – Dina *Kane*?'

'You started Meadow cream, right?'

'You brought in the Dr Lowe stuff to Torch. I kill for that cleanser! It's the only place you can get it outside of London! Wow! I love you.'

'Don't actually kill for a cleanser,' Dina joked. 'But thank you.'

The redhead was beanpole tall and lean, with that clear Irish skin, a dusting of freckles, and Dina could see that she was flawless.

'In my line of work, it's the most vital thing there *is*,' the girl gushed. 'They make you up, like, *every* day. And it all has to come off. I can't *afford* a zit. You have the best stuff that works. Oh my God. Dina Kane.'

'I know, right?' asked a brunette, sidling up to her. 'I'm Erin Lanster. They made me up at Torch and, like, my boyfriend *proposed* that night at dinner.'

'I really don't think one thing happened because of the other, but I'm so glad you liked it . . .'

'Who did your make-up tonight?' asked a blonde. 'Can I get her number?'

'Uh, that was me.'

'Oh my God! Like, wow.'

Ludo laughed, delighted. He'd been in the middle of a crowd of girls like this, but never had their attention been focused on anything else. A crew of pretty chicks paying homage to his woman; he felt more secure than ever in his choice.

'Excuse us, ladies; I have to take Dina to meet our hostess.'

He extricated her and steered her into the centre of the vast room, with a huge fire blazing in a two-sided chimney. There was the sight of the sea, lit up from the enormous open windows, just in front of the stretch of private beach.

'Roxana? I'm Ludo Morgan.'

He introduced himself to a tall, stunning older woman with long, dark hair, wearing a gorgeous tailored evening pantsuit in silk, and teetering heels. Chandelier earrings hung from her lobes, and she looked as wild as a gypsy.

'Hey; good to see you. You've bought the cottage down the road?'

To her it was a cottage – he swallowed his annoyance.

'In Sagaponack. Yes.'

'Well, we look forward to having you around. You should say hi to my husband; he's upstairs playing guitar, I think. Lots of boys.' She laughed. 'Never stopped being a rock star, in his heart. And who's your girlfriend?'

'This is Dina Kane. She works for me at Torch, in the beauty department.'

'Hi,' Dina said, nervously. Roxana Felix was a legend – one of the great supermodels of the nineties. And she still looked incredible.

'I heard you're doing great things over there, Dina.'

'Thank you, ma'am.'

'Ma'am is my mother. Did you make yourself up tonight?'

Roxana was leaning closer, and Dina suddenly, desperately, wanted her to approve. She was a hell of an expert.

'Yes, I did. Do you like it?'

'I do. You have real talent. I've started to use Meadow, by the way.'

Dina flushed. 'How did you know that was me?'

'Oh, my friend told me. He was actually just talking about you. Let's see if I can find him.' She turned around. 'Susan! Joel! Come here.'

Dina gripped on to Ludo. She breathed hard; she felt dizzy.

'Come on, baby,' he whispered.

Desperately, she grabbed a flute of champagne from a passing waiter and tipped it back, downing half of it in a couple of seconds; the icy cold alcohol hit her tongue, bubbling and soothing, promising her a little courage by the time it had soaked into her bloodstream.

She looked good; she knew it. That was important to her. She had a man. She had a job, a career. Success. Time to hold her head up. Dina forced herself to calm her ragged breathing. *Do you want him to see?*

'Dina, Ludo, this is Susan Gaines.'

'Oh! Hiiii!' A tall, older, groomed blonde with talon-like nails painted scarlet and an artfully made-up face smiled at her from a pillar of blue velvet. Dina tried to take her in. She was beautiful, in a way, but plucked and painted to within an inch of her life; diamonds glittered around her throat like stars, and there was a massive ring on her left hand, the size of a marble. Her ears were studded with long, dangling columns – more diamonds – and there was a huge pearl and conch brooch at her ample bosom. Blonde, big-breasted, she said *rich* in every possible way. *Wife. Queen.* Dina felt ill; she swallowed a little more champagne.

'Hi to you. What a pleasure!' Ludo said. 'We've heard so much about you. Looking forward to getting to know you guys better. Dina owes your husband a favour, don't you, honey?'

'Oh, yes. Mr Gaines has been very good to me,' Dina said, weakly.

'Mr Gaines! Come on, you call him Joel, don't you? If you don't, you're going to start,' said Susan. 'Joel! Sugar! It's that couple I was talking to you about. We were discussing you guys *just* this afternoon,' she said, as Joel walked towards them, and Dina could not take her eyes off him.

Her heart thudded against her ribcage; she was dizzy. *Hold on. Keep it together*.

She couldn't let him see. He would laugh, thinking she still wasn't over him. Dina forced a bright smile on to her face with the utmost effort, and threaded her arm through Ludo's, bringing him closer to her.

'Hi,' Gaines said, offering his hand to Ludo.

'Good to meet you, sir,' Ludo said. There was something like awe in his voice, and Dina blushed to hear it. Gaines was the kind of man other men feared and envied, and it turned her on to see them scurry and scuttle about him. To have Ludo do it was an exquisite humiliation. 'My father knows you well, I believe.'

'For a long time.'

'And you sent us Dina. She's quite the worker.' Ludo smiled proudly. 'I should thank you for that, and a lot more, because I got a beautiful girlfriend out of the deal.'

Joel Gaines turned his dark eyes to Dina Kane, looking down at her; she couldn't read their expression. Nor could she move her gaze from his. She was utterly mesmerised. She felt her lack of jewels, of haute couture, of evening make-up. Simple had seemed chic; now she felt like some kind of shepherdess who had wandered into Versailles. Outclassed and out of place.

'Isn't it hard dating somebody that works for you? Office romances are notorious,' Susan Gaines said, conspiratorially. 'All the other girls will complain about how you got the job, Dina – and they'll be after your man. Although I'm sure you quite hold your own!'

'Oh, no. Dina's a great worker. She's really helped in my turnaround of the store,' Ludo said.

Dina wasn't listening. She was looking at Gaines, lost in his eyes like her body was crying out to him. Dimly, she became aware that Ludo was looking at her, and forced herself to break the spell, look at the floor.

'Yes, that's right,' she said, automatically.

'It's interesting that you put it like that, though,' Gaines said, lightly. 'I thought it was Dina, not you, who had turned the store around. I'm sure you wouldn't want to take credit for the way she blitzed your beauty department.'

It was a shock. She hadn't been expecting that, not any of it. Gaines was defending her; he was taking Ludo on. And he knew – he knew about her work. Not a word from him, not an email all these many months, but he still knew all about it, and this was firm praise.

'She submitted plans, sure. I ran with them. And I have been revamping all our other departments.' Ludo didn't bridle, he couldn't afford to, but he was furious. What did Gaines mean by it, at a social gathering? And was this his life, to have his woman upstage him in front of bankers, investors? His anger hardened – at Joel, even at Dina. This charade would be finished by the end of the night, he vowed it. The ring came with a price. 'Isn't that right, Dina?'

She was put on the spot.

'Is it, indeed?' asked Gaines, as if idly curious.

'I . . . Yes.' She could not fight with Ludo, not right now. She was with him, here, as his girlfriend. That meant loyalty, or go home. 'Many of the suggestions came from Ludo, and he's the one working the rest of the store . . .'

'And I'm in charge of social media, development and purchasing,' Ludo said, curtly. 'I run our press campaigns. Perhaps you saw me in *Vogue*?'

'I did! I did!' Susan squealed. 'I swear, that's what I was show-ing Joel, like, just today! It was amazing! You looked fantastic. You've done wonders; your father must be proud as hell, young man. And you, Dina, you have a *great* boss. I think Ludo's going out of his way to talk up her contribution, am I right, Dina? After all, there are a lot of staff who make up that beauty department. I've been there. The make-up artists are to die for. And the girls at the counter are all experts—'

'Yes, and Dina hand-picked them,' Joel said. 'But never mind; I hope the rest of your rebranding goes as well as the beauty department, Ludo. We shouldn't be all business tonight.'

'Hey, thanks,' Ludo said. 'In fact, I was hoping your wife might give me some tips for the summer, now I'm moving in.' He turned to Susan. 'Good restaurants, reliable pool cleaners, that kind of stuff. And perhaps we could all have dinner?'

Dear God, no. Dina groaned.

'Oh, yes! That would be perfect. We'd love to. And we'll get a few friends round to meet you.'

Ludo smiled, that was what he was hoping for.

Susan turned to Dina. 'Sweetie, can I steal him for a second? We have lots to discuss. Joel will look after you.'

Without waiting for an answer, she grabbed a willing Ludo by the elbow and led him over to one of Roxana Felix's cavernous leather couches.

Dina breathed in, a shuddering breath of excitement and fear. She clutched the stem of her champagne flute like it was a lifejacket.

'Oh, yes,' said Joel, softly. 'I'd love to look after you.'

She bridled. 'After you last saw me? You basically told me to drop dead. You implied I had a crush on you.'

'And you didn't?'

The casual, teasing power of his voice . . . She couldn't help it, her body responded immediately, her nipples tautening, her belly warming with blood.

'Don't talk to me that way. I'm with Ludo.'

'So I see.'

'And you're with Susan. Nice dress. Nice jewels.'

He lifted an eyebrow. 'You sound bitter.'

'I guess I just don't understand what you have in common, Joel. And I'm not bitter; I'm angry.' It was tumbling out of her now, and she couldn't stop it, didn't want to. 'You shouted at me; you dropped me. But you wanted me just as much. Perhaps I shouldn't have asked you to meet me, but we both know how you looked at me, Joel Gaines. It's goddamn *cruel* of you to lay it all on me.'

He stared down at her, and his eyes softened.

'Maybe so.'

Her heart leaped. 'So you did want me? You admit it?'

'I wouldn't put it in the past tense.' He glanced over at the couch, where his wife was holding court, and Ludo, like a little puppy, was sitting next to her, making notes in his phone. 'Let's step outside, into the garden. He'll find you. You can say you went for some air.'

Meekly, she followed him, her blood singing, the desire and excitement crackling across her skin like electricity. She had the feeling of being right on the edge with him, of saying things that could never be unsaid. But she didn't want to unsay them. She wanted to speak the truth, let it all out, tell him, plainly, how she felt, and then let the cards fall where they would. It would be a relief, a massive relief, not to have to pretend.

He took her outside, away from the spotlights, across a lawn with a few people on it, and into a garden with hedges; through the darkness, she could see roses and English topiary, lit with candles.

'Stop here.' She did, stumbling after him, her heels sinking into the grass. He stood close to her, really close, his huge, tall, strong body looming over her, in her space, and the eroticism hung about him so hard she could hardly breathe.

'There's something I have to do,' Gaines said, and he drew her in close, his arm around her waist, pulling her tight, and kissed her, full, deep. His strong arms folded around her, his tongue in her mouth, and she was wet, hot and open, moaning with a desire that he swallowed, his lips strong on hers, firm, exploring her, feeling her need, and the warmth of her body stretched all across him.

And then, finally, he let her go.

Dina wiped her hand across her mouth, panting.

'I had to taste you,' he said. 'I've been thinking about it, dreaming about it since we met. You have no idea how hard I've fought to get you out of my system. I wanted to be so foul to you, you'd never speak to me again.'

She sobbed. 'And it worked.'

'No. I couldn't stop thinking about you. I was obsessed. I couldn't even tell my shrink.' He chuckled, without mirth. 'And I haven't even slept with you.'

'Nor will you,' she said, wiping away tears. 'I won't be your piece on the side. Ludo is good to me.'

'You don't love him.'

'And you don't love your wife.'

He sighed. 'I deserved that. I guess I love her enough not to divorce her, after all these years, and two kids together.'

Dina froze; she couldn't disagree with the words, but the pain in her heart was acute, so strong she could hardly breathe.

'Then please do not torture me,' she said. 'Let me make a life.'

'I want to be in touch. I want to be your friend. We don't have to see each other, just talk on the telephone.'

'That's fine.' She wiped her eyes, trying to repair her face. They would have to go back inside. 'Ignoring you didn't work.'

'I get that. Same here. You know I want you; I want to make love to you. I want to turn you inside out. I think about it all the time. I hate to see you with Ludo Morgan.'

'He's a good man,' Dina said, flatly. 'What the hell difference does it make? It would be the same with anyone else.'

'You might be in love with somebody else.'

She shook her head. 'I'm in love with you, Joel. It's stupid and hopeless, but there it is. I know it now. I knew it when you kissed me. So I may as well date a friend. There's nothing better out there for me.'

'Oh, God,' he said. He crouched down, squatting, and put his hands over his head. 'Oh, God. This feels so wrong. I can't; I wish I could. My God. I just want to have you. Only that's not it. I want to talk to you the next day. And every day.'

'You can call me,' she said. 'It's probably unhealthy, but I don't care. If talking is all I can have, I'll take it.'

He stood. 'We must go back. You know, Ludo Morgan is ripping you off. Perhaps you've been too busy to see it.'

'He's backed me.'

'Backed you by signing his own name to every press release. Backed you by ripping off your ideas as his own. He does the interviews; he's the brand. Susan was crass, but that's how people will see you – as a better paid version of a make-up girl.'

Dina slowly turned the idea over in her mind. 'I really don't think—'

'Yes, you do. You just didn't want to admit it to yourself.'

'He gave me a pay rise, a company car. A budget—'

'That's cents on the dollar, baby. You're making the stock of his company soar. Come on, Dina. Don't let this guy screw you. At least not like that.'

'He's not that way. He really loves me, wants me to succeed.'

'So ask him to make you a partner. You deserve it; the company was treading water. You've opened up everything. You should have stock.'

She walked with him, back to the house, back to her life.

'And, Dina, you can do whatever you want, of course you can, but I think you're wrong. Don't make any big decisions while you're on the rebound. You . . . you can find the right man.'

'You really have no say in that, do you, Joel?'

He bowed his head, and they walked back into the house together. She left his side as fast as she could, and went to look for Ludo; he was still sitting there, like a puppy looking up at its mistress.

'Hey, Susan. So sweet of you to take Ludo under your wing! But he's really got to come back to me now, or I'm going on strike.' She flashed a bright smile at the older woman.

'Sure! I hope Joel took care of you.'

'He was the perfect host,' Dina said, lightly. 'Sweet of you both.'

'I'd better get back to him myself. But we're looking forward to seeing you both soon!'

Susan stood up; Ludo did the same and they exchanged air-kisses. Then she smiled benignly at Dina and wandered off into the crowd, looking for Joel. Dina pictured it: the clutching at his arm, the laughing, the rich patroness regaling him with stories of how she'd helped the eager young man. She wasn't looking forward to the rest of the party, not one little bit; socialising was too much.

'Hey! How was it?' Ludo was peppy, full of excitement. 'Please tell me you made friends? Susan was so great. They want to have a dinner party for us next month—'

'Oh, let's not go so fast. You've hardly settled into the house—'

'No time to waste. He can really help me, you know. Joel Gaines is an *incredible* person to know. I'm excited, Dina. Did you get on with him?' His eyes were wide and hopeful.

'I got on fine with him,' she said, dying a little inside.

'That's perfect! We'll be such a hit here. I can't wait. Come on outside, would you?'

She baulked. 'Not the garden – I really don't want to go out there . . .'

'No, Dina – the beach. The ocean. It's romantic, see?'

He gestured out front to the door, and the spotlights on the shore. 'I would really like you to come, OK?'

Dina nodded. 'OK. Sure.' She could hardly turn him down.

'And then maybe . . . maybe we could go home – to the cottage? I'm feeling a bit overwhelmed by all this.'

'Oh no, sweetheart. You're doing great. Believe me, you'll want to come back in after this.'

He held out his hand, and Dina took it. It was clammy with sweat. She followed him out of the packed crowd of beautiful people in their jewels and silks and bespoke suits, grateful at least to be outside, away from everyone, away from Susan Gaines – away from Joel Gaines.

'Come here, where we can see the sea.'

She dutifully followed. She was barely paying attention. Her mind was back in the garden, in Gaines' arms, in the insistent mastery of his kiss.

'Stop – that's enough.'

Dina jerked herself away from her thoughts and looked around. They were just at the edge of the light, and in front of them was the dark, quiet sand of the beach, with the immensity of the ocean crashing on the shore. It was lovely, and soothing, and she wished to God she were almost anywhere else.

'I have something to say.'

She looked at him. She could still hardly pay attention to him. Whatever it was, it could wait.

'Dina, we've been going out for a while now, and each month I feel I'm getting closer to you. You're so beautiful, and stylish, and stunning, and you make me feel great about myself. You're funny and you work so hard. *Too* hard. I'd like your work to be different, to be us, and our family.'

'Our family?' Dina repeated, blankly.

'Yes. The one we can start, any moment now. Once we get married.'

She gasped. For once, Ludo Morgan had taken her completely by surprise.

'You can't believe it, can you? But it's true. Dina, fairy tales do happen. We met by chance, and now, this.' He reached into his pocket and drew out the small Tiffany box; as she looked, transfixed with fear, Ludo flicked it open.

Proud. Smug. Looking up at her for acceptance.

'My God,' Dina whispered. The diamond was huge, the sapphires exquisite.

'Yes. It's true. I want to marry you,' Ludo said. 'What do you say, Dina Kane?'

She didn't hesitate.

'No.'

Chapter Fourteen

'You have a visitor, Mr Kane.'

The therapist put her head round Johnny's door. She wore those green slacks they all wore, with different T-shirts to make them look a little less medical. He hated how she never knocked; you lost your dignity fast in here.

But then he'd lost his dignity a long while ago, somewhere in all the pills and the bottles. Same as he'd lost Brad.

'Show her in.'

There was Dina – and he loved Dina – but Johnny Kane almost hated her, too. So she was spending all her money on him, and for what? To save his body, so he could go back to his shitty life? Without Brad? What the hell was the point?

He was better – maybe. He was bored and depressed, and the anxiety crept all over him, every day, like ants. No college – he was long since a dropout – no job prospects. Of course, Dina would find him something to do, or keep him, but he didn't want to hang round his little sister for the rest of his life, like a bad smell.

Maybe she was a half-sister. Jeez, they were so different, he wondered if his mother had been fucking around long before it became obvious. He was the product of the construction worker with the bottle of booze in his pants pocket, and Dina was the secret daughter of some high-powered mafia boss. Johnny smiled – that would totally fit.

'It's not your sister,' the therapist said. 'It's a man called Johnson. Edward Johnson. Do you want to see him?'

Johnny considered. He didn't know any Edward Johnsons, but he was bored out of his skull and there was nothing to drink or smoke up here.

'Sure,' he said.

The door opened wider and a handsome blond man, around Johnny's own age, thin and well dressed, stood there. He was gorgeous. Man, Johnny hadn't seen any hot guys for a lifetime.

'Come on in,' he said.

'How are you doing?' said the young man. 'I'm a friend of Brad's. I thought maybe you'd like to get out of here.'

Johnny Kane beamed with pleasure.

'Of Brad's?'

'Hey, don't get too excited. He left for Europe with his new boyfriend. But he did want to check up on you. He asked me if I would come see you when you got better, take you home and give you a little fun. He said you've been real short on fun, and you've got your life in front of you.'

'Why would he do that? If he left for Europe?'

The blond shrugged. 'He didn't want to see you himself, said it would be too emotional for both of you. But he did want to look out for you. Brad left a place you could stay in the city, and a list of a few guys to hang out with. At least till you get back on your feet.'

Johnny chewed his lip.

'If he did that for me, he must have feelings . . .'

'Johnny, please. He's rented a furnished place for you for two months – so you can find something. Thought maybe you'd want to organise your own life. It's paid for, but then it runs out. Up to you if you want to live with your sister instead . . .'

'I want Brad's phone number.'

'No can do. He made me promise not to. I think he's serious about this new guy – a Brit. They went to Paris together for a while and they're getting married in London.'

Johnny sank back against the pillows on his bed, despondent. 'Then what do I care?'

'There are other fish in the sea.'

'Like you?' he asked, idly. The boy was so smoothly good-looking; maybe he could be distracted from his broken heart.

'I'm straight.'

'Of course you are.' Johnny sighed deeply. 'And I bet you didn't even have the courtesy to bring me some cigarettes.'

'How wrong you are,' Edward said. He reached inside his jacket and drew out a pack of smokes, then fished into his pants for a lighter; it was solid gold, and monogrammed *EJ*.

Johnny stared. He licked his lips.

'A little smoke's hardly going to kill you. Face it: you aren't drinking anymore. Anyway, since you don't want to come out, I'll leave you here to wait for your sister. Doing well, isn't she? So busy these days . . .'

'Dina always does well.' Johnny stared at the cigarettes. 'You know, there's no smoking in here.'

'I know. They were for the car ride; kind of a celebration. If you checked yourself out . . .'

'Checked myself out?'

'It's not prison.'

'Doesn't Dina have to sign off on it?'

'Dude, I don't know. Is your sister your jailer? Maybe she had you committed? Because then I can't help you.'

He got up and put the cigarettes down on the table. 'Good to see you're in good health. Keep them, but you need to find your own matches.'

Johnny looked round at the little room that had been his oppressive prison for almost a year now, in between hospital visits and bouts in the little cell nobody talked about – the padded one where they sent you to kick.

'Screw it,' he said. 'I've really had enough. I'll come with you.'

*   *   *

Ludo shuddered with fury. He was having trouble believing it.

'No,' she said, just like that.

After that, she tried something softer: not ready, liked him as a partner, wasn't in love with him yet, not sure if it could be anything more. She even tried the line about friends. And then the one about colleagues.

'I'm so sorry. You know, maybe it's for the best, Ludo. I was getting kind of uncomfortable working for you and—'

'No, you weren't. You never had a problem.'

'I just – I liked dating.'

'Liked my money, our restaurants, is what you mean, isn't it?' he said, though he knew how dumb that was. She was turning down millions. 'I hired you; I backed you; I *made* you. I brought you here and you humiliate me like this?'

'Nobody knows. Nobody's out here but us.'

Thank God he hadn't told Susan. 'You'll regret this, Dina. You led me on.'

'Ludo, please. You don't want to marry somebody you don't love . . .'

'How do you know I don't love you? I had a *life* planned for us. You were going to make the best wedding, decorate our beach house. We'd have children. You were going to be the star at home, just like tonight, Dina.' He waved at the beach house, Roxana's glittering party. 'Why the hell not? Are you seeing somebody else?'

'I'm not seeing anybody.'

'Fucking somebody else, then?'

She looked at him, mute in the face of his anger.

'Ludo, I need more credit for my work. You shouldn't have told Susan Gaines that you revamped the store. It's mine. You really need to stop doing press like it's all yours.'

He pressed his fingers to his temples. The girl was insane, clinically insane. She was walking out on a vast fortune – and now arguing with him over her shitty six-figure job?

'Is that what this is about? Your job?'

'It matters to me.'

'You're nuts. I don't believe this. Jesus Christ!' He looked around, snapped the velvet ring box shut and shoved it back in his pocket. 'I think maybe you should just go home.'

'I don't know where the cottage is.'

Ludo stood up. 'I meant go to your home. I'm not interested in being around you.'

Dina almost laughed. 'Ludo, Manhattan is hours away. You brought me here; you have my stuff at your place. You will take me there for the night and you will take me back to Manhattan in the morning.'

'Or what?' he snarled.

'Or I go right back in there and I will make the most horrible scene. And the first person I talk to will be Roxana Felix when I ask her for a spare bedroom and if I can borrow pyjamas.'

He swallowed, hard. It was bitter. Back home, the house-keeper would be waiting with champagne. He had to call her, tell her to get the fuck out and put Dina's stuff in the smallest guest room.

'Fine,' he said. 'And tomorrow the chauffeur will drive you and your case all the way home. And you can start looking for another job. You're fired.'

Dina laughed. 'I will sue you.'

'You don't have the money and you don't have a case. Look at your contract: under a year, still. I can terminate you without cause at any time and pay you two months' salary. And, since you signed off all the documents listing my contribution to Torch, if you start claiming credit, the company will sue you.'

Dina blinked. 'Ludo – you can't do that.'

'I can. I will. It's done. Go wait at the front of the house while I call the driver.'

*　*　*

When she woke up in the morning, Dina Kane felt like she'd got drunk and had the world's worst hangover.

Her head was thumping. Her body ached from poor, stressed-out sleep. For a few moments, she was so groggy she didn't realise where she was.

Then the sound of the sea came faintly in at her window, the small single bed looking out over farmland to the water, and she remembered it all.

She pushed back the covers and sat up in bed. Surely Ludo wouldn't be this much of an asshole. He wouldn't fire her, just because she turned him down – she was the key to everything at Torch. It was her job, her life, her everything . . .

Dina shrieked. Ludo Morgan was standing in the doorway of her room, staring down at her.

'Get dressed,' he said, contemptuously. 'You're leaving in thirty minutes. Or you can walk home.'

She didn't cry. She showered quickly, hating to be naked in a house with him. And then she pulled on clothes as fast as she could from the half-packed case Ludo had dumped in her bedroom: panties, jeans, last night's bra and a T-shirt; screw style, anything that could cover her. Frantically, she closed the suitcase and hauled it downstairs, her dress and shoes from last night shoved inside. Ludo had brought her a pair of flip-flops, for the beach; that was what she would travel home in.

'Enjoy it,' he said, coldly, as she lugged the heavy case across his flagstone path, laid out over a manicured lawn. 'It's the last limousine ride you'll be getting for a while.'

It was a long drive home. Dina sat and thought for most of it. Who could she call? Her mother? What a joke. She had no one.

Maybe a couple of the girls on the shop floor? But she didn't want to put them through it. Ludo was their boss, too; they would be risking their jobs by talking with Dina. She felt ill, frantic that she'd been this stupid. Of course, he was right, the little asshole; her contract had a year's grace period, and they could fire her whenever they liked.

Dina had to go quietly, or Ludo Morgan could make her name mud. She thought of Gaines, of his kiss, of his advice. He was right – goddamn him – he'd seen in a moment what she'd blocked out for months.

And she could call him, if he wasn't in bed sleeping with his wife.

In the end, there was only one person she could talk to: Johnny. The thought of hearing his voice made her happy, made the tears she'd been suppressing well up and drift down her cheek. Somebody was there who loved her, who would not sell her out. Who wouldn't fire her. And who, any minute now, she would get to see again. He was coming home.

Tears trickling down her face, Dina dialled the number.

'Hi. Can you put me through to Johnny Kane's room?'

'One moment please.' Pause. 'Oh, Mr Kane isn't with us anymore, I'm afraid.'

'What? That's impossible. This is his sister, Dina. He hasn't been taken back to hospital?'

'No, ma'am. Mr Kane checked out yesterday, with his friend.'

She dabbed at her face. 'His friend?'

'Said he was a friend of Brad's, or something.'

She relaxed. 'And Johnny was fine to leave?'

'He seemed OK, but you know it is up to the patient. We can't compel them to complete treatment.'

'I've been paying his bills. You can send me the final accounts.'

'Yes, ma'am.'

Dina dried her tears. If Brad had sent somebody for Johnny, that was wonderful news. She thought they were all over, all finished. Nothing could welcome her brother back to the world better than Brad taking him back.

* * *

269

Edward looked around the flat, very satisfied with it. It was scummy, cheap – Red Hook in Brooklyn – and right around drug dealer central. It had been rented in cash for him by Olivia Broadwell, his private investigator, using a fake ID; the owner never saw or met him. The furniture was revolting, but they had cleaned it up, tidied it with throws and pillows and put clean, cheap sheets on the bed. The fridge was stocked with food, and there was a rack of wine – screw-top; easy to open. He had cigarettes, lighters and ashtrays, and cold beers in the fridge, along with soft drinks. Nothing too pushy or obvious.

Most importantly, there were the 'friends' sitting around: male hookers – gay and gorgeous. They made Edward's stomach turn; he hated perversion – scorned everybody not like him. He despised Johnny, that weak, detestable fag with the bitch sister. But he loved what these boys were going to do for him. Olivia's hires; she'd bought them to order: twenty-one through twenty-six, blonds, brunettes, a couple with muscles, mostly smooth-featured pretty guys. There were five of them, all well-paid and known for being discreet.

And following orders.

The orders right now were to show Johnny a *great* time, to party with him and to pretend they were friends with this guy, Brad – just maybe knew him casually – but to talk more about the scene. They'd been instructed not to be found out. Sex – yes; clubs – yes. And as many drugs and as much alcohol as they could take.

Olivia supplied the bonuses: ecstasy, pure coke, high-level heroin – mostly unadulterated. It was on them what they did with it.

'Hey, here he is!' one of them said, as Olivia opened the door. She was unrecognisable, dressed as a graduate student, Iona college sweatshirt, beanie on her head, coloured contact lenses. 'Hey, Johnny! Welcome back. My name's Mark.'

'And I'm Joaquin.'

'David.'

'Justus. How you doing?'

'I'm Karl; I don't really know Brad that well, but what the hell? Welcome home, dude.'

Johnny waved hi, and his eyes lit up. People – *guys*. He looked around at the low-rent apartment like it was paradise.

'All yours for two months,' Edward said, breezily. 'Paid upfront. OK, so, my job's done. There's one more thing, though – can you come into the bedroom a second?'

Johnny followed him in there, while the hookers laughed and catcalled.

'Those boys are incorrigible. Well, look. It's not much, but Brad wanted you to have a fresh start, not be so dependent on Dina while you think about a job. And remember, the rent's taken care of.' He handed Johnny a white envelope, fat with bills. 'There's ten grand in there, plus another two grand in twenties. Please don't contact Brad, though.' He put on a fake air of concern. 'Are you sure you'll be OK with alcohol in the house? We figured, for your friends, not you. And, anyway, you can drink Diet Coke, or moderate it or whatever.'

The sound of beer cans cracking open and young male laughter came from the other room.

'Of course, you can also tell them to pour it away, but it might be a pretty short party. Up to you.'

Johnny's eyes looked hunted. He heard the sound of the booze pouring, the boys having fun. 'I . . . I guess. Like, maybe it'll be OK. If they drink it all.'

'Sweet. And now I've got to split.'

Johnny nodded. 'Hey, thanks, man. When do I see you again?'

'You don't. Brad's farewell gift, you know? Better make a clean break of it. Have fun! I think those guys like the look of you. *Sayonara.*'

And Edward left with a wave, closing the door behind him.

He walked down the stairs as fast as he could, scarf pulled up over his face, woollen hat low on his eyes. There was no doubt now. He was happy to bank on Johnny Kane's weakness.

Nature was tough, and she was going to take her course.

His limousine was heading back to the townhouse when Olivia called.

'You wanted to be kept updated on Dina Kane.'

She never indulged in pleasantries.

'Obviously. Go.'

'She's been fired. Last night. Word went out at Torch today.'

Edward sat up. 'You're kidding me?'

'Not at all. The rumour is that Ludo Morgan, her boss, dumped her. They were dating, remember?'

'Of course I fucking remember.' The only way to get to that bitch had seemed to be through her brother. Morgan was serious about the girl, Olivia had reported; and he was richer than Edward or his father had ever been.

That marriage would have taken her out of his grasp – at least, financially.

'Well, there was a party in the Hamptons. Some sort of scene. We heard from staff at the beach house that she was flung out and fired. Sources at Torch confirmed it this morning.'

'Any press release?'

'All the press has been in Ludo Morgan's name. She's just been fired. Their plan seems to be to replace her and move on.'

Edward thought of Johnny. Was he drinking, right now? Smoking something? How long would it take? And she was at home, crying and wailing, dumped and fired. He felt his cock hardening. Revenge at long last.

'Get something in the gossip columns. Dumped. Scene at fancy party. Trying to pass off Ludo's work as her own. Pattern with the Meadow cream invented by an old man. No respectable guy should date her.'

Olivia paused. 'Maybe I can do something on Ludo and the Hamptons, but the other stuff is boring, at least to the press.'

'Just do what I say,' Edward repeated. 'Use your connections.'

'Very well.'

She hung up.

Edward almost laughed. What a pain in the ass, setting all this shit up, but it was going to be so worth it. The perfect one-two punch. In a moment, in a day, Dina Kane was going to be finished.

'There's nothing you can do.' The lawyer, Marie Costas, was a no-nonsense older woman, and she gave it to Dina straight.

'That can't be true.'

'Get another job.' Costas sighed. 'Look, Miss Kane, I'd be happy to represent you, but I'd just be stealing your money. You have no case. A trial period is just that. For the first year, they get to fire you, no cause needed.'

'Sexual discrimination, though?'

'You signed the contract; you dated freely; this was an open relationship. In court, I can't prove you were compelled to do anything.'

'But they promoted me – gave me five pay rises, all in a few months.'

'Creative differences? Maybe you argued about how to present the beauty department, it doesn't matter. That clause means get out of jail free. I'm an employment lawyer and I have to give you the facts.'

Dina's fist curled around the receiver. 'I saved his store.'

'It doesn't matter. I'm sorry.'

She let out a long, whistling sigh. Johnny was nowhere to be found, Ludo wouldn't even return her calls, and human resources was sending her stuff back to her apartment in a box.

'I suppose I will have to find another job,' she said, slowly. 'Wow. It's going to be hard, starting from scratch.'

'Dina, there's more bad news.'

'What else could there be?' she asked, bitterly.

'Your next job. It can't be in beauty, or style. At least, not for two years.'

Dina actually laughed. 'What? What's that? Beauty is all I know.'

'Your contract included a noncompetition clause. You can't go to work for any other department store, or any existing store in the United States that works in a "competing field", which they define as retail, beauty or fashion.'

She felt a cold wave of fear wash over her. 'You have to be kidding me, Marie. How can I support myself?'

'There are other industries. Maybe you could be a fashion journalist?'

'I make a good six figures.' Dina paused. 'That's insane. Can we challenge that in court?'

'We could, sure. You could make a case, it is too onerous. But it will be a long fight, and Torch has deep pockets. You couldn't start work unless you got a judgement in your favour. Nobody could hire you.'

The pain and disappointment started to mix with fear. She glanced around her new apartment, wondering how long she'd be able to afford it.

'My best advice is that you go see your ex-boyfriend and ask him to let you out of the clause. The firm could release you.'

Ludo Morgan was enjoying the day.

Maybe he'd been lucky. Dina Kane would have been a big mistake.

She wasn't from his world. Couldn't handle it. And all that pushy aggression was getting old fast. He wasn't interested in working hard all day, then coming back to a rival at night.

Dina had a lot of enemies. Lots of rivals. As word leaked out, women had been congratulating him all morning.

'Thank you, Mr Morgan – she was so bossy.'

'Oh, well done, sir. She was always trying to change your orders.'

'She made us work nights. Thank you.'

'Not my place, but I really don't think she was your type,' said the large-breasted blonde girl from mascara, fluttering professionally impressive lashes at him. 'You know – *so* ambitious.'

'Why, thank you – Tara.' He looked at her name badge.

'I'm sure many of the girls thought she was *very* lucky, but she didn't act that way.'

He smiled. He would bang the girl, since she was practically begging for it, but that was about all.

No more employees. No shopgirls. He would head back to the Hamptons and let Susan Gaines fix him up with somebody's daughter.

The calls came in to the office, too: reporters, bloggers, other executives.

'Was it wise to dismiss Dina Kane? She was one of the prime movers on Torch's relaunch, wasn't she?'

'We have a great team, which I head. She was one part of it, but it's time to move on. The company has other plans.'

'Mr Morgan, thanks for taking my call, we just heard the news this morning . . .'

'What news is that?' Ludo asked.

'About Dina Kane. Your beauty director.'

'Oh, Kane. Yes, well, there were a few differences of opinion. We have a terrific team implementing my changes. I'll be appointing a new head of social media soon, to reach out to you guys.'

'You don't really credit Dina—?'

'Lots of people did a lot of good work, and we wish her luck.'

'So your relationship wasn't a part of this?'

'We weren't a good fit, personally or professionally, but I enjoyed spending time with Dina, and hopefully she'll find the right person for her someday soon.'

'OK,' said the woman, tentatively. 'Uh . . . Thank you.'

He gave out the same line all morning, then stopped taking calls. No press release; best not to encourage the idea that she mattered.

Finally, after lunch, there came the call he was expecting.

'Do you want to take this?' his secretary, Eileen, asked. 'It's from Dina Kane.'

Ludo smiled broadly. The anger inside him, from last night, was still clear and bright, cold as a diamond. It was interesting how much he minded her rejection.

But, best of all, he was in a position to do something about it.

'Certainly. Shut the office door.'

'Yes, sir.'

He depressed the red button on his phone.

'Dina Kane.'

'Ludo. I need some help.'

He chuckled. 'Then you've come to the wrong place. I'm not interested in working with you, and your contract is rock solid.'

She paused, and he tried to imagine the turmoil crossing that beautiful face.

'I understand that, Ludo. I think you're making a terrible mistake. We were a good team, professionally.'

'You led me on – probably so you could rise at Torch. You may call that professional, I don't.'

She gasped. 'That's bullshit. You asked me out.'

'And you couldn't wait to say yes. Look, I'm not interested in your little games. I just thank whatever's up there that I avoided a horrible mistake.'

'You sound so bitter,' Dina said, after a pause.

'Bitter? No. You're a joke, and I'm annoyed at the time I've wasted. Now, do run along and play in the traffic. If you're looking for favours, you used up your share long ago, baby.'

'I don't want my job back. I accept you can't work with me. I just need you to release me from the noncompetition clause—'

'So you can go and work for a rival? Drive sales up at Bloomingdales? What, you think I'm dumb? Always under-estimating everybody else, that's you, Dina Kane.'

'Come on, Ludo! Beauty's all I know. Just because we broke up, you want to ruin my life?'

'Enough with the drama queen. Go get a job bagging groceries. I don't give a shit.'

'That clause is totally unfair. It's restrictive—'

'We paid you enough in bonuses to keep you for a couple of years.'

'Not in Manhattan.'

'So move back to Westchester, the suburbs, where you came from. If you don't like the clause, take us to court. Torch has *great* lawyers, Dina.'

She breathed in and out, hard, ragged. He wanted to laugh.

'I'll go to your father. He's the one that hired me.'

'Don't bother. Dad and I have already had this discussion. He's not interested in you working in beauty for anyone else.'

Ah, yes . . . his father. The one cloud over his day. His father had been pretty goddamned furious that he'd fired Dina.

'Ship her down to Los Angeles. We can open a second store; she can run it.'

'Dad! Christ! I can't work with her. She dumped me.'

'Girlfriends are two a penny, Ludo. She's done wonders with the goddamned store.'

'I've seen what she did. I can replicate it. Please don't worry. You can't have me humiliated like that, Dad.'

His father sighed. 'Next time, keep it in your pants. She was *useful*.'

Still, at least he'd agreed: no Dina anywhere else.

'Make sure she doesn't go to Saks. They're already eating our lunch; we don't need Dina Kane making things worse. Or opening a Manhattan branch of Harrods.'

'No, sir,' Ludo assured him. 'Not a chance.'

Now he was glad to be able to rub it in. 'My father specifically asked me to bind you to the noncompetition clause. You will learn that what you did last night has consequences. And your precious career is one of them.'

She spoke slowly, clearly. 'I had no idea you were such a bastard, Ludo, but I promise you – you and your company will live to regret this.'

He laughed. 'Sure, Dina.' He hung up.

Goddamn you, Johnny, Dina thought. *I don't need this right now – I just don't need this.*

She was fighting to keep her head up. The emails were flooding her inbox; there were dozens of Google Alerts on her name. Reporters were calling. There were instant blog pieces, some supportive, others mocking. A lot of jealousy out there. And Ludo, such an asshole; she felt small and stupid ever to have dated him, ever to have thought it was OK.

Yet, even as she cried and tried to control herself, she could not find her brother. Every time she hung up the phone, she looked for news. The rehab was no help.

'We can't give you any assistance, Ms Kane. Yes, we know you paid the bills. But you don't have a power of attorney. Mr Kane was free to leave with whoever he liked.'

'My brother wouldn't just leave me without word.'

'If you get a power of attorney, we can send you videotape of the man who picked him up. Although he wore a hat and scarf . . .'

'Goddamn it!' Dina sobbed. 'He was an addict. He's in danger.'

'Have you filed a missing-person's report?'

'It hasn't even been two days; he's an adult. The cops won't touch it yet.'

'Well, then,' said the receptionist.

'I just want to know the name of his visitor. Please. Just give me a name. They sign a book; how confidential can it be?'

'Miss, please, I've told you, I need some kind of release. You can't ask me to break the law. He warned me against giving out the name, the gentleman.'

Dina's hand gripped the phone. She was suddenly struck with a horrible thought.

'OK,' she said, faintly. 'I'll come back to you.'

Her mother wasn't answering her phone. Dina left four messages, then she called the police. A Sergeant Mukowski listened to her politely and told her he couldn't help her.

'Ma'am, he's not a child. He could be anywhere. Could be on vacation. This could be a boyfriend, from what you say.'

'But can't you at least look for him?'

'No, ma'am. He's not a missing person. Why don't you wait a few days?'

Maybe he's right, Dina thought, as she hung up the phone, yet again. Maybe they were all right. She was worrying for nothing.

But her heart told her different.

She lay on the bed. She wanted to call Joel Gaines, tell him her fears, tell him everything. But she didn't dare.

If Johnny had been kidnapped, the people who had him knew where to find her. But where was the call? Where was the ransom note?

Even as she agonised over her future, the thought – that bad idea in the back of her head – would not go away, would not shift.

It had been years – years. And she hadn't heard a word from him.

Edward Johnson.

Of course, she still had the address, the phone records, tucked away – everything she'd found out from his father, whilst mercilessly screwing him for revenge. She'd hoped that the rage within her would calm afterwards, but instead she'd felt like she was dying inside, a little, every day.

What she'd done had destroyed Shelby Johnson. And his son. She understood now that it also destroyed her.

Workaholism had redoubled. No real boyfriends. No trust; no hope. She had been fixated on the safe . . . until Joel Gaines came along and she was tempted again by another married man – for good this time.

Dina buried her face in her hands. She was a disaster, an emotional cripple. And now she was nothing at work, either.

But her brother was still out there, out there somewhere. Feeling sick, dizzy with fear, she dug out the old number and called it up.

'Johnson residence,' said a voice.

'I want to speak to Edward. Is he there?'

'Who's calling, please? I'll see if Mr Johnson is available.'

Dina felt that surge of hatred again, jolting through her heartbreak. Overprivileged, spoiled little brat; rich guy who'd done nothing to deserve it; pampered prince, laughing at her. Her remorse over his father, what she'd done, that dirty, arid, deceptive sex, almost vanished at the sound of the servant's voice. Jesus Christ! What fucking century were they living in? One where you could bang the help, laugh about it and just walk away.

'My name is Dina Kane. I think he'll remember me.'

'Hold a moment, please.'

She waited maybe thirty seconds, and every one of them, an eternity. He was there, playing with her, making her wait. The acid bubbled in her stomach.

'Dina!' said that familiar voice, too brightly, and she understood at once that he loathed her. 'What a pleasant surprise to hear from you again, and on such a worrying day for you! Or so a little bird tells me.'

'Edward –' she choked down the insults that sprang to her lips – 'do you know something about my brother?'

'Oh, Dina. I know *masses* about your brother. He was kind

enough to enlighten me, all the way back from the rehab facility. It's a long drive, when you're stuck with such a *boring* companion. I can't abide sob stories.'

She shuddered with horror. 'If you've done anything to him – I'll go straight to the police.'

'My dear girl, don't be foolish. I've done nothing to him. He checked out quite voluntarily. The staff will tell you that. He had a very slow time of it up there: no drink; no boyfriends. So, to celebrate his checking out, I gave him some champagne. He asked to be dropped off in Red Hook – quite a party zone, I believe. He was going to visit a few fellows.'

'You gave him alcohol? After all this time?' Her heart thumped wildly. 'Where is he, Edward? For God's sake, this is his life.'

'He's an adult with choices, Dina. There's nothing criminal in it.'

She whispered. 'Where is he? Is he dead?'

'How the hell should I know?'

She sobbed. 'You bastard! I'll call the police—'

'And accuse me of what? Offering him champagne? That's not a hanging offence, even in Manhattan. Think hard, Dina Kane. Do you really want the police to sit down with us? What I did isn't illegal. Blackmail is, however. Do you know what happened to my parents?'

'They are adults, too.'

'Right – isn't it marvellous? Everybody's an adult here! My mother was free to divorce my dad and slide into alcoholism; my father lost his position and became a hippie for the world to laugh at. My mother nearly died, too; forgive me if I don't give a flying fuck about your junkie fag of a brother. Except in so far as it makes us even.'

'I never killed anybody.'

'And nor did I, darling. Not that you can prove, anyway.' The sarcastic lightness of tone dropped away. 'It's on your brother. Or, if you prefer, it's on you. The same as your failure at work, and your failure with your latest ex. See, that's the problem with whores like you: you just fuck around.'

Dina gasped. She hung up, shaking, trembling across her whole body. A wave of panic coursed through her, so strong her legs gave way, and she collapsed on to the couch.

When it passed, she had only one thought.

She picked up her cellphone and dialled Joel Gaines' number.

'Dina.' He answered immediately. 'Give me a second. I'll call you back.'

She waited, miserably, knowing that he was leaving his wife, leaving Susan, to take her call, heading out of their kitchen, or bedroom. Sneaking around.

It was low and dirty, reaching out for Joel, but she had no choice.

The phone rang two minutes later. 'It's me. I heard; I'm so sorry.'

'This is not about Torch. It's my brother, Johnny. He's in trouble and I need help.'

Gaines' voice changed immediately. 'What do you need?'

'He's an addict.'

'You told me his story. What happened?'

'An enemy of mine sprung him from rehab, gave him wine and dropped him in Red Hook. The way he was talking, I guess it was more than wine.' She sobbed. 'He won't tell me where Johnny is and, the way he was saying it, I think he's dead. He was close to death before we got him clean. It wouldn't take much.'

'Presumably Johnny's not answering calls?'

'Nothing. I've tried emails, calls, texts. My mother hasn't heard from him – doesn't seem to care. The police won't get involved, because he's an adult. He's all I've got, Joel.'

'Why would this . . . this enemy do this to you?'

Dina twisted like a butterfly under a pin. The shame of

admitting it to Joel Gaines . . . admitting any of it to Joel Gaines . . . Maybe he would never be hers, but she didn't want him to know. She didn't want to shatter whatever image he had of Dina Kane.

'His name is Edward Johnson.'

'Edward Johnson? The kid, the son of Shelby Johnson?'

'Yes. He's a psycho, Joel.'

'Why would he try to kill your brother?'

She sobbed. 'I . . . I . . . slept with his father, Shelby, to blackmail him.'

There was a long pause and, in that pause, Dina felt all her hopes and dreams sputter out, like a candle that had burned to the very end.

'I can find your brother.'

'Don't you want to hear what happened, Joel?'

His voice was cold. 'No, Dina. You were clear enough.'

She wept.

'Let me find out what happened to Johnny. It may not be tonight. Hold tight. When I know, I'll call you.'

'Joel, please—'

'I'll call you,' he repeated, and hung up.

Dina walked numbly into her bathroom and peeled off her clothes. With an incredible effort, she forced herself to throw them in the laundry basket and step into the shower.

She dried off mechanically and reached for her cotton pyjamas. The toothbrush in her hand was like a lead weight. Just keeping herself upright seemed more effort than she could bear.

Before bed, she reached into her medicine closet and brought out a small bottle of anti-anxiety pills: Valium. A doctor had recommended it once, and Dina had laughed at him. Weakness? That was for other people.

She wasn't laughing now. She took one, swallowing it with difficulty, gulping the water. And then she crawled into her exquisite antique sleigh bed, made up with crisp Irish linen, and lay down in it like she would never get up again.

Chapter Fifteen

Joel Gaines looked at the body bag.

He had put out the word, and taken the call about an hour ago. His anger at Dina – his disgust, his disappointment – it was wide and deep, but he wasn't going to refuse the plea about her brother.

She was desperate; he recognised that. And, if Johnny Kane was alive, Gaines was going to find him.

It didn't take too long for the answer to come back. Not the one he wanted. But he left his office immediately and met the cop at the scene.

The plastic body bag was unzipped, and there was the unmistakable face of Johnny Kane – bruised, skinny, pale in death, but otherwise matching the photo Dina emailed him. The wasted frame of a young man. He'd been a failure in this life, his potential unrealised, killed by a fatal weakness. Stemming from what? The tension of a bad childhood? It had made Dina – and broken her big brother.

Looking at the corpse, Gaines had no doubt that Edward Johnson did more than hand out wine. There were drugs in the system, the medical examiner said, lots of drugs: heroin, methamphetamine, coke. There was recent sexual activity. All of this, for a penniless ex-student with no money in the bank account, kept by his sister.

The apartment had been ghost rented. There were no signs of anything other than a party, and an OD. Nothing forcible; no murder.

He knew all this because he could hire investigators when he had to. And his law enforcement connections were rock solid. Gaines knew people in the police department, in the Mayor's office, throughout the city.

But Edward Johnson could not have tempted Johnny Kane without that huge void in his life. They were screwed up, both the brother and the sister.

He wondered about it – the dead father, the mother who was there in the most literal sense, but not really there for her kids.

'We'll need next of kin to ID the body,' the cop said.

He wanted to spare Dina that. 'No need; I knew Johnny Kane,' he lied. 'I can ID him for you.'

The guy pursed his mouth, but nodded. Everybody knew Mr Gaines: richest man in the city, but stand-up, nonetheless. His gifts to the Benevolent Fund sent hundreds of dead cops' kids to college, every year.

'Hey, no problem. That'd be great; thank you, sir.'

'Joel.'

The cop smiled. 'Joel.'

DOA was a shitty job, always, but you got used to it – so used to it in New York. This guy lightened the load. He would remember meeting Joel Gaines; he was some kind of big shot, man. The muscles were also impressive. The guy must bench like a maniac. He liked that; exercise was no respecter of wallets. Gaines obviously worked for it. Respect. He had no need to work out to get all the chicks fluttering; his bank account would be more than enough to do that.

'Over here, then.' He walked across and pulled the body bag open a little more. The corpse was pale, a little blood and drool dried on his cheek. His eyes had rolled up into his head. Classic OD.

'That's Johnny Kane,' Gaines said, without hesitation. He was glad Dina would never have to see it. 'Did the medical examiner sign off?'

'At the scene. Full autopsy tonight. Then the body can be released.' He hesitated. 'We really do need next of kin for that one.'

'I understand. Thank you, officer.'

Joel Gaines was not a praying man, but he sent a thought upwards – some kind of wish, intent, call it whatever you like – to whoever was out there, that somebody loved this boy now.

Dina. Her name shoved itself into his mind. *Dina loved him. Dina looked out for him.*

He didn't want to give her credit right now. Didn't want to think good thoughts. She was a low-life; what his wife said was true; what that schmuck Ludo Morgan said was true.

The shock of her words hit him like a fist.

I slept with his father, to blackmail him.

That was what all the jealous bastards said about Dina Kane, that she was a user, a gold-digger, that she latched on to rich men. Shelby Johnson – by her own admission. Who now could believe her story over Meadow? Maybe she took that old chemist guy, Dr Green, for a ride like the rest . . . Stole his idea. And then at Torch . . . she winds up, in two minutes, banging the owner's son.

A job she got via him.

And he was a very rich man, too.

Loser. Idiot. It's a pattern. You're meant to be good at patterns.

He was like some drunk asshole in a strip club, going, 'She likes me!' because the girl shakes her ass nearest to the dollar bills. What a fool! What an idiot. Of course, he was way too old for her. And to think he had gulled himself into believing . . .

Believing that she loved him.

The struggling, the wrestling, the way he'd become so

dissatisfied that the torpor of his marriage was suddenly smothering to him – none of it had any point, because Dina Kane – so beautiful, so smart and so strong – was a self-confessed predator.

There's no fool like an old fool. Wasn't that what they said?

He didn't know why he felt so angry. Hadn't he vowed that kiss was the end? He was staying true. He wasn't going to sleep with Dina, see Dina, anything. They could be friends; they could talk.

And, within one day – this.

What a difference twenty-four hours made. After the party, and the kiss, he had been utterly unable to sleep. He had no desire for Susan, not even enough for the mechanics of sex. He'd told her he was exhausted, and he'd lain down in bed, staring at the ceiling.

And, the next day, he was staring at his cellphone from the moment he walked out of the shower. Waiting for her to call. Willing her to call.

When he heard the news that she'd been fired, his heart leaped. How pathetic – to be pleased that she'd broken up with Ludo Morgan, and was free again. He wasn't free – would never be free – but he rejoiced all the same. And when she didn't call him for help on her business, did not seek his protection, didn't ask him to extend his arm, Joel Gaines was bitterly disappointed.

He recognised the illogic. The selfishness. The dog in the manger. But he wanted – how he wanted – to ride into battle for her and show her what real power meant.

She would be helplessly aroused by it, he knew it: money and power as a proxy for sex.

But Dina Kane did not call. And, as the minutes ticked by, he found himself falling ever more hopelessly in love with her. The bravery of it – the standing on her own two feet – not coming to him, not begging.

When she finally called, it was late, and he assumed she just wanted comfort.

But Dina asked for his power, after all. Wanted it for something he could not refuse. And the price was telling him the truth.

He would have loved to have had that day over again. He'd have given a million dollars, ten million dollars, not to have heard Dina Kane say those words to him.

Johnny Kane was dead. And, for a moment, Joel Gaines envied him. There was nothing true in this world, nothing beautiful.

As he walked away, towards the limousine, that aggravating voice in his head corrected him.

Her love for her brother, her care for her brother was true and beautiful.

Johnny Kane didn't fit Dina's pattern. He couldn't help her career, or give her money. He was a cost centre, without prestige or usefulness. But Dina had been devoted to him. Devoted enough to spend money, even when she hardly had any.

Joel was not looking forward to the stop he had to make.

She was waiting when he knocked on her door.

'Dina, it's me. Open up.'

In a second, the door was wrenched open. She looked worse than Joel had ever seen her. That beautiful face was grey and lifeless. Her eyes were red; her hair was unwashed, unbrushed. She looked like she hadn't eaten in a day. She was gaunt, listless. Not a scrap of make-up on her.

'Joel,' she said, and her whole body teetered and gave way. He reached forward, automatically, and caught her, under the arms. Her head lolled.

'Easy; easy there,' he said, alarmed. He kicked the door shut and guided her to a chair, forcing her to sit. She hadn't fainted, but her head was pressed in her hands. Clearly, it was a dizzy spell. 'When did you last eat?'

'I . . . I don't know.'

'You have to eat, drink. It's low blood sugar. Here.'

He opened her fridge. There was almost nothing in it – a half-empty milk carton, some eggs, some wilting lettuce. 'Jesus. You don't even have orange juice?'

'Joel, please. I can't think about food.'

He felt lost. What did people say about shock? Sweet things – that was right. This was where women looked after men, not the other way around. He filled her electric kettle and hunted in the cupboards till he found a box of teabags and the remnants of a packet of sugar. She stared into space as he fixed her a cup of boiling hot tea and put three sugars in it, stirring it and brewing it, no milk. He didn't trust the milk. She was falling apart, and he was about to help her on the way down.

'Here.' He blew on it a little, to cool it. 'Drink.'

'What did you find out?'

'We're not talking until you've drunk half of that.'

Joel waited. As angry as he was at her and his stupidity, and as much as he wished he'd never heard the name Dina Kane, he could not stand there and see her broken.

She took the mug from him and drank, numbly, not resisting. There was no fire in her anymore. It was nuts, but he felt his heart clenching with emotion. As pallid and dirty as she looked this evening, she was unutterably beautiful to him – vulnerable in a way he had never seen. He could not shake his feelings for her, no matter what he did.

After she had drained most of it, he took the mug from her, so that she wouldn't hurt herself if she dropped it, and knelt down in front of the chair. He took her hands.

'Dina, you will have to be brave. Johnny's dead. I'm so sorry. He died of an overdose, and it was very peaceful.' God knows if it was peaceful or not – he remembered the blood and the drool – but that was what he was going to tell her. 'I identified the body. There were no signs of violence, and it went down as an OD.'

Tears sprang into her eyes, and her thin frame shook with sobs. Great, wrenching, heaving sobs, shocking in their intensity, jolted her out of her numbness and lethargy. He stood there, helpless, with no way to comfort her. In the end, he reached for the kitchen towel and handed it to her so she could mop her face, but the tears continued.

Joel Gaines leaned in and folded his arms around her, wrapping her close, so close, holding her firmly, not letting her slump, until, in the end, her sobs ceased and she was breathing hard, shuddering against him.

'I will take care of everything,' he said. 'They will release the body to you or your mother. The police will inform her.'

'I'll call Mom,' Dina whispered.

'I can have the best funeral home in the city pick him up and arrange any kind of service you like.'

'Catholic.'

'Fine. I give half a million to the Cardinal's appeal every year.'

She looked up at him with the suggestion of a smile. 'But you're Jewish.'

Joel gripped on to that tiny flicker of amusement. 'Baby, I give half a million to everybody important in the city. You buy friends as well as karma.'

'Always at work, aren't you?'

'Aren't we,' he corrected her, but he was thrilled to see this stirring of life.

'I don't know how I'm going to tell Ellen.'

He noted the first name. There was so little there, between mother and daughter; it was sad.

'I'll stay with you. I'm not leaving you right now.'

Dina shook her head; more tears. 'You have to go . . . Your wife . . .'

'My wife can wait.' He pulled out his cellphone and tapped on it. 'I'm just texting her that I'm staying in the city. That's normal on a weeknight.'

She said nothing, and he could see her thoughts dragging back to her admission, and the breach between them.

'You don't owe me anything else, Joel.'

'I didn't owe you this,' he said. 'Go get in the shower. You look awful and you're starting to smell.'

Dina opened her eyes wider, actually shocked.

'We're past the sweet-nothings stage, Dina Kane. Get in the shower. Now.'

She stood up, weakly, and headed to her bathroom. He waited a few seconds, to hear the sound of the water running, then walked in after her.

Dina gasped.

'Chill out, I can't see a goddamn thing with all that steam against the glass.'

Actually, that was not true. He could see the shape of her body just fine; not everything, maybe, just the still-firm curve of that ass, the long hair hanging slick down her back. He bit his lip against the surge of desire and tried to focus. Her clothes were on the floor. He gathered them up and laid out a white waffle robe for her.

'I'm going to wash these. And put new clothes on your bed.'

She said nothing.

Gaines went into her kitchen and found the washing machine. God, she still lived so small, for a girl that could have been married to millions of dollars. This was middle-management stuff, and Dina's brain was way above that level; she was meant to be a superstar, a CEO, a revolutionary.

He flung the clothes in there, added a bag of soap, then went into her bedroom and stripped the sheets from the bed. Dina was a minimalist: just a fitted sheet, pillowcase and a duvet cover in white linen. It smelled bad – of sweat and despair. So he added them to the wash.

Then he charged back into the bathroom. The steam was really up now. Dina said nothing, no word of protest. He imagined she had not eaten all day, maybe longer. Opening her mirrored cabinet, he found shampoo, conditioner and a disposable razor. He opened the door to the stall.

'I'm not looking,' he lied, and extended his hand. 'Take these. All these. Use them. Clean up.'

She lifted them from him. 'OK.'

'When you're done, there's a towel outside this stall, and a robe. Clean your teeth. Then you can go into your bedroom and change.'

'You don't have to do all this.'

'Where do you keep your spare bedding?'

'What?'

'Just answer the question.'

'There's a chest at the foot of the bed.'

He left her then, and went and made the bed, something he had not done since he was a student. The washing machine became a dryer; he was rather proud that he was figuring this stuff out. Her clothes hung in the wardrobe and lay in her chest of drawers: exquisite things, but not many of them. He picked a pair of soft cashmere lounge pants, a bra, panties and a draped jersey T-shirt. It would not be such a disaster if she fell asleep on a couch dressed like that.

Then he called for delivery: Chinese – Manhattan's answer to everything. He got her beef lo mein, for protein and carbohydrates, and a helping of steamed vegetables, and the same for himself. Then he called his assistant.

'Marian, I want you to get a week's groceries for one person delivered, right now. Get the best of everything: Häagen-Dazs, fillet steak, fresh-squeezed orange juice, milk, fruit, smoked salmon, cereals – everything. Tea and coffee. When the guy arrives, have him ring the doorbell but leave it outside. I will unpack myself. Tip him in advance; I don't want to see him. And I want it here fast.'

'Right away, Mr Gaines.' She didn't ask questions. 'What is the address?'

He gave it to her.

'And what name?'

'My name,' Joel said, shortly, and hung up.

He could hear Dina stepping out of the shower. The temptation to go in there, to give her something else, just to see her naked, was overwhelming, but he fought it. Goddamn it; he hated to be here, but he didn't want to leave.

'Do your teeth, like I told you,' he said, loudly.

He heard the sink running as she obeyed him. Right now, she was washed, clean-shaven and doing her teeth: coming back to life because he had ordered it.

Gaines was torn. This was real emotion, not faked. He did not know what to think of her. There was pity, and fury, and jealousy, and disgust, and concern, and admiration, and desire.

No woman had ever made him feel like this. He wondered who was weaker – she or he?

He waited. In a few minutes, he heard her pad to the bedroom, and then she came out to meet him, dressed in the simple clothes, exactly as he'd laid out for her.

'More tea,' he said. 'There's a meal coming. I'm not leaving until you've eaten it. Don't argue with me; I am going to watch you eat.'

'Yes, Joel,' she said. She twisted her fingers, like she was trying to get up the courage to say something else.

'You should ring your mother.'

'Yes.' Dina's gaze broke away. 'Of course; I'll do that now.'

He moved away from her as she made the call. He could hear her voice rise, pleading, arguing with her mother. More tears. The doorbell rang for his Chinese; when he brought it back inside, she was done, and in tears again.

'Here. Sit. Eat,' he said, laying it out on the table before her and fetching them both water. He pushed forward the cartons, just handing her a fork.

She ate, mechanically at first, not appearing to taste anything. He wolfed his down – he was starving – and, after a few moments, Dina began to eat properly, too, and to sip at her water.

Gaines was relieved. She was not likely to kill herself, after all, not once she started to treat herself properly.

The doorbell rang again. Dina started, but he held out his hand. 'Don't worry about it. I'll get it in a second. It's a grocery delivery.'

'I didn't order any.'

'I did. I'm not having you use depression as an excuse not to eat. Your brother is dead, but you're not. And you need to go on.'

'For what?' she said. 'I don't have Johnny. I don't have a job.' She sobbed. 'I don't have you.'

Gaines rose, opened the door and brought the bags in. There were a lot of them – all gourmet. Cinnamon and vanilla coffee beans. Zabar's smoked salmon. Stoneground bread. Artisanal cheeses and honey. Sugar, milk and farm-fresh eggs. Bottles of squeezed orange juice, and an elegant fruit basket, nicely wrapped. It went on and on. Filet mignon steaks, packets of Cheerios, steel-cut oatmeal, Greek yoghurt, smoked almonds, Charbonnel et Walker chocolates.

He unpacked them as she stared. She was almost licking her lips, now, he saw; the taste of food had triggered her suppressed appetite.

'I'll fix us some ice cream,' he said, as he packed away the Twinings tea. 'You will be getting the call that your brother's body is ready, after the autopsy; I want you to let me know. You can text me. Will your mother want to arrange the funeral?'

Dina shook her head. 'Ellen – Mom – she was embarrassed of Johnny by the end. He was her pride and joy, her favourite, but when he came out as gay, she just withdrew. She said she accepted him, but she didn't. I don't think she visited him in the city even one time.'

'And she never switched her affections back to you?'

'She had a new man by then. Somebody who would overlook the past. My mom never really loved either of us. She just covered it a little better with Johnny. But she dropped him like a stone at the first sign of trouble.' Dina's face hardened, a burst of anger surging through the lethargy of her sadness. 'You know, maybe that was worst of all. At least I knew I wasn't loved by the time I left home. She tricked Johnny. She made him believe she cared. And when he needed her most, he found out she didn't. She just loved the idea of a son, not the son she got.' Dina shook her head. 'No, she won't take care of the arrangements; why should she? She'll expect me to do that.'

'Will she attend?'

'She'll come along – not because she gives a damn – to look respectable.'

'Very well.' Gaines paused, to take that in. Whatever sympathy he felt, he couldn't express; Dina would fall apart again. The best thing he could do for her was to take over the situation, lift the burden off her back. That part was easy, and he ploughed ahead. 'I will arrange the embalming and the funeral, in a couple of days. Do you have a preferred cemetery?'

Dina wiped her eyes. 'Somewhere green – in Westchester.'

'Done. Will you come to the funeral mass?'

'Of course I will.'

'Then you need to eat, sleep, exercise. Be there for your brother.'

She nodded. 'I'll try.'

He finished with the groceries, and put out two small bowls of vanilla ice cream. Watching her eat it was unbearably erotic. He needed to get the hell out of here.

'I should go,' he said, as she finished and stood up to clear the table. 'You'll call me when you hear?'

Dina nodded.

'OK then.' He stood to leave, and his legs were as heavy as iron. This felt wrong, walking out on her. But he had no more excuses to stay.

'Joel, I want to thank you – for trying to help Johnny, for finding him and . . . and giving him dignity. I don't think I could organise anything well right now.'

'It's fine, Dina.'

'And for helping me. For coming here and . . . all this.'

'We were friends.'

Tears sprang fresh to her eyes. 'Please don't say that. Don't say *were*. Say *are*.'

He twisted. 'Look, it's not the time to talk about it. If you're grateful to me, don't make me talk about it now. I want you better. I want you healthy and well.'

'You can't forgive me? Let me tell you the story – the whole story. Everything that happened.' Her voice cracked, and she looked at him, openly pleading, imploring him. 'Joel, I can take it if you don't love me and you don't want to be with me. But I can't bear it that you should think so ill of me. I know what I did was wrong. But you need to understand what happened, why it all happened. I beg you, Joel; I beg you.'

'Who gives a damn what I think? Just live your life, Dina; be well.'

'I give a damn. Right now it means everything to me.'

'Why?'

'Because I'm in love with you.' She shrugged. 'I just don't care anymore; I can't hide it anymore. Even though I know there's no point, I need you to like me – I need that at least.'

'I do like you.' *God help me*. 'I like you very much.'

'Then you'll let me talk to you? And, if you feel the same after that, I'll accept it. I won't bother you again.'

He nodded. 'OK, Dina Kane. Here's the deal: if I see you at your brother's funeral, and you look well, and strong, and put-together, we will go someplace quiet for coffee afterwards, and you can tell me everything. Enough?'

She breathed out – a long, ragged sigh of relief. 'Enough.'

He leaned forwards and, with incredible restraint, kissed her on the cheek. Then he let himself out of her apartment, closing the door behind him.

Chapter Sixteen

The funeral was two days later, on a warm day, in a beautiful church in Bronxville. Dina wore black. She stood with her mother and Ellen's new husband, Oliver. Joel Gaines was the only other mourner.

Nobody had been able to track Brad down. Gaines was struck by the smallness and loneliness of it all. Ellen Kane never put her arm round Dina; she cried a little, but her daughter seemed destroyed.

The priest was sensitive, and kept the mass short. Johnny's corpse was beautifully embalmed and dressed, giving him a serenity he never had in life. But Joel had ordered the casket closed; he wanted Dina's last memory of her brother to be of a warm, living body – a young man getting better.

Oliver, the stepfather, seemed disengaged. He patted his wife's back and shook Dina's hand. Gaines could not see him attempting to make conversation. What a lonely, sad little family they were.

He stood at the back. There were limousines waiting outside the church: one for the casket, one for the family and the priest, and a third for him. He had ensured everything would be done perfectly. There were white and yellow roses atop the casket, and beautiful displays in various colours, labelled with love from Dina, from Ellen, from Oliver, and from himself. As the priest finished the final words, Gaines slipped out of the church to double check everything was ready. He wanted it to be seamless.

Immediately, he saw it. Leaning up against the old brick walls, the extra floral arrangement – a heart – stuck out like a sore thumb. It was made up of garish red and orange carnations, ridiculously huge; clearly designed to be noticed.

Gaines quickly walked over and checked the label.

So glad to have met Johnny. Dina, you deserved him. Love and kisses, Edward Johnson.

His heart thudded. *She was right.*

His driver had come out of the limo and walked over to him. 'Everything OK, Mr Gaines? Some goons got here just a minute ago and brought this thing up. Took two of them to carry it.'

'Get rid of it, Carlos. Now.'

'Yes, sir.'

Gaines ripped off the label, and Carlos hefted the huge arrangement up and hauled it away, round the back of the church; he heard him stamping on it.

At that moment, the church doors opened and the pallbearers came out with the coffin; the priest followed, and the three family members walked behind. Dina lifted her head, looking for him; tears had streaked her face and make-up, but she smiled at him, gratefully.

Gaines crunched the card in his pocket as they climbed into the limousines. His driver came back; he was ex-Special Forces, like all Gaines' personal employees.

'It's in a trash can. Anything else?'

'No. Thanks. Just take me to the cemetery.'

They buried Johnny Kane with final honours in the best plot money could buy, under a spreading oak tree, in the quietest part of the grounds. Gaines had ordered a simple gravestone, with a cross, and the name and dates. Dina threw earth on to the coffin, and a white rose Gaines had made available for her. The priest said prayers, and then they all walked back, quietly, towards the cars.

'Thank you so much, Father,' Dina said, when they had come to a stop by the limousines.

'God bless you, my child.'

She turned to her mother. 'Momma, I'm not riding back with you and Oliver. Mr Gaines is taking me to the city.'

'Suit yourself, Dina. It was certainly a beautiful ceremony, Father.' Ellen presented one gloved hand, as though she wanted it kissed.

Dina walked with Gaines to his waiting car. He opened the door, and she slid in, on to the seat.

'Take us to the office,' Gaines said.

'Very good, sir,' Carlos replied.

Joel pressed a button, and a soundproof, bullet-proof security screen slid up between them and the driver. Now they were as good as alone.

Dina kissed him on the cheek. 'Joel, thank you so much. That was an incredible relief for me. Thank you for arranging it all. I am in your debt forever.'

He shrugged. 'Least I could do. I'm sorry.'

She leant back against the soft pewter leather of his limousine seats. 'I feel like I could sleep for days. Emotion – it's exhausting.' Her eyes moistened. 'My poor Johnny.'

'Maybe you should see somebody – a counsellor. Grief hits you in waves, that's what they say.'

She shook her head. 'I don't think there's any shortcut. I'll be mourning Johnny for the rest of my life. But I still have to live it out.'

Gaines looked her over. He was truly done now; the brother was buried, and he couldn't hide behind the Good Samaritan schtick any longer. She was still thin, but clearly had been eating healthily. Her hair was washed and she had simple make-up on. Dina was back from the dead.

Now he had to decide where he was, in her life. If anywhere.

'You're looking at me.' Dina stared back at him, boldly. 'I'm not the mess I was a couple of days ago. Thank you for that, too.'

He nodded.

'But we also had a deal. You told me that, if I kept it together, you'd at least give me the chance to explain.'

His voice was cold. 'Slept with a rich man to blackmail him? An older man? A man my age? I don't think there's an explanation in the world that can take that away.'

'Joel – you said you'd hear me out. Over coffee.'

'This car is completely private. He can't hear a thing. Tell me now, Dina, because I don't think I can take any more game playing. My life has been on hold for you – because of the past, pity, whatever reason – but I'm nobody's sucker, girl, not even yours. So, if you have something to say, tell me right fucking now.'

She was taken aback by his anger. All the care, all the comfort – she had got used to it. But now that he saw she was well – coping – he was turning that fire back on her.

Dina responded. It was good; it felt good to be challenged. Gaines was treating her like a person, not a patient. Sympathy and kindness weakened her; aggression, a fight, she knew how to rise to.

'When I was growing up, it was rough. My dad died early, and my mom . . . My mom didn't really care for me.'

He nodded, said nothing.

'At school, the boys would try to feel me up and kiss me and stuff, and the girls didn't really like me, so basically nobody hung out with me. Except Johnny. He was my only friend. He couldn't stand up to Mom, though; he was always weak. I don't blame him; it was his way.'

She swallowed. She wanted this to come out just right, just well enough to convince Joel Gaines that she was serious, not guilty, that she was still worth his love, his lust, his patronage – whatever was going; whatever tiny part of him could be hers.

'My mom started drinking when she got a little older. And men started to come around at night. Different men, in cars, from the Family.'

'The Family?'

'My dad worked a Mafia construction site. They provided for the widow; it's good for morale. Anyway, I knew these guys were using my mom, turning her into some sort of hooker. They were all married.'

I'm married. The unspoken fact hung in the air.

'What did you do?'

'Everybody knew the local Don, where he lived. I got a bus; I went to see him. At his gatehouse, his bodyguards felt me up when they patted me down. Really groped me – touched me. I was fifteen and they made me feel like meat.'

He digested that. 'And the *capo*?'

'He listened to me. After that, somebody came by the house and spoke to my mom. No men came by ever again, and she never drank another drop. I think he told her he would kill her. Anyway, she never gave me another affectionate word after that.' Dina smiled slightly. 'There hadn't been too many before. I mean, she almost hated me; maybe she did hate me. She thought I had ruined her life – no parties; no fun. Before I had even turned eighteen she was ready to throw me right out of the house.'

He could no longer keep up the cold shoulder. 'Goddamn. That's hard.'

'She gave everything to Johnny – paid for his Catholic schooling, his college. I had to go to public school; there was no money for me to go to college, although I had the grades. She wouldn't take a loan on the house or anything. Swore she needed it all. I had to threaten her, too, to give me some cash for a deposit on my first rental.'

'What did you say?'

'That I would go back to the Don. After that, she ponied up. I would have gone to thank Don Angelo personally, except his guards probably wouldn't have stopped at feeling my ass.'

'No. Probably not.'

'They have this fucked up code. Kids get immunity – mostly.'

'So then what?'

'I moved to the city. No college; high-school diploma; small pot of money. I worked round the clock, waitressing. I got very good at it, helped my diner out by bringing in new customers, but, you see, all the men mostly leered at me. They'd proposition me. They'd offer me money to fuck them. I never had a boyfriend at school. I was eighteen and I didn't know how to date.' She paused. 'I started hating men, I guess.'

'I'm sorry.'

'I flung myself into work – I wanted to, and I had to. This guy who runs a coffee chain gave me a break, made me a junior manager of a café. It was uptown, near Columbia. I always wanted to study there; even though I was running the books at the café, it wasn't college-level stuff. I'd serve coffee to kids my own age, just a little older, and it felt like I'd be serving them all my life. All these rich, preppy kids. And the boys were the worst. It was exactly the same as the diner, except they didn't just leer, they laughed at me – took bets on who would be first to bang me. This one bastard – he totally humiliated me, and I poured coffee on him.'

Gaines laughed. He was gripped. 'I bet you did.'

'And, just when I was feeling sick, this guy, Edward, came up to me. Only he'd given himself a fake name: Edward Fielding. He acted really disgusted and sympathetic. He treated me with respect.' She choked back tears. 'It was the first time any boy had treated me with respect. We dated, and eventually I went to bed with him. Then he ditched his cellphone number and his fake name, and he vanished – completely vanished. I gave my virginity to a guy who just screwed me and walked out.'

'What happened?'

'Nothing – until he turned up at the coffee shop, with his friends. You see, he wanted to prove to them he'd fucked me. I was a bet.'

Gaines was starting to understand.

'I laughed it off, told the boys Edward had been drunk – too drunk to get it up. He denied it, of course; they argued; we argued. I heard one of them say his name – Johnson. That made me see red and I threw coffee on all of them. The café fired me, right away. So, then I had no job, no money left, and some guy – the first guy I'd ever trusted – had used me like a tissue. It was so funny to him, Joel, so goddamned amusing. That's when I started looking him up, finding out how I could hurt him. He's an only child; Mommy is a society queen; Daddy is this banker who wants to be a politician and who's buying his seat. Edward Johnson hurt me with sex, and I wanted to hurt him back. I wanted to humiliate him, like he did me. When the father was ready to jump me, I took full advantage: I screwed him; I photographed him; I sent his wife the pictures. Maybe it was whorish. I sold myself – not for money, but revenge. You've got to understand, Edward had already made me feel like a whore. So what was the fucking difference?'

The bitterness and anger in her tone was thick with regret.

Gaines asked a question to which he didn't want to know the answer: 'Money, Dina? You were out of a job, so you asked them for money?'

She shook her head. 'God – not that kind of whore. I wanted to put Edward Johnson in my position, let him see how that other half lived.'

'You're saying you *didn't* demand any money?'

'Hell, no. I told Shelby to step down from the campaign, and

Edward was to drop out of college. Beyond that, I didn't give a damn. I just wanted to take from him that life that made him so smug, so entitled. So, it was blackmail, if you like, but not for money. For justice. As I saw it, back then.'

Gaines took a full breath in, like he could drain all the oxygen from the world.

'You know what happened to the Johnsons?' he asked.

She flushed. 'I didn't care. I know – I know how that sounds. But I didn't think about it more than that. Edward told me when I called him about Johnny.'

'Shelby Johnson dropped off the face of the earth. There was a divorce, and he went to "find himself" in Florida. The wife started to drink. She's in Florida now, too, in a rehab camp. The family were a laughing stock.'

'I understand that. I didn't think . . . I didn't care.'

'Dina, your beef was with Edward, but you destroyed his parents to get to him.'

She bowed her head. 'I blamed them, for raising him. I hated them all. Rich bastards. I know it was wrong, now. The mother never did anything to me. And I seduced the father. He was unfaithful, but I tempted him pretty hard, as hard as I knew how. I understand if you despise me for it.' She sobbed. 'I despise me.'

'It was wrong, but I can see why you did it.' Gaines leaned back, next to her, his shoulders relaxing against the car seat as he let out the long-held tension in his body. 'You didn't ask for them to fall apart like that, though you should have been more careful.'

'I wanted them to divorce. I was angry – so angry. Maybe Edward was unlucky. He was just the last and worst in a long line.'

'And you snapped.'

Dina sobbed.

'What you did to his parents is bad news, Dina. You should try and set that right.'

She raised her head and looked at him. 'How can I? It's over.'

'You can try. Use your ingenuity.'

Dina was startled out of her crying. She'd never even thought of that, not for a moment. Put it right? Could she? Was there anything she could do?

Joel Gaines sat next to her, the most surprising man she had ever met. *Put it right.* No therapist would ever say that. It would be, *explore your feelings* or *write a letter and burn it.*

'And Hector Green? And Ludo?'

'Hector happened just as I told you, Joel. I deserved half of that cream. It was my idea. His whole store was my idea – all the expansion of it. It was where I learned to run a beauty business, and I took that into Torch.' She shook her head. 'I don't know what happened to Hector, who got to him, or why he changed.'

'You didn't have a relationship with him? Sleep with him?'

She laughed aloud. '*Hector*? He was about ninety. No, and he never asked. He just got tired, and greedy. I was ready to take the Green Apothecary to the heights, but he just wanted a little money and then to be left alone. It's not always that way with men, the sexual thing. I just haven't been lucky.'

'And Ludo Morgan?'

'You weren't available.'

He looked at her.

'I'm serious. Hell, Joel, I'm tired, too. I feel like Hector Green, right now. I can't dance around things anymore. I had fallen in love, and it was a disaster; you brushed me off. I don't blame you – you were married. The worst you did was flirt with me a little. I packed more into it than was there. But you hit me hard; I can't lie. I needed something to get over you, something that wasn't just a job. My career path was a little erratic, shall we say. I had made money – from Meadow, from our deal. But also some from the Green Apothecary, and quite a lot from real estate. Maybe I wasn't the most normal girl in the world. But I wanted to take a break from all the pushing, all the struggle to be someone.' She put her hand up to her face and dashed away tears. 'A weak moment, maybe. I just wanted . . . to get a job, and then get a boyfriend. A normal boyfriend, who wasn't you.'

'Is Ludo Morgan normal?' Gaines looked at her. 'He was the boss. His daddy owns the company.'

Dina shrugged. 'Torch became very consuming.'

Joel grinned. 'A pattern, Dina. Did you notice that? Even when you say you won't push yourself, you can't help it.'

'You might have a point. Anyway, Ludo solved a major problem for me. He was at work. That was part of it. I didn't have to take time out. And, after Edward, I insisted he date me in public, and he had no problem with that. So I guessed it was OK.'

He looked at her. 'But it wasn't OK, was it?'

She shook her head. 'I liked him; I didn't love him. I thought maybe love would grow. But we didn't fit – romantically; in bed it was just like going through the motions. Maybe that's what sex is.'

Gaines shook his head. 'Not if you're doing it right.'

'Well, I'm hardly going to be anybody's test case. So . . . at the party, when I saw you and you warned me he was trying to steal my work . . . And you kissed me . . .'

'I'm sorry,' Gaines said. He wasn't.

'Right after that, he took me out to the beach and proposed.'

For the first time, Joel sat up straight. 'What?'

'He got out this huge diamond ring and asked me to marry him, and said I should quit my job and just be with him.'

There was a long pause.

'You turned him down?'

'Obviously. And, when I said no, he wanted me to walk back to Manhattan. It was only when I threatened to make a scene at the party that he decided to be more reasonable. He said I could stay in his spare room, and that I was fired. Next day, he airbrushed me from all the company literature. Not only that, but it turns out I had a non-competition clause in my contract. And he's enforcing it. I can't work for anybody else.'

'You didn't mention that.'

'Johnny was missing. I didn't care.' Dina breathed out. 'Thanks for letting me talk, Joel. Now you know the whole thing. Ugly or not, that's my life.'

Gaines said nothing for a few moments.

'I jumped to conclusions,' he said. 'I apologise, Dina. If you were some kind of gold-digger, you were offered the entire mine with Ludo. But you turned him down. Ambitious – yes; desperate – yes. Gold-digger? No.'

She smiled sadly. 'Funny thing is, until he fired me, I kind of felt bad for him. He said I led him on, and maybe I did. I just didn't realise how little I cared for him till that night.'

'And you can't settle?'

'Apparently not.'

Gaines looked out of the window. 'Midtown. We're coming up to my offices. I have to get to work; I've been away far too long.'

She lowered her head. 'I understand. Thanks again.'

'We have to talk some more. I need time to figure this all out. One thing I can say is that I don't think badly of you, Dina. You messed up, but you're amazing.' He pressed the button, and the window slid back. 'Carlos, I'm getting out here. Afterwards, take Ms Kane anywhere she wants to go, OK?'

'Yes, sir. Of course.'

Gaines opened the door; as he did so, he reached back and squeezed Dina's hand.

When she got home, Dina went straight to her bedroom. She peeled off her mourning clothes and changed into her running gear.

It was a warm, beautiful day outside, and she had nowhere to be. She started running; a couple of blocks west was Central Park and, two minutes inside the perimeter, it was like being in another world.

There was music in her headphones, but she paid no attention to the playlist. Her mind was on Joel Gaines, and his words, and how he'd held her hand. His forgiveness – could he forgive what she'd done to somebody else? – buoyed her, excited her. The depression was lifting, and it was spring, and there was a future.

She loved Joel. God, the relief of admitting that to herself – and to him! She loved him. She wanted to be with him, and nobody else but him. There would be no more Shelbys, no more Edwards or Ludos. Unless and until she fell out of love, Dina decided, she wasn't going to try and date anyone else.

With every step she pounded on the hard paths, every stride she ran under the canopy of trees, she felt lighter, better. Her heart would fix itself. Joel liked her; he'd kissed her. Even if he wasn't hers, that was something. She could try to be a better person, get some therapy, not see herself as the victim.

So she didn't like Susan Gaines – fine – but if Joel was happy in his marriage, Dina needed to back off. So she wouldn't marry; it wasn't the only thing in life, right?

What was the point of being into beauty, if you couldn't look at yourself in the mirror?

Her heart was racing, thumping. It felt good to run, to sweat, to be alive. This was her therapy, her confessional. Dina let her thoughts go, abandoned herself to the sheer joy of movement.

When she arrived back in her apartment, panting but content, everything seemed a lot clearer.

If she couldn't have Joel, it was time to focus on something else she loved.

Like business. And sticking it to Torch and Ludo Morgan.

And, as for Edward Johnson, she would figure that out later. He had as good as killed her Johnny. Did she deserve it? Johnny certainly didn't. But Dina had no thoughts of blood, of payback.

He hurt her. She hurt him. Johnny was dead. Where did that cycle end?

The most revenge she could have would be to succeed – to get rich, to live well, to make a mark – and not need a single man to do it.

Dina loved Joel. But she didn't want to *need* him, not anymore.

And she had the perfect idea for what to do next.

'I . . . It's certainly a very healthy balance sheet.'

The banker's name was Raul Benitez and he was fifty-eight years old. Not everybody got into his office. There were too many time-wasters out there. He made loans to small businesses on behalf of Luisitana Bank; they were a Brazilian outfit, trying to expand into North America, and they were minnows out here.

He was tasked with bread-and-butter banking: selling money to little guys who would repay it and spread the word. No giant financial punts, just a solid basis within the community.

Somewhere much, much higher up the tree, in Lima, his boss wanted to turn them into Santander. But they were starting here, at the bottom.

Benitez only saw business owners with a certain amount of assets, a plan and a proven track record. These were mostly men in their late thirties to mid fifties. He had lent to some female-owned shops, too: cafés, manicure salons, eyebrow places.

This girl was different. She was fifteen years younger than anybody else he had seen. She had no roots in the community; she wasn't Korean or Hispanic. She was beautiful, like a model, but disturbingly cold, and she had the strangest résumé he had ever seen.

But she had a plan. And she had some wealth – money in the bank, and a very nice apartment. And she was willing to risk it all.

'Torch is a very big name in retail right now.'

'Because of me,' Dina said.

He pushed his spectacles towards the end of his nose, raised bushy eyebrows. 'Is that a little bit of an exaggeration, perhaps, Señorita Kane?'

'No, it isn't. I revamped the beauty division. All their sales flow from that.'

'Then why were you fired?'

He saw people taking credit every day. She was less believable when she praised herself like this.

'Because the boss's son wanted to marry me, and I turned him down.'

Benitez looked at her.

She leaned towards him, over the desk.

'Does your wife shop at Torch, Señor Benitez?'

He nodded.

'I joined that store six months ago. Ask her when she started to shop there.'

'Very well.' He glanced down at her financial statement again. Everything was in place: all the bank statements, six months' expenses. 'You have very good security. For a million dollars, we will need to have a lien against the apartment.'

'I understand that. This is the way I want to launch. You only have that chance once.'

He licked dry lips. 'It would be by far the largest loan I have ever approved.'

'I picked your bank because you need a home run,' Dina told him. 'You are scraping by on these tiny loans. You need a star client, for the publicity. It could make you.'

'And a million-dollar loss could break us, too.'

'No chance of that. My apartment is worth much more to you.'

He sighed. 'I'll ask my wife. Somebody will call you this afternoon.'

'Very good.' She stood up and, somehow, in her silk blouse and modest skirt, she was more of a powerhouse than all the older, suited males he was used to. 'I'm in a hurry, Señor Benitez. I don't want to have to head down the road to Chase.'

Dina Kane let herself out of his office. But he had the feeling he would be seeing much more of her.

Benitez took his lunch out to the park. He liked it there, especially on these hot days Manhattan specialised in, which reminded him of home.

There was a great little place just by the Hudson, with a wide running track the joggers raced up and down all day long, and a green garden on one side, with a few fountains and benches. New York was very good at that, carving out green islands in the forest of glass and concrete. This was almost a sea garden, with hardy, silver-grey plants and grasses that could take the swell and spray from the great river, the blasting summer heat and the winter freeze and pounding winds.

There were a couple of benches he liked. He could think here. Nature found its way. And so did women, so did beauty.

As he wolfed his sandwich, he looked idly at the women racing down the track. Some were heavy, just starting out – good for them. Most of them, though, were in tight Lycra, neon sneakers, their hair caught back in ponytails. Now he took time to notice, almost all of them were made up – even to run.

It was huge, the market in America. Especially in this city. Manhattan was goddamned expensive. If you lived here, you had money – enough to buy all kinds of beauty products.

He called his wife. What the hell? She had been noticeably more attractive, less frumpy, since she'd started shopping at Torch.

'Cristina, it's me.'

'*Hola*, baby.'

'I have a strange question. When did you start going to that department store uptown? Do you remember?'

His wife paused. 'Maybe six months back. When that new girl

came in and revamped it. I heard from my girlfriends we should try it, and we all took a cab together.'

'That new girl?'

'Oh, there was this kid they hired. It was all over the blogs and magazines. Then you stopped hearing about her. Whatever; she did a marvellous job.'

'You have been looking wonderful lately. But then, you always did,' he lied.

In truth, Torch had transformed his wife; she'd got rid of the harsh blond hair dye, the layers of mascara and bright red cheeks. The new light stuff she wore on her face, the olives and brown shadows that picked out her eyes, and the gloss on her lips made her look years younger. She was wearing less and looking better, and he loved it. They were having more sex; it felt like they were closer than they'd been in years.

'Why do you ask, sweetie?'

'You won't believe it. The girl you were talking about – she was in my office this morning, asking for a loan.'

'Get out!' his wife said. 'Really?'

'She wants to start her own beauty store – with a website and big poster advertising.'

'Wonderful!' His wife seemed thrilled. 'Can't wait to go. You're approving the loan? Congratulations.'

'I haven't decided yet. It's a million dollars.'

'Oh, Raul. If you want to be the sucker who passes her up, go ahead. But, trust me on this – she knows just what she's doing.'

He leaned back against the bench. 'How can you be so sure? You've never even met her.'

Cristina laughed. 'No, honey, I *wear* her.'

He blew her a kiss and hung up. Then he crumpled up his sandwich wrapper with the meal half-finished.

Break time was over. He wanted to do this deal, before somebody else got the chance. Time to gamble.

* * *

Her phone rang at ten to three exactly.

'Yes?'

'Your loan is approved, Señorita Kane. When can you sign the paperwork? We can set a date next week.'

'I'll be back in your office in twenty minutes.'

The ink was dry before close of business; Dina Kane had a new corporate account, and a million dollars was winging its way to her.

She worked from home. No point hiring an office, and she would need every red cent of that money. Nothing was going to be wasted.

First, the store: it could be small, but it had to be beautiful – and right in the heart of town. Nothing else would do.

But it was easier said than done.

Dina tried everything conventional. She registered with all the commercial brokers, listened as they tried to sell her snake oil, but flagship sites were far too much, charging rents that would have eaten up her loan in two months.

'Well, you want the centre of town? That's what it costs,' said Roxie, a broker, standing in the middle of a small vacant space on Fifty-Third and Lex.

'This is the third business to shut here in two years. There just isn't the foot traffic. Won't the landlord consider a lower rent?' Dina pleaded.

'Honey, one tenant fails, another takes his place. This is Manhattan. He wants what he wants.' Roxie shrugged. 'Look, with your budget, I would suggest Harlem. Or Brooklyn. Or maybe something industrial, like off Tenth Avenue, or First—'

'I'm selling make-up,' Dina said.

'Sephora sells make-up – on Fifth Avenue. South of Saks.' Roxie sniffed. 'I wish you luck, honey, but you ain't Sephora.'

After two months wearing out her shoe leather, Dina was truly desperate. Nothing would happen without an anchor store.

Maybe the landlords were all correct; maybe she should go someplace cheaper. She travelled out to Brooklyn and looked at Cobble Hill and Prospect Park; she went to the outer streets in Manhattan, off the beaten track, looked at places in Chinatown, a former pawnshop near the jewellery district. Some of those spaces were bigger, cleaner, but they were also in Siberia, as far as she was concerned. And the ones in town were in the wrong area.

Yes, dammit – she wanted to be Sephora. But she didn't have any of the money, or the connections, or the corporate clout that it took.

Sometimes, after a full day's hunting for a retail space, Dina was so frustrated she felt like crying.

Maybe she should give it up. Perhaps online was the way to go.

But there were a billion online sites for make-up and skin care. Dina thought of the Green Apothecary, of Meadow, of turning Torch around. She was convinced in her bones that a store – a real place, a home – had to come first, and it had to be right there, in the news, where she wanted to be. This was the first time Dina had ever worked for herself, and she was a hell of a demanding boss.

It has to be big. It has to be perfect.

At night, she would fall asleep and dream of a flagship store, a landmark, a palace of light and digital displays. Nothing she could achieve – not yet; not for years. But, in the mornings, there was always another meeting with another realtor; another boarded-up shop in another scummy area, off the beaten track.

'You don't want much, do you, Ms Kane?'

Gunther Fassbaum was losing patience with Dina. He'd shown her ten stores already within her modest budget. At first, she seemed the real deal: an ambitious young comer with bank backing; an entrepreneur in a hurry. But he was starting to think she was just wasting his time.

'Centre-town premises, long lease, five to ten per cent rises, and you don't have much to start with in the first place. Maybe we're not the right agency for you.'

'But I can move fast.' Dina looked around the former boutique, another own-label clothes store on Lexington Avenue – too quiet, too old money. This place had been a vanity project; people saw Dina Kane Cosmetics the same way. 'And I don't need it to come with bells and whistles. I can fix up a scruffy place myself. I just want the right terms and the right location.'

'But you don't want to pay the right price.'

'It doesn't even have to be big. I'm not looking for a lot of square footage here, Mr Fassbaum. I'd take a small boutique in the right spot, any day.'

He stared. 'Miss, for you, the right spot is Times Square. I don't mean to be rude, but I've shown you some genuine bargains and you're still not satisfied.'

Dina's eyes widened. She took a step backwards.

'Are you OK?'

'I'm fine. Fine.' She tugged at her jacket. 'Look, bear with me, Mr Fassbaum. I appreciate you showing me this space. I . . . I'm going to do some more research and come right back to you. I hope that's all right.'

'It's quite all right,' Fassbaum said, to her departing back. Then he pulled out his Blackberry and erased Dina Kane from his contact list.

Goddamn time waster. He felt like an idiot.

Dina ran to the subway and got on the express to Times Square. She felt her heart beating, her pulse racing.

For you, the right spot is Times Square.

Of course it was. The centre of Manhattan: the neon skyscrapers, the moving advertisements, the giant billboards and stock tickers – the beating heart of the richest, most powerful, most *beautiful* city in the world. Was that nuts? Billboards here cost two hundred thousand dollars a month, and that was just for the signage, before you spent one cent on electric screens. She could hardly afford market rent for a goddamn storefront.

And yet . . . And yet . . . Times Square: it was her home, it had to be, it just had to be. The train slid into the station and she rushed out, joining the throng of tourists and commuters, all that foot traffic, the most you could imagine. Here was the heart of everything, and of Dina Kane.

She walked around the square. It wasn't, of course – wasn't square. A sort of diamond-shaped space, everything that looked directly on to it counted: Paramount Pictures, Toys 'R' Us and ABC's flagship studio building. But Dina wasn't disheartened; she looked elsewhere – at the other subway stations, how people came here, where they travelled. Broadway was reserved for the fancy shows, but Seventh Avenue had a couple of diners . . . office buildings . . . and a subway station, right there. And, as Dina looked around, the answer was staring her in the face.

If 'staring' was the right word. Perhaps 'poking' was more accurate. There, right in front of her, was a silhouette of a bare-breasted woman with cartoonishly erect nipples. It was just a little store frontage, all black, with a faded red carpet and a sign, calling it a *Gentleman's Establishment*, inviting her to come downstairs.

Dina watched that entrance for twenty minutes straight. Not a single customer. This was an eyesore – a remnant from Times Square's sleazy past. It had to be rent controlled, and there was no doubt in her mind that the city would love to lose it.

She picked up the phone and called Fassbaum.

'What do you want?'

'I think I might have found somewhere. On Seventh Avenue. A strip club.'

'Why would the tenant want to give his business up?'

That was what she didn't know just yet, but she was determined to find a reason. 'Maybe I can make him a better offer. Can you run the address and see who rents the space?'

There was a heavy sigh. 'I'm busy.'

'Just for doing a few searches, I'll buy you a coffee and give you two thousand dollars in cash. Not the firm's commission – just your cash.'

There was a pause. 'I'll come back to you.'

Within ten minutes, her phone rang again. 'Find another strip club. This one's a non-starter.'

'Why? Who's got it?'

A beat. 'Some people from Westchester.'

'Westchester?' Dina repeated. Why would suburban hicks want a strip joint in Times Square?

And then it dawned on her. 'What kind of people? Italian people?'

'Do your own research. And keep your goddamned coffee.'

Dina hung up, ecstatic. She knew exactly who Fassbaum meant. What a blast from the past! She hailed a cab, heading home to do just that – work on her computer; do her research. She would need it for the presentation she would make tomorrow.

At nine a.m. precisely the next morning, Dina put her laptop in its carry case, headed out of her building and walked towards the nearest subway. She would go to Grand Central and work on the way. There was no time to waste. This company needed to launch within the month.

And that meant taking risks.

Chapter Seventeen

'There is a girl at the gatehouse, Don Angelo, asking for admittance.'

The mafioso looked up at his valet. This kind of thing was unusual, these days. His wife and children had long since been moved to a mansion outside of Bronxville, where they enjoyed the local schools and suburban life. He wanted to head into the city, but there was too much business in Westchester. Leaders who took their eyes off the ball wound up ousted, and that usually meant dead.

It wasn't machine-gun drive-bys outside steak houses anymore, either. Law enforcement was far too good for that. When somebody got whacked, it was far more subtle, more terrifying. Bad medicine. A heart attack. Yachting accident. The boys were getting smart.

Angelo had plans, and was executing them. As much of the junk stuff as possible, he was selling off, dumping, losing. Discipline was necessary amongst the soldiers; made men knew to keep their mouths shut, even amongst themselves. He was experimenting with online gambling, where the big money was made. The older, bloodthirsty types were pensioned off – buy them waterfront condos in Florida, mansions in La Jolla, even estates in Tuscany, in the old country – divide and rule.

Things were changing, and he liked it that way.

But there were privileges he wanted to keep. Business-men were afraid of him, afraid to say no. That mattered. He'd wiped guys out, didn't give a fuck about that. And girls never refused him, either. They opened their legs the way developers opened their wallets.

But he called for them, not the other way round. He didn't like pieces of ass turning up without appointments. They whined for favours, money, help. Some of the girls dared to think they could have a relationship. He wasn't like other men, though; they were warned off, and it usually only took one go. A friend paid them a visit, had a word. After that, the girl kept her mouth shut.

He enjoyed that – the basics – power, pussy, the fear he inspired in other men. Even while he legitimised, he kept all those things good and close. Besides, the boys expected it of a Don. They were all taking chances; that was the life.

'Which one?'

'None of the regular girls. Says you've seen her before. A beauty, though.' Tony kissed his fingers. 'Maybe twenty-four; a great-looking lay. She says she wants to do business. We can find some business for her . . .'

'Name?'

'Diana something. Diana Kane. Something like that.'

Don Angelo shook his head a little. 'That name rings a bell. Send her into the office.'

'You want company?'

'I think I can handle a twenty-four-year-old, Tony.'

'OK, boss.' His consigliere made a face. The killers came younger these days, and never like you'd expect. What if the girl had a needle? A pill? Angelo was his responsibility; anything happened to him, Tony was in trouble. And he had a wife and two daughters at home – they needed their dad – and the *famiglia* was unforgiving when it came to a *capo*. Which this urbane son of a bitch still was.

322

He pressed a button on the phone. 'Send her to the house. She can be shown to the office.'

They waited. A minute later, the girl arrived. Tony smacked his lips again. *Hell, what a great ass on that chick. A beauty – real classy.* He would put her rate at thousands an hour; a girl for high rollers on Wall Street. She was wearing demure clothes, which made her even sexier: a knee-length sweaterdress in cream cashmere and light brown flats. Her legs were bare, tanned, and her hair was twisted on top of her head in a bun. She had green eyes, and she carried a cute chestnut leather bag and, incongruously, a laptop in a case.

The computer would have run through the scanner. They put one in last year – same standard as you had in courthouses and public schools. Don Angelo took no chances.

'Do I know you?' Angelo said.

He lifted a finger, and Tony reluctantly took himself out of the room. He would hover outside, and that was OK. Angelo didn't think the girl was here to fuck, although he toyed with the idea of making her do just that. She certainly was gorgeous.

But not a hooker. You could go as high-end as you liked – and the fresh-faced girls always came the most expensive – there was always some desperation behind that pretty smile, some stress from alcohol and drugs and self-loathing. There was none of that in this girl's features. She wasn't in the life. And that made him more curious.

'You saw me once before, Don Angelo. Do you remember?'

'I see lots of people.' But then he did remember, and he started with surprise. 'Wait – you're the daughter . . . That guy on one of my crews.'

'Paul Kane. Yes.'

'You had a problem with your mother. I fixed it.'

'Yes, sir, you did. Thank you, Don Angelo.'

He liked that, liked it a lot. It was sexy, hearing the girl call him *sir*, the submission laced into it. He started to feel aroused.

She should be careful what she was playing with. She was older now, fair game.

'I know the men that knew my father were grateful you respected one of your own,' Dina said, like she could read his mind.

Boom! The start of a hard-on shrivelled right up again. Angelo almost laughed, she was playing the game so well.

'Nicely done.'

'Excuse me, sir?'

'You understand me. Don't waste my time, pretty girl, I'm a lot busier than you are.'

She smiled, ducking her head in acknowledgement, and he almost liked her for it. His was a pretty segregated society; he didn't have women friends, didn't mix with them outside of church and parties. This was something new, and he was kind of enjoying it.

'I would like to do some business with you, Don Angelo. Just something small.'

He pushed back his chair. His office was wood-panelled, filled with old leather-bound books he'd never read and Roman antiques his wife liked to shop for. The computer and phones were the only concessions to modernity. There were none to femininity.

'You have no business with me, girl. You understand, you are lucky to be Paul Kane's daughter. You're alone and you're tempting. Try not to be so stupid. Clearly, you're not Italian.'

Now Dina laughed. 'No. Irish. My father never got made, never got close. Anyway, don't be so sure about what business I do or don't have, Don Angelo. Things changed for me after I came to see you.'

'Unless you won the lottery, honey, they didn't change enough.'

'I moved to the city, launched a face cream, sold my share for half a million dollars. I bought and sold a few apartments. I ran the beauty department at a big department store.' Don Angelo settled back in his chair; she now had his full attention. 'They fired me after six months, even though I turned their shitty store around, because I refused the owner's son when he proposed marriage.'

'Why did you do that?'

'Didn't love him.'

Angelo chuckled. 'How old fashioned! Go on.'

'There's a noncompetition clause in my contract, so I can't take another job in the industry. Instead, I'm starting my own business. I'll be great at it; it's what I know.'

'And you've come back to me for funds.'

'No, sir. I've got the money.'

Dina Kane had surprised him for the third time that day.

'You don't want money?'

'You have a strip club operating out of a dark half-store in Times Square, just north of the main drag, and right by the Seventh Avenue subway.'

'It's a gentleman's club. It's legal, honey.'

'It might be legal, Don Angelo, but it's attracting attention. Women are starting to picket it. There's a city councillor trying to make a case out of it: flagship city icon, that kind of thing. You don't want a politician on the make crawling over your business, talking to the IRS.'

She had a point. This was simmering in the background; nothing much had happened lately, but it was a problem. He was looking to get out of strip joints altogether. They were too sleazy, too obvious. Money these days was in garbage collection, and construction, still.

'And you want the space?'

'I can't afford to pay market. But how about you lease it to me for six months? Three hundred thousand, with an option to buy the space after that – mid-point between our two appraisals. Reasonable appraisals.'

'Three hundred thousand? Don't be a comedian, honey. This is Times Square real estate. I can sell that lease to anyone.'

'Yes, but it's a small, ground-level piece of Times Square – mostly basement. Yes, you can sell, but it will take you another six months to find a kosher buyer, and they'll do inspections and all that crap. Lease it to me, and I will have the painters in there tomorrow. It's done, and your headache is taken care of.'

'You're too far under market.'

'Three hundred thousand for three months, then. By that time, I'll know if it's working. Beauty is a fast business, Don Angelo. You hit or you don't.' She laughed. 'No pun intended.'

He grinned, openly. She'd done it; she had won him over. She wanted the space – a prime-location dump – and she would take it without questions.

It didn't occur to him to challenge whether or not she had the cash. She obviously did; there was just that confidence about her.

'I want it all upfront,' he said.

Dina sighed. That was a huge chunk of her capital. 'Very well – if you agree to the right-to-purchase clause. I can make money out of this space; but, the thing is, Don Angelo, you can't. It's just too visible – which is why I want it.'

'How much money did you raise, kid?'

She hesitated. If she told him, would he ask for more?

'A million dollars.'

Screw it. You didn't lie to the Mafia. Not ever. No disrespect.

He lifted an eyebrow. 'No shit? Maybe you are Italian, after all.'

'I can email you a rent-to-buy agreement tonight, Don Angelo, and wire the money to any account you want.'

'Hold your horses,' he said, slowly. This girl was interesting, very interesting. She was a comer, and he was now taking inventory of her perfect make-up, her chic dress. She came from a shit-hole in Westchester and had made it, or close to, within a couple of years. *I can make money out of this space.* Yeah, he bet she could – many millions. And he wanted some. 'I'll give you the purchase clause, at your own appraisal price. But I want in. Five per cent.'

Dina Kane sat bolt upright. 'No deal.'

'What? You're saying no deal?'

'I won't give you five per cent. I won't give you any per cent.'

Angelo frowned. 'Don't fuck with me. You will give me what I tell you to give me. Be glad I don't make it ten.'

'I'm serious. This company is clean. I want to buy something from you at a fair price. My offer is speed, no questions. I don't want you looking down my neck for the next twenty years.'

'This isn't the old days. You've been watching too many films. Nobody's going to come round demanding protection money every month. I want in to a legitimate business. And I have the store you need.'

Dina shook her head. 'Sir, you don't understand. I wouldn't partner with you. I wouldn't partner with *anybody*. Dina Kane is my name, my company. Nobody touches it.'

'And you're willing to give up Times Square?'

She pulled her shoulders back. 'If I have to.'

Angelo relaxed against the soft leather of his chair again. 'Aren't you afraid of me?'

'No. You don't go after people on a whim. Besides, I don't have much to lose. No family. No husband.' Dina shrugged. 'This is what I want, my way or not at all.'

He shook his head. 'You're in the wrong business, kid. You should come and work for me. No – don't say anything – it was a joke. You can email me the contract.'

She breathed out. 'Thank you, Don Angelo. I won't forget it.'

He didn't laugh at this, as he would have from some other kid. Dina Kane might be Governor some day.

She got up to leave. 'You know, last time I came to see you, the goons in your gatehouse made me spread my legs and they patted me down, felt me up.'

His face was expressionless. 'They do that again this time?'

'I told them that, if they touched me, I would make sure you killed them.'

Angelo smiled. 'You should have been a man.'

Dina rode the train home, full of hope. Her computer was on her lap, and she tapped away on it, oblivious of the angry stares of other passengers trying to enjoy their magazines.

She was working.

She knew a handful of good lawyers already – guys she'd worked with at Torch – and one of them was now drawing up a simple rent-to-buy contract, which would be with her in an hour.

She was writing down her products – the stock she would carry in order to give the perfect combination of space, luxury and choice. Not too much choice. Big names might not work with her. That was OK. Dina Kane, Inc. would supply a new vision in cosmetics: incredible beauty that worked. Stuff you couldn't get anyplace else.

The transformation of that space would be a piece of cake. She wouldn't replicate Torch – they might sue. Besides, the bar was filthy and gloomy, with no natural light. She had a vision, and four apartments had taught her how to realise it.

On her screen, the vision started to take shape: golds, creams, clear lighting; staff in chic uniforms of fitted shift dresses or dark suits. Dina Kane would be a one-stop shop, with everything in it irresistible. She would cherry pick the best products, lay them all out, offer more free samples than anyone else and source the most gorgeous accessories. There would be a small men's grooming department, themed to remind customers of James Bond: photos of muscled men in Savile Row suits, Floris aftershave, real badger-hair shaving brushes and solid gold cuff-links. Goddamn, it was exciting. She wanted the place to scream *luxury*; and, more than that, *vacation*. To buy a lip gloss at Dina Kane would be like stepping into another world. There would be beautiful shopping bags and pale green and gold ribbon for women's purchases, thick gunmetal for the guys . . .

The billboard: she would buy the space, design it herself. The cheapest agency in town could put it together – Dina would control the image. She knew exactly when to put it up, when to launch, how to sell.

Electricity crackled through her veins. By the time she stepped out of the train at Grand Central, she was almost running, her cellphone fixed to her ear.

The space was ready for her by lunchtime the next day. Angelo could move fast, too. All of the strippers had left; the cheap, wine-stained tables and chairs had been cleared away; the scummy patrons had gone. Signs were still up in the window: a sad Martini glass in neon light tubing, with a nude girl's silhouette poking up from it, her breasts like olives on a cocktail stick.

That was OK. That was fine. Dina breathed deeply, taking in the scent of old beer, desperation, sweat and darkness. It was heady perfume. This scumminess was the reason she'd pulled off the deal.

'You know . . . it is what it is.' The caretaker was a jaded old guy, who had seen tenants come and go. 'The girls perform and the men pay.'

Bare electric bulbs revealed the squalor: peeling paint, mould in the ceiling corners, ripped up linoleum on the floor. There was a dirty glass booth where girls had squirmed and humiliated themselves for drunk men at two in the afternoon. Behind a faded red velvet curtain, fringed with red tassels, was a hideous enclave of glitz: wide red banquettes, cushioned to hold two people; fake plastic marble on the floor; low-light electric torches on the walls. Dina shoved from her mind the humiliations that must have happened here, the dirt and the sex and the hatred and the sale of flesh.

She looked, and, as the caretaker coughed his embarrassment behind her, a warm smile broke across Dina's face.

'I love it,' she said. 'It's perfect.'

'Lady, you're crazy,' he said.

'My guys will be in tomorrow. And so will I.'

The old man shrugged. She wanted this shit-hole, she could surely have it.

Dina worked. She set her alarm for five a.m. and went running, pounding along the streets of Manhattan while it was still dark. There were others with her, of course – the bankers, the lawyers – all those high-powered men and women who needed to start early. Dina loved it, the excitement of the city that never sleeps crackling under her feet.

She wasn't even tired. She was full of adrenaline.

The music pumped in her headphones, but she was paying no attention. Already, her mind was running on Dina Kane, Inc. The name was registered, the company incorporated, she had a blank website – it made it seem real. There was a bank account and she could hire staff, source products, get deep into it.

Within a month, she wanted to have something to show Joel Gaines. Not to ask for his help – never again – just to show him.

And it needed to be under the radar – a surprise – so Ludo Morgan, Edward Johnson, none of those bastards could come after her.

The first person she had to call was Piotr Ilyich. His crew knew her, had renovated her last three apartments. They were cheap, hard working and preferred cash. Besides, they liked a client who paid up and gave directions.

She never wasted Piotr's time on materials or finishes. Dina always knew exactly what she wanted.

The run was over. She headed back inside, showered, dressed and blow-dried her hair. A simple sweater dress, flats and her best make-up – Dina was a walking billboard.

She called Piotr. It was half six now; he would be up.

'Dina!'

'It's your favourite client.'

'I would say it's a bit early, but it's you. Moved house again?'

'Better than that. It's an office, mostly underground, needs a full gut job, an architect and a plumber.'

He sighed. 'I would – for you – but we are about to start a job uptown. An old lady's penthouse, on Eightieth Street. Big money.'

'Put her off. Say you need another permit. This is only going to take you a month, and there's two hundred thousand in it. Small space; tricky.'

He whistled. 'Two hundred thousand?'

'To include an architect – three days' work. I know what I want; he can draw up plans for it.'

'And where is this amazing office you intend to waste so much cash on?'

'Times Square. It won't be a waste; it's the start of my empire.'

He laughed. 'I think I believe you.'

'You know a good architect? He has to be good.'

Two hours later, they were at the site. Piotr came with Arek, the chief of his workmen, and a young woman, skinny with lanky, mousy hair, thick glasses and sallow skin. She was in her early thirties; older than Dina and, judging by the clothes, poorer.

'Hi. I'm Dina.' She looked at the girl. 'You work for Arek?'

'Natalya,' the woman said, shaking hands. She looked over at Piotr.

'Natalya is our architect.'

Dina bridled.

'She fled from Russia, where she worked at one of the top

firms. She was a star designer; helped with Naberezhnaya Tower in Moscow.'

'Why did you leave?'

'Husband,' the woman said.

'Natalya has little English. Her former husband is well connected to one of the oligarch families. He beat her and, when she left, she did not want to stay there. Now she has come here as a student.'

'She's legal?'

'She came on a nanny visa. Works all hours for a rich family on the Upper West Side. They treat her like a slave, but at least she has a sponsor. Four children and a house to clean. She cleans like maid, cooks like servant, but she has an advanced degree, a good career.'

'How is she here?'

'The family is on vacation. They don't want to pay for the extra air ticket. She's good, understands structure.'

Dina looked carefully from man to woman. 'What is in this for you, Piotr?'

'Natalya is my second cousin's daughter.' He shrugged. 'In Russia, we take family very seriously.'

'Translate,' Dina said. 'If she does this well, I will help her. No more housekeeping.'

Piotr spoke quickly to Natalya, and her eyes lit up.

'I want the office waterproofed. The whole place must be wired for internet and LED throughout. Spots in the ceiling and walls. Backlighting. Bulbs must be natural daylight, and we want climate control. Solid glass steps here. I want light wells drilled in from the ceiling, to bring natural light into the space, maybe tunnelled from the walls. The look is to be that of an urban garden. Air-hanging plants, ferns, a small rockery – greenery everywhere. In the back, I want a perpetual fountain, and tiny, luminescent fish swimming in a rock pool. There will be mirrors on every shelf, lit with smaller daylight bulbs, so that girls can make up.'

Piotr was talking as fast as he could. Natalya nodded.

'Every surface will be light, so that the space seems more open: glass, blond wood, cream and caramel marble, with specks of greenery and warm sandy pebbles. When a woman walks out of the chaos of Times Square – even in winter – I want this to be warm, moist, calming, soothing. She breathes out; she relaxes.'

'*Da*.' Natalya looked around, and Dina could tell her eyes were cataloguing the dimensions.

'Make sure the design is expandable. There's a Hooter's restaurant right above us; I'm going to want to buy that too.'

Piotr shook his head. 'You steal our strip clubs; now Hooter's too? Typical woman.'

Dina ignored him. 'Here are the materials I want. I brought samples – left over from my own apartments.'

She unzipped the heavy canvas bag she'd brought with her and laid out samples – chips of golden brown marble, blond Swedish wood, a hunk of sparkling, tempered glass, some mirrors, white limestone . . .

Natalya looked up at her. Her dull skin was already luminous; her face was bright with excitement. She nodded eagerly and spoke in a peal of Russian, words tumbling out of her.

'She says she understand very well, your vision. It will look beautiful. She says you bring California to New York – water and desert. She want you to know most important is electrics and water. Then light wells. She will give you drawings. We can make it.'

Dina smiled slightly, and the older girl nodded eagerly and clasped her hand.

'She says you very alike. You will see what Russia can do. She already create in extreme environment. You make this extreme beauty.'

'Extreme beauty,' Dina said, softly, rolling the words on her tongue. '*Extreme beauty*. I love it.'

'I do not understand,' Piotr said.

'Pay her. She will need your men to start today; she can tell them what to do as she draws. I don't have a minute to lose. The plumbers and electricians should be here right away.'

'Very good.' He had learned not to argue.

'And, Piotr, one other thing. I will give you extra money; hire a tutor for Natalya. Have him here, round the clock. I want her to learn English. We can work together.'

He spoke to the young woman, and she nodded, again, harder.

'I am intelligent. I learn English,' she said. 'Learn fast. Make building.'

'She's exactly what I need. Tell her I will be talking to an immigration lawyer. And I want her to have the basic drawings for the conversion ready in one month.'

Natalya reached out and grabbed Dina's hand. 'Boss,' she said. 'Boss.'

The days went by, dementedly. Dina sunk herself into it. There was the website, which she needed to be better, cooler, than anything else on the web. She hired some kids from NYU, and showed them her brilliant ideas.

'First, it needs to be easy to pay.'

They all sat there, in a cramped little room in the Times Square space, trying to block out the sound of the drilling and hammers.

'What was this place?' Damian Black, web guru, had thick glasses, skinny jeans and Converse trainers. He didn't see a lot of sun, but the dense, narrow darkness they were plunged into was something else.

'A strip club. This was the cloakroom,' Dina Kane said, matter of factly.

'I see.' They were sitting round a long, narrow table, made completely of Perspex, with laptops and a huge router plugged into the wall. 'What's it going to be next?'

The alcove was barely four paces wide, and the table took up most of it. Plunging, slippery black stairs led down to the hole where the men were working.

'You can't even fit customers in here. It's a useless space.'

Dina smiled tightly. 'Nothing's useless. This will be a giant wall of high-res screens, projecting our slogan and showing clips of ordinary women, their faces being made over with the products we stock. You won't see the hands of the make-up artist, just beauty appearing on the skin. Different women – all ages, all races – and, beside them, popping up in bubbles, some of the products we use.'

There was a moment's silence.

'Goddamn,' Damian said. 'That's fucking cool.'

'There will be men in there, too – groomed, shaved – looking sharp, like James Bond. We have a male section.'

'What's the slogan?'

Damian's partner was Cliff Green. He was just as brilliant, maybe a little more of a businessman. And this girl had his antenna up.

'Dina Kane – Extreme Beauty.'

He exhaled. 'I fucking love it.'

'It's perfect for New York,' Damian said.

'And building my site is going to get you guys where you want to go, believe me. I don't have the cash to go hiring the blue-chip firms, those tired old bastards with fancy offices. My architect is a Russian refugee. My first store is a basement strip club. You guys are students. But, together, we are going to build an empire.'

It could have sounded hokey, in the tiny dark room with the drills and the plastic table, but the young men were drinking in her every word.

'Everybody on this team is making their name. You're about to debut the smoothest site since Net-A-Porter. Since Sephora. You got it?'

'Shit. We're taking notes.'

'So –' Dina rose up and started to wave her hands, like she was literally building castles in the air – 'this website is the business. The store is going to be amazing – and there will be more stores, bigger stores – but the website is where we make our money. Chanel doesn't make money through ten-thousand-dollar suit jackets; it makes money through No. 5 sold in every airport concession in America.'

'Right.'

'So let's start with the basics: it's so easy to pay. Customers can use PayPal. They only need to log in once, then they stay logged in for six months. Credit cards are automatically retained, unless the opt-out box is selected. Password – six characters – anything you like. Understand?'

They nodded furiously.

'Next, Extreme Beauty is immersive. First, you organise the products by type. I'll give you the categories. Next, as soon as something pops up, I want videos of its application – just like the fashion sites show women walking in the clothes – consumers want it. We will have ten-second before-and-afters.'

'Yeah. Cool.'

'With every product, we add in partners. "Goes great with . . ." and two other things pop up. I will give you the list. There's also, "Best suited to . . ." and categories: blondes, African-Americans, oily skin, whatever.'

The boys were typing now, barely looking up from their screens.

'We want women to linger on this site – to play on it. Every image can be tacked to Pinterest – they all link back to us.'

'Great.'

'Search. You can search for product category, by your hair colour and type, by your skin colour and type, by new products, by most wanted, and the last category I'm doing is "Toys for Girls". That's like our personal recommendations. There will also be Extreme Style, the men's section, and gifts – stuff that works for everybody.'

'OK. OK. This is going to be a big site – lot of real estate; lot of usage.'

'I have the money. Animation must be smooth. Recommendations must fade in. I want you to think of this as the hottest make-up site you ever saw.'

'My girlfriend is going to freak,' Damian said.

'Dude, shut up. You don't have a girlfriend.'

'I will after this.' And he grinned.

'You can sign up and, after you spend a certain level, you become a VIP and get discounts, makeover vouchers and free samples.'

'OK.'

'There needs to be a community section. It'll be moderated; girls can send in photos of themselves using the products, offer their endorsements and suggestions. No reviews, though; I don't need spammers marking the stuff down. Everything on Dina Kane is going to be perfect – if it's properly used. Do you get it? Are you with me?'

They nodded furiously.

'This is more than a place to buy cosmetics. It's full of videos, bubbles, games, makeovers, enchantment. It's Aladdin's cave. It's immersive. You know, Net-A-Porter built a billion-dollar business selling purses that cost a thousand bucks. There are a lot more women out there who can buy a top-line lipstick at thirty dollars. You know why Net-A-Porter works? Because it's not work. They show the product on a woman. They video the product on a woman. You search by size and colour and they tell you what goes with it. Rich women are busy; they love it; it's like a personal shopper on their computer. Understand?'

They nodded. She could sell ice to Eskimos, and the two gamer freaks were suddenly all about the cult of mascara.

'So, you guys start. Send me links to the alpha pages. Use dummy items and prices.'

'Absolutely,' Damian said. 'Yes, Ms Kane.'

Dina smiled at that. She liked it.

The site was coming; the store was coming. The last piece of the puzzle was the billboard, but Dina wanted to wait on that. Everything would be exquisite, the way she'd wanted it for Torch – no, more gorgeous, better. She was doing things her own way, not limited by Ludo or other departments or anything else.

But it started and ended with quality. Perfection.

Dina would only sell the best. That meant cherry-picking from a range, just like the big stores did from the fashion collections. It meant limiting big, powerful companies, who wanted you to take their whole stock, including the stinkers. She had to curate it, do the customers' work.

Painstakingly, in between trips to the building site, conversations with Natalya in her halting English and meetings with the kids ploughing through her site, Dina Kane sunk herself into the world of beauty.

She tried to remember that wonder she'd first had with Hector at the Green Apothecary, when she was just a customer and everything he had was fusty and dust-covered and imported – but it *worked*.

As Dina toured stores, pored over make-up websites and underground beauty blogs, and scoured the magazines, she tried to forget everything she knew. In jeans and a T-shirt, she was just another girl with a pretty face. She went for free makeovers – everywhere except Torch; sat on little stools in Nordstrom and Bloomingdales, trying samples; took some days to spa at Bliss and Elizabeth Arden; wandered around Sephora and the boutiques in the West Village; she even studied the drugstore shelves.

What did women want? So much choice; so little time. It was all in the thrill of discovering a new wonder product, the thing you had to have – BB cream; Meadow; Great Lash mascara; Eight Hour cream; Chanel No. 5 – the blockbusters and their funky new cousins: Bobbi Brown's shimmer bricks; Urban Decay's nails . . .

Dina studied the executives swooping on the premier lines,

the younger women lingering, like kids in a candy store, trying several items, shopping as leisure. She listened to the chatter from the shopgirls making her up, followed the gossip on the websites. Everybody was looking for that new big thing. Minimalists, who wanted a small bag of reliable cosmetics; maximalists, fashionistas who loved to experiment; girls in the middle, who were just impulse buyers, influenced by the full-page ads in the women's magazines that week – there were so many types of girl, and Dina wanted to cater to them all, to own them all. Dina Kane was going to be different; taking herself back to that lover of beauty, that young girl . . . this was key.

The guys at the building site asked if she'd stopped working when she turned up with her shopping bags tied with pink ribbons, her face fresh from a makeover.

'I never stop working,' Dina said, and headed back out to the stores.

She tried to recall her first trip to Saks, her first muslin face cloth and Eve Lom cleanser, her first Bobbi Brown bronzer, the tight, bright Beauty Flash Balm by Clarins, Issima's Midnight Secret when she hadn't slept through the night. It was more than vanity; it was exciting – a thrill – to use her own face as a canvas, to be the artist. This was luxury she could afford.

Beauty was your best self. Beauty was armour; it was a weapon; it was a sign of great taste, grooming, elegance. Even a waitress could save up for that special Touche Éclat radiance and concealer. And then there was the joy of the drugstore find that beat all the boutiques – her Maybelline Great Lash mascara, which stayed on all night, didn't smudge, didn't run, beat her weary tears.

She was selling excitement. She was selling confidence. She was selling art. And everything for sale at Dina Kane had to be *great*. Just so goddamn good that a girl knew that *anything* she bought in the store, on the site, was quality. No fail.

She was asking American women to trust her taste. She was saying that this was important to women, and she could help.

Chapter Eighteen

She worked hard enough that every waking moment was spent sunk in Dina Kane. The visits to corporate headquarters were the worst.

'I'm sorry, Ms Kane, our brand has a stocking policy. It's the same for every store.'

'We like your ideas but we can hardly make an exception for a tiny premises in Manhattan.'

'If you take the primer, you have to take our Fashionista Mascara range. You can't just select.'

Dina sat in the offices of yet another cosmetics house and argued with a head of sales – fifty-five years old, with steel-grey hair and make-up free.

'Mrs Zagar, I assure you that being stocked at Dina Kane will be a mark of quality for every brand that works with us. Your best products will receive global attention. Their sales will shoot into a new stratosphere.'

'That's very nice, but they are bestsellers for a reason.'

'I don't want all your bestsellers. Some of them are no good.'

'Excuse me?' the older woman said.

Dina shrugged. 'Your Absolute Riches tinted moisturiser is chalky and your Forever Lips range dries hard on the mouth, leaving cracks. These are heavily supported by marketing, Mrs Zagar. The company didn't put any marketing behind the primer, and it sold by word of mouth. Appearance on the Dina Kane roster will *be* word of mouth.'

'Please, Ms Kane. I agreed to see you because we liked your work with Meadow. We hoped to offer you a job.'

'I have a noncompetition clause.'

'Well then I can't see what else we can do together.'

'I want you to license me to sell six products. I guarantee you that in one year those six products will make up a third of your revenue. You will be able to increase production, and drop from the manufacturing process those items not making you money.'

The girl's zeal was so all consuming that Mrs Zagar actually paused for a minute. On her computer screen, she tapped quietly, pulling up a list of the company's best and worst sellers. The marketing spend was beside each one. She noted that the primer had had hardly any.

Dina knew her stuff. Well, it was to be expected, with her background at Torch, learning from Ludo Morgan, who now had such a great reputation.

'What do you think are our worst sellers?'

She kicked herself for asking, for showing interest. Who cared what the girl thought? That was market confidential information she couldn't possibly have access to.

'Easy. Your Fashionista Mascaras, for one.'

Hannah Zagar jumped, but recollected herself. 'You guessed that because I told you it was part of the deal.'

'No, ma'am. I guessed that because the formulation is clumpy and the brush smudges. The colours are far too bright. Other worst sellers are your lip stains – again, the pigments are too bright. Your tinted moisturisers are being remaindered every-where because they're overpriced and chalky, and you're behind on the BB cream revolution. Your self-tanner comes out orange. Your whipped foundation is jar-packed; it oxidises right away when exposed to the air, and that means it goes too brown in about two weeks. Plus, your Tempting Trios in eye colour aren't tempting, because nobody goes for pops of colour on the lids – you're not selling T-shirts.'

Hannah Zagar glanced at her screen. The girl had called every one correctly.

'And the bestsellers?'

'Primer. Bronzers. Your cream peach blushes are translucent and unique on the market. If I might make a suggestion, you should rebrand them, and sell them as a double cheek and lip gloss. They can be dabbed on the lips, and last longer than regular gloss. Bronze cheek powders that work on eyes too are nothing new, but blusher for the lips is a good one.'

Hannah sat up, and looked at Dina very carefully.

'How did you come by this information? Have you had access to our servers?'

'No, ma'am. I just know make-up; I really know it.'

The head of sales chewed on her lip. Their company needed a break. Dina Kane was more correct than she knew; they had more misses than hits, and even clever advertising was not getting their products out of stores. They had good buy-in, but complaints from the boutiques that their lines were sitting on the shelves.

She had long argued they should cut the fat and just sell what worked. Now this young woman had penetrated deep to the heart of it, in a single meeting.

'How can you make the claim that being on your site will sell our products that way?'

'Because I only work with the best. Women will know they can trust Dina Kane for their cosmetics. It's the same way I got a reputation for Meadow – the same way I turned around Torch – only now there's nobody else holding me back.'

'And if I say no?'

'I still won't stock your other products. I'd rather sell fifty brilliant cosmetics than four hundred mediocre ones.'

Hannah Zagar considered it. 'I don't know, Ms Kane. It's

taking a great risk – even though I have found you very impressive.'

Dina said, impulsively, 'I can prove it to you, Mrs Zagar. I'll make you over, using nothing but Dina Kane, Inc. stock.'

She started. 'What? I'm not interested personally, Ms Kane. My younger days ended some time ago.'

'Allow me to try. Just as an experiment. You can wipe it off immediately afterwards.'

'You are joking.'

'Not at all. Women have to see it to believe it – cosmetics houses, too.'

Hannah Zagar resisted the impulse to steal a look at her reflection in the glass walls of the meeting room. She always dressed neatly, but she was in her early fifties. That was all there was to it – age was age. Right?

She laughed. 'I tell you what, Ms Kane. Come back here after lunch with a bag of your products. If you can turn me into a glamour girl, we'll take a chance on your store and your site. But don't hold your breath.'

Kane was cocky, confident, but a little too presumptuous. Hannah Zagar didn't mind that – she had been ambitious too, when she was younger. She would teach the girl not to overreach, and give her a valuable business lesson.

Her good deed for the day.

'How long is this going to take?'

Hannah's chair was away from the mirror. They had set up in a little-used bathroom on the top floor – she hardly wanted to make a spectacle of herself – which had a large window, as Dina had asked for natural light. She had returned with a disappointingly small make-up bag, the primer was the only product of theirs. Any fantasies Hannah was secretly harbouring about being transformed evaporated, but, then again, she had agreed to go through with this farce.

'I'll only need a few minutes. May I shape your eyebrows? It stings slightly, but it will look very good on you. I'll be using Perfection Tweezers, which we'll be stocking.'

Hannah sighed. 'OK. But get on with it. Really, I must get back to work. This was a mistake.'

Dina said nothing; she leaned in over the older woman with the tweezers, plucking and shaping. She moved very quickly, and Hannah waited, although she winced once or twice. There was no chatter. In a few moments, Dina was wiping something soft across her brows. She added a touch of primer, and then dusted some eye shadow lightly over the lids – one, two strokes of the brush, different shades. Dina worked across her whole face: eyes, cheeks, lips. Then, after just a few minutes, she stood back.

'That's it,' she said.

'That's it?' Kane had barely spent eight minutes on her face. 'You think this will make a difference?'

'Dina Kane stocks only the world's best products. Take a look for yourself, Mrs Zagar.'

The younger woman watched her expectantly, and Hannah reluctantly turned her chair around to face the bathroom mirror.

She gasped.

The face staring back at her was unrecognisable. Not younger – just better, so much better. Her skin was smoother, and the foundation on top of the primer gave her an elegant, even glow. Her pale cheeks had a light shimmer of bronzer on them, which brought out her high cheekbones; her eyebrows, thick and beetling, were lifted into elegant arches that widened her whole look. Her eyes, pale blue, suddenly popped in her face, with light brown shadow on the lids and a little chestnut on the creases. The shadows under her eyes had vanished, making her look lively and alert. She was wearing lip gloss – an attractive, natural peach – and it wasn't bleeding into the lines around her mouth, which was why she had given up wearing it. As she stared,

Hannah now remembered Dina dabbing powder there, and primer, and then two coats of gloss.

She breathed in, stunned. Taking in this version of herself.

'Primer – your primer – is very helpful on the mature face, but you still don't need much, just the right foundation, bronzer, powder and gloss. I would add mascara at night.'

'My husband won't believe it.' She wished the day was over already, so she could rush home and surprise him. 'I . . . It's incredible.'

'You could look even better if you dyed your hair to cover the grey and got a chic cut. I can recommend you a great salon for your type.'

'Really? Could you?' Hannah stopped herself – she was sounding like a teenager. But Dina Kane had transformed her, literally transformed her, in minutes.

'Of course. Can I have the primer? And my selection?'

'Ms Kane,' Hannah Zagar said, unable to look away from her reflection, 'you can have anything you want.'

Joel Gaines sat in his office, staring into space.

Below him was the great expanse of Manhattan. This view had always inspired him: the city, pulsing with life and money. Power ran through its crosswalks. This was where the great deals were done, where American fortunes were made. This was where he'd changed his life.

He had crushed the opposition. And when things at home were stressful, or boring, or frustrating, it didn't matter; he could come to the office.

Glass walls, installed custom by his architect, had been designed to mercilessly intimidate the guy on the other side of the desk. And for his own pleasure. He wanted to be looking down on it all, like a bird of prey in his eyrie – literally, at the pinnacle.

But today, he didn't see the view. He was just staring into nothingness.

Dina Kane. He could not forget her. Get over her. Get past her. She was the most remarkable, the bravest chick he'd ever met.

That scene in the cab, where she'd made her peace, said her goodbyes – it was too much emotion, too heavy for him. But still, he'd been expecting a call. A text. Something.

Dina Kane had vanished off the face of the earth. Nothing. It was like she'd never come into his life at all.

He worked and went home. The boys were at college. The younger one had come home that weekend, played some tennis. His wife swam and went to the beauty salon, attended a house party, threw a lunch for their friends. Gaines had sat around, unable even to socialise. When he looked at Susan, all dressed up, wearing her jewels and heavy make-up, talking to him about couples therapy and working on himself, he felt a suffocating depression.

But that was commitment, that was marriage. Why couldn't he deal with it?

His phone rang.

'Yes?'

'Sir, I wanted to remind you: you have therapy with Dr Fallon in fifteen minutes.'

Therapy. He was usually never late. It decompressed him, helped him relax, but he could not speak of Dina, and it seemed pointless right now, so pointless – talking about his life, instead of doing something about it.

'Cancel it.'

'Yes, sir.'

'Cancel all my meetings. I'm going home.'

There was a pause at the end of the line. 'But, sir, you have a partnership meeting on L'Audace. You have Goldman coming in on the Durant deal – their senior VP. And you're expected in the Mayor's box at the opera tonight, for the opening of *Der Rosenkavalier*. You accepted that invitation months ago . . .'

'Doesn't matter. I'm going home.'

'Are you sick, Mr Gaines?'

'I'm not sick. I hope you're not deaf.'

'No, sir. Very good, sir. I'll cancel your meetings.'

He walked to the executive elevator, the one that went directly down to the lobby, and below, to the garage. The shaft was designed for exactly that reason: so Gaines could get in and out, if he chose, without seeing another living soul. It was pure Master-of-the-Universe stuff, and today he was glad of it. He just had no desire at all to see his secretary's curious face right now, like he was a crossword puzzle she had to crack.

It was funny, he thought, as the elevator car whisked him down, down into the floodlit open space of their senior executive garage, that the one person he wanted to talk to about this was Dina Kane. But he couldn't talk to her.

Not yet.

Not till it was done.

'I think you should know about this, Mr Johnson.'

Edward sighed. He had just finished smoking a joint, a deep, mellow feeling was stealing over him, and he really didn't want any hassle from Lena just now. Bills, unfinished accounts: it was all from the past.

His mother was due back up from Florida tomorrow. He had persuaded her that staying in the townhouse – *his* townhouse – would be wrong. It was, after all, the site of her addictions. She would occupy his old apartment. In the end, he was going to persuade her to move out of state permanently.

There was no way he would allow her back to take what was his. His parents screwed things up; it was Edward's time now.

The stock portfolio was doing well, under the manager he had hired. He had a plan: to marry, and then sell either her house or his and buy a beachfront place in the Hamptons. That would rent out for a million a year, and there was his income for life. Edward had decided that work was – well – too much like work.

Women were the cause of all his problems; women could solve them. A rich spouse. It was one of the oldest transactions: his name for her cash.

He was already having some success. Back in the social circle, invited to all the parties, Edward Johnson was no longer a pariah. Crazy father? Drunken mother? So what? He had the house, and did you ever *see* such a perfect gem? There was private money. He was a trust fund, baby. He was a catch for some lucky girl.

Most of the best set wouldn't date him – the pretty blondes with the long limbs and white teeth, swinging their tennis rackets and setting their cap at the hedge-fund guys, the investment bankers. But that still left a lot of rich pickings. The ugly chicks, the girls who were overweight with the dull skin and disappointed eyes, they were there for the plucking. They were the nervous ones, the aggressively political girls – camouflaging the pain of not being wanted with activism and ideology.

Edward was careful. It wouldn't do to leave a trail of broken hearts. So he threw parties and dinners, and invited a good selection of the richest wallflowers from Wall Street – ugly chicks with great financial résumés. He was sociable, he didn't hit on them, taking his time to scope them out.

His plan now was to date just one, maybe two, if that didn't work out. He would be remiss if he didn't get some chick to the altar in three dating partners.

First, he had to ensure they really were solvent. Not just pretend rich, like him. Was there a solid trust fund in the girl's own name? Were her parents the kind of crazy liberals that left their money to foundations? Did she have her own house, income, stock portfolio? Were the parents achingly rich? Were there brothers and sisters? Who had she dated before?

It took time, and it was work Edward didn't want to contract out. If the slightest whisper got back to any of them, he was ruined. He investigated public records and gossip columns, chatted to friends about his own investments, drew them out . . .

Some wine, cigars for the men, moving on to a private smoking club where the scent of cigars, money and fine cognac all mingled together. By the end of a month of socialising, he had three women picked out, and had already dined with two of them alone.

The room came back into focus and he remembered Lena was in front of him, one of the only staff he had retained in the house: the cook. You couldn't get rid of a brilliant cook that worked cheaply. Edward liked his food, and there was something so *colonial* about having servants.

'Yes? What?'

He was filled with foreboding. What had she seen? What would she say to his mother? Perhaps he'd been stupid, keeping her around.

'It's on the computer.'

He stared at the older woman. 'I'm not going to the computer. What is it?'

'Well, sir, it's on one of the blogs. As Mrs Johnson is coming back . . . You wouldn't want her upset . . . I think there may be some publicity tomorrow about a *certain person*. Perhaps if you can get her to delay her return just one more week, it might be better.'

'A certain person? Is my father returning?'

'Oh. No, sir. Nothing like that.' Lena twisted her hands. 'It's just, you know, that awful young woman. Dina Kane.'

The shock hit Edward like a physical punch to the chest. 'What? What did you say?'

'Dina Kane, sir, if you remember.'

He remembered. 'But she was fired. Ruined. She can't work again. What are they saying on the fucking computer?'

Lena winced. 'Sir, please . . .'

Edward bit his lip. Rage was simmering, he could feel it, that old rage he thought had gone, it was just lying in his blood, waiting for a spark to ignite it. He felt dizzy, sick, like his careful world was shattering – shattering *again* – just as he was putting it back together.

'Tell me,' he hissed.

'That she's opening a store.'

'For Torch?' Had that jerk off, Ludo Morgan, taken her back?

'No, sir. Her own store, they say. And a website. It's happening tomorrow. All quite secret, but the blogs are leaking now.'

Edward Johnson stared. 'Lena, you read the beauty blogs?'

His cook was a mature woman, but she was slender and dark haired, somewhat elegant. He supposed he had never looked at her as a person before.

'I . . . Sometimes. Yes, sir. Sometimes.'

He took in her dress. It was dark and well cut, and her hair had a short, fashionable shape to it.

'And I read up on the news when that girl was fired, sir, and you were very pleased.'

'I hardly noticed,' snapped Edward.

'Oh. I'm sorry, sir. I suppose I thought you might. Never mind – my mistake.'

She made to move away. Edward forced down the bile, the impulse to grab her and shake her by the shoulders.

'Lena, wait! If you think it might upset Momma, I should like to know the details. I'll go and sit in the study. Can you email the piece to me?'

'Yes, sir. Of course. Can I go?'

He waved his hand and dismissed her. 'Yes. And I'll eat out tonight.'

'Very good, Mr Edward.'

The last thing he wanted right now was chatter with this woman: discussing Dina Kane . . . giving something away . . .

She scuttled off, and he forced himself to wait, to pour a large whiskey from the decanter into a cut-crystal glass, so that he was not rushing off to his office. He didn't want to give Lena clues.

This was important; he didn't yet know why, but it was important to him.

Dina Kane was off limits.

He sipped the whiskey, neat, feeling the alcohol burn against his tongue and his lips. He allowed the tang of it to slow his anger, make him stay there, to work through the spurt of rage. Agonisingly slowly, he drank one finger of the golden-brown spirit and it relaxed him a little.

Then, finally, he headed off to his study.

The computer was there before him. His email box was blinking with the link from Lena.

Edward clicked on it, sucking in his breath, and read.

Big launch tomorrow. Dina Kane vanished from the scene when she got fired by Torch – but now she's back in a big way. Dina has been doing more than just counting her savings in the piggy bank. She's opening an exclusive new boutique in Times Square, selling top-rated beauty finds. Dina Kane, Inc. is aiming to be the new Sephora, but Dina has added a new twist: the walls of her ultra-chic basement getaway sport scrolling videos of real women being made over by the products on sale. It's hypnotic – as is the underground oasis Kane and her architects have built. You won't believe how the tiny space, formerly a strip club, transports you to an underground jungle, serene with waterfalls, white woods and natural lights. But every inch is beautifully used, with fewer products on shelves than normal, yet each one a standout. Kane has found some of the best freelance make-up artists in the city, and samples are available with larger purchases. Her base range is high-end. We predict a riot – and that's before we even consider her stunning website.

The preview, which bloggers were shown, of DinaKane.com got most of us very excited! Expect a wider range of first-class beauty finds, brushes and accessories, and – more than that – a masterclass in Kane's natural look on every page. Just like a designer fashion site, she breaks new ground for make-up by including video tutorials with every item. That's right — see your Bobbi Brown Brick in Pink Quartz applied to the face, or an African-American model experimenting live with IMAN's BB Crème! DinaKane.com is too cute. And it suggests other 'pieces' you might want to go with your purchases . . . An Urban Decay eye shadow palette matches beautifully with a Chanel bronzer; do you need a Shu Uemura brow pencil with those Kevyn Aucoin brushes?

I don't like hype, here on Unfashionista, but I think we may just be seeing the next big name in beauty — and, in the next days and months, we'll find out!

Edward read the review twice, three times. There were pictures of some kind of spa with make-up in it, a hanging garden, a waterfall, bright daylight flooding a basement. It looked architectural, stunning, inviting — deeply rich.

Toys for girls — wealthy girls. He wanted to kill her. How the hell . . . ? How had this happened? With what money? It had barely been more than a few months. How did she get up this fucking fast? *Times Square*? His head was spinning. How had she found the stock? Wasn't there a clause? A fucking clause that stopped her working?

Dina Kane was supposed to be falling apart in a corner somewhere. He'd intended to finish the job, get her addicted, get her fucked up, just like her worthless brother, after he was done at home. Managing his mother and picking a girl — those were his priorities. Settling the money, the finance, the easy way.

Once he had a rock-solid prenup and title to the new wife's assets, Edward planned to go looking for Dina. The dead brother was meant to be a warm up.

He had to think. But the rage was rising inside him, rising into a frenzy. Impotent and enraged, Edward thumped at his desk.

The phone rang.

'Yes?' he barked.

'Edward? Oh, it's Janet . . . Is this a bad time?'

'Janet? Jesus! I'm busy!' One of his girlfriends. He tensed with annoyance.

'Oh. Oh, OK; I'm sorry to have bothered you.'

This was Janet – *his* Janet; if he worked hard enough, she was his ticket to comfort and fortune. What the hell was wrong with him?

'No, Janet, wait. Wait . . .' Panicking, he tried to force some calm into his voice. 'It's a fine time to talk, don't worry—'

'It's OK. I didn't expect to be shouted at.' Janet was teary down the phone, reproachful, exactly what he hated in women. 'We've only been out once, I mean . . .'

'Yes – absolutely. I didn't mean to snap; I'm sorry. Can I take you out tonight to apologise?'

There was a pause. 'I'm busy tonight.'

'Tomorrow night?' He kicked himself under the desk, now he was chasing, sounding desperate.

'I have a date with Peter Lucas tomorrow night. We can talk some other time – *maybe*,' she said, and hung up.

'Goddamn it!' Edward shrieked. He slammed down the phone and buried his head in his hands.

Peter Lucas was his rival; a poor but sleekly handsome young guy on a full scholarship to Columbia, he was invited to parties as a guest, getting a taste for the high life. He specialised in the rich, ugly chicks, although he dated around, not settling on any one of them. Edward knew he was after Janet, but hadn't worried. At least Edward had a good name, had his own townhouse, a presence on the Upper West Side. Lucas was some pretty schmuck from Brooklyn.

But he was soft-spoken. *Greedy, not pathological.*

Pathological. Edward had wondered – every now and then – in the days after he'd found out that Johnny Kane OD'd . . . But so fucking what? *If I'm pathological, Dina Kane made me so.*

354

He would watch the launch tomorrow. He didn't kid himself that it would fall flat.

Dina Kane was his disease. And Edward Johnson needed it cured.

Their home in the Hamptons was truly magnificent. He had spent many happy days here. And Susan had built up the estate, planning the garden, the tennis courts, looking after their boys and the dogs. Perhaps they were detached, but they had been a team.

The sprawling mansion reached out, through its Italian front garden with four interlinked saltwater pools, down to a stretch of private beach, one of the largest in Sagaponack. He would sit here with his phone and make calls, with the ocean crashing before him, feeling calmer, feeling the intensity of triumph at his success: a wife and children who would never want for anything; being able to afford any toy he chose – even his own jet, although he only kept a modest Gulfstream V.

Joel drove to the house. He didn't park the Lexus in the garage; he left it right in front of the front door, which was open slightly. Maria, his housekeeper, was dusting along the marble staircase.

'Where is she?' he said.

'Out in the garden, señor. I think she just finish tennis.'

'Very good. I need to talk to her privately. Tell the staff to give us some space, OK?'

Maria lifted a brow. 'Yes, Mr Gaines.'

She knew better than to ask her boss what he was doing. When Gaines spoke like that, nobody questioned him.

He waited there a little, as she scurried away, listening to the sound of workers quietly moving to the back wing of the house. And then he walked outside.

Susan was bending over some rose bushes with her secateurs. She always liked clipping fresh roses from the garden; they grew all kinds, a riot of colour, across the spectrum, with flowering

355

from May to August. Picking flowers was as close as she ever really got to getting involved, but it helped her to believe she had a green thumb. And, indeed, she had a good eye, telling the gardener what to plant, the cook what to make and the housekeepers how they should store Joel's things. She ran a tight ship at home and, as a chief of staff, he had no complaints; as a mom, she was fine.

It was just their marriage that was dead. As he breathed in, feeling the weight of pain across his chest, of what he was about to do, Joel Gaines suddenly understood that he had been aching for years. It wasn't just the sex, as routine and dull as that was, scratching an itch; it was the lack of adventure, of passion – for him, for life. They never argued politics. They never talked late into the night, not unless it was about the kids. He had friends, business deals, his sons: that was his life. Plus this lovely, comfortable home, which had become a prison.

'Susan,' he said.

She stood up straight, surprised. 'Honey! I wasn't expecting you till tonight. What happened? The office close early or something? Look –' she thrust a bouquet at him: pale green and cream roses – 'I thought these for your study. You like them?'

God almighty, but this hurts. He took the roses, laid them down on the grass.

'Susan, I have something to say to you. It's important. Can we sit down somewhere? Go inside?'

She blinked at his tone. 'What? Why? Are you sick?'

'I'm not sick. But we need to talk. Can you come into the study with me?'

Looking anxious, she followed him indoors, into his downstairs study. It had a window looking out on to the garden, but it was small and private, and he could close the door.

'Joel, you're scaring me.'

'Please sit, Susan.'

She did, on the burgundy love seat, and he faced her on the

hard English oak chair he used at his desk, turning it to look directly at her.

'We've lost our money?' Her face was grey with anxiety. 'Something at work? Oh, God, Joel, you're not into some kind of Bernie Madoff thing, or anything . . . ?'

'No. Nothing like that. Susan, there is no good way to say this, so I'll just come out with it. I want a divorce.'

She slumped. 'What? What did you say?'

'I want a divorce. I'm in love with someone else, and our marriage has been miserable for years now. We've been living separate lives – emotionally, at least.'

Tears sprang to her eyes, and that made Joel feel awful, sick. The powerful weapon of tears. He didn't love Susan; he couldn't spend the rest of his life with her. But having to hurt her was dreadful.

'What are you talking about? We're not *miserable*. We have two kids. We have a lovely life!'

'Our boys are grown, Susan. Yes, the *life* is lovely –' he gestured around the garden, warm in the sun, at the roses and the sea beyond – 'but *you're* not in love with me anymore. Are you?'

'I am!' she protested.

'You're not, Susan. You don't want me in bed; you don't ask me to come home and spend time with you. We live very beautifully, but we live separate lives. I work; you do . . . your thing – socially and otherwise.' He could hardly say, *Shopping, yoga, Pilates, visiting the salon.*

Her tearful face was hardening now – to anger. 'You said you're in love with someone else. You *cheated* on me? The mother of your children? How could you do that?'

Gaines didn't deny it. 'I'm sorry.'

There had been no sex, but there was intent. Flirtation. Bonding. Love, even. Could he say he hadn't cheated on her?

'What is her name?' Susan hissed. 'Tell me that bitch's name!'

He swallowed. 'Dina Kane.'

There was no point in hiding it; she would know soon enough.

Susan blinked. 'What? Dina Kane? That girl Ludo Morgan dumped? *The girl at the party?*'

'Yes. It was after that night that I fell in love with her.'

Susan looked around wildly. 'But, Joel . . . you can't do this. *We're* married. You made *vows* to me. We have kids. I've always been honest and faithful . . . and you're leaving me?' She was frowning with rage but not crying anymore; her face was red; she was screeching. 'It's just a mid-life crisis! You're an old man to her, an old man with money. Don't you get it? She's playing you for a fool. You can't throw away our *family* for this!'

'Susan –' he wanted to take her hand, to calm her down, but didn't dare – 'please. Dina didn't ask me to do this. She doesn't even know I'm doing it. I haven't spoken to her for weeks.'

'Don't defend that slut to me!'

'I want you to understand this is about us . . . first. For years now, we haven't had a real marriage. You reject me in bed.'

'Lies! I never turn you down.'

'And you never ask me, either. It was always a duty to you, Susan. Do you realise, in all these years together, you never once came to me and asked me to take you to bed?'

She flushed. 'I'm not built that way. It's up to you to lead . . .'

'Men want to be desired, just like women do. Susan, you don't ask me to come back home here unless there's an event, or a party. You never come down to Manhattan to spend time with me in the season.'

Susan Gaines bit her lip. 'But you never said you wanted it!'

'I need you to take the initiative, not simply act like a secretary that runs the Hamptons house. Look, we have wonderful children together, Susan, but once they were grown, you just weren't interested in me. I always thought you were a great mom. But I want a wife, a partner . . . More than this.'

'Well, you never complained to me.'

He winced; that was true.

'If you were unhappy, why didn't you say anything? What are you going to tell our children? *My* children?'

Joel sighed, long and deep. 'Yes. You're right. I should have said something. But I didn't know how much I missed being loved until I found a girl who really did love me.'

'Bullshit! You're going to throw away twenty years together for a gold-digger?'

'Susan, look me in the eyes. Are you in love with me? Do you love me?'

For a few seconds, he held his breath. If she said yes, she loved him, he couldn't really go through with it. Not yet. Not after twenty years. There would have to be counselling, and trying again, and what his sons deserved. He was afraid, fearful she would say yes. He loved Dina Kane, and he had finally done this, and now he wanted to pursue her, openly, and desperately. But if Susan said she loved him . . .

The moment hung in the air, and time seemed to slow down, to freeze.

Susan lifted her head and stared at him. There was a long, long pause, and then she crumpled, folding on the couch.

Joel felt the wave of relief crash over him, merciful obliteration.

'You think you'll get away with this?' She was flushed with anger now. 'Humiliating me like this, with some slut?'

'Dina's not a slut.'

'This is *my* house. She's never setting foot in here. I've been married to you for twenty years; don't think you're just going to give my home to her!'

'Be reasonable, Susan. We can work all that stuff out.'

But she was lost in her rage now, and nothing he said could change it.

'I want the money, you goddamned bastard! You owe me.'

'You'll get half of everything, Susan.' That much was easy. 'Including this house. I'm not going to cheat you.'

'You should give me more than half. You should give me all of it.'

He shook his head. 'The lawyers will do their thing. But I wanted you to know that you will get half of everything. I'm sorry, Susan.'

'I hate you!' she shrieked. 'Get out of my goddamned house!'

And Joel Gaines got up, left the study and walked out of the house, and out of his old life.

A day later, Joel Gaines was sitting on a weather-beaten green bench in JFK park in Cambridge, Massachusetts, gazing out at the river and trying not to look at the mutinous face of his son.

'So that's it, Dad? You can't be persuaded?'

'I'm sorry, Noah. We fell out of love. It happens.'

'When it happens, you guys are meant to work on it. Twenty years – that should mean something.'

'It does. I just . . . I can't be unhappy for the rest of my life, Noah. I'm sorry.'

'And you think this girl really loves you? You're a very rich man.'

'I know. She's different.'

'Family is supposed to be forever,' his son said. 'I don't want to meet her. I don't want to know.'

Joel breathed in. 'Noah, I love you and your brother very much. I always will. But you can't sentence me to a life of misery. You're an adult now, making your own decisions. I can't say if it'll work out between me and Dina, but I can say that, when I asked your mom if she loved me, she didn't say yes.'

'Have you spoken to Seth?'

'This morning.' His older son had shouted at him, railed, called him a moron; it was preferable to this quiet disappointment. 'He was mad, too. I'm sorry.'

'Not sorry enough.'

Joel squared his shoulders. 'Noah, I'm not yet fifty. You can't seriously think I owe it to my adult kids to continue in a loveless marriage.'

His son kicked at the gravel on the path, his head bowed.

'Maybe it's not loveless, Dad. Maybe she was hurt and that's why she didn't say it. It might be you needed to work things out.'

'That would just prolong the pain.' He blew out air, like he was lifting a heavy weight. 'I'll always be your father, and I'll always love you.'

There was a silence, a heavy beat that hit him in the gut like a fist.

'We love you too, Dad. But we have to be there for Mom right now.'

Noah reached across and gave him an awkward hug. Joel patted his son on the back, running his hands up and down his spine as he'd done when Noah was a baby.

'That's fine, buddy. You do everything you have to. I'm still going to be around.'

And he breathed out because, in the end, after this was all done, and the anger was spent, when Susan had her settlement and maybe another man, Joel believed it would be OK.

It was done; it was over.

He was in the car, driving mindlessly, glad of the monotony, back to the city, trying to let the task clear his mind. The pain was real, but so was the relief; those iron chains, the ones that had locked him down for the last ten years, were shattered, broken. He was a free man.

There was no question of what he would do next: go to his apartment; dump the car; call his business partner; call a lawyer. That was the housekeeping taken care of.

And then . . . Joel Gaines was going to find Dina Kane, wherever the hell she was, and tell her he loved her, and take her to bed. That was the only certain thing in his life, and the one thing he was holding on to.

Chapter Nineteen

Dina sat with Natalya in the bar of the Victrix. It was late. She never usually drank, but tonight they had a bottle of champagne between them: Cristal, the house brand of Manhattan's most luxurious hotel. They were drinking from cut-glass flutes, and she was finally relaxing.

It was over. Win or lose, she couldn't do any more. The money was mostly spent; there was just enough left for a month's expenses. She had a handful of staff: make-up artists she trusted; girls who could stand at a register and also socialise; there were the geeks running the website, and, now the store was built in record time, there was Natalya – a friend.

They had seen each other daily for weeks as the underground club transformed from sweat-soaked strip joint to an architectural jewel. Even the city inspectors had been impressed. Dina had spent real money on an immigration lawyer, and got Natalya into the system as an applicant for a professional visa; she quit nannying for the family that treated her like a slave. Piotr was right: she was a star. She jumped at Dina's vision for the space, working and reworking everything, directing plumbing, engineering, everything perfectly. And something else: she was as hard a worker as Dina was, herself. Each night, she left at eight p.m. for a night class in English and, when Dina visited the site, if Natalya was alone, she found her plugged into her earbuds, talking to herself aloud, doing English on her phone, teaching herself around the clock.

By the third week, she was arguing with the suppliers – in broken English. By the fourth, she was talking haltingly to Dina. Natalya applied herself not just a few nights a week, but day in, day out. She plunged into the language like Dina flung herself at the business. And now her English was passable.

Dina admired it. She loved Natalya's work ethic and the clear way that she understood and executed Dina's own creative vision. The space was light-filled, just as Dina dreamed, temperate and warm, with water cascading down the rock sculpture, daylight pouring in and the beauty products mounted on the shelves like jewels. The limited space was maximised with light and mirrors, and everything said *luxury* and *simplicity*. In addition to her clear architectural skills – bringing that sense of space, light and peace to a small underground room – Natalya had a flair for design, interpreting what Dina wanted to do and sourcing the exact pieces that could make it happen; she took her time, but the perfect modern stools showed up, the right blond woods, the clean, pale-grey tiles, mirrors to reflect the piped-in sunshine . . .

The space was transformed. First, the cleanup, then the wires, the plumbing, the light-well and the glass. Next, the interior element: neutral colours, recessed lighting, the LED displays, a waterfall and bright, open shelving for customer space and comfort, designed so nobody would have to jostle to see the stock.

There were stools, brush bars, testers and pots of wipes. There were alcoves for the make-up artists to work on clients. The web address of the store was everywhere, scrolled on the walls, on the sides of shelving, on their newly printed stiff paper bags with the pale green and gold ribbon. And the men's corner was a gorgeous contrast in slate greys and black marble, with dark green leather and old-fashioned grooming products; a Manhattan

Wall Street shark could come in here and pick up solid gold cufflinks, some Floris aftershave, or Hermès Eau d'Orange Verte shower gel, and feel himself well groomed in the capitals of Europe – feel himself a gentleman. Natalya had down-lit the old world into the new, so that they melded beautifully together. And Dina's web designers, kid geeks that they were, loved it, too; they took photographs, blogged it and styled it right into the site; DinaKane.com carried through that seamless look.

Another bonus: Natalya was good with money. Dina found that out early on, when she heard her screeching at the contractors in Russian.

'I talk them budget,' she haltingly explained. 'I tell, they not pay at end if spend too much now. Waste wood if not planks cut right.'

Dina looked at the floor, and saw what she meant – the wide Swedish blond planks were not fitting right at the end of the room.

'Waste money,' Natalya said, frowning. 'Stupid fault.'

Dina laughed.

'What wrong?'

'Sorry – no – you're absolutely right. It's just the English.'

'Working on that,' Natalya said.

'I know. It's fantastic. I'll leave you to it.'

As they progressed, Natalya brought her budget breakdowns, every day, on a spreadsheet – everything from wages to MetroCard expenses. She listened avidly as Dina outlined her vision for the store, for new stock, for the uniforms of the staff.

'Plain beige dresses. Short sleeves; fitted waist; knee length. Any designer they like, prêt-à-porter, and we pay. Dina Kane says chic, not straightjacket.'

'I like this. Everything must say *style*.'

'Creams, golds, beige, neutral: that's the design of the wrapping paper, the tissue, the ribbons and the gift boxes. Kane Men is dark grey and burnt gold.'

'Also very good.' Natalya nodded. 'Russian men like very much, the oligarchs who want London style. Your taste very beautiful.'

'Do you have a boyfriend?'

Natalya's shoulders hunched up defensively. 'No time; I work here all day, English all night, and everyone here is married. Or maybe stupid.'

Dina laughed. 'Piotr's friends, you mean?'

Natalya shrugged. 'It's the community. When you want to be ambitious, you cannot take off time for – what you say? – Frivolous . . . Messing round.'

'You need a private life, otherwise you'll burn out.' Dina looked round the store; the last of the workmen was heading out. 'Mikhail, it's OK – I'll lock up.'

'Fine, miss.' He nodded his head, just glad to be getting back home.

Dina walked up the stairs and shut the door from the inside. Now they could not be disturbed. 'Natalya, do you have five minutes?'

The older girl immediately hunched. 'Why? What is wrong?'

She's used to being attacked, Dina thought. *She thinks I'm going to pack her up and ship her back to the spoiled kids and the slave-driving parents. Or stiff her on her wages with an immigration threat.*

'Nothing. Nothing at all. Your work is incredible. I would just like to practise on you.'

'Practise?' Natalya shook her head. 'I do not understand.'

'The make-up booths; the styling – would you consider being a guinea pig for this process? I'd like to make you up, and maybe also do your hair. And dress you. No charge,' she said, hastily. 'All on the company.'

Natalya winced. 'You must need me do this?'

'No, not at all. Not a job requirement. You don't have to, not in any way.' Dina ventured a smile. 'I just think . . . you might enjoy it.'

'Enjoy it,' said Natalya, as if this were a foreign concept. 'You think?'

'I do. And I was hoping that, when we are through here, you might consider working for me. Not as an architect. I'd like you to help me run the company. If –' she corrected herself – '*when* we get new stores, bigger ones, you can design them, but mostly I just want your business input. I have plans – across America, and then into Europe. Why not?'

Natalya gasped with pleasure.

When her face lights up like that, Dina thought, *she can be truly beautiful*. She understood better than she could speak, and the hope in her eyes was something to see.

'Yes. Wonderful. Thank you.' She struggled for the right words. 'I very alike you. Not so imagination, but working hard. And your business good one. I understand American women; they love all this things.'

'Well . . . if you want to be number two at Dina Kane,' Dina said, slowly, 'maybe you really do need to let me at you, after all. My first management hire has to be well made up, beautifully dressed. They will take photographs when we launch.'

Natalya considered this. 'Yes, OK. I understand this.' Then she frowned. 'But now is time for my English class.'

'Fine. Tomorrow, no architecture. Meet me at Daniel Gibbons, the hairdresser. Here's the address. See you there at nine.'

Daniel didn't open his doors till half ten, but he loved Dina, and she knew he would fit her in. Besides, once she explained, he'd see that this was going to be fun.

The next morning, she met a nervous Natalya at the salon.

'You just lie back,' Dina said. 'Daniel will do all the work.'

Natalya's Russian face tightened; the shutters in her eyes came down. 'Fine,' she said.

Dina fed her magazines, but her face was impassive. Daniel washed, and cut, and shaped her hair, exactly as Dina told him;

367

her style was legendary, and he was happy to be the instrument in her hands.

'Shape it into a flame. It's fine and thin, so it should hold that shape. Cut the edges diagonally across the face, and end it just below the collarbone. And I want it lightened. Highlights, till she's a good caramel blonde, with just a couple of truly fair streaks, OK? Not framing the face – scattered, not symmetrical. This has to be an easy cut she can just blow-dry and go. Are you with me?'

'That's going to look fabulous. Leave it with me.'

After they were done, Dina didn't let Natalya look in the mirror. She put her in a cab and took her straight to Saks.

'You're a size four.'

'How do you know?'

'I can tell. Come with me.'

They visited DKNY, Hervé Léger, Prada and Ralph Lauren. Then she crossed the street to Uniqlo and picked up jeans and puffer jackets in a rainbow of colours, with soft cashmere sweaters. Lastly, at Columbus Circle, they stopped at Cole Haan, and Dina took out her credit card.

'You're a seven. You need more shoes, but this will do for summer – heels, courts and flats. I love these, they have the same air cushioning they put in the Nike shoes.'

'I don't understand.'

'You will.' The girls were laden down with shopping bags. Dina hailed a cab for her apartment. 'Just come with me.'

Once there, she pulled out a fitted dress in red, some hose and a pair of platform pumps, and sent Natalya into the spare bedroom to change.

'Yes. Wonderful,' Dina said when she reappeared. The red dress woke her up, clinging beautifully to the slim curves of her body, and the pumps made her look model thin. There was no bag, but Dina figured she could pick up one of those tomorrow. She caught Natalya glancing around, trying to see a mirror. 'Not yet. The reveal is the whole fun of it.'

The older girl looked doubtful.

'Just sit on the chair. We're nearly done, and then I'll get you a cab back to Brooklyn, OK? And you can take the afternoon off.'

Natalya sighed. 'Yes, Dina, OK. You not be too long.'

It was quick work. She applied BB cream, two shades mixed together, and highlighted Natalya's slim cheekbones with a dusting of Bobbi Brown's Pink Quartz Brick in gold and rose. There was no point going heavy; Natalya was a dark blonde with a fair skin, and natural would always suit her. Dina used the most basic cosmetics: light brown eye shadow from Mac, a single coat of lash-separating Maybelline mascara – drug-store cheap – and a Revlon glittering lip gloss in clear, to give a wet look to her lips.

'OK. Stand. Come to the mirror,' she said, taking the girl into her own bedroom, to the full-length French antique that stood there by the bed. 'This is how you should look.'

Natalya stared at the mirror, as if spellbound. She reached her hands up to her new hair and touched it, gingerly. Then she smoothed down the dress and turned. She walked closer, examining her face.

Then she said something in Russian. And then she burst into tears.

That was the start of their friendship. Natalya became even more confident, stronger. She looked wonderful, and the men on the crew propositioned her, but she said no. Each day, she attended work in a casual, chic outfit, fitted to her body, and experimented with make-up the way Dina instructed her to.

Within a month, she had a boyfriend: a doctor. He was from Texas, working paediatric oncology at Mount Sinai.

'How did you meet?'

'At the theatre. I go for my English. He had the next seat. His friend is not coming; she gets called into hospital. I was wearing the red dress,' Natalya said, happily. 'He asked me out the next day. And so I like him, very much.'

'That's great.'

'It's you, Dina. It's this.' She gestured at herself. 'Maybe I'm not so beautiful, like you, but I feel beautiful – for me. It gives me confidence to know I can look this way.'

Dina grinned. 'Great. That's exactly what we're going for.'

'Confidence makes me happy. And he tells me all the time I am beautiful, but not just this, also brave and clever. He loves my story.' She giggled, and it was strange to hear that light laughter from Natalya. 'He even likes the accent. Isn't that crazy?'

'Not crazy. I'm glad for you.'

'I can't know if we are to get married yet.' She smiled. 'But I like being with him, getting to understand him.'

Dina hugged her. 'Oh, seriously, that's perfect, Natalya. Take it slow. I'm thrilled for you.'

But there was an ache under the words, because Dina didn't have anyone, couldn't have anyone. The mad work of setting this company up was slowing, her days were slowing, and now, when she wanted it least, Dina was thinking about Joel Gaines once again.

There would not be anyone else. And when Natalya talked about her doctor, Jesse, it sent the old longing rushing back through Dina's veins.

She hadn't called him, hadn't been weak. But he hadn't called her, either.

There was nothing, just silence. No emails, no texts. It was as if none of it had happened, or as if it had happened to someone else, long ago. In another life.

She dreaded the days after the launch. When things settled down, and she had time and space to herself, and Dina Kane, Inc. was growing, but more slowly, then how would she stop thinking about Joel? How would she manage to get a grip on herself?

But, for now, she just hugged her new friend.

* * *

Tonight, she was glad to be with Natalya. It had been a very long day. At nine p.m., her deputy forced her to put away her cellphone and stop talking to the beauty bloggers and fashion PRs and editor types who were all due in Times Square at nine a.m. tomorrow; their little space would be full to overflowing. Dina had to parcel out invitations, and that made it better. She now had a b-list of smaller bloggers and magazines, due in an hour later, at ten.

'Starting small is unfortunate. But you made it into a virtue,' Natalya said.

Her English was almost perfect now. The two girls chinked glasses.

'I think it'll go well.' Dina shrugged. 'Scrub that. I know it will.'

'Your cash on hand is very low. Your apartment is the security?'

'I'm not worried,' Dina replied. She took a long, cool drink of the champagne, playing with it, letting the bubbles crackle around her mouth. 'Dina Kane, Inc. is going to work. We will double our financing within the month.'

Natalya shook her blond head, admiringly. She was wearing a chic little brown dress and comfortable ballet flats in burnt orange: perfect for the coming days of fall, for New York's warm September. Style was something she was learning, along with her English; she felt accomplished, beautiful – reborn, almost. Dina believed in her, and she was starting to believe in herself again.

Every day, she thanked God for her cousin Piotr, who had brought her to this woman.

'How can you have such certainty?'

'The products are good. The design is good.' Dina drank a little more. 'I'm good. We've worked the insider beauty press relentlessly. It's a story because of Ludo and Torch, and the products and the store back it up.'

'They ran a server test on the website. Do you really think you're going to get all those hits?'

Dina nodded. 'We have to be ready. If we crash on day one, it will be a disaster.' She thought for a second of Edward Johnson. 'And there could be a cyber attack, who knows?'

'You've spent so much on that website.'

'It matters more than the stores. That's beauty now, Natalya – global. Somebody could log in in Auckland and get our stuff. We will ship it to Reykjavik. Every girl has a dream; we want to inspire them. Even those who can't afford it: we want them on that site, playing our videos –' her eyes lit up – 'learning how beauty works, the canvas of the face.'

'But if they can't afford it—'

'Maybe one day they will grow up and be able to. Or suddenly get a better job. We want them to sink into beauty with Dina Kane.' She drank a little more, feeling a sudden rush of pleasure, of triumph. Her dream was here – and she had made it, against all odds, against everything. The launch, the money – it seemed like an afterthought. This was her dream for other women, and it was coming true.

'I understand.'

'Beauty was my escape. I want it to be their escape, too.'

Natalya drained her glass. 'You will be very successful with it, Dina. And I can't wait to work with you.' She glanced at her watch. 'I should go; Jesse's shift is ending. I'd like to be back for him.'

'Of course.' The girls hugged. 'See you tomorrow,' Dina said. 'Be there at eight?'

'Seven thirty,' Natalya promised her.

She knew she should probably get up and leave, too. But Dina didn't want to move, not just yet. She was tired, happy, enjoying her champagne.

'Have a great night.' She kissed Natalya goodbye, and tipped the glass to her mouth, savouring it. And then she took out her phone. Maybe there were some bloggers she could call, some last minute work she could do . . . just while she finished one more flute of the ice-cold, glittering froth of a wine.

There were no messages on her phone. But there was a text. From Joel Gaines.

Where are you? We need to talk.

Dina breathed in, hard. Her hand gripped the side of the bar; her head swayed. Carefully, she steadied herself so the others around her – the couples, the businessmen standing around in knots, socialising – wouldn't see it.

She paused, then tapped out a reply.

I can't bear it, Joel. Please. It's a big day for me tomorrow.

His reply came through almost immediately.

Ten minutes, that's all. Where are you?

Dina took her glass and swallowed a large gulp of the champagne, tossing it quickly down her throat, letting it burn.

She shivered. What if she said no? She would be off her game, thinking about him, obsessing, on one of the most important days of her life. If Joel was here, she had to deal with him. Talk to him now. Get it out of the way.

Tomorrow she needed to concentrate.

He could come to her. She was on Central Park South, right in the heart of Manhattan. Not her apartment, where her bedroom was. Where she might do something stupid.

I just said goodnight to my friend. I was leaving, but I'm in the bar of the Victrix. Call me, or I can wait for you for fifteen minutes.

There was a pause. Dina held her breath, wishing it didn't matter so much. But it did. She was in suspended animation, staring at the screen.

My garage is a block away. I'll be with you in five minutes, Dina. Don't leave.

She texted back OK and sat there, sipping slowly. Time passed like treacle. She could not think, could not concentrate, could not act her age. When Joel appeared, would she have any dignity?

Frenzied work had distracted her, but they were close now, almost at the end. She had nothing to hide behind. And her feelings for Joel were beating at her resistance, relentless as the tides.

She was past dignity, maybe. One text from him and her body was on fire. Joel Gaines had only kissed her once. If he wanted more tonight, Dina had no idea how the hell she was going to turn him down.

And then, there he was, walking in through the door from the lobby, paying no attention to the wait staff talking to him. He was moving fast, the hugeness of that body, the spread of his chest, the power of it, striding towards her in his suit, like nothing could stop him; purposeful, intent.

Dina was immediately wet and aroused, absolutely responsive to him. Her body crackled with adrenaline, as though she'd been shocked.

'Joel,' she whispered.

She could hardly speak. Joel was right in front of her. His body was close to hers, in her space again. Towering over her. Looking down on her. She trembled; she couldn't say a word.

'Dina –' he grabbed her hand, fiercely – 'I love you. I've loved you for a year, maybe more. I want you. I cannot stop thinking about you. You're stronger than everything. I have to be with you. That's it. I have to be.'

Tears sprang to her eyes. 'But you're married.'

'I asked Susan for a divorce. It's done. I left the house. I told the boys. They're grown, and I want to be with you.' He clutched her hands. 'As soon as the papers come through, we can get married. Yes? Tell me yes.'

The tears brimmed over, running down her cheeks. She swayed where she sat, and Gaines put out an arm to support her. 'Yes,' she whispered. 'Yes. Why?'

'Because I couldn't take the rest of my life thinking about you, and not seeing you. Wanting you, and not having you. Because

I never met a woman like you. Because you are the girl I should have married first. I don't want a roommate; I want a lover, a friend, a challenge. I want you, and none other. You understand?'

She nodded. 'Yes.' Her face was in her hands, sobbing.

'Let's go home.'

'I have to get the check . . .'

Joel gestured to the barman. 'Put this on my account.'

'Yes, sir, Mr Gaines.'

The small display of power thrilled Dina. She couldn't help herself. Her body shuddered at his touch as he slipped her off the stool. The rest of her champagne lay on the counter, but she already felt drunk, almost high.

'Where shall we go?' she asked, as they stood at the coat check, and Gaines slipped his hands around her waist, her shoulders, touching her everywhere as he put the garment on her. 'Your place or mine?'

'Yours,' Gaines replied, immediately.

His apartment would need to be cleaned out, all of Susan's things returned: the framed photos of them together, the detritus of a failed marriage. Dina's neat, ambitious little place was perfect; she had won it on her own, succeeded on her own. It was small, beautiful, an up-and-comer's apartment. Everything he'd wanted to be, once, a long while ago. Everything he admired in her.

'Fine.' She kissed him, melted into him.

He felt himself stiffen, harden. He had to get her into a taxi. 'Dina. Not here. Let's go.'

Edward knew he was drunk. But that was fine, because he had cut it with cocaine – lots of cocaine. It made you see things clearer. He felt big now, confident; he could do exactly as he liked. And mostly what he wanted was to deal with Dina Kane.

Once. For all. Forever.

He'd sent Lena home, and the night housekeeper. And then he'd looked, and read, and drank, and pulled it all close into him. Dina Kane, Inc., the new wave, the next big thing, was launching tomorrow. Times Square. Tickets like gold dust.

Once he got good and drunk, it seemed he had to cut it. That was what the coke was for. It had been a while, but Edward still kept his stash. And, tonight, he needed to use it.

The bad feelings left him; he woke up, became powerful and strong again. Dina Kane, a ten-minute diversion, had derailed his whole life. He saw that clearly now. And, even as he was getting back on track, the bitch was returning from the grave to fucking haunt him.

It was time to be done. To get it over with.

He barely registered what he was doing as he walked upstairs to the bathroom cabinet and took out the Klonopin and the plastic gloves – little cheap plastic gloves, the kind that came with a packet of hair dye. He found a small bottle of whiskey and a long, sharp knife. He had a gun, too, but that was messy, that led to all kinds of annoying things, like splatter patterns on the wall; the FBI worked things out that way. Edward was smarter than them; he had seen the TV shows, all the cop series. He was no fool.

He'd killed Philippe, and Johnny Kane – or helped them on their way, at least. Both the assholes had got drunk themselves, taken pills themselves. So Philippe didn't know what he was doing, but Johnny did – fool; weak little fool.

Both of them, far too trusting. He knew that Dina Kane wouldn't be making that mistake. He'd have to be careful with her.

There was a key – that was the thing. Olivia had provided him with a copy – no questions asked. He could let himself into her new apartment, wait for her, jump her. One hand over the mouth, force the pills down her throat, pour the alcohol in after it. Maybe he'd leave her in the bath, knife in her own hand – her prints on it. She would slit her own wrists. He giggled; that was a neat trick to do when unconscious, but Edward would be happy to lend a little assistance before she was fully passed out. Olivia told him the apartment building had a security guard and cameras in the lobby, but they were turned off at night; they were just for show.

Why hadn't he done it before? It seemed crazy now. Stupid fears about getting caught. He wouldn't *be* caught. When Edward Johnson took care of them, they stayed down. No questions after Johnny, none after Philippe. Why would some bitch from Westchester be any different?

He snorted more coke, got a cap and muffler and a large coat, and walked out in to the night. It was only twelve blocks to Dina's apartment. He entered the front door purposefully, grunting at the guard and walking straight ahead. The man was reading a magazine, not paying attention. There were corridors and an elevator bank. She was on floor sixteen and, with the drug pumping through his veins, Edward Johnson rode up to the right floor.

Adrenaline mixed with the coke. What if she was there? In? And by the door? She was a hermit, that bitch, a fucking hermit; she hated men; never saw anybody. She was probably there, working, waiting . . . He'd have to move fast, jump on her. That was OK. That was fine. Edward didn't want to think it through. He took out his key, opened the door, entered the apartment and shut it behind him.

He listened. He didn't call out – didn't want the neighbours to hear anything.

It was silent. Silent as the grave; silent as her grave. He giggled. Funny. There was nobody here.

Just to make sure, he walked through the place, checked it out. Empty.

There was a large wardrobe in the bedroom. That's where he would go. He had more coke, of course; it was with him in a silver vial. And he could afford to swallow a little of the whiskey.

He had a celebratory swig and a snort. Then he opened the wardrobe door, climbed inside, and sat down comfortably on its base. Using his phone for a light, he put on the gloves, opened the pillbox and laid the knife next to it.

Everything was ready.

Dina felt like her hands didn't work. She couldn't find her keys; she was opening the bag, fumbling, kissing. Joel's hands were on her, possessively, running up her legs, her thighs, under her skirt, cupping her ass. She was wet, helplessly aroused.

'God – help me. I can't . . . I can't . . .'

He took one hand away from stroking her through the thin, damp cotton of her panties, found her key, unlocked the door and shoved her through it.

It closed, heavy, behind them.

'My bedroom's this way,' Dina said.

He was already lifting her shirt over her head, popping the bra undone with practised ease, feeling her full breasts that tumbled out into his hands, her nipples painfully erect. She was so hot for him, he could feel the blood rushing into her belly, her womb literally heating under his hands.

'Fuck the bedroom.' Gaines thrust her on to the floor, ripping the clothes from her, tearing the skirt down, the panties off. 'You aren't getting that far.'

Dina moaned. He tore off his clothes, too, impatiently, buttons ripping, his tie yanked from his neck. He kicked his shoes off, kissing at her neck, her face, raking his teeth and lips across her throat. She split her legs, wide, willing, desperate to feel him inside her. There was nothing but desire now, pure lust – not love, not friendship – just his power, his might, the strength of his body moving over her.

'Joel!' she gasped. 'Oh, God! Please. Please.'

Inside the wardrobe, Edward Johnson thought fast.

There were two people in this apartment. And one of them was a man. They were fucking, so they were naked.

He had a knife.

But the man seemed sober. And, underneath the glittering bravado of the coke and booze, Edward was a coward.

His body was skinny, even lanky. Any halfway decent guy could take him. That was the problem. And the voice outside sounded familiar.

Joel Gaines.

Fucking shit scared, Edward started to shudder. Gaines, the goddamned *billionaire*. Gaines, who was built like an army tank, who pumped weights like a Marine drill sergeant on a good day.

He ran through scenarios in his mind. Lurching out, drunk, high, with his little knife. It had seemed big when he was planning on slashing Dina's wrists while she was passed out in the bath. Now it was a fucking penknife. He would stab at Gaines, maybe hurt him. Then the big man would grab his wrist, break his arm. That was the thing with women: they were so soft, so weak. All those TV shows with karate-kicking female detectives – Edward laughed at them. Even a puny man could grab a woman, subdue her, wrestle her to the ground. It was muscle mass; it was power.

But against Gaines? No. Gaines would fight, and Dina would scream, and get to a phone.

He was trapped. He had to do something. If he left the wardrobe, they would hear him, probably. They were distracted, but they would notice someone trying to get out the door. There was a fire escape, if he could open the windows . . .

Terrified, Edward peeled off the thin plastic gloves and stuffed them in his underpants. The ludicrous smallness of this hit him. He wept with self-pity in the closet. The clonazepam was in its bottle. Maybe he could get to a window, drop that outside . . . For now, he hid it in an inner jacket pocket. The whiskey . . . It wasn't a crime to have whiskey. The knife . . . Jesus, the knife.

He grabbed a cardigan and used it to scrub the knife clean, then, holding it in the fabric, he opened the door as slowly as he could and tossed it under the wardrobe, all the way to the back of the wall.

It was no good. If he stayed here, she'd find him in the morning. He had to get out. He needed to get out . . .

She felt him against her – hard, urgent, forcing her legs apart still wider. Dina groaned with pleasure; she felt dizzy, almost unable to hold herself back. She was gasping every time he touched her, no matter how light, how soft . . .

Gaines pulled back. Dina felt the air on her skin, the rush of it where his body had been.

'What?' she whimpered, and not with desire. 'What is it?'

He sprang back from her, naked, crouching. His body was incredible – strong, knotted with muscles. Even in her dismay, Dina was stunned by it.

'Cover yourself. Get a phone. There's someone here. In the apartment.'

At that moment, there came a cry from the bedroom – a weak, mewling cry, sobbing, pathetic.

Dina gasped in horror and grabbed her dress, tugging it over her head.

'Who's in there?' Gaines barked. He lifted his trousers with one hand and slipped them on. 'Answer me or we call the police. And I'm coming to get you. I have a gun.'

Dina looked wildly at him but he shook his head.

'Don't shoot!' It was a shriek. 'Don't shoot, please! It's me – Edward Johnson. I'm unarmed. Don't kill me!'

'Don't you fucking move,' Gaines said.

He gestured, and Dina, hot, flushed, scrambled to pull on underwear, cover herself properly. Then she moved towards the bedroom door, but Gaines was ahead of her, his body covering hers, protecting her.

He lifted one leg and kicked the door open. A perfect, strong extension. The wood splintered and shattered in the middle.

Edward Johnson was sitting there on the bed, hunched, sobbing, tears and mucus streaming down his face. He was swaying, and there was a stench of alcohol, and powder was scattered around him.

'How the fuck did you get in here?' Gaines demanded. 'Get down on the fucking floor. Spread your legs and arms. *Now.*'

Meekly, Johnson obeyed. He looked so weak, flopping to his knees, then his belly, prostrating himself before Gaines and Dina.

Joel ran his hands quickly and efficiently across his body, pulling out the vial of meds. 'Clonazepam. You stink of booze. Where is it?'

Johnson said nothing. Joel kicked him, hard, between the legs. There was a whooshing sound as he sucked in his breath and then a high-pitched gasp of agony.

'Jesus! Jesus ...'

'He wants nothing to do with you. Where is it?'

'In the closet . . . I have nothing . . .'

Gaines placed one foot on Johnson's neck. Dina was staring, stunned, but he ignored her. He took inventory of the wardrobe; there was a bottle of whiskey, opened, a little drunk. Johnson had been on it for hours before this bottle, clearly. There was powder on his lip.

'What else did you bring?'

'What? What do you mean? Don't hurt me! I came here to confront Dina!'

'You came here to kill Dina,' Gaines said. His foot moved down on Johnson's neck. 'Like you killed her brother. What else, fucker?'

'Nothing else . . . I swear!'

'If I ask the question again, you're dead. You think anybody is going to give a shit that I defended a woman from a home invasion?' Gaines pressed harder, half-choking Johnson. 'Confession time, Edward. Right now.'

'Ugh – knife . . .'

Dina was shaking with fear and shock.

'Where's the goddamned knife, Edward?'

'Under the closet.'

Gaines looked at Dina. 'Check it, sweetheart. I don't want to move off him.'

Dina dropped to the floor. Gaines pressed harder. 'Close your eyes. Don't even look at her.'

'There it is. Oh my God, Joel.' She reached underneath and pulled it out, showing it to him.

He lifted Johnson up by the back of his neck and threw him on the bed.

'You are a pathetic, worthless junkie.' He reached out and grabbed Edward's hair, tilting his head backwards. 'Look at that: coke on your lip. You killed Johnny Kane with it, and now you've started killing yourself. Tell me how you got in here.'

'I had a key,' Edward said, weeping with fear. 'Somebody made it – someone in the underworld. I don't have their contact anymore. If I look too hard for them, they'll pop me.'

Dina moaned. He had a key. If she hadn't been with Joel, she'd have been dead.

'It's you,' he said, suddenly, wiping his eyes and hissing at her. 'You bitch – it's all you! The way I am. You split my family. You made my mother sick. My father – you might as well have killed him.'

'Bullshit, Edward!' Gaines said. 'You don't give a fuck about anybody except yourself. When did you last call your father?'

'I . . . We don't speak.'

'And your mother? You're not the only one that can do research. You packed her off to Florida and all of a sudden she signs the family trust over to you, am I right? You own the townhouse now?'

'How do you—?'

'I know. I watched you. I watched Dina.'

'She blackmailed my father; she's a whore. You know that? She's a goddamned whore. Fucked me for my money—'

Gaines punched him in the face. Dina squealed, and Edward spat out teeth, blood, and crumpled on the bed.

'She's more than you'll ever be.'

'Joel . . . Joel, he's nothing. He's over.' Dina clutched on to him. 'I'm sorry for what I did to your parents, Edward. I was so angry.'

'Say it to them, if you want. He doesn't care about either of them. He's a fucking psychopath.'

Dina moaned. 'I don't care. Let him go; let him go.'

Joel held her hands. 'If you do that, what woman does he kill next? This one is dangerous, Dina. Your brother? You? God knows who else! He broke into this apartment. We need to call the police.'

She gripped him. 'I can't think. My – my company launches tomorrow.'

'Let's hope they serve good coffee,' Gaines said. 'We're going to be up late tonight.'

Edward sat there, rocking on the bed, twisting his fingers. 'You can't do that – call the police – I'll tell them you hit me. I'll tell everybody what you did to my father. You're a whore, Dina Kane; I still have the pictures. Try running your precious business when that comes out.'

Dina held on to Joel and looked at Edward, the malicious, seething wreck of him, and then looked at the knife, shining, sharp, free of blood.

'Joel's right. Do your worst. We don't care. We need you off the streets – before you hurt anyone else.'

She held up her phone. 'Nine-one-one? Yes, I need the police. I'm in my apartment with a man who just tried to kill me. And I'm pretty sure he killed my brother, too.'

* * *

It was past midnight when they finally got back home – his place – Dina couldn't face her own. She walked past the pictures, and Gaines apologised, but she held up one hand.

'Stop. I don't care. That was the past.'

He took her face in his hands and kissed her, again and again, and she felt the warmth returning, like he was blowing on embers, fanning them back into flame. The heat that she thought was gone came back to her; she pressed herself against him.

'No.' Joel bent down and kissed her on the mouth. 'He's been arrested. He tried to kill you. It's not the time, baby.'

She moaned. 'Joel – I've waited so long.'

'We both have. But tomorrow you launch your business. You need to sleep, wake up and do that. I'll still be here. The first time we make love has to be when you're calm, rested, when you've thought it through. Not right after somebody tries to murder you.'

Dina laughed. 'Sweet talker.'

'If you want me when you wake up, I won't put up a fight.'

She kissed him back. The exhaustion, the nervousness was coming back to her. 'OK, OK. But I want to sleep next to you.'

'Deal.' Gaines bent down and scooped her up in his arms and carried her into the bedroom; she nestled against him, and he felt her slump. After he'd laid her down on the bed, within minutes, she was asleep, like a child after a long journey.

He watched her sleeping face for a few seconds, then placed a throw across her body and lay down next to her, closing his eyes, comforted by the quiet sounds of her breathing.

The early morning light was streaming into the room, the red sun of dawn. Dina woke, glanced around, realised where she was – who she was with.

And what was going to happen today. Everything. All of it.

Joel first.

She slipped the throw off her, careful not to wake him, and stripped nude. Then she padded into his wet room and turned on the shower, cleaning herself. She wasted no time; within a minute, she was rough-dried, back in his bed, slipping under the covers this time, pressing herself against him.

His eyes flicked open.

'That's a hell of a wake-up call.'

'I love you,' Dina said. 'I still want you.'

Gaines ran his hands firmly over her whole body. Feeling her calves, her breasts. Cupping her ass.

'Ohhh . . .'

He pulled the covers back; she was there, under him, naked. This was the first time he had ever seen her body clearly. Goddamn, but she was beautiful.

He knelt across her, stripping his own clothes off, piece by piece. And, as he slid his fingers from her breasts to her knees, Dina gasped with longing.

'Patience is a virtue,' he said, and teased her lightly with one finger, just grazing her, back and forth, as his other hand grasped her hands, holding them over her head. She was wet, so wet, and her belly was literally hot, warm with blood under him. She bucked and lifted herself to him. She was beside herself with longing, and he wanted to laugh with the triumph and love of it.

'Oh my God!' Dina gasped. 'Oh Joel! Please . . .'

And his knee nudged her legs apart, and he took her, swiftly, hard, his mouth on hers, kissing her, bearing down on her, and her body dissolved in a wave of bliss, so intense and wonderful that it blew everything away.

Chapter Twenty

A buzz rippled through the crowd.

Dina Kane certainly knew how to make an entrance.

There was a portion of the street roped off with ribbon – a precious thirty-minute easement granted by the city, delighted to have another strip club removed from Times Square. And the space was completely full.

The Dina Kane, Inc. blog had been up for a week – promising samples, makeovers and all kinds of goodies to the first hundred customers. She had more than two hundred women milling around the avenue now, annoying commuters, spilling on to the street.

Among the crowd were tens of New York beauty bloggers – and not just the big ones, the giants from Makeup Alley and the rest. Dina had sent personal invites to all her favourites, the underground anarchist beauty sites, the one that focused solely on the over-sixty-fives, the gay beauty blog, the Urdu-only site for Asian skin . . . She had spent those months as a shopper delving deep into the bones of Manhattan's beauty addicts, and the result was a heady mix of eclecticism, ethnic beauty, impoverished students and Social Registry housewives from the East Side.

Every few minutes, her staff – the best make-up artists she'd poached from Torch, the sales consultants Natalya had signed off on – emerged from the gleaming entrance to the Dina Kane store, handing out free goodies: a lip balm from Scotland, a new mascara from California, fragrance samples from a tiny house in Austria. The journalists from the women's magazines, roped off separately, watched and scribbled. There was a palpable sense of excitement.

And it wasn't just them. Three camera crews were pointed at her tiny storefront: all local TV, but clearly Dina Kane was getting a name for herself, was worth watching. An ageing reporter in Versace, a doyenne of the gossip columns, hung around too, gawping at the commotion for a single shop, unable to report on the embarrassment he had predicted for Ludo Morgan's ex-girlfriend.

They were expecting a limousine, a big black monster, or a Lincoln Town Car at the very least.

But suddenly there was a light ringing of a bell – a bicycle bell – and Dina Kane had arrived. The custom-painted green and gold bike contrasted with her stunning outfit; she wore some beige leggings, rammed into chestnut high-heeled boots, a fitted cream silk shirt and a simple gold bracelet. As the flashbulbs popped and snapped, Dina Kane took off her helmet – letting her dark hair fall loosely down her back.

The photographers purred. The women breathed out. She was beautiful. She was stunning. Her young face was made up, lightly, nothing too heavy: a sheer mousse foundation, golden eye shadow, bronzer on her cheekbones, clear lip gloss and a separating mascara that made her eyes pop. Her teeth were white as she smiled, and she looked healthy, attractive, young and confident.

'Dina! Where's the limo?' a journalist shouted.

There was a mike stand set up on the pavement in front of her, and Dina Kane approached it, laughing, her helmet under one arm.

'No car. This is New York! We bike. We love fitness – it's the best blusher you can't buy.'

All the women laughed. The flashbulbs popped once more.

'Ladies and gentlemen, if you'll just look over there – Dina Kane, Inc. has come to Times Square.'

She pointed and, above them, to the right, a huge rectangle thirty storeys high suddenly blazed into light.

DINA KANE, it said. *BEAUTY*.

The company logo and website address flashed up, and then a smooth morph of a slender forty-five-year-old's face, with make-up being applied, becoming groomed, beautiful. It was replaced by a plus-sized teenager, an African-American mom cradling a baby, and a blonde twenty-six-year-old – all with the Dina Kane message scrolling behind them.

There were *oohs* and *aahs*, and when Dina was satisfied they had gazed, transfixed, long enough, she spoke into the mike again.

'And now, I'm so happy to say that Dina Kane, Inc. is open for business. All women are beautiful – we hope to help show that to the world. Thank you – and enjoy yourselves.'

She lifted a hand, and the glass doors slid open; the wall at the top of the stairs played makeovers, and women stumbled in from the street, rushing down into the gorgeously appointed space.

Dina handed her bike to an assistant.

'Ms Kane, they're ready for you,' Natalya said, walking up to her.

She was beaming with pride. The store looked incredible, the crowd was wonderful, and the neon billboard at the heart of Times Square – a third of the budget, just on that, and they could only have it for a week – meant it was major league. 'The press want to talk to you – about Ludo Morgan, you understand, as well as the store and the site. They want to discuss Torch and Joel Gaines. And there was some arrest this morning . . . ?'

Dina turned around and smiled at the little knot of journalists, looking directly into the TV cameras.

'Of course,' she said. 'And I'll happily make a statement. For now, though, we have Dina Kane customers waiting. Excuse me, OK? I need to go and serve them.'

And she disappeared down the wide stairs into the brightly lit underground oasis of beauty that was to be Dina Kane's new home, shaking hands, calling out greetings.

Natalya looked down after her boss and saw the women mob her as she walked into the store, applauding, pressing round her with compliments, already holding up face creams, asking questions. Behind her, the press pack was following; they were pursuing her down those stairs like she was a celebrity already.

She felt a frisson of excitement. It was only a store, but it was a damned good one. Casually she flicked open her cellphone and pressed the icon for the Dina Kane, Inc. app – it took her directly to the online store, which opened for business the moment the retail one did.

Already, she could see a few golden *sold out* banners.

Something was starting, right now. The result of one girl betting on herself, completely. And Natalya had a feeling it was going to be big – very big.

She breathed in deeply, and followed her boss down into the store.

Epilogue

The launch was a complete success.

Within forty minutes, shoppers had cleared the stock from the showroom, and within an hour they'd taken all their reserves. Natalya had runners out to their suppliers for more; and the press had to wait, and watch Dina Kane do business.

It was quite something. They reported the success, live, like financial reporters counting down to the closing bell.

And Dina did not disappoint. As soon as she'd shaken hands with the last customer, she walked up the stairs and back out to Times Square, where the cameras had been set up for filming.

Joel Gaines came down from his office. He watched discreetly from across the square. There was a scrum of media there now, and Dina faced the cameras head on.

'Good morning,' she said. 'Thank you all for coming to cover the opening of our store. I'm sorry I couldn't get to your questions earlier, but, as you can see, we've been a little busy.' There was a ripple of laughter from the hacks; Gaines shook his head, admiringly. She had them eating out of the palm of her hand. 'Let me pre-empt some of your questions. I'll try to be as frank as possible.' Now they were rolling their eyes; nobody did frank, not in Manhattan, not where money was at stake. But Dina Kane stood tall and unafraid, and she kept talking. The effect was mesmerising.

'Edward Johnson has been arrested for trying to kill me,' she said. 'There's going to be a trial, and I can't prejudice it.'

'Is it true you slept with his father?'

'Yes, it is true.'

There was a gasp of surprise from the press pack. She *admitted* it?

'I did so for revenge. Although it was years ago, I still regret that very much. I would like to apologise to Mr Johnson, and his wife, and his family.'

'Revenge for what? What did he do to you?'

'So you slept with father and son?'

'Look this way, Dina! Over here!'

'What else can you tell us?'

'Absolutely nothing whatsoever.' She smiled brightly. 'The legal process will take its course. I'm sorry I can't go any further.'

There was a clicking of bulbs and a whirring as cameras were trained towards her, boom mikes shoved in her direction.

'Why were you fired from Torch, Dina?'

'You'll have to ask Ludo Morgan that.'

'The company says there's a non-compete clause in your contract – that you can't work for anyone else. They're going to sue Dina Kane, Inc.'

'How typically male,' Dina said.

That provoked shocked laughter from the women there – journalists and style editors.

'Let them try. The suit will be baseless. I'm not working for Dina Kane. I own Dina Kane.' She flashed another strong, brilliant smile. 'By all means, let Torch try to compete.'

'But Ludo Morgan has so much power in retail! Torch have all the financial muscle!'

Dina lifted her head and looked around. Gaines stiffened; she had seen him, standing back there, gazing out at her. She winked at him, and his heart turned over with pleasure and love. To be at the start of this journey with her . . . And their journey – their journey together . . .

'They do have a lot of muscle.' Dina gestured towards the bright doors of Dina Kane, the electronic makeovers dancing, a little crowd outside as fresh boxes of stock were being carted hurriedly down the stairs. 'But I've never worried too much about brawn. I'm going to put my faith in beauty.'

And she raised one manicured hand to the press pack, and walked across Times Square, towards her first store, and her new life.

Acknowledgements

No book is a solo project, and I have been fortunate to be edited by Imogen Taylor and to have the endlessly patient Michael Sissons as my agent. Fiona Petheram, Robert Caskie and Isabel Evans have all shepherded me at PFD; I also want to thank Jateen Patel. At Headline, Emily Furniss in publicity and Emma Holtz have been working on the team and I am grateful to everybody who put *Beauty* together in record time with an amazing cover.

And finally, thanks to you for reading it – ultimately all stories are a collaboration between the writer and the reader. Dina's adventures happen in your head, and that's the true beauty of this novel.

"You could take a problem to Big Earl and he would sit there and listen to you spill out a lifetime's worth of troubles. He'd nod patiently like it was all new to him, even though he was a man who had seen a lot in his life and had probably heard your particular kind of blues a hundred times over. After you were done, he'd rub his huge hands across the white stubble that stood out against the coal black of his skin and he'd say, 'Here's what we're gonna do.'"

About the Author

Edward Kelsey Moore lives in Chicago with his partner of many years. Having trained with some of the world's finest musicians, he has travelled widely and recorded extensively during his lengthy career as a professional cellist. Edward's literary work often reflects both his life as a musician and his upbringing as the backsliding son of a Baptist preacher. His short fiction has appeared in several literary magazines and on Public Radio. Like Dora in *The Supremes at Earl's All-You-Can-Eat*, Edward is also an avid gardener; like Odette, his horticultural projects are not always successful. *The Supremes at Earl's All-You-Can-Eat* is Edward Kelsey Moore's first novel.

Find out more on Edward's website at
www.edwardkelseymoore.com
or Facebook page www.facebook.com/
EdwardKelseyMooreauthor
and follow him on Twitter @edkmoore.

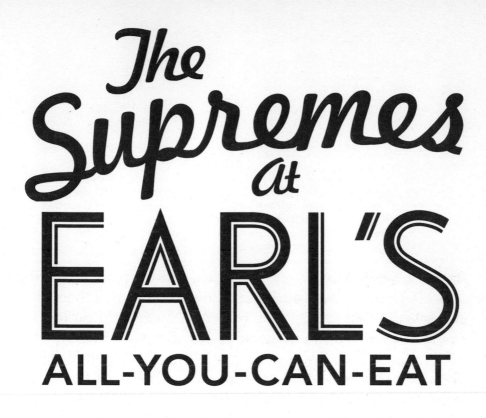

The Supremes At EARL'S ALL-YOU-CAN-EAT

Edward Kelsey Moore

HODDER &
STOUGHTON

First published in the United States of America in 2013 by Alfred A. Knopf,
an imprint of The Knopf Doubleday Group
A division of Random House, Inc.
First published in Great Britain in 2013 by Hodder & Stoughton
An Hachette UK company

1

A CIP catalogue record for this title is available from the British Library

Trade Paperback ISBN 978 1 444 75802 3
Ebook ISBN 978 1 444 75730 9

Printed and bound by CPI Group (UK) Ltd, Croydon, CR0 4YY

Hodder & Stoughton policy is to use papers that are natural, renewable
and recyclable products and made from wood grown in sustainable forests.
The logging and manufacturing processes are expected to conform
to the environmental regulations of the country of origin.

Hodder & Stoughton Ltd
338 Euston Road
London NW1 3BH

www.hodder.co.uk

For Mom and Dad

Chapter 1

I woke up hot that morning. Came out of a sound sleep with my face tingling and my nightgown stuck to my body. Third time that week. The clock on the dresser on the other side of the bedroom glowed 4:45, and I could hear the hiss of the air conditioner and feel its breeze across my face. I had set the temperature to sixty before going to sleep. So common sense said that it had to be chilly in the room. Well, common sense and the fact that my husband, James, who lay snoring beside me, was outfitted for winter even though it was mid-July. He slept like a child – a six-foot, bald-headed, middle-aged child – wrapped in a cocoon he had fashioned for himself out of the sheet and blanket I had kicked off during the night. Just the top of his brown head was visible above the floral pattern of the linens. Still, every inch of me was screaming that the room was a hundred degrees.

I lifted my nightgown and let it fall, trying to fan cool air onto my skin. That accomplished nothing. My friend Clarice claimed that meditation and positive thinking eased her path through menopause, and she was forever after me to try it. So I lay still in the predawn darkness and thought cool thoughts. I summoned up an old summer memory of hopping with the kids through the cold water jetting from the clicking yellow sprinkler in our backyard. I pictured the ice that formed every winter on the creek that ran behind Mama and Daddy's house in Leaning Tree, making it look like it was wrapped up in cellophane.

I thought of my father, Wilbur Jackson. My earliest recollection of him is the delicious chill I got as a little girl whenever Daddy scooped me up in his arms after walking home on winter evenings from the carpentry shop he owned. I recalled how cold radiated from Daddy's coveralls and the way it felt to run my hands over the frost-coated hair of his beard.

But Daddy's shop had been gone for ages. The Leaning Tree property, creek and all, had been the domain of various renters for half a decade. And my children were each at least twenty years beyond dancing in the spray of a sprinkler.

No thoughts, at least not the ones I came up with, proved capable of icing down my burning skin. So I cussed Clarice for her bad advice and for making me think of the old days – a certain recipe for sleeplessness – and I decided to head for the kitchen. There was a pitcher of water in the Frigidaire and butter pecan ice cream in the freezer. I figured a treat would set me right.

I sat up in the bed, careful not to wake James. Normally, he was as easygoing a man as you'd ever meet. But if I woke him before dawn on a Sunday, he would look at me sideways all through morning service and right up until dinner. So, in order not to disturb him, I moved in slow motion as I stood, slipped my feet into my house shoes, and made my way to the bedroom door in the dark.

Even though I had made the trip from our bed to the kitchen thousands of times in pitch blackness, what with sick children and countless other nighttime emergencies during the decades of our marriage, and even though not a stick of furniture in our bedroom had been moved in twenty years, I rammed the little toe of my right foot into the corner of our old mahogany dresser not five steps into my journey. I cussed again, out loud this time. I looked over my shoulder to see if I had awakened James, but he was still snoring away in his linen wrappings. Hot and tired, my toe throbbing in my green terrycloth slip-ons, I had to fight the urge to run and wake James and insist that he sit up and suffer along with me. But I was good and continued to creep out of the room.

Other than the faint growl of James snoring three rooms away, the only sound in the kitchen was the bass whoosh made by the lopsided ceiling fan churning above my head. I turned on the kitchen light and looked up at that fan wobbling on its axis. With my toe smarting, and still longing to distribute my bad humor, I decided that even if I couldn't justify snapping at James about my hot flash or my sore toe, I could surely rationalize letting off some steam by yelling at him for improperly installing that fan eighteen years earlier. But, like my desire to wake him and demand empathy, I successfully fought off this temptation.

I opened the refrigerator door to get the water pitcher and decided to stick my head inside. I was in almost to my shoulders, enjoying the frosty temperature, when I got the giggles thinking how someone coming upon me, head stuffed into the refrigerator instead of the oven, would say, "Now there's a fat woman who is completely clueless about how a proper kitchen suicide works."

I grabbed the water pitcher and saw a bowl of grapes sitting next to it looking cool and delicious. I pulled the bowl out with the pitcher and set them on the kitchen table. Then I fetched a glass from the dish drainer and brought it to the table, kicking my house shoes off along the way in order to enjoy the feel of cold linoleum against the soles of my bare feet. I sat down at what had been my place at the table for three decades and poured a glass of water. Then I popped a handful of grapes into my mouth and started to feel better.

I loved that time of day, that time just before sunrise. Now that Jimmy, Eric, and Denise were all grown and out of the house, the early hours of the day were no longer linked to slow-passing minutes listening for coughs or cries or, later, teenage feet sneaking in or out of the house. I was free to appreciate the quiet and the way the yellowish-gray light of the rising sun entered the room, turning everything from black and white to color. The journey from Kansas to Oz right in my own kitchen.

That morning, when the daylight came it brought along a visitor, Dora Jackson. I clapped my hand over my mouth to stifle a squeak of surprise when I first caught sight of my mother strolling into the room. She came from the direction of the back door, her short, wide body waddling with an uneven stride from having her left leg badly set by a country doctor when she was a girl.

People used to call us "the twins," Mama and me. The two of us are round women – big in the chest, thick around the waist, and wide across the hips. We share what has often been charitably called an "interesting" face – narrow eyes, jowly cheeks, broad forehead, big but perfect teeth. I grew to be a few inches taller, five foot three. But if you were to look at pictures of us, you'd swear we were the same woman at different ages.

My mother loved the way she looked. She would strut through town on her uneven legs with her big breasts pointing the way forward, and you knew from looking at her that she figured she was just about the hottest thing going. I never came to love my tube-shaped body the way Mama loved hers, but learning to imitate that confident stride of hers was probably the single smartest thing I ever did.

Mama wore her best dress that Sunday morning, the one she usually brought out only for summer weddings and Easter. It was light blue with delicate yellow flowers and green vines embroidered around the collar and the cuffs of the short sleeves. Her hair was pulled up, the way she wore it for special occasions. She sat down across from me at the table and smiled.

Mama gestured with her hand toward the bowl of grapes on the table and said, "Are you outta ice cream, Odette?"

"I'm trying to eat healthier, maybe take off a few pounds this summer," I lied, not wanting to admit that I was think-ing of the grapes as a first course.

Mama said, "Dietin' is a waste of energy. Nothin' wrong with having a few extra pounds on you. And you really shouldn't drink so much water at this time of day. You were a bedwetter."

I smiled and, in a childish show of independence, drank more water. Then I tried to change the subject. I asked, "What brings you by, Mama?"

"I just thought I'd come tell you about the fun I had with Earl and Thelma McIntyre. We was up all night goin' over old times and just laughin' up a storm. I had forgot just how funny Thelma was. Lord, that was a good time. And that Thelma can roll a joint like nobody's business, tight little sticks with just enough slack in the roach. I told her—"

"Mama, please," I interrupted. I looked over my shoulder the way I always did when she started talking about that stuff. My mother had been a dedicated marijuana smoker all of her adult life. She said it was for her glaucoma. And if you reminded her that she'd never had glaucoma, she would bend your ear about the virtues of her preventative vision care regimen.

Other than being against the law, the problem with Mama's habit, and the reason I automatically glanced over my shoulder when she started talking about that mess, was that James had worked for the Indiana State Police for thirty-five years. Mama got caught twenty years back buying a bag of dope on the state university campus on the north end of town, and as a favor to James, the head of campus security brought her home instead of arresting her. The campus security chief swore he'd keep it under wraps, but things like that never stay quiet in a little town like Plainview. Everybody knew about it by the next morning. It tickled Mama to no end when her getting busted became a sermon topic at church a week later. But James didn't see the humor in it when it happened, and he never would.

I was eager for Mama to get back on track with the story of her evening with the McIntyres, skipping any illegal parts, because foremost among my mother's many peculiarities was the fact that, for many years, the vast majority of her conversations had been with dead people. Thelma McIntyre, the excellent joint roller, had been dead for twenty-some years. Big Earl, on the other hand, had been just fine one day earlier when I'd seen him at Earl's All-You-Can-Eat buffet. If he had indeed been visiting with Mama, it was not good news for Big Earl.

"So, Big Earl's dead, is he?" I asked.

"I imagine so," she said.

I sat there for a while, not saying anything, just thinking about Big Earl gone from the earth. Mama gazed at me like she was reading my mind and said, "It's all right, baby. Really. He couldn't be happier."

We found out about Mama seeing ghosts at a Thanksgiving supper back in the 1970s. Mama, Daddy, my big brother Rudy, James, Jimmy, Eric, and me – I was pregnant with Denise that fall – were all gathered around the table. In keeping with tradition, I had done all of the cooking. Flowers Mama understood. She had the best garden in town, even before she devoted a plot to her prized marijuana plants. Food Mama never quite got the hang of. The last time Mama attempted to cook a holiday meal, we ended up feeding her black-and-gray glazed ham to the dog and dining on hardboiled eggs. The dog took one bite of Mama's ham and howled for six hours straight. The poor animal never quite recovered. So I became the family chef at age ten and we ended up with the only vegetarian dog in southern Indiana.

That Thanksgiving supper had started off real nice. I had cooked my best feast ever and everybody loved it. We joked and ate and celebrated having Rudy at home. My brother had run off to Indianapolis as soon as he graduated high school, so we didn't see much of him and my boys barely knew their uncle. Everyone was having a good time, except for Mama, who was testy and distracted all afternoon. She got more agitated as the meal went on, mumbling to herself and snapping at anyone who asked her what was wrong. Finally she stood up from the table and hurled the butter dish at an empty corner of the dining room. She shouted, "Goddammit to hell!" – my mother can cuss a blue streak when the inspiration hits her – "Goddammit to hell! I have had just about all I can take from you, Eleanor Roosevelt. Nobody invited you here and it's time for you to go." She shook an accusatory index finger at the corner of the room where the stick of butter, avocado-green plastic butter dish still adhered to it, slid down the wall, leaving a shiny trail like the path of a rectangular snail. Mama looked at the astonished faces around the table and said, "Don't give me that look. She may have been the perfect little lady when she was in the White House – all lace doilies and finger bowls – but since she died, she ain't done nothin' but show up here drunk as a skunk, tryin' to start some shit."

Later, Jackie Onassis came to see Mama, too, but she was much better behaved.

Daddy reacted to Mama's ghosts by trying, unsuccessfully, to persuade her to see a doctor. James and I worried about her in private, but pretended in front of the kids that there was nothing odd about their grandma. Rudy decided that Indianapolis wasn't nearly far enough from the craziness of his family, and he moved to California a month later. He has lived there ever since.

Mama reached across the kitchen table and poked at my arm. "You're gonna get a kick out of this," she said. "You know that woman Earl was livin' with?" "That woman" would be Big Earl's second wife, Minnie. Mama couldn't stand Minnie, and she refused to utter her name or acknowledge her marriage to Big Earl.

"Thelma says that woman set up a fountain in the front room where Thelma and Earl used to have the hi-fi. Can you imagine that? Do you remember how nice that hi-fi was? Best I ever heard. And they saved up for a year to get it. We sure had us some parties to remember in that house."

Mama watched me eat a few more grapes and then said, "Earl said the nicest things about you. He was always so crazy about you, you know. And I don't need to tell you how much he loved James."

James loved Big Earl, too. Earl McIntyre was the closest thing to a father James ever had. James's daddy was a low-down, dirty son of a bitch who ran out on him and his mother when James was barely more than a toddler. James's father stuck around just long enough to leave a few nasty scars and then hightailed it out of town a few steps ahead of the law to inflict more damage somewhere else. The visible scar on James was a half-moon-shaped raised leathery line along his jaw made by a razor slash intended for James's mother. The deeper, invisible scars he left on James, only I saw. Only me and Big Earl.

After James's father ran off, Big Earl and Miss Thelma

took it upon themselves to see that James's mother always had food on the table. When the All-You-Can-Eat, the first black-owned business in downtown Plainview, opened in the mid-1950s and Big Earl couldn't have been making a dime, he hired James's mother as his first employee. And they kept her on the payroll long after emphysema had made it impossible for her to work. More important, the McIntyres kept an eye on James, so he wouldn't end up like his daddy. I'll be forever grateful to them for that.

That's how Big Earl was, a good and strong man who helped other people to get stronger, too. All kinds of folks, and not just black, loved him. You could take a problem to Big Earl and he would sit there and listen to you spill out a lifetime's worth of troubles. He'd nod patiently like it was all new to him, even though he was a man who had seen a lot in his life and had probably heard your particular kind of blues a hundred times over. After you were done, he'd rub his huge hands across the white stubble that stood out against the coal black of his skin and he'd say, "Here's what we're gonna do." And if you had sense, you did whatever it was he said. He was a smart man. Made a little money, kept his dignity, and still managed to live to be old – something a black man his age in southern Indiana shouldn't have been able to do. Something many had tried to do, but failed at.

Now, if Mama's word was to be trusted, Big Earl was dead. But that was a mighty big "if."

Mama said, "What was I talkin' about? Oh yeah, the fountain. Thelma said the fountain in her front room was six feet tall, if it was an inch. And it was made up to look like a naked white girl pouring water out of a pitcher onto the head of another naked white girl. Who comes up with that kind of stuff?"

I poured another glass of water, and thought. Mama was often wrong when it came to her perceptions of the world, physical or ghostly. And she'd said many times herself that ghosts could be tricksters. The whole thing about Big Earl being dead could have been a prank played on Mama by a tipsy, belligerent Eleanor Roosevelt. I decided to put it out of my mind until later when we'd meet our friends for our standing after-church dinner date. We were gathering that Sunday, as we always did, at the All-You-Can-Eat. Little Earl and his wife, Erma Mae, had taken over running the restaurant several years back, but Big Earl still came in nearly every day to help out his son and daughter-in-law. One way or another, I'd have my answer come evening.

Mama asked, "So why are you up drinkin' all this water at this hour?"

"I woke up hot and needed to cool down," I said, taking another swig. "Hot flash."

"Hot flash? I thought you were done with the change."

"I thought so, too, but I guess I'm still changing."

"Well, you might wanna get that checked out. You don't wanna change too much. Your aunt Marjorie started changin' and kept it up till she changed into a man."

"Oh, she did not and you know it."

"Okay, maybe she didn't switch all the way over to a man, but Marjorie grew a mustache, shaved her head, and took to wearin' overalls to church. I'm not sayin' the look didn't suit her; I'm just sayin' you can draw a straight line between her first hot flash and that bar fight she died in."

I ate a grape and said, "Point taken."

We sat in silence, me thinking about Big Earl in spite of telling myself I wouldn't, and Mama thinking about God knows what. She stood up and walked to the window that looked out onto the side yard. She said, "It's gonna be a truly beautiful Sunday morning. I love it hot. You should get some rest before you go to church." She turned away from the window and said, talking to me like she used to when I was a kid, "Go on to bed now, git."

I obeyed. I put my glass in the sink and replaced the half-empty bowl of grapes and the water pitcher in the fridge and headed back toward my bedroom. I turned around and said, "Say hi to Daddy for me."

But Mama had already slipped out the back door. Through the window, I saw her slowly making her way through my sorry excuse for a garden. She stopped and shook her head with disapproval at the stunted stalks, insect-chewed vegetables, and pale blooms that made up my pitiful little plots. I knew what I would hear about on her next visit.

Back in the bedroom, I climbed into the bed and squeezed in close to my husband. I propped myself up on one elbow, leaned over James, and kissed the rough scar on his jaw. He grunted, but didn't wake up. I lay back down and pressed myself against his back. Then I reached around and brought my hand to rest on James's stomach. Squeezed against my man in the center of our king-size bed, I fell asleep listening to the rhythm of his breathing.

Throughout the year that followed, I thought about that Sunday morning and how Mama's visit had cooled me down and cheered me. Even during the worst of the troubles that came later, I smiled whenever I recalled that visit and how sweet it had been for her to come by, looking all done up in that cute sky-blue dress I hadn't seen in the six years since we buried her in it.

Chapter 2

I was born in a sycamore tree. That was fifty-five years ago, and it made me a bit of a local celebrity. My celebrity status was brief, though. Two baby girls, later my best friends, came along within months of me in ways that made my sycamore tree entrance seem less astonishing. I only mention the tree because I have been told all of my life that it explains how I ended up the way I am – brave and strong according to those who like me, mannish and pigheaded to those who don't. Also, it probably explains why, after the initial jolt passed, I wasn't much troubled when my dead mother showed up for a chat.

I started out life in that sycamore because my mother went to see a witch. Mama was smart and tough. She worked hard every day of her life right up until she dropped dead from a stroke while she was winding up to throw a rock at a squirrel that was digging up bulbs in her showplace of a garden. All of Mama's toughness had evaporated, though, when she found herself halfway through the tenth month of her pregnancy, wondering if it would ever end. Seven years earlier, Rudy had been born right on schedule. But three lost babies followed my brother, none of them managing to remain inside my mother's womb for longer than a few months. Now I had come along and refused to leave.

Before she went to see the witch, Mama tried all kinds of things her country relatives told her to do to get the baby to come. My grandmother advised her to eat hot peppers with every meal, claiming that the heat would drive the baby out. Mama did it for three days and ended up with indigestion so severe that she was fooled twice into thinking she was in labor. Two times, she and Daddy went to the colored hospital in Evansville, and both times she came home with no baby.

My mother's sister whispered to her that the only way to get the baby out was to have sex. Aunt Marjorie said, "That's how it got there, Dora. And that's the only sure way to get it out."

Mama liked the sex idea, if only just to pass the time while waiting, but Daddy was less than enthusiastic. She was twice his weight even before her pregnancy, and when she straddled him in his sleep one night demanding satisfaction, the terrified look in his eyes as she hovered over him made her back down from the sex solution and look to sorcery instead.

Like I said, that was 1950, and back then a fair number of people in Plainview, black and white, consulted a witch from time to time. Some still do, but nowadays it's only the poorest and most superstitious of folks, mostly the ones who live in the little Appalachian clusters outside of town, who will admit to it.

Mama went to the witch expecting a potion or a poultice – poultices were big among witches – but what she got instead were instructions. The witch told her that if she climbed up into the branches of a sycamore tree at straight-up noon and sang her favorite hymn, the baby would come.

Witches were like that. They almost always mixed in a touch of something approved by the Baptist church – a prayer, a spiritual, or a chant warning about the godlessness of Lutherans – so people could go to a witch and not have to worry that they'd pay for it down the line with their immortal souls. It absolved the clients' guilt and kept the preachers off the witches' backs.

So, on a windy afternoon, my mother hauled a rickety old ladder out to a sycamore tree by the woods behind the house. Mama propped her ladder against the tree and climbed up. Then she nestled herself in the crook of two branches as comfortably as was possible considering her condition and began to sing.

Mama used to joke that if she had chosen something more sedate, something along the lines of "Mary, Don't You Weep" or "Calvary," she might not have given birth to such a peculiar daughter. But she dug her teeth into "Jesus Is a Rock" and swayed and kicked her feet with that good gospel spirit until she knocked over the ladder and couldn't get back down. I was born at one o'clock and spent the rest of the afternoon in the sycamore tree until my father rescued us when he got home from his shop at six. They named me Odette Breeze Jackson, in honor of my being born in the open air.

As it often happened when a child was born under unusual circumstances, old folks who claimed that they'd been schooled in the wisdom of the ancestors felt called upon to use the occasion to issue dire warnings. My grandma led the chorus in forecasting a dreary future for me. The way she explained it, if a baby was born off of the ground, that child was born without its first natural fear, the fear of falling. That set off a horrible chain reaction resulting in the child's being cursed with a life of fearlessness. She said a fearless boy had some hope of growing up to be a hero, but a fearless girl would more than likely be a reckless fool. My mother also accepted this as fact, although she leaned more toward the notion that I might become a hero. It should be remembered, of course, that Mama was a grown woman who thought climbing a tree in her tenth month of pregnancy was a good idea. Her judgment had to be looked at with suspicion.

Nearly everyone, it seemed to me, believed that coming into the world in any manner that could be seen as out of the ordinary was a bad omen. People never said, "Congratulations on managing to deliver a healthy baby while you were stuck in that rowboat in the middle of the lake." They just shook their heads and whispered to each other that the child would surely drown one day. No one ever said, "Aren't you a brave little thing, having your baby all alone in a chicken coop." They just said that the child would turn out to have bird shit for brains and then went on to treat the child that way even if the kid was clearly a tiny genius. Like the doomed child born on the water and the dummy arriving among fowl, I was born in a sycamore tree and would never have the good sense to know when to run scared.

Not knowing any better, I listened to what I was told about myself and grew up convinced I was a little brown warrior. I stomped my way through life like I was the Queen of the Amazons. I got in fights with grown men who were twice as big as and ten times meaner than me. I did things that got me talked about pretty bad and then went back and did them again. And that morning I first saw my dead mother in my kitchen, I accepted that I had inherited a strange legacy and visited with her over a bowl of grapes instead of screaming and heading for the hills.

I know the truth about myself, though. I have never been fearless. If I ever believed such a thing, motherhood banished that myth but quick. Still, whenever logic told me it was time to run, a little voice whispered in my ear, "You were born in a sycamore tree." And, for good or ill, the sound of that voice always made me stand my ground.

Chapter 3

Clarice and Richmond Baker claimed seats at opposite ends of the window table at Earl's All-You-Can-Eat and waited for their four friends to arrive. The restaurant was an easy walk from Calvary Baptist and they were always first to show up for after-church supper. Odette and James Henry's little country church, Holy Family Baptist, was farthest from the All-You-Can-Eat, but James was a fast driver and, being a cop, unafraid of getting speeding tickets. So they usually arrived next. Barbara Jean and Lester Maxberry were members of grand First Baptist, the rich people's church. It looked down on Plainview from its perch on Main Street and was closest to the restaurant, but Lester was twenty-five years older than the rest of the group and he often moved slowly.

Clarice caught her reflection in the window glass and imagined that she and Richmond must resemble a luminous peacock and his drab mate. She was hidden, neck to kneecaps, beneath a modest, well-tailored beige linen dress. Richmond, leaning back in his chair and waving hello to friends seated at other tables around the room, demanded attention in the pale gray summer suit Clarice had set out for him the night before along with his favorite shirt, a cotton button-down that was the vivid ultramarine of aquarium rocks.

He had always worn bold colors. Richmond had such a Ken-doll handsomeness about him that the women in his life, first his mother and then Clarice, couldn't resist the urge to dress him in bright hues and show him off. On the occasion of Richmond's first date with Clarice, his mother had adorned her teenage son in a peach jacket with white rope trim ornamenting the lapels. A getup like that would have gotten any other boy in town ridiculed and called a sissy – it was still the 1960s, after all. But Richmond Baker sauntered up Clarice's front walk and managed to make that outfit look as masculine as a rack of antlers. Clarice often pictured that loose, powerful way he walked back then before the surgeries stiffened him. It was as if he were constructed entirely of lean muscle strung together with taut rubber bands.

By coincidence, Clarice had chosen a peach skirt for that first date. Her skirt matched Richmond's prissy jacket so perfectly that everyone who saw them out on the town later assumed they had planned it that way. Clarice and her mother had peeked through the curtains and watched him step onto the front porch. Her mother, who was as excited as Clarice was, had dug her fingers into Clarice's arm until her daughter pulled away from her. All the while, her mother had gushed that their matching ensembles were a sign Clarice and Richmond were made for each other.

Clarice, though, had already seen all the signs she needed. Young Richmond had a handsome, almost pretty face with a small, well-shaped mouth and long eyelashes.

He had a football scholarship waiting for him at the university across town. He was a preacher's son, his father having been the pastor of their church before moving on to a larger congregation just across the state line in Louisville. And he had those beautiful hands.

She had been in awe of his hands long before they brought him glory for palming a football in high school, college, and a professional career that had lasted only one season.

By the time he was eleven years old, Richmond was using his already large paws to show off for the girls by pulling walnuts from the low-hanging branches of the trees that lined the streets between the schoolyard and their neighborhood. He would make a grunting, grimacing production of crushing the nuts between his palms until he tired of his solo act and joined in with the other boys who ran in his pack, tossing the walnuts at the girls as they ran home squealing and laughing.

The children had named the walnut trees "time bomb trees" because when the nuts were past their prime they turned black and made a quiet ticking sound on hot days. Years later, she often thought it was fitting that her earliest recollection of the boy who would become her husband was a memory of him lobbing time bombs in her direction.

Lit by the afternoon sun from the window at the All-You-Can-Eat, Richmond Baker still looked like a square-jawed young football hero. But Clarice was doing her best not to look his way at all. Every time she glanced at her husband, she thought back to the hours she had sat up worrying until he finally staggered in at 3:57 that morning. The sight of him brought to mind those horrible, slow-passing minutes of waiting and then the time spent lying in bed beside him after he finally got home, pretending to sleep and wondering whether she possessed sufficient upper-body strength to smother him with his pillow.

At breakfast, he had dragged himself into the kitchen, scratched his private parts, and told her a tale that she knew was a lie. It was the old reliable story of having to work late and finding that every phone within a ten-mile radius was broken. For the new millennium, he had updated his excuse to include cellular phones mysteriously losing their signals. He deserved some credit for keeping up with the times, she thought. After he told his lie, he had sat down at the kitchen table, blown a kiss in his wife's direction, and tucked himself into the breakfast she had prepared for him, attacking it as if he hadn't eaten a meal in weeks. Screwing around, Clarice thought, must stimulate the appetite.

Before church that morning, Clarice had mulled over her situation and decided that her problem was that she had gotten out of the habit of ignoring Richmond's little lapses; he had been on such good behavior for the past couple of years. She figured that if she just avoided looking at Richmond through breakfast, morning service, and maybe during the walk to Earl's, she could relocate that old wall in her brain she used to hide behind at times like this. Then she'd soon be back to merrily pretending things were just fine, as she had done for decades. She had gazed at the kitchen floor through breakfast. She had stared at the stained-glass windows during church. She counted the clouds in the sky and the cracks in the sidewalk on the way to the All-You-Can-Eat. But the remedy didn't work. The throbbing at her temples that bloomed each time she watched Richmond's pretty, lying mouth spread into a grin told her that she needed more time before she could step back into the old routine, the way her husband apparently had.

Clarice heard a deep male voice whisper, "Hey there, gorgeous." She looked to her right and saw that Ramsey Abrams had slithered up beside her. He placed one hand on the table and the other on the back of her chair, and then he leaned in until his face was just inches away from hers.

Ramsey had been Richmond's number one running buddy for years, the two of them continuing to sow their wild oats together long after they were married and the fathers of several children between them. With his nose nearly touching hers, Clarice could see that the whites of Ramsey's eyes were laced with bright red veins. She detected the odor of stale rum on his breath.

She began to create a picture in her head of how the previous evening had started. Richmond would have been in his office at the university where he and Ramsey both worked as recruiters for the football team. Ramsey shuffled in and said something along the lines of "Come on, Richmond. Just join me for a quick drink. I'll have you home by ten. You can stay out till ten, can't you? Your woman ain't got that tight a hold on your balls, does she?"

She had no real evidence that he had been the instigator of Richmond's night out, and she knew Richmond was perfectly capable of getting into mischief all on his own.

Still, Clarice itched to slap Ramsey's stupid face and tell him to get back across the room to the table where his son Clifton – the son who had been in and out of jail since he was thirteen, not the other son who sniffed airplane glue and touched himself inappropriately in women's shoe stores – and Ramsey's bucktoothed wife, Florence, sat glaring at each other.

She said, "Ramsey, you keep sweet-talking me like that and I'm going to have to try and steal you away from Florence."

He laughed. "Baby, I sure won't stop you from trying. Just don't tell Richmond."

Clarice said, "Ramsey, you are so naughty," and she slapped his hand in that way that men like him interpreted as *Please do go on, you sexy bad boy.* Then he leaned in closer and kissed her on the cheek. She let loose a kind of girlish squeal, the sound of which made her want to kick herself. No, not only herself, but her mother, too, for drumming this business of responding to male attention with adolescent giddiness so firmly into her head that it was automatic now.

She delivered another slap to Ramsey's hand. This time, she accidentally allowed her true feelings about him to creep into her gesture. He let out a very sincere "Ouch!" and snatched his hand away before walking toward Richmond's end of the table. As she watched Ramsey rubbing his knuckles, her headache eased just a bit.

Ramsey pulled a chair up close to Richmond and the two of them started whispering in each other's ears, stopping occasionally to bellow with laughter. Clarice imagined the content of the conversation passing between them and her thoughts turned violent again. She picked up her fork from the place setting, twirled it like a cheerleader's baton with her left thumb and forefinger, and thought about the sense of fulfillment she would gain if she walked to the other end of the table and plunged that fork into Richmond's forehead. She pictured the look of amazement that would spread over his face as she grabbed hold of his jaw to get better leverage, and then twisted the fork 180 degrees counterclockwise. That fantasy felt so dangerously good that she forced herself to put the fork back down on the table. She told herself, again, to look away.

Her gaze was drawn to the center of the table then, and she noticed the new tablecloth for the first time. The restaurant, apparently, had a new logo. At the center of the tablecloth, and all the others in the room, a painted wreath of fruits and vegetables spelled out "All-You-Can-Eat." Inside the circle of produce was a pair of shiny red lips with a bright pink tongue protruding from them.

Clarice could see Little Earl's tacky fingerprints all over this. He had inherited his father's kind disposition, but not much of his good taste. And she suspected that, even though the place was no longer legally his, Big Earl wasn't going to be happy with this innovation. Those nasty-looking lips and fruits and vegetables – particularly the suggestive cherry and cucumbers that spelled "All" – were going to have the more conservative patrons in an uproar. Clarice was thankful that her pastor wasn't a regular customer; she could easily imagine him calling for a boycott.

She couldn't believe she hadn't noticed the new tablecloths the instant she walked in. They definitely hadn't been there a day earlier when she had eaten lunch at this same table with Odette and Barbara Jean. She was so familiar with the All-You-Can-Eat, and it had changed so little over the years, that she could usually tell if one chair was out of place. This was how much Richmond had put her off her game.

Clarice and her friends had been meeting at the window table at Earl's for almost forty years – since right about the time they were nicknamed the Supremes. Little Earl had wild crushes on all three of them back then, and he had tried his best to seduce them with free Cokes and chicken wings. Clarice was sure that, if he had been a little more persistent, it would have eventually worked on Odette. That girl was always hungry. Even when she was a child, Odette ate like a grown man.

Clarice's first memory of Odette was of watching her stuff fistfuls of candy into her mouth and then wipe her sticky hands on her dress in kindergarten. Odette always wore hideous homemade dresses with crooked seams and mismatched patterns. Clarice still remembered their first conversation. Since Odette's maiden name was Jackson and Clarice's was Jordan, alphabetical order demanded that they sit next to each other throughout most of their education. Odette had reached over from her desk and passed Clarice a piece of taffy in class one day. Clarice said to her, "That's the ugliest dress in the whole world."

Odette replied, "My grandmama made it for me. She's real good at sewin', but she's blind." She popped another piece of candy into her mouth and added, "This ain't the ugliest dress in the world. I'm gonna wear that one tomorrow."

And she did. And it was. And they'd been friends ever since.

Little Earl's wife, Erma Mae, walked, ass first, through the swinging doors that led from the kitchen, carrying a tray of food. Erma Mae had the largest head Clarice had ever seen on a woman. When she was in high school, that huge, round head, coupled with her tall, bony body and flat chest, earned her the nickname Lollipop. Marriage to Little Earl, and access to all that good free food, had thickened her out from her hips on down, so the nickname hadn't stuck. Putting on all that extra weight was probably not the healthiest thing for her, but it did help to balance out that giant head, which Clarice supposed must bring Erma Mae some solace.

Erma Mae placed the tray on the buffet table and then plopped down on one of the two wooden stools next to the gleaming stainless-steel steam tables from which she and her husband oversaw their domain every day. She made eye contact with Clarice after she settled onto her stool, and she waved at her.

When Clarice waved back, Erma Mae stood and performed a little pirouette to display her new apron, which, like the tablecloths, had that awful lips logo on it. Clarice mouthed, "I love it," and thought, *Hope you're watching, Richmond. This is how you tell a convincing lie.*

Erma Mae yelled, "Belinda!" and her daughter rushed in from the kitchen. Erma Mae pointed toward Clarice and Richmond, and Belinda picked up a pitcher of iced tea and headed to their table. Clarice was fond of Belinda. She was a darling girl, and smart, too. She had won enough scholarship money to pay for a full ride at the university.

Unfortunately, she was also the mirror image of her big-headed mother at that age. If you squinted as she walked toward you, you'd swear a brown party balloon was floating your way.

After Belinda poured Richmond's tea, she accidentally nudged his glass with the pitcher, causing the glass to fall to the floor. She let out a yelp and said she was sorry. Then she started going on about how clumsy she was. Belinda pulled a kitchen rag from her apron pocket and moved to wipe up the spill, but Richmond stopped her. "And risk ruining that fancy new apron? I wouldn't be able to live with myself," he said as he took the rag from her. He dropped to his knees to clean up the mess. Belinda continued apologizing as he worked, and she poured him another tea using a glass taken from one of the other place settings at the table.

Watching Richmond kneel in his best summer suit at the feet of that awkward, plain girl just to make her feel good caused Clarice's bad memories of the previous night and morning to recede a little. That was Richmond. About the time she built up a good head of steam thinking of the many ways he had disappointed her, he'd go and remind her of what she loved about him. She watched him swirl that rag over the rutted oak floor and couldn't help but think of how those same wonderful hands had comforted their children and changed as many, if not more, of their diapers as hers had. Those hands had also spoon-fed her father – three times a day, every day – for the last weeks of her father's life, when he was too frail to lift a spoon and too proud to allow Clarice or her mother to feed him. *That* Richmond, the kind and selfless one, was the only

Richmond she had seen for two years. But the other Richmond, the one who lied and cheated, had reappeared, and no number of kind words or gallant gestures could erase him from her mind.

Belinda left, carrying the tea-soaked cloth and still looking flustered, but grinning. Richmond returned to his chair and gulped from his glass. Clarice tasted her tea and discovered that it was so sweet she couldn't stand more than a sip. Richmond, who was diabetic, had no business drinking any of it. But when she looked his way, she saw that Richmond was not only guzzling the sweet tea, he was using it to wash down a piece of pecan pie that someone, probably that damn Ramsey Abrams, had slipped to him.

This was part of the dance they did each Sunday. Richmond sneaked fatty, sugary treats that were off his diet and Clarice played the role of the frustrated mother, running to the other end of the table to pinch his ear and demand that he hand it over to her. The game always ended with Richmond batting those long lashes of his at her until she permitted him a spoonful of whatever he was sneaking. Then she would return to her chair, theatrically rolling her eyes about what an ill-disciplined boy her Richmond was.

But Clarice was in no mood to play along with him this time. She watched him chew the pie and wash it down with sweet tea, and she kept her mouth firmly shut. She told herself that this time she wasn't going to lift a finger to stop him. He could put himself in the hospital again, if he wanted to. If he didn't care, why should she?

Old habits evolve into reflexes, though, and Clarice found that she couldn't stop herself. She raised her tea glass high in the air with her right hand and then tapped it with the nail of her left ring finger to get his attention. She said, "Richmond, too sweet."

He pushed his lower lip out and unleashed the sad eyes, but he slid his glass of tea and the small plate containing the pie away from his place setting. Then, performing his part of their little ritual to perfection, he grabbed his fork and took one more quick bite of the pie. Then he winked at her.

Clarice had learned her husband was a diabetic two years earlier when she received a phone call from the hospital saying that he had been found in his university office in a coma and might not make it. He was in intensive care for weeks, and for months afterward he was nearly helpless – no feeling in his feet, no strength in his beautiful hands. When she finally got him home, she prayed, bullied, sweet-talked, and seduced, anything to get Richmond well again.

She succeeded magnificently. He was up and about far sooner than his doctors had anticipated. And when he recovered, he expressed his gratitude for the care she had given him to anyone who would listen. He would actually stop strangers on the street and say, "This woman saved my life; made me a new man."

And Richmond *was* a new man. For the first time in their marriage he was actually the husband Clarice had always pretended he was. All the love she had for him, the affection that had felt so inconvenient for so long, suddenly didn't seem misplaced. It was a second chance at life, a wonderful rebirth for both of them.

It lasted two years. Two fine years.

A petite woman in a knee-length tan dress and black patent leather pumps walked past Clarice and strode up to Richmond. She leaned over to say something into his ear, giving Clarice and half the dining room a view of her tiny backside.

The vise around Clarice's forehead tightened again. There she is, Clarice thought, the reason Richmond didn't make it home until nearly sunrise.

With her eyeglasses stowed away in her purse, Clarice couldn't identify the woman whispering to her husband. She reached to retrieve her glasses, but stopped herself. The only people who saw her bespectacled with any regularity were her piano students. That concession to middle age had come only after she had detected a slight decline in the general level of her students' playing that was caused, she came to realize, by her inability to see subtle technical lapses – an intermittently flattened finger, a wrist that dipped at just the wrong moment, a transient raised shoulder. Few people even knew that Clarice owned glasses, and she certainly wasn't about to give Richmond's latest partner in fornication the pleasure of seeing her looking matronly. Not today.

Clarice leaned back, hoping that a little more distance would bring the woman into better focus. She teetered on the rear legs of her chair until she felt that she was on the verge of toppling over backwards. Only the thought of Richmond's current bit on the side laughing at her as she lay with her back on the floor and her best Sunday pumps pointing at the ceiling forced Clarice to sit up straight again.

Attempting not to squint so blatantly that Richmond

and the stranger might notice, Clarice strained to see the other end of the table. Whoever the woman was, Richmond responded to her with a wide smile that displayed even, capped teeth that were the eye-straining white of new aluminum siding and took years off his face.

Right then, Clarice felt something crack inside of her. The look of admiration on Richmond's face as he flirted, right in front of her, with this skinny tramp in her polyester dress was just too damn much to take. Clarice had gone decades without making scenes, no matter how great the provocation. But now, at their window table at the All-You-Can-Eat, in front of some of their oldest friends, she was primed to leap into uncharted territory.

Before she had time to think about what she was doing, Clarice stood from her chair and shouted, "Richmond!" loud enough that the restaurant grew quieter as the people at the surrounding tables stopped their conversations to look her way. But her chance to let thirty-five years of pent-up outrage come flooding out evaporated when the woman whispering to Richmond turned in her direction and Clarice saw that it was Carmel Handy. She was good-looking, nicely shaped, well-groomed, and at least ninety years old. The schoolboy smile Clarice had seen on her husband's face had been just that. They'd both had Miss Carmel as their ninth grade English teacher.

That her prime suspect turned out to be Miss Carmel was, Clarice had to admit, one hell of an ironic twist. Carmel Handy was, at that time, Clarice's personal hero because of the local legend about her marriage.

The tale people told was that William Handy once took off on a weeklong whoring excursion. When he got home, Miss Carmel confronted him and told him the only excuse he could possibly have for disappearing like that was that he must have forgotten where he lived. So she recited their address, 10 Pine Street, aloud. And, to make it memorable, she punctuated the telling with three blows to Mr Handy's head with a cast-iron skillet. She didn't kill him, but she changed him from Big Bad Bill to Sweet William overnight.

That had happened before Clarice was born, if it happened at all. Rumor had a way of becoming permanently entangled with fact in small towns like Plainview. But, to this day, angry wives in southern Indiana evoke the legend of "the Skillet Lady" whenever they want to get their husbands' full attention.

Richmond and Miss Carmel both stared at Clarice, waiting for her to explain her outburst. She stared back at them, trying to come up with words. But no words would form. All she could think about was how satisfying it must have been for Miss Carmel to remind her no-count husband where he lived by clobbering him on the head once for each of the three syllables of their address. Since Richmond and Clarice lived at 1722 Prendergast Boulevard, she assumed that her satisfaction would be four times sweeter.

As she had so many times in the past, Odette came riding to Clarice's rescue. Through the window, Clarice saw James and Odette's car squeezing into a small space directly across the street, in front of the two-story white clapboard house Big Earl had moved his young family into not long after he opened the All-You-Can-Eat.

Clarice lowered herself into her chair and said, "Hi,

Miss Carmel, how are you, dear?" Then, to Richmond, "Honey, Odette and James are here."

Miss Carmel said hello to Clarice and then went back to chatting with Richmond, who was still teacher's pet after forty-three years. The customers seated nearby stopped staring and resumed their conversations when they saw that nothing exciting was going to happen.

For reasons Clarice could never understand, Odette and James insisted upon traveling around town in a microscopic ten-year-old Honda when James had full access to a much roomier and more presentable state police department vehicle. It looked even worse now because Odette had packed on at least ten more pounds that year; and that was on top of the extra fifty she'd been carrying since the Nixon years. The sight of them extricating themselves from that tiny car – Odette, as round as a berry and dressed in one of those shapeless muumuus she favored, and James, skeletal and over six feet tall – was such a spectacle that Clarice couldn't help but imagine she was taking in a circus act.

As she watched Odette and James walk toward the All-You-Can-Eat, Clarice asked herself how on earth she had ended up being the one Supreme who turned into her mother. Odette might look like Dora Jackson, but she was as different as she could be from her mother, who had always scared Clarice a bit with her talk of ghosts and her countrified brusqueness. And with all of her wealth, civic-mindedness, and charitable deeds, Barbara Jean was about as far as she could get from living the sad, desperate life her mother had lived.

Clarice had been the one to follow her mother's

example. She had become a pillar of her church, striving for biblical perfection at all costs. When her children came, first Ricky, then Abe, and, finally, the twins, Carolyn and Carl, Clarice had made sure that they were the cleanest, best-dressed, and most polite children in town. She had acted the part of a lady, even when every last particle of her being yearned to spit, curse, and kill. And she had grown up and married her father.

Chapter 4

Clarice Jordan Baker was the first black child born at University Hospital. It was reported in black newspapers as far away as Los Angeles. Clarice's mother, Beatrice Jordan, encased the news clippings of the glad tidings in ornate gold frames and placed them strategically around her house. No guest could sit at the Jordans' dining table or use their toilet without being aware that the family had once made history. The clipping over the mantel in the living room was snipped from the front page of the *Indianapolis Recorder*. The caption beneath the photo read "The New Negro Family." The article about Clarice's birth heralded the arrival of the "new Negro family of the desegregated 1950s." Her father, attorney Abraham Jordan, was missing from the picture.

Beatrice worked as a nursing assistant at University Hospital. She got it into her head one day that her child would be born there, instead of at the colored hospital an hour away in Evansville where everyone in Leaning Tree had their babies. Fortunately for her, this wild idea coincided with the arrival of Dr Samuel Snow, who had come to Indiana State University at Plainview from New York City that year to preside over the ob-gyn department. Dr Snow let it be known when he came to the hospital that, under his leadership, access to the department would no longer be restricted by race. The university agreed to his demand, believing he would get over that bit of New York–style eccentricity once he got settled in southern Indiana and gained an appreciation for how things worked there. But Dr Snow did not change his mind, and Beatrice, on the job well into her pregnancy, arranged to repeatedly waddle across his path and allow him to believe he had handpicked her – instead of the other way around – for the honor of making history at University Hospital.

In Beatrice's retelling, the minor complications of Clarice's birth were elevated to terrifying hours during which she and her baby balanced on a knife's edge between survival and doom. When Beatrice sensed in her daughter some resistance to acknowledging her mother's wisdom, she trotted out the tale of how her solid judgment was the only reason the two of them hadn't died in a substandard Evansville clinic. Clarice heard the story so often in her childhood that it became as familiar to her as "Cinderella" or "The Pied Piper." When relating the long version of the ordeal she suffered giving Clarice life, Beatrice often employed overripe fruit as stage props. For the short version, she simply pressed the back of her hand to her forehead and whispered, "It was a horror show."

Freshly snatched from death's door or not, an hour after Clarice was born her mother was fully made up, coiffed, dressed in a satin bed coat, and propped up in her hospital bed, ready for the photographers who had gathered to snap pictures of the inspirational middle-class colored family. But Mr Jordan couldn't be found. By the time he was located, sharing an intimate moment with one of the

hospital cleaning ladies in a supply closet, the photographers had taken their snapshots and gone. That cleaning
lady may or may not have been the woman who gave him
the syphilis he passed on to his wife, sterilizing her and
ensuring that Clarice would be an only child; Abraham
was never quite certain.

And so it went, from the time Clarice was old enough to
understand what was what until her father was too sick to
get into trouble. Abraham Jordan cheated and lied. Beatrice
prayed, consulted with her pastor, prayed again, and then
accepted each deception with a smile. Clarice watched
and learned.

Unlike her mother, who had been taken by surprise,
Clarice had received fair warning about Richmond. Just
before Clarice's marriage, Odette had a frank talk with her
friend that forced Clarice to open her eyes and see just how
much Richmond had in common with Abraham Jordan.
Clarice had nearly called off the wedding, but, because she
loved Richmond so, she chose to rely upon the counsel of
her mother and the same pastor whose guidance would lead
Beatrice into a life consumed by bitterness. Clarice had
weighed her options and – like a fool, she later saw – she
had decided to make a deal with Richmond that allowed her
to clamp her eyes shut again. The deal was, so long as
Richmond didn't embarrass her by being indiscreet the way
her father had been, she would accept him as he was and go
on as if everything were perfect.

They both stuck by the terms of their agreement, but
Clarice's definition of indiscretion shifted over the years.
At first, she told herself she could handle his missteps if he
was at home and in bed beside her at a decent hour every

night. But that didn't even make it through their first year. So she decided late nights were okay, as long as no strange women called the house. When she gave up on that, she settled for not being confronted with physical evidence.

As it turned out, Richmond was good about leaving no evidence. Clarice never had to scrub lipstick stains from his shorts or brush face powder from his lapels. She never contracted any diseases. And unlike her father, who had cast his seed around with the abandon of malfunctioning farm equipment, Richmond was careful. Clarice was never greeted at her front door by a younger woman clutching the hand of a child who had Richmond's pretty mouth.

That Sunday afternoon at the All-You-Can-Eat, between the ex-ample of her parents and the years she had spent honoring her part of her deal with Richmond, Clarice told herself that, given time, she could find her way back to that blissful state of mind in which the absence of sexually transmitted diseases and not having bastard children dropped off at her door were sufficient proof of her husband's love and respect. She was wrong.

Chapter 5

Idid my best not to dwell on my sunrise conversation with Mama, but it was on my mind all through morning service and during the drive to the All-You-Can-Eat. When we got to the restaurant, I tried not to be obvious about it as I studied Big Earl's house, searching for signs of unusual activity. But everything was quiet. There were no cars in the driveway except Big Earl's Buick. No somber-faced men stood smoking on the front porch. No one was visible through the parted living room drapes.

Inside the restaurant, I scanned the room for Big Earl. It was his habit to spend Sundays zigzagging his way between the tables, chatting with the customers. I didn't see him, so I turned toward the buffet to look for Little Earl or Erma Mae. I caught sight of Erma Mae sliding off of her stool and walking into the kitchen. I decided to take her presence and the calm at the house across the street as good signs about Big Earl's well-being. Feeling optimistic and a little annoyed with Mama for getting me all riled up with her ghostly insider information, I followed James to our table.

Richmond was waving goodbye to Carmel Handy and Clarice sat staring at the cutlery with a peculiar look on her face when we joined them. James took a seat next to

Richmond and the two of them jumped right into a conversation. I didn't have to listen in to know what they were saying. They had been discussing the same two topics since 1972. They either talked about football or boxing. Specifically, they talked about famous athletes of the past and how they might fare against famous athletes of the present. When Lester arrived, the conversation would get heated. Each week he loudly declared that Joe Louis, the Brown Bomber, could have taken on Ali and Tyson together, and single-handedly whupped an entire football team. If Richmond or James disagreed with him, Lester would grow frustrated and begin to bang his walking stick against the nearest table leg, insisting that his age and wisdom made him the better judge.

Clarice perched on the edge of her chair, showing off her best charm school posture and wearing an expression that was supposed to be a smile. Clarice has a long, handsome face with lovely, round eyes and a wide, nicely shaped mouth. But that day her lower jaw was pushed forward, her eyes were squinted, and her lips were pressed together like she was trying hard to keep something in. I hadn't seen that face in a while, but I knew it well. And I had a good idea what its return meant. I had to fight to keep myself from going down to the other end of the table and slapping the shit out of Richmond. But it was none of my business. And I knew from experience that my interference would not be appreciated.

Before she married Richmond, I went to Clarice and told her some things that I thought she should know about her fiancé. No rumors, no guesses. I sat with my oldest friend on the couch in her parents' living room and described seeing Richmond late the night before kissing a woman who lived around the block from me and seeing his car still parked in front of her house that morning. It hurt me to say it, loving Clarice like I do. But Clarice used to claim that, when it came to matters of men, she wanted her friends to give her the cold and honest truth, even if it was painful. I was young then, just twenty-one, and I didn't understand yet that nearly all of the women who make that claim are lying.

Clarice being Clarice, she took my news about Richmond with such sweet grace and calm that I didn't realize I'd been relieved of my matron of honor duties and thrown out of her house until I was standing on her front porch with the door bumping against my ass. But the next day she was at my house holding an armful of bride magazines, acting like our conversation had never happened. I was her matron of honor after all, and I never said another word to her about any of Richmond's shenanigans from then on.

After we got through our kisses and hellos, I asked Clarice, "Seen Big Earl today?"

She said, "No, why do you ask?"

"No reason. He was just on my mind," I said, which was the truth, if not the whole truth.

Clarice said, "I'm sure he'll be in pretty soon. That's a man who truly does not understand the idea of retirement. Besides, I get the feeling he prefers being here on Sundays since *she* doesn't work on the Sabbath."

Clarice nodded toward the only vacant table in the room. It sat in a back corner and was covered with a shiny gold tablecloth that was decorated with silver stars and moons and symbols of the zodiac. At the center of the table sat a stack of tarot cards and a crystal ball the size of a large cantaloupe. A forty-year-old framed eight-by-ten photograph showing Minnie McIntyre decked out in sequins and feathers acting as a magician's assistant to her first husband, Charlemagne the Magnificent, was propped up behind the tarot cards and crystal ball. From that table in the back of the All-You-Can-Eat, Minnie operated her fortune-telling business. It was her claim that, since his death, Charlemagne had reversed their roles and was now working as her assistant and guide to the spirit world.

In spite of my own encounter with a traveler from the afterlife just that morning, I didn't believe for a second that Minnie had any such connections. It wasn't just that her predictions were famous for being way off; I knew just how inaccurate the dead could be from years of hearing Mama complain about how her ghosts often fed her a line of crap. The thing with Minnie was that her predictions almost always had a nasty edge to them that made it seem like she was more interested in delivering insults disguised as prophecies and manipulating her naïve customers than she was in communing with the other side.

Inaccurate and ornery as she was, Minnie had been in business for years and still had a steady stream of customers, many of whom were the sort of people you'd think would know better. Clarice doesn't like to admit it, but she was once one of those customers.

In a fit of bridal jitters, Clarice went to Minnie for a tarot reading the week before she married Richmond. Big Earl's first wife, Thelma, was still alive then, and Minnie hadn't yet sunk her teeth into Big Earl. So Clarice dragged

Barbara Jean and me to the run-down house out near the highway bypass where Minnie used to tell fortunes. She swore us both to secrecy, since seeing a fortune-teller was just a hair's breadth away from consorting with Satan to the folks at Clarice's church. Inside that nasty shack, we inhaled jasmine incense and listened while Minnie told Clarice that her marriage to Richmond would be joyful, but, having drawn an upright Hermit and a reverse Three of Cups, she would turn out to be barren and would look fat in her wedding gown. Clarice worried herself sick throughout her first pregnancy. And for years she couldn't bring herself to look at what turned out to be lovely wedding photos. Four healthy children and three decades later, Clarice still wasn't feeling inclined to forgive Minnie.

Clarice pointed her index finger at Minnie's table and said, "Stepmother or not, Little Earl shouldn't have that old fake in this place. There have got to be laws against that kind of thing. It's fraud, pure and simple." She took a swig of iced tea and twisted her mouth. "Too sweet," she said.

I prepared myself for one of Clarice's lectures on the moral failings of Minnie McIntyre. When Clarice was in the kind of mood she was in that day, she enjoyed identifying flaws, moral and otherwise, in everyone except the idiot in the blue shirt at the other end of the table. My friend had a multitude of gifts. She played the piano like an angel. She could cook, sew, sing, and speak French. And she was as kind and generous a friend as anyone could hope for. What she didn't have much of a knack for was placing blame where it should truly lie.

Clarice's church didn't help her disposition much.

Calvary Baptist wasn't full-blown Pentecostal, but it still managed to be the Bible-thumpingest and angriest church in town. So Sundays were bad for Clarice even without Richmond misbehaving or Minnie's name coming up in the conversation. Calvary's pastor, Reverend Peterson, yelled at his congregation every week that God was mad at them for a long list of wrongs they had committed and that He was even madder about whatever they were thinking of doing. If you weren't in a foul temper by the time you left a Calvary Baptist service, it meant you weren't listening.

At my church, Holy Family Baptist, the only hard-and-fast rule was that everyone should be kind to everybody. That view was way too casual for the Calvary congregation, and it drove them straight up the wall that we didn't take a harder line on sin and sinners. The Calvary crowd were equally disgusted with Barbara Jean's church, First Baptist, where the members proved their devotion to God by doing charity work and by dressing up like they were on a fashion runway every Sunday. The old joke was that Holy Family preached the good news gospel, Calvary Baptist preached the bad news gospel, and First Baptist preached the new clothes gospel.

Clarice didn't begin a recitation from her catalog of the ways Minnie's behavior offended her, though. A glance through the window provided her with something new to complain about. Pointing outside, she said, "There's Barbara Jean and Lester. You know, she really should call when she's going to be this late. It's not right to worry everybody like this."

Clarice was mostly letting off steam, but she had a point.

The summer heat tended to aggravate Lester's various health problems. And there was quite a list of problems. Heart, lungs, liver, kidneys. If it was still in Lester's body, it was going bad. They often appeared for supper an hour late after having to pull their car over for Barbara Jean to kick-start one of Lester's vital organs with a remedy from the portable clinic she kept in her pocketbook.

So, when I turned to watch Barbara Jean and Lester Maxberry making their way toward the restaurant, I was surprised to see Lester moving much more energetically than usual. Dressed in a white suit and matching white fedora, Lester's usually round back was straight, and he hardly leaned on his ivory walking stick at all. He lifted his knees high in that almost military way he did when he was feeling spry. It was Barbara Jean who slowly shuffled along, frowning with each step.

Barbara Jean wore a snug-fitting bright yellow dress and a yellow hat with a brim at least three feet wide. Her calves were encased in white go-go boots that had three-inch heels. Even from half a block away I could see that the boots were paining her. With every step she took, the corners of Barbara Jean's mouth turned down a little more, and she occasionally stopped walking altogether to take a deep breath before soldiering on.

Clarice said, "Oh, for heaven's sake, would you look at that." She pointed toward our approaching friend. "No wonder they're so late. She's wearing that yellow dress again. That thing is so tight she can barely breathe, much less take a full step. And would you look at the shoes she's trying to walk in. Those heels are six inches, if they're an inch. I tell you, Odette, Barbara Jean has got to accept the fact that she is a middle-aged woman and she can't wear the things she wore when she was twenty-two. It's unseemly. We really should have a talk with her about that. She needs an intervention real bad." She sat back in her chair and crossed her arms over her chest.

Clarice would never say a word to Barbara Jean about the way she dressed, and we both knew it. Just like she and Barbara Jean wouldn't tell me to my face that I was fat, and Barbara Jean and I wouldn't remind Clarice that her husband was a dog. These were the tender considerations that came with being a member of the Supremes. We overlooked each other's flaws and treated each other well, even when we didn't deserve it.

When Clarice got to carrying on the way she was, it always came back to one thing: Richmond. When he was up to no good, Clarice grew fangs that filled her mouth with bitterness. Mostly she swallowed the poison, but sometimes it came seeping out.

"I'll tell you one thing," Clarice said, "I wouldn't be caught dead in that dress." Clarice was nowhere near as big as me, but she was solidly built, no matter how she starved herself. If either of us was ever foolish enough to try and force ourselves into Barbara Jean's sexy little dress, death *would* most likely be the outcome.

The only thing I didn't like about Barbara Jean's and Lester's outfits was that they made my stomach growl. I was ravenous and, with her in that yellow dress and him in his cream-colored suit, they got me thinking about a slice of lemon meringue pie.

Truth was, Barbara Jean looked lovely in whatever she wore. She'd been the prettiest girl in our high school and she became the most beautiful woman I'd ever seen. In middle age, it's still difficult to look away from her. Every single feature of her face is striking and exotic. Looking at Barbara Jean makes you think that maybe God is a wonderful, ancient artist who decided one day to piece together all his loveliest creations and craft something that put his other works to shame. Unfortunately, God neglected to prepare men for his good work. Men had behaved very badly because of my friend's beauty, and, the world being unfair, Barbara Jean had often paid the price.

Barbara Jean and Lester came into the All-You-Can-Eat and brought along a gust of hot air that quickly overwhelmed the feeble air conditioner that hummed and sputtered above the doorway. People sitting near the door looked at Lester like they wanted to take a good whack at him with the walking stick he was using to hold the door open for his wife, who was several steps behind him on account of her impractical choices in wardrobe and footwear.

Barbara Jean came limping to the table issuing apologies. "I am so sorry we're late. Morning service went long today," she said as she sat down, unzipped her boots under the table, and sighed with relief.

Clarice interrupted her, saying, "Let's eat." Then she stood from her chair and marched toward the steam tables.

The men followed Clarice to the food while I waited for Barbara Jean to squeeze herself back into her boots. When she was done, we walked to the buffet line. Along the way, Barbara Jean leaned over and whispered in my ear, "Richmond back at it again?"

"That's my guess," I said.

We took plates from the carousel at the near end of the

four steam tables – one for main courses, two for side dishes, and the fourth for desserts. Then each of us did what we did every week. Skinny James piled his plate with some of everything. Richmond hid food that was off-limits to him because of his diabetes beneath layers of green beans and roasted carrots. Lester ate the old folks' selections, easy-to-chew dishes enhanced with added fiber. Clarice hadn't allowed herself a piece of anything fried since she was twenty-eight, and that day was no exception. She ate minuscule portions of low-fat items. Out of consideration for Clarice, Barbara Jean, who could eat anything and never gain a pound, ate only low-fat foods so it wouldn't seem like she was rubbing the difference in their metabolisms in Clarice's face. I, as always, divided my plate equally between main courses and desserts. Vegetables take up too much space on a small plate.

When we got to the end of the line, the men headed back to our table. The three of us women stopped to say hello to Little Earl and Erma Mae, who had come in from the kitchen and were sitting side by side on stools at the far end of the last steam table.

I said, "Hey, Little Earl. Hey, Erma Mae."

They answered together, "Hey, Supremes."

I inquired about their health, their children, and Erma Mae's elderly mother. I asked Little Earl for the latest on his sister Lydia and her husband, who ran a diner in Chicago that was almost identical to the All-You-Can-Eat. After being assured that all of those people were fine, I got around to the question I really wanted an answer to.

I asked, "How's your daddy doing, Little Earl?" trying to sound casual about it.

"Oh, he's great. Eighty-eight next month and gonna outlive us all, I 'spect. He should be comin' by sometime soon. Here lately he'll sometimes sleep in, but he won't miss an entire day's work, that's for certain."

"'Specially not on a Sunday," Erma Mae added, nodding her head toward Minnie's empty fortune-telling table. She said that for Clarice's benefit since the two of them were kindred spirits on the subject of Minnie.

At that moment the front door opened with a loud scrape. Little Earl looked toward the door with an expression of boyish expectation, like he really believed that just speaking of his father would conjure him up. But Big Earl didn't step into the restaurant. Instead, Minnie McIntyre stood in the threshold, holding the door open and letting a hot, moist draft into the room that made the nearby patrons groan in discomfort and give her the evil eye.

Minnie's costume of the day was a deep purple robe decorated with the same astrological signs that adorned her corner table. She wore gold Arabian-style slippers with curled-up toes, a necklace made of twelve large chunks of colored glass, each representing a birthstone, and a white turban with a silver bell jutting out from its top. The bell, she claimed, was for Charlemagne the Magnificent to ring whenever he had a message for her. He was very consistent. Charlemagne rang every time Minnie lowered her head to count a client's money.

Minnie walked into the restaurant, taking long, slow strides and holding her arms outstretched, palms toward the ceiling.

Little Earl left his stool and met her at the cash register. He sighed and said, "Miss Minnie, please, we talked about this. I just can't have you doing your readings on Sundays. The Pentecostals'll have my ass."

Minnie said, "You and your precious Pentecostals will be happy to know that you won't have to worry about me or my gift much longer." She wiggled her head from side to side as she spoke, making her bell ring repeatedly. She lowered the range of her normally high-pitched voice to a deep rumble and said, loud enough for nearly everyone in the place to hear, "Charlemagne says I'll be dead within a year."

Most people in the restaurant, having heard Minnie announce grave prophecies that failed to come to pass many times, paid her no mind. Clarice, Barbara Jean, and I stuck around and waited to hear what else she had to say.

Little Earl said, "Why don't I make you some tea, get you calmed down?"

"There's no calmin' me down; I'm facin' the end. And don't pretend you're sad to see it. You've wanted me out of the way ever since I married Earl." She pointed at Erma Mae and added, "You, too. I dare you to deny it."

Erma Mae was never one for lying. Instead of responding to Minnie, she yelled toward the kitchen, "Belinda, bring some hot tea for Grandma Minnie!"

Little Earl led Minnie behind the register and guided her onto his stool. In a soft, soothing tone of voice he said, "Yeah, that's right. Have a cup of tea, and then I'll walk you back across the street. You, me, and Daddy can talk this whole thing out."

She made a kind of a squawking noise and dismissed him with a wave of her hand. "There's nothin' to talk out. A year from now, I'll be dead."

Clarice was tired of listening to Minnie's ramblings. She whispered in my ear, "My food is getting cold. Are we about done listening to this old fake?"

Minnie screamed, "I heard that!" She was old; but you had to hand it to her, the woman still had excellent hearing. She leapt from the stool and lunged at Clarice, ready to dig her purple polished nails into Clarice's face.

Little Earl held her back and got her onto the stool again. She immediately burst into tears, sending black trails of mascara down her copper cheeks. Maybe she'd been faking it for so long that she'd started to believe herself. Or maybe she really had talked to Charlemagne. Fake or not, we all could clearly see that this was a woman who believed what she was saying. Even Clarice felt bad watching Minnie break down like that. She said, "Minnie, I'm sorry. I shouldn't have said that."

But Minnie wasn't ready to hear apologies or be consoled.

"I knew this was gonna happen. Nobody cares what happens to me. As soon as Charlemagne told me that I'd be dead within a year of Earl, I knew I'd get no sympathy."

Little Earl, who had been patting his stepmother on the back while she wailed, took a step away from her and said, "What?"

"Charlemagne came to me early this morning and said that I would follow Earl to the grave within a year. Those were his exact words."

Now the restaurant grew quiet as people began to catch the drift of what she was saying.

"Are you saying that Daddy is dead?"

"Yeah, he died last night while he was sayin' his prayers. Between that and my bad news from Charlemagne this morning, I've had a terrible, terrible Sunday, let me tell you."

Little Earl grabbed Minnie's shoulders and spun her on the stool so she faced him directly. "Daddy died last night . . . and you didn't call me?"

"I was gonna call you, but then I thought, *If I call 'em, they'll feel like they've got to come over. Then there'll be the preacher and the undertaker and maybe the grandkids. With everybody makin' such a fuss, I'll never get a lick of sleep.* So I thought it out and figured your daddy would be just as dead if I got a good night's rest as he'd be if I called you and didn't get my sleep. So I just let it be."

James, Richmond, and Lester came over from the window table then and joined us. No one said anything, and Minnie sensed that it wasn't an approving silence. She looked at Little Earl and Erma Mae and said, "I was just tryin' to be considerate. Y'all need your sleep, too."

When the crowd around her remained quiet, she let loose with another wail and a new round of tears. She said, "This is no way to treat a dyin' woman."

Little Earl began to untie his apron. He said, "Is he at Stewart's?" Stewart's is the largest black mortuary in town and it's where most of us are taken when our time comes.

"No," Minnie said, "I told you I let it be. He's upstairs beside the bed. And that wasn't easy on me, neither. I hardly got seven hours of sleep, him kneelin' there and starin' at me all night."

Little Earl threw his apron to the floor and ran out of the door toward his father's house across the road. James was right on his heels.

Erma Mae began to sob. She came around the buffet line and launched herself straight into Barbara Jean's arms, passing by Clarice and me even though we were both closer friends of hers than Barbara Jean. I wasn't surprised or offended, though. And I was sure Clarice wasn't either. Everyone knew Barbara Jean was the expert on grief.

As Barbara Jean held Erma Mae and patted her trembling back, I looked through the window and across the street. James and Little Earl were just arriving at Big Earl's home. They rushed up the front stairs and right past Mama, who stood near the porch swing. Big Earl and Thelma McIntyre sat on the swing holding hands, Miss Thelma's head on her husband's shoulder. I could tell from Mama's familiar gestures that she was telling one of her jokes. I had seen those particular movements a hundred times. I knew which joke she was telling and that she was now at the punch line. Right on cue, Big Earl and Miss Thelma doubled over laughing, stomping their feet on the painted boards of the porch floor and falling against each other on the swing. Even from dozens of yards away, I could see the sun reflecting off the tears that ran down the cheeks of Big Earl's grinning face.

Chapter 6

Erma Mae cried on Barbara Jean's shoulder as a crowd of friends surrounded them murmuring words of sympathy and support. Barbara Jean felt a hand stroke her back and she turned her head to see Carmel Handy standing behind her, shrunken and bony in her best Sunday dress. Barbara Jean knew what the first words out of Miss Carmel's mouth would be and she held her breath, bracing herself to hear them. Miss Carmel didn't disappoint. In her high-pitched, feathery voice she said, "Sweetheart, did you know you were born on my davenport?"

Barbara Jean's mother, Loretta Perdue, was drunk when she gave birth on the living room sofa of Miss Carmel, a woman she had never met. Her friends had thrown her a baby shower that day at Forrest Payne's Pink Slipper Gentlemen's Club, where she worked as a dancer. She often told Barbara Jean how she only drank whiskey sours when she was expecting because everyone knew that drinking beer during pregnancy would make your baby nappy-headed. "See, honey," she would say, "your mama was always lookin' out for you."

Loretta had plans to give her daughter, and herself, a leg up in life. After reading the news of Clarice's birth in the newspaper, and seeing how people went on about it, she decided that her child would be the second black baby born at University Hospital. Clarice's mother was just the wife of a shady lawyer and no better than she was, Loretta figured. Now that the color barrier had been broken, she would just show up at the hospital when the first pain hit and take her rightful place among a higher class of folk. Like most of Loretta's schemes, it didn't work out that way.

Things went wrong for Barbara Jean's mother when the man she had arranged to see that evening sprung a surprise on her. She'd told him five months earlier that he was going to be a father, and he had seemed to be pleased about it. Or rather, he was pleased Loretta was not going to tell his wife. She was content merely to accept a small monthly payment in exchange for her discretion. This same arrangement also suited each of the three other men Loretta had informed that they were the father of her unborn child.

Loretta had set up a meeting with Daddy no. 4 (going by the order in which she had told them about her pregnancy) at a quiet roadside diner in Leaning Tree after the baby shower. At the diner, she was going to remind him of just how fair she was being and then, when she had him feeling appropriately grateful to her for being such a good sport, she would casually mention just how much easier a new Chevrolet would make life for her and his child. If she worked it right, by sunset she would have a new car and he would travel back to his wife and family in Louisville thanking God that he had knocked up such a reasonable woman.

She seated herself at a booth and drank coffee to

come down from her whiskey sour buzz and waited for Daddy no. 4 to join her. When he stepped through the door with Daddy no. 2 right behind him, she knew that the jig was up.

As the men approached, Loretta, always quick on her feet when cornered, made one last desperate move to hold her plan together by playing one daddy against the other. She said, "I'm sorry, sweetheart. I've tried so many times to tell him that I love you and it's all over with him, but I was just too scared. He's so mean; I didn't know what he might do to me and our baby." She said it to both of them, hoping each would assume she was talking to him alone and that she could slip out of the diner while they fought over her. Later, she could separately thank both the conquering hero and the valiant loser for defending her honor, assuring each that she loved only him. With luck, after the dust settled, her plans could go forward unchanged.

Loretta was a stunning beauty, and she knew it. She thought it was only logical that men should fight over her, and they often did. When she got sick with the cirrhosis that killed her at thirty-five, the hardest thing for her – harder than dying, Barbara Jean thought – was saying goodbye to her beauty. Loretta died hard and she died ugly. Liver disease whittled away her cute, round face and bountiful figure to nothing – a mean turn of fate for a woman who, as one of her men described her, "looked like she was made out of basketballs and chocolate pudding."

Daddies no. 2 and no. 4 presented a united front in the diner, with Daddy no. 4 doing most of the talking. He told her she'd never get another dime from either of them, and he carried on as if he were some sort of genius detective for single-handedly figuring out her plot. The truth, blurted out by Daddy no. 2, was that Loretta had been the victim of her customary bad luck. The fathers had ended up seated next to each other at Forrest Payne's joint, and after they had sucked down enough of Forrest's watered-down liquor to loosen their tongues, they started bragging about their women. It didn't take them long to realize that they were each bragging about the same one.

Forrest Payne had pretensions of running a gentlemen's club instead of a country strip joint and whorehouse, so he greeted every customer at the door dressed up in his signature canary-yellow tuxedo. Then he escorted them to their seats with all the flourish of a French maitre d'. Since he didn't trust anyone else to handle the door and the cover charge money, Loretta knew it had to have been Forrest himself who had seated the daddies next to each other. This, in spite of the fact that she had left explicit instructions that none of her baby's fathers should be placed within ten feet of each other. For the rest of her short life, Loretta blamed Forrest Payne for ruining her.

Daddy no. 4 leaned across the table and wagged his finger at Loretta's nose. He said, "I was too smart for you, li'l girl. You been outplayed at your own game."

Loretta stared at Daddy no. 4, who had once been her favorite, and wondered what it was she had ever seen in him, with his wide, lopsided mouth and his strange, Egyptian-looking eyes. Then she thought about the ring he had bought for her, a decent-sized ruby with tiny azure sapphires arranged around it in a daisy pattern, and she recalled why she had put up with him. She slid her hands from the table so he wouldn't see the ring and get it in his head to demand its return. When she tried to pawn it a year later, she would find out the stones were glass.

Daddy no. 2 surprised Loretta by bursting into tears. He buried his face in his hands and wailed as if he'd been stuck with a sharp stick, blubbering on about his lost son. Daddy no. 4 put his arm around his new friend and then put both of their feelings about Loretta into words. He leaned toward her and launched into some very loud and creative name-calling. The other customers in the diner looked their way, wondering what the commotion was about.

Loretta was a firm believer that, if a woman was smart, she acted like a lady by the light of day no matter what she did after sunset. This situation, one daddy crying his eyes out and the other loudly exploring the limits of his vocabulary, was just the kind of thing that got you ostracized by decent folks – the kind of people she planned to be spending her time with as soon as she'd had her baby in University Hospital and elevated her status. Loretta hurried away from the booth and, for the benefit of anyone who might have been listening, said, "I can see that you two do not intend to behave like gentlemen. I shall not stay and risk losing my poise due to your crass behavior." What she said to herself was "Fuck this. I still got Daddy no. 1 and Daddy no. 3."

She headed back toward Forrest Payne's place to cuss him out, and was halfway there when her water broke. She made her way to the best-kept house on the block, thinking that its owners would be likely to have a telephone – not everyone did in 1950. Mrs Carmel Handy, a schoolteacher Loretta would have known if she hadn't left school

in the sixth grade, owned the well-landscaped brick bungalow she chose to stop at. Miss Carmel answered the
insistent knocking at her door and found herself confronted
with a very attractive, massively pregnant young woman
supporting herself against the doorjamb.

Between groans of discomfort, the girl said, "Hi, I'm
Mrs Loretta Perdue, and I was admiring your front yard
and thinking that whoever lived here must be a person of
class and would surely have a telephone. I myself have a
telephone, but I'm a ways from home and I'm not feeling
well. So, if you don't mind, I need you to call my friend,
Mr Forrest Payne, at his place of business and tell him to
come get me and drive me to University Hospital where I
plan to have my baby like folks of substance. It's the least
Forrest could do since my situation is entirely his fault."

Because she had been in the middle of pressing her hair
and she didn't want to stand there with her door open for
any passersby to see her with her head half done, Carmel
Handy permitted Loretta to enter her home. Careful not
to burn Loretta with the still-smoking straightening comb,
she helped her into the house. In her foyer, Miss Carmel
listened politely as Loretta recited Forrest Payne's telephone number, all the while thinking how funny it was
that this girl was trying so hard to make Forrest sound like
anything but the pimp everyone in Plainview knew he was.

Miss Carmel led Loretta to her living room sofa to rest
while she made the phone call. But instead of calling
Forrest Payne – she wasn't about to have her neighbors
see that man coming and going from her house, thank you
very much – she called a nurse who lived down the block.

The nurse brought Barbara Jean into the world right

there on the sofa while Carmel Handy made the first of a dozen phone calls she would make that day to tell her friends what had happened in her home and to extol the benefits of plasticizing your furniture. That first call began "Some girl just popped out another of Forrest Payne's bastards right in my front room," starting a rumor that would follow Barbara Jean for the rest of her life.

The baby was named Barbara Jean – Barbara for Daddy no. 1's mother and Jean for Daddy no. 3's.

When Loretta's child was first handed to her, she took note of the infant's lopsided, half-smiling mouth and the almond-shaped eyes, already fully open, that were tilted up at the corners like an Egyptian's. Loretta recognized that face instantly and said to herself, "Ain't this some shit. It was No. 4 all along." Then she turned to Mrs Handy and said, "Got any whiskey?"

On a September morning fourteen years later, Miss Carmel read Barbara Jean's name aloud from the roster in her ninth grade English class. After placing her clipboard down on her desk, Miss Carmel walked over to Barbara Jean and, for the first time, uttered the words that would begin most of their encounters for the next four decades. "Girl, did you know you were born on my davenport?"

Once Barbara Jean had married Lester and his business had taken off, most of the town lined up to kiss her ass in order to get on Lester's good side. But Carmel Handy continued to greet her that same way. Barbara Jean supposed it spoke well of Miss Carmel's character that the wealth she came into didn't change her old teacher's behavior toward her one bit. But she still hated her for it. It shamed her to admit it, but Barbara Jean felt relieved when, in her eighties, Miss Carmel developed the habit of telling each black woman around Barbara Jean's age who crossed her path that she was born on her sofa. Eventually, the tale of the baby born in her front room became so bound up with Miss Carmel's short-circuiting brain that nearly everyone forgot that the story was rooted in fact or had anything to do with Barbara Jean.

Carmel Handy's block was one of the first to be demolished when housing developers and the university bought up most of Leaning Tree in the 1980s and '90s. On the day they bulldozed that little brick bungalow, Barbara Jean drove over to Miss Carmel's street and drank a champagne toast in the front seat of her new Mercedes.

As she stood in the All-You-Can-Eat at the center of an expanding circle of grief over Big Earl's passing, Barbara Jean listened to Carmel Handy reminding her, yet again, of her low origins. Barbara Jean thought then of the taste of the champagne she sipped that day in her car as she watched the workmen scratch Miss Carmel's home out of existence. That delicious memory helped her not to scream.

Chapter 7

The night before Big Earl's funeral, Barbara Jean dreamed that she and Lester were walking along a rutted dirt road on a cool fall day. They exhaled clouds of white mist while rust, yellow, and brown leaves floated around them in a circle, as if they were at the center of a cyclone. Because of the storm of leaves, Barbara Jean was just barely able to make out the path ahead of them. She held Lester's arm tight to keep from twisting her ankle in the tire tracks embedded in the road. Even in her dreams, she always wore heels.

After a time, the leaf storm around them thinned enough to reveal a river ahead. On the opposite shore, a small boy waved. Then, just as they lifted their hands to wave back, a woman in a silvery, iridescent gown appeared, hovering in the air above their heads. The woman said, "Lester, the water is frozen. Just walk on over and get him. He's waiting." But it was November or December in the dream and the river was clearly only half frozen. Barbara Jean could see the bubbling and churning current just beneath the brittle surface of the ice. She dug her fingers into the rough cloth of her husband's winter coat to keep him from going out onto the river. As Lester's sleeve escaped her grasp, Barbara Jean woke up with her pulse racing and both of her arms reaching out for Lester.

She'd had that dream, or one nearly identical to it, for years. Sometimes it was spring or summer in the dream and, instead of a dangerously thin layer of ice, it was a decrepit rope bridge with rotted wooden slats that spanned the water. But she always dreamed of the same road, the dirt trail that had once formed the western border of Leaning Tree. It had been paved ages ago, or so Barbara Jean had been told. She hadn't gone near it in years. She always dreamed of the same waving boy, her lost Adam. The woman in the air also never varied. It was always her mother.

Barbara Jean awakened from her dream with a sore back from being curled up for hours on one of the two Chippendale wingback chairs that sat by the fireplace in the library of her home. The chairs had been reupholstered, at frightful expense, with burgundy crushed-velvet fabric adorned with a fleur-de-lis pattern that matched the design of the library's hand-painted wallpaper. Every spring at the Plainview Home and Garden Walk, people made a big fuss over those chairs, and Barbara Jean loved them. But they were hell on her lower back if she sat in them for too long a time.

Barbara Jean and Lester's house stood at the intersection of Plainview Avenue and Main Street. A three-story Queen Anne giant with a turret at its northeast corner and six separate porches, it had once been called Ballard House, and still was by most of the inhabitants of Plainview over the age of fifty. It was built in 1870 by a local thief named Alfred Ballard who looted some of the best homes in the vanquished South during the Civil War and returned to Plainview a rich man. Mr Ballard's descendants lacked his business sense and his ruthlessness. They failed to add to their fortune, wasted the money Ballard had left them, and eventually lost the house to the tax man. In 1969, after he expanded his lawn care business to Kentucky and got a contract to tend all of the state-owned properties in the northern half of the state, Lester bought Ballard House for his young wife and their son, Adam. It was a gutted, falling-down mess at the time, and although she loved the house, Barbara Jean had no clue what needed to be done to put it back together. Clarice, though, had been raised by her mother with the assumption that she would one day oversee a grand home. So Barbara Jean turned every decision in the renovation process over to her friend. Barbara Jean stood back and watched as Clarice transformed her massive shell of a house into the kind of showplace Clarice would have lived in if fate, in the form of a three-hundred-pound, corn-fed Wisconsin linebacker with blood in his eye, hadn't stepped in and transformed Richmond from a potential NFL legend into a recruiter at a university whose football glory days were long past. Out of respect for her friend, Clarice never accepted a bit of credit for her hard work. Instead, she patiently tutored Barbara Jean, teaching her everything she knew about art, antiques, and architecture. Between the practical experience Barbara Jean gained from tending to the needs of her extravagant old home and from Clarice's guidance, she eventually surpassed her instructor's level of expertise.

When she stood from the antique chair to stretch her lower back, Barbara Jean's Bible tumbled to the floor. After she'd had dinner with Lester, counted out his pills, and put him to bed, the evening had become a blur. She didn't recall that she'd been reading the Bible before she fell asleep. It made sense, though. She tended to drag out the Good Book when she was in a dark mood, and the shadows had closed in around her that night, for sure.

Clarice had given Barbara Jean that Bible in 1977, just after Adam died. Lester had become frightened when his wife stopped speaking and eating and then refused to come out of Adam's room, so he called in Odette and Clarice. They got right to work, each of her friends administering the cures they trusted most. Odette mothered her, cooking wonderful-smelling meals which she fed to her by hand on the worst days. And, during the long hours she spent sitting in bed beside Barbara Jean while her friend cried onto her broad bosom, brave Odette whispered into Barbara Jean's ear that now was the time to be fearless.

Clarice came brandishing a brown suede-covered Bible. It was embossed with Barbara Jean's name in gold letters on its front cover and had "Salvation = Calvary Baptist Church" printed on the back. For weeks, Clarice read to her about the trials of Job and reminded her that the fifth chapter of Matthew promised "Blessed are they that mourn, for they shall be comforted."

But both of Barbara Jean's friends had come bearing medicine for the wrong illness. More than courage or piety, what she needed, what she would scour Clarice's Bible forwards and backwards searching for over the many years that followed, was a clue as to how to get out from under the boulder of guilt that rested on her chest and forced the breath out of her. Well intentioned as it was, Clarice's gift just armed Barbara Jean with a long list of good reasons to be seriously pissed off at God while the weight of her guilt ground her into powder.

Barbara Jean was finally able to leave Adam's room after she and God came to an understanding. She would continue to smile and nod through services every week at First Baptist just as she always had, and she wouldn't call Him out for being as demanding and capricious as the worst two-year-old child, ready at any moment to reach out with his greedy hands and snatch whatever shone brightest. In exchange for this consideration, Barbara Jean asked only that God leave her alone. For decades, the pact worked out fine. Then, with Big Earl's sudden passing, God reminded Barbara Jean of who He was. Bringer of death, master comedian, lightning bearer. He made it clear to her that He had no intentions of honoring the terms of their truce.

Barbara Jean put the Bible on the eighteenth-century candle table next to her chair and walked to the mirror above the fireplace to inspect herself. She didn't look too bad – a little puffy, but nothing some time with an ice pack wouldn't take care of. Also, the sun wasn't up yet, so she still had time to get a little rest to ensure she would look good for Big Earl. And she was determined to say goodbye to her friend looking her very best.

She had laid out her outfit for Big Earl's service earlier that evening, before heading into the library. Out of respect, she would wear a black dress. But she chose magenta shoes, a matching belt, and a white hat with clusters of red and black leather roses around its wide brim to go with it. The little black dress was cut well above the knee and had a tiny slit on the right seam. Clarice would hate it and would have to bite her tongue to keep from saying so. But Barbara Jean wasn't wearing it for Clarice. She was wearing it for Big Earl.

When she was a teenager and was ashamed of having to wear her mother's flashy, trashy hand-me-downs, Big Earl made a point of telling Barbara Jean that she looked pretty every time he saw her. Not in a dirty old man way or anything. He would just smile at her and say, "You look divine today," in a way that made her feel as if she were wearing haute couture. Or he would see her come into the restaurant in one of her mother's shiny, too-short skirts and he'd turn to Miss Thelma and say, "Don't Barbara Jean look exactly like a flower." Anywhere else in town, she might have been dirt, but inside the walls of the All-You-Can-Eat, she was a flower.

Long after Barbara Jean had choices and knew better, she would occasionally pick one of the brightest and the tightest from her closet and sashay into the All-You-Can-Eat on a Sunday afternoon just to give Big Earl a reason to grin and slap his knee and say, "That's my girl." On those days, she left the All-You-Can-Eat feeling twenty years younger than when she'd walked in. So, for Big Earl she was going to squeeze into a black dress she wouldn't be able to take more than a shallow breath in and she was going to look damn good in it, or die trying.

Barbara Jean knew she should get to bed, but she didn't feel sleepy, just a little woozy still from the vodka. She didn't remember getting the bottle from the liquor cabinet, but there it was on the table next to the Bible. That was her pattern. When her mind was too full of thoughts – usually about the old days, her mother or her son – she would reach for either the Bible or the bottle and end up with both in her lap before the night was over. She would sit in one of her burgundy chairs and drink vodka from one of the antique demitasse cups Clarice had found for the house. She sipped and read until the memories went away.

Barbara Jean always drank vodka, partly because whiskey had been her mother's drink and she swore she'd never touch it. Also, vodka was safe because people couldn't smell it on you. If you stuck to vodka and you knew how to control yourself, nobody talked trash about you, no matter how many times you filled your demitasse cup.

She put the cap back on the vodka bottle and returned it to the liquor cabinet. Then she took her cup and saucer to the kitchen and left them on the counter for the maid to deal with in the morning. When she returned to the library to turn out the lights, she contemplated reopening that troublesome Bible. She was in just that kind of mood, and it wouldn't take long. After a few vodkas, Barbara Jean's form of Bible study was to close her eyes, open the book on her lap, and let her index finger fall onto the open page. Then she would read whatever verse was nearest the tip of her nail. She had done this for years, telling herself that one day she would land on just the right thing to turn on some light inside her head. But, mostly, she spent countless nights learning who begat whom and reading of the endless, seemingly random smitings the Bible specialized in.

She thought about the day to come and decided to go on up to bed. Rather than disturb Lester, who was a light sleeper, she would lie down in one of the guest rooms. If he asked in the morning why she hadn't come to bed, she would tell him that she had gone straight to the guest room after staying up late to pick out her outfit for Big Earl. If she looked well rested enough, maybe he wouldn't suspect that she had spent yet another night in the library drinking and stocking up on ammunition for her ongoing battle with God.

Barbara Jean removed her shoes before she left the library so the sound of her steps wouldn't create a racket as she crossed the herringbone parquet floor of the grand foyer. She climbed the stairs slowly and carefully, recalling one of her mother's warnings about the missteps that could prevent Barbara Jean from accessing the better, more respectable life that Loretta had been cheated out of. Loretta had said that if a woman fell down the stairs, people would always gossip that either she was a drunk or her man beat her. And you couldn't have them saying either thing about you if you wanted to get chummy with the type of folks who could actually do something for you. That was the way Loretta had divided up the world, into those who could or could not do something for her. And she spent most of her life designing plots to wrest the things she wanted from the people who she believed possessed them. In the end, it did her no good.

In her stocking feet, Barbara Jean crept along the second-floor hallway of her house. She tiptoed past the bedroom she shared with Lester. Then she passed by the guest rooms. The door to Adam's room drew her to it as surely as if it had stretched out a pair of arms and pulled her into its embrace. She opened the door and stared into the room at the familiar low shelves crammed with out-of-date toys, the small desk strewn with faded crayon drawings, the miniature chair with a pale green sweater slung over it as if its owner might dash into the room at any second to retrieve it. Everywhere she looked there were things that she had sworn to her friends she had thrown away or given away decades earlier. She knew she shouldn't go into this room; it did her no good. But she still had a stagger in her step from the vodka. And she comforted herself with the knowledge that, in the morning, she probably wouldn't recall experiencing the ache in her soul and the fire in her brain that always led her to this same place.

Barbara Jean stepped inside and shut the door. She curled up on the short bed, atop cowboys and Indians on horseback engaged in endless pursuit of each other across the comforter. She closed her eyes – not to sleep, she told herself – just to rest and gather her thoughts before going to one of the guest rooms for the few remaining hours of the night. Moments later, Barbara Jean was on that dirt road again, clutching her husband's arm while her shimmering mother floated above their heads whispering, "He's waiting."

Chapter 8

Big Earl's funeral was held at Clarice's church, Calvary Baptist. He wasn't much of a churchgoer himself, but his daughter-in-law's family had worshipped at Calvary for almost as many generations as Clarice's people. It seemed like the perfect choice until the place started to fill up and it became clear that the university's football stadium was the only building in town that could have comfortably accommodated everyone.

Each pew of the church was packed with mourners. Hundreds of folks who couldn't get seats crowded the outer aisles, leaning against the white plaster walls. Small clusters of people who weren't able to squeeze inside the church stuck their heads into the opened side doors of the sanctuary, amen-ing Reverend Peterson's homily and bobbing their heads to the music along with those of us on the inside.

Denise, Jimmy, and Eric sat in the row behind their father and me. Without having to be asked, all three of our kids had arrived that morning to comfort James and to pay their respects to the man who was the only grandfather they'd ever really known, since my father passed when they were still little. They'd traveled to Plainview from their homes in Illinois, California, and Washington to be with us, and I was happy and proud that they'd come.

Although the Calvary Baptist approach to faith was a bit hard-assed for my taste, I was glad the service was there. For my money, that church is the prettiest in town. Calvary is only half the size of First Baptist, but it has a dozen beautiful stained-glass windows, each one portraying the life of an apostle. The windows extend from the floor all the way up to the vaulted ceiling and, when sunlight hits the glass, a rainbow is projected through the sanctuary onto a mural of the Crucifixion on the wall behind the baptismal pool.

The highlight of the mural is the sexiest picture of Jesus you've ever seen. He has high cheekbones and curly jet-black hair. His bronzed, outstretched arms bulge with muscles and He has the firm stomach of a Brazilian underwear model. His mouth seems to be blowing kisses to the congregation and His crown of thorns is tilted so He has a Frank Sinatra cool about Him. It all comes together in a way that makes you wonder if Jesus is about to ask you to join the church or to run outside for a game of beach volleyball with Him and a dozen of His hot biblical friends.

At Little Earl's request, Clarice played two pieces on the piano after Reverend Peterson's eulogy. One was an arrangement of "His Eye Is on the Sparrow," and the other was a piece that the program identified as a Brahms intermezzo. Both were lovely, but she had everyone in the church crying their eyes out at the end of the Brahms.

Clarice is one hell of a piano player. Beyond turning on the stereo, music has never been my thing, but even I can hear that something special happens when Clarice sits down at the piano.

When we were kids, we all thought she was going to be

famous. She won contests and got to play with the Indianapolis Symphony and the Louisville Symphony while she was still in high school. Conservatories across the country offered her full scholarships, but she stayed in Plainview because of Richmond. He repaid her by break-ing her heart. He joined the NFL and left her behind without so much as a goodbye. Then, right after Clarice made plans to move to New York and launch her career, Richmond was back in town with a crushed ankle and no future in football. He swore his never-ending love for her and begged for forgiveness and nursing. The following year she was his wife, and ten months after the wedding she gave birth to their first child. Not long after that, the other children came and Clarice began her career as a local piano teacher.

Staying in Plainview and giving up on the future we'd all expected her to have was Clarice's choice. It wasn't some crime committed against her by her husband. And I never once heard her complain that she felt she'd missed out on anything. But as I watched my friend at the piano rocking to an internal beat below steamy Jesus, I couldn't help but think that we were all getting a peek at a great treasure Richmond Baker had selfishly snatched from the world to keep as his own.

Three of Clarice and Richmond's four children sat alongside mine. Like my kids, Carolyn, Ricky, and Abe had also come long distances. Only Carl, Carolyn's twin, didn't make an appearance, in spite of the fact that his wife, who he had told he would be in Plainview for the week, had called Clarice's house several times that morn-ing trying to reach him. Even as she played, Clarice kept looking over her shoulder, searching for the face of her youngest son in the crowd. But I was sure that, deep down, she knew he wouldn't be coming. Carl could be anywhere. And wherever he was, he wasn't likely to be alone. Handsome Carl was the pretty apple that hadn't fallen far from Richmond's big, dumb tree.

After seeing Big Earl laid to rest next to Miss Thelma, we kissed our children goodbye and watched them hurry back to their busy lives. Then James and I drove home to pick up the food I'd made for the funeral dinner and headed over to Big Earl and Minnie's house.

No, just Minnie's house now. Big Earl had lived across the street from the All-You-Can-Eat since I could remember, and this sad, new reality was going to be tough to get used to.

We found the widow situated on the porch swing surrounded by sympathetic well-wishers. Minnie made it clear that no one would be granted admission without first being given a recounting of the visit from her spirit guide and the prediction that her death was coming sometime over the next 360 days. So we stood in the heat while she acted out the tale again. Then, as soon as decency allowed, James and I offered our condolences for her husband's passing and for her own upcoming demise and ran inside.

The place had changed a good deal since the days when I had spent a lot of time there. But that was to be expected. My memories were mostly from attending countless childhood parties in these rooms with Little Earl and our school friends. And the last time I'd stepped beyond the front door had probably been twenty years earlier, on the occasion of Miss Thelma's funeral.

The interior was now a combination of the old and the new. Everywhere I looked, decorations and furnishings from the era of the first Mrs McIntyre battled it out with things obviously brought in by the second wife. The old oak table I'd eaten at many times still took up most of the dining room's floor space, but an enormous, glittering gold-plated chandelier hung above it now. The chandelier had hundreds of clear glass lightbulbs with jittery orange lights bouncing around inside of them to suggest candle flames. It was definitely a Minnie addition.

Family pictures and framed needlepoint scenes crafted by Miss Thelma shared the walls with photographs and posters of young Minnie dressed in a sparkling one-piece bathing suit. In the photos, Minnie stood onstage flourishing a handful of playing cards or staring at the camera in open-mouthed pretend surprise as Charlemagne the Magnificent levitated her above his head.

I had never understood why Big Earl married Minnie. They couldn't have been more different in terms of their dispositions, and I never witnessed a moment of anything that looked like true affection between them. But looking at the old pictures of her that adorned the walls, the mantel, and just about every other visible surface, it made a little more sense to me. In those pictures, she was glamorous and desirable, an exotic and magical creature with an air of mystery. We had all thought of Big Earl as a father figure and a friend. But hadn't he been a man, like any other? Maybe when he saw Minnie, he didn't see the spiteful old woman who now sat on the front porch greeting guests with "Thank you for coming. Did you know I'll be dead in a year?" Maybe Big Earl looked at her and saw a gorgeous, smiling showgirl freeing a squirming rabbit from a hat. Maybe seeing Minnie that way had helped him get through those lonely years until he was back with Miss Thelma. I hoped that was the way it had been for him.

I caught sight of the fountain Mama had told me about during her visit to my kitchen earlier in the week. It took up a quarter of the floor space in the living room and was even more of an eyesore than Mama had made it out to be. It was six feet high, and the two naked maidens Mama had described – one crouching, the other standing over her dousing her with water from a pitcher – were life-size and realistically detailed. Rose-colored lights shone on the fountain from sconces on the wall above and behind it, giving the smooth marble surface of the statues the glow of pink skin. One of the lights submerged in the pool of water beneath the statues' feet was malfunctioning. The light flickered on and off and made it appear as if the statues were quivering.

A voice said, "Hard to look away, ain't it?" I turned and saw Thelma McIntyre standing next to me. Ever the lady, Miss Thelma was dressed for her husband's funeral in a tasteful black mourning dress. Her face was covered by a veil.

I nodded in agreement, but didn't say anything out loud to Miss Thelma. I had decided as soon as Mama left my house that first night that I was going to keep any ghost sightings to myself. I didn't want to put James through what we had all gone through with Mama, her driving us to distraction by keeping up an almost constant dialogue with one invisible friend or another. Also, I was perfectly happy to do without everybody thinking I was out of my mind and giving me that *poor thing, she can't help it* smile that the local folks had given my mother after word got around that she thought she was talking with the dead.

Another voice called out, "Over here, Odette" from the direction of the dining room. I turned, half expecting to see another dead friend. Instead, I saw Lydia, Big Earl's daughter, waving me over to a ten-foot-long table of food that sagged under the weight of countless covered dishes. With Miss Thelma tagging along, I brought my addition to the feast to Lydia in the dining room.

While I helped Lydia shift things around to make room on the table for my platter, James declared himself starving and began to pile food onto a plate. Mama, Big Earl, and a well-dressed white woman who I didn't recognize right away made their way through the crowded room toward Miss Thelma and me. People stood shoulder to shoulder in the room, but Mama and her friends glided across the space easily, squeezing between the guests in a way that made them appear to blink in and out of sight like Christmas tree lights.

When she got to the food table, Mama started to count. "One, two, three, four, five, six. That's six hams. Two smoked, two baked, a boiled, and a deep-fried. Very impressive." Mama was of the generation that believed you showed your respect for the deceased with a tribute of pork. She turned to Big Earl, who seemed to be genuinely moved by the pork shrine in his dining room, and said, "Six hams. Earl, you were truly loved."

Just then, Lydia pulled the foil off the dish I had brought. She bent over and took a long, deep sniff. She said, "Mmm, honey walnut glazed and spiral cut. Bless your heart."

Mama yelled, "Seven!" and Big Earl appeared to blush a little bit.

I realized that Barbara Jean and Lester were at the other end of the table when I heard Barbara Jean slap her husband's hand and say, "Stop right there. Strawberries make your throat close up." He received another slap when he reached for a different fruit platter and had to be warned about the countereffects of citrus on his ulcer medication.

Mama asked, "Has Lester been sick?"

I couldn't help but chuckle. Asking if Lester was sick was like asking if it was likely the sun would come up in the morning. His vital organs had gone into a state of semi-retirement ages ago. I was surprised that Mama had forgotten.

Seeing my reaction, Mama said, "I know he's been sick. I meant has he been extra bad off?" She pointed toward Lester as he and Barbara Jean sat down next to James in the living room. The strange white woman, who had just moments earlier been standing beside Mama and Big Earl, had followed Lester to his chair. She stood next to him, studying him closely as he began to eat his wife-approved plate of food. Mama said, "It's just that she's not usually interested in people unless they're about to pass over. She hovered around your daddy for an entire month before he died."

I recognized the woman then and let out a little squeak in spite of myself. Standing there in the living room in her fox stole was the regal former first lady, Mrs Eleanor Roosevelt. I suppose I shouldn't have been surprised to see Mrs Roosevelt. She moved in with my mother right after Daddy passed, so I heard about her antics nearly every day during the last nineteen years of Mama's life. And I had no reason to believe they'd parted company. Still, there are some people you just don't expect to come across in an old friend's living room.

Mama said, "Eleanor ain't good for much these days – can't be, the way she drinks and carries on – but she's got a real knack for knowin' who's about to go."

I whispered, "Well, tell her she's likely to have a long wait. Lester's been kicking at death's door for more than ten years, but it never opens up for him."

Clarice and Richmond came in burdened with yet another ham, and Clarice was immediately set upon by people eager to tell her how they had loved her piano playing at the service. After she escaped her admirers, Clarice came to the table and passed her ham to Lydia. Mama moved away then, presumably to tell Big Earl, who had wandered off somewhere with Miss Thelma, that the ham count was up to eight. Clarice saw the fountain in the living room and groaned. "Would you look at that? What that woman has done to this house is a crime." She stopped herself; her good upbringing wouldn't allow her to go on an anti-Minnie tirade in the woman's own home an hour after Minnie's husband had been put into the ground.

We filled our plates and joined Barbara Jean, Lester, and James in the living room. When we got there, Lester was complaining that the blinking light in the fountain's pool was beginning to give him a headache. "Probably a loose bulb. Wouldn't take but three seconds to fix." I expected Barbara Jean to warn Lester away from any notions he might have had about fixing the underwater light in the fountain. It would be just like Lester to splash around in that water and come up with some sort of microbe that landed him in the hospital for a week.

But Barbara Jean was staring at something else. Her eyes were locked on the picture window and on the crowd gathered around Minnie out on the porch. Something she saw there caused a look to come over her face that was a mixture of amazement and terror. I was certain for a moment that I wasn't the only person in the room newly able to see ghosts. Slowly, like she was a puppet being hauled upright by tightening strings, Barbara Jean began to rise from her chair. In her trance, she didn't seem to remember that she had a plate of food on her lap and I had to lunge and grab the plate before it slid onto the floor.

Clarice saw me snatch the plate from the air and asked, "What's going on?"

Then we looked to where Barbara Jean's gaze was focused, and we both understood. There, among the circle of cinnamon and mahogany faces surrounding Minnie on the front porch, was one white face. It was a face I recognized, one that I never thought I'd see again. Almost thirty years had passed since Clarice and I had last laid eyes on him, but we both knew it was Chick Carlson. His black hair was streaked with gray and he was thicker around the waist now. But he had just grown out of boyishness when he'd left Plainview, so that wasn't a surprise. Even from where I sat, I could see the pale blue of his eyes and see that he was, in middle age, a mature version of the beautiful kid Clarice had proclaimed "King of the Pretty White Boys" on the day we got our first look at him in 1967. Barbara Jean and Chick had loved each other deeply and foolishly, the way only young people can do. And it nearly killed them both.

As Chick leaned over to take Minnie's hand and offer condolences, Barbara Jean, wobbling a little on her red high heels, stepped away from us and toward the front window.

Then things got crazy.

A loud noise in the room drew everyone's attention. It was a kind of a low-pitched "whoop," like the short, insistent bark of a large dog. After that, there was a loud pop and the lights went out. It was still midafternoon and plenty of light came in from the windows, but the sudden dimness made people gasp anyway. Then we heard a series of thudding noises, another barking sound, and a splash.

Lester stood next to me now. His best black funeral suit was sopping wet and his sleeves were rolled up. He said, "I was just trying to fix that damn light in the fountain." He looked down at himself, dripping water onto the carpet. "I guess I fell in."

He held up his right hand for me to see. The tips of his fingers appeared to be singed. "Hurt my hand, too. That light must've had a short in it." Mama came up and stood between me and Lester. His brow wrinkled in confusion and he said, directly to Mama, "Dora, is that you?"

Mama said, "Hey Lester, nice to see you again."

I said, "Oh, shit."

Miss Thelma, Big Earl, and Mrs Roosevelt walked up to us then. Miss Thelma handed a lit joint to Mama, who offered it to Lester. "Take a hit, baby. It'll all make sense in a minute."

Lester, whose suit had completely dried in the previous

few seconds, continued to look uncertain about what had happened. But he said, "Yes, I think that sounds good," and took the joint from Mama.

Someone called, "Barbara Jean," and she turned around where she stood, just a few feet from the front window. The crowd parted between Barbara Jean and the corner of the room that contained the fountain. Now she and I both saw what most of the people in the room had already seen. Lester was on the floor, half in and half out of the now-darkened fountain, the two marble statues lying on top of him.

Barbara Jean ran to Lester's side as Richmond threw the large statues off of him like they were made of cotton balls instead of stone. James shouted for someone to call 9-1-1 and moved in to start CPR. I knew it was too late. Lester – the true Lester, not the wet shell being pounded on by my well-meaning husband – was already shaking hands with Eleanor Roosevelt and telling her how much he had always admired her good works.

Mama turned to me and said, "I gotta tell ya, I'm surprised."

No one was looking my way, so I answered her out loud. "Well, you said Mrs Roosevelt was good at picking out who was about to die."

"Oh, not that. I figured all along she was right about that. I just always assumed it would be Richmond who'd die underneath two naked white girls." Mama walked away then, not interested in the commotion taking place at the foot of the fountain.

I went over and joined my friends. Clarice had her arms around Barbara Jean, both of them seated on the floor. I got down on my knees beside them and grabbed ahold of Barbara Jean's hand. She stared at Lester's body as it rocked under James's futile effort to revive him. She shook her head slowly from side to side and said, in the soft tone of a mother gently scolding a much-loved, naughty child, "I can't take my eyes off you, can I? Not for two seconds."

Chapter 9

Clarice and Odette moved in with Barbara Jean after Lester died. For the last bit of July and on into August, they made sure she got dressed and ate something every day. They slept on either side of her in bed for the first few nights. Not that Barbara Jean slept much. Every night, they heard her creep out of her room and down the stairs to sit alone in her library. She would return to the bed just before sunrise and pretend later that she'd slept through the night.

Barbara Jean hardly spoke at all. And, when she did, not a word of it was about Lester. Most of her time was spent pacing the house, stopping in her tracks every so often to shake her head like a sleeper trying to wake up from a nightmare. She was in no shape to be left alone or to make any decisions. And there was so much that had to be done.

Clarice and Odette were surprised to learn that, although Lester had spent many years fighting off various near-fatal illnesses, the only preparation he had made for his passing was a short will leaving everything to Barbara Jean. So while Odette saw to Barbara Jean, Clarice could be depended on to organize the service and interment. She planned everything from Lester's burial suit to the menu for the funeral dinner. She accomplished it all with a gracious smile, even swallowing her temper when dealing with the pastor and higher-ups of First Baptist Church – a piss-elegant crowd if ever there was one, all of them eager to demonstrate to his widow just how deeply they adored the wealthy deceased. It was quite an undertaking, but burying any signs of contention and making sure that everything moved smoothly and looked exactly as it should was what Clarice had been raised to do. And Clarice was glad that her unique skills, gained at considerable personal expense, could be put to use to help her friend.

When a rich man dies, the vultures descend quickly. And Lester had been wealthier than anyone had imagined. He'd been Plainview-rich back when he was courting Barbara Jean. He became Louisville-rich not long after they got married. And, it was learned, he died Chicago-rich/New York-comfortable. Lester's greedier relatives were knocking on Barbara Jean's door for a handout well before the first fistful of dirt hit the lid of Lester's coffin. One previously unknown cousin came by claiming Lester had promised to fund her Hawaiian vacation. A great-niece wanted to interest Barbara Jean in "a surefire business opportunity" that just needed "a little start-up money." Several of Lester's leering male relations dropped by, basted in Old Spice, all prepared to provide guidance and a strong shoulder for the beautiful widow to weep upon.

This sort of situation, Clarice thought, was precisely why God made Odette. When the corners of Odette's mouth turned downward and her eyes narrowed, nobody stuck around to see what was coming next. She stood guard over Barbara Jean, sending anyone who posed a potential threat running for their lives with just a glance. And she did it all while battling through hot flashes that set her on fire almost every night.

The Supremes were in residence at Barbara Jean's for three weeks. Odette left each day to spend time with James, but always came back to be with Barbara Jean at night. Clarice went to check on Richmond a few times that first week, intending to cook his dinner and monitor his diabetes. But the fifth time she stopped by the house and failed to find him in or see any sign that he had come home at all since she'd been at Barbara Jean's, she asked herself why she was doing it, and couldn't come up with a good answer. So that day Clarice made sure the freezer was stocked with a month of meals, then she left Richmond a note saying she would return when Barbara Jean was okay. She stayed away for the next two weeks, limiting her contact with Richmond to one daily phone message that always went unanswered.

The morning after declaring temporary independence from Richmond, Clarice sat down at the piano in Barbara Jean's sitting room after breakfast. The piano was a Victorian beauty, a Steinway square grand with a rosewood cabinet. Clarice had ordered it herself during the initial renovation of Barbara Jean's mansion. It was a fine instrument and Clarice thought it was a shame that its role of late was merely decorative. She ran a finger over the white keys and then the black and was pleased to discover that it was in tune. She began to play.

The music drew Barbara Jean to the room, closely followed by Odette. They listened and then applauded when she finished. "That was nice," Barbara Jean said. "Sort of happy and sad at the same time."

"Chopin. Perfect for any occasion," Clarice said.

Barbara Jean rested her elbows on the piano. "Remember how Adam used to imitate you?"

"I sure do," Clarice said, twisting her mouth to feign offense.

Barbara Jean turned to Odette. "Adam used to do the best imitation of Clarice after his lessons. He would hunch over the keys and sway and moan. It was the funniest thing in the world, watching him work up all that passion while he played – what was it? 'Chopsticks'?"

"'Heart and Soul,'" Clarice said.

"That's right. 'Heart and Soul.' The first time he did it, Clarice and I both laughed so hard we ended up on our knees crying. It was a hoot."

Odette had heard that story on the day it happened and hundreds of times since, but Barbara Jean was laughing and it sounded too good to put a stop to it.

Barbara Jean said, "He loved music. I bet he could've been really good."

"Absolutely. He was musical. He had a natural facility. Adam had it all."

"Yes, he did," Barbara Jean said.

Barbara Jean talked about Adam for the rest of that morning. "Remember how he loved to draw? He'd spend hours up in his room with his crayons and colored pencils." "I'll never forget how he taught Odette's boys to dance like James Brown. I can still see Eric shuffling across the floor in his training pants." "Wasn't he the most dapper little boy you ever saw? Never knew a boy to fuss over his clothes like he did. One scuff on his shoes and he'd pout all day."

The following morning and the next few began the same way. They had breakfast, and then Clarice played the piano. Then Barbara Jean talked about Adam, allowing memories of him to pull her back into her life. Eventually, there was so much conversation and laughter that it seemed as if the three of them were guests at an extended slumber party. Except, at this party, talking about men was carefully avoided. No Lester Maxberry. No Richmond Baker, which suited Clarice fine. And definitely no Chick Carlson, whom Clarice and Odette were both pretending they hadn't seen at Big Earl's house after the funeral.

In spite of the circumstances, on the mid-August morning when Barbara Jean thanked Odette and Clarice for their support and kindly, but firmly, ordered them out, Clarice was sorry to leave. She told herself at the time that her reluctance to end the slumber party was because she'd had such fun with her friends, reliving a part of their shared youth. Later, she admitted to herself that she was frightened of what she knew in her heart she would find when she got home.

When Clarice stepped inside her front door after two weeks away, she called out Richmond's name to empty walls. None of the food she had prepared for him had been touched. And the sheets on their bed were as fresh as they'd been when she had put them on over a fortnight earlier.

When Richmond came home two days later, he gave her a peck on the cheek and inquired about Barbara Jean.

"She's better," Clarice answered. "Are you hungry?"

He answered yes, and then kissed his wife's cheek again after she told him that she would prepare ham steak and roasted potatoes, one of his favorite meals.

Richmond showered while Clarice hummed "Für Elise" and cooked his dinner. He never offered an explanation about where he'd been sleeping, and Clarice never asked him for one.

Chapter 10

Odette, Clarice, and Barbara Jean became the Supremes in the summer of 1967, just after the end of their junior year of high school. Classes had been out for only a couple of weeks and Clarice was at Odette's house preparing to go to the All-You-Can-Eat. Big Earl occasionally opened up the restaurant to his son's friends on Saturday nights. The kids thought of it as adventurous and grown-up, getting out of Leaning Tree and into downtown Plainview for an evening. A night at the All-You-Can-Eat was their first taste of adult liberty. In truth, they had escaped their homes and their parents to sip Coca-Cola and eat chicken wings under the most watchful eyes in town. They couldn't have been more strictly monitored anywhere else on the planet. Big Earl and Miss Thelma had a talent for identifying and neutralizing troublemakers, and no kind of teenage mischief got past them.

Mrs Jackson tapped on Odette's bedroom door as Clarice rummaged through her best friend's chest of drawers searching for something to liven up, or cover up, those dreadful dresses Odette always wore. The blind grandmother who had made her clothes back when she was a little girl was dead, but her grandma's style and taste lived on in Odette's sorry closet. Mrs Jackson said, "Before y'all go to Earl's, I want you to run this over to Mrs Perdue's house for me."

She held out a cardboard box wrapped with twine. Grease stains covered most of the box's surface, and it emitted an aroma of burnt toast and raw garlic. Even Odette's three cats, all strays that had sensed her true nature beneath her get-the-hell-away-from-me exterior and followed her home to be adopted, shrank away from the odor of the package. They yowled and bolted out of the open doorway.

Odette took the box from her mother and asked, "Who is Mrs Perdue?"

Mrs Jackson said, "You know, your little friend Barbara Jean's mother. Her funeral was today, so I baked a chicken for the family."

Clarice looked at the clock and felt that she had to say something. She had made plans to meet Richmond and one of his buddies at 7:00. It was only 5:30, but Clarice knew from experience how long it could take to transform Odette from her usual self into someone a boy might want to wrap his arm around. There simply wasn't time for anything else.

Clarice was indignant. She was a good girl. She got excellent grades. Hardly a season passed without her piano playing winning her a prize or affording her a mention in the newspaper that would join the articles about her birth that adorned the walls of her parents' home. Still, she was monitored every hour of her day. All of her socializing took a backseat to the four hours of piano practice she did daily in preparation for the two lessons she had each week with Zara Olavsky, an internationally renowned piano pedagogue who taught at the university's music school. She was required to check in hourly whenever she was away from home. And she had the earliest curfew of any teenager in town.

Her parents grew even more vigilant that year, with Richmond in college and Clarice still in high school. There were no dates at all unless she double-dated with Odette. Clarice was certain that, with Odette's gruff personality around boys and those horrible outfits she wore that growled "*keep away*," her parents viewed Odette as walking, talking virginity insurance. Not that Odette's face was all that bad. She could be cute in the right light. And her figure was decent, top-heavy and round. Lord knows there were plenty of boys who longed to slip a hand down her blouse. But no boy wanted to cop a feel off the fearless girl. She was just more trouble than she was worth. Richmond had called in all kinds of favors to get his college friends to go out with her. Pretty soon he was going to have to start paying them.

But Richmond had a date for Odette that night and Clarice's parents had agreed to allow her to stay out an hour later than usual. It was going to be a perfect evening. Now Odette's mother was trying to ruin it.

Whining often worked on her own mother when she wanted out of an unpleasant chore or wanted her curfew extended, so Clarice gave it a try with Dora Jackson. She said, "But, Mrs Jackson, we're going to the All-You-Can-Eat and Barbara Jean lives the other direction and I've got on heels."

Odette mouthed, "Shut up." But even though she knew

from the look on Mrs Jackson's face that she should stop talking, Clarice piped up with "And besides, Barbara Jean is not our friend. She's nobody's friend, except the boys she runs around with. And she stinks, Mrs Jackson. She really does. She drowns herself in cheap perfume every day. And my cousin Veronica saw her combing her hair in the bathroom at school last year and a roach fell out."

Mrs Jackson narrowed her eyes at Clarice and said, slow and low, "Odette's gonna take this chicken over to Barbara Jean to show that child some kindness on the day of her mother's funeral. If you don't wanna go, then don't. If you're worried about your feet, borrow some sneakers from Odette. If you're worried about roaches fallin' off of her, then step back if she gets to flingin' her head around. Or maybe you should just go on home."

The only thing Clarice could think of that was worse than delaying her date with Richmond to run this ridiculous errand Mrs Jackson couldn't be dissuaded from was the idea of going back home and, with her chaperone otherwise occupied, being forced to stay in and keep her mother company all evening. Seeing her plans with Richmond fading away, Clarice rushed to save them. Speaking quickly, she said, "No, ma'am. I'll go with Odette. I didn't really believe that roach story. Veronica likes to make stuff up."

Mrs Jackson left the room without another word, and Odette and Clarice headed to Barbara Jean's.

Plainview is shaped like a triangle. Leaning Tree comprises its southeast section. To get to Barbara Jean's house, the two girls had to walk south along Wall Road and then along side streets into the very tip of the triangle's corner.

The wall that gave the road its name was built by the town when freed blacks started settling in Plainview after the Civil War. A group of town leaders led by Alfred Ballard – whose house Barbara Jean would one day own – decided to build a ten-foot-high, five-mile-long stone wall to protect the wealthy whites who lived downtown when the race war they expected finally came. Though further north, the poor whites were on the east side of the wall with the blacks, but the town leaders figured they could fend for themselves. When the new inhabitants proved less frightening than predicted, commitment to the wall project faded. The only section of Ballard's Wall that made it to the full ten-foot goal was the portion that divided Leaning Tree from downtown. The rest of the proposed wall ended up as isolated piles of rocks, creating a dotted dividing line through town.

That part of the story of Leaning Tree was pretty well accepted as fact by everyone. Plainview's children were taught that bit of local history in school, with the aesthetic aspects of the wall replacing much of the racial politics. But the history taught in school and what black children were taught at home took off in radically different directions at the subject of the naming of Leaning Tree.

In school, they learned that early settlers called the southeast area of town Leaning Tree because of a mysterious natural phenomenon – something about the position of the river and the hills – that caused the trees to lean toward the west.

At their dinner tables, the children of Leaning Tree were told that there was no mystery at all to the crooked trees. Their parents told them that, because downtown was on higher ground, Ballard's Wall cast a shadow over the black area of town. The trees there needed sunlight, so they bent. Every tree that didn't die in the shadow of that wall grew tall, top-heavy, and visibly tilted. A name was born.

Barbara Jean's house was on the worst street in the worst neighborhood in Leaning Tree. Her street was only eight blocks from Clarice's house, only five from Odette's. But as they turned onto Barbara Jean's block, Clarice surveyed her surroundings and thought that this place might as well have been on the far side of the moon for all the resemblance it held to the landscaped, middle-class order of her street or the quaint charm of Odette's old farmhouse, with its fanciful octagonal windows and scalloped picket fence, courtesy of Odette's carpenter father. In this neighborhood, people lived in tiny boxes with warped and splintering siding, peeling paint, and no gutters. Noisy, nappy-headed children ran naked over lawns that were mostly dirt accented with patches of weeds.

Barbara Jean's house was the best on her block, but that wasn't saying much. It was a little brown shack whose paint had faded to a chalky tan color. This house was only better than its neighbors because, unlike every other house on the street, the glass in all of its windows seemed to be intact.

Odette climbed up the two steps from the walkway and rang the bell. No one answered, and Clarice said, "Let's just leave it on the stoop and get going." But Odette started banging on the door with her fist.

A few seconds later, the door opened just wide enough for Clarice and Odette to see a big man with red eyes and blotchy, grayish-brown skin staring at them. His nose was flat and crooked, as if it had been broken a few times. He had no discernible neck, and most of his face was occupied by an unusually wide mouth. His shirt strained against his belly to stay fastened. He topped it all off with hair that had been straightened and lacquered until it resembled a plastic wig from an Elvis Presley Halloween costume.

He squinted against the sunlight and said, "Y'all want somethin'?" His words whistled through a gap between his front teeth.

Odette lifted the box and said, "My mama sent this for Barbara Jean."

The man opened the door fully then. He stretched his mouth into a smile that caused a prickly sensation to travel across the back of Clarice's neck and gave her the feeling he was about to take a bite out of her. She was relieved that they could finally hand off the box and get the hell out of this neighborhood. But the man stepped back into the dark beyond the doorway and said, "Come on in." Then he yelled, "Barbara Jean, your friends is here to see you."

Clarice wanted to stand on the front stoop and wait for Barbara Jean to come outside, but Odette was already walking through the front door and waving at her to follow. When they stepped into the front room, they saw Barbara Jean looking surprised and embarrassed to have two girls from school she hardly knew walking into her house.

Barbara Jean wore her funeral clothes, a too-tight black skirt and a clinging, shiny black blouse. Shameless, Clarice thought. During the walk to Barbara Jean's, Clarice had admitted to herself that this mission of mercy really was the only right thing to do. But as she silently critiqued Barbara Jean's sexy mourning outfit, another side of Clarice's nature leapt to the forefront and she began to eagerly anticipate describing Barbara Jean's getup to her mother and her cousin Veronica. Their reactions would be priceless.

The living room was crowded with showy, ornate furniture that was all well past its prime. With each step, a plastic runner protecting the bright orange carpet crunched beneath their feet. The place looked as if someone with a little money, but not much taste or good sense, had once lived there and left behind all their stuff.

Odette walked over to Barbara Jean and held out the box. "We were sorry to hear about your loss. My mama sent this. It's a roast chicken."

Barbara Jean said, "Thank you," and reached for the box, looking eager to hasten her visitors' departure. But the man grabbed the box away just as Odette handed it to her. He said, "Y'all come on into the kitchen," and walked toward the back of the house. The girls didn't move, and from the next room the man shouted, "Come on now." Obedient girls that they were, they followed.

The kitchen was in worse shape than the two rooms Clarice and Odette had passed through to get to it. The floor was so chipped they could see the tar paper underneath the linoleum. Dirty dishes were heaped in the rusted metal sink and piled on the cracked wooden countertop. The red patent leather seat covers of the kitchen chairs had all split open and dingy white stuffing bulged out of the open seams.

Where, Clarice wondered, were the aunts, female

friends, and cousins who were supposed to descend en masse to cook, clean, and comfort after a tragedy? Even the lowliest, most despised second or third cousin in her family would have merited at least one afternoon of attention on the day of their burial. But no one had bothered to come here.

The man sat at the table and motioned for them to sit with him. The three girls sat down and stared at each other, not knowing what to say. He turned toward Odette and said, "Tell your mama that me and my stepdaughter sure appreciate her kindness." He reached out then and patted Barbara Jean's arm, causing her to flinch and scoot away from him, her chair making a loud scraping noise as the metal feet dug into the scarred floor.

Clarice wanted to get out worse than ever, but Odette wasn't doing anything to move the process along. Odette just watched the man and Barbara Jean closely, as if she were trying to decipher a riddle.

The man poured a shot of whiskey from a bottle of Old Crow that sat in front of him on the table. Then he picked up his smudged glass and drained it in one swallow. Clarice had never seen a man drink straight whiskey and she couldn't help gawking. When he noticed her staring, he said, "Sorry, girls. Where's my manners? Barbara Jean, get some glasses for our guests."

Barbara Jean put her hand to her forehead and sank a little lower in her chair.

Odette said, "No, thank you, sir. We just came to drop off the food and get Barbara Jean. My mother said to bring her back to our house for dinner and not to take no for an answer."

Barbara Jean looked at Odette and wondered if she was crazy. Clarice kicked Odette hard under the table with the point of her shoe. Odette didn't yelp or react at all. She just sat there smiling at the man, who was pouring his second drink.

"Nah, I don't think she should go anywhere tonight," he said, his wide mouth twisting into a nasty expression that made Clarice's stomach tighten up. She got the feeling that something bad was about to happen, and she set her feet beneath her so she could run if she needed to. But the man relaxed his mouth back into his cannibal grin and said, "Barbara Jean's been through a lot today and she should stay home with her family." He looked around the room and made an expansive, circular motion with the whiskey bottle as if he were indicating a corps of relatives scampering and fussing around them. Then he put the bottle down and touched Barbara Jean's arm again. Again, she recoiled from him.

Odette said, "Please let her come. If we come back without her, Mama'll have Daddy drive us back over to get her. And I hate riding around town in the back of that police cruiser. It's embarrassing."

"Your daddy's a cop, huh?"

"Yes, sir. In Louisville," Odette said.

Clarice couldn't stop her jaw from dropping open at the sound of Odette lying with such conviction.

The man thought for a few seconds and had a change of heart. He rose from his chair, staggered badly, and stood just behind Barbara Jean. He leaned forward and squeezed her upper arms with his large hands. Then he rested his chin on the top of her head. He said, "No need to put your daddy through the trouble of comin' by. Your mama's right. My little girl should be around women tonight. Jus' don't stay out too late. I don't like to worry."

He stood there for a while holding on to Barbara Jean's arms and swaying while she looked straight ahead. Finally, she said, "I've got to change," and she slid sideways out of his grasp. The man was thrown off balance and had to grip the chair to keep from toppling forward onto the table.

Barbara Jean walked just a few steps away and opened a door off the kitchen. She went into the smallest bedroom Clarice had ever seen. It was really just a pantry with a bed and a battered old dresser in it. And the bed was a child's bed, far too small for a teenager. Clarice watched through the partially opened door as Barbara Jean pulled off her tacky black blouse. Then she picked up a bottle of perfume from the dresser and repeatedly squeezed the bulb, spraying her arms where the man had touched her as if she were applying an antiseptic. When she caught Clarice's reflection in the mirror above her dresser, she slammed shut the door.

The man straightened up and said, "Y'all scuse me. I gotta take a leak." He shuffled away, but stopped at the kitchen door and turned back to Clarice and Odette. He winked and said, "Be good and don't drink up all my whiskey while I'm gone." Then he continued out of the room. A few seconds later, they heard him relieving himself and humming from down the hallway.

When they were alone, Clarice took the opportunity to kick Odette again. This time Odette said, "Ouch, quit it."

"Why did you do that? We could've been out of here and gone."

Odette said, "We can't just leave her here with him."

"Yes, we can. This is her house."

"Maybe, but we're not leaving her alone with him right after she buried her mother."

There was no use arguing with Odette once she got a notion stuck in her head, so Clarice said nothing more. It was clear to her that Odette had looked at this cat-eyed, stray girl and set her mind on adoption.

When Barbara Jean emerged from her cramped cell, she was wearing a glittery red blouse and the same black skirt. Her hair, which had been pulled back and pinned up, now fell around her shoulders in waves, and she had applied lipstick to match her blouse. She may have stunk of cheap perfume, but she looked like a movie star.

The man came back into the room. He said, "You look just like your sweet mama," and Barbara Jean looked at him with a hatred so strong that Clarice and Odette felt it like a hot wind sweeping through the room.

As the man fell into his chair and reached for the bottle, Barbara Jean said, "Bye, Vondell." She was out of the kitchen and headed down the hallway before Clarice and Odette had begun their farewells to the bleary-eyed man at the table.

Outside, they stood in front of the house looking at each other. Clarice couldn't stand the silence. She lied the way she'd been taught to do after meeting someone's unpleasant relative. "Your stepfather seems nice."

Odette rolled her eyes.

Barbara Jean said, "He's not my stepfather. He's my mother's . . . He's nothing is what he is."

They walked about a half a block together, quiet again.

Barbara Jean spoke after a while. "Listen, I appreciate you getting me out of the house. I really do. But you don't have to take me anywhere. I can just walk around for a while." She looked at her watch, a dime-store accessory with yellow rhinestones surrounding its face and a cracked, white patent leather band. "Vondell's likely to be asleep in another couple hours. I can go back then." To Odette she said, "Thank your mother for making the chicken. It was real nice of her."

Odette hooked an arm under Barbara Jean's elbow and said, "If you're gonna walk, you might as well walk with us. You can meet the latest victim Clarice's boyfriend has dragged over from the college to distract me while he tries to get down her pants."

"Odette!" Clarice screamed.

Odette said, "It's true and you know it." Then she tugged Barbara Jean in the direction of the All-You-Can-Eat. "Oh, and Barbara Jean, whatever you do, don't eat any of my mama's chicken."

When her mother and her cousin later asked Clarice why she had become friendly with Barbara Jean that summer, she would say that it was because she got to know and appreciate Barbara Jean's sweetness and sense of humor and because she had felt a welling up of Christian sympathy after gaining a deeper understanding of the difficulties of Barbara Jean's life – her dead mother, her dreadful neighborhood, her sad little hole of a bedroom, that man Vondell. And those things would one day be true. Within months, Clarice's mother and cousin would learn that any petty criticism or harsh judgment of Barbara Jean would be met with icy silence or an uncharacteristically blunt rebuke from Clarice. And Clarice would eventually confess to Odette that she felt tremendous guilt about having been the source of many of the rumors about Barbara Jean. Her cousin might have started the rumor about the roach in Barbara Jean's hair, but Clarice had been the main one spreading it around.

But at the time, even as she listed in her mind the more noble reasons for making this new friend, she knew that there was more to it. At seventeen, Clarice was unable to see the true extent to which she was ruled by a slavish devotion to her own self-interest, but she understood that her primary reason for becoming friends with Barbara Jean was that it had benefited her. On the night she and Odette dropped off that putrid-smelling chicken, Clarice discovered that Barbara Jean's presence was surprisingly convenient.

When Clarice, Odette, and Barbara Jean walked into the All-You-Can-Eat, Little Earl ushered them to the coveted window table for the first time. A group of his pals was sitting there, but he chased them off, saying, "Make way. This table is reserved for the Supremes." After that, every boy in the place, even those who Clarice knew had told some of the most outlandish lies about Barbara Jean and what she'd supposedly done with them, came to the window table to stutter and stammer through their best adolescent pickup lines.

Richmond showed up with James Henry in tow a few minutes after the girls had been seated. Clarice made a mental note to give Richmond hell later for bringing him. James was the worst of all the regular guys Richmond had scrounged up for Odette. He was nice enough, and he'd had a fondness for Odette ever since she'd beaten two teenage boys bloody when she was ten after they'd called him "Frankenstein" because of that ugly knife scar on his face. But he was, Clarice thought, the most boring boy on the face of the earth. He barely made conversation at all. And when he did, it was pathetic.

The only topic James talked with Odette about at any length was her mother's garden. He worked for Lester Maxberry's lawn care business and he came to their dates armed with helpful hints for Odette to pass along to Mrs Jackson. James was the only boy Clarice knew who could sit in the back of a car parked on the side of a dark road with a girl and talk to her about nothing but composted manure.

Worst of all, James was always exhausted. He had to be at work early in the mornings, and he took classes at the university in the afternoons. So just when the evening got going, James would start nodding off. Odette would see his head droop and she would announce, "My date's asleep. Time to go home." It was intolerable.

Odette had a slightly different view of James Henry. He might have been the worst double-date choice for Clarice's purposes, but Odette was content with him. She thought it was kind of sweet how he dropped off to sleep during their dates. How many other boys would let themselves be that vulnerable in front of a girl – mouth open and snoring? And he had excellent manners. James had become a frequent visitor, never failing to come by and personally convey his thanks to Dora Jackson for the food she regularly brought to his home after his mother became

housebound with emphysema. This in spite of the fact that
Odette had witnessed James wisely burying her mother's
half-raw, half-burned pork chops beside his house one
day. She assumed, hoped, that all of the meals her mother
gave the Henrys ended up underground as well. Still, each
inedible bundle was greeted with undeserved gratitude
from James.

Odette knew just enough about men to have her guard
up at all times. So she hadn't eliminated the possibility
that, underneath it all, James might be as horny and stupid
as his friend Richmond. But she was willing to tolerate his
head falling onto her shoulder occasionally while she
figured him out.

Richmond and James wound through the crowd of boys
gathered around the window table. James behaved the
same way he always did. He sat next to Odette, compli-
mented her homemade dress, inquired about her mother's
garden, and then yawned. Richmond was another story.
To Clarice's surprise and enjoyment, Richmond, by then a
college football hero, felt threatened by all of the
testosterone-dizzy boys surrounding his girl, even though
they were really there for Barbara Jean. Ordinarily, he was
content to sit in the center of the throng, entertaining the
boys who came by the table to laugh at his jokes and to
hear tales of his record-breaking freshman year on the
team. Clarice felt that she had his full attention only in
those brief moments when they found themselves alone.
That night, though, Richmond spent the entire evening
with his arm draped around her shoulders, whispering in
her ear and being extra attentive to her in order to clearly
stake out his claim.

Barbara Jean was like magic, Clarice thought. The more boys came by to get a close look at her, the more territorial Richmond became. That night was a wonderful evening of flirting, dancing, and nonstop free malts and Coca-Colas from admirers. When James drifted off to sleep and it came time to leave, Big Earl had to intercede to forestall a fistfight over who would see the Supremes home.

As they left the All-You-Can-Eat and headed for Richmond's car, Clarice whispered to Odette, "Barbara Jean is our new best friend, okay?"

Odette said, "Okay." And by the end of the summer, that's the way it was.

Chapter 11

Six weeks after Big Earl's funeral, my summer break ended and I returned to my job. I was food services manager at James Whitcomb Riley Elementary School, which was a fancy way of saying "head lunch lady." Normally, I enjoyed getting back to work and starting the new school year. But that fall was a tough one.

James was still adjusting to life without Big Earl being there for him. I often caught him reaching for the phone, only to set it back down again as a brief shadow of pain traveled across his face. Whenever that happened, I knew who he'd been thinking of calling. I'd done the same thing for months after losing Mama so suddenly. James's mother had died relatively young, but she had wasted away for years and James had learned to live without her long before she passed. Losing a parent, and that's what Big Earl had been to James, in the blink of an eye was a new kind of loss for James and it was going to take him some time to work it through.

Barbara Jean was bad off, too. She tried to put up a good front. She wasn't hysterical or even teary-eyed, and she looked as perfectly put together as ever. But it was easy to see that Lester and Big Earl passing right up on top of each other like they'd done had laid her low. She was living deep in her own thoughts and pulling herself further away from Clarice and me every day.

Clarice had her hands full with Richmond. He was back to his cheating ways with a vengeance. It was like the old days. Richmond catted around, not caring who knew. People barely acquainted with him and Clarice openly gossiped about it. Clarice pretended not to notice, but she burned so hot with anger at him some days that I hoped, for both of their sakes, that Richmond was sleeping with one eye open.

And me. After slacking off for a while, my hot flashes were back big time. More nights than not, the early hours of the day found me cooling myself in the kitchen and shooting the breeze with Mama, instead of sleeping. I loved Mama's company, but the lack of sleep was taking a toll on me. I felt run-down and I looked, as my mother bluntly put it, "like shit on a cracker."

By the middle of October, I'd had my fill of feeling bad, so I went to my doctor and rattled off a long list of symptoms. I told him about my hot flashes and my fatigue. I complained that I was getting forgetful and, James claimed, irritable. I wasn't willing to tell him the main reason I had decided to see him. I had no desire whatsoever to explain to my doctor that I'd made my appointment because former first lady Eleanor Roosevelt had been showing an awful lot of interest in me lately. I remembered, all too well, how she'd orbited around Lester right before he electrocuted himself, and it had me feeling antsy.

At first Mrs Roosevelt had only visited me along with Mama, but then she started turning up by herself. Some mornings I would walk into my cramped office off of the cafeteria at Riley Elementary and there she'd be, asleep in one of the rusty metal folding chairs or stretched out on the floor. Occasionally she'd pop up out of nowhere and lean over my shoulder as I did the food orders over the phone. I made up my mind to see the doctor after Mrs Roosevelt greeted me every morning for a solid week, grinning wide and offering me a swig from her flask. (Mama had been right about Mrs Roosevelt and the drinking. That woman was at her flask morning, noon, and night.)

Mrs Roosevelt and Mama sat in the corner of the examining room during my checkup and during the tests that came afterwards. They came with me again a week after that first appointment and listened in as my doctor, Dr Alex Soo, told me that I had non-Hodgkin's lymphoma.

Alex was my friend. He was a chubby Korean man, about a year younger than my son Jimmy. When he took over my old doctor's practice several years back, I had been his very first patient.

Alex came to town just after my Denise left the house, and as soon as I laid eyes on Alex's round, smooth face I decided to mother the hell out of him, whether he wanted it or not. When I found out that he lived alone and had no relatives nearby, I badgered him into spending the holidays with me and my family. It was an annual tradition now. Sometimes, if Alex wasn't careful, he'd slip and call me "Ma."

Now this kind young man sat twisting his fingers behind a mahogany desk that seemed too large for him. He worked hard at not looking me in the eye while he rattled off the details of what was happening within my body and what needed to be done to stop it. The next step, he said, was to get a second opinion. He'd already made an appointment for me with an oncologist at University Hospital who was "one of the most highly regarded in his field." He used terms like "five-year survival rate" and "well-tolerated chemotherapy cycles." I felt sorry for him. He was trying so hard to remain calm that his voice came out robotic and full of bottled-up emotion at the same time, like a bad actor playing a soap opera doctor.

After he got done with his speech, he let out a long sigh of relief. The corners of his mouth curled up slightly, like he was proud of himself for making it over a big hurdle. When he was able to look at me again, he started in offering his most optimistic prognosis. He said, "Your general level of health is very good. And we know a lot about this kind of cancer." He went on to say that I might be lucky. I might be one of those rare people who sailed on through chemotherapy with hardly any side effects.

His words were meant to comfort me, and I appreciated it. But part of my mind had already left the office. In my head, I was telling my anguished kids not to worry about me. They were adults now and scattered all over the country, but still in need of parenting. Denise was a young mother, still filled with fear and worry over each stage of her children's development that defied the books she had believed would bring order to motherhood. Jimmy and his wife were both hell-bent on getting ahead and would work themselves to death if I didn't nag them into taking an occasional vacation. And Eric, he was as quiet as his father, and no one but me, who had listened over the phone as he cried his heart out over lost love more than once, knew that he felt everything twice as deep as his brother or sister.

From the moment I told the Supremes I was sick, Clarice would try to take over my life. First she'd want to take charge of my medical treatment. Then she'd get on my very last nerve by trying to drag me to her church for anointings and such. And Barbara Jean would just get all quiet and accept that I was as good as dead. Seeing her grieving for me ahead of time would bring back memories of all she's lost in her life, and it would depress the hell out of me.

My brother, in spite of being raised by our mother, had grown up and become a man who believed that women were helpless victims of our emotions and hormones. When he found out I was sick, he would talk to me like I was a child and pester me just like he used to when we were children.

And James. I thought of the look I used to see on James's face in that horrible, gray-yellow emergency room light whenever one of the kids suffered some childhood injury. The smallest pain for them meant despair for him. Whenever I came down with a cold or flu, he was at my side with a thermometer, medicine, and an expression of agony on his face for the duration. It was like he'd pooled up all the love and caring his father had denied him and his mother and was determined to shower it onto me and our children ten times over.

I made up my mind right then that I'd keep this whole thing to myself for as long as I could. There was still an outside chance that it was all a false alarm, wasn't there? And, if this chemo was indeed "well-tolerated," I might be able to tell everyone about it at my leisure. If I was lucky, in five or six months I could turn to James and my friends one Sunday at the All-You-Can-Eat and say, "Hey, did I ever tell you all about the time I had cancer?"

When I didn't say anything for a while, Alex spoke faster. believing he had to provide me with some sort of consolation. But I wasn't the one who needed to be consoled. Behind him on the windowsill of his office, Mama sat with both of her hands pressed to her face. She was crying like I had never seen before.

Mama muttered, "No, no, this can't be right. It's too soon."

Mrs Roosevelt, who had been lying on the sofa against the wall of Alex's office, rose and walked over to Mama. She patted Mama on the back and whispered in her ear, but whatever she said didn't do the trick. Mama continued to cry. She was crying so loud now that I could barely hear the doctor.

Finally, forgetting my vow not to talk to the dead in the presence of the living, I said, "It's all right. Really, it's all right. There's nothing to cry about."

Alex stopped talking and stared at me for a moment, assuming I was talking to him. He apparently took my words as permission for him to let go because within seconds he was out of his chair and crouching in front of me. He buried his face in my lap, and I soon felt his tears soak through my skirt. He said, "I'm so sorry, Ma." Then he apologized for not being more professional as he blew his nose into a tissue I pulled from the box on the corner of his desk and handed to him.

I rubbed his back, pleased to be comforting him instead of him comforting me. I bent forward and whispered,

"Shh, shh, don't cry," into Alex's ear. But I said it staring ahead at my mother as she sobbed into Eleanor Roosevelt's fox stole. "I'm not afraid. Can't be, remember? I was born in a sycamore tree."

Chapter 12

Clarice turned around in her chair to get a good look at the newly redecorated All-You-Can-Eat. It was just before Halloween and the restaurant was dressed up for the holiday. The windows were draped with cotton cobwebs. A garland of crepe-paper skulls surrounded the cash register. Each table was decorated with a center-piece of tiny orange pumpkins, gold-and-green striped gourds, and a small wicker basket filled with candy corn. It wasn't the prettiest display Clarice had ever seen, but it did at least cover up that awful restaurant logo on the tablecloth.

No matter how she felt about the new logo, it was clear that this affront to her sensibilities wasn't going anywhere anytime soon. The kids from the university had discovered Little Earl's T-shirts with the big red lips, pink tongue, and suggestive fruits on them. Now a constant stream of young people came into the All-You-Can-Eat to giggle and buy the risqué restaurant merchandise. Little Earl was making a small fortune.

The Supremes, Richmond, and James were all in their usual places by the front window. For Barbara Jean's sake, they had tried shuffling things around after Lester died – moving the men to the opposite end one week, shifting

James to the center and Richmond to Lester's seat the next. But it was no use. The more they tried to avoid seeing it, the stronger they felt Lester's absence. Barbara Jean finally called a halt to the musical chairs, saying that she preferred to keep things the way they had always been.

Everyone was tired that week. Richmond yawned every few minutes – which was no surprise to Clarice since he'd been out all night again. Barbara Jean hadn't been fully awake since Lester died. She pretended that she was okay, but her mind wandered constantly and Clarice always had the feeling when she talked to her that Barbara Jean was only half there. James had been sleepy since childhood. And Odette actually fell asleep at the table that afternoon.

Clarice was exhausted from having spent most of the night playing the piano. She had begun to rely on music to get her through those nights when Richmond did his disappearing act. Instead of sitting up stewing over where her husband was, she had taken to playing the piano until she was too worn out to think. The previous night Clarice had begun playing Beethoven sonatas at midnight, and the next thing she knew she was underscoring Richmond's arrival home at six in the morning with an angry fugue. Now her fingers ached and she could hardly lift her arms.

She poked Odette on her shoulder with her fork and said, "Wake up. You're starting to snore."

Odette said, "I wasn't sleeping. And I certainly wasn't snoring. I never snore." James heard her say that and let out a snort. "I heard every word you said. You were talking about how you surprised yourself yesterday with how much Beethoven you could still play from memory. See, I was listening."

"I finished telling that story ten minutes ago, Odette. Since then I've just been watching you sleep. Are you feeling okay?"

Odette sidestepped Clarice's question. "I'm sorry," she said. "Work is really taking it out of me. The children get unrulier every year. And the parents, well, they're just impossible. It seems like all the kids are on some sort of restricted diet that their parents have to come in and explain to me. And you'd better believe they make sure I know they'll sue me and the school district, too, if their little darlings ever get near a peanut or a grain of refined sugar. It's like they were bred in a lab somewhere, all of them allergic to this and intolerant of that. And try keeping those kids from trading candy loaded with chocolate and nuts this close to Halloween. It's enough to drive you crazy."

Barbara Jean said, "The kids haven't changed, Odette, you have. You're getting old."

"Thank you both. It's such a joy to come have Sunday supper and find out I'm a decrepit old woman who snores. Why I continue to hang out with you witches I will never understand."

Clarice laughed and said, "You hang out with us because we're the only ones not too scared of you to tell you that you snore and that you're old. But don't feel bad about it. We're all in the same boat."

At the other end of the table Richmond said, "Now *that* is a nice car."

Everyone turned and saw the car Richmond was

admiring. It was a steel-gray Lexus, polished to perfection, with windows tinted so dark you couldn't see who was behind the wheel.

No one spoke, each person at the table feeling the absence of Lester right then. He would surely have taken over the conversation at that moment. Lester had loved cars. He would have said that the Lexus was okay to look at, but way too small. From the 1970s onward he complained that luxury cars were disappointing now that they'd "taken the size out of 'em." Every year, he took a tape measure with him to the Cadillac dealer and bought the longest one on the lot regardless of color or style.

The Lexus moved forward at no more than three miles per hour. Just a few steps in front of the car, a heavyset young woman in a blue sweatshirt and blue sweatpants that were darkened to black from perspiration jogged in slow motion, struggling to lift her feet from the pavement.

Barbara Jean asked, "Isn't that your cousin's girl?"

Clarice said, "Yes, that's Sharon." The driver's-side window of the Lexus slid down and Veronica stuck her head out of the window. She yelled something at her daughter that the spectators in the restaurant couldn't hear.

"What on earth is Sharon doing?" Odette asked.

"I think she's exercising," Barbara Jean said.

Clarice said, "A big girl like that shouldn't run. It's suicidal."

The car stopped and they watched as Veronica double-parked and got out. She walked up to her daughter, who stood doubled over gasping for air in the street, and wagged a finger at her. Sharon poked out her lower lip and then began to run in place in front of her mother's car. Veronica gave her panting daughter a thumbs-up and headed toward the All-You-Can-Eat.

Odette groaned. "Oh, Lord, not her. Your cousin is the last thing I want to deal with today."

Odette had longed to strangle Veronica since 1965. But she had resisted the impulse, for Clarice's sake. Clarice didn't feel much fondness for Veronica, but they were blood. She was stuck with her, in spite of the fact that her cousin had been a thorn in her rear as far back as Clarice could remember. And now she was worse than ever, the perfect example, Clarice thought, of what happens when a pile of cash gets thrown on top of a raging blaze of ignorance.

Veronica's family had been the last of the Leaning Tree old-timers to sell out to the developers and it paid off big for them. Given half a chance, Veronica would expound for hours about what a visionary her father had been for holding out the way he did. The truth was, Veronica's father hated his wife so much that he preferred to keep the family poor rather than sell the property and see her live comfortably. Like Clarice's mother and many of the devout women of her generation, Clarice's aunt Glory had believed divorcing her husband and taking her rightful half of everything he owned would buy her a trip to hell, so her husband knew he had her stuck. He planned to torture her with his presence for decades. What he didn't plan on was dropping dead of a heart attack in the middle of one of their nightly arguments. Glory skipped her husband's funeral service to meet with a real estate lawyer.

She moved next door to her sister Beatrice in an Arkansas retirement village a week later.

Now Glory, Veronica, and Veronica's family were all living off the big chunk of money that they had received for the property, which Clarice hoped Veronica thanked the Lord for every night since she was married to a man who was borderline retarded and couldn't feed a bowl of goldfish, much less an entire family, on the piddling amount of money he made. Of course, like most of the poor folks from Leaning Tree who had lucked into the first real money of their lives when they sold their land, Veronica's clan of morons were burning through the money as quickly as they could. Clarice had no doubt Veronica would show up on her doorstep pleading for a handout sometime in the near future.

Veronica had a distinctive walk that was characterized by rigidly straight legs and jerky movements. She took fast, short steps – not quite running, not quite walking. Just the sight of her cousin trotting toward the window table that afternoon made Clarice ache to slap Veronica with her open palm. But instead of slapping her, Clarice said, "Veronica, darling, what a lovely surprise." Then the two of them made kissing noises at each other.

Clarice prepared herself to hear Veronica brag about her new car, but Veronica had other fish to fry. Without saying a word of hello to anybody – that was *so* like her – she started talking.

"I figured I'd catch you here. I've got wonderful news. Guess what it is." Clarice was about to say that she couldn't possibly guess what her cousin's news was when Veronica yelled out, "Sharon's getting married!"

Clarice said, "Congratulations. I didn't even know she was seeing anybody."

"It was a whirlwind romance. She met him four weeks back and the two of them hit it off right away. And here's the amazing thing, it was all foretold. I went to see Miss Minnie for a reading last month, and she told me that Sharon would meet a man and fall in love that very week. And wouldn't you know it, she met the man of her dreams at church the next Sunday." She wrinkled up her nose at Clarice and said, "That'll teach you to doubt Miss Minnie's powers. She hit the nail right on the head with this one. He was just who she described to me, tall, handsome, well-dressed. I took one look at him and told Sharon, 'Go introduce yourself. That man is your future husband.' A few dates later, she was asked to become Mrs Abrams."

Veronica had been a true believer in Minnie's abilities since she'd gone to see her for the first of many readings a few years earlier. Clarice was convinced her cousin went to see Minnie that first time for the specific purpose of getting under Clarice's skin, since Veronica knew full well how Clarice felt about the fortune-teller. At that reading, Minnie predicted that Veronica's husband, Clement, would have an accident of some sort. As it happened, Clement ended up in the hospital that same day after injuring himself at work. That was all the proof Veronica needed. Now she took everything Minnie said as the complete gospel truth. Clarice had reminded her, as nicely as she could, that predicting an accident for Clement wasn't such an impressive feat. He worked construction and, being a blithering idiot, he sliced, punctured, or burned himself on a weekly basis. It was the inevitable result of putting that fool in the same room with band saws, nail guns, and blowtorches. You didn't have to have second sight to see it coming. But Veronica was convinced that fate, having already showered her with much-deserved cash, had now provided her with her own oracle to go along with her imagined social prominence, and she wasn't hearing anything to the contrary.

Richmond said, "Sharon's marrying Ramsey Abrams's boy?" When Veronica nodded yes, Richmond looked right and left to see if anyone was within earshot and then whispered, "I don't want to talk bad about the boy, but does Sharon know about the stuff with him and the ladies' shoes?"

"Not *that* Abrams boy," she snapped. "Sharon's marrying the other brother." Clifton, the Abrams boy now engaged to Sharon, had spent his teenage years getting stoned and committing petty theft. As an adult, he had spent more time in jail than out. It seemed likely to Clarice that, if the Abrams boy had proposed to Sharon, it was because he was trying to get his hands on her mother's money before it ran out.

When no one said anything, Veronica seemed to guess what was on all of their minds. She added, "Clifton's changed. Been saved by the Lord and the love of a good woman."

Veronica looked over at Minnie's fortune-telling table. "I was hoping to catch Miss Minnie between appointments to get a quick reading. I want to find out what her spirit guide says before I pick the wedding date. I told Sharon I'd take care of all the plans so she can concentrate on losing weight. I want her to look just like her sisters did at their weddings."

Clarice said, "That's so sweet of you," but she thought something else. She thought of how Sharon's older sisters were two of the ugliest women she had ever seen, having inherited their mother's heavy brow and too-close eyes and their father's huge ears and sunken chin. Thin as the older girls were, Veronica would be doing her youngest no favor by making her look like her sisters.

The door opened again and Minnie McIntyre, draped in a black cape with dozens of silver eyes pasted all over it, swaggered into the All-You-Can-Eat. Since her husband's funeral she had taken advantage of Little Earl's soft heart and guilted him into allowing her to do Sunday readings. Of course, he was also less concerned about offending his more conservative customers than he had been before, now that his All-You-Can-Eat merchandise was such a big hit with the college crowd.

Veronica said, "I'm glad you're here, Miss Minnie. I was hoping you had a few minutes free today."

Minnie didn't answer Veronica. She turned to the occupants of the table and said, "I suppose y'all have heard about my latest prediction coming true. Charlemagne has opened the gates to the world of shadows to me now that he knows I'll be coming to join him soon." She crossed her arms over her chest and looked toward heaven the way she always did now when she talked about her approaching death.

Clarice couldn't stop herself from rolling her eyes. Minnie saw her, and she looked for a moment as if she might punch Clarice. But just then, a woman waved at her and called her name from the client chair at Minnie's table.

Minnie said, "Veronica darlin', I've got this one readin' to do and I can help you right after."

She took two steps away in the direction of her table, but then turned around, forcing her cape to swirl dramatically around her. She said, "You know, Clarice, I had a vision last night that I was all set to tell you about. I saw Richmond embracing you on a foggy beach, and I was sure that there was a romantic journey in your future. Funny thing is, when the fog cleared up, I saw that the man in my vision was Richmond, but the woman wasn't you. Isn't that strange?"

She stood there grinning, both she and Veronica waiting to see how Clarice would respond. But Clarice didn't tear up or even do Minnie the honor of casting an angry glance at Richmond, who was busy dragging a spoon across his empty plate and pretending not to hear what was being said just a few feet away. So the fortune-teller twisted her mouth in annoyance and marched off across the room toward her client.

Veronica raised her right arm in the air and snapped her fingers several times. When she attracted Erma Mae's attention she mouthed, "Iced tea." As she seated herself in the table's empty chair, she muttered, "And don't take a year to bring it." Then she turned to Clarice and said, "I didn't just come here to see Miss Minnie. I wanted to ask you to help me with the wedding, Clarice. You did such a nice job on your daughter's wedding that I thought of you immediately when Sharon got engaged. The first thing I said to Sharon was 'Let's call Clarice and have her do your wedding the exact same way she did Carolyn's, except without the shoestring budget.'"

Clarice exhaled slowly, smiled, and said, "You're a doll to think of me, Veronica. But I'm sure you and Sharon will be able to plan a beautiful wedding without my help."

Odette, who had been unusually quiet all afternoon, spoke up. She said, "Yes, Veronica, none of us will forget that Easter pageant you organized over at First Baptist. It was spectacular." Barbara Jean put her head down and covered her laughter by pretending she was coughing. And Clarice made a mental note to buy Odette an extra nice Christmas gift for bringing up Veronica's Easter pageant just then.

A couple of years earlier, Veronica had played on the fears of the board at First Baptist that their Easter pageant would be outshined by the white folks at Plainview Lutheran. The Lutherans had recently started adding some real sparkle to their Easter show – live lambs and a candlelight processional. She promised them that, if they handed the event over to her, she would produce an extravaganza that would leave the demoralized Lutherans hanging their heads in shame.

From the moment Veronica's daughters started the show with an interpretive dance, the whole thing was a disaster. Veronica's older girls were no more coordinated than they were pretty. And poor Sharon, who had been known to become out of breath just lifting a two-liter Pepsi bottle to her lips, got heart palpitations and had to sit down and rest in the middle of the routine.

The highlight of Veronica's show, a dramatization of Christ's ascension into heaven, was ruined when the winch used to carry Reverend Biggs up into the rafters got stuck and left him dangling in a harness thirty feet in the air. It took hours for the fire department to get him down. And the worst part was that no one had any doubt the Lutherans would hear all about the whole debacle.

Veronica slid her glass of iced tea, untouched since Erma Mae brought it to her, a few inches further away from her so she could rest her elbow on the table as she presented her back to Odette. To Clarice, she said, "I was thinking you could come with me tomorrow to look at invitations and some swatches for the girls' dresses."

Clarice didn't want to spend an extra minute with Veronica. The holidays weren't that far off and she would be stuck with her at family gatherings soon enough. But she also had an awful feeling that this was a little taste of justice coming her way. She had sought Odette's counsel when helping to put together Carolyn's wedding, and she had initially been sincere in asking for it. Denise's ceremony, which Odette had helped to plan, had been lovely. But once Clarice got going, she hadn't been able to stop herself from taking note of each detail of Denise's wedding and then doing her best to ostentatiously outdo them all. Now Veronica was asking for advice, and Clarice knew without a doubt that her cousin would one-up everything Clarice had done for her Carolyn's nuptials.

Clarice was reminded then of what she found most insufferable about Veronica. Her cousin had an awful way of making her look at her own worst traits just when she didn't want to see them. Whenever Clarice was around Veronica, she had to acknowledge that in Veronica she saw herself. It frightened her a little to think that the primary difference between them was the moderating influence of Odette and Barbara Jean.

Thanks to Odette stepping in again, Clarice didn't have to commit to helping her cousin that afternoon. "Veronica," Odette said, "I think maybe Sharon's ready to get back to her run." They looked outside and saw that Sharon had left the car behind and was moving down the block with renewed determination in her stride.

Veronica said, "You can't keep that girl away from her jogging. I had some trouble persuading her to get with the program at first, but now she's devoted."

Not a second later, Sharon veered off the street and straight into the front door of Donut Heaven bakery.

Veronica grumbled, "That girl," and ran out of the restaurant. She hopped into her new car and drove a third of a block up the street to the donut shop. She dashed inside and came out seconds later, dragging Sharon with her. As her mother wrestled her into the car, Sharon cradled one of Donut Heaven's bright pink boxes against her chest as if it were a newborn baby.

Odette cleaned the last bit of gravy from her plate with a dinner roll and said, "That woman ruins my appetite." Then she gnawed the gristle from the end of a pork chop bone.

They left the All-You-Can-Eat earlier than usual that day, all of them pleading fatigue. For the rest of the evening Clarice thought about Minnie's vision. She wasn't becoming a convert or anything like that. She knew that it took no psychic ability to envision Richmond with another woman. Hell, it didn't even take a good pair of eyes. What she thought about was how peculiar it was that having that nasty woman rub Richmond's behavior in her face in public had hardly had any effect on her. If such an incident had occurred a few months earlier, she'd have taken to her bed for days. But, even as it happened, the only sensation Clarice had been aware of was a fierce desire to be alone with her piano.

Chapter 13

After Lester's business was sold and all of the money issues had been seen to, Barbara Jean decided that she needed some sort of regular activity to give shape to her days. So she found a job. Then she found another. And another. All three were volunteer positions; still, it was the first time she'd had to report to work since she'd polished nails and administered shampoos at a hair salon when she was a teenager. On Mondays and Wednesdays, she delivered flowers to patients at University Hospital. Out of respect for her recent loss, the volunteer coordinator assigned her to the maternity ward, where she mostly encountered happy new parents and avoided the terminally ill. It wouldn't have mattered, though. They could have thrown death in her face all day and Barbara Jean wouldn't have blinked. With the help of an occasional sip from the thermos of spiked tea she always kept with her – it wasn't practical to bring her demitasse cups from home – she had turned off the part of her that grieved. And she wasn't about to turn it back on.

Every Friday morning, Barbara Jean went to First Baptist and did office work. She answered the phone, filed and made copies, all the things she had once done for Lester when his business first took off. After the office closed, she went downstairs to the church school and led Bible study class for new members. Even her pastor, Reverend Biggs, was impressed with Barbara Jean's biblical knowledge. Finally, she thought, all of those drunken nights in her library with Clarice's gift Bible were of some use to her.

On Tuesdays, Thursdays, and Saturdays, she worked at the Plainview Historical Society Museum. The museum, which consisted of a greeting area and three small rooms, each dedicated to a period of Plainview history – Indian Territory, Civil War, and Modern – was a twenty-minute walk up Plainview Avenue from her house. Her primary responsibilities were to sit at a desk in the greeting area, hand out brochures, and say, "Please wait beneath the Indiana state flag generously donated to the museum by the descendants of famed Hoosier president Benjamin Harrison. A tour guide will be with you momentarily."

Sometimes she was called upon to don a frontier wife costume and pretend to churn butter or stir imaginary food in a plastic pot over a papier-mâché fire, if the usual frontier wife volunteer couldn't make it. When no guests were at the museum, which was most of the time, she sat, sipped from her thermos, and read fashion magazines.

There were many days when her two sentences guiding the museum guests to their waiting place beneath the flag were the only words to cross her lips from sunrise to sunset. Those days were her favorites. She saw the other Supremes two or three times a week, and that was all the conversation she felt she could handle.

Walking back to her house from the museum, she followed Plainview Avenue as it rose toward the center of town and the intersection of Plainview and Main, where her house stood. If she turned her head to the left and peered downhill, she had a perfect view of the remnants of Ballard's Wall and the entrance to Leaning Tree Estates, as the housing development that now occupied her old neighborhood was called.

One early November day as she left the museum for home, she looked down at Leaning Tree. The tall, contorted trees of her old stomping grounds lent even more drama to the landscape now that they'd shed their leaves. She stared at their hunched-over skeletons. They were more impressive to her now than ever. Those trees had all adapted and thrived in the face of the grave insult that had been done to them. If she'd been inclined to ask God for anything, it would have been to make her more like the leaning trees.

She had done her best to adapt. In the three months since Lester's death, she had organized her time so that she was on the move nearly all day, every day. And wasn't that what everyone said widows should do?

But now, studying those crooked, old trees, Barbara Jean had to admit to herself that she had failed to thrive. No matter how activity-filled her days were, it was her nights that owned her. That night, she entered her fine home and heard the voice of her mother whispering bad advice and viperous recriminations in her ear. And after managing to fall asleep in her bed, she was wide awake within an hour, believing that she had felt Lester shift positions in the bed and then heard his congested cough coming from the bathroom. *Was it pneumonia again?*

She got out of bed and wandered the three floors of her

house, hoping that she might find it calming. But it didn't work; it never did. Adam filled the space every bit as much now as he had when he was alive. She heard his footsteps running from room to room on the third floor, where Lester's home office had been before the stairs became too much for him. Adam played up there that night just as he had thirty years earlier. The dark, cluttered storage rooms and mazes of filing cabinets held no menace for an adventurous boy who was never frightened, even when he should have been. The sound of Adam humming to himself in the TV room off of the kitchen as he polished that collection of shoes he was so fond of echoed through the first floor. She caught sight of him at the piano in the sitting room, waiting for his aunt Clarice to come by to give him his lesson. The museum that his bedroom had become seemed to have taken over the second floor. All of the other bedrooms were merely anterooms ushering her into the one room on the floor that mattered.

Only the library, with its waiting bottle and book, was a sanctuary from the spirits that haunted her. And that room offered no refuge after she collapsed into a drunken, exhausted sleep in her Chippendale chair. As soon as she nodded off, they returned. Loretta, Lester, Adam, and now Chick.

By the start of her senior year of high school, Barbara Jean was spending most of her time with Clarice and Odette. She hung out at one of their houses every day after school, doing homework, listening to records, and gossiping until at least eight. That way, when she got home she could tiptoe past Vondell, who was pretty much guaranteed to be passed out on the couch by then. On weekends, when it was harder to avoid Vondell, she worked at a hair salon that one of her mother's old friends owned, and slept at Odette's.

Barbara Jean never stayed over at Clarice's house. Mrs Jordan always went out of her way to be polite and kind to Barbara Jean, but she couldn't go so far as to allow the daughter of Loretta Perdue to spend an entire night in her home. Barbara Jean was initially surprised that Clarice's mother even allowed her to enter her front door, as Mrs Jordan was widely thought to be equal parts sanctimonious and stuck up. But she welcomed Barbara Jean's visits. When Barbara Jean better understood the workings of Mr and Mrs Jordan's marriage, she felt comfortable in assuming that Mrs Jordan's friendliness was the result of her relief at seeing that at least one of the town's bastards looked nothing like her husband.

It was a Saturday night. The three girls were at Clarice's house listening to records when the phone rang. Mrs Jordan called up the stairs for Clarice, saying that her cousin Veronica was on the line. Odette and Barbara Jean followed Clarice down to the kitchen where the phone was and watched as she listened. She hardly spoke at all, just shook her head and gasped, "No," and "You're kidding." When she hung up the phone, she turned to Odette and Barbara Jean and said, "Veronica says there's a white boy working at the All-You-Can-Eat."

Back then, no white people ever wandered into the All-You-Can-Eat. And it was unheard of for a white person, even a teenager, to work for a black man. So this was major news indeed. Five minutes after Clarice hung up the phone, the Supremes were on their way to Earl's.

When they arrived at the restaurant, they found the largest Saturday night crowd they had ever seen. Every table was full, except for the window table that, on weekends, was now permanently reserved for them. They had to squeeze through the crowd to get to their station. What with Clarice's music prizes, Richmond being the local football hero, and Barbara Jean looking the way she did, the window table was normally the center of attention at Earl's. But that night nobody glanced their way. Everyone was there to see the white boy.

When he stepped out of the kitchen with Big Earl, the crowd grew quiet. All that could be heard was an occasional whisper and the voice of Diana Ross cooing "Reflections" on the jukebox.

The white boy did not disappoint. He was tall and thin with wide shoulders and narrow hips. His skin was so pale that he looked as if he hadn't been in the sun in years. His hair was Shinola black and somewhere between wavy and curly. His pronounced cheekbones and high-bridged nose reminded Barbara Jean of the faces of statues she had seen in school art books. His round eyes were an icy blue. Later, Barbara Jean would remember looking at those eyes and thinking, *This must be what the sky looks like if you see it through a diamond.* He followed Big Earl from table to table, taking drink orders, clearing dishes, and wiping up spills. All the while, no one in the entire restaurant made a sound. They just watched him.

It was Odette, never embarrassed to say what she thought, who broke the silence. "That," she said, "is one pretty white boy." Several people heard her and began to snicker. Then conversations started again and the atmosphere returned to something closer to normal.

Clarice said, "I have to disagree with you, Odette. What we have here is the King of the Pretty White Boys." Barbara Jean giggled, but she thought that maybe it was true. It made perfect sense to her that, if she stared at him for long enough, a jeweled crown would appear on top of his head, maybe with an accompanying trumpet salute, like in the Imperial Margarine commercial on TV.

When Big Earl came to the window table accompanied by the King of the Pretty White Boys, he said, "Hey girls, let me introduce you to Ray Carlson. He's gonna be workin' here."

The boy mumbled, "Hi," and gave the table a wipe, even though it was clean.

The Supremes were saying hi to him when Ramsey Abrams, who had overheard Big Earl's introduction, hollered out from a couple of tables away, "You related to Desmond Carlson?" And the place went quiet again.

Desmond Carlson and a few other rednecks were the reason blacks couldn't walk along Wall Road any further north than Leaning Tree. Desmond and his crew drove their pickup trucks over the northern end of Wall Road on their way from their houses to downtown and to the backcountry bars that dotted the landscape outside of Plainview's town limits. Poor, uneducated, and faced with a world that was changing in ways they couldn't understand, Desmond and his buddies were perpetually one or two whiskey shots away from stupidity and violence. It was their habit to hurl insults and beer bottles from their cars at anyone with dark skin they found on the section of the road they had laid claim to.

His friends were content to cause trouble at night. But if Desmond encountered a Leaning Tree resident on Wall Road at any time of the day, he would yell out, "Get off my fuckin' road, jig," or some other comment that made his viewpoint clear. Then, laughing, he would aim his truck at whomever he had caught trespassing on his road so that they had to jump into the ditch at the side of the road to avoid being sideswiped.

Half of the town was scared to death of Desmond, who was always drunk, always angry, and – rumor had it – always armed. The Plainview police were in the scared half. They used the fact that Wall Road was university property and therefore technically under the jurisdiction of the Indiana State Police as an excuse to avoid having to confront Desmond and his buddies, who all had much bigger guns and were much tougher than the police. The university cops were only equipped to deal with drunken frat boys and they weren't about to get in the middle of a local squabble that might ignite a civil rights battle. So the residents of Leaning Tree walked a half mile out of their way, around the southern end of Wall Road and onto side streets that led to Plainview Avenue, whenever they left home for downtown.

Ramsey Abrams asked again, "So, what is it? You related to him, or not?"

Ray Carlson said, "He's my brother," and a wave of cursing and grumbling moved through the room.

Ramsey said, "Damn, Big Earl, what'd you go and let him in here for?"

Big Earl turned a hard eye on Ramsey and said, "Ramsey, both your brothers is in jail and you don't see me checkin' your pockets for silverware every time you leave here, do ya? I figure Ray here deserves the same chance."

That was that. Big Earl had told everyone how it was going to go down, and there was to be no arguing. Ramsey made a loud snorting noise to show his disapproval and went back to his food. Everyone else returned to eating, dancing, and flirting, the business of being teenagers.

Every so often someone came to the window table to whisper about the white boy. Little Earl told the girls that Ray had come by the restaurant trying to sell chickens he had raised. He said his father gave Ray a meal and then offered him a job on the spot, without the boy even asking. Ramsey came over to repeat his belief that it was a shame Big Earl had given a job to a white man that a black man should have had. Veronica came by and said that the girls at her table agreed he was cute, but thought he had no ass. Odette replied, "Who cares what he looks like walking away when he looks that good coming at you." And the night went on that way.

Later in the evening, Barbara Jean watched Ray Carlson as he cleared the table next to hers. As he worked, small white feathers began to fly through the air around him. Every time he moved his arm, another feather flew. She wasn't sure what was going on at first, but finally she saw that the feathers were coming from him. Hundreds of tiny white chicken feathers were stuck to his shirt and pants. Did he sleep with those chickens he raised?

Ray shed so much as he wiped the table that Richmond

Baker made his entrance through a cloud of white. Richmond reached out with one of his big hands and snatched a floating feather out of the air, then another. In addition to being a college football star, Richmond was a twenty-four-hour smartass. He took a look at the molting boy and cracked, "Hey, Big Earl, I see you went and hired yourself a chicken." From that day forward, Ray was Chick.

All evening long, Barbara Jean watched Chick work. He was a sight to see. He moved quickly and gracefully, gliding between the tables and maneuvering around the whirling couples as they spun in front of the jukebox in the corner where Big Earl had rearranged the tables to make room for dancing.

The only time Chick and Barbara Jean acknowledged each other directly after their introduction at the table came just before the girls went home that night. Clarice wanted to have one more dance with Richmond before leaving, so Barbara Jean was sent up to the jukebox to choose a song. She had just picked a tune and turned around to go back to her table when she found herself staring right into Chick's face.

Both of his arms were loaded with dirty dishes as he headed toward the kitchen door just a few feet away. The strain of lifting the plates made the muscles of his skinny arms stand out. Barbara Jean noticed for the first time that he had a dimple in his chin. She had to clasp her hands behind her back to keep from reaching out and pressing that delicate indentation with her forefinger.

Neither of them said anything for a few seconds. Then he said, "Hi," and smiled at her. She said hi back and took in that face of his again.

That was the end of their conversation. Just then, a dancer bumped him from behind and the stacks of dirty plates, silverware, and cups that he had balanced on his arms tilted forward and headed straight for the floor. Barbara Jean had to jump back to keep from being hit by the bits of food and shards of broken ceramics that went flying. The noise was tremendous, and when they saw what had happened, several boys cackled and pointed as if it were the funniest thing they had ever seen.

Big Earl came rushing over then. And that was when Barbara Jean saw something. It was just the briefest exchange, but it taught her lessons about both Big Earl and Chick, the first men she would love. Chick was already on his knees piling up the plates and garbage when Big Earl got to him, all six and a half feet of him still moving fast. Chick's reaction was to bring his forearm up defensively over his face and say, "I'm sorry. I'm sorry."

Barbara Jean recognized that posture and that reflexive apology and the feeling of waiting to be hit that went along with it. She understood then at least one part of Chick's story.

Big Earl knelt down beside him and used his great paw of a hand to pull Chick's arm away from his face. He wrapped an arm around the King of the Pretty White Boys and gave him a quick squeeze. Though the music was loud, Barbara Jean heard him clearly say, "It's all right. You're all right here. Ain't nobody here gonna hurt you." Then he helped Chick pick up the dishes.

The entire scene took less time to play out than it took Aretha to spell out "R-E-S-P-E-C-T" and Barbara Jean stood a few feet away watching it all. As Big Earl and Chick cleaned up the mess and then headed into the kitchen together, Barbara Jean thought for the first time in her life that she had truly been cheated by not having had a father.

More than three decades later, after she saw Chick standing on the porch at Big Earl's funeral dinner and after Lester was dead and gone, Barbara Jean had every evening to sit alone and think. She used many of those hours to return to the night she first saw Chick at the All-You-Can-Eat. She played it over countless times in her head in a way she hadn't done in ages. Every time she thought about it, she asked herself whether things might have turned out differently if she hadn't gone to the jukebox that night, or if she had just walked away when those plates hit the floor instead of standing there and learning just enough of Ray Carlson's story to set in motion the schoolgirl process that transformed pity into love. She asked herself if maybe there was some way she could have seen what was coming and avoided it. After each round of those thoughts, she would end up in her chair in the library curled up with her vodka bottle, wondering if she would ever be able to stop rolling that same old stone up the hill and just accept that what had happened was her fate. She had inherited her mother's luck.

Chapter 14

I got a second opinion about my condition on the Friday after Halloween. Again, Mama, Mrs Roosevelt, and I had to sit through a speech about non-Hodgkin's lymphoma. This time nobody cried, though.

Mama said I should talk to James as soon as I got back home, but I ignored her advice. I still wanted to hold on to the fantasy that maybe I could get through my treatment and never have to tell him. Hadn't Alex Soo said that some rare patients got through chemo like they were taking an aspirin? Well, maybe he hadn't said exactly that, but I decided to believe he had. I made up my mind to put my trust in the part of James's nature that never noticed when I got new clothes or when I gained pounds or lost them. Okay, so far only *gained* pounds, but the opposite was likely to be true, too. I decided to count on the same cluelessness that used to make me want to shake James by the throat to be my friend now.

I slept late that next morning. Life being funny the way it is, the hot flashes that had been keeping me awake at night for months stopped the day after Alex Soo told me I might be dying. When I walked into the kitchen, the first surprise was the smell of coffee. I had learned decades ago that James didn't understand the science of coffee making.

Whenever he brewed up a batch, he ended up with sludge or piss water, nothing in between. So he was forbidden to touch the coffee machine.

But that morning a glass carafe full of coffee rested on a cork trivet in the center of the kitchen table. My mug, a brown and white mess of clay coils fashioned by the tiny fingers of the grandkids and presented to me the previous Christmas, was there on the table, too. And at his usual spot at the table, behind a coffee mug that matched mine, sat James, who was supposed to be working that day.

He sat at attention with his back completely straight and his hands clasped together in front of him atop a wicker placemat. He stared at me for a moment and then said, "What's wrong?"

I started to say, "Nothing," but he held up a hand to stop me. He asked again, slower this time, "Odette, what's wrong?"

I never lie to James – well, not often, at least. I poured a cup of pale brown coffee for myself and I sat down next to him. I exhaled and began, "You know those hot spells I was having? Turns out it was more than the change."

Then I told him everything that both of the doctors had told me. James listened to me without saying a word. The only time he interrupted me was when he scooted his chair back from the table and patted his thighs with his palms, a gesture that had been a signal for me to climb into his lap in the early days of our marriage.

I laughed. "It's been a long time since I sat in your lap, honey." Running my hand over my round stomach, I said, "This might be the end of that chair."

But James didn't laugh at my little joke. He patted his

thighs again and I went over to him and sat. As I talked, he squeezed me tighter and tighter against his body. By the time I reached the end, explaining what I knew of my treatment, our faces were pressed together and I could feel tears rolling down my cheeks.

I cried for the first time since hearing Dr Soo tell me I had cancer. I wasn't crying for the life I might be leaving. Months of talking to Mama had taught me that death didn't have to mean leaving at all. I cried for James, whose heart I might break, for my beautiful, scarred husband who continued to hold me even though his legs must surely have already gone numb under my weight. My tears fell for this strong man who surprised me by managing not to weep, even though I knew from our decades together that he must be screaming inside. I cried for James, who never expected, or needed, me to be that fearless girl from the tree, just me.

He wiped my face with a paper napkin and asked, "So, when do we start treatment?"

"Tuesday," I said. I had made plans to start on Tuesday because that was usually James's late day at work. I wanted as much time as possible to get myself together afterwards, in case my first day was rough.

He caught on immediately that I had planned to use his work schedule as a way to maneuver around him. He said, "Decided to do it on my late day, huh? Sneaky. And a little cowardly, I've got to say." But he didn't look too angry. And he didn't let go of me.

He asked, "What time do we go to the hospital?"

"James, you don't have to come. There's a service at University Hospital that'll drive me home if I don't feel good."

He acted like he hadn't heard me. "What time on Tuesday?"

I told him, and it was settled. He would take Tuesday off from work and go with me to the hospital for my first treatment.

James said, "If you don't tell Clarice and Barbara Jean soon, you won't have to worry about any cancer. They'll kill you themselves when they find out. You wanna call 'em now, or do you wanna call the kids and Rudy first?"

I said. "I've got a better idea. When do you have to go in to work?"

"I told 'em I'd be in around noon, but I'll call in and stay here with you."

"No, I won't need you for the whole day, the morning'll do." Then I began to unbutton his shirt.

James might sometimes be slow on the uptake, but he read my intentions right away. "Really?" he said.

"Sure. Who knows how I'm going to feel after Tuesday. We'd better get it while the gettin' is good." I kissed James hard on his mouth. Then I slipped off of his lap and reached out for his hand to pull him up from his chair.

As we walked to our bedroom, our hands clasped together so tight that it hurt, I thought, *How on earth could I ever have underestimated this man?*

After I told Clarice about my chemotherapy routine – each cycle would be five days long, followed by a few weeks of rest before the next cycle started – she drew up a chemo calendar that designated who – James, Barbara Jean, or Clarice – would be in charge of me on each treatment day. She did several hours of research to determine the best foods for fighting cancer and designed a diet for me. Then she arranged for weekly deliveries of vitamin- and antioxidant-rich groceries to my house. She hired a personal trainer for me. A thick-necked former marine sergeant who worked on injured football players at the university, he showed up at my door one afternoon barking out orders and vowing to whip me into shape. And she penciled me in for a laying on of hands at Calvary Baptist's Wednesday night prayer meeting, which was no small feat seeing as Reverend Peterson didn't even consider the members of my church to be Christians, and felt that praying over us was a waste of energy.

I appreciated her efforts. But I had to show Clarice that she wasn't going to boss me through cancer the way she wanted to, even if I had to be a bit childish and ornery about it. I shifted my appointments around until Clarice's detailed schedule became meaningless. I blanketed the healthy foods Clarice chose for me with butter and bacon crumbles. And the personal trainer, well, he yelled at me one time too many. The last I saw of Sergeant Pete, he was running from my family room with tears in his eyes. Of course, I outright refused to go to Calvary Baptist for the laying on of hands. I tried explaining to Clarice that I always felt worse leaving her church than I did when I walked in and I didn't think that boded well for the healing process. Thoroughly exasperated, Clarice looked at me like I was crazy and said, "Feeling bad about yourself is the entire point of going to church, Odette. Don't you know that?"

I stopped by Barbara Jean's house and told her about my diagnosis over a cup of tea in her library. She was silent for so long that I asked, "Are you all right?"

She started to say "How long have you got?" or "How long do they give you?" But she thought better of it after the first two words came out and she turned it into "How long . . . have you known?"

We talked for an hour, and I think, by the time I left, she had come around to believing I had at least a small chance of surviving.

My brother, Rudy, said that he would come to take care of me as soon as he could get away. I told him it wasn't necessary, that I was fine and had plenty of people looking after me. And I joked with him, as I did each year, that Southern California had thinned his blood too much for him to handle Indiana in the fall or winter. But my brother, who is old-fashioned to the point of annoyance, kept insisting that he would come. He only relented after I handed the phone over to James and let my husband convince Rudy that a levelheaded man was in charge of me.

Denise cried for just a minute or two, but she soon calmed herself and accepted my word that things weren't too bad. Then she took my cue and settled in to talking about the grandchildren. I heard Jimmy's fingers tapping at the keyboard of his computer as I told him. Facts had always comforted him, and he was on his way to becoming a lymphoma expert by the time we said goodbye. Eric hardly said a word to me over the phone, but he was in Plainview for a surprise visit a few days later. Eric was at my side every second for a week and, even as I snapped at him to quit breathing down my neck, I loved having him at home again.

Everything considered, they all took the news of my

illness as well as possible. Even as I grew sicker, proving to everyone, and ultimately to myself, that I wasn't going to be that rare patient who sailed through chemotherapy without so much as a tummy ache, my people propped me up. I think it made everybody feel more optimistic about my chances for recovery to see that I was determined to charge through my disease just like I charged through everything else in life. My friends and family found few things more comforting than the sight of me with my fists up and ready for battle.

Chapter 15

A month before Little Earl's eighteenth birthday, a cute girl at school told him that he looked like Martin Luther King. Then she let him put his hand under her blouse in the name of Negro solidarity. That led Little Earl to celebrate his birthday that November with a costume party so he could dress up as Dr King in hopes of encountering more young women who were passionately devoted to the civil rights movement.

Clarice, Odette, and Barbara Jean made plans to dress up as the Supremes since their friends, families, and even some of the teachers at school were now calling them by that name. They spent weeks working on their costumes. Odette did most of the sewing, stitching together glossy, gold, sleeveless gowns. They used hot glue to attach glitter to old shoes. And Barbara Jean's boss at the salon loaned them three acrylic wigs with identical bouffants for the occasion.

On the night of the party, the plan was that they would each get dressed at home. Clarice had been given a used Buick after a third piano lesson with Mrs Olavsky was added to her weekly schedule and her mother decided that she'd had enough of chauffeur duty, so Clarice was to pick up the other girls at their houses for the ride to the All-You-Can-Eat. Clarice parked in front of Barbara Jean's house and she and Odette went to the door to fetch her and some accessories for their costumes. Barbara Jean had offered to dip into her inheritance of fake furs and oversized plastic jewelry to help them complete their ensembles.

They were standing on the porch when Clarice saw an odd expression come over Odette's face. She didn't know what Odette was reacting to. Maybe it was a sound or a smell. But Clarice had just raised her hand to knock on the door when Odette said, "Something's wrong."

Before Clarice could say anything, Odette pushed right past her and turned the knob. The door opened and she rushed inside. Not taking the time to think about the possible consequences, Clarice followed her, both of them moving in a kind of a shimmying shuffle because of the restrictions of their outfits.

Barbara Jean, wearing her shiny gold gown, sat in a threadbare maroon overstuffed chair in a corner of the living room. Her bare feet were tucked beneath her and she clutched her wig in both hands, pressing it to her chest. The fake furs and costume jewelry she and her friends were going to wear that evening rested in a pile on the floor in front of the chair. She didn't look up as Odette and Clarice came into the room.

Vondell, her stepfather or whatever he was, stood beside Barbara Jean's chair. He had disappeared a month earlier, making Barbara Jean's life easier and giving her the hope that she might not have to deal with him anymore. Between free meals at Odette's and Clarice's houses, the tips she made at the salon, and the low rent on the dump she lived in, Barbara Jean had been able to afford a teenager's dream. She had a house of her own and complete independence.

But now Vondell was back and he looked even worse than he had the last time they had seen him. His stubbly graying beard had grown thicker, and his processed hair had grown out so it was nappy at the roots and matted at the ends. And then there was that odor of his that permeated the room, that sharp blend of cigarettes, whiskey, and poor personal hygiene.

He glared at Odette and Clarice for a minute. Then he said, "Barbara Jean, you didn't tell me we was gonna have company this evenin'." That wide, froglike mouth of his broadened into a grin as he talked, but no one in the room sensed a bit of goodwill in him.

Odette said, "Hello, sir, we're going to a birthday party tonight and we just came to get Barbara Jean." She looked at Barbara Jean in the chair and said, "Come on, Barbara Jean. We don't wanna be late."

But Barbara Jean didn't move. She just glanced up at Vondell and then stared at her knees again. The big man had lost his smile now. He glared at her, daring her to rise from the chair.

Clarice joined in and said, "Yeah, we have to finish up our hair and nails at my house and . . ." She lost her nerve and didn't finish. No one was listening to her anyway. The battle was on, and it was being fought between the other three people in the room.

There was a long silence during which Clarice heard only the big man's breathing and the sound of the plastic carpet runner crunching beneath her feet as she inched backwards toward the front door. Then Vondell said, "I think y'all best get movin'. Barbara Jean ain't goin' out tonight."

The tone of his voice scared Clarice half to death and she ran to the door. But Odette stayed put. Odette looked back and forth from Barbara Jean, still cowering in the shabby chair like a scared two-year-old, to the hulking man who had moved closer to Barbara Jean and was now stroking her hair in an imitation of fatherly affection that caused acid to rise in Clarice's stomach.

Odette said, "I haven't heard what Barbara Jean wants us to do. If she wants us to go, she can say it herself."

Vondell took a step toward Odette and put his hands on his hips to puff himself up. He was careful to keep a smile on his face so she would know he wasn't taking her seriously. "Li'l girl, I told you to leave *my* house. And, believe me, you don't want me to have to say it again. Now, get a move on before I put you over my knee and teach you some manners."

Vondell had Clarice scared, but the look Odette gave him now frightened her almost as much. Odette's eyes narrowed and her mouth twisted. She lowered her head as if she were preparing to ram into him headfirst. Clarice could see that even if Odette didn't scare Vondell, she definitely surprised him. When he saw the change in her posture, he jerked back away from her a little before he could stop himself.

Odette, talking louder now, said, "Barbara Jean, do you want to stay here or come with us?"

Barbara Jean didn't answer at first. Then, almost too quietly for anyone to hear, she whispered, "I want to go with you."

Odette said, "Well, that settles it. She's coming with us."

Vondell didn't speak to Odette, but turned his attention to Barbara Jean instead. He moved beside her again and grasped her right forearm in his big hand, pulling her half-way out of the chair so awkwardly that she would have fallen to the floor if he had not been supporting her with the strength of his hold. She let out a gasp of pain and Vondell growled, "You best tell these girls to go on home, or you gonna be in some real trouble. I fixed your mama's uppity ways and I can do the same wit' you."

Odette's voice dropped an octave and she very slowly said, "If you don't want that hand broke, you'd better get it off of her right now."

Clarice got swept up in the moment and put in her two cents. "She's coming with us," she said, trying to act like Odette.

But Clarice wasn't born in a tree. When he took a couple of quick steps in her direction, she hopped backwards and let out a squeal. Odette moved, too, but she moved side-ways to stand between Vondell and Clarice.

He said, "What you gonna do, call your daddy? You know, I asked around about your daddy after the last time you was here, and I heard he ain't no cop at all. What I heard was that you was that child born in a tree and you ain't supposed to be 'fraid of nothin'. Maybe it's time somebody gave you somethin' to be scared of." He moved closer to her and pushed out his chin.

Odette stepped away from him then and came over to where Clarice stood with her fist clinched around the handle of the door, ready to escape. Vondell laughed at her and said, "That's a good girl. Run on home." Then to

Clarice he said, "You can come back sometime if you wanna, baby. But leave that crazy fat bitch at home."

A few feet away from Clarice, Odette stopped, yanked the wig from her head, and tossed it to her. Clarice caught it out of reflex and then watched in bewilderment as Odette spun away from her and said, "Clarice, unzip me."

When Clarice didn't say anything or do as Odette had told her, she said it again. "Unzip me. I spent too much time making this dress to get this asshole's blood all over it."

She fixed her eyes on Vondell and said, "You're right about me. I am the girl who was born in a tree. And you're right about my father. He's not a cop. But he was the 1947 welterweight Golden Gloves champion. And from the time I was a little girl my boxer daddy has been teaching me how to deal with dumb-ass men who want me to be afraid. So let me thank you now, while you're still conscious, for giving me the opportunity to demonstrate some of the special shit my daddy taught me to use on occasions like this.

"Now, Clarice, unzip me so I can take care of this big bag of stink and ignorance, once and for all."

With fingers that shook so badly she could hardly grab hold of the zipper, Clarice did as she had been commanded. She pulled the zipper down and Odette's shiny gown slid off of her and formed a shimmering pool at her feet. Wearing just a white bra and floral-patterned panties, Odette lifted her fists and danced her way toward Vondell, already floating like a butterfly and apparently prepared to sting like a bee.

For a moment, Vondell stood gaping at her, eyes wide,

mouth open. Then, to Clarice's amazement, he started to back up. First one step, then another. He tried to act as if he were in charge, calling her a string of filthy names and threatening to hurt her. But Clarice could see from the way his eyes darted left and right searching out an escape route that this short, chubby teenage girl had him unnerved.

Odette kept moving toward him and he kept backing away. He moved across the living room floor, his feet shuffling across the orange carpet. His hands gripped the backs of the heavy, mismatched furniture he was careful to keep between himself and Odette. When he had backed completely out of the room and into the hallway that led to the kitchen, he yelled out, "I ain't got time to be dealin' with this crazy shit. Go on, get out. I don't care where you go. You ain't none of my concern." He moved out of sight then, and a few seconds later they heard the rear door of the house open and slam shut.

Odette maintained her Golden Gloves stance for what seemed like an hour, but was probably less than a minute. When Vondell didn't return, she brought her fists down, shaking out her shoulders as if she'd just gone ten rounds. Then she walked toward Clarice, who was still frozen at the front door. Stepping into the circle of golden fabric she had shed onto the floor earlier, Odette said, "Clarice, could you give me a hand getting back into my dress?"

After Clarice packed Odette into her gown, the two girls went to Barbara Jean, who sat in the maroon chair staring at Odette with awe. Clarice picked up the imitation fur stoles and dime-store jewelry from the floor while Odette helped Barbara Jean up from the chair. Odette said, "Come on, Barbara Jean, we've got us a party to go to."

The three girls squeezed into the front seat of Clarice's car for the drive to Little Earl's party. They were about a third of the way there when Clarice finally found words. She said, "That was incredible, Odette. I had no idea your father taught you how to box."

Odette snorted and said, "Box? Daddy's never weighed more than a hundred ten pounds his entire life. Who the hell was he gonna box? Vondell would've broken my neck if he'd decided to fight me."

During the rest of the ride to the All-You-Can-Eat, Clarice fought to keep her eyes on the road and not stare at her insane friend in disbelief. Barbara Jean gazed out of the car window and periodically gasped, "Holy shit."

They had fun at the party that night. They flirted and lip-synched Supremes songs. They watched Little Earl, in a costume consisting of his best Sunday suit and a Bible, try to use the "I Have a Dream" speech as a pickup line. They admired Chick Carlson.

Girls approached Chick all night. Freed from convention by their costumes, they forgot for that evening that they were on opposite sides of a racial divide and constantly interrupted his busboy duties by asking him to dance. Clarice, Barbara Jean, and Odette got a kick out of watching him hop across the floor in his cowboy costume – his everyday clothes plus a bandana. And they giggled as, regardless of the song, he treated each girl to a two-step – the only dance that country white boys knew back then.

Late in the evening, Odette went missing for a while. She returned to the window table with Big Earl and Miss Thelma, who promptly shooed away all of the kids, except Barbara Jean, Odette, and Clarice. Then, after seating themselves on either side of Barbara Jean, they told her that she would be moving into the room that their daughter, Lydia, had vacated when she left Plainview two years earlier. They didn't ask her opinion or entertain other options. Each of them held one of Barbara Jean's hands and informed her that Lydia's room was hers that night and for as long as she wanted.

Barbara Jean protested just long enough to show that she had good manners. Then she agreed. So that evening, courtesy of Big Earl, Miss Thelma, and Odette, Barbara Jean had a family for the first time in her life. And Clarice came to understand that she had a friend who could perform miracles.

Chapter 16

Between them, Lester and Barbara Jean owned four vehicles when he died. When she learned that Odette was sick, Barbara Jean donated Lester's truck and his year-old car to the American Cancer Society. She thought it might buy her friend some good luck. That left her with her Mercedes and an old Cadillac.

Lester had bought the Cadillac new in 1967, the first in a long string of Caddies he bought over the years. He babied it, keeping it looking as if it had just rolled off the dealer's showroom floor until the day he died. It was the only one of his cars he never sold or gave away when newer models came out. The car hadn't been touched since the last time Lester drove it. It just sat in the garage taking up space and reminding Barbara Jean of the past.

One day when she arrived at the museum to work a volunteer shift in her butter-churning outfit, Barbara Jean discovered that a sign had been posted near Benjamin Harrison's flag. The sign asked for volunteers to contribute something to the annual Christmas auction. She offered the Cadillac.

Judging from the shocked reaction she received when she contacted the committee putting together the auction, a mint condition 1967 Fleetwood was a little more than they had in mind. They had been expecting donations more along the lines of handcrafted needlepoint chair cushions, beeswax candles, or gift baskets full of home-made strawberry preserves in quaintly bonneted jars. But once they understood that Barbara Jean really intended to donate the car itself, not a ride in it or some sort of leasing arrangement, they eagerly accepted her gift. In return, she took them up on their offer to have a room of the museum, the one with the Indian artifacts, renamed the Lester Maxberry Exhibition Hall. They had wanted to name the room after Barbara Jean, but she declined the honor. The Fleetwood had been Lester's baby. And he had been the one with happy memories of it, not her.

Barbara Jean had been living at Big Earl and Miss Thelma's house for about a month when she first saw the car. She was walking home from her job at the salon when she saw a crowd gathered across the street outside the All-You-Can-Eat. Clarice stepped out of the knot of people and called her name.

When she got closer, she saw that the dozen or so people in the street were clustered around the nicest Cadillac she had ever seen. In fact, it was the only brand-new Cadillac Barbara Jean had ever seen outside of TV commercials. It was a beauty, so shiny that it was hard to look directly at it in the afternoon sun. It was sky blue, and the brilliant gloss of the car's paint job reflected the clouds above so perfectly that looking down at the hood almost made you feel dizzy, as if you didn't know which way was up. The back end of the car was long and so sleek that it seemed likely you would cut your finger if you ran it along the sharp fins. Occasionally one of the people circling the car in admiration would lean in to exhale on the bright finish and watch the oval of their condensed breath appear and then evaporate.

Only one person in the crowd dared make any real physical contact with the car. That was the Cadillac's owner, Mr Lester Maxberry.

Barbara Jean knew Lester, of course. He was famous. At one time or another, he had employed half of the boys in her high school in his landscaping business. James Henry worked for him all through high school and his two years of college. James worked for Lester so long that everyone expected him to take over the business one day. They went on expecting it until James surprised them all by becoming a cop.

Lester sometimes came into the All-You-Can-Eat with James and sat with the young people at the window table. He was always nice, courteous, and charming in an avuncular way. He would talk sports with the guys, or dispense advice, or compliment the girls. But he usually didn't stick around for long. He would say, "Let me get going, so you young people can enjoy your evening," and then he'd tip the fedora he always wore and leave while they objected.

Barbara Jean enjoyed Lester's company, but she never thought of him in a romantic way, even though just about every other woman she knew did. He had a small, compact body and a long face with droopy eyes that most of the girls thought were sexy. He also had a slight hesitation in his stride from an injury he had received while he was in the service, but he layered it over with so much cool and self-confidence that it seemed like a stylish accessory. Lester was light-skinned and had curly, but not kinky, hair at a time when there weren't many attributes considered more important than fair skin and good hair.

Lester stood at the prow of his automobile with one foot on the front bumper and his hip leaning onto the driver's-side quarter panel. He wore navy blue pinstriped pants, a dress shirt the same sky blue as his new car, and a black fedora with a blue feather in its band. He must have been cold. It couldn't have been more than forty-five degrees on that December day. But he looked perfectly comfortable posing there, smiling and showing off his car.

When he saw Barbara Jean, Lester stood and said, "Hey, Barbie, what do you think?"

She said, "It's slick, real slick." She immediately regretted that answer. "Slick" sounded so stupid and childish, just the wrong thing to say to a man like Lester Maxberry. She corrected herself. She said, "It's a gorgeous car, truly gorgeous," and felt better.

"Wait till you see this. This is the best part." He walked around to the driver's side of the car and then leaned into the open window. He pressed the horn, and after it sounded he turned around with a big grin on his face. The horn had been modified so that it honked out the first three notes from the chorus of Smokey Robinson's "Ooo Baby, Baby." The crowd gathered around the car went nuts, some of them singing, "Ooo, *Ooo*-ooo."

Barbara Jean was squeezed off to the edges of the crowd by the boys who pushed forward to ask car questions or just to hear the horn again, so she went into the All-You-Can-Eat to say hi to Miss Thelma. By this time on a Saturday she could usually be found in the kitchen of the restaurant starting the baking for Sunday's after-church rush.

Barbara Jean walked through the dining room and headed down the hallway that led to the storeroom and the rear of the kitchen where the baking table and ovens were. Before she got to the kitchen, the door to the storeroom opened and Chick Carlson stepped out. She acknowledged him with a nod and kept walking. But when she came closer to him, she saw that he had a cut on his forehead.

She knew that she shouldn't ask. She knew that it was none of her business. But she asked anyway.

She pointed to the cut just below his hairline. "What happened?"

He said, "My brother, he gets mad and . . ." He stopped himself and looked embarrassed, as if he hadn't intended to say what he had said. He bit his lip and stood there turning redder and redder.

She didn't recognize it at the time, but something started between them at that moment, an irresistible need to say and do things before common sense could intervene and hold them back. That need would stretch out over far too many years. And she would live to regret it.

Barbara Jean slipped off her jacket and rolled up the sleeve of her blouse. She pointed to three small scars on her arm and said, "My mother hit me with a belt buckle."

He said, "I'm sure she didn't mean it."

"Yes, she did. She used to hit me a lot when she was drunk. But you're half right; she didn't mean to give me the scars. She was just so drunk that time that she didn't realize she'd grabbed the wrong end of the belt when she swung it."

He came closer to her then and reached out and touched

her scars with the tip of his finger. "It looks like a face. See?" He ran his finger over the longer arc-shaped scar on the bottom, "That line looks like a mouth and these two smaller ones up here are like eyes."

With that slight touch, suddenly they couldn't stop talking. Words that they had kept bottled up while they stared at each other across the dining room of the All-You-Can-Eat came rushing forward. They didn't flirt or tease each other with coy chitchat the way other teenagers might have done in the same situation. The things they told each other were the things that only they could share.

She said, "My mother drank herself to death."

He said, "My father died in jail. When I was a kid they told me it was a heart attack, but I found out later he got knifed in a fight. My mother ran off about the same time. I barely remember her."

"I never met my father, but there are two guys who think I'm their daughter."

"You can't see it because of my hair, but I've got a five-inch scar on top of my head from getting stitches after my brother hit me with a brick for taking food from his refrigerator."

"When I was fourteen, my mother twisted my arm until she dislocated it because I left the house with no makeup on."

Chick said, "Big Earl lets me stay in the storeroom here because he found out I was living in the shed at my brother's place and sharing it with the chickens."

She held up her hand and said, "Okay, you win." Then they both started laughing.

That was when she did it. She took a step toward him

and kissed him on his mouth. She leaned into him until he fell back against the wall. Then she kept pressing against him, wanting to be as close to him as she could be.

She didn't know why she was kissing him, she just knew that she had to, the same way she had to tell him things she hadn't yet told Odette or Clarice, stuff about her mother and her various fathers. With him, those truths just came tumbling out.

When she started to think about the foolishness of what she was doing and began to pull away, he wrapped his arm around her waist and squeezed her even tighter to him. They stood there in the back hallway of the All-You-Can-Eat kissing each other until they were both dizzy from not breathing. They only stopped when they heard someone calling Barbara Jean's name.

Chick released her waist and Barbara Jean stepped away from him until her back met the opposite wall. They were there, grinning at each other across the hallway, when Clarice ran in and shouted, "Barbara Jean, come on! Lester wants to take us for a ride in his new car. He asked especially about you."

She said, "Hi, Chick," and then pulled Barbara Jean down the hallway, stopping only long enough to give Barbara Jean a chance to pick up the coat she had cast off in order to show her scars. As she grabbed her coat, Barbara Jean glanced back for one more look at Chick's beautiful, smiling face. Then she was off to take her first ride in Lester's blue Fleetwood.

The chairman of the museum's Christmas auction committee was Phyllis Feeney. She was a nervous, pear-shaped woman who used her hands so much when she talked that she looked as if she were speaking sign language. When Phyllis came to get the Cadillac, she brought along her husband, Andy, who was stocky and jumpy like her. Phyllis was even more animated than usual that day, fidgeting and playing with her hair. She relaxed quite a bit when the title to the car was handed over and she was assured that Barbara Jean wasn't going to back out of the deal at the last second.

Barbara Jean escorted them to the garage, where Phyllis handed the keys to Lester's blue Cadillac over to her husband. Then Phyllis climbed back into the Ford they had arrived in and drove off. Andy slid behind the wheel of the Fleetwood and brought the giant engine to life. He rolled down the window and said, "She purrs like a kitten."

He put the car in reverse and drove out of the garage. Just as he got to the end of the driveway, Barbara Jean called out, "Andy, hit the horn!"

"What?" he asked.

"Hit the horn. It's the best part."

He did it, and when he heard the three notes of the horn rise and fall he said, "Oh man, I love this car. I'm gonna have to bid on it myself." He waved at Barbara Jean and turned down Plainview Avenue.

For a good five minutes after he was out of sight, Barbara Jean could still hear Lester's car off in the distance singing, "Ooo, *Ooo*-ooo."

Chapter 17

Odette, Barbara Jean, and Clarice sat talking in the infusion room of the hospital. Clarice, who couldn't resist judging décor wherever she was, approved of the room. It was pretty, if you ignored the medical equipment. The lighting was less harsh than in the rest of the hospital. And the muted pastel flowers on the wallpaper complemented the comfortable cherry wood and brown leather chairs that stood beside the treatment lounges. Unfortunately, there wasn't much that could be done to beautify an IV pole. Looking in any direction reminded you of precisely why you were there.

It was just before Christmas, but the room wasn't decorated. The only signs of the holidays were the red Santa Claus hat worn by the gum-popping duty nurse who kept watch from a desk in the corner and the blinking Christmas tree pin on the collar of Barbara Jean's yellow hospital volunteer smock.

Barbara Jean wore her smock even though she wasn't working that day. There was a limit of one visitor per patient during chemo, so Barbara Jean wore her volunteer outfit to look official enough to get around the rule. Clarice sometimes borrowed the smock from Barbara Jean so she could visit along with James on the days he came with Odette.

To pass the time that morning and to distract Odette during her treatment, Clarice showed the other Supremes the twelve fabric swatches Veronica had dropped off at her house the previous evening. Veronica had begged and flattered Clarice into agreeing to assist her in planning Sharon's wedding, and she had given Clarice a list of tedious chores to perform. In spite of herself and in spite of Veronica, Clarice found that she was pleased to have this wedding-related work to do. She needed as many diversions as possible to keep her from dwelling on Odette's health and Richmond's errant penis. And there were only so many hours a day she could practice the piano before her knuckles complained. Her latest job was to submit her written opinion on each of the fabric swatches Veronica had brought to her. Every single one of the swatches was a subtly different shade of green crushed velvet.

Clarice said, "I'm supposed to help choose the material for the bridesmaids' dresses from these. Can you imagine? Wrapping up Veronica's unfortunate-looking daughters in any of these fabrics is just plain cruel. And green is Veronica's favorite color, by the way, not Sharon's. Sharon wanted peach, but Veronica told her nobody could tell the difference between peach and pink, so it would look like just a run-of-the-mill pink wedding. Veronica decided the wedding would be green and white, and that was that."

Odette and Barbara Jean agreed that slapping green crushed velvet on the homeliest girls in town was an insane notion. Barbara Jean pronounced it "child abuse" and Odette, enjoying her curious-bystander-to-a-highway-pileup role, said, "I can't wait for that wedding." Even the duty nurse, who had been pretending not to listen in, stared at the swatches as Clarice waved them in the air. She stopped chomping her gum long enough to mouth "Pitiful."

Clarice explained that she had to get the fabric judging out of the way quickly in order to concentrate on a more complicated chore. She was supposed to find a flock of white doves to be released as Sharon walked down the aisle.

"Veronica saw it on TV and now she just has to have it. Have you any idea how hard it is to find trained white doves? And of course it's all because I had that bubble machine at Carolyn's wedding. Everything's like that with Veronica. Carolyn had bubbles; Sharon has to have white doves. Carolyn had a broom-jumping; Sharon's going to have laser lights that spell out 'Clifton and Sharon' above their heads during the ceremony and then switch to read 'Hallelujah!' when they're pronounced husband and wife."

Barbara Jean said, "Lasers? Really? You'd think she'd want to steer away from special effects after that Easter pageant went so wrong."

"I guess she feels like she's safe since there are no plans for any of the wedding party to fly through the air. Not yet, at least."

They were laughing so loudly at the memory of poor Reverend Biggs hovering in the rafters of First Baptist that they just barely heard the hiss of the automatic door to the infusion room announcing that someone had entered. Odette looked up and smiled. Barbara Jean and Clarice turned around and saw Chick Carlson.

Chick wore a tan overcoat with a university ID clipped to the collar. He lifted the ID in the direction of the nurse when she approached him to ask who he was there to see, and she nodded at him and let him pass. He walked toward the Supremes until he stood at the foot of Odette's lounge. He said, "Hey, everybody," greeting them as if it were just another day at the All-You-Can-Eat in 1968.

Odette said, "Hey, Chick. I can't get up and hug you, so you'd better come to me." He stepped closer to Odette, leaned down, and kissed her on the cheek. He turned toward Clarice and she reached out and shook his hand. Then, after a pause that was just a little too long to feel comfortable, Barbara Jean said, "Hello, Ray. It's been a long time."

Odette sat up as much as she could on the infusion lounge and took in her old friend, getting her first good look at him in almost thirty years. He reminded her of a seasoned hiker who had just stepped in from a brisk stroll on the mountainside. His cheeks were red and his gray and black waves of hair had either been tousled by the wind or he had spent hours with a stylist that morning to give him the air of a gracefully aging action-movie star. Odette caused his cheeks to redden even more by saying, "All these years and you still look good enough to eat."

She told him to pull up a seat, but he claimed that he was already running late and couldn't stay long. Chick said he had seen James on his way in to work that morning. James had filled him in on Odette's condition and told him where he'd find her.

Odette asked, "So what brings you back to us after all this time?"

"I'm in charge of a research project," he said. "We're working with birds. Raptors, actually – hawks, owls, falcons. They converted the old tower for us." He waved his hand in the direction of the tower even though there was no window in the room and in spite of the fact that the Supremes, like everyone else in town, knew exactly what tower he was talking about.

The tower was all that was left of a tuberculosis sanatorium that had once occupied the land where the hospital now stood. TB patients had been brought there to take the fresh air cure. Five stories tall, it stood atop a rise at the edge of the campus and was visible from nearly any vantage point in town. Now Chick, the boy who had always been covered with feathers, kept birds there.

"You really should see what the university has done with it," he said. "The facility is incredible. Twice as big as the space I had in Oregon."

"Oregon?" Odette said. "I thought you went off to school in Florida."

"I did, but I only lasted a few months there. Too hot for me. After a year, I transferred to a graduate program in Oregon. The college offered me a teaching job after I finished and I ended up staying till I came back here."

Odette, who was never shy about obtaining information, proceeded to grill him. Within a minute or two, she'd found out that Chick had lived in Plainview since the summer, had been married and divorced twice with no children from either marriage, and lived in one of the new houses in Leaning Tree.

Chick felt himself beginning to sweat. Since the day he accepted the job that meant returning to his hometown, he had thought about what he would say when he crossed paths with the Supremes. He prepared a short speech, a few sentences about his life in the Northwest followed by a brief description of the work that had brought him back to Plainview. But he had envisioned reciting his carefully practiced patter to the Supremes in a safe environment like a grocery store loaded with distracted, chatting customers or a busy street corner. Now, because of a chance meeting with his old buddy James that morning, he found himself fumbling through a scattered version of his little speech in a hospital room whose walls seemed to be inching toward him more quickly with each passing second. He had been thrown hopelessly off balance by Odette's questions, this place, and the presence of Barbara Jean, still painfully beautiful after what seemed like a million years and like no time at all.

Chick veered away from his prepared remarks, speaking faster and faster. He described, floor by floor, the state-of-the-art veterinary facility that was housed in the tower. He told them about the two graduate-level courses he taught at the university and how the brightest of his students now formed the eager young staff that assisted him in his work with the raptor project. He detailed the plans for releasing the first breeding pair of rehabbed falcons sometime that coming summer. After he had listed the names of each of the eight birds in the project and related the story of how each name was chosen, he realized that he had been talking for ten minutes straight and he stopped himself. He said, "I'm sorry. You get me started talking about my project and I don't shut up."

Odette said, "No need to apologize, it's nice to hear that you like your work." Then she laughed. "But tell me, Chick, what is it with you and birds?"

He grinned, then stuffed his hands inside the pockets of his coat and shrugged his shoulders. For a moment, he was once more the shy, pretty boy they had met almost forty years earlier.

No one said anything for a few seconds. Barbara Jean, Odette, and Clarice did some throat-clearing and fidgeting. Chick stood staring down at the floor, making it apparent that he had prepared only a few lines of dialogue for this meeting and, having exhausted them and followed them up with some nervous rambling, had no more conversation left in him.

Barbara Jean filled the silence with something that surprised them all. She said, "I saw you after Big Earl's funeral."

Startled by her own words, Barbara Jean let out a little gasp and her eyes grew large. She looked back and forth from Odette to Clarice several times in quick succession. Clarice thought for a moment Barbara Jean might ask which one of them had spoken. Of course, it would never have crossed either of her friends' lips. Clarice and Odette had carefully avoided discussing the day of Big Earl's funeral – the day of Lester's death – for months. And they had never once told Barbara Jean that they had seen her staring out of the window at Chick just before Lester decided to perform those ill-fated electrical repairs.

Chick and Barbara Jean locked eyes, but said nothing. Clarice began to prattle on about what a good friend Big Earl had been to all of them. Odette nodded in agreement. Barbara Jean clasped her hands together in her lap to stop them from shaking.

Finally, Chick said, "Well, I'd better get going."

Odette made him promise that he would come by her house for a visit, and polite goodbyes were exchanged. Then Chick took a couple of steps in the direction of the door that led out to the hallway. Before leaving the room, he turned around and added, "It's really nice to see you all looking so lovely."

It seemed to both Clarice and Odette that his last remark was aimed directly at Barbara Jean.

As soon as Chick left the room, Barbara Jean slumped forward in her chair and buried her face in her hands. She took two or three deep breaths and then sat up straight again. She announced, "I'm going to get some coffee. Anybody else want some?" Before either of her friends could answer her, she rose and rushed toward the door. Odette gestured with her head for Clarice to follow, and she did.

Clarice found Barbara Jean standing with her forehead pressed against a window just down the hall, her breath fogging the glass with each exhalation. She walked up to Barbara Jean and stood beside her.

Clarice asked, "Are you all right?"

Barbara Jean replied, "He looked good, didn't he?"

"Yes, he did look good. Grew up to be a handsome man."

"No, I mean he looked like his life was okay. He didn't look like his life was sad or ruined or anything."

Clarice said that yes, Chick looked as if his life had been fine, not knowing where Barbara Jean was going with all this.

Barbara Jean said, "Yes, he's done all right. He's done real well. Works for the university now. Teaches. Likes his work. Ray's all right." It sounded to Clarice as if Barbara Jean were trying to convince herself.

It is truly a wonder, Clarice thought, how that old devil inconvenient love can rear its head and start messing with you when you least expect it. She'd have bet a million dollars Barbara Jean didn't want to feel anything for Chick, the man she'd loved before she was old enough to know any better. But it was written all across her face. Game over, story ended. Barbara Jean was stuck with affection that just wouldn't die, no matter how hard life and time had tried to kill it. Oh sister, Clarice thought, I know just how you feel. Barbara Jean and Clarice stayed there for several minutes gazing out of the window. They had a view of the hospital parking lot and the redbrick tower where Chick was presumably now settling in for a day of tending to his birds. Clarice watched clusters of students walk up the hill toward the main part of the campus, the vapor of their breath rising around them in the cold December air. In the distance, she could see the crosses atop the steeples of First Baptist and Plainview Lutheran. She saw the preening copper rooster on the weather vane that capped the turret at the northeast corner of Barbara Jean's house rising over the tops of trees that had lost all but the most tenacious of their leaves. Further off, she could see the remains of Ballard's Wall and the tidy roofs of the new houses of Leaning Tree.

Plainview was lovely. A sprinkling of snow had fallen and turned the town into a postcard-perfect scene, ready to be photographed for the university's catalog or committed to needlepoint. She was about to say as much to Barbara Jean when something new came into view that caused them both to stiffen.

A white Chrysler, its sunroof open in spite of the chill, pulled into the parking lot and stopped at the doors just below where they stood. A man got out of the car and greeted the young woman who ran out of the building to meet him. He walked around to the passenger side of the Chrysler and opened the door for the woman. She lost her hat – a replica of the wide-brimmed, floppy style popular in the 1970s – to a gust of wind as she bent to climb into the car. The man caught the hat for her, gracefully snatching it from midair. He glanced left and right, like a criminal checking for witnesses. Then he playfully swatted the woman on her behind with the hat. She took her hat from him and, with a toss of her long black hair, hopped into the Chrysler.

The man was Clarice's husband.

Barbara Jean kept her face pointed forward and said nothing. But she watched Clarice out of the corner of her eye.

Clarice stared at the car as it left the parking lot. She felt more embarrassed for Richmond than for herself as she watched him roar out of the lot and onto the road that led downhill to the highway, peeling rubber like a rowdy high school boy. The sound of his screeching tires was so loud that they heard it through the thick plate-glass window.

After the car had disappeared from sight, Clarice said, "He claimed he was going to be in Atlanta to scout recruits with Ramsey Abrams for the next two days."

Barbara Jean, still not looking directly at her, said, "The girl works in the hospital gift shop. The flowers I take to patients on my volunteer days get delivered to the gift shop first. I see her at least two times a week when I go there to sort the flowers. Her name is Cherokee."

"Cherokee? Like the Indian tribe?"

"No, Cherokee like the Jeep. Her father owns a car repair shop and he takes his work home, apparently. She has brothers named Tercel and Seville."

"You're kidding me."

"Nope. Cherokee, Tercel, and Seville Robinson."

Clarice said, "You see? This is why I can't hate Richmond, no matter what he does. Just when I want to break his neck, the man always finds a way to make me laugh."

Barbara Jean reached out and grabbed hold of Clarice's hand, saying, "Let's go back and see if Odette's finished." They left the window and walked back down the hallway toward the infusion room swinging their clutched hands like a pair of five-year-olds.

Just before they got to the door, Clarice said, "Chick Carlson and this Cherokee woman both in one day. I swear, Barbara Jean, sometimes this town is just too damn small."

"Clarice, honey," she responded, "you have just said a mouthful."

Chapter 18

On the evening of December twenty-first, Clarice answered the ringing telephone in her living room and heard a familiar voice. It was a sweet, tenor sound with a subtle lisp, like a choirboy who had been born with the tongue of a snake. It was the voice of Mr Forrest Payne.

Instead of hello, he said, "She's here."

Clarice didn't need to ask what or whom he was talking about. She answered, "I'm sorry. I'll be right over."

From the other end of the line, she heard the *snick-snick* of a cigarette lighter being struck. Then Mr Payne, the vile whoremonger with the lovely speaking voice, said, "Merry Christmas, Clarice. God bless you and your family." He hung up before she was forced to return his kind wishes.

Clarice arrived at the Pink Slipper Gentlemen's Club fifteen minutes after receiving Forrest Payne's call. Her mother stood on a small hill just east of the parking lot. Tall and thin, Beatrice Jordan looked elegant in the black, sable-trimmed sheared mink coat that Clarice's father had given her twenty years earlier after doing something especially humiliating to her, the details of which Clarice was never privy to. In hands covered by her bright red leather Christmas gloves, Beatrice held a megaphone. She bellowed, "You are a child of God. Stop what you're doing. Your sinful ways will bring a storm of hellfire down upon you. Come to the Lord and you will be saved."

Clarice had heard her mother's hilltop sermon dozens of times. It always began the same way, "You are a child of God. Stop what you're doing. Your sinful ways will bring a storm of hellfire down upon you. Come to the Lord and you will be saved." After that, a Bible verse. As Clarice approached her on her hill, her mother broadcast Romans 8:13. "For if you live according to the sinful nature, you will die; but if by the Spirit you put to death the misdeeds of the body, you will live." Beatrice was especially fond of the more ominous verses.

Clarice's mother's first Pink Slipper bullhorn sermon occurred during a visit home not long after she'd moved away following her husband's death. Clarice had been at home awaiting her mother's arrival. Anticipation had just transformed into worry, causing her to station herself at the front window to watch for her mother's rental car, when the phone rang. Pretty-voiced Forrest Payne had told her that her mother was at his place with a mega-phone. She hadn't believed him until he carried his phone outside so she could hear her mother's amplified voice crackling out warnings of damnation.

Mr Payne had said, "Clarice, I'm calling you instead of the police out of respect for the many years your daddy, God rest his soul, served as my attorney." But she suspected it was really out of respect for the fact that her father had spent so much money at the Pink Slipper that Forrest Payne should have named a room, or at least a memorial stripper pole, in Abraham Jordan's honor.

After Clarice persuaded her mother to stop sermonizing that first time and got her back to her house, Beatrice informed her daughter that she was finally ready to openly acknowledge her deceased husband's infidelities. But she also made it clear that she had entered into a new type of denial. She refused to hold Abraham responsible for any of his misbehavior. Instead, she blamed his cheating on the loose women and poorly chosen male friends who she believed had led him down a sinful path. She focused her righteous fury on Forrest Payne and his little den of iniquity out on the edge of town.

So, once or twice a year, Clarice's mother, the epitome of all things ladylike and proper, stopped by Forrest Payne's Pink Slipper Gentlemen's Club armed with a megaphone and an unquenchable thirst for revenge. It is terrifying, Clarice thought, what marriage can do to a woman.

Making the situation even worse, Beatrice didn't recognize Clarice at first. When she saw that Clarice was walking toward her instead of going into the club, she took her daughter for a fresh convert. She pointed the megaphone at Clarice and said, "That's right, sister, turn your back on that house of evil and listen to the Word." Seeing, finally, that it was Clarice, Beatrice said, unamplified, "Hi, sweetheart, I suppose he called you again."

Clarice nodded yes.

"Well, I was just about finished here anyway." But she wasn't done quite yet. A truck pulled into the parking lot just then and the driver, a heavyset, bearded man in a cowboy hat who moved as if he had already had a few drinks, walked falteringly from his vehicle toward the fuchsia front door of the club. Beatrice lifted her mega-phone again and squawked out, "You are a child of God. Stop what you're doing. Your sinful ways will bring a storm of hellfire down upon you. Come to the Lord and you will be saved." When the man disappeared inside the Pink Slipper, she tucked the bullhorn under her arm and descended her hill.

She stopped just in front of Clarice and looked her up and down. Clarice was wearing the gray down parka and snow boots she had thrown on to go fetch her mother after receiving Forrest Payne's phone call. Beatrice frowned as she took in her daughter's ensemble. She said, "I can't believe you allow yourself to be seen in public like this. These people may be the lowest of God's creatures, but that doesn't mean they won't talk."

Clarice quietly mumbled to herself, "I love my mother. I love my mother." She knew she was going to have to remind herself of that often over the next several days. This Christmas season was going to be rough, with Odette being sick, Barbara Jean walking around half in a coma, and Richmond behaving more like Richmond than ever. She wasn't in the mood to have her mother's special brand of crazy piled on top of it all. Clarice gave serious thought to marching into the Pink Slipper and doing her best to persuade Forrest Payne to have Beatrice locked up for trespassing and disturbing the peace. Let the county jail have her for the holidays. That would serve her right.

Clarice hugged her mother and said, "Merry Christmas."

The following morning as she cooked breakfast, Clarice discussed the day's itinerary with her mother. She had scheduled several things: hair appointments for them both, visits to old family friends, shopping excursions for last-minute gifts, and a grocery store trip for the meal they had to prepare for Clarice's children and their families. There were also all sorts of holiday events going on at Calvary Baptist if more was required to keep Beatrice busy. It was important that Beatrice always have something to do. Left to her own devices, her fingers began to itch for her bullhorn.

Things would become easier when the kids arrived the next day. Ricky would be with his wife's family this year, but Clarice and Richmond's other children were coming. Abe was bringing along a new girlfriend for his grandmother to exhaustively interview and disapprove of. Carl would have dozens of pictures to show Beatrice from the latest exotic vacation spot he had taken his wife to as penance for his latest transgression. Carolyn's four-year-old son, Esai, who had inherited Clarice's musical genes, could be relied upon to occupy his great-grandmother with hours of singing and dancing. God bless him. The child could go all day, if needed.

Beatrice wore dark red lipstick that left a vivid imprint on the white mug from which she sipped Earl Grey tea. She always came to breakfast in full makeup. Because it involved a rare excursion into the use of coarse language, Clarice never forgot her mother's opinion about being seen, even in your own home, without your face done. "Honey, it's the equivalent of dropping your pants and taking a dump in the fountain outside of Town Hall." As a goodwill gesture toward her mother and to avoid aggravation, Clarice had been sure to apply lipstick herself that morning.

Her mother asked, "What were you playing last night?"

Clarice apologized for waking her. The piano was in a music room that was off the living room. The bedrooms were upstairs at the opposite end of the house – far out of earshot, she thought.

"No, no, you didn't wake me. I just got up in the night to go to the bathroom and I heard you. I sat on the stairs for a while and listened to you play. It was beautiful. Took me back to when you were a youngster. I used to sit on the stairs at the old house for hours listening to you practice. I have never been as proud of you as I was then, listening to my baby girl overpower that big piano. You really had a gift."

Her mother seldom passed out compliments, even backhanded ones. Clarice took a moment to enjoy it. Then she said, "It was Beethoven, the *Waldstein* Sonata. I've gotten into a habit lately of practicing Beethoven in the middle of the night when I can't sleep."

Beatrice took another sip of tea and said, "You know, I've always thought it was a terrible shame that you gave up on your music."

Here we go, Clarice thought. "I hardly gave up on music, Mother. I have two dozen piano students, and I have former students performing all around the world."

Her mother dabbed at her lips with a napkin and said, "That's nice, I suppose. But what I meant was that it's a shame you never did more, after showing such promise. You never made those recordings when that man asked you to. What was his name? Albert-something, right?"

"Albertson. Wendell Albertson."

"That's right. You really should have made those records."

When Clarice was a sophomore at the university, she won a major national competition. Wendell Albertson, who was the head producer at what was at that time the leading classical music label in the country, was one of the judges. He talked to Clarice after the competition and told her that he wanted to record her. His idea was that she should record all of the Beethoven sonatas over the coming year. He had wanted to market her as a female André Watts, a pianist version of Leontyne Price. But Richmond was injured not long after the competition, so the recording was put off until later. Then Richmond and Clarice became engaged and the recording was delayed again. Then there were the children. Her piano teacher, Mrs Olavsky, had greeted the news of Clarice's first pregnancy by shaking her head and saying, "All these years, wasted," before slamming the door to her studio in Clarice's face.

Clarice hadn't wanted to believe that it was over for her, but time had proved her teacher right. All those years of work, both hers and Mrs Olavsky's, had been wasted. Though she tried not to, Clarice thought of the career she had thrown away whenever she suffered through a sloppy, poorly phrased performance from one of her weaker students. And she mourned that lost life even more keenly each time she watched one of her especially gifted pupils escape Plainview for a fine conservatory, leaving her behind to ruminate over her missed opportunities.

Beatrice said, "You know, I often wonder what would have happened if you'd gone ahead and made those records."

"I haven't given it a thought in years," Clarice said. That was only half a lie because there *had* been years, mostly when the kids were young, when she hardly ever thought about having passed up her big chance. But now it was on her mind during each one of those nights when she sat up playing the piano. Lately, as she charged through the angriest Beethoven passages, she found herself wondering what would have happened if she had been stronger or braver and walked away from Richmond when she'd had the opportunity. But then there wouldn't have been the children, and what would her life have been without them? She stirred the grits in the saucepan and tried to think of Christmas shopping.

The phone rang and Clarice pulled the last strips of bacon from the skillet before going to answer it. After she said hello, she heard a young woman ask, "May I please speak to Richmond?"

Clarice was about to call him to the phone, but she heard the sound of water running in the bathroom at the top of the stairs, so she said, "I'm sorry, Richmond isn't available right now. Who may I tell him called?"

There was a pause, and then the woman said, "I was just calling to confirm my meeting with him today." Another pause. "This is Mrs Jones."

Mrs Jones. Clarice had to roll her eyes at that one.

Clarice said, "I'll be sure to deliver the message, Mrs Jones." She hung up and went back to stirring the already overcooked grits.

Her mother had tired of discussing Clarice's failed musical career. She began to complain about her Arkansas neighbor, Clarice's aunt Glory, another of her favorite topics of conversation. Aunt Glory was petty. Aunt Glory was ill-tempered. Aunt Glory was unwilling to listen to constructive criticism. And, worst of all, Aunt Glory had set such a bad Christian example in her own home that Veronica had fallen under the satanic influence of a fortune-teller.

She said, "Veronica hasn't been right since she left Calvary and went over to First Baptist. Those First Baptist folks are all show and no substance. Watch and see how fast they drop her after she burns through that money she got from the Leaning Tree place. Mind you, they're still a step ahead of that primitive Holy Family bunch. I know your friend Odette goes there, but honestly, they might as well be snake handlers."

The ache behind Clarice's eyes that had started when Forrest Payne called a day earlier throbbed a little harder with each word that came from her mother's mouth. What made it worse was the fact that Clarice had expressed similar sentiments about her cousin and about her friends' churches countless times. Just like Veronica, her mother had a way of reminding Clarice of how alike their thinking was, and seeing the similarities between them made her more and more uncomfortable as time passed.

Richmond burst into the kitchen with a wide, welcoming grin on his handsome face. He was dressed in black slacks and a maroon knit shirt that was tight enough to display the muscles he worked so hard at maintaining. He kissed his mother-in-law on her forehead and sat down next to her.

He winked and said, "Good morning, Bea. How's the second-prettiest girl in the world doing today?"

Beatrice giggled and said, "You are a darling man, taking the time to sweet-talk an old woman like me."

"You haven't aged a day since I met you, and that's the truth," he said, gaining another giggle in reply.

To Clarice, Richmond said, "Sweetheart, I have to spend the day in Louisville with Ramsey talking to a football coach and a kid we're scouting. Depending on how things go, I might not make it back for dinner."

She nodded and brought Richmond his bowl of grits and a plate with two scrambled eggs and bacon. He said, "Thanks, babe," and began to eat.

She walked across the kitchen and got the pot of coffee from the machine and brought it back to the table to pour it into his mug. Maybe it was because her mother distracted her from her task by asking about Odette's health, or perhaps because her mind wandered off to her plans for the day, or because she caught a glimpse of the self-satisfied smirk on Richmond's face, but the coffee Clarice poured missed Richmond's mug entirely. Half of the pot spread onto the table and the other half splashed into Richmond's lap. It wasn't until he screamed, "Damn it!" and jumped up from his chair that she realized what she had done.

In a voice so high-pitched and breathless from shock that she sounded as if she had been the one doused with steaming hot coffee, Clarice cried out, "I'm so sorry! Are you okay? Let me get something to wipe that off."

He pulled the steaming fabric of his pants away from his thighs with both thumbs and forefingers. "Don't bother. I've got to get out of these. Jesus Christ, Clarice." He left the kitchen and hurried up the stairs.

Beatrice didn't say anything to Clarice as she watched her daughter clean up the mess she had made. She just finished her cup of tea and ate her breakfast – one slice of dry toast and one poached egg, the same breakfast she'd eaten every morning Clarice could recall.

Clarice, having lost her appetite, placed the food she had planned to eat into a plastic tub and tucked it into the refrigerator along with the eggs and milk.

Richmond came down again as Clarice put the last of her breakfast away. He was wearing gray pants and an annoyed expression now. He said, "I'm running late. I've got to go."

"But you've hardly had anything to eat," Clarice said.

He pulled his coat from the rack by the garage door. "That's okay. I'll get something later."

"Richmond, I really am sorry about the coffee."

He blew a kiss at his wife from across the room and went through the door.

Beatrice retrieved her compact from the pocket of her red-and-green Christmas cardigan and reapplied her lipstick. Then she said, "Clarice, I think you should have a talk with Reverend Peterson. That always helped me when things were bad with your father and our little problem."

Clarice's mother called her father's serial infidelities their "little problem." It bugged Clarice to no end whenever she described it that way, but she felt that she couldn't rightfully say anything about it. She knew it was hypocritical of her to be bothered by her mother giving Abraham Jordan's cheating a comfortable euphemism when Clarice herself had spent decades pretending Richmond's "little problem" didn't even exist. But that didn't stop her from wanting to shout at her mother to shut the hell up.

Beatrice said, "Reverend Peterson has had a lot of experience. Believe me, there isn't a thing you can say that'll shock him. He can help you deal with all this anger."

"I'm not angry."

"Clarice, what you have to concentrate on is that this is all a part of God's plan. Sometimes we women have to suffer an unfair amount to gain the Lord's favor. Just remember that you're paying the toll for your entrance into the Kingdom. Reverend Peterson explained that to me years ago, and I haven't had a moment of anger since."

That just about beat all, Clarice thought. Her father was long dead and her mother still felt sufficiently irate about his behavior to warrant traveling with her holy megaphone. And *she* was passing out anger-management advice? *Watch out, old woman, or I'll brew an extra hot pot of coffee just for you.*

Clarice said, "Thank you for your advice, Mother, but I'm really not angry. Things are the same with Richmond as they've always been. We're fine."

"Clarice, dear, you just scalded the man's crotch and threw away his insulin."

"Threw away his insulin? What are you talking about?"

Her mother pointed at the trash can. Clarice went to it and pressed the foot pedal that lifted the lid. Sure enough, atop eggshells, coffee grounds, and discarded wrappings of different sorts was the box that contained Richmond's insulin supply, the box that sometime during the past ten minutes she must have removed from its place in the refrigerator door and tossed into the trash.

She picked up the insulin and stared at it for several seconds. Then she put the box back into the fridge. She took off her apron then and said, "Mother, I think we'll go shopping a little bit later."

Clarice left the kitchen and walked through the dining room, past the living room, into the music room, and to her piano. She ripped into Beethoven's *Appassionata* Sonata and forgot about everything, for a while.

Chapter 19

During the week after she saw Chick at the hospital, Barbara Jean couldn't keep her mind in the present day. She chatted with Erma Mae at the All-You-Can-Eat on Wednesday afternoon and found herself glancing down, fully expecting to see Erma Mae's son, Earl III, clinging to his mother's apron with sticky hands. It was only after several seconds of bewilderment that Barbara Jean recalled that Earl III – or Three, as everyone called him – had long since grown up and said goodbye to Plainview, like most of his generation. That Friday evening, a pack of laughing college students passed her on the street as she walked home from the museum, and she ogled them until they noticed that she was watching and returned her stare while chuckling and whispering to each other. In her embarrassment, she nearly chased after them to explain that she had momentarily misplaced a few decades and had been searching through their crowd for the younger faces of her middle-aged friends. The sight of a young interracial couple strolling, hand in hand, down Plainview Avenue on Saturday night spun her into a state of near hysteria, fretting over threats to the couple's safety that had largely vanished years earlier. Each memory triggered by these encounters pushed her toward a bottle, a flask, or her thermos of spiked tea. The good memories weighed her down just as heavily as the bad, and they all demanded to be drunk away, even though some of those memories really were wonderful.

After Barbara Jean kissed Chick in the back hallway of the All-You-Can-Eat, she fell into a pattern. She would wait until Big Earl, Miss Thelma, and Little Earl were asleep, and then she would look out of her bedroom window to see if the light in the storeroom across the street at the restaurant was on. If it was, she slipped out of the house and went to see Chick.

They sat on his bed, surrounded by sixty-four-ounce cans of green beans and corn, and they talked until one or both of them couldn't keep their eyes open any longer. When they weren't talking, they were kissing – it was just kissing, at first. And every moment was heavenly.

If they couldn't meet at the All-You-Can-Eat, they would sneak over to the backyard of Odette's house and press themselves together in the seclusion of the vine-covered gazebo in her mother's garden. At Barbara Jean's insistence, they even traveled over shadowed routes to his bully of a brother's property a few times. They went into the shed where Chick had lived with his chickens and they kissed passionately on his old feather-covered cot. It was like a purification ritual, and the danger of the situation made it all the more irresistible.

Chick was a year out of high school then and he was thinking about college, mostly because Big Earl kept telling him that he was too smart not to. Big Earl said the same thing to Barbara Jean.

Barbara Jean liked the idea of college, but she couldn't imagine what she would study. She didn't have a passion like Clarice had with her piano. She got okay grades and she liked school enough. But Loretta had drummed it into her head since she was a child that she was going to marry a rich man. And that required a specific kind of preparation, a kind that you didn't need college to achieve.

Barbara Jean's mother taught her to dress in the manner that she associated with glamour – everything shiny and/or revealing. To make sure Barbara Jean talked like a high-class woman, her mother put belt lashes across her back if she dropped *g*s from the ends of her words, the way Loretta did. Barbara Jean and her mother joined First Baptist Church because the richest and lightest-skinned black people in town went there. Her mother weighed her every week to make sure her weight was always within man-catching range – something she and Clarice shared in common, Barbara Jean later discovered.

Barbara Jean thought it was funny that, when she finally did find a rich man, Loretta's life lessons had proved useless. All that had mattered was that she pass his family's skin color test. When she was introduced to Lester's mother, the old woman held a brown paper bag up to Barbara Jean's cheek and, judging her just a smidge lighter in comparison, said, "Welcome to the family."

During the winter of Barbara Jean's senior year, she wasn't thinking about her education, or marrying rich, or anything. She was crazy in love with a white boy who was poorer than anybody she knew. Loretta must have been spinning in her grave.

Even as she fell more deeply in love with Chick, Barbara

Jean saw more of Lester. She was too naïve and too blinded by her feelings for Chick to even notice that the hours she spent with Lester were also a kind of dating. He often showed up at the All-You-Can-Eat with James and sat for a while at the window table with Barbara Jean and her friends. But Barbara Jean never thought anything of it. Everyone, it seemed, put in time at the window table. Little Earl, that obnoxious Ramsey Abrams, Clarice's silly cousin Veronica. Even Chick became a regular guest at the table when he wasn't on duty, since he and James had become good buddies.

Sometimes Lester drove his young friends to Evansville and other nearby towns in his beautiful blue Cadillac, treating them to dinners they could never have afforded on their own. Always, he was a perfect gentleman. Lester never so much as held Barbara Jean's hand, much less made any sort of advances. She enjoyed his company and was flattered that he wanted to be her friend.

Clarice told Barbara Jean several times that Lester was interested in her, but Barbara Jean didn't pay much attention to her. Barbara Jean shared Odette's opinion that Clarice, already having scripted her own happy ending with Richmond, was now eager to write one for everybody else.

On a January night in 1968, Lester took James, Richmond, and the Supremes out for a ride in his Cadillac and then to dinner at a nice place in Louisville to celebrate Richmond having broken a passing record at the university. Barbara Jean enjoyed herself. The food was good and the restaurant was the most glamorous place she had ever stepped inside of. But she couldn't wait to get back to Chick. It was Chick's birthday and she had saved up to buy him a Timex wristwatch with a genuine leather band, which she thought back then was the height of elegance. She kept an eye on James all through dinner, waiting for his yawning to signal that the evening was over. But James didn't start to fade until 10:00, and it was nearly 10:30 when they began the forty-minute drive back to Plainview.

When Lester dropped Barbara Jean off, she found Odette's parents in Big Earl and Miss Thelma's living room. Laughing and bobbing their heads to a scratchy old record playing on the stereo, they waved hello to Barbara Jean through a haze of bluish-gray smoke as she climbed the stairs to her bedroom. The four of them stayed up late that night, the way they always did when they got together. When the Jacksons finally went home at around 2:00, Big Earl and Miss Thelma went straight to bed. They fell into loud snoring not five minutes after their bedroom door closed. For the thousandth time that night, Barbara Jean looked out the window to see if the storeroom light at the All-You-Can-Eat was still on. It was, so she tiptoed down the stairs and went to see Chick.

He was sitting on his narrow bed looking down when Barbara Jean walked into the room with the gift box in her outstretched hands. She rushed over and sat beside him. She said, "I'm sorry. I couldn't get over here any sooner." She was going to explain about the Jacksons visiting until late, but he looked up then and she stopped talking.

Chick had a red-and-blue bruise on his chin and his lower lip was split. She didn't need to ask who had done it.

She said, "Why'd you go over there?" and then immediately wished she hadn't said it.

She reached out and wrapped her arms around his shoulders. He tried to pull away at first, but then he relaxed and laid his head against her neck. He talked quietly in her ear.

"I ran into my brother's girlfriend, Liz, this morning. She said Desmond had been talking about how he wanted me to come back home. She said he'd been in a good mood for a while, not drinking as much and stuff. Plus, Liz's got this little girl. She's not my brother's kid, but she calls me Uncle Ray. And Liz said her daughter was asking why her Uncle Ray didn't come see her over Christmas." Chick shrugged. "She asked me to come by for supper. So, I went.

"Desmond was already pretty drunk when I got to the house, but he was joking and kidding around like we used to do sometimes. Then he lost it halfway through supper. He's like that. Changes real quick."

From years with Loretta, Barbara Jean knew how a drunken meal could go all crazy with no warning. One sip too much and a switch inside got flipped from off to on, and then things went bad fast.

"Nothing really started it, but all of a sudden he was yelling at Liz that she was a whore and was cheating on him. He threw his plate at her, so Liz grabbed her kid and took off before he could throw another one. Then he started in on me. He said he heard a rumor that I was working for a – a colored man."

Chick said it in a way that made it clear to Barbara Jean that "colored man" hadn't been the term his brother had used.

"Desmond said he wasn't gonna let me shame him in front of his friends. And then he started swinging.

"I'm getting better, though," Chick said. He raised his hands and showed her his scraped and bleeding knuckles. "I got in a few good ones myself this time." He tried to smile and grimaced because of his busted lip.

All the air seemed to go out of him then. He pulled away from Barbara Jean and stared down at his hands as they rested in his lap. Shaking his head, he said, "It's all shit. It's all just a bunch of shit."

She reached out and lightly stroked the bruise on his chin, remembering how the touch of his fingers had forever transformed the belt buckle scars on her arm into a smiling face. She kissed his mouth, avoiding the swollen part of his lip. She kissed him again and again. Then she put her hands on his waist and carefully pulled his T-shirt up over his head. There were more bruises on his chest and on his skinny arms and she leaned over and kissed those, too.

Chick put his hands on the sides of her face and kissed her now. Then he reached down and began to unbutton her blouse.

They undressed each other as if they had been doing it for years, no fumbling or rushing. And when they were both naked, they slid beneath the covers of his bed.

Barbara Jean was more experienced than Chick was. But her knowledge of intimacy had come too early and under bad circumstances, courtesy of evil men. She realized from the moment that she and Chick pulled the blankets over their bodies that this was as different from those other times as it could be. And that difference made it seem like her first time, too.

They wound themselves together over and over again, in a blur of arms and legs, lips and hands. When, finally, they were so ragged from exhaustion that they could do no more than lie with their mouths inches apart, each inhaling the other's breath, Barbara Jean forgot all about the passing of time and fell asleep in his arms under the pile of tangled linens.

When Barbara Jean awakened, he was gone. She sat up in the bed and looked around the tiny room, at the giant cans of corn, lard, and beans that were stacked to the ceiling against slatted wood walls, at the lamp he'd made from a Coca-Cola bottle and other bits scavenged from the trash cans behind the hardware store. She began to panic, thinking that she had made an awful mistake. She heard her mother's voice in her head saying, "I told you, girl. That's how men are. They get what they want, and then they run."

The panic fled when Chick tiptoed back into the room, still naked, carrying a big dish of ice cream with two spoons sticking out of it.

Seeing that Barbara Jean was awake, he grinned at her. "It's my birthday. We've got to have ice cream."

His smile fell away when he saw Barbara Jean's face. He said, "Are you okay? You aren't sorry, are you? You aren't sorry we did – you know, what we did, are you?"

"I'm not sorry. I just thought for a second that you'd left, that's all."

Chick sat on the edge of the bed and kissed her. He tasted like vanilla and cream. "Why would I go anywhere? You're here."

She took the ice cream dish from him and placed it on

the bedside table he had made by stacking old fruit crates. She kicked off the blankets and pulled him toward her. They both laughed as she sang, "Happy birthday to you, happy birthday to you," into his ear while he settled his weight on top of her again.

Barbara Jean and Chick were sharing melted ice cream when they heard the back door of the restaurant open. Someone rattled around in the kitchen as they listened. Then the radio came on and they heard Miss Thelma humming.

Barbara Jean knew she should have been frightened of being discovered there with Chick. And she knew that she should have thought she had done something wrong. She had learned at least that much from Sundays at First Baptist Church. But she couldn't manage to feel the slightest bit bad about the best night of her life.

They stayed there in bed together listening to the clanking of pots and pans and enjoying the sound of Miss Thelma's out-of-tune vocalizing. They finished the melted ice cream and kissed, silently celebrating their new lives on a planet all their own.

An old-timey blues song came on the radio and Miss Thelma began to sing along: "My baby love to rock, my baby love to roll. What she do to me just soothe my soul. Ye-ye-yes, my baby love me . . ."

Chick threw back the covers and hopped out of the bed. He stood beside the bed and began to dance, slowly moving his narrow hips in a widening circle while turning away from Barbara Jean to wave his tiny ass in her direction. He grinned back at her over his shoulder, mouthing the words of the song as he moved.

Barbara Jean had to pick up the pillow and press it against her mouth to keep Miss Thelma from hearing her laugh as Ray Carlson, the King of the Pretty White Boys, danced for her. She laughed so hard she cried. All the while her spinning, seventeen-year-old brain replayed the same thoughts: *My Ray. Ray of light. Ray of sunshine. Ray of hope.*

Barbara Jean thought of her mother. But now, for the first time ever, thinking of Loretta didn't make her feel bad. She thought about what Loretta would say if she had been able to tell her about this night. Her mother would have said, "Well, it looks like you are your mama's daughter after all. Your stuff was so good you done made a white boy jump up naked and dance the blues."

Chapter 20

I didn't exactly sail through my treatments the way I'd fantasized, but the side effects weren't as bad as I'd been warned they could be. My stomach was a mess sometimes, but mostly I was able to eat like I always had. My skin dried out, but didn't crack and bleed. I was tired, but not so weary that I had to quit my job or even miss a Sunday at the All-You-Can-Eat. Though it was brittle and broke off with the slightest tug, I kept a fair amount of my hair. Best of all, I celebrated Christmas week without a single visit from Eleanor Roosevelt. By the time of our New Year's Day party, I was full of optimism and ready to kick up my heels.

Our annual January get-together was a long-running tradition, going back to the first year of our marriage. The truth, even though he denies this, is that the first party was an attempt by James to prove to his friends that I wasn't as bad a choice of a mate as I seemed. Richmond and Ramsey – and others, most likely – had warned James that a big-mouthed, hot-tempered woman like me could never be properly tamed. But James was determined to show them that I could, on occasion, be as domestic and wifely as any other woman. I suspect that he's still trying to convince them.

What James *has* proved is that people will flock to a party hosted by a troublesome woman as long as she lays out a good spread. The party got a little bigger with each passing year, and lately we can count on seventy-five to a hundred folks showing up throughout the course of the day.

I normally cooked for a solid week in anticipation of my guests arriving, but that year James fought me, insisting that I conserve my strength and have the whole thing catered by Little Earl. We battled it out until we finally came to a compromise. Little Earl covered the savory. I did the sweet, with some help from Barbara Jean and Clarice.

My friends worked harder than I did to put the party together. Clarice even brought her mother by to lend a hand with the baking. Mrs Jordan – who, with her bull-horn nonsense, was giving Mama a run for her money in the race to be considered the nuttiest woman Plainview had ever produced – was a real asset in the kitchen once she got past her revulsion over the cheapness of my serving platters. I appreciated her coming by to help, but her habit of stopping to thank Jesus at every step of the cooking process got old real fast. We thanked Him for every ingredient, the utensils, even the oven timer. Being around her reminded me of something Mama liked to say: "I love Jesus, but some of his representatives sure make my ass tired."

On New Year's Day, the guests started showing up around three o'clock. My sons, my daughter, and my grandkids did all of the greeting. Denise was bossy, ordering her older brothers around like she always had. Jimmy argued with his sister over the slightest thing: "The coats go in the middle bedroom." "No, they don't. They go in the guest bedroom." Eric ignored them both and acted just as thrilled to be having company over as he did when he was six years old. I half expected him to grab one of the guests by the hand and demand that they accompany him to his room to see his train set. Seeing my fully grown offspring together, falling back into the roles they had played as children, was a load of fun for me, although I'm sure my son-in-law and daughter-in-law were counting the seconds until they could escape my house and get back the adults they'd married.

James's police friends arrived first. The younger men who worked under James came at the precise moment the party was scheduled to start, like they were appearing for morning roll call. Mostly fresh-faced, beefy white boys – there were still no women in his unit – they came bearing flowers, in the company of skinny girlfriends who wore extremely low-cut blouses. As always, the first-timers looked stiff and uncomfortable until the good food, plentiful beer, and a few country songs mixed in with the R&B on the stereo loosened them up.

My brother stomped through the living room and threw himself on me like an overly friendly Labrador. Rudy spun me around and inspected me. "You don't look much worse than usual," he said. Then he gave me a brotherly punch in the arm and a kiss on each cheek.

Rudy's wife, Inez, stepped closer, slapped him on the wrist, and chastised him for being too rough with me. Then she hugged me so tight she squeezed the breath out of me. Inez might be a dainty thing – she's my height and no more than a hundred pounds – but every last bit of what's there is muscle. Rudy likes to pretend his wife is helpless, and she plays along. But I wouldn't want to be the one to make Inez mad. The three of us did some fast catching up before I passed them along to James and said hello to the newest guests.

Richmond, Clarice, and her mother, Beatrice, arrived at the same time as Veronica and her mother, Glory. Beatrice, Glory, and Veronica all wore elaborate, floor-length gowns. It was their habit to overdress for every occasion. They came to picnics dressed for a day on a yacht. They showed up at graduation ceremonies done up as if they were attending a coronation. They always wanted their hosts to understand that they were either on their way to or on their way from a much more important gathering.

Beatrice and Glory made a big show of not speaking to each other due to an argument they'd had on the phone that morning. Whenever the two elderly sisters came within five feet of each other, they snorted and sniffed like riled-up horses before stalking off in opposite directions.

Barbara Jean caused a stir when she sashayed in packed into a hot pink dress with a plunging neckline. The young cops looked away from their dates and stared in appreciation at this woman twice the age of their girlfriends. Barbara Jean went straight to the drinks table and hit the vodka with an intensity that worried me.

My doctor, Alex Soo, came in with a hefty woman on his arm. She was as loud as he was quiet, and she had a laugh like a rooster's crow. She parked herself beside one of the food tables and soon made it clear that her goal for the day was to break the world record for consuming the most deviled eggs in one sitting. I liked her right off.

Ramsey Abrams and his always angry wife, Florence, arrived with their sons, Clifton and Stevie, and their future daughter-in-law. Like her mother, grandmother, and great-aunt, Sharon was dressed in the style of touring royalty. From the moment she stepped in the door, she signaled her intent to spend the evening flouncing around in her party dress while gesturing wildly with her left hand to show off the expensive engagement ring Clifton had given her. The naïve girl was completely oblivious to the way her shady fiancé broke out in a sweat when she brandished that rock anywhere near one of the many cops in attendance.

I sure wished Ramsey and Florence had used common sense and left Stevie at home. He clearly wasn't over that shoe thing of his, or his airplane glue habit either, judging from his glassy eyes. He stared at the feet of every woman who walked past with an expression on his face that reminded you of a stray dog outside of a butcher shop. It gave people the creeps.

Clarice's daughter, Carolyn, who is good friends with my Denise, stretched her Christmas visit out a few extra days and came to the party with her husband and her son, who was carried in already sound asleep in his father's arms. Carolyn had gone way out of her way to find a man who wasn't the least bit like her father. She married a Latino intellectual who teaches physics at a college in Massachusetts. He's small, much shorter than Carolyn, and he's had the doughy body of an idle middle-aged man since he was twenty-two.

When Richmond realized that Carolyn was getting

serious about the intellectual, he did everything he could to divert Carolyn's interest in the direction of someone he thought would be more suitable for her. He scoured the campus until he found two replicas of himself in his virile prime. Then he dragged both men to a big Memorial Day picnic at his house, where he paraded them in front of Carolyn like a couple of prize bulls. In a turn of events that I'm sure Richmond will still be trying to sort out on the day he dies, Carolyn stayed with her egghead while the two Richmond clones began a romance with each other on that Memorial Day that is still going strong more than a decade later.

Mama appeared, along with Mrs Roosevelt, late in the evening. They both looked like they'd been to several other parties already that day. Mama's eyes were bloodshot and Mrs Roosevelt, who was wearing a cone-shaped silver and gold paper hat that was attached to her head with an elastic band, seemed to have forgotten her usual good manners. She waved in my general direction as she staggered in. Then she plopped down onto a footstool and began to snore.

When Mama spotted Rudy, she squealed, "Look at my boy. Ain't he the handsomest thing?" Rudy's a dear, but he's mostly ears, nose, and belly. Pretty, my brother is not. I said nothing.

After Mama finished making a fuss over Rudy, she commenced to making a nuisance of herself by following me around the house as I performed my hostess duties. "Oh, there's the Abrams boy," she said when she saw Ramsey. He was standing much too close to the girlfriend of one of the young cops and getting dirty looks from the girl's date and from his wife, who scowled at him from a few feet away.

Mama said, "You know, it's sad when you think about it. He's probably just overcompensatin' for a very small penis. All of the Abrams men have little dicks. That's why they're so short-tempered. His poor father and uncle were the same way, had practically nothin' down there at all."

I silently prayed that my mother would spare me the details of just how she'd come across that bit of information about the Abrams men.

I noticed Clarice sitting on the couch next to her mother and aunt. She was frowning like she had a toothache and her attention was focused on some point way off in the distance. The fingers of both her hands were tapping away on her lap like she was playing an invisible piano. If her mother didn't get out of town soon, Clarice was going to snap.

When I came over to offer to freshen up their drinks, I saw that Clarice's mother and her aunt Glory had started speaking to each other again. They were having a good time now, arguing about who would be more surprised to be left behind after the Rapture, the Catholics or the Mormons.

Mama sneered at them. "I know you and Clarice are friends, but you can't tell me you don't wanna slap the livin' shit outta that mother of hers. Talk about somebody with her head stuffed way up her own ass. And that sister of hers is just as bad. As far back as I can remember, Beatrice and Glory been usin' Jesus as an excuse to be bitches." She wagged her finger at them and, like they could hear her, said, "That's right, I said it!"

Veronica waved me over to where she was holding court, showing Sharon's wedding planning book to a group of women who were too polite to walk away. She pointed to a page in the book that held a magazine clipping with a picture of a bride floating on a rug in midair down the center aisle of a church. Veronica said, "I'm thinking Sharon should make a magic carpet entrance. It's all done with lights and mirrors. Isn't it something?"

I agreed that it was something, all right, and tried to ignore the fact that my mother was next to me shrieking with laughter at the idea of big Sharon floating to the altar.

Over Mama's continued cackling, I heard Veronica discussing the trouble she was having finding a suitable affordable home for the newlyweds. Sharon had another year at the university, and her fiancé, Clifton, Veronica claimed, would be going back to school soon. So after the wedding, which Veronica and her psychic had determined should happen on the first Saturday in July, she would settle them into something nice, but reasonably priced, here in town.

James, ever helpful, walked by just then and said, "You know, Veronica, we don't have a tenant in the house in Leaning Tree."

If I hadn't been holding a tray of pigs in blankets, I'd have knocked James upside his head. I had nothing against Sharon. It wasn't her fault that she'd inherited her father's intelligence and her mother's personality. It was the thought of Veronica traipsing in and out of Mama and Daddy's house that made my pressure rise.

I gave James my *back away quickly* look. But he'd been immune to my hostile glances for ages, so he wasn't put off his stride for a second. He just went right on being helpful.

He said, "We just put a new roof on it and painted it. And the last tenant took good care of the garden. It's not like it was when Miss Dora was living, but it's not bad."

It turned out I didn't have to worry about the prospect of having more Veronica in my life. Veronica wrinkled her nose and said, "Thanks, James, but I didn't spend all those years working to get out of Leaning Tree just to send my baby daughter back there."

Mama let out a snort. "Talk about a nerve. I guess she's too good for my house now. She oughta try to sell that bullshit to some folks who don't remember where she came from. And what kind of 'working' did she do to get outta Leanin' Tree? All she did was outlive her lowlife daddy. Odette, tell her your mama's back and that she's fixin' to haunt the fuck outta her. Go on, tell 'er."

I hadn't seen Minnie McIntyre come in, but I heard the tinkling of a bell and turned to see her standing just behind me. Minnie had taken to wearing her fortune-telling turban with its tiny silver bell all the time. She said that, because she was so near death, Charlemagne the Magnificent had more messages for her than ever. So she wouldn't miss one of those messages, she made sure to always have her bell at the ready. My first thought was *Oh great, now Mama will never shut up.*

When Mama was alive, just the sight of Minnie McIntyre was enough to start her cussing and spitting. I prepared myself to hear her let loose with a foul-mouthed tirade. But Mama was watching Denise as she attempted to corral my grandkids. She wasn't thinking about Minnie. Mama heard Denise call her daughter by her name, Dora, and I thought she was going to fall out on the floor.

Mama was in my business so much that I had forgotten she wasn't a daily part of my children's lives, too. She hadn't seen them in years and didn't know her great-grandchildren at all. Now she'd discovered that she had a cute little namesake running around and it had knocked the wind out of her sails. She went silent and tottered off behind the kids. After all the shocks she'd handed me, it was kind of nice to see Mama taken by surprise for a change.

Barbara Jean stood talking with Erma Mae on the other side of the living room from me. She nodded her head and pretended to listen to whatever Erma Mae was saying to her. But I could see that she was staring at my grandkids, especially my grandson William, just as hard as Mama was. Barbara Jean did that from time to time, saw boys around eight or nine years old and couldn't draw her eyes away from them. I knew she was thinking of Adam. How could she not? Sure, Adam and William looked nothing alike. My grandson inherited my roundness and cocoa skin, and Adam was a buttercream-colored string bean. But they shared that same wild energy and heartbreaking sweetness that little boys have in those brief years before your presence bores and annoys them and they can't abide an embrace. Barbara Jean's boy would never grow out of that phase.

Barbara Jean watched my grandson as he zipped through the room, tormenting my cats with an overabundance of affection and charming guests with his big smile. When my son-in-law sensed that William was becoming too rambunctious for the crowd and carried his giggling and squirming son out of the room under his arm, Barbara Jean looked like she might cry. I'd have bet good money that she was seeing Lester and Adam just like I was, remembering how Lester couldn't resist hoisting Adam in the air whenever that boy was within reach. If Lester'd had his way, Adam's feet would never have touched the ground. Barbara Jean walked away from Erma Mae then, heading in the direction of the vodka.

That year's party was the biggest ever. It was like everybody we'd ever met came by to say hello. Or, more likely, they came to say goodbye. Nothing like a little touch of cancer to get folks to feel all sentimental about you, whether they cared for you or not. But by midnight most of the guests had left. Mama retired to the family room to coo over her great-grandkids, who had collapsed on the couch alongside Clarice's grandson by then. I was dead on my feet and longed to stretch out and rest, but I went into the kitchen to do some cleaning up. I opened the kitchen door to find my Denise and Clarice's Carolyn washing dishes, laughing and talking the same way they had done when they were girls. I stood there for a few seconds watching them – both of them smart, strong, and happy. Well, I thought, looks like Clarice and I did at least one thing right.

A hand touched my shoulder and I turned to see Richmond. He whispered into my ear, "Listen, Odette, Clarice and I are leaving, and we're taking Barbara Jean. She's had a little too much to drink."

I followed him out of the kitchen, through the living room, and into the front hallway, where Clarice was helping Barbara Jean into her coat. The quiet mood Barbara Jean had been in all day had given way to gloominess. Her watery eyes and the haunted expression on her face seemed even bleaker because of the pink dress that mocked her now with its youthful cheeriness.

I gave her a quick hug and said, "I'll call you tomorrow."

Barbara Jean tried to say good night, but her words came out in a jumble. Clarice and Richmond each grabbed one of her arms and guided her out. They were followed by the oh-so-proper Mrs Jordan, who glared at Barbara Jean and clucked, "Unseemly. Entirely unseemly."

I stepped out onto the front porch and watched as Clarice and her mother got into the front seat of Richmond's Chrysler while he helped Barbara Jean into the back. After he got Barbara Jean settled in, he shut the door and trotted over to her car and hopped inside. They drove off, Richmond leading the way in Barbara Jean's Mercedes.

I stayed on the porch for a few minutes, enjoying the cold air after so many hours inside the warm, crowded house. Mama joined me, and Mrs Roosevelt came out just after Mama. The former first lady had sobered up and her famous warm, toothy smile was firmly in place as she snuggled up against me.

Mama said, "I hate to see Barbara Jean like that. I think maybe there's trouble comin', don't you?"

I didn't answer for a moment. I was distracted because, for the first time in all of her visits, Mrs Roosevelt seemed to have actual physical presence. I felt the weight of her body leaning against mine. And, in the chilly air of the evening, the warmth that emanated from her was almost uncomfortably hot. She and I now truly shared the same world. *This can't be good,* I thought.

When I finally answered Mama, I said, "Yeah, I believe trouble's coming."

Chapter 21

If you ever wanted evidence that I wasn't as fearless as the rumors made me out to be, all you had to do was look at the way I handled Barbara Jean's drinking. Without even discussing it, I joined in a coward's pact with Clarice and didn't say a word about it for years. Both of us were afraid that if we confronted it head-on we'd find our friendship toppling over like a tower of children's blocks.

Not dealing with Barbara Jean's drinking turned it into an invisible fourth member of our trio, a pesky, out-of-tune singer who Clarice and I just adjusted to over time. We learned not to call Barbara Jean on the phone after nine at night because she wasn't likely to remember the conversation. If she was going through a bad spell, we would say that she was "tired" and we rescheduled anything that we might have had planned so we could do it when she was feeling more energetic. It went on like that for years, and the whole time I convinced myself that we weren't doing her any harm by not confronting her about it. She would go through periods when she was tired more days than not, but those episodes were always followed by longer periods when she was fine.

I told myself that it was Lester's place to step in and say something if it was going to be said. He was her husband.

But Lester was gone now, and for the first time in ages, Barbara Jean had been drunk in public. I tried to tell myself that what had happened at my party had been typical New Year's Day excess. Who hadn't tied one on celebrating a new year at some point in their lives?

But this was different. And Clarice and I both knew it, even if we hadn't said anything. Barbara Jean had that darkness about her in a way that I hadn't seen since she lost Adam. And it didn't seem like she was going to shake it anytime soon.

I entered 2005 recognizing that one day soon, while I still had the chance to do it, I was going to have to risk toppling that tower of blocks.

Barbara Jean's drinking got bad for the first time in 1977, during that horrible year after little Adam died. For a long stretch of months she was drunk more than she was sober. I would stop by her house and find her hardly able to stand. She maintained a good front when she was out among strangers, though; people talked about how well she was holding up. If I hadn't known her like I did, I'd have agreed. But I heard the occasional slurred word coming into her speech earlier and earlier in the day. I saw how she wobbled on those high heels she loved to wear.

And poor Lester. World War II had only succeeded in adding a hitch to his step, but his son's death defeated him. He turned into an old man that year. The first in a long list of chronic ailments – a kidney problem, if memory serves – made its appearance just a month after Adam's funeral.

Lester dosed himself with work the same way Barbara

Jean medicated her sorrow with alcohol. With Adam gone, Lester started taking more business trips, staying away from home longer. And when he returned, he looked more exhausted and more miserable.

When he had Adam, Lester's work energized him and kept him young. Barbara Jean might have seen her son as a future painter because of his elaborate crayon drawings or a musician because he was such a natural at the piano, but Lester knew that his boy was meant to work with the land like his daddy. On the weekends and during Adam's summer break from school, Lester brought his son with him whenever he had jobs around Plainview. Lester joined in doing the sort of grunt work that was customarily left to low-level employees so that Adam could see and understand every aspect of the business he would inherit one day. And Adam had loved every minute of it. Dressed in his overalls, he followed his father everywhere, planting, digging, and raking with his miniature tools.

Now that he wasn't creating something to hand over to his son, there was no reason for Lester to touch a shovel or lift a rake. His body withered along with his spirit, and his life's work turned into a numbers game. He made deal after deal and piled up cash like he thought it might make him and Barbara Jean happy one day.

Even though they were from different generations and even though the one thing, or so it had always seemed to me, that bound them as a couple was gone, Lester and Barbara Jean stayed together and sometimes managed to look like all that money really was bringing them happiness. Richer, sicker, sadder, and older, as the shock of Adam's death faded, they built new lives.

It was during that awful first year that the Supremes and the fragile new life Barbara Jean and Lester were building nearly came to an end, with some help from Richmond Baker.

We were at our table at the All-You-Can-Eat on a Sunday afternoon. Clarice's twins were seated in their highchairs between her and Richmond. Denise was on James's lap, making a macaroni and cheese sculpture. The other children were at a table of their own just a few feet away, within snatching distance.

Clarice tried to keep up a conversation between yawns. The twins had really knocked the stuffing out of Clarice in a way the older two hadn't. She could barely keep her eyes open some days.

Barbara Jean looked divine that Sunday in a dress of layered taffeta that was traffic-cone orange. Big Earl stood and applauded her when she walked into the restaurant. Lester was out of town again, so she was alone. She was relatively steady on her feet, but she talked in an uneven, overly careful way that telegraphed her drunken state to those of us who really knew her.

During that meal I watched as a curious and troubling scene played out. We were discussing the latest round of renovations going on at Barbara Jean's house. It was one of the few activities that seemed to really interest Barbara Jean around that time. Things started going funny when she said, "What I need to do right now is get a carpenter in there to do some work in the bedroom closets. Somebody put in metal shelves at some point, and those things are coming down practically every day. One of them almost took my head off last night."

Richmond said, "You don't need to hire anybody to do that. Lester can take care of that with an electric drill and some masonry screws in no time."

Barbara Jean shook her head no. "Lester's gone for the next two weeks and I've got to do something about it right away." She laughed and said, "I think that for everyone's safety I'd better not try to do it myself."

Richmond, the charitable Mr Fix-it, said, "I'd be happy to come over and help you out."

Barbara Jean leaned across James to pat Richmond's arm. "Richmond, you are a lifesaver."

The thing with Richmond was that he *would* help a friend in need without giving it a second thought. As much as he annoyed me, I had to admit that he really was that guy who'd hand you the shirt off his back. Unfortunately, when an attractive woman was involved, Richmond would hand her the shirt off his back and then toss her his pants and underwear, too.

Alarm bells went off in my head when Richmond turned his *at your service* smile on Barbara Jean. I looked at Clarice and James to see if they were hearing the same warning signal I was. But Clarice was focused on the twins, not her husband. And James was bouncing Denise on his knee and not paying a bit of attention to anything else that was happening at the table.

That night at home I stewed over what I'd heard earlier at the All-You-Can-Eat. I told myself it wasn't any of my business and that my friends were responsible adults. They would come to the right decisions on their own. And even if they didn't do the right thing, it wasn't my place to step in. Finally, when it was clear that turning things over in my mind was going to ruin *Kojak* for me, I told James that I had an errand to run and I left the house to act upon my true nature.

I smelled Richmond before I saw him. Since he was a teenager, he'd worn the same lemony, woody cologne. It always marched into the room several seconds before he did. I was waiting in the shadows, sitting in one of the wicker rockers on Barbara Jean's front porch when he stepped up to the door.

I said, "Hello there, Richmond," just loud enough for him to hear me.

He jumped, put his hand to his chest, and said, "Odette, you damn near scared me to death." Then he asked, "What are you doing here?"

"Just enjoying the night air. What about you, Richmond? What brings you by Barbara Jean's tonight?"

He produced a smile that I would have believed was innocent through and through if I hadn't known him better. He said, "I told Barbara Jean I'd come by and take a look at those shelves of hers that keep falling."

"That's truly sweet, Richmond. But I've got some bad news for you."

"What's that?"

I pointed to the sack in his hand and said, "Looks like you were in such a rush to come over here and be a Good Samaritan that you went and picked up the wrong bag. Instead of your drill, you accidentally grabbed a bottle of wine. Must be the stress of dealing with the twins."

He lost his smile then and said, "Listen, Odette, it's not what you're thinking. I was just—"

I interrupted him. "Richmond, why don't you come over here and sit with me for a minute."

He hemmed and hawed, saying that he should probably get back home.

"Just for a minute, Richmond. Really, I insist."

He groaned and then took a seat in the chair next to mine, falling into it like a teenager who'd been called into the vice-principal's office.

He placed the bottle of wine on the floor between his feet and said, "Odette, I was just paying a friendly visit. Nothing's happened and nothing's going to happen. But Clarice might get things mixed up. You aren't going to tell her, are you?"

"No, Richmond, I'm not going to tell Clarice. But you and I have to have a conversation because there's something I need to tell you."

I rocked back and forth in the chair a few times to think about what I wanted to say. Then I said, "If I weren't married to a man everyone loves, I probably wouldn't have a true friend in this world, except Barbara Jean and Clarice."

He said, "That's not true. You're a perfectly charming woman."

I waved off the compliment, saying, "Richmond, you have lovely manners. I've always admired that about you. But you don't need to waste time blowing smoke up my ass. I know who I am."

I continued, "I'm a tough woman to be around. I don't try to be, I just am. I don't know how James deals with me. And to top it off, I was never pretty enough for people to overlook me being a pain in the ass."

He started to interrupt once more, but again I stopped him. "Please, Richmond, let me go on. I promise to get to the point.

"I know that you probably think I don't like you. Maybe Clarice told you that I warned her not to marry you." In the dim light from the street lamps out on Main Street, I saw an expression of surprise on his face. "She didn't tell you, huh? Well, I did. I told her you'd always be a cheater no matter how hard she tried to change you and that she was better off without you. I shouldn't have said it, but I did. That's kind of my way.

"But I want you to know that I really don't have anything against you. And I understand why Clarice loves you. You're polite. You're funny. When I watch you with your children, I see a kind, warm side of you that is absolutely beautiful. And, even though I hate to admit it, you are one of the best-looking men I've ever laid eyes on."

He relaxed then. A discussion of his physical attractiveness was something Richmond had always been comfortable with. "And I love Clarice, I really do."

"I believe you. But what you need to understand is I'll do absolutely anything to protect the handful of people in this world who truly love me. And, Richmond, if you follow your dick and go in this house with Barbara Jean, she'll never be able to see herself as a decent human being again. She'll come to her senses tomorrow and hate herself for letting it happen. It'll eat her alive, almost as bad as losing Adam. Clarice will eventually figure it out and feel more humiliated than she has ever felt with any of your other women. And then, Richmond" – I reached out and placed my hand on his muscular forearm – "I will have to kill you."

Richmond laughed and then said, "Okay, Odette, I get it. I'll stay away from Barbara Jean."

"No, Richmond, I don't think you really get it yet." I squeezed his arm tighter and said, very slowly, "I am as serious as a heart attack. If you ever come sniffing around Barbara Jean again, I will kill you dead."

I held his gaze and added, "I won't want to. And it will bring me no pleasure to do it. But, still, I will kill you."

Our eyes locked for several seconds and I watched the last traces of a smile leave his face as he took in that I was telling him God's honest truth.

He nodded. "I understand."

I patted his arm and said, "Well, this has been real nice. I don't know about you, but I feel a whole lot better."

I pushed the sleeve of his shirt a few inches higher on his wrist and read his watch in the faint light. "And would you look at that," I said, "I can still catch the end of *Kojak*." I stood and stepped to the edge of the porch. "Why don't you walk me home?"

Richmond picked up the bottle and came along with me, down the stairs and onto the stone walkway that led to Main Street. I looped my arm around his and said, "It really is a lovely evening, isn't it?"

I looked over my shoulder as we turned onto the sidewalk. Just for a second, I caught sight of Barbara Jean peeking out of an upstairs window at me and Richmond, a man who now understood me in a way that even James didn't, as we strolled away from her magnificent house.

Chapter 22

After saying goodbye to her last piano student of the day, Clarice went to visit Odette. Late February had brought with it a spell of false spring. Temperatures were almost twenty degrees above normal and she felt energized by the warm weather.

Odette was having a bad month. She didn't complain, but Clarice could see that she had practically no energy. The previous Sunday at the All-You-Can-Eat, Odette had terrified everyone at the table by leaving an entire pork chop untouched on her plate at the end of supper. So Clarice decided to drop by bearing a slice of peach cobbler, a bag of gifts, and some decent local gossip she'd picked up. (Rumor had it that Clifton Abrams, less than five months from marrying Sharon, had something going on the side.)

Everyone in town was celebrating the unexpected warm weather by airing out their homes. For the first time in months, Clarice passed by open door after open door as Plainview's residents welcomed in the unseasonable breeze. Odette and James's front door was also open, and standing on their porch, Clarice peered through the screen door and saw them in their living room. James sat on the sofa and Odette sat on the floor in front of him with her back to him and her legs stretched out on the rag rug. She petted an enormous calico cat that Clarice didn't recognize. Odette still picked up strays, so this one could have been added just that day. Two other cats lounged across her shins. Her eyes were closed and her head was tilted back. James, who had half a dozen bobby pins squeezed between his lips, attempted to coax Odette's hair into a semblance of the style she'd worn it in most days for the last three decades, pulled into a tight bun on the back of her skull.

Odette had lost a lot of hair by that time, and what was left didn't want to cooperate with the twisting and tugging of James's long, clumsy fingers. Repeatedly, he would lift one of the remaining tendrils of hair only to have it slip away from him or simply break off at the root and float down onto Odette's shoulder.

When a particularly large clump of hair came off in his hand, he spat out the bobby pins and said, "I'm sorry."

She said, "That's okay. Most of it's already come out anyway." Then she reached back and grabbed his shirt and pulled him down toward her. She kissed him on the mouth.

When Odette released her husband, she looked at him with a softness in her face that Clarice only saw when Odette looked at James. It was a warm glow that never failed to make her look pretty.

Through the screen, Clarice watched James redouble his efforts to style Odette's hair. She had just raised her hand to knock when she heard Odette chuckle and say, "Clarice is gonna be thrilled when I go bald. She's been wanting me to cover up this mess on my head with a wig since we were in the eighth grade."

Clarice knew that Odette hadn't meant anything unkind by that remark. She knew that Odette would happily say the same thing directly to her with a broad smile on her face. But that knowledge didn't help her at that moment. All she wanted to do was rush inside and shout to Odette that she loved the sight of her just as she was – good hair, bad hair, or no hair. But Clarice didn't move. She couldn't.

Was it possible that she had allowed the person she loved most in the world to believe that she saw her as something other than beautiful? And she did love Odette most of all. More than she loved Richmond. And, she asked the Lord to forgive her even as she thought it, as much as she loved her own children. Words Clarice had spoken to Odette over the decades rang in her ears, obliterating any other sounds or thoughts. "Do something about your clothes." "Fix your hair." "Let me help you with your makeup." "If you could just take off twenty pounds, you'd have such a cute figure."

A wave of shame struck her so hard that she pulled her knuckles away from the wood frame of the door and backed off of the porch. She walked to her car as quickly as she could and drove away with the shopping bag containing two pre-styled wigs, now destined for the Salvation Army, resting on the passenger seat.

Clarice was at her piano, trying not to think, when Richmond came home a couple of hours later. He surprised her by announcing that he would be spending the evening in, something he hadn't done on a Saturday night in months. They had dinner – leftovers since she had thought she would be dining alone and hadn't cooked anything that day. Then they cuddled together under a throw blanket on the living room sofa and watched a movie he had picked up from the video store. Later, Clarice would recall that the movie had probably been a comedy. She would carry with her a hazy memory of Richmond laughing just before things took a turn.

Clarice couldn't concentrate on the movie enough to laugh or cry. She was still dwelling on her visit to Odette and James's house. She watched her handsome husband and thought, *Would you do that for me? Would you do my hair for me if I was too sick to lift my arms and do it myself?*

The answer she came up with was a decisive yes.

Yes, Richmond would style her hair if she was sick. He would do it for her and do it with no complaints. And he would probably do it well. Those big, beautiful hands of his were capable of anything he put his mind to doing with them.

But she also knew that one night, as Richmond combed through her hair, their phone would ring and he would go to answer it. After he hung up, he would return to her with a lie already worked out to explain why he had to leave for just a little while. She would sit, hair half done, smiling in her sickbed, and pretend to believe his lie as he scooted out the door. If she was lucky, there would be no mirror in the room in which she might catch a glimpse of her face contorted into an imitation of that lovely, soft expression that came over Odette's face so naturally when she gazed at James.

That vision was in Clarice's head when she stood up from the sofa, walked over to the television, and turned it off.

Richmond said, "Hey, what are you doing?" He lifted

the remote from where it rested on his lap and pointed it at the television. But Clarice was standing in the way and the set wouldn't respond.

When she didn't move, he asked, "What's going on?"

She said, "Richmond, I can't live with you anymore." It came out easily and sounded totally natural, even though her heart was pounding so hard she could barely hear her own voice.

He said, "What do you mean?"

"I mean I'm tired. I'm tired of you, tired of us. Mostly I'm tired of me. And I know I can't live with you anymore."

He let out a long sigh and set down the remote. Then he spoke to her in the low, calming tone people reserve for interactions with hysterical children and brain-damaged adults. "Now, Clarice, I'm not sure what's gotten into you that you think you need to make this fuss right now, but I want you to know that I'm sympathetic. You've gone through a lot lately with Odette being sick, your mother's problems, and whatever's going on with Barbara Jean. And I understand that the change can hit some women extra hard, mess up your hormones and everything. But I think you should remember what the truth is. And the truth is, I've never pretended to be anything other than the man I am.

"Not that I'm claiming to be perfect. Listen, I'm more than willing to accept my portion of the blame for a situation or two that may have hurt you. But I have to say that I believe most women would envy the honesty we have between us. At least you know who your husband is."

She nodded. "You're right, Richmond. You never pretended to be anyone other than the man you are. And that might be the saddest part for me. I really should have helped you be a better man than this. Because, sweetheart, the man you are just isn't good enough."

That came out meaner than she had intended it to. She really wasn't angry – well, no angrier than usual. She wasn't sure what she felt. She had always assumed that if this moment ever came she would be yelling and crying and trying to decide whether to burn his clothes or glue his testicles to his thighs while he slept, the way women on afternoon TV always seemed to be doing to their unfaithful men. Now mostly she felt fatigue and a sadness that left no room for histrionics.

Richmond shook his head in disbelief and said, "Something's not right about this. Really, I'm worried about you. You should get a checkup or something. This could be a symptom of something bad."

"No, it's not a symptom," Clarice said, "but it might be the cure."

Richmond hopped up from the sofa. His shock and confusion had faded. Now he was only mad. He started to pace back and forth. "This is Odette's idea, isn't it? It's got to be her idea, all the time you've been spending with her."

"No, this idea is all mine. Odette's idea was to castrate you back in 1971. Since then she's kept quiet on the subject of you."

He stopped pacing then and tried a different approach. He walked over until he stood close to her. Smiling his slickest, most seductive smile, he put his hands on her arms and began to stroke them up and down.

"Clarice, Clarice," he whispered, "there's no need to go on like this. We can work this out."

He pulled her to him, saying, "Here's what I think. Let's plan a little trip together. Maybe go see Carolyn in Massachusetts. Would you enjoy that? I could buy you a new car and we could make it a road trip. Just you and me."

His mouth was at her ear now. "Just tell me what you want me to do, baby. Tell me what I can do." This was Richmond at his best, Richmond the lover. That part of their relationship had always been perfect. But now, when she thought about his extraordinary abilities in the arena of lovemaking, she was forced to think about the countless hours he'd spent honing those skills with other women.

Clarice put her hand on his chest and pushed him away. She shoved him harder than she meant to and he lost his balance for a second. She was shocked by how good it felt to see him stagger, on the brink of crashing ass-backwards into the glass-topped coffee table.

She said, "Evolve, Richmond. What I want you to do is *evolve*."

He started pacing again, faster this time. "I don't get it. All these years and you pull this on me now. You had plenty of time to say something if you weren't happy. This is on you, Clarice." And more softly, to himself, "This is not my fault."

She could see the gears turning as he tried to figure a way out of this. When he couldn't come up with a way to turn things around, he settled on rage. He stalked up to her and bent over so his square chin was just inches from her nose. His breath hot on his wife's face, Richmond said, "And I'll tell you something, Clarice, I'm not moving out. This is my house every bit as much as it is yours. More, actually, since *I* paid for it. So, you'd better think this foolishness through a little more."

He crossed his arms over his broad chest and stood up straight, looking satisfied that he'd made his point successfully and put her tantrum in its proper place.

Clarice walked out of the living room then, and headed toward the stairs and their bedroom. She said, "That's okay, Richmond. You're welcome to stay here. I'll leave."

That night, after stopping by Odette's place to pick up the keys, Clarice carried a suitcase of clothes and a cosmetics bag into the front door of Mr and Mrs Jackson's old house in Leaning Tree. When her piano was delivered two days later, Clarice inaugurated this new phase of her life by playing Beethoven's melancholy, powerful, and joyful *Les Adieux* Sonata and allowed the second love of her life to reassure her that she'd done the right thing in leaving the first.

Chapter 23

Despite Clarice's pleas, her parents maintained their insistence that Odette chaperone all of their daughter's dates throughout her senior year of high school. Barbara Jean was as disinterested in dating boys as boys were eager to date her, or so it appeared at the time. So she often came along to keep Odette company. From Clarice's standpoint, the situation was tolerable when it was just the Supremes and Richmond out for the evening. Richmond, the lone male among a group of females, enjoyed the appearance that he was keeping a harem. And Odette and Barbara Jean were good about giving her some time alone with Richmond. The arrangement was upended when Barbara Jean began to decline Clarice's invitations in order to spend more time with Chick. Claiming she had taken on extra hours at the salon, Barbara Jean withdrew from the foursome.

So Richmond dragged James Henry along again. Late nights out came to an end and conversations about topsoil resumed. Even on the rare occasions when Clarice was granted an extended curfew, usually as a reward for a well-reviewed piano performance or as a way to end her relentless begging, the presence of sleepy James was guaranteed to cut the evening short. Finally, after one too many nights of getting back home before ten o'clock, Clarice put her foot down and demanded that Richmond find some-one for Odette who kept grown-up hours. That was when Richmond began bringing Ramsey Abrams along to serve as Odette's date.

Ramsey was a night owl, but he was also an idiot. Odette spent the evenings she was paired up with him cruelly mocking the stream of inane blather that poured out of him. And if Ramsey noticed her sharpening her claws on him, he was content to ignore it for the opportunity to spend a few hours ogling Odette's breasts.

Odette didn't appear to be bothered by James's absence from date nights. She only asked Richmond once what had become of James, and that single inquiry was phrased as a question about the health of James's mother. After Richmond told her that Mrs Henry was no better or worse as far as he knew, Odette didn't ask about James again.

Switching out James for Ramsey worked fine as far as Clarice was concerned. She and Richmond saw more of each other than they'd been able to for a long time. They stayed out later, usually meeting at Earl's and then going for a ride or to a party or somewhere in Louisville when they had time. Ramsey had just enough sense not to make the potentially fatal mistake of copping a feel off Odette, and she seemed amused to have Ramsey around to insult. Everybody won.

After several late nights with Ramsey, Odette and Clarice showed up at the All-You-Can-Eat one Friday night in March assuming that Ramsey and Richmond would be waiting for them at the window table. Instead, James Henry sat in the chair to Richmond's left.

Clarice walked over to the table and said hello. Then she took Richmond aside to express her disapproval. She said, "What is *he* doing here?"

Richmond said, "It'll be all right, I swear." In response to her raised eyebrow, he added, "The thing is, James really likes her. He found out I'd been bringing Ramsey along for Odette and he got so mad I was scared he was gonna take a swing at me."

He was exaggerating just a bit. Richmond hadn't really worried that he'd be attacked when James barged into Richmond's dorm room the night before. Either of Richmond's biceps was nearly as big around as James's waist, so even if James had violence on his mind, Richmond knew any danger posed by him was minimal. Still, Richmond had been amazed to see James that agitated. It wasn't James's way.

James had worked like a grown man to help support himself and his mother since he was thirteen years old. In high school, when Richmond and the other guys were playing sports or sharing a bottle of rotgut whiskey in the woods, James was likely to be at home cooking and cleaning. And James never showed any sign of being justifiably pissed off about any of it or even seemed to notice that he was being cheated, not that Richmond saw, at least. But there James had been, jabbing his bony finger into Richmond's chest and yelling about Odette Jackson, of all things. Richmond had wanted to laugh, but instead he promised James he would help him.

Richmond put his big hands on Clarice's arms and slowly slid them from her shoulders to her elbows and back again, trying to massage away her anger.

He said, "It'll be good, really. I told James exactly what to say to her. I gave him some great lines to use. And I filled him up with coffee before we got here. It's going to work. Trust me."

When they got back to the table, James was saying, "So tell your mother she should put herbs in her perennial border to keep pests down." Then James sat back and began silently studying Odette the way he always did after he had run out of gardening talk, as if he were a scientist and she was something rare he'd spotted growing in a petri dish. Odette stared back at James, her mouth set in a scowl. If he had tried any of those good lines Richmond claimed to have given him, Clarice assumed that they must not have worked.

As they sipped pop and ate chicken wings, Richmond and Clarice tried to keep some sort of conversation going. But neither Odette nor James talked. James just watched Odette with a mixture of affection and curiosity while she squinted back at him with an expression that approached fury.

Richmond talked about maybe driving down to Louisville and checking out a dance club he had heard about. Clarice suggested that they stop by a secluded place by the river on the way back.

The plans for the evening were just about finalized when Odette blew up. "What the hell is wrong with you, James Henry?" She leaned toward him until their noses were just inches apart and said, "I'm so sick of you staring at me like I'm gonna sprout another head all of a sudden. This is how I look, James. If you don't like it, you can just go stare at somebody else." She sat back in her chair then.

"Now, you got something to say? Or do you just wanna stare some more?"

James looked surprised and then embarrassed. He broke eye contact with Odette and watched the tabletop for a few seconds. Then James said, "I love you. And I've been thinkin' that if you ever get married, it should be to me."

Odette, Richmond, and Clarice all said, "What?"

He said it again, "I love you, Odette, and I've been thinkin' that if you ever get married it should be to me."

Richmond threw both of his hands in the air in disgust. He said, "I swear to God, Clarice, that is *not* one of the things I told him to say."

Odette narrowed her eyes at James. Clarice could tell that Odette thought he was making fun of her.

But James just sat there, still watching her. Only now he sported a grin on his face, as if he were proud of himself for finally having his say.

Right then, at their table at the All-You-Can-Eat, Clarice saw Odette rendered speechless for the first and last time of their long friendship. Clarice watched as Odette scrutinized James for a good long while. That was when she saw it for the first time, that softness in Odette's face. The lines on Odette's forehead disappeared, her jaw relaxed, and the corners of her mouth tilted up just the tiniest bit. Clarice understood then that she had witnessed more than one unusual sight that evening. She had also seen something Odette was afraid of. All this time, her tough friend had been frightened that this scarred boy might not love her the way she loved him.

Odette had seen enough movies and heard Clarice rhapsodize over Richmond often enough to know that there were things a young woman was supposed to say at a time like this. She tried her hardest to think of one of those things, but nothing came to her. Her mouth dry and her pulse racing, she sensed the onset of what she guessed was panic. But when Odette looked at James's satisfied smile, she was comforted by the certainty that he wasn't a man who would ever need long-winded reassurances or grand pronouncements of affection. And that made her want to wrap her arms around him and hold on till he begged her to let him go.

Odette covered James's hand with hers and nodded her head a couple of times. She said, "Okay then, James, just so's we understand each other."

Chapter 24

Barbara Jean knew that Clarice leaving Richmond and returning to Leaning Tree didn't have anything to do with her; it had been a long time coming. Still, it felt like another piece in the conspiracy the whole world was engaged in, a sinister plot to drag her back into the past and lock her up there. Here they were, the Supremes, gathering again in Leaning Tree, in the same house where they had talked, laughed, and sung along to records on Odette's pink and violet portable record player forty years earlier.

Driving to and from Odette's old house – Clarice's house, now – Barbara Jean saw the Leaning Tree of her girlhood all around her, instead of the one that existed in the present day. Out of the corner of her eye, she spotted landmarks that hadn't stood in decades – Abraham Jordan's law office, the five-and-dime where her mother bought her cosmetics, the carpentry shop Odette's father had once owned. They were there, more real than the large homes and cute, overpriced boutiques that had replaced them, until she blinked her eyes and made them vanish.

The people of the past continued to visit her as well. And when they came – Lester, Adam, Loretta, Chick, Big Earl, Miss Thelma, the other Supremes and herself as young girls – Barbara Jean gave in completely to the past and let the force of it pull her drunken mind along as if it were caught in the tide under the surface of the frozen river she now dreamed about every night.

Lester asked Barbara Jean to marry him on April Fool's Day in 1968. At first she thought he was kidding.

Lester had taken the Supremes, Richmond, and James out to dinner. Being a Monday, it had been an early night. James worked mornings. The girls had school.

Barbara Jean was the last to be dropped off at home that night. Lester parked outside Big Earl and Miss Thelma's house, and she waited for him to jump out of the car and come around to open her door the way he always did. But Lester sat gazing forward as the Cadillac idled. So she said, "Well, good night, Lester," and she reached for the handle to open the door.

Lester put a hand on her shoulder and said, "Hold on a minute, Barbara Jean. There's something I want to talk to you about." He left his hand on her shoulder, the most physical contact they'd ever had, and began to speak.

"Barbara Jean," he said, "I've been trying hard not to make a fool of myself about this, but I'm sure by now you know that I have feelings for you."

She expected him to grin and shout "April Fool!" But he continued with a straight face, and she realized, with as much fear as interest, that he was serious.

"You probably think of me as an old man—"

"No, I don't, Lester," she interrupted.

"It's okay. You're young. When I was your age I thought forty-two was ancient. But, here's the thing. Forty-two isn't really all that old. And you've always seemed like someone more mature than your years. So, I've been thinking that maybe you and me could spend more time together."

When she didn't respond, he added, "Just so you understand, I'm not talking about just messing around or something. I'm talking about you and me really being together. What I want is a wife, Barbara Jean."

She didn't know what to say, so she just nodded and thought, *Boy, were you right about this one, Clarice.*

"You'll be done with school in a couple months and you've probably been thinking about what's ahead for you."

Lester was wrong about that. While Barbara Jean had been raised to always have an eye out for the next opportunity – "You got to be a forward-thinkin' woman if you wanna get anywhere in this world," her mother always said – she had done nothing but try *not* to think about the future since the day she first kissed Chick Carlson in the hallway of the All-You-Can-Eat. And it was becoming increasingly difficult to do. Practically every night, Chick whispered his dreams to her as she lay in his bed with her head resting on his chest. Chick had been reading about cities where they could be together. He made it sound so easy, so possible. They would slip off together to one of the mixed-marriage Promised Lands, maybe Chicago or Detroit, and everything would be perfect. Barbara Jean wanted to fantasize along with him, but where Chick imagined minor inconveniences that they could link arms and breeze right past, Barbara Jean saw impassable obstacles of race, ignorance, and rage. So she let Chick talk about an idyllic tomorrow, but she blocked out his words and only listened to the sound of his heartbeat.

Lester continued, "I just want you to know that I'd like to be a part of your thinking. I've got a fair amount of money. And if things go the way I believe they will, I'll have a lot more soon. I could certainly take care of you and give you anything you might want. Not that I'm trying to buy you, or anything like that. I just thought you should know that I can take care of you right. I could even buy you Ballard House and fix it up for you, if you want. I remember how much you said you liked it."

"I did?" Barbara Jean asked, not recalling having said any such thing.

"Yeah, that first time you rode in my car, when we passed by the house you said, 'Look at that place. I'd love to live in something like that.'"

Barbara Jean had thought that very thing every time she passed the house, but she didn't realize she had ever said it out loud. But Lester had heard her and remembered all these months later. It touched her heart.

"You don't have to decide anything right now. I know this probably isn't what you were expecting to hear from me today," he said. "I'm going to be away in Indianapolis for the next week and a half to do some business. You can think about it and give me an answer when I get back."

The only words Barbara Jean could think to say were "Thank you, Lester." So she left it at that.

Lester took his hand away from her shoulder. Then he leaned in and planted a kiss on her cheek. He slid away from her and hopped out of the car. Then he walked around to the passenger side and opened it. Again, she said, "Thank you, Lester."

She hurried up the walkway to Big Earl and Miss Thelma's house without glancing back and she let herself in. As she climbed the stairs to her room, Barbara Jean thought of her mother. When Loretta was dying, she had spent hours looking back at her life and listing the ways the world had wronged and cheated her. The main thing she had been denied was "a man who could look me in the eye and swear that he'd be my man forever and that he would always do right by me and my baby." Now, after what Lester had just said to Barbara Jean in his car, she heard the voice of her mother panting in her ear, "This is it, girl, what we been waitin' for."

When she got to her room that night and peered out of the window, she saw that the light was on in the storeroom of the All-You-Can-Eat. But she pulled down her window shade and didn't go to see Chick.

For two days, Barbara Jean kept what Lester had said to her all to herself, hoping that an answer would come if she thought about it long enough. She stayed behind her locked bedroom door and avoided everyone. If asked, she claimed to be sick, which was half true because holding her secret inside made her stomach churn throughout each of those days. And her shade remained drawn, because she knew that if she stared too long at the storeroom light across the street, she would run to Chick and the decision would be made for her.

Finally she had to let it out, so she called a meeting of the Supremes. In the gazebo behind Odette's house, the very one that she and Chick had sneaked off to so many times, she told Odette and Clarice about Lester's proposal.

Clarice was overjoyed. She said, "See? See? I told you Lester was interested in you. You told him yes, didn't you?"

"I told him I'd think about it."

"What's there to think about?" Clarice asked. "There's not a colored woman in town who wouldn't jump at the chance to have Lester. Veronica's been trying to get him to notice her since she was thirteen. You'd better lay claim to him while you can, or somebody else'll beat you to it."

Odette didn't say a word while Clarice went on and on about Lester's proposal as if it were the greatest thing that had ever happened to anyone in the world. Barbara Jean thought that Clarice sounded as excited about this as she did when she talked about herself and Richmond. Clarice stood up from the wooden bench that lined the lattice walls of the gazebo and walked in a tight circle, already planning Barbara Jean's wedding.

Clarice named ten girls from their high school, in descending order of height, who would make the best bridesmaids. She rattled off a full menu of foreign-sounding foods Barbara Jean had never heard of, freely spending Lester's money.

Barbara Jean asked her to stop, saying that she had to think about it. Clarice countered, "Lester is a nice guy, and he has all kinds of money. He's a little on the short side, but he's handsome. I don't see what's holding you back. Do you, Odette?"

That was when Odette said it, just as casual as can be. "Well, Barbara Jean's in love with Chick."

Clarice said, "Chick? What are you talking about?"

"They've been together for months. Don't you have eyes, Clarice?"

Barbara Jean stared at Odette, unnerved by what her friend had just said. Being in love with James seemed to have imbued Odette with a hypersensitivity to other people's feelings that hadn't been there before. This new, greater power of observation, combined with Odette's tendency to say what was on her mind, made her kind of spooky in addition to being a pain in the neck.

Clarice turned to Barbara Jean and asked, "Is that true?"

Barbara Jean was going to lie, but she looked at Odette's face. Odette cast her open, accepting gaze on Barbara Jean and the truth came on out. Barbara Jean described the first time she kissed Chick. She told them about the nights they had shared in the storeroom. She repeated to them what Chick had said to her about the two of them running away together to Chicago or Detroit, how couples like them weren't a big deal there and they could get married.

Odette said, "You should go talk to Big Earl, see what he has to say about it."

"I can't do that. What am I going to say? 'Guess what, Big Earl, I've been sneaking out of the house you invited me into and going over to fuck the white busboy in your storeroom.' I can't have him thinking of me that way. I can't have him thinking I'm like . . ."

Barbara Jean stopped there, but Clarice and Odette both knew how that sentence ended.

Clarice always thought of herself as the most practical of the three of them. She said, "Chick's sweet. And he's good-looking. But he's got no money and no prospects that I can see. Plus, there's his brother to think about."

They had all seen Desmond Carlson driving slowly past the All-You-Can-Eat in his red truck at least once a week over the past several months. He never came inside the restaurant to cause trouble; Big Earl wouldn't have tolerated anything like that, and Desmond knew it. But if he caught sight of his brother through the window as he cruised by, he made obscene gestures and called his brother out to fight before eventually giving up and speeding away.

Clarice said, "That crazy redneck brother of Chick's will track you both down and kill you even if you make it to Chicago or Detroit."

Barbara Jean didn't respond to that because the truth of it was clear. And it wasn't only Desmond Carlson. There were plenty of folks in Plainview, black and white, who'd happily have seen Chick and Barbara Jean dead rather than see them together. That was just how things were.

When the silence stretched out a while longer, Clarice assumed that the debate was over and that Barbara Jean had seen that she was right. She went back to planning a huge spectacle of a wedding for Barbara Jean. Clarice kept it up during the ride from Odette's house and didn't stop until Barbara Jean jumped out of her car in front of Big Earl's.

In her heart, Barbara Jean knew Clarice was right; there was only one choice that made good sense. But the gorgeous picture Clarice painted of a hand-embroidered wedding dress with a ten-foot lace train battled an even more exquisite image in Barbara Jean's head, the vision of what she truly wanted.

In the years that came later, Barbara Jean would

imagine what might have happened if she had been more like Odette when she was young. Maybe if she'd had more courage, she could have told common sense to kiss her ass and run straight at that sweet vision of a life with Chick in Detroit or Chicago or anywhere. Maybe if she had been braver, her boy would have lived.

Chapter 25

On April 4, 1968, the night after Barbara Jean talked with Odette and Clarice in Mrs Jackson's gazebo, Dr Martin Luther King, Jr, was murdered in Memphis. Both Chicago and Detroit, the potential escape routes for Chick and Barbara Jean, went up in flames.

Barbara Jean, Miss Thelma, and Little Earl watched TV as a parade of solemn white male faces tried to explain to white America just what had been lost that day. Big Earl came home late that night. As soon as he'd shut the front door, Miss Thelma asked, "Where you been? I saw the lights go out over across the street almost an hour ago. You had me worried."

"I drove Ray to his brother's place," he said.

"What? You went over there with them crazy-ass hillbillies? Are you outta your mind?"

Big Earl said, "Those folks are too damn happy to be thinkin' about me, or Chick, or anything but their good news. Besides, there was some trouble over at the restaurant, and I didn't want him to be there by himself all night."

Miss Thelma saved Barbara Jean from having to ask what had happened by saying, "What kinda trouble?"

"Not much, just Ramsey and some of his friends actin' stupid. They lost what little sense they have and decided they had to beat down a white man. So Ramsey started in on Ray."

Barbara Jean's heart began pounding so hard that she was sure everyone in the room could hear it.

Miss Thelma asked, "Ray all right?"

Big Earl laughed. "He's fine. Odette and James was there, and they stepped into it. Make that girl mad and you got somethin' fierce on your hands. I had to pull her off of Ramsey myself. And he's gonna have a nasty black eye tomorrow. That'll teach 'im not to act a fool."

"No, it won't," Miss Thelma said.

Big Earl nodded. "You're right. It won't."

"You shoulda brought Ray over here to stay, 'stead of takin' him to his brother," Miss Thelma said.

"I asked, but he said he didn't wanna come. Something's goin' on with him."

When Big Earl said that, Barbara Jean could've sworn he was staring at her. But she told herself it had to be her imagination; she hadn't been able to think straight since Lester had asked her to marry him. As she sat with the McIntyres and took in replay after replay of the ugly story on the TV news, she thought about the boy she loved, sitting in a cold shack in a section of town where people were at that moment firing shotguns into the air in celebration.

Plainview shut down in the days after Dr King was killed. The university was so afraid that its handful of black students would start a riot that classes were canceled. Some white neighborhoods put up barricades. People were afraid to travel about, so businesses temporarily closed their doors. Some business owners who had seen what was happening in big cities around the country stayed in their places twenty-four hours a day with shotguns on their laps, waiting for looters. Big Earl was one of the few people who understood from the beginning that Plainview wasn't going to explode. He kept his restaurant open every day.

The afternoon after Dr King died, Barbara Jean stopped by the All-You-Can-Eat. Clarice met her just inside the door. She grabbed Barbara Jean's arm and pulled her toward their window table, where Odette sat waiting. After she led Barbara Jean to her seat, words rushed from Clarice's mouth. "I'm so sorry, Barbara Jean. The only person I told was my mother."

Barbara Jean didn't understand what Clarice was saying at first. But she figured it out fast enough when she glanced around and realized that most of the eyes in the room were on her. She realized then that she was looking at a restaurant full of people who knew her secrets.

"Jesus Christ, Clarice," she said.

"I'm sorry, I'm so sorry. Everybody was so upset last night. I was trying to think of good things to keep our minds off of the bad stuff on TV and it just slipped out. Mother said she wouldn't tell, but she must've told Aunt Glory and Aunt Glory must've told Veronica. And, well, you know that Veronica. She's got such a big mouth."

Odette spoke for the first time. "*Veronica's* got a big mouth?" Then Odette slapped Clarice's arm so hard it made her cry out, "Ouch!"

Veronica and two other girls from school started walking their way. As they came closer, Clarice whispered, "I never said a word about Chick, I swear to God. Just Lester."

Veronica smirked that way people do when they know more of someone else's business than they should. She said, "So your work paid off, I guess. I've got to hand it to you. It didn't even look like you were trying. So, when's the wedding?"

Her friends joined in asking questions. They didn't really care if Barbara Jean responded at all. This was the stage of gossip when getting the facts from the horse's mouth only interfered with the fun of it all.

Barbara Jean couldn't have answered anyway; she was too busy looking around the room for Chick. Until then, the notion of becoming engaged to Lester had been kind of like a fantasy to her, an interesting story to share with her best girlfriends. Now it was out in the world, the property of others, not just Barbara Jean and the other Supremes. It was something real. Now it had the power to hurt people. She excused herself from the window table, brushing past Veronica and her friends on her way to Chick.

He was sitting on the corner of his bed when she walked into the storeroom. He wore his food-stained work apron and his hair was covered with a net. Before Barbara Jean could say anything, he spat out, "Were you going to tell me about it, or were you just going to invite me to the wedding?"

"I didn't tell you about it because I knew you'd get upset. And there was really nothing to say. I didn't tell Lester I was going to marry him."

"What did you tell him, then?"

"I told him I'd think about it."

Chick stood up from the bed then and said, "*Think about it?* What's there to think about?"

"There's a whole lot to think about, Chick. There's my life to think about. There's my future to think about." In the voice of her mother, Barbara Jean heard herself say, "I've got to be a forward-thinking woman. And a forward-thinking woman looks out for herself."

Chick's voice cracked as he spoke. His usual deep, smooth tone went high, almost childlike. "I thought you were going to let *me* look out for you. I thought you were going to be with *me*."

"I can't be with you, and you know it. We've been back here playing around and pretending like it could work out, but we both know it can't."

"We can get married. It's been legal here for two years."

"Legal's one thing. What they'll beat you down and string you up for is another."

"Then we'll get married and go someplace else. We've talked about it before. We could go to Chicago or Detroit. There are couples like us there and nobody even thinks a thing about it."

"Haven't you heard the news? The Promised Lands are on fire. If we tried walking down the street together in Chicago or Detroit, we wouldn't make it half a block before our heads got busted open."

He said, "I'll figure out a way to make it work. There are plenty of other places we can go."

"No, there aren't, and you know it. The best we can hope for is to run away somewhere and find somebody like Big Earl who'd let us hole up in a little dump of a room like this." She gestured around the storeroom. "And what about your brother? He's been driving up and down the street for months now waiting for his chance to catch you outside alone just because you work for a black man. Now you want to tell him that you're going to have a black wife? Do you honestly think he'd let you shame him by marrying me? You think he wouldn't hunt you down and hurt you worse than he ever has? And wherever we go, we'd be lucky to get through a day without getting spit on. Chick, you don't know what it's like to have everybody look down on you, point at you, and treat you like you're less than nothing. You think you know, but you don't. I lived that way almost all my life until this last year and I can't go back to it. I can't."

"What are you saying, Barbara Jean?"

She took a deep breath and tried to hold back the tears that wanted so badly to come out, and then she said what she had avoided saying all week. "I'm saying I'm going to marry Lester."

Chick didn't try to, or couldn't, stop tears from flowing down his cheeks as he yelled, "You love me. I know you love me," making it sound like an accusation.

She answered automatically and honestly without thinking. She said, "Yes. I love you." Barbara Jean felt her will beginning to dissolve. She wanted to grab him and pull him into the bed with her with no thought of who might find them together. But then she felt the hand of her mother pushing her toward the door of the room just as surely as if Loretta had been alive and breathing. As Barbara Jean backed out of the storeroom, Loretta used her daughter's mouth to say, "But love ain't never put a bite of food on any table."

She couldn't face her friends or the gossipmongers in the dining room of the All-You-Can-Eat, so Barbara Jean slipped out the back door. In the alley behind the restaurant, she felt her stomach lurch and she had to bend over and gasp for air. When she got her nerves and her stomach calmed down, she walked around the block. Then she hurried over to the alley behind the next street, so she could enter Big Earl and Miss Thelma's house from the back and not be seen by her friends at the restaurant. By the time Barbara Jean let herself into the back door of the house, she had started to feel a little bit better. She told herself that she had done the right thing for herself, and for Chick, too. This was the first step into a new and improved life, the life she deserved. But she hadn't anticipated what that old comedian God had in mind for her.

Chapter 26

I never thought I'd live to see the day when Clarice walked out on Richmond. I'd thought of them as a couple since we were children and he would tease her by hurling walnuts at her and yelling "Time bomb!" as she ran away. They were lovers before any of us knew what lovers were. Now Clarice had gone and shocked me by moving to Leaning Tree. I couldn't help but join the crowd who studied them like they were a couple of curiosities in a traveling freak show.

Many things were still the same. Clarice and Richmond got together each Sunday to attend morning services at Calvary Baptist. They still came to the All-You-Can-Eat and sat at their usual places at the table.

But Clarice had given up pretending to have a good time at Calvary. The hardcore, fire-and-brimstone services she once used as a yardstick to measure all other churches with – and find the others lacking – weren't bringing her the same satisfaction anymore. She'd started complaining about how judgmental the congregation was encouraged to be – which, frankly, I'd always thought was one of the things she enjoyed most about the place. And she didn't bother to hide her annoyance with Reverend Peterson, who had met with her twice already to remind her of her duties as a Christian wife and to express his disappointment at her "unfortunate recent behavior." She had some especially harsh words for Calvary Baptist and her pastor after she opened the weekly bulletin at church and found her name on the prayer list alongside the names of misfits, troubled children, and other notorious backsliders from the congregation.

There were physical changes, too. I had called upon Barbara Jean's old hairdressing skills one Saturday and had her shave what was left of my hair until it was just a bit of black and gray fluff clinging to my scalp. The second I vacated the makeshift barber chair we'd set up in my kitchen, Clarice hopped into it and ordered Barbara Jean to cut her hair almost as short. She claimed she did it because, after fifty years of dealing with heat, rollers, chemicals, and pins to keep her long hair perfectly styled, she wanted something that required less maintenance. But Barbara Jean and I both thought she did it to get back at Richmond for having her name put on the backsliders' prayer list. She'd kept her hair long for years because he liked it that way. Now Clarice was determined to show him that she had laid claim to her own head in more ways than one.

I could tell that Clarice was filling at least some of her post-Richmond time with music. She had fallen back into her habit of humming quietly to herself and absentmindedly tapping out piano fingerings on whatever surface her hands happened to land on, a practice we'd teased her about back when we were young and she was still performing regularly. Clarice was more cheerful and more relaxed than I'd seen her in years, maybe ever.

Richmond changed even more than Clarice. Without his wife around to dress and tend to him, our stylish, pressed, and polished Richmond was revealed to be a color-blind man who clearly didn't know how to operate a steam iron. Richmond, who had always been so easygoing and relaxed, now spent most of our Sunday suppers staring at Clarice and chewing on his lower lip. Depending on his mood, he either ate the most diabetic-friendly things on the buffet, showing his plate to Clarice for her approval, or he took heaping bowls of sweets from the dessert table and dug into them with a fury while glaring at her. But he couldn't get a rise out of her. The most Clarice would say in response was "Try not to kill yourself. It might upset the kids."

The biggest change, though, was that now it was Richmond, not Clarice, who presented a fantasy to the world about their relationship. He had spread the word that Clarice had rented Mama and Daddy's old house in Leaning Tree because so many of her piano students lived in the new subdivisions over there. Everyone who knew them knew that she had moved out, but he insisted on repeating the fiction that Clarice went to her studio in Leaning Tree to practice and teach every day and then came back to him each night. I always thought I'd enjoy seeing Richmond get a good hard kick in the ass, but it was sad to see the mighty Richmond Baker reduced to spreading such tales.

Like his attitude toward Clarice, Richmond's feelings about me changed from week to week. He didn't know whether he should blame me for Clarice leaving him and react with open hostility or see me as a way back into his wife's good graces and ladle on the sweet talk. That week, as we sat waiting for Barbara Jean to arrive at the All-You-Can-Eat, he was being overly polite to me, inquiring about my health and complimenting a dress he must've seen a hundred times before. It all came across as awkward and forced. Poor Richmond didn't wear desperation well.

I heard Clarice issue a groan and I looked over my shoulder to see her cousin walking across the street toward the restaurant in the company of Minnie McIntyre. Minnie was swallowed up by her new fortune-telling outfit, a dramatically oversized silver robe that billowed out around her in the breeze as she crossed the street. Veronica, all done up for church, moved alongside Minnie with her jerky half-running walk. Together they looked like a Fourth of July parade float and the local beauty queen who'd just fallen off of it.

They entered the restaurant and Minnie headed for her fortune-telling table. Veronica took a detour in our direction. She had her daughter's wedding book under her arm. This was the "official wedding book." Twice as thick as the duplicate book she had given to Clarice, it overflowed with bits of paper and cloth.

Veronica said to Clarice, "I've got all kinds of stuff to tell you as soon as my reading's done." She took two steps away and then hustled back. "Let me show you this one thing, though."

She sat in Barbara Jean's chair and then dropped the heavy book down on the table. It made a loud thud and caused the tableware to teeter so wildly that all of us had to grab our water glasses to steady them. She opened the wedding book and said, "I went to Madame Minnie and told her about the problems I was having over at First Baptist about the wedding. Can you believe that after all I've done for them they refused to let me release doves inside the chapel? I explained to them that the doves were from Boston and were sophisticated and all, and that these doves would just as soon die of embarrassment as make a mess. But they wouldn't listen.

"Well, I talked to Madame Minnie about it and she told me to take a drive and the answer would come to me. I did what she said, and I found my answer at the corner of College Boulevard and Second Avenue. Here it is." She tilted one end of the wedding book so we could all see a brochure she'd clipped in. On the cover of the brochure was a picture of a two-story white building whose entrance-way was framed by several tall columns. Parked outside the building was a white carriage hitched to two white horses with white feathers attached to their heads. The caption beneath the picture read "Garden Hills Banquet Hall and Corporate Meetings Venue."

Veronica said, "Isn't it perfect? The inner courtyard can seat almost as many people as First Baptist. And we can have the ceremony, cocktails, sit-down dinner, and danc-ing all in the same place."

"The courtyard? Isn't that outside?" Clarice asked.

Veronica rolled her eyes and said, "Of course it is. That's why it's called a courtyard, Clarice."

Clarice ignored the eye-rolling. "You want to have a wedding outdoors in southern Indiana? In July?"

Veronica said, "I have to have it outside. Truth is, the banquet hall wasn't much happier about the doves than the church was. They were going to charge me an arm and a leg for a cleanup fee if I had the wedding inside. Not that money is an object, mind you. I consulted Madame Minnie about the weather and Charlemagne assured her it would be perfect. Also, the laser lights will look better outdoors."

Clarice said, "It's bad luck not to get married in a church."

"No offense, cousin, but you had your wedding in a church and look where it got you," Veronica replied.

Of its own free will, my hand started moving toward an overfilled glass of water that sat dangerously close to the edge of the table just to Veronica's right. I was an inch away from accidentally tipping the glass into Veronica's lap when Clarice grabbed ahold of my arm. She moved the water glass to a safer spot on the table and warned me with her eyes not to give in to immaturity again. Minnie approached the window table then, her silver robe rustling as she swept across the floor. Veronica said to her, "I'm sorry to keep you waiting, Madame Minnie. I just had to tell them about the exciting things happening with the wedding. It's really all her doing," she said, pointing at Minnie. "Everything is happening just like she foresaw it."

Minnie pointed her nose toward the ceiling and said, "I am only partially of this earth. My true essence is already on the spirit plane."

I was glad Mama wasn't hovering around that day. I wouldn't have been able to keep a straight face. Of course, Mama would have started cussing and carrying on as soon as she heard Veronica say "Madame Minnie."

Veronica chimed in, "And get a load of this." She opened the wedding book to a different page and pointed to a newspaper ad that she'd pasted inside. The ad was for a hypnotherapist in Louisville. "Madame Minnie has a friend who does hypnosis. I've been taking Sharon to see him and, let me tell you, it's a miracle. She's dropping pounds right and left. The hypnotist puts her in a recliner, lights some scented candles, whispers in her ear for a while, and she walks out terrified of starchy foods. That girl sees a crouton on top of her salad and she runs screaming from the room." Veronica clapped her hands together and grinned so broadly that we saw every filling in her teeth. "Sharon can almost fit into the gown I picked out for her."

Minnie took a bow to acknowledge her latest accomplishment. The bell on her turban rang, but it was drowned out by the sound of the bell over the doorway of the restaurant as Yvonne Wilson, one of Minnie's longtime regulars, entered.

Yvonne was pregnant with her seventh child. Two of her older girls, both dusted in powdered sugar from chin to waist courtesy of the Donut Heaven treats they were eating, tagged along behind her. Yvonne had been one of Minnie's fortune-telling customers for years and was one of the few who were dumb enough to actually heed her advice over the long haul. Minnie had told Yvonne a decade earlier that she would have a baby who was so beautiful and talented that he or she would make Yvonne and her boyfriend into showbiz millionaires. Yvonne foolishly believed Minnie and commenced to pop out baby after baby, waiting for the miraculous moneymaking child to arrive. With every birth she would run to Minnie and ask, "Is this the one?" Each time, Minnie would take her money and then tell her that Charlemagne said to try again. Now Yvonne had six homely, untalented children, and she still hadn't figured out that Minnie was playing a mean-spirited trick on her.

Yvonne walked up to Minnie and, rubbing her belly, said, "I had a dream last night that this one was tap-dancing on the hood of a gold Rolls-Royce. I need a reading right away."

Veronica said, "You go ahead, Yvonne, I've got some other things to show Clarice. I'll get my reading after you."

Yvonne thanked Veronica and ordered her daughters, whom she had optimistically named Star and Desiree, to sit quietly at a nearby table and wait for her. Then she followed Minnie to the crystal ball in the corner.

When they were gone, Veronica said, "Here's the big news. Sharon's going to be the first in town to have the Cloud Nine Wedding Package." She opened the wedding book to the page with the banquet hall brochure. She removed the brochure from the book and showed us a picture on the back cover. It appeared to be a photograph of a huge pink marshmallow squeezing through a doorway.

"That's the cloud," Veronica said. "The party enters and leaves through a lavender-scented pink cloud. Everybody in New York is doing it."

She shared more details about the Cloud Nine Wedding Package, dwelling particularly on its high cost. She told us how every aspect of the wedding had been timed to perfection. She peppered her conversation with catty little comments about Clarice's daughter's wedding that Clarice pretended not to notice.

I'd had just about enough of Veronica and was about to

make another try at dumping the glass of water in her lap when Clarice spoke up during a brief pause in Veronica's monologue. She glanced at her watch and said, "I wonder what's keeping Barbara Jean."

Veronica said, "I figured she must be sick. She didn't come to church today."

Clarice raised an eyebrow and looked in my direction. "Maybe she was just too tired to go today."

Veronica shrugged and said, "I see Madame Minnie is finishing up. I'd better get going. I'll call you tonight, Clarice." Veronica left us and trotted across the room to where Yvonne Wilson was thanking Minnie and corralling her daughters.

Clarice said, "How Veronica can waste her money on such idiocy is a mystery to me."

From across the room Minnie yelled, "I heard that, Clarice!"

That old woman's good hearing never ceased to amaze me.

Fifteen minutes later, Barbara Jean still hadn't appeared. Clarice and I debated whether we should go over to her house and see how she was doing – I was for, Clarice was against. I had just about talked Clarice into getting a quick bite from the buffet and then walking over to Barbara Jean's when we looked out the window and saw her car pulling up on the other side of the street.

The Mercedes crawled slowly into a parking space, thumping the curb repeatedly as she backed up, drove forward, backed up, drove forward in a vain attempt to straighten out the car in a space that could have fit four vehicles of its size. She stopped with the front passenger side tire up on the curb. Barbara Jean sat there for a long while, looking straight ahead. We watched her, wondering what was going on. Then we saw her slump forward until her forehead came to a rest on the steering wheel.

Clarice and I both got up and went out, running across the street to the car. Clarice got there first and opened the driver's-side door. I went around to the other side and climbed in.

Barbara Jean was weeping and rolling her forehead back and forth on the top edge of the steering wheel. She asked, "How could this happen? How did I end up like this?" But she didn't seem to be addressing anyone in particular. When she looked up at me her lovely, exotic eyes were bloodshot and her breath had the sweet, grassy odor of whiskey, something I'd never known her to drink.

It was a raw, early spring day and there were just a few people out on the street, but they were beginning to look in our direction. We were also attracting attention from the All-You-Can-Eat across the way. Clarice shut the driver's-side door of the car and came around to my side. She leaned down and whispered in my ear, "Odette, she's wet herself."

I looked over and saw that, sure enough, the pale green of Barbara Jean's skirt was stained dark with urine from her waist nearly to her knees. I took the keys from the ignition and told Clarice to stay with Barbara Jean. Then I went back to the restaurant to tell James what was happening. I handed off her keys to him and asked him to deal with her car. I went back outside and pulled our car up between Barbara Jean's Mercedes and the All-You-Can-Eat's windows so Clarice and I could transfer her to my car out of eyeshot of the restaurant's curious patrons. Once we got Barbara Jean into the backseat of my Honda, Clarice and I drove her back to her house, cleaned her up, and then put her to bed.

We waited four hours for Barbara Jean to wake up. Clarice and I spent the time chatting about Richmond, the garden at the house in Leaning Tree, the music she was playing now that her piano technique was back, my chemo – everything but what had happened earlier across the street from the All-You-Can-Eat.

When Barbara Jean came down from her room, Clarice headed into the kitchen and began to search through the refrigerator for something to fix for dinner. As Clarice boiled up noodles, she settled into some familiar, comfortable denial. She said, "Barbara Jean, you're going to be just fine. You just have to make sure you get enough rest and enough to eat. It's a nutrition issue, mostly."

I wanted to join in and make the same excuses we had always made rather than deal with what was staring us in the face. But things had changed now. I was a sick woman who saw ghosts. I didn't have the strength or inclination to lie anymore.

I said, "Stop it, Clarice. We've all gotta put an end to this right here and now."

I turned to Barbara Jean, who sat across from me on a chrome-and-leather stool at the butcher-block kitchen island. "Barbara Jean, earlier today you got drunk and got behind the wheel of your car. You could've killed somebody. You could've killed a child." Both Clarice and Barbara Jean gasped when I said that. And, looking back, I suppose that it was just about the meanest thing I could've

said. But I was on a roll and I wasn't going to let politeness
interfere with what I had to say, what I should have said so
many years earlier.

"You drove drunk and you pissed on yourself in public,
Barbara Jean. There's no way to pass that off as anything
but what it is.

"The way I see it, now that Lester's gone, this is my
business." I gestured at Clarice. "*Our* business, because we
both love you."

Barbara Jean spoke for the first time since I'd started the
off-the-cuff intervention. She said, "Today was a hard day,
Odette. You don't understand."

"You're right. I don't understand. I probably can't. My
husband's healthy. My children are alive. I'm not saying
you don't have cause. I'm saying you're an alcoholic who
pissed her panties in downtown Plainview. And I'm saying
that I can't watch you do this to yourself. I've got enough
on my hands dealing with *my* disease. I can't deal with
yours, too. The cancer's all I can handle right now."

"Odette, please," Barbara Jean said.

But I had played the cancer card, and I wasn't ashamed
to follow through. I said, "Barbara Jean, I might not live to
see you have that moment of clarity that tells you to stop
drinking on your own. So I'm telling you, loud and clear.
You're gonna put a stop to this shit before it kills you.
Tomorrow, Clarice and I will pick you up and drive you to
Alcoholics Anonymous."

The AA thing just came to me all of a sudden and I had
no idea where we'd find a meeting. But even though
Plainview was a small town to those of us who'd grown up
here, it was really a small city now, especially if you added

in the university. And every city in the country had at least one AA meeting a day, didn't it? I added, "If you're not ready and waiting when we drive up, I'm washing my hands of you."

Clarice cried out, "Odette, you don't mean that." Then, to Barbara Jean, "She doesn't mean that. She's just worked up."

She was right. I couldn't really have washed my hands of Barbara Jean, but I was hoping that Barbara Jean was too messed up to know that. I drove the point home. I said, "Barbara Jean, I won't spend what might be my last days dealing with a damn drunk. I've got too much on my plate."

I couldn't think of anything more to say to Barbara Jean, so I turned to Clarice. "And, speaking of plates, what's with those noodles, Clarice? I didn't get my supper today and I'd better put something in my stomach."

We ate and didn't talk about AA for the rest of the evening.

Aside from putting together a good meal from the odds and ends in Barbara Jean's refrigerator, Clarice did a nice job of keeping our minds off what had happened. She made us laugh talking about Sharon's wedding, which we decided to start calling "Veronica's wedding" since that was more accurate.

Clarice said that, for Sharon's sake, she was trying to inject some small touches of good taste into the spectacle Veronica was designing. The more she talked, the more excited she became. It reminded me of how she'd gotten such big kicks, and big disappointments, out of planning Barbara Jean's wedding and mine.

She claimed to be a fan of understatement now, but decades earlier Clarice had tried to convince both Barbara Jean and me that we had to have at least a dozen bridesmaids because it was unlikely you could get your picture in *Jet* magazine with any fewer. She'd also insisted that we had to have our ceremonies at Calvary Baptist instead of our own churches because Calvary's beautiful stained glass and the painting of sexy Jesus above the baptismal pool made for the best wedding photos.

Clarice's wedding to Richmond did get covered in *Jet* – because of his football career and her historic birth and piano prizes. But things didn't go as she'd planned for Barbara Jean and me. I married James in my mother's garden with just Clarice and Barbara Jean as bridesmaids.

The day after our high school graduation, Barbara Jean married Lester in the pastor's office at First Baptist with just Big Earl, Miss Thelma, and Lester's mother in attendance. The big wedding Clarice had dreamed of for her was out of the question since Barbara Jean was well into her fourth month with Adam by then and was starting to show.

Chapter 27

AA meetings made Barbara Jean want to drink. She sat and listened to people whine about the hardships that had led them to gather in a basement room of the administration building at University Hospital, where they were served the harshest coffee Barbara Jean had ever tasted – but good pastries, thanks to Donut Heaven. They'd tell their tales of woe and Barbara Jean would think, *I can top that*. But she never said anything herself during those first meetings, nothing honest, at least. She went twice a week, and at the end of each meeting she left feeling that she was fully justified in having a little cocktail as a reward for having sat through it. Still, she declared her AA experience a success because she now drank about half as much as she had been drinking before. At least it seemed like half as much to her.

She patted herself on the back for throwing out most of the alcohol in her house. Though, naturally, she had to keep some beer and wine on hand for guests. And she saw no reason to toss out the whiskey, since she hardly ever drank that anyway. She stopped carrying around liquor in her thermos to her volunteer jobs, most days. She didn't drink before 5:00 p.m., more often than not. And she let the calendar determine the extent of her late-night drinking. She only drank on dates that had some particular importance – holidays, birthdays, special anniversaries, things like that. So, if she was drinking every night, it was just because it was April. That month being a minefield of significant dates was hardly her fault.

On April 11, 1968, one week after Dr King was shot dead, Miss Thelma tired of watching Barbara Jean mope around the house and struggle to keep her food down. So she sent her to the clinic at University Hospital. The next day, which was the day Lester was due back to hear Barbara Jean's answer to his proposal of marriage, she returned to the clinic and learned that she was pregnant.

Barbara Jean was seventeen, no husband, no family – more or less the same situation her mother had faced in 1950. But Barbara Jean was relieved when she found out. By the time she walked the distance from the clinic to the All-You-Can-Eat, she actually felt joyous. The decision she had made to choose Lester was suddenly unmade. She had leaped off a tall building and discovered that the pavement was made of rubber. Marrying Lester was out now. Chick and Barbara Jean would have to create a life together somehow. Detroit, Chicago, Los Angeles. Any city, burning or not, would have to do.

When she got to the All-You-Can-Eat, the after-work rush was on. Barbara Jean saw Little Earl running from table to table taking drink orders and clearing plates, but she didn't see Chick. She walked through the dining room and down the back hallway and looked into the kitchen. Still no Chick. Big Earl was alone there, so busy slinging pots and pans around that he didn't notice her sticking her head in. She went to the storeroom then.

Barbara Jean knocked lightly on the storeroom door and whispered, "Ray?" No one answered. She pushed open the door and walked into the dark room. Groping along the wall, she found the light switch and turned it on. Everything of Chick's was gone. The bed was there, but it was stripped of its sheets and blankets. His books and magazines were no longer stacked on the homemade shelves. His clothes were missing from the hooks Big Earl had screwed into the walls. She stepped further inside and turned in a circle as if she might find him secreted away in a corner of the tiny room. The one thing she did find was the Timex she had given him for his birthday, a day that now seemed as if it were a thousand years in the past. The watch rested atop a stack of cans at the side of the bed surrounded by tiny bits of glass from its smashed crystal. She picked up the watch and squeezed it tight, feeling the broken glass bite into her palm.

She heard Big Earl's rumbling voice behind her. "Barbara Jean, you all right?"

"I was looking for Ray," she said.

Big Earl walked into the storeroom, making the space seem even smaller with his massive presence. He stood there wiping his hands on his apron and said, "Ray quit last night, baby. Said he was movin' on."

Barbara Jean managed not to shout when she asked, "Did he say where he was going?"

"No, he just said he had to go." He put a hand on her shoulder. "Maybe this is the best thing for you two, for now, at least."

Barbara Jean nodded, not knowing what to say. Then she took off. She hurried out of the All-You-Can-Eat and headed up the street. First walking, then running, she went in the direction of Main Street and then over to Wall Road. She had a hard time remembering the way, but eventually she found the winding gravel and dirt route that led to the house Chick had once shared with his brother.

She was covered in perspiration and gasping for breath when Desmond Carlson's place came into view. She saw the big red truck Desmond used to chase people off Wall Road sitting on a bald patch in the center of the overgrown field of weeds that passed for a front lawn. The sun had set by then and the property was dark except for the pulsating blue light of a television shining through one of the windows. She hurried out back and found the rundown old shed that Chick had called home. For the second time that night, Barbara Jean searched an empty room. The moonlight beaming in from the open door provided just enough light for her to see that the few personal belongings she had taken note of on her previous visits when she and Chick had come there to lie together on his narrow cot had vanished. The two posters of eagles in flight, the photograph of his mother and father, the ratty blue sleeping bag covered with crudely cut rectangular patches – all of it gone.

But then, just when she thought she would lose her mind from despair, she turned and saw him standing in the doorway. She shouted, "Ray!" and ran the few steps to him.

Not Ray, she realized when she was close enough to

smell the sour odor of his sweat and feel his breath on her face.

Desmond Carlson reached up and pulled a chain to light the bare bulb that hung from the ceiling so that they could both see each other. The thing that struck Barbara Jean about Desmond, whom she had never seen up close before this moment, was how much he resembled Ray. They had the same height and build, although Desmond was considerably heavier around the waist – a drinker's body. Their features were similar, but the mouth Barbara Jean had known so well as a feature of Chick's face was misshapen on his brother due to a white scar that ran from just below his nose to the cleft in his chin. And Desmond's nose looked slightly off-kilter, the result, she imagined, of a long-ago fight. Still, the life he led had only damaged him slightly. This man, who had caused so much turmoil and become the symbol of everything scary and evil in the world to her, was pretty.

Desmond looked Barbara Jean up and down two times – slowly, making a show of it. Then he snorted and said, "Now I see what it was had Ray goin' over to the coloreds. Didn't know he had it in him. I always figured him for a sissy."

Barbara Jean wanted out of there and away from this man, but she stayed calm long enough to ask, "Where's Ray?"

"Your little boyfriend's gone. Ungrateful bastard ran off and said he ain't comin' back." He smiled at her then. But there was no friendliness or humor in his expression, and she moved away from him as far as the space allowed. He said, "But listen, sweet thing, if it's white meat you've got a taste for, let me show you what a real man's like." Then he lunged at her and pressed her against the wall with his body. He ground his crotch against Barbara Jean's hip, all the while snickering like a mean-spirited child playing a game. He stopped laughing when she brought her hand to his crotch, grabbed him and twisted as if she were wringing out a wet dish towel. He hit the floor with Barbara Jean's fist still between his legs, gripping and turning.

She let go, leaped over him, and ran out of the shed. She flew across the yard, hearing him cuss and threaten as she escaped. "I'm gonna kill you, bitch!" he shouted.

Barbara Jean was back on the gravel road when she heard the sound of an engine firing and knew that he was coming after her. She darted down narrow, muddy streets that she had never seen before, hoping to hide from Desmond. She ducked behind trees and crouched in gullies to stay out of sight. More than once her pursuer's truck passed just a few feet away from her face as she knelt in tall weeds at the side of the road.

Finally, after thinking she would be lost forever in this unfamiliar and inhospitable part of town, Barbara Jean found her way back to Wall Road. From there, it was just a twenty-five-minute walk back to Big Earl's house.

It was probably the thunderous pounding of her heart that kept Barbara Jean from hearing the sound of the engine as it approached from the rear. She didn't realize that she was being followed until the headlights behind her caused her shadow to lengthen on the road ahead. She started to run again, but she only had two steps left in her. She was just too damn tired.

She glanced toward the side of the road where it

sloped down into a deep gully and then dark woods. If she could get out of the light and into the trees, she might be all right. She could hide, maybe even all night if she had to.

No. No hiding, she decided. For just a little while she had to become somebody else. Until this was over, no matter how it ended, she had to be somebody fearless.

Barbara Jean turned toward the headlights that had now come to a stop just a few yards away from her. Then she brought up her fists, ready to fight. She whispered to herself, "My name is Odette Breeze Jackson and I was born in a sycamore tree. My name is Odette Breeze Jackson and I was born in a sycamore tree."

But no one approached. She heard nothing for several drawn-out seconds. Then the quiet night air was filled with the sound of a car horn's blast. The horn played out, "Ooo, *Ooo*-ooo."

Lester.

Inside the blue Cadillac, Lester explained that he had gone to the McIntyres' to see her as soon as he returned to town. He had arrived at the house just in time to cross paths with Big Earl as he came rushing out of the door on his way to look for Barbara Jean. They had talked, and Lester persuaded Big Earl to go back to the All-You-Can-Eat while he tracked her down. After being pointed in the direction of Wall Road, that's just what Lester had done.

Barbara Jean didn't say a word all the way back to the house and Lester asked her no questions. When they pulled up outside Big Earl and Miss Thelma's, Lester performed like the gentleman he was. He opened the passenger-side door for her and accompanied her up the front walkway. As they reached the porch steps, Lester asked, "Have you given any thought to what we talked about?"

She started to laugh then. She laughed so hard at God's good joke on her that she had to hold on to the wrought-iron step railing to keep from falling over. Tears rushed down Barbara Jean's face and she struggled to breathe. When she could talk again, she said, "I'm sorry. But you're going to think this is funny, too, when I tell you . . . Lester, I'm pregnant. I'm going to have Chick Carlson's baby. And I just spent the evening running and hiding behind trees, trying to get away from his crazy-ass brother. So, you can take that proposal back and count yourself lucky." Barbara Jean climbed the three steps to the porch and then turned around, expecting to see Lester scrambling back to his Cadillac.

But Lester didn't walk away. He looked up at her and asked, "What do you want to do?"

"What I want doesn't matter. Chick's gone. Now I've got to make plans for me and my baby. My mother managed to do it on her own. I figure I can't do a worse job of it than she did."

Lester said, "I really meant it when I said I wanted to marry you, Barbara Jean. I've loved you since I first laid eyes on you, and that hasn't changed. We can get married tomorrow, if you want."

She waited for Lester to think about what he had just said and return to his senses. But he just stood there. She could only think of one thing to say. She asked the question her mother would have wanted her to ask. "Lester, can you look me in the eye and swear that you'll forever be my man and that you'll always do right by me and my baby?"

Lester stepped up onto the porch beside her and placed a warm hand on her stomach. "I swear," he said.

So Barbara Jean married Lester, the man who had the right answer to her mother's question.

Chapter 28

Each spring, Calvary Baptist Church held a tent revival. It was a tradition that Richmond's father started during his years as the pastor of the church, and it continued after he moved on. The revival was famous in Baptist circles throughout the Midwest. It attracted a huge crowd of the faithful every year and provided a boost to the church coffers during the long drought between Easter and Christmas. Clarice couldn't remember a year of her life that she didn't attend.

The revival always began on a Friday night with the raising of the tent. A makeshift stage was set up for the choir. Hundreds of folding chairs – ancient, splintering, torturously uncomfortable things Clarice believed had been designed to remind the congregation of the suffering of Christ – were brought in. Then there was a prayer service to get everyone worked up for the thirty-six straight hours of preaching, singing, and soul-saving that would follow. The revival culminated in a mile-long procession from the tent site on the edge of town back to Calvary.

Richmond's status as both a church deacon and the son of the revival's founder guaranteed that he and Clarice always had good seats. On opening night that year they sat in the front row. Richmond was in a snit that day over

Clarice's continued refusal to come back home, so Clarice sat between Odette and Barbara Jean and gave James the honor of sitting next to Richmond. The arrangement had the effect of further worsening Richmond's mood. He sat with his lower lip poked out and only looked in Clarice's direction to scowl at her.

Clarice still saw plenty of Richmond now that she had moved out. He stopped by the house in Leaning Tree a few times a week. "Where's my orange tie?" "How does the oven timer work?" "Where do I take the dry cleaning?" He always seemed to need something.

If he was on good behavior – not too whiny or argumentative – Clarice would invite him in. Richmond was good company. And she loved him. She had never loved any man except Richmond. Well, there was also Beethoven, but he didn't really count. The problem was, just as soon as Clarice started to think about Richmond's good points – how charming he could be, how he made her laugh – he would switch into seduction mode. His midnight eyes would flicker on and his voice would take on a quality that made her imagine that she smelled brandy and felt the heat of a roaring wood fire.

But whenever Clarice thought about having Richmond stay the night – a pleasurable thought – an image came into her mind that made her push him out of the door. It was that picture in her head of James trying, and failing, to style Odette's hair. That image just wouldn't allow her to step back into the life she had lived for so many years.

It was nearly midnight that first night of the revival and Reverend Peterson was wrapping up his sermon. Reverend Peterson always spoke first on opening night before handing off the podium to visiting preachers. His sermon that night was a good one. He told the terrifying story of the Great Flood from the perspective of one of Noah's nonbelieving neighbors. The speech climaxed with a vivid description of the doomed neighbor, knee-deep in swirling, filthy water, banging on the side of the ark and begging Noah to let him in. Reverend Peterson added color to the story by imitating the squawks, neighs, and moos of the animals. Of course, Noah could do nothing but wave goodbye to the terrified sinner as he sailed away with the righteous and the noisy animals.

The Noah's Ark sermon was typical of the Calvary Baptist experience. It was not a gray-area kind of church. Every Sunday, church members sat and listened to their pastor as he gave them the latest message from an angry God. They left the sanctuary certain that Calvary Baptist and Reverend Peterson were the only things standing between them and an eternity of suffering in hell. Calvary's parishioners fully expected that, like Noah, they would be waving goodbye to everyone in Plainview who didn't go to Calvary Baptist when Jesus shipped them all off to join Him.

When Reverend Peterson finished, the crowd was in an uproar of shouting, amen-ing, and speaking in tongues. The church nurses, in their starched white uniforms and white gloves, rushed through the tent to tend to women who had collapsed with the Holy Ghost.

In spite of the barn-busting sermon Reverend Peterson delivered that night, Clarice surprised herself by thinking that maybe it was time she left some of this bad news and rage behind. Sitting there listening to the angriest choir in town as they spat out "It's Gonna Rain," she thought that maybe she should branch out and give something else a try.

Having ended his sermon, Reverend Peterson made a plea to the unrepentant sinners in the crowd to come forward and receive the Lord's blessing before it was too late. He walked back and forth in front of the wailing choir and warned, "It won't be water, but fire, the next time." As he returned to his lectern to introduce the next speaker, there was a commotion in the back of the tent.

A woman's voice shouted, "Let me testify! Let me testify!"

Clarice and everyone else in the front row turned around to look, but there were too many people standing and gawking for them to see all the way to the back. The tent grew quieter and a wave of soft murmuring spread slowly from the rear to the front as the woman moved up the center aisle toward Reverend Peterson.

She was young – around twenty-five, Clarice guessed. The woman's gravity-defying cleavage hovered above a neon-green tube top that was just wide enough that it wasn't illegal. Below her exposed navel, she wore tight-fitting vermillion shorts that were so revealing Clarice imagined the woman had borrowed them from an emaciated eleven-year-old. The tube top and the shorts she wore were both made of shiny, wet-looking latex. With each step she took, the movement of latex abrading latex caused a high-pitched squeaking noise to pierce the air. Her hair was pulled back from her face into a fall of glossy black ringlets that hung down to the middle of her back.

Clarice leaned close to Barbara Jean and whispered, "Hair weave."

She replied, "Implants."

The woman staggered and stumbled up toward the stage and Reverend Peterson. His bushy, silver eyebrows climbed a little closer to his receding hairline with every step she took in his direction. Clarice wasn't sure if the woman's staggering was due to her being drunk or due to the fact that she was only wearing one shoe and had a thick layer of mud up to each ankle.

When she reached the lectern, the woman snatched the microphone away from an astonished Reverend Peterson. "I just had a miracle happen and I need to testify." She yelled her words into the microphone and feedback from the sound system caused everyone to clamp their hands to their ears. "Just a little while ago, after my shift at the Pink Slipper Gentlemen's Club, I was doin' a private perform-ance out in the parking lot in the back of a Chevy Suburban when I heard a voice. Clear as a bell the voice said, 'You are a child of God.'

"Now, at first I just ignored it 'cause I thought it was my customer. He's one of my regulars and he carries on like that – always God this, Jesus that, Sweet Lord the other."

Reverend Peterson's face registered panic and he made a grab for the microphone. But the stripper was faster. She hopped away from him and continued her testimony.

"The voice said, 'You are a child of God. Stop what you're doing.'

"I still thought it was my customer, so I got up off the floor of the Chevy and said, 'Fine. I don't gotta keep doin' what I'm doin'? Just give me my damn money and I'll go home.'

"But then, I heard the voice again. This time it said,

'Your sinful ways will bring a storm of hellfire down upon you. Come to the Lord and you will be saved.'

"I knew then that it wasn't my customer at all. It was an angel sent from heaven to tell me to change my life. So I got out of that SUV and I followed a light I saw off in the distance. I crossed Highway 37 and went through a patch of trees, even lost a shoe walkin' across a muddy field. But I kept goin' until I found this here tent. Now I'm here and ready to give up my sinful ways like that angel's voice told me to. If that ain't a miracle, I don't know what is."

The crowd erupted in praise of the stripper's miracle. People shouted, "Amen!" and the choir started to sing out twice as loud as they had before.

Encouraged by the response of her audience, the stripper went on with her testimony. "The second I walked into this tent, somethin' changed inside my heart. All of a sudden, I started to think about all the fine things God had done for me. I started to think maybe He seen me safely through all the dangerous, sinful things I did for a reason.

"And believe me, there's a lot of scary stuff out there. Hell, you go out for one night's work and you could end up with the herpes, the AIDS, the syphilis, the Chinese chicken flu, or the Ebola virus." She poked long, crimson nails into the air as she used her fingers to count off the diseases.

Reverend Peterson made another attempt to snatch the microphone away from the young woman, but again she was quicker. Like the performer she was, she gave her audience more of what they wanted. She said, "And I tell you, the way some of these men are, they don't care about protectin' themselves, you, or their wives and families.

They only care about their own pleasure. They wanna act like it's thirty years ago, before shit got so serious. I'm tellin' you, you gotta be a safety-first kinda gal if you wanna live long. You know what I do when some asshole tries to talk me into doin' something stupid? I look him dead in the eye and say, 'Honey, you think we're gonna fuck ourselves right back to 1978? This is some magical pussy all right, but it ain't no damn time machine.'"

On that note, several people moved in to restrain her, allowing Reverend Peterson, at last, to retrieve his microphone. The stripper was promptly helped off the stage by one of the church nurses and two representatives of the New Members Committee. As she was led past Clarice, Richmond, and their friends, the woman stopped for a second, turned toward Richmond, and said, "Hey, Richmond, you gettin' saved, too, baby?" before stumbling away with her keepers.

Everyone near the front of the tent, except for Richmond, who had buried his face in his hands, turned to stare at Clarice to see how she would react to the newly saved stripper greeting her husband like an old friend. But Clarice had something else on her mind. She was thinking about the miraculous voice that had summoned the stripper from the back of the Chevy behind the Pink Slipper Gentlemen's Club with the all-too-familiar words, "You are a child of God. Stop what you're doing." Clarice wondered how long her mother and her bullhorn had been back in town.

Chapter 29

The morning after Richmond's stripper friend signed up to have her soul saved, Clarice heard a knock at her door. It was just before nine o'clock in the morning, so she assumed that it was her first student of the day arriving early for her lesson. From the piano bench where she was having her tea, Clarice called out, "Come in." Beatrice Jordan and Richmond marched into the living room.

Beatrice pointed at her daughter's chopped-off hair and grimaced. For several seconds, she stood in the center of the room regarding Clarice as if she'd just discovered her dancing naked in a crack house. Richmond wore a smug expression on his face as his mother-in-law said, "Clarice, would you care to explain yourself?"

In the past, this was the point at which Clarice would revert to behaving like an obedient little girl. She would make nice and apologize to her mother for whatever she had done, just to get Beatrice off her back. But living alone in her own house, even for such a short amount of time, had changed her. Clarice found that she couldn't react like her old self. She said, "I've already explained things to Richmond. And I believe that's all the explaining I need to do."

Her mother spoke softly, as if she believed someone

might be listening in. "Everyone at Calvary Baptist is talking about you. How could you do this? You made a vow before God and everybody."

"So did Richmond. Did you have a talk with him about his vows?" Clarice said, feeling heat rise from her neck onto her face.

"It's different for men, and you know it. Besides, Richmond is not the one who ran out on his marriage; you are. But listen, it's not too late to fix this. Richmond is prepared to go see Reverend Peterson with you to work this out."

"I don't think so," Clarice said. "I've seen where Reverend Peterson's advice leads. And no offense, but I don't intend to spend my golden years shouting at whores through a megaphone."

She felt guilty for that low blow when her mother's eyes began to glisten with tears. But Clarice had been mad for a good long time and a lot nastier things than that were waiting to come out. To keep from saying those things, she took a deep breath and then a drink from her cup of tea. The tea was too hot for the big swallow she took and it scalded all the way from her lips to her stomach. It hurt so much that it took her breath away for a few seconds, but the time she spent recovering from burning her tongue stopped her from saying some of the meaner things that were swirling around in her brain.

Clarice said, "Mother, I love you, but this has nothing to do with you. This is between me and Richmond, and I think I've made it clear to him where I stand. I'm done with things the way they were. I'll go back home, *or not,* when I see fit."

Beatrice whimpered quietly and said, "Honestly, when I think about how hard I fought for us both to live when you were born." She put the back of her hand to her forehead. "It was a horror show." When that didn't produce the desired effect, she changed tactics. In the tone of voice she used when delivering her parking lot sermons, she declared, "Ephesians says, 'Wives, submit yourselves unto your own husbands as unto the Lord.' What do you say to that?"

Clarice snapped, "I say God and I will just have to hash that one out between the two of us. My submitting days are over."

Richmond spoke for the first time. He said, "I talked to the kids, and they're shocked that you've done this. They're very upset and confused."

Clarice said, "You must have talked to four different kids than the ones I talked to. When I told Carolyn, Ricky, and Abe that I'd moved out, they were just surprised that it had taken me so long. And if Carl's upset, it's because he's too much like you and he knows it. The way I see it, I've done him a favor I should have done years ago. Now maybe he'll think about the crap he's pulled on his wife and realize it might come back and bite him in the ass one day."

Richmond turned to Beatrice and said, "See? It's like I told you. She's talking more like Odette all the time."

Beatrice nodded. "I've always known that girl would cause trouble one day."

Clarice's mother believed that a woman showed that she was well brought up by doing three things: dressing impeccably, enunciating like an East Coast debutante, and starving herself to the edge of unconsciousness for the sake of her figure. So, Odette had never made sense to her. But Beatrice had chosen the wrong time to start in on Odette, Clarice's sick friend who had stepped in time and time again when Clarice needed her and had now even supplied her with a home. The little bit of restraint Clarice had managed to get hold of was in danger of slipping away. She narrowed her eyes at her mother and her husband and prepared to let loose. But just as her scalded tongue was poised to toss forth a red-hot string of long-overdue words, Clarice was distracted by the sound of light tapping coming from the front door. Clarice stood from the bench and said, "My student is here."

When Clarice rounded the piano on her way to admit her pupil, Beatrice saw for the first time what her daughter was wearing. Beatrice let out a whimper and turned her face away.

During Clarice's first weekend in the house, she had gone down to the basement to put some things away and came upon a box full of old clothes that had been left behind by one of the previous tenants. Odette had rented the house, furnished, to visiting faculty members at the university. They tended to be an earthy lot and the clothes in the box reflected what Clarice thought of as the academic fashion sense – shapeless, hippie-style items made of cotton and hemp. To celebrate her emancipation, she ran the old skirts and blouses she had found through the washer and dryer and started wearing them.

The skirt Clarice wore that morning was made of a faded blue-and-white-checked fabric. It had a high waist that was embroidered with blue and green stick figures.

Strands of puka shells that hung from the fringed hem grazed the floor when she walked and made a rattling noise.

Beatrice pointed at her daughter and said, "Oh dear Lord, first her hair, and now a peasant skirt. Richmond, we're too late."

It took every ounce of willpower in Clarice's body to keep from lifting the hem of her skirt and revealing that she was wearing a pair of Birkenstock sandals that she had purchased a few days earlier at a shop near the campus where young saleswomen who didn't shave their armpits or wear makeup sold comfortable shoes and artisan cheeses. She continued past her stunned mother and husband and went to the door, where she was greeted by Sherri Morris, a gap-toothed nine-year-old girl whose bad practice habits and resultant sloppy technique gave Clarice fits for an hour each week.

Sherri said, "Good morning, Mrs Baker. I love your skirt."

Clarice thanked the girl and made a mental note to put a gold star in her étude book that day no matter how poorly she played. She told Sherri to go to the piano and warm up on some scales while she said goodbye to her guests.

At the door Richmond whispered, "We can finish this discussion at the revival tonight."

"Sorry, I have students until late in the day today. I'll be too tired to go back to the revival tonight."

Richmond sighed and looked at Beatrice as if to say "See what I've been dealing with?" To Clarice, he said, "Fine, we'll talk at church tomorrow."

"If you really must talk to me, I'll see you at the

All-You-Can-Eat after church. I won't be at Calvary tomorrow. I'm planning to stop by the Unitarian church for services this week," she said.

Clarice said that purely for spite. Although she had talked to Odette about maybe giving Holy Family Baptist a try, Clarice had no intention of going to the Unitarian church that Sunday. She was furious that the two of them had come over to gang up on her and preach at her, so she wanted to shake them up. Besides, there was something about putting on a peasant skirt and puka shells that made Unitarianism pop into your head.

Her mother moaned and leaned against Richmond for support. Clarice felt guilty for an instant. She knew that her mother would just as soon have seen her hook up with one of the polygamist congregations that were rumored to thrive in the hills outside of town as hand her soul over to the Unitarians.

But even though she had said it out of spite, Clarice started thinking that it might not be such a bad idea to try out the Unitarians. Why not? She was certainly in the mood for something different from the bitter mouthful she'd been chewing on for all those years.

As Beatrice crossed the threshold of the front door, still clinging to Richmond, she said to Clarice, "I'll pray for you." Clarice marveled at how her mother had managed to make it sound like a threat.

Richmond mouthed, "See what you've done," and led his mother-in-law back to his Chrysler.

Clarice closed the door behind them and went to her student, who proceeded to brutally massacre a helpless Satie piece. She kept the promise she had made to herself to give Sherri a gold star, and the girl left happy at the end of her lesson.

Clarice's roster had expanded since her move. The wealthy families of new Leaning Tree were thrilled to have a locally famous piano teacher within walking distance. And Saturday was her longest teaching day. By that evening, she was exhausted. She made herself a fresh cup of tea and went back to the piano to play a little something to wash away the sound of her students' uneven perform- ances – a kind of musical sorbet.

She had just settled onto the bench when sharp hammer- ing at the front door abruptly ended the night's quiet. When she looked through the keyhole, she expected to see Richmond or her mother back for another round. Instead, Reverend Peterson stood on the porch. His dark, wrinkled face managed to appear sorrowful, beseeching, and pissed off all at the same time. She reached to turn the knob and allow him in, but then thought better of it.

Maybe it was more displaced anger, but she couldn't help but think that Reverend Peterson's counsel was some- thing she was better off without. His track record was pretty bad, she thought. She had followed his directions for years and had ended up believing that, in a woman, self-respect was the same thing as the sin of pride. And his advice to shut up and pray while her husband made a fool of her by screwing everything in sight had helped to keep Richmond a spoiled boy instead of the man he might have grown up to be. Okay, it might have been a stretch to blame Reverend Peterson for that, but she wasn't in the mood to play fair.

Fair or not, thinking clearly or not, hell-bound or not,

Clarice turned around and walked back to her piano. She sat down and, to the beat of the insistent rapping on the door, began to play Brahms's rapturous B Minor Intermezzo. As she played, she felt the stress of the day begin to fade away. Clarice thought, *God and I are communicating just fine.*

Chapter 30

After months of good test results, my medicine stopped working. So my doctor started me on a different regimen. The first treatment with the new medication made me far sicker than I'd been on the worst days with the old formula. And when I stopped feeling sick, I started feeling weak.

My bosses had been real nice about adjusting my work schedule to accommodate my chemo, but with this new treatment kicking my ass the way it was, I had to ask for a leave of absence. They – the principal of the school and the food services coordinator from the school board – were very understanding and told me I could take as much time as I needed before coming back. But I could tell by the looks on their faces that they weren't expecting me to return.

One morning, just after James left for work, I had a bad spell – feverish and achy all over. I was glad it hadn't happened when he was still there. It was next to impossible to get James out the door if he thought I was in trouble. If I didn't look okay to him, he'd dig in his heels and declare that he wasn't about to leave me alone. Then he'd sit staring at me like an orphaned puppy until I convinced him that I felt better.

Of course, James didn't need to worry about me being

alone. The kids called daily to check up on me and kept me talking for hours. Rudy called a couple of times a week. Barbara Jean and Clarice were in and out all the time. And Mama drifted in every day to keep me company. She was there that morning when I shuffled out of the bathroom with a cool towel on my head.

"You've lost weight," Mama said.

I looked down and saw that my nightgown was roomy now where it used to bind me. I was able to grab a handful of cloth at my waist and twist it in a half circle before the material was tight against my stomach.

"Isn't this something, all the time I wasted wishing I was able to take some weight off, and all it took to do the job was the teensiest little touch of cancer. Looks like I'll get the last laugh on Clarice for making fun of me holding on to those old, out-of-style clothes in the attic that nobody ever thought I'd fit into again. I'm gonna wow 'em at the hospice in my parachute pants and Nehru jacket." I laughed, but Mama didn't.

I waved two of my cats away from their resting places on the living room couch. Then I lay down, pulled a quilt over myself, and adjusted the couch pillows to support my head. The cats reclaimed their spots near my feet as soon as I settled in. Mama sat on the floor beside me with her legs crossed, Indian-style.

After lying there in silence for a while, I said, "I guess this is when I'm supposed to start praying for a miracle."

Mama shrugged. "You know, I don't think I much believe in miracles. I think there's just what's supposed to happen and what's not, and then goin' along with it or standin' in its way."

I said, "Hmm, I'll have to think about that. I like the idea of a good miracle every now and then."

She shrugged again and, after a few seconds, said, "I've got to say your James has been more wonderful than I imagined he could be through this whole thing. Not that I ever thought bad of him. I just didn't know he'd be this good."

"I'm not surprised at all. James is being exactly who I knew he'd be. I'm lucky."

"We're both lucky, you and me. I got your daddy and you and Rudy. You got James and those sweet kids."

"And the Supremes," I added.

Mama nodded. "That's what you'll think about when you pass, you know. How good your man was, how you loved your children. How your friends made you laugh till you cried. That's what flows through your mind when the time comes. Not the bad things.

"I don't know if I was smilin' or not when you found me dead in my garden, but I should've been. At the end, I was thinkin' about you and your grandmama and how she'd put you in those horrible dresses she made that you loved so much. And I thought about how good it felt to kiss your daddy.

"I don't recall hittin' the ground after throwin' the rock at that squirrel. I just remember havin' those sweet thoughts and then seein' your daddy standin' over me, stretchin' out his hand to help me up. When I got to my feet, my garden was more beautiful than ever – no damn tulip-bulb-eatin' squirrels in the afterlife. Wilbur and me hadn't walked more than five feet before we ran into your aunt Marjorie. She was doin' one-arm pushups and lookin' more like a man than ever. Her mustache had filled in real nice and she'd taken to waxin' it and twistin' it at its tips. Looked good on her. My big brother was there, too, all decked out in his army uniform, wearing all those shiny medals the government mailed home to us after the war. And the first person to say hello to me was Thelma McIntyre. She handed me a big fat doobie and said, 'Hey, Dora. Take a hit off this. And don't bogart it the way you always do.' It was lovely."

I hoped Mama was right. There had been so many beautiful days with James and the children and the Supremes, so many days I wanted to carry with me when I crossed over into whatever came next. And if I could shed the bad times like a dry, ill-fitting skin, that would be nice, too.

I always feel guilty when I think back to my worst day ever because others lost so much more than I did. Still, that day is there in my memory as the worst. And I believe, no matter what happens to me from here on out, that day will forever have its hooks in my mind.

Barbara Jean had just set out coffee for Clarice and me in her kitchen when the doorbell rang. It was the first weekend of May 1977 and the three of us were planning a birthday party for my Jimmy. All of our children had their parties at Barbara Jean's. Clarice and I had both moved away from Leaning Tree and into new developments with small lawns by then. So letting the kids loose in Barbara Jean's spacious yard, with its topiaries and flowering trees everywhere, was like setting them free in an enchanted forest.

Clarice's children were at home with Richmond. My

three were at Mama and Daddy's house being bribed into good behavior with candy bars and potato chips. Barbara Jean's Adam was at Mama and Daddy's, too – at least that's what we thought. He'd left about half an hour earlier for the fifteen-minute walk to Mama's house. This was a period of time when no one thought twice about a child of seven or eight walking a familiar path alone in Plainview. It was the last day of that era.

Lester answered the doorbell and I was surprised to hear James's voice. In that big house the kitchen was half a block away from the front door, so I couldn't make out exactly what they were saying. I don't know if it was the tone of James's voice or Lester's that drew the three of us into the foyer to see what was going on, but I knew something terrible had happened the second I saw James's face.

The first thing I thought was that it was one of our kids, or maybe Mama or Daddy. Then Lester, who'd had his back to us, turned around. Right away, I knew. So did Barbara Jean.

Lester's skin had gone gray and I could see him wavering on his feet like he was standing in the center of a whirlpool. James, who was wearing his Indiana State Police uniform, stood in the doorway with another trooper, a big white guy with a smooth red face who kept his eyes focused on the floor in front of him. James reached out and held on to Lester's shoulder to keep him upright.

Barbara Jean said, "Lester?" Tears began to fall from Lester's eyes as he stood supported by James. Barbara Jean turned to James and asked, "What's happened to Adam?"

It was Lester who answered her: "He's dead, Barbie. Our boy is dead."

And then Barbara Jean screamed. She screamed like she was trying to cover up every other sound in the world. I had never heard anything like that, and I hope to God I never will again. She started to stumble backwards, her feet losing traction and her arms flailing like she was suddenly standing on ice. The white cop stepped forward to keep her from falling, but I had her already. We fell back together against the wall and then slid down to that elegant parquet floor. She stopped screaming and started making a low, pained moan while I squeezed her against my body and Clarice knelt beside us stroking Barbara Jean's hair.

I heard Lester asking, "Where?" I heard James answer, "North end of Wall Road."

Lester protested that it had to be a mistake. Like all the black children in town, Adam had been warned. He'd been told, time and time again, that bad people drove on that part of Wall Road. It couldn't be Adam.

But James shook his head. "There's no mistake. It's him, Lester. It's him."

Lester stood up straight and knocked James's hand from his shoulder. "I have to go see," he said. Then he started for the door.

The white trooper tried to stop him. "Mr Maxberry, you really shouldn't. This isn't something you want to see." But James pulled a windbreaker from the coat tree near the door – it had started to sprinkle outside – and handed it to Lester, saying, "I'll take you." The men left while the three of us huddled on the floor.

By the time Lester and James came back, Barbara Jean was in her bedroom, lying with her knees drawn up to her chest. We lay beside her in the bed, me clutching her hand

and Clarice praying, while Barbara Jean gasped out Adam's name over and over like he'd hear her wherever he was and come on home. When she heard the sound of the front door opening, Barbara Jean hopped out of bed and ran downstairs, chasing after the one last bit of hope that it had all been a mistake and she'd discover pretty little Adam standing in the front hallway waiting for her.

We found James and Lester in the library. James stood by the fireplace watching his old friend and former boss pace the room and strike his head with his balled fists. Lester's face wasn't gray anymore; his light brown skin was purple with anger.

Lester said, "You know he did it. You know he killed my boy."

James tried to calm him. "Lester, please just take a breath and sit down. They're over at his place right now. I promise we'll get to the bottom of it. I'm telling you, it's not like it used to be."

Lester snorted. "There's nothing to get to the bottom of. You know he did it. If you cops won't do something, I swear to God I'll take care of it myself."

James said quietly, "Lester, please don't let anybody but us hear you say that."

Lester turned to Barbara Jean, his voice almost unrecognizable in his grief and fury. "Desmond Carlson murdered our Adam. He hit him with his truck on Wall Road. Hit him so hard our baby got tossed against a tree." Lester started hitting himself in the forehead again as he croaked out his words. "His neck snapped, Barbie. That fuckin' redneck piece of shit broke our baby's neck."

Barbara Jean let out a grunt and doubled over like she'd

been punched in the stomach. Then she ran from the room. She was up the stairs and back in her bedroom before Clarice or I could get our feet moving. We went up after her when we heard the screaming start again.

Later that night in bed, James and I stared at the ceiling while he explained to me what had happened to Adam. James said Adam had been on his way to Mama's house when he was hit. He was eight years old and knew that he was supposed to go the long way from his house to get to Grandma Dora's, but Adam was an adventurous boy. The temptation of taking the shortcut had, apparently, been too great. And the risk of punishment hadn't stopped him. James said, "I guess we haven't done a good enough job of making them afraid."

James said Lester was right about it being Desmond Carlson. There were tracks in the muddy road that led directly from the place where Adam was hit to the unnamed street that wound through the woods and led to a neighborhood of only five houses, one of them Carlson's place. Desmond, who had been falling-down drunk when the police got to his house, claimed his truck had been stolen the day before and he hadn't gotten around to reporting it. The truck was nowhere to be found and Desmond's girlfriend was backing up his story. Even after the police had located the truck later that evening, hidden in the woods less than a mile from his house, its grille streaked with blood, he'd stuck to his tale that he didn't know a thing about what had happened to little Adam.

Desmond had probably been playing the same game of chicken he had been playing with blacks along Wall Road for years. This time he'd just gotten too close. Or maybe Desmond had simply been so drunk he couldn't keep his truck in a straight line and it was just horrible luck all the way around. After all, Adam was so fair-skinned that most people seeing him would think he was a tanned white child. The *why* of it didn't matter. The result was the same.

"We'll get him, though," James said. But he didn't sound too certain to me.

James was quiet for a while. Then he said, "Adam was lying on his side against a tree. I thought Lester was going to die when he saw him. He made this terrible sound like he couldn't breathe out, just in. Then he dropped down beside Adam and grabbed ahold of him and just rocked back and forth in the dirt and mud with him."

"Oh, James," I said, reaching out to touch my husband's arm.

"When I finally got him onto his feet, he just stood there wheezing and staring down at Adam. Then he said, 'Where's his shoes?' Over and over, he kept asking where Adam's shoes were. He wouldn't leave or let them take Adam away until we found the shoes.

"We poked around, looking in the weeds and under-brush for what seemed like forever, and the whole time Lester's wailing louder and louder, 'Where's his shoes?'

"It was the coroner's assistant who finally found them. They were twenty feet away at the side of the road, little white sneakers, just sitting there side by side, like they'd been polished and set out for him by his mama. Lord, Odette, I've seen some bad things since I've had this job, but as long as I live I don't believe I'll ever forget watching Lester put those shoes on that poor dead baby's feet."

James mumbled, "His face was okay. The back of his head was bashed in and his neck was broken. So was one leg and probably an arm. But his face was okay, so they'll be able to have an open casket if they want to. That's something, I guess."

James and I rolled over toward each other in the bed and we pressed our foreheads together. We both shook with tears of grief over Adam and sorrow for our friends. And we cried with guilty relief that this thing, the monster that all parents fear most, had swiped near to us with its sharp and merciless claws, but had not carried off one of our own babies.

Neither of us got any sleep on the night of that worst day. Both James and I were up and on our feet at least once every hour, prying open the doors of our children's bedrooms to watch them as they slept safe in their beds.

Chapter 31

The second round of chemo with the new drugs gave me an even fiercer ass-whupping than the first round. To make matters worse, in May the great love of my life deserted me. It wasn't James. It was food that left me. I woke up one morning with a sour taste in my mouth that wouldn't be scrubbed away with a toothbrush or rinsed out with mouthwash. Worse than that, nearly everything I ate tasted like tin. And what didn't taste like tin, I couldn't keep down.

Mama and Mrs Roosevelt greeted me when I came into the kitchen. That morning's breakfast was a cup of watered-down coffee – my stomach wouldn't take full-strength anymore – and a small bowl of oatmeal that I couldn't persuade myself to eat.

For the first time in my life, my doctor was concerned that I was losing too much weight too quickly. I wasn't skinny by any stretch of the imagination, but I had lost several more pounds in a short period of time and I didn't see any way I was going to slow down the weight loss. Food and I just weren't getting along.

When I gave up on my oatmeal and rose from my chair at the kitchen table to toss the remainder away, Mama said, "You know what you need? You need some herb."

"What?" I asked.

"Herb. Marijuana, ganja, buda, Tijuana tea, pot, bud, skunkweed, giggleweed, wacky tobacky, kif, reefer."

"Stop showing off. I know what you're talking about."

"Whatever you wanna call it, that's what you need," Mama said. "It'll fix that appetite of yours right up."

I didn't want to admit it, but I'd been thinking the same thing for a few weeks. I'd been on the computer researching it when James wasn't around, and I'd been thinking maybe medical marijuana might be the thing to get me back on track. Unfortunately, I didn't live in a state where I could get it legally.

I said, "You may be right, Mama, but it's not like I can go to the drugstore and order some. And please don't tell me to go over to the campus and hang around at the frat houses. We both know where that leads."

"Scaredy-cat. I thought you weren't supposed to be afraid of nothin'," Mama teased.

I wasn't going to be baited that easily. "I mean it, Mama. James has had enough to deal with lately. I'm not about to get arrested and add to it."

Mama let out an exaggerated sigh. "I won't get you arrested, Miss Priss. Get dressed and come on with me."

Once we were in the car, Mama guided me along the familiar route from my house to her and Daddy's old place in Leaning Tree. She instructed me to park the car on the street, rather than in the driveway, and follow her around to the back. She led me and Mrs Roosevelt behind the house and toward what remained of her once-magnificent garden. It had been a damp spring and my feet sank into the wet ground as we walked. I could hear Clarice playing the piano inside and I was thankful that she was occupied. I certainly didn't want her to see me sneaking through the yard and ask me what I was doing: "Oh, hey, Clarice, my dead mama, Eleanor Roosevelt, and me were just heading out back to fetch some marijuana."

We stepped onto the cobblestone garden path and passed the gazebo. It was already green with clematis and honeysuckle vines, though they hadn't bloomed yet. We passed the roses and alliums and walked through the vegetable garden, which was untended and going wild that season. I hacked with my forearms at the tall reed grass and miscanthus Mama had grown at the back of her garden to keep prying eyes from spotting the illegal crop that James and I had pretended not to know about. A sad thought came to me then that brought our entire journey into question.

With as much gentleness as I could muster, considering I was panting with exhaustion by then, I said, "Mama, you do realize that you've been gone for a long time now and nobody's taken care of your special plants in years. I don't think we're gonna find anything still growing back there."

"Hush," she said. "We ain't goin' there." We trudged on several more yards and then turned. Ahead of us was an old tool shed that I'd forgotten all about. It was a short structure, more the height of a child's playhouse than a work shed. But Daddy had been a small man and he had made this shed for himself. It made me happy to see that it still stood and that, even though the vestiges of its white paint were long gone, leaving the bleached pine boards exposed, it looked solid. My daddy built things to last.

Mama instructed me to open the door of the shed. It took some effort because, although only a sliding wood bolt kept the door shut, reed grass and honeysuckle – which would smell divine in a month, but was now just an invasive pest – had nearly swallowed the building. I yanked repeatedly at the door until it opened just wide enough for me to squeeze inside.

We entered the shed to the rustling sound of small creatures scurrying for cover. Mama said, "Over there," pointing at the back wall.

I climbed over an ancient push mower and a rusted tiller, and then stood staring at the wall. All I saw were cobwebs, mouse droppings, and corroded garden tools hanging from a pegboard. I asked Mama what exactly I was looking for and she said, "Just slide that board over to the left and you'll see."

I curled my fingers around the edge of the pegboard and gave it a vigorous shove. I didn't need to try so hard, as it turned out. The board slid over on its metal track so easily you'd have thought it had been oiled that very day. Behind it, I saw an old plastic spice rack that was screwed into the wall. In the cubbyholes of the rack were small glass jars, each of them filled with brownish leaves and labeled in Mama's neat, loopy handwriting with a name and a date.

I picked up random jars and read the labels: "Jamaican Red–1997," "Kentucky Skunk/Thai Stick Hybrid–1999," "Kona–1998," "Sinsemilla–1996." There were around two dozen of them.

I reached for a jar that read "Maui Surprise," and Mama said, "Oh no, no, honey, put that one back. That Maui'll blow the top of your head clean off. We'll start you off with somethin' tamer." She pointed an index finger at a jar in the lower right-hand corner of the rack and I pulled it out.

"Soother–1998," I read aloud from the jar. "They're all kind of old. You think they'll still be good?"

"Trust me. An hour from now you'll wanna kill anybody standing between you and a bag of pork rinds."

I slipped the jar into my pocket and was about to slide the pegboard back in place when Mama stopped me. "Wait a minute. We need that and that." She gestured toward a small shelf below the rack. On the shelf, I found rolling papers and a box of wooden matches. I grabbed them, covered Mama's secret stash with the sliding pegboard, and left the shed.

Mama suggested that I take my herbal cure in the gazebo, but I had another idea. I stomped through more reeds and climbed the hill at the back end of the property. I stopped when we stood beneath the sycamore tree where I was born fifty-five years earlier.

Mama and I sat on the cool ground and rested our backs against the tree. Mrs Roosevelt, who seemed to have been energized by our walk in the spring air, spun in a circle like Julie Andrews at the beginning of *The Sound of Music,* and then did some cartwheels.

Mama said, "Pay her no mind. If she gets your attention she'll never stop."

When I opened the jar, the vacuum seal broke with a noise that sounded like someone blowing a kiss. I lifted it to my nose and inhaled. It smelled like rich soil and newly cut hay, with a dash of skunk spray laid on top. It was as fresh as if it had been picked that day. Mama might not have been able to cook worth a damn, but she sure as hell knew how to can.

Mama started in instructing me. "What you need to do is grab ahold of one of the bigger buds and roll it between your fingers to get the seeds and stems out. Then—"

I interrupted her. "Mama, I think I watched you do this enough times over the years to figure it out." Then I began to roll the first joint I'd rolled in my life.

To my embarrassment, it turned out to be a lot harder to do than I'd imagined. Mama had to guide me through the entire process. It was made worse by the fact that the papers were so old that they cracked whenever I bent them, and the saliva-activated adhesive refused to activate. But I finally produced a functional cigarette. The old sulfur matches worked just fine, and soon enough I found myself inhaling the sweet, pungent fumes of Mama's Soother.

I had never smoked marijuana before and had only smoked tobacco once in high school, when Clarice and I had proclaimed ourselves bad girls for a day and each coughed our way through a quarter of a cigarette before giving up. But in ten minutes that tinny taste in my mouth was fading away, and I was starting to feel pretty damn good. I had to hand it to Mama: she had named the Soother just right.

I looked up at the leaves of the tree. They were still the pale green of spring, and they shivered in the breeze against the background of the blue sky.

"Beautiful," I said. "It looks like a painting. You know, Mama, I think it's *all* like a painting."

"What is?"

"Everything. Life. It's like you're filling in a little bit more of a picture every day. You stroke on color after color, trying to make it as pretty as you can before you reach the edge of your canvas. And if you're lucky enough that your mama had you in a sycamore tree, maybe your hand won't shake with fear too bad when you see that your brush is right up against the frame."

Mama said, "You're stoned."

"Maybe, but I think this is the loveliest spot on my canvas. When the end comes, I think this is where I'd like to be. Right back here where I started out," I said.

"I don't like to hear you talk like that. Makes me think you're givin' up. You probably won't have to think about dyin' for a long time."

Mrs Roosevelt, who now knelt beside me after tiring of turning cartwheels, shook her head and frowned as if to say "Your mother may think you've got time, but I say you're a goner." Then with the grace of a jungle cat, Eleanor Roosevelt hitched up her skirt and scrambled up the trunk of the sycamore and into its branches until she was nearly at the top of the tree. She put a satin-gloved hand up to her brow to block out glare from the sun and proceeded to scan the horizon – looking for mischief to get into, no doubt.

I said, "I don't dwell on it, or anything. But when I think about it, this is always the place that comes to mind when I imagine the end. I like the idea of making this big ol' jumble of a life into a nice, neat circle."

Mama nodded and looked up at the sky with me.

I don't know how long we sat under the sycamore staring up at the passing clouds, but I called a halt to it when my behind started to go numb and the damp of the ground began seeping through my hose. I pushed myself up, using the tree trunk for leverage. After I straightened and stretched, I brushed the dirt from my rear end and said, "Well, I guess we'd better head on home."

Mama and I – Mrs Roosevelt chose to stay up in the tree – began to walk back through the garden. My first few steps on the soft, uneven ground were not too steady. Mama commented, "I think your nerves might be a little too soothed for you to drive right now. Let's go sit in the gazebo for a spell." I agreed, and we walked back toward the house.

The open side of the six-sided gazebo faced the rear of the house, so we couldn't see into it as we approached it from the back. Even from the front, it was impossible to make out more than a narrow slice of the dim interior from outside. So we had no way of knowing who was inside when we heard the unmistakable sounds of love-making – a man's low grunts, a woman's sighs – emanating from the gazebo as we came closer to it.

Mama said, "Sounds like Clarice and Richmond are gettin' along better these days."

I turned away from the gazebo and walked as fast as I could toward the house and the driveway that led back to the street. I was even less eager to come across Clarice and Richmond in this situation than I was for Clarice to catch me foraging for marijuana.

I had just about made it to the driveway when I heard

the back door of the house open and then heard the sound of Clarice's voice. She called out, "Odette! Glad you came by. I was just going to call you to ask you over for lunch."

Confused, I looked back at the garden. Clarice followed my gaze and then we both heard muffled voices. A head stuck out from the entrance of the gazebo and looked back at us. Clarice came and stood beside me and we watched a young man come in and out of view inside the gazebo as he hopped from one side of the structure to the other, struggling ungracefully to get back into his drawers. The young man was Clifton Abrams, the fiancé of Clarice's cousin Sharon.

Mama shook her head with pity as she watched Clifton hurry to cover his nakedness. Holding up her thumb and forefinger spaced about two inches apart, she said, "Poor boy has the curse of the Abrams men. Did you notice?"

A woman's head popped out and peered at us, then receded into the shadows. We heard more shuffling as the two of them bumped around, climbing into their clothes. The young woman was not Sharon.

I glanced at Clarice, wondering, but not saying, *Who the hell is she?*

Clarice read my mind. "Her name is Cherokee."

"Like the Indian tribe?"

"No, like the Jeep. Come on in and I'll tell you all about her. I've got some leftover turkey breast. You hungry?"

My stomach growled at the mention of roast turkey and I was surprised that I was able to honestly answer, "Yes, as a matter of fact, I am hungry."

We left the garden and strolled back toward the house. Mama came along, saying, "Told you your mama knew how to fix up that appetite." With that, the three of us stepped together through the back door of Mama's old house.

Chapter 32

Barbara Jean's AA sponsor was a man named Carlo who taught speech therapy at the university. A pudgy tanning booth devotee whose carrot-colored skin had the texture of an alligator purse, Carlo was a few years younger than Barbara Jean, but he looked a lot older. He had an unusually long, pointed nose, a wide jaw, and eyes that bulged a little. Still, in spite of having an odd collection of features that seemed to be fighting for dominance of his face, Barbara Jean thought he wasn't a bad-looking guy. Somehow it all worked together, the different unpleasant facets canceling each other out.

Carlo lived with his partner, another former drinker who sometimes came to meetings with him. Barbara Jean chose him to be her sponsor because he was gay. During some of her late nights, she watched television shows that featured gay guys who were perpetually shopping and making witty conversation. She thought a sponsor like that would be a lot of fun. Barbara Jean was disappointed to discover that Carlo must have been watching different TV shows. She liked him enough, but, blunt and serious, he was as different from those men as she was from the sassy, wisecracking black women who populated TV Land. Carlo, as it turned out, was a big gay pain in the neck.

Right about the time Barbara Jean convinced herself that she had fully mastered the AA thing, Carlo called and asked her to meet him. They arranged to get together at a coffee shop near the campus. It was a dark, cramped place with bookshelves lining every wall, designed to cater to the student population. Their meeting took place early in the day, just after the morning rush of harried graduate students had left. Barbara Jean came armed with a shopping list, ready to begin the fun part of their relationship.

She arrived at the coffee shop first and found a seat at one of the tables, which were all made from recycled industrial cable spools. When Carlo sat down across from her, she greeted him by saying how happy she was that he had called and that she had been thinking it would be nice for the two of them to get together for brunch, but hadn't gotten around to asking him over to the house.

He interrupted her. "Barbara Jean, it doesn't appear that I'm the right sponsor to help you to take your recovery seriously."

"Why do you say that?" she asked.

Carlo crossed his arms over his chest and stared at her. One of his eyebrows rose. "Your eyes are fucking blood-shot and you're drunk right now."

She put her hand to her chest and gasped to let Carlo know how offended she was. She would have stood up from her chair and stormed out of the place if she hadn't been just the tiniest bit buzzed and afraid that she might fall on her face in front of him.

"I can't believe you would say such a thing to me."

Barbara Jean slipped her sunglasses onto her face, blowing a quick breath into her hand to check for the telltale odor of liquor as she adjusted the frames. "I don't know how much more seriously I can take my sobriety. That damn Serenity Prayer is on my lips practically all day long. And I've been going to three meetings a week for two months now. *Three* meetings."

He scrunched up his long nose and said, "Are you sure you haven't been going to one meeting a week, but getting there so drunk you're seeing triple?"

Barbara Jean felt a tear trickle out from behind her sunglasses and travel down her cheek. She grabbed a napkin from the table and wiped it away as quickly as she could.

Carlo softened his tone, which was contrary to his nature and, she knew, hard for him. He said, "Look, Barbara Jean, I like you a lot. You're good company and you're a nice lady. But I'm not helping you. And, frankly, it's not good for me to be around someone who continues to drink the way you do. Especially someone I like as much as I've come to like you."

Barbara Jean struggled to find something to say. She mumbled a few words about how wrong he was and how it hurt her that he didn't believe her. But her heart wasn't really in the lie anymore. She leaned back in her chair and said, "Some folks have a good reason for drinking, you know. A damn good reason. I want to tell you a story. And after I'm done, you look me in the eye and tell me that I shouldn't take a drink every now and then."

She took a sip of the coffee she had spiked with a healthy splash of Irish whiskey from her silver flask before he'd arrived at the coffee shop. Then she told Carlo a tale she had never told Odette or Clarice.

The night of Adam's funeral, Odette and Clarice stayed on after everyone else had left Barbara Jean's house. After they'd helped her maid to clean up after the guests who had filled the house with far more food and sympathy than Barbara Jean could handle, she rushed them out the door. Lester, who was just a few weeks away from the first of many hospitalizations that were to come, collapsed onto the bed the second he was out of his black suit. As soon as he began to snore, Barbara Jean slipped out of the house.

She went to see Big Earl. It was cool and misty outside that night, but there he was, smoking a cigar and rocking on the porch swing, when she came up the walk to the house. It was as if he'd been waiting for her. When she stood beside him, he looked up at her and said, "Baby, you should go on home."

"I need to know where he is," she said, not bothering to say his name. Though Chick never set foot in the All-You-Can-Eat or made any attempt to see her, Barbara Jean knew that he had been back in Plainview for at least two years. She had spotted him coming and going from the McIntyres' house, and she had overheard Little Earl saying that Chick was a frequent visitor now that Miss Thelma was sick.

Big Earl said, "You and Ray ain't talked in nine years. Won't nothin' be helped by talkin' now."

"I need to see him. And I know you can tell me where to find him."

"Be careful, Barbara Jean. You ain't in the shape to make a

good decision right now. You need to give it some time before you do anything that might cause you more heartache."

"*More heartache?*" She laughed at the thought of that, and Big Earl winced at the sound of her laughter, which to his ear sounded like a shriek of hysteria. She said, "I've got to talk to Chick and I'm going to do it tonight. Will you tell me where he lives? Or do I have to drive out Wall Road past the place where my little boy died and ask Desmond Carlson where I can find his brother?"

Big Earl stared down at his feet and slowly shook his head. Then he looked up at Barbara Jean and told her the address. As she left, he said, "Be careful, baby. Be careful."

Chick lived on a block near the university that was mostly student housing, little square boxes painted dinner-mint colors. Was he in school? She didn't really know anything about his life since he'd returned to Plainview. Was he married? Was she about to awaken a family? She sat in her car across the street from his house, staring at the place until a light came on in back. She decided that was her signal, just like the light in the storeroom of the All-You-Can-Eat she had once watched for from her bedroom. She crossed the street and knocked on the door. The noise of her fist striking wood was the loudest sound on the street at that late hour.

Chick opened the door and drew in a sharp breath when he saw her standing in the harsh light of the yellow bulb that hung over the front stoop. "Barbara Jean?" he said, as if he thought he might be seeing things. He didn't move, so she opened the screen door and walked in, brushing past him.

She stepped into a small, tidy living room that was furnished with two metal folding chairs, a beaten-up old couch upholstered in cracked brown patent leather, and a desk that was piled high with neatly stacked papers and books. Against one wall were two tables that supported six cages and an elaborate system of lights. Each cage contained an identical small bird with gray, red, and white striped feathers, pretty little things whose sad cooing echoed in the quiet room.

Chick saw her looking at the birds and said, "I'm studying them at the university. I'm working on this project . . ." His voice tapered off and they stared at each other.

There he was, just inches away from her again after all those years. Ray Carlson. Ray of light. Ray of sunshine. Ray of hope. Ray, who had danced naked for her to an old, dirty blues song.

The room was hot, warmed by the lights over the cages, and he was shirtless. He was still thin, but broader across the chest than he'd once been. *He's still beautiful,* she thought, *just like our son was.* She turned her back to him, afraid all of a sudden that she wouldn't be able to say what she had come to say if she was looking at him.

"Barbara Jean," he said, "I heard about your—"

Still with her back to him, she interrupted. "I just want to know one thing. Did Desmond kill him because of us? Did he kill Adam because he was your son?"

She waited for his answer, but he said nothing. After several seconds, she turned around and looked at him. His mouth hung open in a face that was slack with shock. His jaw twitched with little movements, but no words came out. When he finally said something, it was so quiet she could hardly distinguish it from the cooing of the birds. "I didn't know."

"You didn't know?" she cried out, surprising herself that she had any more anger left inside of her. "How could you not know? Didn't you ever look at him?"

Every time Barbara Jean looked at Adam, she saw Chick. His profile, the shape of his body, the way he moved. It was all Chick. Clarice and Odette saw it, too. She could tell by the way they stared at Adam sometimes. If other friends and acquaintances didn't see the resemblance, it was probably because they couldn't have imagined a man doting on a child who wasn't his the way Lester had doted on Adam. And Barbara Jean understood Lester's family not seeing it. They had taken their cue from Lester's late mother, who saw her light-skinned grandchild and thought of nothing but rejoicing over the new infusion of café-au-lait-colored blood into the veins of her family line. But how Chick could not have known that Adam was his son was impossible for Barbara Jean to comprehend.

Chick said, "I couldn't look at him. When I came back and heard that you and Lester had a son, I couldn't look at him. Or you either." His voice growing more tremulous, he said again, "I didn't know."

She knew then that she should just go home. She knew that words could only make things worse. But Barbara Jean couldn't stop herself from speaking the truth to Chick, just like she couldn't stop herself from telling him the story of her life in the hallway of the All-You-Can-Eat back when she had first realized that she loved him.

"I married Lester because you took off and I had to make a life for myself and your child. I married him because it was that or die because I couldn't be with you. Maybe I was wrong to marry him. Maybe I was cruel to you. Maybe this is my punishment for spending nine years waiting for you to knock on my door and come take me and Adam away, even though Lester loved our son as much as any father could and loves me more than I deserve. Maybe this is God's judgment for every bad thing I ever did."

He stepped toward her then and wrapped his arms around her. He pulled her into his body and she inhaled the scent of him, familiar and strange, perfect and wrong. She wanted to embrace him and squeeze him to her, but her body wouldn't cooperate. She stood stiff and straight with her arms crossed over her chest like a corpse inside a coffin.

He asked in a voice ragged with sorrow, "What can I do, Barbara Jean? What can I do to make it better?"

It just came out, the simple truth of what she wanted at that moment. "Kill him. If you want to do something for me, if you want to do something for our son, you'll kill Desmond." Barbara Jean twisted out of his arms and stepped away from him. Brushing off the stray gray, red, and white feathers that had transferred from his body to her black sweater, she said, "I've got to get back to my husband. He's not well." She left him standing with his arms reaching out for her.

The police were back at Barbara Jean's house the next day. They were Plainview police officers this time instead of the Indiana State Police. They talked to Lester for a while in the foyer and told him they wanted him to come with them. Barbara Jean refused to let him leave the house without her. She made such a fuss that they put her in the squad car along with her husband. The police drove them out of downtown Plainview and onto Wall Road. She closed her eyes as they passed the place where Adam had been found.

The Plainview chief of police stood in the side yard of Desmond Carlson's house, one of a dozen cops milling around – the entire Plainview police department back then. Three of the policemen were loading Desmond's body onto a stretcher when the car carrying Barbara Jean and Lester drove up. At least Barbara Jean thought it was Desmond. She hadn't seen him up close in nine years. And he was barely recognizable now, with half of his face gone.

They separated Lester and Barbara Jean then. The chief of police talked to Lester ten yards away from her while a patrolman asked Barbara Jean where her husband had been the previous night and early that morning.

That was when James drove up along with the white state trooper who'd come to the house with him to tell Barbara Jean and Lester about Adam. They moved fast, their police cruiser skidding in the mud. The questioning ended as soon as James approached. Lester came over and stood next to Barbara Jean while James spoke with the police chief for several minutes. Then James walked over to his friends and said he would drive them home.

On the way back to the house, James apologized for the trouble and explained that he didn't hear about it right away because Desmond's neighborhood was part of the Plainview cops' jurisdiction, while Wall Road, owned by the university, was the territory of the state police. He assured them that, after the investigation, it would be concluded that Desmond, overcome with guilt, had killed himself with a shot to the head. James said, "That'll turn out to be the best thing for everybody."

When the car pulled up in Barbara Jean and Lester's driveway, the white trooper shook Lester's hand and whispered, "I would've done the same thing if it'd been my boy."

It began that day, the rumor that Lester had killed or engineered the death of Desmond Carlson. Eventually, Lester seemed to believe it himself. But Barbara Jean knew the truth. Out at Desmond Carlson's place, while the policeman questioned her about her husband's whereabouts, she had stared down at her feet and watched several delicate gray, red, and white feathers, just like the ones she had brushed from her sweater at Chick's the night before, float across the ground.

That night was the first Barbara Jean spent curled up on Adam's little bed and the first time in her life she had been drunk.

When she finished talking, Carlo looked at Barbara Jean with an expression of pained empathy on his face. "Whatever happened to this guy Chick?"

"What do you mean?"

"I mean did he get arrested or anything?"

"No. He just disappeared. I found out later that he went to Florida, but I never heard from him. And I didn't see him again until this past summer."

"Is he here now? In Plainview?"

She nodded.

Carlo reached across the table and patted her hand.

"You can do something about this, you know. You can work your eighth and ninth steps."

When he saw that, even after months of going to meetings, Barbara Jean had no idea what the eighth and ninth steps of AA were, he sighed with exasperation. In a voice that made his annoyance clear to her, he said, "Make a list of all persons you have harmed, and become willing to make amends to them all. Then make direct amends to those people wherever possible, except when to do so would injure them or others.

"This Chick guy seems to be on your list, so you should go see him."

She agreed that she would, not knowing if she meant it or not.

Carlo said, "I'll see you at the ten-thirty meeting tomorrow." Then he got up and left the coffee shop. She watched her sponsor walk away, this chunky man who was so comfortable doling out unpleasant truths. Barbara Jean thought, not for the first or last time, that she must have some special kind of bad luck. She'd gone searching for a witty shopping companion and ended up with a gay Italian version of Odette.

Two nights after her meeting with Carlo, that moment of clarity Odette had tried to knock into Barbara Jean's head after she had embarrassed herself so badly outside the All-You-Can-Eat finally came. And to her amazement, it came in her library, in her Chippendale chair.

Without alcohol, her body fought sleep. Feeling ants crawling beneath her skin and unable to even imagine rest, she returned to her beautiful Chippendale chair and the Bible Clarice had burdened her with decades earlier. She did what she had done more times than she could count. She opened the book to a random page and dropped her finger. Then she read what she had landed on.

John 8:32. "And ye shall know the truth, and the truth shall make you free."

Common as salt, as the old folks used to say. And Barbara Jean had found her fingertip pointing to this passage often enough over the years that it ordinarily held no meaning for her. But that night, John 8:32 started her thinking.

Maybe if she'd had a couple of good stiff drinks in her at that moment or if she'd had one more day of sobriety, she would have ignored this familiar verse. In either case, Barbara Jean might have simply closed up the book and gone back to bed for another stab at sleep. But she was freshly dried out and ready for a revelation. She thought later that it was likely any verse would have done the job, but that night it was John 8:32 that rolled around in her mind until it transformed from an adage into a command. Before she returned to her bed, that verse demanded and received a promise from her that she would face Chick. She would acknowledge out loud that she had used him, that she had transformed him, the father of her child, from the sweetest man she had ever known into her instrument of vengeance against his own brother. Then she would have to ask him, "What can I do to make it better?" just as he had asked her all those years earlier.

Chapter 33

Before things turned ugly, Clarice, Veronica, and Sharon sat enjoying iced tea and friendly conversation beneath a patio umbrella on the enormous redwood deck that wrapped around the back of Veronica's house. The deck was the first in a long series of alterations Veronica had inflicted upon her redbrick ranch house after she and her mother split the money they received for the property in Leaning Tree. It occupied two-thirds of her backyard and rightfully belonged on the Pacific side of a California oceanfront mansion. The other changes were fashioned after Barbara Jean's huge Victorian. She had added on a small turret, two colorfully painted front porches, and a widow's walk. The result of the renovations was a structure that combined the worst aspects of a Southern California beach house and a San Francisco bordello. Behind her back, Clarice called Veronica's home Barbie's Malibu Whorehouse.

With the words "Sharon, there's something I have to tell you," the atmosphere of conviviality evaporated. After Clarice told Veronica and Sharon the story of finding Clifton Abrams nude with a woman in the gazebo, she was called a liar in stereo. Then Veronica began to pace the deck, her heavy footsteps echoing like hammer blows as she stalked across the redwood beams.

Veronica recited a list of offenses Clarice had committed against her over the years. She started in 1960 and worked her way forward, spelling out just how Clarice had wronged her in each decade of her life. The most heinous crime, Veronica said, had been Clarice keeping her at arm's length while publicly embracing Odette and Barbara Jean as if they were her sisters. "It says a lot about your character, if you ask me, throwing over your own family for a foul-tempered, smartass fat girl and a whore's daughter."

Sharon said, "Mmm, hmm."

Clarice knew from experience that a young woman in love could derive great comfort from sticking her head in the sand. So instead of addressing Sharon, she said to Veronica, "This relationship between Sharon and Clifton has come along pretty fast. I'm just saying that there are things she hasn't learned about him yet, and she should learn those things before she marries him."

Veronica shrieked, "Minnie warned me you would try to interfere with things. I bet you've been itching to pull this for months. You can't stand for anybody else to be important. It always has to be about you." She singsonged, "Clarice and her piano. Clarice and her football star." Then she coughed out a rough-sounding laugh and said, "You're a fine one to come around here with marriage advice. Why don't we ask Richmond how he appreciated coming in third on your list behind *the Supremes*?" She put her finger to her chin, pretending to be deep in thought, "Oh yeah, that's right, we can't ask him. He put you out. Didn't he, Miss Marriage Expert?"

Clarice turned to Sharon. "I really didn't come by to

upset you or cause trouble." Sharon responded with a groan of skepticism. "The thing is, I *am* the expert on this. I know what it means to spend your life with a cheating man. And the only reason I'm here telling you this is that I care about you and I don't want to see you go through what I've been through."

Veronica put her hands on her hips and cocked her head to one side. "Because you care so much about Sharon, I won't un-invite you to our wedding. But your services as assistant wedding planner will no longer be needed. I'll have your wedding book back now, thank you very much." She dramatically extended her arms and held out both hands, palms up, as if she thought Clarice had the twenty-pound book in one of her pockets and might conceivably slip it out and hand it to her.

When Clarice pointed out that she didn't have the book on her, Veronica said, "Well, you can bring it by later. Leave it on the front stoop, if you please. I don't think you and I need to have any further interaction." Then she opened the sliding glass door and strode inside with Sharon at her heels.

As she disappeared into the house, Sharon called out over her shoulder, "People will be talking about my wedding for years to come."

None of them knew then just how right Sharon was about that.

When Clarice got back to Leaning Tree, she did some work in the garden to sweat the lingering frustration from her tussle with Veronica out of her system. Then she bathed and started to cook her dinner. She cracked eggs and pulled leftover potatoes and fried onions from the refrigerator for a frittata. Since she'd been on her own, her meals tended toward that kind of thing – simple dishes that Richmond had refused to eat because of their foreign-sounding names or had rejected as "girl food" because they lacked red meat.

Clarice was whisking eggs when Richmond knocked on the front door. She saw him on the porch and thought, *Lord, this is the last thing I need today.* She opened the door and prepared herself for a fight.

"Hello, Richmond. What do you want?"

He smiled and said, "Is that any way for a wife to greet a husband who comes bearing a gift?"

He held up an envelope in his right hand and waved it back and forth in front of his face.

"What's that?" she asked.

"Like I said, it's a gift. A birthday gift."

"It's not my birthday. You must have me confused with some other woman."

He pouted. "Come on, Clarice, give a man a break. I know when your birthday is. This is an *early* present."

"Sorry. It's been kind of a rough day. Thanks for the present." She held out her hand to take the envelope.

"Aren't you going to invite me in?"

Clarice sighed, still not in the mood to be bothered. But years of childhood etiquette training kicked in and she couldn't be rude any longer. She said, "Come on in," and he followed her into the living room.

They sat together on the couch. Like most of the furniture in the house, it dated back to the 1960s. The springs beneath the cushions had long since given up the ghost, and Richmond's weight caused him to sink so far into the couch that his knees came close to his chest. He handed Clarice the envelope and she tore it open.

She began to read the letter he had given her, but she couldn't make sense of what she was seeing. "What *is* this?" she asked.

"It's what it looks like."

What she held in her hands was a letter from Wendell Albertson, the music producer who had invited her to record all of the Beethoven sonatas for his label more than thirty years earlier. She said, "Is this some kind of a joke? Wendell Albertson would have to be a hundred years old, if he's alive at all. And I know his record company is long gone."

"The record company is gone, all right. But Albertson's alive and well. He's not that much older than we are. You were only, what—twenty, when you first met him? Everybody over thirty was old to us then. Anyway, as you can see, he's still working and still remembers you."

In the letter, Mr Albertson expressed his surprise and pleasure that Clarice had contacted him after all these years. He also thanked her for the "wonderful recordings" that had accompanied her letter to him.

"What letter? What recordings?" she asked Richmond.

He said, "Well, the letter is what you might call a 'loving forgery,' but the recordings are yours. I took the tapes from your recitals over to the audio lab at the university and they made them into disks for me. And I sent the disks to Albertson." He leaned back and sank even further into the couch with a self-satisfied smile on his face.

Clarice shook her head. "Oh Richmond, I know you

meant well, but you really shouldn't have done this. Those tapes are ancient. I don't play like that anymore."

"No, you play better than you did," he said. "I've been listening. Every time I come by here I sit outside on the porch before I knock, or sometimes after I say goodbye, and I listen to you. You play better than ever, sweetheart, you really do."

The last part of the letter from Wendell Albertson discussed possible dates for Clarice to come play for him in New York. Assuming that went well, they would talk recording dates and discuss his idea of marketing her as a resurrected prodigy.

She put the sheet of paper down on the coffee table in front of her and said, "I honestly don't know whether to kiss you or spank you."

Now was the time for Richmond to test the waters by saying "You could do both," or something along those lines. Because he didn't, she leaned over and kissed him on the mouth. Then she gave him another kiss because, even though what he'd done was crazy, it was also the kindest thing he had ever done for her. She picked up the letter and read it again just to make sure she hadn't imagined it.

"So, do you like your birthday present?" he asked.

"You know, I think I do like it. It'll probably blow up in my face. But I like it. Thank you, Richmond."

"You're welcome. I'm glad to see I can still make you happy."

Clarice kissed him once more, on the cheek this time. Then she thanked him again.

Richmond said, "Well, I'd better get out while I'm

ahead." He scooted forward on the couch, beginning the process of extricating himself from the cushions. He stood, grunting as he put weight on his bad ankle.

Clarice walked a few steps toward the door with him, but then stopped him with a hand on his arm. "You don't have to go. Stay for dinner. I'm making a frittata."

"That sounds nice. You know how I love fri-tta-ta." He pronounced it "free tah-tah," drawing it out so that it sounded both silly and dirty. She gave his arm a playful punch and he accompanied her into the kitchen.

After dinner, they sat on stools at the kitchen counter and talked. Clarice described her afternoon at Veronica's house to him. He filled her in on the latest about the football team and how their prospects looked for the upcoming season. She told him that Odette was getting worse and that it scared her. He bragged that he was on schedule with his diabetes medication nearly every day now and was becoming a champion clothes ironer. She told him about going to the Unitarian church and how she thought maybe it was just right for her. Clarice even related to him the tale of finding his girlfriend Cherokee in the gazebo with Clifton Abrams.

Richmond laughed until tears came to his eyes at her description of Clifton hopping around naked, trying to get back into his underpants. But he took exception to her calling Cherokee his girlfriend, insisting that he had given up all of his women in an effort to become a better man. This included, he claimed, the girls at the Pink Slipper Gentlemen's Club. He said that his only recent visit to the club had been for purely theological purposes.

In response to her laughter, Richmond raised his right

hand as if he were taking the Boy Scout Oath. "No, really. Tammi, the girl who showed up at the last revival meeting, has been doing biblically themed pole dances on Monday nights at the club. Last week she danced the tale of Eve's expulsion from the Garden of Eden and gave every cent she made to the New Roof Fund at church. What kind of Christian would I be if I didn't show up and support a young convert preaching the Word?" He swore that he had left the club, alone, the second the dancer and her python exited the stage. He said, "You told me to evolve, remember?"

"I remember. But please don't change everything. You've still got your good points," Clarice said. She wondered if she was flirting with him now from force of habit or because she actually sensed something was different about him.

She thought back to her conversation with Veronica then. She said, "Richmond, tell me something. Do you feel like I neglected you or made you a low priority in my life because of Odette and Barbara Jean?"

The expression on his face said that he thought she had thrown him a trick question or was laying a trap. "Why do you ask that?"

"Something Veronica said to me today made me wonder."

He thought about it for a while and then said, "You know, if you'd asked me that question a few weeks ago, I'd have said yes. But that would have been to get you to feel guilty and maybe come back home. But, honestly, I was always glad you had the Supremes. I think it made me feel okay about running with Ramsey and all my other . . . well, *activities*, let's say. When it came to you and me, I never felt anything but loved, and that's the truth."

"Thanks, Richmond. I appreciate you saying that. That was really sweet of you."

"What can I say? I'm a sweet guy. That's why you married me, isn't it?"

Remembering the early years of their courtship and the fever that had swept over her whenever she looked at Richmond or even thought about him, Clarice said, "Not exactly."

"No, I suppose it was having your mother on my side that sealed the deal for me."

"Partly. But, to be honest about it, the thing that really made up my mind for me was something Big Earl said."

"Big Earl?"

"Mm-hmm. I had already talked to Mother, Reverend Peterson, even that old fraud Minnie, and I was still wavering. So I went by the All-You-Can-Eat one night to talk to Big Earl. Odette and Barbara Jean both swore the man was a genius, and I had always liked him. So I figured, *why not*?"

"Big Earl stuck up for me, did he?"

"He said that when you grew up you'd be a fine man."

Richmond swallowed hard and his mouth spread into a slightly sad smile. "Damn, I miss that old man."

Clarice had done a little paraphrasing for the sake of the evening's mood. What Big Earl had actually said was, "Clarice, honey, I truly believe that in about twenty-five years, Richmond Baker is likely to show himself to be as fine a man as this town ever turned out. Till then, you might be in for a rough ride." With that fever in her blood,

Clarice had decided to hear what Big Earl said as a glowing endorsement. It was years before she realized that she had ignored a warning in favor of an optimistic prediction. And that prediction had been quite optimistic. Big Earl had seen Richmond's turnaround coming in twenty-five years. As usual, Richmond was dragging himself in late.

Neither of them said anything for a while. Then Richmond glanced at his watch. "I guess now I've really got to go."

Clarice reached out and patted his cheek with her hand, allowing it to rest there for a few seconds to enjoy the familiar sensation of his beard stubble against her open palm. She thought for a moment and then said, "Don't go. Stay over."

His eyebrows rose and he asked, "You mean it?"

"Yeah, why not? We're married, aren't we?"

As he hopped off of his stool, he smiled that fun, nasty smile she had always loved. Then he hooked an arm around her and pulled her to him. They kissed through the kitchen, the hallway, the living room, and up the stairs.

Clarice had thought that it would be like old times, she and Richmond together enjoying that type of married folks' lovemaking that was a mixture of passion and efficiency gained from familiarity. But it was better than it had been before. Living alone for the first time in her life had changed her perspective. She didn't have to see Richmond as a disappointing husband anymore. In her house he was her lover, there at her request, for her pleasure. In that department, Richmond never disappointed. And without the burden of having to play the wronged wife, Clarice could be his lover, too – a free woman who wore peasant skirts and comfortable shoes and gave as good as she got in bed.

She woke up in the morning to find Richmond already awake. He was lying on his side, his right elbow on the mattress, his head propped up by his hand. "G'morning," he said.

She stretched and yawned. "Good morning to you, too."

He pecked her lightly on the lips and whispered, "Glad you're awake. I didn't want to take off before you got up. I have to be at a meeting in a couple hours."

Clarice nodded. "Sorry you have to go."

"Me, too." He slid out of the bed and went across the room retrieving his clothing, which they had flung from wall to wall in the heat of the moment the night before. Once he had gathered all of his clothes, he sat on the edge of the bed and started to dress. It was a reverse striptease Clarice had seen thousands of times. It was always done in the same order. Right sock. Left sock. Underwear. Pants. Belt. Shoes. Then, finally, the undershirt and shirt were slipped over his massive and still firm upper torso and arms. Richmond had a strong sense of what his best features were and he didn't like to cover up the good stuff too quickly.

He was just about to pull on his pants when he said, "Listen, while you were sleeping I was thinking there's no need for you to have to pack up all your things. We can hire somebody to box up your clothes and whatever else you brought over. And later in the week we can have the piano movers come. How's that sound?"

"What are you talking about?"

"Your move back home. We can hire someone to pack your things."

"I'm not moving back home, Richmond."

He'd had his back to her; now he stood and turned around. Richmond, clad in his boxer shorts and socks, stared at Clarice with an astonished look on his face. "What do you mean you're not coming home? I thought – well, after last night and what happened . . ." He gestured back and forth from his bare chest to her naked body in the bed to illustrate his point.

She sat up in the bed. "Richmond, last night was a lot of fun, but I see no reason to come back home. I like it here. And this short amount of time we've been apart isn't enough to fix forty years of both of us making foolish decisions. You know that."

His eyes grew big and he raised his voice. "You knew that if we went to bed together I'd think you were coming home, and you went ahead and let me think that."

"I'm sorry if that's what you thought. But nothing's changed, except we had a really good night."

Richmond stood beside the bed with his mouth opening and shutting. He looked like a giant brown fish that had been thrown onto dry land. He clutched his pants against his chest as if he had suddenly grown modest and was trying to cover himself. With his empty hand, he pointed at Clarice and stammered out, "Y-y-you led me on and used me. That's what you did. You made me think we were going to be together again and you used me."

She thought about it for a few seconds and realized that he was right. She had known what he would think about the two of them after last night, and she had pushed that knowledge aside because she wanted him, the way she had always wanted him. Some other day, maybe she'd have felt guilty. But that morning, she was completely unable to keep herself from grinning, and then giggling at the thought that she had used Richmond.

Towering over her beside the bed, Richmond looked as indignant as Clarice could remember seeing him. But then she saw his face gradually break into a smile and he began to chuckle along with her. He laughed harder and harder until he wobbled on his feet and collapsed onto the bed next to her.

"You had me over for dinner, screwed my brains out, and now you're getting rid of me at sunrise. I can't believe this. You turned me into a one-night stand. No, it's even worse. You actually had me believing we were going to be together. Holy shit. I'm not your one-night stand; I'm your mistress." He whacked his forehead with his hand and shook his head. "Ramsey's always telling me, 'Man, Clarice is gonna turn you into a woman if you give her half the chance.' And after forty years, it's finally happened."

Still snickering, Clarice put a leg over him and straddled his hips. "We don't have to tell Ramsey about it. We can keep it our dirty little secret." Then she kissed him hard.

He stayed for another hour.

On his way out later that morning, she told him she would call him about getting together for dinner soon. At the door, she swatted him on his firm, round ass and kissed him goodbye.

After she put the teakettle on and popped bread into the toaster, Clarice reread the letter Richmond had brought her the night before. She thought to herself that if this was what it was like to have a mistress – a night of thoughtful gifts and good sex, then your lover is out of your hair by breakfast time – Richmond's behavior over the past few decades made a lot more sense to her.

Chapter 34

Sharon's wedding took place on the hottest day south-ern Indiana had seen in decades. Spring had come early that year and the trend of record temperatures that had begun in February continued into the summer. The mercury registered right at one hundred and five degrees that afternoon and the humidity was just as awful. Only Richmond wasn't panting from the exertion of climbing the slight incline that led to the Garden Hills Banquet Hall and Corporate Meetings Venue from its parking lot. The Supremes and James began gasping for air within yards of their cars. The journey from the parking lot to the banquet hall was made worse by the fact that the high temperature had caused the tar on the asphalt of the lot and driveway to become tacky so they had to work hard just to lift their feet from the ground.

They stopped at the front steps of Garden Hills to take in the enormity of the place. The pictures from Veronica's wedding book hadn't done it justice. The building was a half a block long. The huge white columns supporting the second-floor verandah that stretched across the width of the structure were far more massive than the photo had let on. Nothing else in town, aside from the larger buildings on the campus, approached this place in size.

The banquet hall was a part of "the other Plainview," the Plainview that those who had grown up there didn't recognize. This imposing tribute to Greek Revival belonged to the new town that was being built by the university and by Plainview's newer residents, people who worked in Louisville and saw little of the town outside of the routes from their bloated homes to the pricey specialty shops of modern-day Leaning Tree. Every one of the people gathered in front of the building thought the same thing. They were becoming outsiders in their own town.

Barbara Jean said, "It looks like something straight out of *Gone With the Wind.*"

Clarice snapped her fingers. "That's it. I've been trying to think what this place reminded me of, and that's it. It's Tara, caught in a fun-house mirror. What a sight."

Odette said, "Would somebody please explain to me why any self-respecting black couple would want to get married in a giant plantation house? That's messed up."

Barbara Jean shook her head. "I tell you they're asking for trouble not getting married in a church. Everybody knows that's bad luck."

"My words exactly," Clarice said.

Two young men exited the building and gawked at Barbara Jean as they passed by. Clarice and Odette silently agreed with their judgment. Barbara Jean looked fantastic. She had toned down the color palette of her clothing over the previous few months. She hadn't exactly turned into a wallflower, but the days of the wild outfits seemed to have come to an end. And it wasn't just her clothes that were different. Sobriety seemed to be doing wonders for her. Who could have imagined that Barbara Jean could become more beautiful? But a few months without liquor had managed the impossible. Odette and Clarice both told her all the time how proud they were of her, but in typical Barbara Jean fashion, she refused to take any credit for what she had accomplished. She would mutter some catchphrase like "One day at a time," and then change the subject. But Barbara Jean had been resurrected and that was plain to see.

"Let's get inside. It's too hot out here," James said, meaning that it was too hot for Odette to be outside. James was more vigilant than ever that summer – part nurse, part mother bear, part prison guard. He was also more aware than anyone that Odette had lost more weight and more strength. She fought on like a champion, though, refusing to acknowledge that anything had changed. Her husband and her friends admired her warrior spirit, but couldn't help but feel like Odette was rubbing her legendary fearlessness in everyone's faces. When they looked at Odette, they all knew it was time to feel scared. They battled with the urge to shake her until she came to her senses and was as frightened as they were.

The lobby welcomed the Supremes, James, and Richmond with a blast of frigid air that made each of them sigh with relief. A pretty young hostess with bright red hair and an exaggerated English accent greeted the wedding guests at the reception desk. She said, "Good afternoon. We are delighted to have you here at Garden Hills Banquet Hall and Corporate Meetings Venue. Please follow the corridor to the doors that lead out to the courtyard for the Swanson-Abrams nuptials," and pointed out the way for them. Her instructions were accompanied by flamboyant arm waving. She wore a tight gray skirt and a very low-cut frilly white blouse. Her breasts jiggled with each of her grand movements. Richmond did an admirable job of staring at the ceiling instead of ogling the girl as his nature would surely have had him do. Clarice had to give the man an A for effort.

Unlike Richmond, who was going all out to prove that he was a changed man, Clarice wasn't certain what degree of exertion on her part was appropriate where her marriage was concerned. The new Clarice enjoyed having Richmond as her secret lover – she hadn't told her friends that he'd been spending nights with her. But the old Clarice, the one who knew all of the rules and yearned to follow them, had staged a reappearance. Somehow Clarice had gone from reveling in her newfound freedom and sensuality to feeling guilty about her vain pursuit of pleasure. She had even begun to take pride in sending Richmond away at the times she most wanted him to stay. Funny how easy it was to tap into all of that – the guilt, the shame, the anger. *You can take the girl out of Calvary Baptist, but you can't take Calvary Baptist out of the girl,* she thought.

At the end of the hallway, two young men in white uniforms stood stationed beside massive oak doors. When the Supremes, Richmond, and James approached, the men shoved open the doors, exposing a vast and spectacu-lar courtyard. Second – possibly – only to Barbara Jean's prizewinning gardens, this was the most elaborately land-scaped property in town. Intricately sculpted evergreens lined the courtyard's redbrick walls. Lacy vines trailed from stone pots that sat atop pillars that had been distressed in the style of Roman ruins. Luridly bright flowers of every variety surrounded the wedding guests.

Barbara Jean grabbed Clarice's arm. "This is incredible. They must swap out these plants every week to keep them looking like this."

The garden was something to see, all right. Unfortunately, the direct sunlight that helped the flowers remain so beautiful was not greeted with much approval from the wedding guests. The sun beat down on them and, as more people arrived, their shared suffering soon became the number one topic of conversation. Erma Mae and Little Earl McIntyre stepped into the courtyard just behind the Supremes, both of them frantically fanning themselves with their hands. Erma Mae grumbled, "Outdoor weddin' in July. Your cousin's tryin' to kill us all, Clarice."

Erma Mae wore a violet straw hat that Clarice thought was cute. But that hat didn't provide a bit of shade to her great, round head. Erma Mae's cheeks and ears baked in the afternoon sun. She continued to curse Veronica as she and her husband headed to their seats.

To ensure Odette's comfort, James had been toting around an enormous insulated bag full of just-in-case supplies all summer. By the time the Supremes and their spouses had traveled down the brick path that divided the courtyard in half and seated themselves on creaky white wooden chairs, James had dug into the bag and pulled out five chilled bottles of water and a couple of battery-operated personal fans. He handed each of his friends a bottle of water and gave fans to Barbara Jean and Odette. In return, James received heartfelt thanks and an apology from Richmond for having teased him about carrying a purse for the past month.

Refreshed by the water and puffs of air from the tiny fans they passed back and forth to each other, Barbara Jean and Clarice ventured from their seats to take a closer look at the flowers. They took a few steps toward the nearest bed, but stopped when they were still about five feet away after discovering that they weren't the only admirers of the flowers. Dozens of bees floated from bloom to bloom in lazy arcs – a picturesque summer scene, best appreciated from a safe distance. When they discussed it later, they all agreed that the bees had been an omen.

The two uniformed employees who had opened the courtyard doors for the guests reappeared, each carrying an oscillating electric floor fan. When they placed the fans in opposing corners of the rectangular seating area and turned them on, the crowd burst into applause. The effect was mostly psychological, though. Humid hundred-degree air was still humid hundred-degree air, even with a two-mile-per-hour gust behind it. But the slightest of breezes was cause for celebration on that day.

The tiresome elevator music that had been piped in via speakers placed throughout the flower beds stopped. The redhead who had greeted everyone at the front door entered the courtyard and asked the crowd to be seated in order that the service might begin. James glanced at his watch and nodded his approval. "Right on time."

The speakers blasted out music again. This time it was Pachelbel's Canon in D. Clarice muttered to herself, "How unimaginative can you get." Then she admonished herself for being mean.

The large oak doors opened again and Reverend Biggs stepped through. He was followed by Clifton Abrams and his groomsmen – Clifton's shoe freak brother Stevie and two shifty-eyed, scowling young men. The groomsmen slouched in their ill-fitting, rented tuxedoes with matching green cummerbunds and emerald bowties beneath a bridal arch that was covered in chartreuse carnations. Behind them, a fountain in the shape of a gigantic fish spat water high into the sticky air.

Odette leaned toward Clarice and said, "Is this a wedding party or a police lineup?" Clarice responded, "You are just awful," even though she had been thinking the same thing.

The doors opened again and Veronica's mother walked out on the arm of her favorite granddaughter's husband, a heavyset young man who stopped every few seconds to wipe perspiration from his eyes with his free hand. Glory's green dress wasn't very flattering, but she seemed unaffected by the heat. In fact, she looked far healthier and cheerier than when Clarice had last seen her. Glory and Clarice's mother, who was boycotting Plainview until Clarice left "that Unitarian cult" she had joined, hadn't spoken in several weeks due to yet another theological spat. From the looks of things, not talking to Beatrice had been good for Glory. There was, Clarice thought, a lesson to be learned in that.

Minnie McIntyre strutted down the aisle after Glory. In keeping with the color scheme of the wedding, Minnie wore a kelly green suit, making it the first time in months she had been seen in anything other than one of her fortune-telling outfits. She slowly walked, unescorted, down the brick path toward her chair in the front row. On her way, she acknowledged acquaintances in the crowd with a slight dipping of her head. She frowned each time she did it. It was clear to all spectators that her signature move was unsatisfying to her without her turban and bell.

The groom's parents, Ramsey and Florence Abrams, came next. Ramsey grinned as if he were filming a toothpaste commercial. Florence smiled, too, though it was difficult to tell with her. For years, Florence had twisted her facial features into an expression more suggestive of having encountered an unpleasant odor than experiencing joy. The muscles responsible for smiling had atrophied long ago. However, her customary pained smirk seemed to be less agonized than usual that day.

Just after Ramsey and Florence were seated, the music changed to Handel's "The Arrival of the Queen of Sheba," which had been Clarice's suggestion for use as the bridal march. Veronica appeared.

Clarice was forced to admit that Veronica looked nice. Green wasn't a good color for anyone else in the wedding party so far, but it looked good on her. Veronica smiled, waved, and occasionally mouthed hello to guests as she proceeded down the aisle with her jerky, fast gait. When she passed Clarice, Veronica made a show of pointing her chin toward the sky to remind her cousin that she had not forgotten the clash they'd had on Veronica's backyard deck when Clarice passed along the story of catching Clifton in a compromising position with another woman.

Veronica's grand procession was marred by a sudden outburst when she was nearly at her seat. Florence Abrams began to scream and run back and forth in front of the bridal arch. No one could hear what she was yelling at first. But the cause of the commotion became evident when Florence ran past Reverend Biggs, who was outfitted with a lapel microphone. She yelled, "I'm stung. I'm stung!" and she clutched her left forearm where a bee had just stung her. A few seconds later, Florence was down on the ground, still screaming. It was very frightening because everyone who knew Florence at all well knew that she was severely allergic to bee stings.

Ramsey promptly fetched his wife's EpiPen injector from her pocketbook and administered a shot of epinephrine so Florence wouldn't choke on her tongue in front of three hundred wedding guests. After tending to his wife, he walked over to Reverend Biggs and shouted into the pastor's lapel that they'd been through this many times before and that Florence would be just fine. Florence remained on the ground for a while, though, until the injection took effect. All anyone could see of her was her feet sticking out from a bed of sky-blue phlox.

Odette leaned across Clarice, who had the aisle seat, in order to get a better look. Always immune to hysteria, Odette said, "I sure do like her shoes."

To a round of applause, Florence was hauled up from the ground and helped back into her seat. Then the reverend, groom, and groomsmen took their places and the speakers came to life again, blasting out a loud drumroll.

The doors opened and suddenly the scent of lavender overwhelmed the fragrance of the flowers. Out came the pink cloud. It wasn't quite the round, cottony ball it had appeared to be in the brochure advertising the Cloud Nine Wedding Package. Because of the fans blowing on it, the cloud looked more like an undulating blob of fiberglass insulation, tendrils of which flailed threateningly in the hot air and then evaporated.

One at a time, Sharon's sisters filed out of the fog. Each of them wore the same neon-green crushed-velvet dress with balloon sleeves and puffy bows ringing the waistline. Only Veronica would conspire to make those homely young women wear such terrifying monstrosities. Watching the bridesmaids lumber down the aisle, Clarice thought, *I know I can't be the only one here thinking "Gorillas in the Mist."*

The bridesmaids were followed by the flower girl, Veronica's nine-year-old granddaughter, Latricia. Veronica had chosen Latricia because she was the prettiest of her three granddaughters and consequently her favorite. Clarice had tried, as diplomatically as she could, to talk Veronica out of that decision. Latricia was a cutie, but no one would ever accuse her of being the least bit intelligent. Latricia's flower girl technique amounted to running several quick steps, then stopping suddenly. Every time she stopped, she dug her hand deep into the green toile-covered wicker basket she carried, took out a fistful of green carnation petals, and flung them as hard as she could directly into the face of whoever sat nearest to her. She kept this up until her mother, the matron of honor, bellowed, "Latricia, cut it out! Now!" Latricia completed her walk at a steady pace. But along the way, she glared at the wedding guests and stuffed flower petals into her mouth.

Odette said, "That is not a bright child."

A trumpet fanfare began and Reverend Biggs raised his

arms to let the guests know that they should stand for the entrance of the bride. Sharon emerged from the pink cloud on the arm of her father, Clement.

Her appearance was greeted with oohs and ahhs from the guests.

"My goodness, she's so thin I wouldn't have recognized her. She looks adorable," Barbara Jean said.

It was true. Sharon looked divine. With the aid of her hypnotist, Sharon had wiped fifty pounds off her figure in just a few months. The gown her mother had purchased several sizes too small for her now fit perfectly. Though Clarice had sworn to herself that, as a part of her new life, she had given up on diets forever, she couldn't help but think that when she and Veronica started speaking again she would have to ask for that hypnotist's phone number.

The trumpet music ended and a syrupy, string-heavy tune began to stream from the speakers as the doors closed behind Sharon and her father. A few steps beyond the pink cloud, Sharon slowly raised her bouquet to her veil-covered face and began to sing "We've Only Just Begun" into a microphone that was hidden among her flowers.

The song was clearly a Veronica touch, Clarice thought. A girl of Sharon's age would never have chosen an old Carpenters' song, popular long before her birth, to sing at her wedding. And Sharon certainly wasn't singing it as if it were a personal favorite. All around the courtyard, people squirmed in their seats and grimaced in response to the bride's voice. The newly slimmed Sharon may have looked like an angel in her ivory-colored, form-fitting bridal gown, but she sang like a screeching demon freshly released from the deepest pit of hell. Clarice thought, *Why, oh why, didn't Veronica spring for a few voice lessons in addition to Sharon's hypnosis?*

Right on cue, a dozen white Bostonian doves fluttered away from a cage hidden behind the spitting fish fountain as Sharon wailed, "A kiss for luck and we're on our way." About ten feet up in the air, the doves formed a circle and flew in formation in response to whistled cues from the bird wrangler, who crouched behind one of the taller pseudo-Roman pillars. The effect was impressive enough to draw scattered applause.

Unfortunately, that impressive moment didn't last long. As Sharon caterwauled her way toward her groom, a dark blur appeared overhead and streaked toward the doves. In a scene reminiscent of *Mutual of Omaha's Wild Kingdom*, an enormous gray-and-brown falcon snatched one of the doves away from the formation and zipped off with it clasped in its talons. The dove wrangler began frenzied tooting, presumably calling the other eleven birds back to their cage. But the doves kept flying higher. They had already sensed the arrival of the second hawk. It descended upon them an instant later and reduced their number to ten.

The remaining birds, shrieking loudly, returned to their trainer. He secured them inside a large cage and then hustled them away from the courtyard. The location of the two missing doves was made clear to the assemblage by the twin streams of white feathers that lazily drifted down from a tall maple tree just on the other side of the wall. Occasionally a feather floated onto the courtyard and was struck by the red light of the laser that spelled out "Sharon and Clifton," imbuing the white feathers with an eerie, bloody-looking tinge.

Shocked, Sharon gave up on her vocalizing and walked the rest of the way down the aisle with her father to the sound of the instrumental accompaniment of the song.

Reverend Biggs tried to get things back on track. He began his homily with a brief reference to the circle of life. Then he artfully segued into his prepared speech.

But, like so many things that day, the reverend's remarks went unfinished. Not long after Reverend Biggs began speaking, the big oak doors creaked open once again. All of the guests turned their faces toward the back, hoping they might feel the sweet breath of cool air escaping from the indoors for a moment. No one got any relief from the heat, but they did get another look at the pink cloud. Then they saw four uniformed policemen step through the fog and onto the brick path. The policemen appeared to be embarrassed when the doors shut behind them and they realized that hundreds of wedding guests sat staring at them. The policemen moved off to one side, trying to make themselves less conspicuous. But they'd been seen, and their effect was immediate.

One of the groomsmen shouted, "It's the cops, man!" Then he and the unsavory-looking character next to him took off running. The groomsmen leaped over shrubs and bushes, finally escaping the courtyard through an emergency exit. Opening that door activated an alarm, and the thick air was filled with shrill screeching. Clarice turned toward her friends and said, "I don't know about you, but I prefer this to the singing." Odette and Barbara Jean nodded in agreement.

The police didn't make a move to pursue the grooms-men. They stared directly at the groom. Clifton Abrams responded to their attention by shoving Reverend Biggs out of his way and running through the tea roses and across a perennials bed. He made a dash for a clematis-covered trellis that stood against an outer wall. Once there, he began to climb. The police chased after him. They grabbed him by his ankles before he could make it over the wall and wrestled him down into a patch of black-eyed Susans.

Florence Abrams let out a loud cry and fainted. She crumpled to the ground so that, once again, all that could be seen of her was her feet sticking out of the phlox bed. Clarice said, "You're right, Odette, those really are cute shoes."

The policemen handcuffed Clifton and carried him out. Sharon followed them, howling, "Clifton! Clifton!"

Little Latricia skipped along after Sharon, tossing green petals high into the air.

Odette said, "They really should get that child some help."

Veronica let loose a stream of obscenities the likes of which none of the Supremes had heard since Odette's mother passed. Veronica cornered Minnie McIntyre near the bridal arch and made quite a scene shouting about the faulty information her oracle had provided. She yelled, "Where's my perfect day, dammit?!" Veronica's husband and daughters had to restrain her while Minnie escaped, running into the pink cloud after the cops, the groom, the bride, and the flower girl.

Rather than stick around Garden Hills for canapés and

quiet gossip, Odette, Barbara Jean, and Clarice decided to adjourn to the All-You-Can-Eat for ribs and loud gossip. They stuck around just long enough for James to put on his law enforcement hat and get the lowdown from one of the cops who had arrested Clifton. Then they walked to their cars in silence, each of them trying to digest what they had just witnessed.

They were in the parking lot when Barbara Jean interrupted the quiet that had fallen over the group, saying, "Well, that just goes to show you what happens when you don't have a church wedding. It was bound to end badly."

Clarice said, "No, that's what happens when you're foolish enough to listen to Minnie McIntyre's advice."

James said, "No, that shows you what happens when the groom is dumb enough to mail a wedding invitation to his pissed-off ex-girlfriend when she knows he has outstanding felony warrants for drug possession and grand larceny in Louisville. The detective said some girl named Cherokee walked into the police station last night waving the invitation in the air and saying, 'If you'd like to apprehend a fugitive felon, I know where he'll be tomorrow at three.'"

Clarice stopped where she was standing and began to laugh. She said, "I feel sorry for Sharon, I really do. But I've been holding in a giggle ever since Florence got stung by that bee."

The floodgates opened. Barbara Jean joined Clarice, laughing so hard that she cried. Richmond chuckled into one hand and held his stomach with the other.

They all stopped laughing when they noticed that Odette had slumped against James. The two of them slowly sank down onto the hot pavement. Odette appeared to be only half-conscious. And James looked even more stricken than she did as he cried out her name.

Clarice and Barbara Jean rushed to Odette's side and saw that her eyes were flickering open and shut. Before she completely lost consciousness, Odette mumbled something that they could have sworn was "Back off, Mrs Roosevelt."

Chapter 35

I was on my feet hooting and howling and preparing to lie about feeling sorry for Veronica when the air around me turned to milky water. Then I was sitting on the asphalt. Everyone except for Mama and Mrs Roosevelt, who both popped up just as the air went to liquid, began to move in slow motion and fade away. I told Mrs Roosevelt to back off, but she cast sorrowful puppy eyes at me and moved closer.

Then I was in the ICU. For six days I lay there, not exactly awake and not exactly asleep. I wasn't in pain. I wasn't frightened. And Lord knows I wasn't lonely, not with the constant stream of guests who came and went – James, my pastor, the other Supremes and Richmond, my doctor, nurses, to mention a few. And that was just the living. Sometimes the room was packed to bursting with Mama, Eleanor Roosevelt, Big Earl, Miss Thelma, and other friends from the spirit world.

Mostly, I felt tired and blazing hot, hotter than I had ever been when I'd had those bad night sweats at the start of my illness. I had a powerful urge to shake off my tired body like it was a heavy, scratchy wool coat and walk away from it feeling light and cool.

Sometimes the air around me would clear and I'd

mumble a few words. Always James was there to respond. He'd grin down at me in my bed and say, "Hey there. I knew you'd come back," and then we'd exchange a few words. But the flood would come again and he'd suddenly be unable to hear what I was saying to him even though I was shouting at the top of my lungs. Whenever that happened, Eleanor Roosevelt would frown and cover her ears and Mama would say, "Stop all that yellin'. You'll wake the dead." Then, each time she made that joke, she'd giggle like it was the first time she'd said it.

On my first day in the hospital, I learned from listening in as Dr Alex Soo talked to James that, for the first time in months, cancer wasn't my most serious health problem. I was suffering from an infection. My heart and lungs were distributing sickness throughout my body and the antibiotics weren't halting it. I was, in Alex's words, "gravely ill."

The rooms in the Intensive Care Unit formed a square around a large nurses' station. Every room was the same: one bed, one chair, one window on the outside wall, three inner walls made of glass. Unless the curtains that lined the walls of each room were pulled shut, I could see into every room in the ICU. I didn't need to peek to know who lay in the other beds, though. My neighbors were up and about every bit as much as they were in their beds. The lady confined to the bed next door to mine regularly left her physical self behind and roamed the corridors performing elaborate dances with a fan of white ostrich plumes. The ancient man across the way from me withered away as a ventilator breathed for him. But I also saw him as a broad-chested, yellow-haired fisherman who politely tipped his lure-covered cap at his fan-dancing neighbor whenever he passed by her on the way to his secret fishing hole. They stepped out of their diseased or broken bodies and had a good old time until they were drawn back to their flesh by a rush of hormones or some medication that suddenly kicked in.

I only left my body behind when I slept. When I was truly asleep, not just incapacitated by sickness or floating in a fever dream, I always traveled to the same place. I relaxed, alone, at the foot of my sycamore in Leaning Tree. Leaving that spot, with its view of the silvery creek I'd played in as a child and the twisted trees that bordered Wall Road, and returning to ghosts and grief in my hospital room was the hardest part of those six days.

I learned from those days in the hospital that if you really want to hear the secret details of people's lives, all you need to do is lapse into a coma. It's like opening up a confessional booth and inviting all comers. People kept showing up and telling me things that they couldn't bring themselves to tell me when I was responsive.

Clarice started the confession ball rolling when she stopped by on my second day in the hospital. She walked into my room all full of optimistic chitchat. She told James about people she'd known who had recovered after being in far worse condition than I was in, and she went on about how she was sure I'd be up and about in time to accompany her and Barbara Jean to New York City when she went to play for the record producer there. Then she took a good look at James, baggy-eyed and haggard, and ordered him to go to the cafeteria for something to eat. As soon as he was gone, she sat on the edge of my bed and confided that she was sleeping with Richmond again.

Barbara Jean and I had long since figured that one out, but Clarice was having such a nice time with her secret that we didn't want to ruin it for her by letting on that we knew. Unfortunately, Clarice had made the mistake of talking to her mother about it. Now Mrs Jordan had Clarice worried that she was headed for hell. Her mother put it in her head that having sex with her own husband while refusing to be his wife in any other way was the height of wantonness.

Clarice said, "Maybe I should just go back home. I love being on my own in Leaning Tree, but it can't be that simple, can it – just doing what you want because it feels good? Mother always says, 'Happiness is the first sign you're living wrong.'"

Mama, listening in, said, "I've always liked Clarice, but right now I wanna slap the shit outta her. Don't she know how lucky she is, havin' that good-lookin' man at her beck and call like she does? She needs to stop this damn whinin' and get to work on a how-to book. There's about a billion women who'd pay good money to learn how they could be in her position. Your father was a good man, but if I coulda had him when I wanted him and then sent him away when I'd had my fill, I'd have been too busy thankin' Jesus to worry whether I was committin' a sin. Poor Clarice, that mother of hers did a real number on her."

Considering the peculiarity of Mama's legacy to me, that struck me as the pot calling the kettle black; but, out of respect, I didn't say so.

Clarice also confessed to trying to outdo my daughter Denise's wedding when she planned her own daughter's ceremony more than ten years ago. She said the guilt had been preying on her mind ever since she'd started helping

Veronica put together that mess of a wedding for poor Sharon. If I could've, I'd have sat up and said, "Tell me something I don't know, why don't ya?" Then I'd have said, "We've been together too long to worry over trivial shit like that, sister. Forget about it."

Richmond came by later that same day and showed that side of him that made Clarice, and so many other women, melt in his presence. He rattled off jokes and stories until he coaxed a genuine smile from James. Then, just the way Clarice had done, Richmond practically tossed James out of the room, insisting that he go get some dinner.

Once we were alone, Richmond got to confessing. And, let me tell you, when Richmond Baker started listing the whos, whats, and wheres of the wrongs he'd done, he drew quite a crowd. The dead, Mama and Mrs Roosevelt, and the almost-dead, my colleagues from other beds in the ICU, couldn't get enough of him. They bellowed with laughter and giggled from embarrassment as Richmond confided some of the carnal sins he'd committed. Mama was quieter than I could ever remember seeing her, uttering only the occasional "Oh my." Mrs Roosevelt pulled a bag of popcorn out of her oversized black alligator pocketbook and munched away like she was at a Saturday matinee. Every now and then someone grunted in disapproval, but they all stuck around to hear every single word of it.

When Richmond was done telling a string of the dirtiest tales I'd ever heard, he stroked my hand and told me that he couldn't imagine the world without me, which touched my heart. Then one last confession. He told me that he'd been terrified of me for years, which made me even happier.

He finished up by talking about Clarice. He went on about how he was so in love with her and how he didn't think he could go on living if she didn't come back home. "I love her so much, Odette. I don't know why I do the stuff I do. Maybe it's an addiction, like alcohol or cocaine."

Mama thought the addiction theory sounded like an excuse. She'd never had patience for what she called "the navel-gazing of philanderers." Mama slapped the side of Richmond's head with the bong she'd been sharing with Mrs Roosevelt – he didn't feel it – and said, "Shut the hell up. You're not addicted. You're just a horndog, you stupid sonofabitch. Odette, tell him he's a dog and that he should just do the decent thing and carry a Victoria's Secret catalog into the bathroom and take care of business when that mood strikes, like every other God-fearing married man in America. Tell him, Odette."

Of course, I wasn't about to tell Richmond something like that, even if I could have. There are some things even I won't say.

It turned out that even the dead still had things to confess. On my third day in the hospital, Lester Maxberry visited me. Or rather, he came to watch Barbara Jean visiting me. He strolled into my room dressed in a spring walking suit that was the color of orange sherbet. His short pants were cut mid-thigh and he wore knee socks and suede espadrilles that were the same shade of light blue as his old Cadillac.

Barbara Jean sat in the visitor's chair while James sat on my bed beside me. The ICU allowed two visitors at a time but, oddly, provided just one chair per room. I did notice, though, when the fan dancer passed away surrounded by six family members, that they relaxed the two-visitor rule when they figured you were about to die. James and Barbara Jean talked about my condition, the weather, and the new volunteer job Barbara Jean had taken. She taught reading to poor kids from the tiny hill towns outside of Plainview. "There are so many more hours to the day when you stop drinking," she said.

While they talked, I took the opportunity to converse with Lester. I said, "Hey, Lester, you're looking sharp."

"Thanks, Odette. Clothes make the man, you know."

"Nope, it's the other way around, my friend. Have you been doing all right?"

Lester nodded, but he wasn't really paying any attention to me. He watched Barbara Jean with the same affection and longing he'd had for her when he was alive. "She's still the loveliest thing I've ever seen. And I've seen some amazing sights over these last eleven months."

"Has it been that long, Lester? I swear it seems like yesterday the six of us were together at the All-You-Can-Eat."

"Sneaks up on you, doesn't it? It's been almost a year." He continued staring at Barbara Jean. "I should never have married her."

"Why would you say that?" I asked.

"It wasn't right. She was practically a child and I was a grown man. I should've known better. Did know better. But when I saw that she was desperate because of the baby, I couldn't stop myself. I told myself it was okay because she'd come round to loving me over time."

"I'm pretty sure she did, Lester."

"Maybe, but mostly she was grateful. And gratitude's not a thing to build a marriage on. I was old enough to know that. She wasn't. Odette, I felt bad about that every day we were together, but it didn't stop me from holding on to her."

"Did you ever tell her that?"

He said, "No." Then he grinned at me. "But you can. The next time you talk to Barbara Jean, you can tell her I'm sorry, that I should have been stronger. Will you do that for me?"

Only someone as over-gentlemanly and overly moral as Lester Maxberry could let a thing like that eat away at him for decades. Any other man would say, "All's fair in love and war," and spend the rest of eternity bragging about how he'd managed to get the most beautiful girl in town to be his wife. I told Lester that I had it on good authority, both medical and ghostly, that I probably wouldn't be talking to Barbara Jean again in this life. But he kept at me until I promised I'd say something to her if I got the chance. Then he thanked me and went back to silently watching Barbara Jean.

The next morning, Chick Carlson dropped by and caused an even bigger fuss in the ICU than Richmond had. The nurses at the station, all full-grown women, fanned themselves and fell against each other in mock swooning after he walked by. When he came into my room, Mama eyed him up and down and nodded her approval. Even Mrs Roosevelt sat up straight and fluffed up her fox stole. Decades had passed, but Ray Carlson was still the King of the Pretty White Boys.

Chick gave my hollow-eyed, gaunt husband the once-over, and then did what all my friends had done. He badgered James into abandoning his vigil long enough to go get something to eat while Chick watched over me.

When James left, Chick sat in the visitor's chair and began to chat with my silent body. He started talking about the All-You-Can-Eat and Big Earl, all that stuff from the distant past. He'd been by my house several times over the months since he'd first visited with me in the chemo room, and every time he sat down with me he'd wanted to relive or analyze the old days. He was just as caged up in the past as Barbara Jean.

That day in the ICU, he also shared a tale with me that made me wish I could sit up right then and call Clarice on the phone. He told me all about how his tower project at the university had successfully released two rehabbed peregrine falcons just that previous Saturday. He described in beautiful detail how his birds had taken flight in front of news cameras and impressed donors. The birds, he said, were majestic and awe-inspiring.

I thought about the two hawks who had swooped in on Sharon's wedding that same Saturday and said to myself, "Majestic, awe-inspiring, and *hungry*."

Outside at the nurses' station, I heard one of the nurses saying, "Hi there, Mrs Maxberry." The staff all knew Barbara Jean from the many visits she had made to the ICU when Lester was in the hospital to have something removed, reattached, repaired, or replaced. When Barbara Jean entered my room, Chick hopped up like the seat of his chair had been electrified. They exchanged greetings and then stood there staring at each other. They were like teenagers at a school dance – both of them eager to say something, neither of them knowing how to say it.

Chick claimed that he'd just been leaving, even though he'd told James he would stay until James returned. He said, "It's nice to see you, Barbara Jean." Then, through my glass walls, I watched him walk past the giggling nurses on his way to the elevator. Every fifth or sixth step, he looked back over his shoulder for another glimpse of the most beautiful woman in town.

Barbara Jean sat in the empty visitor's chair and chewed her lip for a while, then she began to talk. The bedside confessional was open for business again.

"My sponsor, Carlo, says I need to talk to Chick. He says I need to make amends; it's one of the twelve steps. See, I did something terrible that I never told you about."

Then Barbara Jean told me a story about going to see Chick on the night of their son's funeral and how what she'd put in motion that night had eaten away at her soul for all the years since. When she got to the end of her story, she was crying hard. Her tears caused her makeup to streak and rain down onto her powder-blue blouse in brown and black droplets that she never made a move to clean up.

Just when you think the world can't hold any more surprises for you, I thought. Unlike most of the people I knew, I had never believed the rumor that it was Lester who'd shot Desmond Carlson. Even though Desmond had killed little Adam, Lester Maxberry couldn't have pulled that trigger. Former soldier or not, Lester was no killer. Truth was, I had always assumed it was Barbara Jean who'd done it, probably because that's what I would have done. Also, the way she'd fallen apart right after, with the drinking and all, she'd seemed as much guilt-ridden as grief-stricken. I had just misjudged where the guilt was coming from.

James came back as Barbara Jean attempted to put her face back together, cleaning up trails of mascara with a handful of tissues. Misreading the situation, my good James knelt on one knee beside my friend and patted her shoulder. He said, "Don't you worry, Barbara Jean. She'll pull through."

She stuffed the tissues back into her pocketbook and said, "I know she will. It all just gets to you sometimes." She pecked James on the cheek and left the room, making her way through the crowd of people, all invisible to her, who'd been eavesdropping on her conversation.

Mama wept as she watched Barbara Jean go. "All that pain. That part of livin' I surely don't miss."

I closed my eyes, though I can't really say for certain that they'd actually been open, and fell asleep. I journeyed again to Leaning Tree, the glistening creek, and my sycamore.

When I woke up, it was dark outside and James was snoring in the visitor's chair. Mrs Carmel Handy, the retired schoolteacher who'd once set her husband on the path to righteousness with the aid of a cast-iron skillet, stood at the foot of my bed. I was surprised to see her. I'd never had anything against Miss Carmel, but she hadn't had much use for me when I was a student in her classroom, and that hadn't changed in the decades that passed afterwards. But there she was, all dressed up, visiting me in the hospital. Then I saw her talking to

Mama and knew that Miss Carmel had taken the boat across to the other side.

I said, "Hello, Miss Carmel. I didn't know you'd passed. I would've sent a ham to your family, if I'd known."

"Just happened today. And, let me tell you, it came as quite a surprise. I was in the middle of cleaning up after supper and I came down with what I thought was a touch of indigestion. Next thing I knew I was getting up from the kitchen floor and my arthritis was gone and my real teeth were back. Then, something drew me right here. And now I know why. Listen, I have a small assignment for you."

The Skillet Lady came closer and whispered a message that she wanted delivered to James. Just like I'd explained to Lester, I told her that I probably wouldn't be talking to any living people again. But she got me to promise I'd try.

I slept and dreamed through the fifth morning – I was doing more of that every day. But I was aware of my kids' presence in my room that afternoon. Denise, Jimmy, and Eric walked in, all full of hope and good cheer. They updated James on the grandkids, their spouses, their lives. They did all the things I'd have wanted them to do to make their father feel better. I was so happy and proud that I used every bit of strength I had to swim up through the water and fog in my mind so I could thank them. It worked for a little while. I got out a few words – my only words to live people that whole day. But after I spoke each of their names aloud, I faded away again. Then my children's composure wilted like the straggly flowers of my garden. Eric's lip began to tremble. Jimmy started to sniffle. Denise's eyes leaked tears. My big boys each laid their heads on one of their sister's shoulders and sobbed. The spectacle was made even more heartbreaking by the fact that Jimmy and Eric had, respectively, seven and eight inches of height on Denise, so they had to crouch down to be comforted. This was the sight I had feared seeing. I was relieved when they dissolved into gray as I fell asleep again.

When I woke up, my room was filled with the warm light of the afternoon sun. It was also packed with people. James held my hand. He had such thick stubble on his face I wondered if maybe more than one day had passed while I slept. My three kids stood next to their father with their hands linked like they used to do when they crossed a street together as youngsters. Barbara Jean and Clarice were perched at the foot of my bed, both of them massaging my legs. Richmond and my brother, Rudy, stood behind Barbara Jean and Clarice with bowed heads. My pastor stood on the opposite side of the bed from James, reading from the Bible in a voice that sounded way too loud in the small space of my crowded hospital room. It was clear from the miserable expressions on everyone's faces and the fact that the nurses had suspended the two-visitor rule that all of these folks were there to say goodbye.

Beyond the ring of sniffling, praying people, my dead acquaintances gabbed without bothering to lower their voices. Among the chatting ghosts stood my father, fit and hardy in his sawdust-sprinkled coveralls. When Daddy realized that I was aware of my surroundings again, he made his way through the crowd to my bedside. He said, "Hey, sweetheart, I see you're back. You had a rough night, baby."

Lester, looking dashing in a rust-colored three-piece

suit and leaning on a gold walking stick, took his place next to Daddy then and said, "I hate to bother you, Odette, but I think maybe this might be a good time to talk to Barbara Jean like you said you would."

Daddy snapped, "This is hardly the time for her to be thinkin' about that, Lester."

Carmel Handy disagreed. "She made promises and she needs to keep them. That was one of the most important lessons I taught my students. *Honor your word.*"

Mama said, "If she's going to talk to anybody, I think she should start with that cheater." She pointed at Richmond. "I got my request in first."

They all started to argue. All those dead folks putting in their two cents about what I should or shouldn't do with the end of my life. Mrs Roosevelt was the only one who kept out of it. She just sat cross-legged atop a steadily beeping machine to the side of my bed and hummed to herself.

I tried to ignore them and concentrate on my own plans. During that last long nap, I'd been thinking about the way this endgame should play out. If I could work it right, these needy ghosts might get some satisfaction, too.

I had to wake up, completely, just for a little while. But that was a tall order. My body didn't want me anymore. The more I tried to wake up, the more my flesh tried to push me out. I wrestled and wrestled, latching on to every reviving thought I could muster. I reached way back and pictured Mama, young and brassy, shouting for me to get my ass out of bed for school. I smelled the bad coffee James distilled on cold mornings. I splashed my face with the frigid water from the creek behind Mama's garden. I thought about the one thing I wanted to do more than anything else and I tried to draw strength from it.

In front of me, a tiny pinpoint of clear air appeared in the haze. In my mind, I ran for that open spot and pulled at it with my fingers until I could stick my head through. Then I kicked and pushed back toward my old life while Lester, Miss Carmel, and Mama shouted out encouragement.

The first thing I said was "Everybody, shut up."

My pastor looked surprised and offended and stopped reading. I was actually talking to the dead people in the room, still fussing and yakking, but I didn't know how many words I had left in me, so I didn't waste them on the reverend's hurt feelings.

At the sound of my voice, creaky and hoarse, James shouted my name and started kissing my face.

Denise ran out and fetched Dr Soo. A few seconds later, Alex squeezed into the room with a nurse at his side and probed me with a cold stethoscope.

James said to the doctor, "See, I told you my girl wasn't done yet." But the frown on Alex's face as he reviewed my vital signs said that he didn't believe there was any need to celebrate.

The bucktoothed, tipsy Angel of Death agreed with the doctor. When we made eye contact, Mrs Roosevelt shook her head solemnly. Then she whispered, "It will happen today."

But she didn't need to warn me. I could see that milky water, thicker and darker than before, forming again at the edges of my vision. So I got down to business.

With a voice weak from not being used, I croaked out,

"James, you look terrible and you smell bad. Alive or dead, I won't have you going to seed. And listen, Carmel Handy is here and she wants you to know that she died yesterday."

"Day before," she corrected.

"Sorry, day before yesterday. She's on her kitchen floor. She wants you to talk to your cop friends and see to it that none of them start the rumor that she died with a skillet in her hand. She refuses to leave this world with people making jokes about her."

Of course, I knew full well that the time for Carmel Handy to worry about people joking was in the seconds before her skillet met the side of Mr Handy's head. But she seemed satisfied with what I'd said to James. She said, "Thank you, dear."

Now that I'd completed her assignment, I waited for her to leave. I figured once you did a ghost a favor they would fade away or maybe pop like a soap bubble that had been pricked with a pin. That was how it worked in the movies, at least. But Miss Carmel was no Hollywood ghost. She stayed put, looking relieved but excited about what might happen next.

Worried expressions spread around the room like a virus. James was frightened. His concerned gaze went back and forth from me to Alex Soo. "Sweetheart, did you say Carmel Handy is dead, *and* she's here?"

"Yes," I said. "I didn't want to worry you with it, but I've been seeing dead folks for a year now. I know it's probably not what you want to hear, but I think we both knew it might happen sooner or later."

From the back of the room, Mama hollered, "Hey,

Odette. Tell Richmond what I said about taking care of those urges!"

"Richmond, Mama says . . ." I stopped to think about what to tell him. I was not about to utter the words "carry a Victoria's Secret catalog into the bathroom" to Richmond Baker. I said, "Mama says you need a new hobby. She suggests you take up reading.

"And, Clarice, Mama also says you should count your blessings for having Richmond around to do the thing he's best at and not having to deal with the bullshit that comes along with living with him. Right now she wants to slap you, but I think she'll get past it if you promise to forget about what your mother says and just use Richmond till you use him up."

Clarice looked mortified, and it pleased me to see that I could still embarrass her after so many years. When she recovered enough to speak, she said, under her breath, "Barbara Jean, I think she's got brain damage."

"Call it brain damage if you need to, Clarice. Just do what Mama says, or we'll both haunt you."

I spoke more carefully to Barbara Jean. "Lester's here and he wants me to tell you something. He feels bad that he got you to marry him when he knew you didn't love him. He says it wasn't right and he should've done better by you since he was so much older. He's asking you to forgive him."

Barbara Jean didn't look the least bit surprised or upset by what I'd said. I knew that she was worried about me, but I could also see that she still wore the remnants of the despair I'd seen on her face two days earlier when she'd talked to me about Chick and his brother Desmond. And

I supposed that, after the haunting she'd gone through over the years, a message from her dead husband was nothing.

Barbara Jean said, "Tell Lester he was good to me . . . to us. He's got nothing to feel bad about. I'm glad I married him."

Lester let out a sigh. He tipped his hat to me and then, like Miss Carmel, sat watching.

James said, "So, you say you've been seeing dead folks for a year?"

"Just about," I answered.

Big Earl, Miss Thelma, and Daddy yelled out in unison, "Tell James we said hey."

I relayed the message. "Daddy, Big Earl, and Miss Thelma all say hey."

James twisted his mouth and rubbed at the scar on his face, the way he often did when he was deep in thought. No doubt he was remembering Mama and her endless public conversations with dead folks. But my James is as adaptable as any of those bowing trees along Wall Road. The frown melted from his face and he nodded his head. "Okay then." Addressing the room, he called out, "Hey, Pop Jackson. Hey, Big Earl and Miss Thelma."

James never ceases to amaze me.

I felt like I was drifting away again and I forced myself to breathe deep and concentrate on staying in this world a little while longer. When I got a second wind, I spoke again, my voice even fainter and hoarser than before. "Now I'd like to have a little family time. Reverend, Alex, nurse, would you mind giving us some privacy?"

They didn't look pleased about it, but they cleared out

like I asked. After they left the room, I said, "The rest of y'all can go, too," talking to the ghosts. But only Lester and Miss Carmel complied. Lester performed a low, courtly bow and then offered Miss Carmel his arm. She wrapped her hand around his elbow and walked toward the door with him. As they left the room, I heard her say, "Lester, did I ever tell you that your wife was born on my davenport?"

I talked to Rudy and my children. "I need y'all to do something." When they stepped forward, I said, "I need you to take my husband home and make sure he's fed and bathed."

James shook his head no. "I'm not leaving you."

I said, "James, I promise you won't come back here and find me dead." I could see that he was mulling it over, wanting to believe me. For insurance, I issued commands to Rudy and my giant sons. "Carry him out if you have to, but take him home."

Eric, Jimmy, and Rudy glanced at each other and then at James, wondering what to do. James let them off the hook, like I thought he would. He said, "Okay, I'll go home and get cleaned up. But I'm coming right back." He said to the Supremes, "Call me if anything happens." Then he kissed my forehead and left with Denise, Jimmy, Eric, and Rudy.

"Clarice, I want you to pick up a couple things for me. I want you to get that violet housecoat you gave me last Christmas from my bedroom chest of drawers. I'd have asked James, but Lord knows what he'd bring back. And I also would kill for a piece of Little Earl's peach cobbler. Would you run by the All-You-Can-Eat and get me a piece?"

Thrilled to think that my appetite had returned, she said, "Sure, I'll go." Then, to Barbara Jean, "I won't be long."

When Clarice was gone, I said to Barbara Jean, "I've got one thing to say to you, Barbara Jean, and it's not coming from any dead person. It's coming straight from me. You need to go see Chick. And not just for the 'making amends' stuff." Her mouth dropped open then as she realized that I had heard and remembered the things she'd said to me a couple days earlier while I was swimming around in that world between worlds.

She wrung her hands for a moment and then, recovering, said, "I'll talk to him soon. I promise. I've just been waiting till I'm strong enough."

"Go now. And after you've settled the past, deal with the here and now. It's time to see how this thing between you and Chick is supposed to play out, once and for all."

Barbara Jean said, "It's too late for any of that, Odette. Years and years too late."

The dead people in the room with us piped up, yelling that I should tell my friend she was wrong. It was never too late, not until you've passed out of this life and maybe not even then.

I told Barbara Jean, "My mama and daddy and Big Earl and Miss Thelma all say you're wrong." I left out Eleanor Roosevelt because I knew the mention of her would tilt the whole thing from eerie and otherworldly right over into crazy. Then, just like I'd played the cancer card to send her off to AA, now I played the dying card. "Barbara Jean, you've got to talk to Chick and set it all straight. Lay every bit of it out in the sunlight, the whole truth. I won't rest in peace unless you do this one last thing for me." I was shameless.

Barbara Jean tugged and twisted the fabric of the loose skirt she was wearing as she sat thinking at the far end of my bed. For a while, I wondered if she still might refuse. Then she walked over to me and kissed my forehead. "Okay, I'll go." She didn't sound eager, but she did at least seem resigned to doing what I'd asked. And that was enough. When she left, Mama, Daddy, and the McIntyres accompanied her, pressed close to her sides like they were propping her up.

I was alone then with Richmond Baker and Mrs Roosevelt.

Richmond rocked back and forth on his heels, looking like he'd rather be anywhere else on the face of the earth at that moment. He said, "Listen, why don't I go get the doctor for you." Then he moved toward the door.

"No, Richmond. I need you to stay."

Eleanor Roosevelt whipped out her popcorn bag again, preparing to hear more juicy stuff from Richmond.

He slumped back in my direction. "Odette, I don't know how much of the stuff I said the other day you remember, but let me just say that I know I've been a bad husband, and maybe I've been a bad friend, too. Can I just tell you I'm sorry for everything and leave it at that? You don't have to tell me what *they* say." He looked around the room like he was expecting floating white sheets to emerge from the walls and shout "Boo!"

With the little bit of voice I had left, I said, "Oh, for God's sake, Richmond. I don't want to talk to you. I just want your muscles. I need you to close the door and all the curtains. And then, when I get these tubes out of me, I need you to grab that wheelchair out in the hallway, bring it in here, and help me get in it. Then you can take me to your car. And if anybody tries to stop you, I need you to be big, black, and scary."

A loud sigh of relief escaped Richmond when he realized that I hadn't kept him around so the two of us could have a heart-to-heart. As he reached for the curtains that were clustered in one corner of the room, he said, "Thank God. I just about pissed my pants wondering what you and your ghosts might come up with next."

Chapter 36

It wasn't until Barbara Jean walked the short distance from the hospital to the tower where Chick worked and saw the puzzled, slightly alarmed expression on the face of the young woman at the reception desk that she remembered what she was wearing. When James called that morning, she had just gotten dressed for a volunteer shift pretending to churn butter in front of a busload of schoolchildren in the Plainview Historical Society Museum's frontier farmhouse re-creation. James had hardly been able to get the words out, but he told Barbara Jean that Odette's doctor had said she was too weak to fight off the infection. She wasn't expected to live through the day. Without changing clothes, Barbara Jean headed straight over to the hospital as soon as she hung up the phone. Now, hours later, she followed the receptionist's directions to the elevator through a maze of workstations and found herself on the receiving end of even more curious looks. People swiveled around in their desk chairs to watch her pass by in her high-collared blouse, long gingham skirt, and tight, pointy-toed leather boots.

The ground floor of the tower was so cluttered with small work cubicles, file cabinets, and tall shelving units that the round shape of the building was completely obscured. But when Barbara Jean stepped out of the elevator, the space she entered was as different from the first floor as it could have been. The fifth floor of the tower was one large open room with a fourteen-foot ceiling that was supported by massive rough-cut wooden beams. The tall windows that dominated the exposed brick walls allowed in so much afternoon sunlight that she had to squint for a moment so that her eyes could adjust to the brightness.

She saw a long wooden desk at the far end of the room. It was very old and a little beaten-up, but freshly waxed. Behind the desk, which was crowded with stacks of books, Ray Carlson stopped shuffling papers when he caught sight of her.

Two beautiful and haughty peregrine falcons scrutinized Barbara Jean from inside their large cages as she passed by them on her way to Chick. The plank flooring creaked beneath her old-fashioned boots with each step, providing an accompaniment to the soft rustling noises of the birds flexing their wings and moving along their perches.

Chick stood and came around the desk to greet her. "Hi, Barbara Jean. This is a nice surprise." A quizzical expression crossed his face as he looked her up and down, taking in her anachronistic outfit.

She saw him staring and said, "I'm supposed to be pretending to churn butter."

He had no idea what she was talking about, but he nodded as if what she said had made sense.

For several awkward seconds, Barbara Jean stood in front of Chick regretting that she hadn't rehearsed something to say to him during her walk from the hospital. She was struck now with a strong urge to run back to the elevator. But she thought about the promise she had made and, instead of running away, looked directly into Chick's eyes, hoping the force that had always moved her to give voice to her feelings when she was near him, whether or not she should, would take over. She said the first thing that came to mind: "Odette—"

He put his hand to his heart and interrupted her. "Is she gone?"

"No, no, she's not gone. She's awake, even speaking. But she's saying some strange stuff."

He smiled. "Well, being that it's Odette we're talking about, saying strange stuff could be a good sign."

"Maybe, maybe not. Her doctor was sure she wouldn't make it through the day and I don't think he's changed his mind."

"I hate to hear that," he said. "Well, let's hope she surprises him." He gestured toward two high-backed, copper-colored leather chairs that sat facing his desk. "Would you like to sit down?"

She answered, "Yes, thank you," but her feet carried her past the chairs and on toward one of the tall windows instead. Chick followed her and stood by her side, so close that their arms almost touched.

From the window, Barbara Jean could see the hospital where Odette lay. She thought about Odette, and she tried to draw strength from imagining how her brave friend would approach this. Odette would get right to it, Barbara Jean thought. So she did the same.

She said, "I'm an alcoholic, just like my mother was. It's a struggle, but I haven't had a drink in a while." That was something she hadn't meant to say, something she had never said outside of an AA meeting. But, after it had been said, it felt like as good a way to start as any.

He furrowed his brow, as if he were searching for the proper response to what she had just blurted out. He settled on "Congratulations. I know how hard that is."

"Thank you. I came to see you because they tell us at AA that we have to make a list of the people we've harmed and try to make amends."

His head jerked back a little and he looked confused. "You want to make amends? To me?"

Barbara Jean nodded. "I know how bad I hurt you and—"

He interrupted her again. "You don't need to feel bad about any of that, Barbara Jean. You were just a kid. We both were." He paused. "And we were in love."

"That's what makes it worse, Ray. That's the thing I used to think about when I sat up at night drinking. I knew you loved me, or at least that you had loved me once upon a time, and I used that. I think maybe I could have gotten past the guilt if I'd done the honest thing and shot Desmond myself. But, instead, I took your love for me and I twisted it to make you pull the trigger. Now, both of us have had to live with it. I can't even imagine what that must have done to you."

Chick remained silent. His only response was to slowly shake his head back and forth.

Barbara Jean wondered why she wasn't crying or shouting, or something. Lord knows she felt as if she were bursting at the seams. But at the same time, she was strangely calm. Well, not calm, she thought. More like purposeful. She could feel something, or someone, willing her on. She imagined voices whispering in her ear saying that every word she spoke was moving her incrementally closer to a place she wanted to be.

She went on. "According to the twelve steps, making amends shouldn't injure the person you've harmed. So I hope and pray that saying this and dredging it all up again doesn't hurt you more. It's just that I want you to know that I'm sorry for what I made you do. And if there's a way I can make it up to you, I'd like to."

Chick's shoulders slumped and his face looked weary. In a tone of voice that sounded as if he were apologizing, he said, "I didn't kill Desmond."

His words took a moment to register and, when they did, Barbara Jean still couldn't accept them. She found herself focusing on his eyes again. She felt sure that, even after all of the years that had passed, she could still read the truth there if she stared hard enough.

It was there, all right. Her throat went dry and she brought her hand to her mouth to smother an escaping gasp. She whispered, "Oh Lord, you're telling the truth."

She took a few steps and fell into the chair he had offered her earlier. Part of Barbara Jean accepted that what Chick had said was true. But another, maybe stronger, piece of her had memorized every second of the morning the police had taken her and Lester to Desmond Carlson's place. That memory, as vivid to her that afternoon as it had been decades earlier, made her mistrust anything that threatened to alter the script of the movie she had played over and over in her head for years.

She said, "But I saw feathers from those birds in the

cages at your house. They were all over the ground at Desmond's place that day. Gray, white, and red feathers. There was nothing that looked like that just flying around town. You had to have been there."

Chick came away from the window then and slid the other leather chair closer to hers so that, when he sat, their knees were just inches apart. The room had grown warmer since she had arrived, the air-conditioning unable to compete with the July sun, but her hands had gone icy. They trembled as if she had laid them onto the surface of the frozen river in her dreams. Chick surprised Barbara Jean by reaching out and pressing her cold fingers between his warm palms.

Speaking quietly and slowly, Chick said, "I was there. But I didn't kill him. I went over to see Desmond late that night after you left my house. I didn't really know what I was going to do. In my mind I pictured strangling him with my bare hands. But when I got to Desmond's place, he was already dead on the porch with his rifle lying beside him. I don't know for sure what happened, but his girlfriend Liz's father walked up to me at Desmond's funeral and bragged right to my face that he'd shot Desmond for beating Liz one time too many. He was falling-down drunk when he said it, so maybe it was true, maybe not. My brother spread a lot of misery in his life, and a long list of people wanted him dead. I suppose it's even possible that Desmond did it himself, like the police decided. But I doubt it.

"All I can tell you for sure is that what you believed . . . Well, that's what I hoped you'd believe. I thought maybe that way you wouldn't hate me, maybe you would believe I'd done at least that one thing for our son."

Barbara Jean sat frozen in the leather chair, going over what he had just said. She sat motionless for so long that Chick asked her if she was all right and offered to go get some water for her. She said, "I'm fine, Ray." But in her mind, she was trying to sort out her new role as an exonerated prisoner. What do you do when your cell door suddenly swings open? How do you embrace freedom when you've never known it? How do you forgive yourself for serving as your own jailer for three decades?

The easiest thing – and the smartest thing, she suspected – would have been to leave then. But being cut loose from the familiar ground of her guilt somehow made going further less scary.

She took a deep breath and said, "Odette told me I had to come talk to you and see how this thing between you and me is supposed to end. She said it was time to tell the whole truth, lay everything out in the sun once and for all. And she said Big Earl and Miss Thelma agreed with her."

Chick looked confused. "What?"

She continued without explaining. "Tomorrow I'll call my sponsor, Carlo, and I'll tell him about today. He'll probably say, 'Barbara Jean, you should have stopped at making amends. You can't trust what you're feeling right now. Years of drinking have pickled your brain and left you stuck where you were when you were a kid.' Or he might say that I'm like a lot of drunks, nostalgic for a sweet past I just imagine I lived.

"But Odette and Big Earl never led me wrong. And since I know the truth, I'm going to say it. That way I can go back over to the hospital and tell my friend that I did what she told me to do. And if that's the last thing I get to tell her, I think I'll be able to look back and not have any regrets. And believe me, I've learned about regret the hard way."

At that moment, Barbara Jean felt that it wasn't just Odette pushing her to talk. All of that ghost business must've gotten under her skin because the voices she had heard whispering in her ear from the time she walked into Chick's office were louder now. The voices encouraged her. "Tell it, girl." "Preach!" "Speak the truth and shame the devil." And Barbara Jean would have sworn on that Bible in her library that had been her companion and nemesis for so many years that one of those voices was Big Earl's.

She kept her eyes on Chick's handsome face and said, "Ray, I loved you that day I kissed you that first time in the hallway at the All-You-Can-Eat and I've never stopped. I loved you when I was sober and when I was drunk. I loved you when I was young and still love you now that I'm old. I thought it would change, or I'd grow out of it one day. But all these years later, after all kinds of people and things have come and gone in my life, that one fact, foolish or not, hasn't changed even the tiniest bit."

She stopped and, except for the occasional chirp or caw from the birds, the room was quiet. There was really nothing more to say. She let out the breath that she hadn't been aware she was holding.

While she talked, Chick had aimed his gaze downward and stared at the floor. Now he released her hands and slid his chair away from hers. As he got up and moved away from her, Barbara Jean told herself that it was fine, *she* was fine. She had done what she needed to do, what Odette had insisted she do. If it ended with this, with Chick stepping away from her, that was okay. At least this time they would part with the whole truth being the last thing spoken. What mattered was that she would know how the story ended, like Odette had said.

Barbara Jean lifted her eyes from the empty chair Chick had vacated. He had moved a few feet away and now stood just to the side of his desk. The afternoon sun blazing into the windows backlit him, turning him into a silhouette. She couldn't see his face. But she heard his voice, strong and exquisitely out of tune, when he opened his mouth and started singing.

"My baby love to rock, my baby love to roll. What she do to me just soothe my soul. Ye-ye-yes, my baby love me . . ." He sang louder and louder, gyrating his hips and pivoting around until he was wiggling his narrow rear in her direction.

She heard herself let out a howl that had been waiting too, too long to come out. She applauded, clapping her hands together until they ached, as Ray Carlson, King of the Pretty White Boys, swayed in the sun and danced the blues.

Chapter 37

By the time Richmond brought me to the house in Leaning Tree, I was holding on to just a tattered corner of the world of the living. I had used up all of the energy I had left in me explaining to Richmond what I needed him to do, and I spent most of the drive from the hospital resting my head against the car window, watching the scenery go by.

Throughout that short ride, I kept picturing James and how he was going to react when he found out I'd run off the moment I got the chance. He'd be good and mad at first. He would ask Richmond why he helped me do this foolish thing and Richmond would shrug those big shoulders of his and say, "She told me to." James would cuss, maybe even take a swing or two at his friend. But he'd think it over and forgive Richmond, eventually.

I hadn't exactly lied to James. I'd promised him he wouldn't come back to the hospital and find me dead. And that was the truth. He would be angry with me for a while, but then he'd admit to himself that I would have found a way to do what I wanted no matter what. And then he'd acknowledge that he couldn't have brought himself to help me do it. Yes, James would understand what I'd done. He couldn't stay married to me for thirty-five years without learning to roll with the punches. He might even laugh about it someday, maybe turn it into a funny story to entertain the grandkids with when they're older: "Hey, did I ever tell y'all about that last crazy thing your Grandma Odette did?"

Richmond helped me out of the car and into the wheelchair we'd borrowed from the hospital. When he wheeled me back behind the house we crossed paths with my father. Daddy looked up from the 1960s-style riding lawn mower he was tinkering with. He saw me and smiled. Then he wiped his hands on a red shop rag that was covered with black oil stains and he waved at me.

Richmond and I bumped along the cobblestone path that led past the gazebo. Clarice, bless her heart, had been good about taking care of Mama's garden. It looked better that year than it had in ages. The climbing roses that Mama had trained onto trellises and an arch were in full bloom. The pink and white flowers and rich green foliage provided shade for Aunt Marjorie, who sat under the arch smoking a cigar and sipping gold-colored liquor from a mason jar. She called out, "Hey, Dette." It cheered me to hear that wonderful, unique voice of hers again, that sound that made you imagine she gargled with pine tar and rock salt. But I didn't have time to say more than a quick hello to her. Richmond, a good soldier who knew a thing or two about breaking rules, was intent on accomplishing the mission I'd assigned to him. He quick-stepped behind my chair as fast as his bad ankle would allow.

When we got to the far end of the garden, where it was too over-grown for him to continue to push the wheelchair, Richmond stopped. He came to my side, slid one arm under my back and the other beneath my knees, and lifted me. Then he carried me up the hill toward my syca-more tree.

At the base of the tree, Richmond put me down with my back pressed against the warm bark of its trunk. He saw that I didn't have the strength to keep my head from falling forward, so he adjusted my position against the tree. Then he lifted my chin so I could look up into the branches and see the green leaves against a blue sky unbro-ken by a single cloud.

I thanked him, but he couldn't hear me.

I let go then of that little bit of the world I'd been hold-ing on to. When hazy liquid flooded in from the corners of my vision, I didn't try to swim against it. I let the tide carry me up toward the branches of the tree where my mother had given birth to me after following a witch's advice so many years earlier.

"Hello, tree, my first cradle, my second mother, the source of my strength, the cause of my struggles. I'm back home."

I saw Mama then. She was wearing her best dress, the light blue one with embroidered yellow flowers and green vines. Her legs were crossed at the ankle, and she kicked her feet out in front of her like she was on a swing set. She shared her tree branch with Eleanor Roosevelt.

I breathed deep and inhaled the smell of the soil, the aroma of the honeysuckle that drifted up the hill from the garden, the faint odor of Aunt Marjorie's foul-smelling cheap cigar. I felt good. Felt like whatever happened next would be just fine. I floated and waited.

I looked around for that welcoming light I'd heard

about, but I didn't see it. Instead, everything around me seemed to glow and shimmer in the sunlight. I heard beautiful sounds – not the voices of dead loved ones, but the laughter and singing of my children when they were tiny. I saw James, young and shirtless, chasing them through Mama's garden. Off in the distance I saw Barbara Jean and Clarice, and even myself when we were kids, dancing to music pouring out of my old pink and violet portable record player. Here I was with my fingers brushing up against the frame of the picture I'd been painting for the last fifty-five years, and my beautiful, scarred husband, my happy children, and my laughing friends were right there with me.

I looked up then to tell Mama how overjoyed I was to see that crossing over was just like she had said it would be. That was when I saw Mrs Roosevelt reach out, pick something from the tree, and then pass it to Mama. I watched as Mama rolled whatever she'd been handed around in her palms before letting it go. It fell from her hands, through the branches and leaves of the tree. Finally, it came down to me where I sat on the ground – or floated in the air, I wasn't quite sure which I was doing. I felt the thing land on my lap.

The object Mama had dropped rested just above my knees. It was small and dark green with blackish-brown spots. I felt the heat it had absorbed from the summer sun coming off of it so strong that I wondered if it might burn clean through the thin robe I was wearing.

Then I felt and heard it tick. Like a time bomb.

I looked back up at the tree again. This time I studied it more carefully. I focused on the shape of the leaves. I squinted and saw that there were clusters of little round fruit covering the tree. I watched as Eleanor Roosevelt tugged another one from the tree and let it fall. This one landed on my head and then bounced off to my right.

"Damn you, Richmond Baker. This is just you all over. I give you one thing to do and you screw it up. And, to top it off, you do it when I'm too gone from the world to yell at you about it. Any fourth grader can tell a sycamore from a time bomb tree. Now here I am with walnuts falling on my head while I'm trying to die the way I want to."

I picked up the walnut from my lap and tossed it at him.

To my surprise, Richmond ducked. Then he backed away several feet.

He started apologizing. "I'm sorry, Odette. A tree's a tree to me. They all look the same."

Another surprise. What I'd believed I had shouted out in a place far beyond Richmond's hearing, I had apparently bellowed directly at him. And he'd heard at least enough of it to know that I was truly pissed. Richmond kept his distance, afraid I might find the strength to toss something else at him.

Throwing something else at Richmond wasn't on my mind, though. I was too busy trying to figure out why I was alive when all the indications were that I was done for. I put my hand to my forehead. I felt hot. But it was the heat from the sun now, not the fire that had been roiling in my blood since the day of Sharon's wedding.

I called up to Mama, "Is this a miracle?"

She raised and lowered her shoulders. Her voice drifted down: "Maybe. Or maybe this is just what's supposed to be."

Richmond assumed I was talking to God, so, preacher's son that he was, he bowed his head. I started to feel bad for yelling at him. He'd done me a big favor, one I couldn't have asked anyone else to do. And it wasn't his fault he screwed it up. That was just his nature.

"I'm sorry, Richmond. I shouldn't have yelled at you, or thrown that walnut either. You've been a good friend, and I appreciate it."

Sensing that the danger had passed, he came closer. Then he sat down next to me in the shade of the walnut tree. The summer afternoon heat was getting to him and he wiped his forehead with a handkerchief he'd pulled from his pocket. "Umm, so do you want me to carry you somewhere else? If you point out the sycamore, I can take you to it."

I pondered what I should do and couldn't come up with a decent answer. "I've gotta tell you, Richmond, I'm not quite sure what to do. I'd only planned the day as far as this. I had it on what I'd taken as good authority that I'd be dead by now."

I turned my face up toward the top of the tree and cut Mrs Roosevelt a dirty look. I was happy to still be a part of the world of the living, but I'd gone to a fair amount of trouble to get myself to my sycamore tree – no, walnut tree, thanks to dumb-ass Richmond – so I could pass in peace. Now it looked like it was all for nothing.

I looked around and saw my sycamore tree about fifty yards away, as twisted and beautiful as ever.

Richmond saw where I was staring. "You want to go over there?"

"I don't think so. It appears I won't be dying just yet.

Let's go back to the hospital. If we're lucky, we might make it before James gets back. If he finds out about this, I might die on schedule after all."

Richmond chuckled.

"I wouldn't laugh if I was you. After James is done with me, he'll want a piece of you, too."

"Well then, we'd better get a move on." Richmond got up on one knee and then bent and scooped me up from the ground.

"Really, Richmond, I don't think you have to carry me. I can probably walk, if you help me."

He began to climb down the hill with me in his arms. "No, no, you're as light as a feather," he lied, grunting with every step.

"You know, Richmond, I see why all the women love you so much. You talk a bunch of shit, but you make it sound good." I wrapped my arms around my accomplice's thick, muscular neck and enjoyed the bouncy ride.

Over Richmond's shoulder, I smiled up at my mother in the walnut tree. She gazed back at me, looking as pleasantly surprised as I was to see me leaving this place alive. Then I focused my attention on that bothersome Eleanor Roosevelt, who had caused me so much concern and vexation throughout the year. I wanted her to know, before Richmond carried me out of sight, that she might have had me worried, but she never had me scared.

I balled my hand into a fist and shook it at Mrs Roosevelt. And, just before Richmond and I reached the tall reed grass at the back end of Mama's garden, I shouted as loud as my hoarse throat would let me, "I was born in a sycamore tree!"

Chapter 38

My first Sunday back at the All-You-Can-Eat came three weeks after I didn't die beneath my tree. The restaurant was packed. Every chair in the place, except the ones waiting for James and me, was occupied. And from the unusual amount of trouble even skinny James had squeezing between the patrons, it seemed to me that Little Earl had added some tables to the dining room to handle the increased numbers.

As we made our way through the crowd, folks greeted me like I'd just returned from the battlefield. Erma Mae rushed up to me and kissed me on each cheek. Ramsey Abrams hugged me – a little too tight and a little too long, as usual. Florence Abrams shook my hand and contorted her face into that wince she believed was a smile. Every step we took, somebody stopped me to say how glad they were that I was on the mend. People had done the same thing when I'd returned to church that morning, and I have to admit I was flattered by the attention.

When we finally got to our window table, I took my seat between Clarice and Barbara Jean. James sat down at the men's end of the table, and we both launched into conversations with our friends.

It was like things had never changed, and it was

completely different at the same time. Clarice, bold and braless in a gauzy, shapeless white dress that she wouldn't have been caught dead in six months earlier, was still the most dedicated gossip I knew. But, courtesy of the Unitarians, she wasn't so filled up with fury now that every story or observation had to have a bite to it. And Barbara Jean was as beautiful as ever in a pearl-gray dress from her new toned-down and sobered-up collection, but she had a way about her that said maybe her soul was truly at peace for the first time in all the years that I'd known her.

I could hear the usual sports talk coming from the other end of the table. But they'd shuffled up things a bit there, too. Richmond had moved over one chair and now sat in the space that Lester had occupied for years. James sat where Richmond used to sit. And Chick Carlson sat in James's old spot.

Barbara Jean didn't talk about the future. She said she planned to take each day as it came. But if you got her alone and pressed her about it, she'd tell you that what was happening – her and Chick together, trying to learn to be happy – was a miracle.

I didn't argue with Barbara Jean, but I'd grown partial to Mama's take on that topic. What we call miracles is just what's supposed to happen. We either go with it or stand in its way. It seemed to me that Barbara Jean had just finally stopped getting in the way of what was meant to be. But what did I know? I'd chosen to go with the flow and I'd ended up letting the drunken ghost of a former first lady convince me that I was about to die.

When we headed to the buffet line, we found the pickings pretty slim. Erma Mae saw me spooning the last of the braised short ribs from a tray. She said, "We'll have some more soon. We thought we'd have a busy day today, but we didn't plan on this kinda crowd showin' up. It's like they all marked the date on their calendars and ran straight over here from church to see the show."

That was when I remembered. One year ago, Minnie McIntyre had announced to everyone that her spirit guide, Charlemagne the Magnificent, had put her on notice that she had a maximum of 365 days to live. Now the All-You-Can-Eat was full of people who'd come to see how Minnie was going to deal with waking up alive a year later.

Little Earl hustled out of the kitchen with an overflowing tray of short ribs. He saw me and said, "Hey, Odette, good to have you back." He put the tray on the steam table with one hand while sliding out the empty tray with the other in one smooth, practiced motion. He said, "It's crazy in here today. Sorry I can't stay and talk." Then he rushed back into the kitchen.

Erma Mae shook her head. "He's not sorry at all. He's tickled pink to have this crowd. Maybe we can persuade Minnie to predict her death every Sunday. That way we could retire in another year." Then someone waved at her from the cash register and she hurried away.

All six of us filled our plates and headed back to our table. As soon as we sat, Clarice said, "I talked to Veronica last night." Veronica had started speaking to Clarice again immediately after everything went so wrong at the wedding. She'd been calling Clarice just about every day since then to vent some steam about what Minnie had done to her with her bad predictions.

"Is Veronica doing any better?" Barbara Jean asked.

"A little. She's still too embarrassed to leave the house, but she got a new prescription for nerve pills and she doesn't talk about murdering Minnie quite so much. Now she does a fair amount of inappropriate giggling instead. It's creepy, but I suppose it's an improvement."

"I'm surprised she isn't here today. I'd think she'd want to be on the scene to hear Minnie try to explain being alive. It might give her a bit of satisfaction," I said.

Clarice said, "No, she's determined to lay low until people forget about the wedding."

"She'll have a hell of a long wait on her hands," I said. "I heard a rumor that the wedding photographer was selling his footage to *America's Funniest Home Videos*."

Clarice and Barbara Jean both squealed, "Really?"

"Well, no," I confessed. "But a girl can dream."

Barbara Jean asked, "What about Sharon? How's she doing?"

Clarice said, "Not so good. I haven't seen her, but, according to Veronica, she's locked herself in her room and only comes out to shoot evil looks at her mother. On top of that, her hypnosis is wearing off, so she's struggling to stay away from the sweets. It's not easy for her, depressed as she is, living with three hundred servings of wedding cake in the deep freezer down in the basement."

Then Clarice said, "Excuse me for a second." She lightly rapped on the table with her knuckles and cleared her throat. When she had everyone's attention, she said, "Richmond," then she extended her right hand, palm up.

Richmond tried his unconvincing innocent look for a few seconds. Then he slid a large serving of banana pudding out from beneath his napkin where he had been hiding it. He stood and brought the pudding to the other end of the table, depositing it in the hand of his part-time wife.

Chick and James laughed at him and started in with the teasing as soon as Richmond sat back down in his chair. But Richmond just grinned and said, "What can I say? My woman wants me to live."

Clarice and Richmond seemed to have come to an understanding. Clarice had gotten over worrying about going to hell for wanting love without misery, and Richmond had given up fighting for a return to the life they had led before she left him. I was happy to see it. I loved Clarice, of course, and Richmond Baker was all right by me, too.

The main reason I'd chosen Richmond to take me out of the hospital and to my sycamore tree was that he was physically the strongest person I knew. Fifty-seven years old and every inch of him still bulged with muscle. Also, of all my friends, Richmond had shown himself the most willing to do things that other people thought were wrong. But it turned out he had some other valuable qualities.

For one, years of sneaking around had taught Richmond how to keep his mouth shut. We made it back to the hospital that day before anyone else returned. I did some apologizing to my doctor and Richmond did some flirting with the nurses. And by the time James, the Supremes, my brother, and my kids came back, an agreement had been struck with the hospital personnel to pretend my escape had never happened.

I thought about telling James what I had done. But I decided it would be better for everyone, especially me, if I didn't. The way I figured it, James had enough on his plate. He was a good husband whose wife had cancer. He was a lawman who had to go on pretending, at least a little while longer, that he didn't know I was smoking marijuana every day. And now James also had to deal with having a chorus line of dead folks dancing in and out of his life. No, that whole thing about my escape to Leaning Tree was something me and my new buddy, Richmond, would keep to ourselves.

Someone shouted, "There's Minnie," and Clarice lost any concern for Richmond's diet, Barbara Jean quit gazing at Chick, and I stopped mulling over my own little secrets. Along with everybody else in the All-You-Can-Eat, we stared out the window at the house across the street.

I scanned the front of Minnie's house and still didn't see a thing. "Where is she?" I asked.

"Look up," Barbara Jean said. "She's on the roof."

Sure enough, there was Minnie. She was crawling, rear end first, out of a second-floor window and onto the wedge of roof above the front porch.

"What on earth is she doing?" Clarice asked as we watched Minnie gain her footing on the slanted shingles. Balancing up there had to have been a tough task since, in addition to her purple fortune-telling robe with the signs of the zodiac pasted all over it and her white turban, she was wearing her satin Arabian slippers with the curled-up toes.

"I believe she's fixin' to jump," I said.

Barbara Jean said, "That's a long way to go to make a prediction come true. If she goes through with it, you have to admire her dedication to her work."

Clarice rolled her eyes. "Oh please, she'll never jump. You know as well as I do that Minnie McIntyre won't die until she contracts some lingering mystery disease that she can whine about for decades till somebody snaps under the strain of listening to her running her mouth and smothers her with a pillow." She snatched a chicken finger off my plate and bit into it.

I said, "Sounds like you've given this a bit of thought, Clarice. What happened to that fresh, mellow outlook on life you said the Unitarians were giving you?"

"I haven't been a Unitarian long," she responded, waving the stub of the chicken finger. "I've still got some work to do."

Always the most charitable of the Supremes, Barbara Jean said, "Someone really should go over there and talk her down."

But no one moved. I'm sure Barbara Jean knew even as she said it that she'd be hard-pressed to find a soul in town who would try to talk Minnie McIntyre out of leaping. In that very room was an assortment of people who would gladly climb onto that roof with her, but only to give her a shove, convinced that they were doing the world a favor by hastening her departure. No, these folks were not a crowd of likely suicide prevention counselors.

Minnie stood now with her arms outstretched like Jesus on the cross, her purple robe billowing in the breeze like the sails of a ship. A particularly strong gust came along and snatched the turban off her head. When she tried to grab for it, she pitched forward so awkwardly that everyone gasped. Minnie wobbled for a few seconds, but soon righted herself. Then she stuck her arms out and struck her martyr pose again, looking angry and defiant as the little wisps of gray hair that poked out from the hairnet she'd worn under her turban danced in the wind.

We all watched for a while longer. Then Little Earl, who had been summoned from the kitchen by his wife, let out a groan. "I guess I better go have a talk with her." He took off his apron and came out from behind the steam tables. But he halted at the front door when he saw that someone had appeared on Minnie's lawn and was having a lively conversation with her.

A slim young woman carrying a pale pink cardboard box labeled "Donut Heaven" under her left arm stood in the center of the lawn. She was wearing a long white dress that looked like it had seen better days. Strips of cloth hung from the ragged hem of the dress, like somebody had taken scissors to it. Stains of assorted sizes and colors dotted the fabric. At first it seemed she and Minnie were having a casual conversation, but then the young woman began to shake an upraised fist in Minnie's direction. Suddenly it was clear that the exchange they were having was anything but casual.

Clarice said, "I can't believe it. It's Sharon."

I squinted and saw that it was, indeed, Sharon, the almost-wife of the now re-incarcerated Clifton Abrams. As I watched, Sharon's movements graduated from testy to furious. Now, instead of a fist, she jabbed her middle finger up toward the old woman.

Clarice said, "I should call Veronica." She twisted around to get at the pocketbook that hung on the back of her chair and fished inside until she found her phone. Then she dialed her cousin.

"Hi, Veronica, it's me. I'm having supper at the All-You-Can-Eat and Sharon just showed up . . . No, she's not having supper with us. She's across the street and it appears she's having words with Minnie . . . Uh-huh . . . And, Veronica, she's in her wedding gown . . . Really? Every day? . . . Well, right now she's just standing there yelling at Minnie with a Donut Heaven box under her arm."

The shriek that came from the other end of the phone line at the mention of Donut Heaven was so loud that Clarice jerked the phone as far away from her head as the length of her arm would let her. When the wailing subsided, Clarice put the phone back to her ear. She listened for a moment and then told Veronica, "I can't really say for sure from this distance, but my guess would be it's the family-size box." Another shriek. This one came and went too quickly for Clarice to pull the phone away. She listened for a few seconds longer and then turned off her phone. Then, to us, Clarice said, "She'll be right over."

We continued to watch the spectacle across the street. The restaurant was so quiet now and Sharon was yelling so loud that we could hear an occasional word even though she was dozens of yards away and separated from us by a thick pane of glass. Her gestures got bigger as she became angrier. She escalated things by opening the donut box, removing a long chocolate éclair, and lobbing it at Minnie like a javelin, which drove the audience in the restaurant to hoots of amusement and shock. The pastry sailed wide of its target and missed by two feet. Minnie made an obscene hand signal back at Sharon and then they screamed at each other for a while longer. Little Earl sighed again and opened the restaurant's front door to go outside and play referee.

Clarice, Barbara Jean, and I glanced at each other, each of us trying to come up with an excuse for following Little Earl across the street that didn't seem like pure nosiness.

Barbara Jean got there first. She said, "I hope Veronica gets here soon. Sharon needs family with her."

Clarice said, "I would love to offer her a shoulder to cry on, but I'm afraid she'd believe I was just butting in. And I wouldn't want Veronica to think I was overstepping. You know how she can be."

"Nonsense," I countered. "When you're a blood relative it's not butting in. It's a family responsibility."

"And a Christian duty," added Barbara Jean.

Clarice asked, "Do you really think so?" She said it like she still had to be persuaded, but she was already standing up to leave, her eyes fixed on the front door.

Barbara Jean said, "I'll go with you . . . for moral support."

Not one to be left out of a mission of Christian mercy, I tagged along. In fact, I nearly beat Clarice to the door.

When we got to Minnie's yard, Little Earl had taken off his All-You-Can-Eat cap and was fanning his face with it. He said, "Miss Minnie, please, just go on back inside the house. We can have a cool drink and work this out."

She said, "Oh, you'd like that, wouldn't you?" Then, addressing us – the Supremes and the other spectators who had decided to leave the All-You-Can-Eat and brave the heat for a closer look at the goings-on – she said, "You'd all love that, wouldn't you. You'd love to have me live through this day and have everybody calling my gift for prophecy into question."

Sharon cried out, "Gift? That's a laugh." Then she flung

a powdered donut at Minnie. Her aim was true that time. She got Minnie in the chest, leaving a chalky white circle of confectioner's sugar on Minnie's purple robe.

Just then, I heard the screeching of car wheels behind us. I thought, *Veronica got here fast.* But when I looked over my shoulder, instead of Veronica's sharp gray Lexus, I saw a rusted old Chevy shuddering to a stop. Yvonne Wilson, the most devout believer in Minnie's fortune-telling abilities, hopped out of the car with a baby in her arms. Her boyfriend and the six underachieving child stars she'd given birth to after Minnie's prediction that one of them would make her rich piled out of the car after her.

Panting for breath, Yvonne sprinted in front of Sharon and gasped, "Don't jump, Madame Minnie! Please don't jump. When I heard you were up on the roof I just about keeled over dead. You can't jump until you see the new baby." Then she raised the infant she was holding high above her head, turning the baby's scrunched-up little face toward Minnie and the sun. "Don't jump until you tell me if this is the one!"

Minnie snarled, "Go away, Yvonne. I can't be bothered with you now."

Yvonne waved the now-crying child in the air. "But I really need to know."

Minnie put her hands on her hips. She twisted her mouth in annoyance and then hollered down, "Charlemagne says no. Try again." Then she extended her arms back out to her sides and scooted the curled toes of her slippers even closer to the edge of the roof.

Yvonne handed off the yowling baby to her boyfriend, who was already carrying another of their offspring. She said, "Dammit! Let's go home." The nine of them piled back into the rusty Chevy and rattled off.

As I watched Yvonne's family disappear in their shivering, smoke-belching car, I found myself thinking of Mama. I wished I could share this with her. If she'd been there, I'd have said, "Mama, this is one of those moments, one of those times that is so good I'll want to carry it with me when I really do cross over one day." I also wished that I could've shared that feeling with Clarice and Barbara Jean in a way that would make sense to them. They did their best with the topic of Mama and the community of ghosts I'd started keeping company with, though we hadn't really talked much about it since I left the hospital.

But maybe there are some things that you don't need knowledge of an unseen world to understand. Just as I was thinking of how I'd like to talk about the wonders of this day with Mama, I felt Barbara Jean hook her left arm around my right. Then, on my other side, Clarice's elbow wrapped around mine.

The three of us stood there on Big Earl's lawn, regarding each other with the kind of expression that could have broken out into a face-splitting grin just as easily as it could have collapsed into tears. A feeling passed between us that didn't need words, an understanding that there was no other place on earth that we should be right then, no one else we could quite so fully share this strange and beautiful day with. We squeezed closer to each other and leaned our foreheads together, forming our own tight, private triangle. Finally, Clarice said, "Let's get back across the street where we can laugh out loud. You don't need to be out in this heat, Odette. And we all know that old fake isn't about to jump."

From the roof, Minnie, with that good hearing of hers, shouted, "I heard that! Don't you call me a fake!" We turned toward her just in time to see her launch herself out into the open air with her long purple painted nails aimed at Clarice, ready to scratch her eyes out.

It seemed to me that it wasn't until Minnie's feet had parted with the metal gutter that she remembered she was up on the roof and not on ground level with Clarice. I clearly recall seeing the expression on her face transform from white hot fury to surprise and terror as she fell. Minnie screamed as she came hurtling down toward the lawn, her purple robe fanning out all around her like a parachute.

As it happened, she didn't hit Clarice or the lawn. She landed on Sharon. The impact caused Sharon to fall back against Little Earl, and all three of them tumbled across the lawn in a purple and white blur. Because the yard sloped slightly toward the street, the Minnie-Sharon-Earl bundle tumbled downhill until it came to a stop against the low yew hedge that lined the front of the property.

The three of them were immediately set upon by rescuers. The first challenge was untangling them from the purple robe and the torn lace of the wedding gown. Then, as a throng of people asked if they were hurt, Minnie shoved helping hands away from her and hopped right up, still ready to take a swipe at Clarice. But as soon as she took one step in Clarice's direction, she crumpled back to the ground and grasped her foot. She howled, "Oww!" Then, pointing at Clarice, she wailed, "You broke my ankle."

Erma Mae, who had come running when she saw Little Earl hit the ground, was checking her husband over for injuries even though he kept insisting that he was just fine.

Tearful and grass-stained, but unhurt, Sharon crawled across the yard on her hands and knees picking up crushed pastries and tossing them back into the pink box.

I heard tires squealing again and I looked toward the street and saw Veronica leaping from her shiny gray car. She trotted over to where Sharon crouched in the grass in her ruined wedding gown and, getting onto her knees, embraced her daughter. She kissed the top of Sharon's head and tried to comfort her, while at the same time attempting to pull the Donut Heaven box from her daughter's grasp.

From the edge of the growing crowd in Minnie's yard, I heard a voice say, "Now that was somethin' to see." I turned, and there was Mama.

Everyone else was occupied. Clarice was trying to prevent a tug-of-war between Veronica and Sharon over the Donut Heaven box. Barbara Jean was playing nursemaid to Minnie. The rest of the crowd was busy discussing what they'd just seen, already starting to exaggerate. So I walked away from the commotion and took off down the street with Mama.

I had seen my mother milling around the hospital during the days between my leaving the ICU and my being released to go home. And later I had noticed her roaming through my backyard, frowning over the condition of my flowers. But we hadn't talked since that day in Leaning Tree when I thought I was going to join her in the afterlife.

Mama said, "You're lookin' good."

"Thank you. I'm feeling all right, considering middle age and cancer."

She said, "Well, you won't have to deal with cancer too much longer. I've got a feelin' you'll be past that soon."

"No offense, Mama, but I think I'm done listening to predictions about whether or not I'll be recovering."

Mama made a face like my remark had stung her. "I'm so sorry about that. Believe you me, I gave Eleanor a piece of my mind for misleadin' you. She swears up and down it wasn't a prank. And I'm inclined to believe her. It was a big blow to her confidence, bein' wrong about you. She took it real hard." Mama whispered, "She's drinkin' like a fish."

I said, "You can tell her I'm not mad. If there's one thing I'm not going to get too angry with somebody about, it's them being wrong about me dying."

Mrs Roosevelt appeared at Mama's side then, like she'd been waiting nearby to hear that all was forgiven. She favored me with a wide, bucktoothed smile and a shy wave.

I nodded to her and we kept walking.

At the corner, we turned around and headed back. When we were about a half a block away from Minnie's house, I saw an ambulance pull up to the curb. I watched paramedics take over tending to Minnie and saw Barbara Jean return to the All-You-Can-Eat now that she wasn't needed. Veronica climbed into her Lexus with Sharon in tow, and Clarice walked back across the street, too.

I told Mama, "Hey, I'm having my last round of chemo on Tuesday – leastways I hope it's my last."

Mama said, "Wonderful. We should have a party. I'll get

everybody together to celebrate – your daddy, Big Earl, Thelma, Eleanor, and maybe your aunt Marjorie."

I said, "How about just you and Daddy. I'd like to keep things a little quieter from now on."

"You're right. That probably would be nicer." Her voice dropped so low I could barely hear her as she added, "Besides, you can't have your aunt Marjorie at the same party with *this one*." She pointed at Mrs Roosevelt, who weaved along beside Mama, sipping from a silver flask that was emblazoned with the presidential seal. "Put the two of them in the same room and it's nonstop arm wrestlin' and drinkin' games."

The paramedics were strapping Minnie onto a gurney as we approached. The hot weather had driven the spectators away. Now only Little Earl remained. As they wheeled her off the lawn, Minnie told her stepson, "Be sure to tell everybody that I had a near-death experience when I hit the ground. And tell 'em all I said it counts as fulfillin' my prediction." I waved goodbye to Minnie as the back doors to the ambulance closed. Little Earl hurried off to his car to follow his stepmother to the hospital.

Now that all of the action was over, I started to feel the sun scorching my skin. I said to Mama, "I've gotta get out of this heat."

"I'll see you on Tuesday, all right?" Mama said.

"All right."

We parted ways then. Mama and Eleanor Roosevelt walked toward the swing on the McIntyres' front porch. I crossed the street and headed back to my friends.

Through the window I saw Barbara Jean and Clarice with their heads together. I suspected they were arguing about whether or not they should ask me if I'd wandered off alone in order to talk to ghosts. At the men's end of the table, Richmond drew laughs from Chick and James as he tried and repeatedly failed to coax small cubes of sugar-free cherry Jell-O onto his spoon without losing them down the front of his gold silk shirt.

James must have felt me looking at him. He turned away from his buddies and made eye contact with me through the glass. He winked.

This was a pretty picture I'd been allowed to paint – my man and my friends all together. It was the best it could be, really, even though the hand that had sketched it was unsure and in spite of the fact that age had washed out some of the colors. And I wasn't about to worry over my picture's frame, not when there was so much more good painting to do.

I reached out to open the door to the All-You-Can-Eat.

Acknowledgments

My most sincere and heartfelt thanks to:

Julia Glass, for her incredible kindness and generosity. My phenomenal agent, Barney Karpfinger, for his encouragement and advice. My editor, Carole Baron, for allowing me to be the beneficiary of her immense talent. My first readers, Claire Parins, Harold Carlton, Grace Lloyd, and Nina Lusterman, for their patience. My father, Reverend Edward Moore, Sr, for a lifetime of lessons in real strength and true goodness. My mother, Delores Moore, for that first library card. And Peter Gronwold, for absolutely everything.

The best books live on in your head long after they are finished. As you read, you are turning the pages faster and faster to find out what happens next, only to feel bereft when you reach the end.

If that is how you feel now, you might like to join us at www.hodder.co.uk, or follow us on Twitter @hodderbooks, and be part of our community of people who love the very best of books and reading.

Whether you want to find out more about this book, or a particular author, watch trailers and interviews, have the chance to win early limited editions, or simply browse our expert readers' selection of the very best books, we think you'll find what you're looking for.

And if you don't, that's the place to tell us what's missing.

We love what we do, and we'd love you to be part of it.

www.hodder.co.uk

 @hodderbooks

HodderBooks

HodderBooks